Saga Six Pack 8

Saga Six Pack 8

By

Sabine Baring-Gould

Hall Caine

Hélène Adeline Guerber

Robert Louis Stevenson

Enhanced Media
2017

The Bondman: A New Saga by Hall Caine. First published in 1890.

The Book of Michael Sunlocks by Hall Caine. First published in 1890.

The Book of Red Jason by Hall Caine. First published in 1890.

The Waif Woman by Robert Louis Stevenson. First published in 1916.

Grettir the Outlaw: A Story of Iceland by Sabine Baring-Gould. First published in 1890.

Greek and Northern Mythologies - A Comparison by Hélène Adeline Guerber. From *Myths of the Norsemen: From the Eddas and Sagas.* First published in 1909.

Saga Six Pack 8. Published by Enhanced Media, 2017. All rights reserved.

Enhanced Media Publishing
Los Angeles, CA.

First Printing: 2017.

ISBN-13: 978-1544724409

ISBN-10: 1544724403

Contents

The Bondman: A New Saga by Hall Caine

"Vengeance is mine—I will repay."

1: Stephen Orry, Seaman, of Stappen

In the latter years of last century, H. Jorgen Jorgensen was Governor-General of Iceland. He was a Dane, born in Copenhagen, apprenticed to the sea on board an English trader, afterwards employed as a petty officer in the British navy, and some time in the command of a Danish privateer in an Alliance of Denmark and France against England. A rover, a schemer, a shrewd man of affairs, who was honest by way of interest, just by policy, generous by strategy, and who never suffered his conscience, which was not a good one, to get the better of him.

In one of his adventures he had sailed a Welsh brig from Liverpool to Reykjavik. This had been his introduction to the Icelandic capital, then a little, hungry, creeping settlement, with its face towards America and its wooden feet in the sea. It had also been his introduction to the household of the Welsh merchant, who had a wharf by the old Canning basin at Liverpool, a counting-house behind his residence in Wolstenholme Square, and a daughter of five and twenty. Jorgen, by his own proposal, was to barter English produce for Icelandic tallow. On his first voyage he took out a hundred tons of salt, and brought back a heavy cargo of lava for ballast. On his second voyage he took out the Welshman's daughter as his wife, and did not again trouble to send home an empty ship.

He had learned that mischief was once more brewing between England and Denmark, had violated his English letters of marque and run into Copenhagen, induced the authorities there, on the strength of his knowledge of English affairs, to appoint him to the Governor-Generalship of Iceland (then vacant) at a salary of four hundred pounds a year, and landed at Reykjavik with the Icelandic flag, of the white falcon on the blue ground—the banner of the Vikings—at the masthead of his father-in-law's Welsh brig.

Jorgen Jorgensen was then in his early manhood, and the strong heart of the good man did not decline with years, but rode it out with him through life and death. He had always intended to have a son and build up a family. It was the sole failure of his career that he had only a daughter. That had been a disaster for which he was not accountable, but he prepared himself to make a good end of a bad beginning. With God's assistance and his own extreme labor he meant to marry his daughter to Count Trollop, the Danish minister for Iceland, a functionary with five hundred a year, a house at Reykjavik, and another at the Danish capital.

This person was five-and-forty, tall, wrinkled, powdered, oiled, and devoted to gallantry. Jorgen's daughter, resembling her Welsh mother, was patient in suffering, passionate in love, and fierce in hatred. Her name was Rachel. At the advent of Count Trollop she was twenty, and her mother had then been some years dead.

The Count perceived Jorgen's drift, smiled at it, silently acquiesced in it, took even a languid interest in it, arising partly out of the Governor's position and the wealth the honest man was supposed to have amassed in the rigorous exercise of a place of power, and partly out of the daughter's own comeliness, which was not to be despised. At first the girl, on her part, neither assisted her father's designs nor resisted them, but showed complete indifference to the weighty questions of whom she should marry, when she should marry, and how she should marry; and this mood of mind contented her down to the last week in June that followed the anniversary of her twenty-first birthday.

That was the month of Althing, the national holiday of fourteen days, when the people's law-givers—the Governor, the Bishop, the Speaker, and the Sheriffs—met the people's delegates and some portion of the people themselves at the ancient Mount of Laws in the valley of Thingvellir, for the reading of the old statutes and the promulgation of the new ones, for the trial of felons and the settlement of claims, for the making of love and the making of quarrels, for wrestling and horse-fighting, for the practice of arms and the breaking of heads. Count Trollop was in Iceland at this celebration of the ancient festival, and he was induced by Jorgen to give it the light of his countenance. The Governor's company set out on half-a-hundred of the native ponies, and his daughter rode between himself and the Count. During that ride of six or seven long Danish miles Jorgen settled the terms of the intended transfer to his own complete contentment. The Count acquiesced and the daughter did not rebel.

The lonely valley was reached, the tents were pitched, the Bishop hallowed the assembly with solemn ceremonies, and the business of Althing began. Three days the work went on, and Rachel wearied of it; but on the fourth the wrestling was started, and her father sent for her to sit with him on the Mount and to present at the end of the contest the silver-buckled belt to the champion of all Iceland. She obeyed the summons with indifference, and took a seat beside the Judge, with the Count standing at her side. In the space below there was a crowd of men and boys, women and children, gathered about the ring. One wrestler was throwing everyone that came before him. His name was Patricksen, and he was supposed to be descended from the Irish, who settled, ages ago, on the Westmann Islands. His success became monotonous; at every fresh bout his self-confidence grew more insufferable, and the girl's eyes wandered from the spectacle to the spectators. From that instant her indifference fell away.

By the outskirts of the crowd, on one of the lower mounds of the Mount of Laws, a man sat with his head in his hand, with elbow on his knee. His head was bare, and from his hairy breast his woolen shirt was thrown back by reason of the heat. He was a magnificent creature—young, stalwart, fair-haired, broad-chested, with limbs like the beech tree, and muscles like its great gnarled round heads. His coat, a sort of sailor's jacket, was coarse and torn; his stockings, reaching to his knees, were cut and brown. He did not seem to heed the wrestling, and there rested upon him the idle air of the lusty Icelander—the languor of the big, tired animal. Only, when at the close of a bout a cheer rose and a way was made through the crowd for the exit of the vanquished man, did he lift up his great slow eyes—gray as those of a seal, and as calm and lustreless.

The wrestling came to an end. Patricksen justified his Irish blood, was proclaimed the winner, and stepped up to the foot of the Mount that the daughter of the Governor might buckle about him his champion's belt. The girl went through her function listlessly, her eyes wandering to where the fair-haired giant sat apart. Then the Westmann islander called for drink that he might treat the losing men, and having drunk himself, he began to swagger afresh, saying that they might find him the strongest and lustiest man that day at Thingvellir, and he would bargain to throw him over his back. As he spoke he strutted by the bottom of the Mount, and the man who sat there lifted his head and looked at him. Something in the glance arrested Patricksen and he stopped.

"This seems to be a lump of a lad," he said. "Let us see what we can do with him."

And at that he threw his long arms about the stalwart fellow, squared his broad hips before him, thrust down his head into his breast until his red neck was as thick as a bullock's, and threw all the strength of his body into his arms that he might lift the man out of his seat. But he moved him not an inch. With feet that held the earth like the hoofs of an ox, the young man sat unmoved.

Then those who had followed at the islander's heels for the liquor he was spending first stared in wonderment at his failure, and next laughed in derision of his bragging, and shouted to know why, before it was too late, the young man had not taken a bout at the wrestling, for that he who could hold his seat so must be the strongest-limbed man between the fells and the sea. Hearing this Patricksen tossed his head in anger, and said it was not yet too late, that if he took home the champion's belt it should be no rude bargain to master or man from sea to sea, and buckled though it was, it should be his who could take it from its place.

At that word the young fellow rose, and then it was seen that his right arm was useless, being broken between the elbow and the wrist, and bound with a kerchief above the wound. Nothing loth for this infirmity, he threw his other arm about the waist of the islander, and the two men closed for a fall. Patricksen had the first grip, and he swung to it, thinking straightway to lay his adversary by the heels; but the young man held his feet, and then, pushing one leg between the legs of the islander, planting the other knee into the islander's stomach, thrusting his head beneath the islander's chin, he knuckled his left hand under the islander's rib, pulled towards him, pushed from him, threw the weight of his body forward, and like a green withe Patricksen doubled backwards with a groan. Then at a rush of the islander's kinsmen, and a cry that his back would be broken, young man loosed his grip, and Patricksen rolled from him to the earth, as a clod rolls from the ploughshare.

All this time Jorgen's daughter had craned her neck to see over the heads of the people, and when the tussle was at an end, her face, which had been strained to the point of anguish, relaxed to smiles, and she turned to her father and asked if the champion's belt should not be his who had overcome the champion. But Jorgen answered no—that the contest was done, and judgment made, and he who would take the champion's belt must come to the next Althing and earn it. Then the girl unlocked her necklace of coral and silver spangles, beckoned the young man to her, bound the necklace about his broken arm close up by the shoulder, and asked him his name.

"Stephen," he answered.

"Whose son?" said she.

"Orrysen—but they call me Stephen Orry."

"Of what craft?"

"Seaman, of Stappen, under Snaefell."

The Westmann islander had rolled to his legs by this time, and now he came shambling up, with the belt in his hand and his sullen eyes on the ground.

"Keep it," he said, and flung the belt at the girl's feet, between her and his adversary. Then he strode away through the people, with curses on his white lips and the veins of his squat forehead large and dark.

It was midnight before the crowds had broken up and straggled away to their tents, but the sun of this northern land was still half over the horizon, and its dull red glow was on the waters of the lake that lay to the west of the valley. In the dim light of an hour later, when the hills of Thingvellir slept under the cloud shadow that was their only night, Stephen Orry stood with the Governor's daughter by the door of the Thingvellir parsonage, for Jorgen's company were the parson's guests. He held out the champion's belt to her and said, "Take it back, for if I keep it the man and his kinsmen will follow me all the days of my life."

She answered him that it was his, for he had won it, and until it was taken from him he must hold it, and if he stood in peril from the kinsmen of any man let him remember that it was she, daughter of the Governor himself, who had given it. The air was hushed in that still hour, not a twig or a blade rustling over the serried face of that desolate land as far as the wooded rifts that stood under the snowy dome of the Armann fells. As she spoke there was a sharp noise near at hand, and he started; but she rallied him on his fears, and laughed that one who had felled the blustering champion of that day should tremble at a noise in the night.

There was a wild outcry in Thingvellir the next morning, Patricksen, the Westmann islander, had been murdered. There was a rush of the people to the place where his body had been found. It lay like a rag across the dyke that ran between the parsonage and the church. On the dead man's face was the look that all had seen there when last night he flung down the belt between his adversary and the Governor's daughter, crying, "keep it." But his sullen eyes were glazed, and stared up without the quivering of a lid through the rosy sunlight; the dark veins on his brow were now purple, and when they lifted him they saw that his back was broken.

Then there was a gathering at the foot of the Mount, with the parson for judge, and nine men of those who had slept in the tents nearest to the body for witnesses and jury. Nothing was discovered. No one had heard a sound throughout the night. There was no charge to put before the law-givers at Althing. The kinsmen of the dead man cast dark looks at Stephen Orry, but he gave never a sign. Next day the strong man was laid under the shallow turf of the Church garth. His little life's swaggering was swaggered out; he must sleep on to the resurrection without one brag more.

The Governor's daughter did not leave the guest room of the parsonage from the night of the wrestling onwards to the last morning of the Althing holiday, and then, the last ceremonies done, the tents struck and the ponies saddled, she took her place between Jorgen and the Count for the return journey home. Twenty paces behind her the fair-haired Stephen Orry rode on his shaggy pony, gaunt and peaky and bearded as a goat, and five paces behind him rode the brother of the dead man Patricksen. Amid five hundred men and women, and eight hundred horses saddled for riding or packed with burdens, these three had set their faces towards the little wooden capital.

July passed into August, and the day was near that had been appointed by Jorgen Jorgensen for the marriage of his daughter to the Count Trollop. At the girl's request the marriage was postponed. The second day came nigh; again the girl excused herself, and again the marriage was put off. A third time the appointed day approached, and a third time the girl asked for delay. But Jorgen's iron will was to be tampered with no longer. The time was near when the Minister must return to Copenhagen, and that was reason enough why the thing in hand should be despatched. The marriage must be delayed no longer.

But then the Count betrayed reluctance. Rumor had pestered him with reports that vexed his pride. He dropped hints of them to the Governor. "Strange," said he, "that a woman should prefer the stink of the fulmar fish to the perfumes of civilization." Jorgen fired up at the sneer. His daughter was his daughter, and he was Governor-General of the island. What lowborn churl would dare to lift his eyes to the child of Jorgen Jorgensen?

The Count had his answer pat. He had made inquiries. The man's name was Stephen Orry. He came from Stappen under Snaefell, and was known there for a wastrel. On the poor glory of his village voyage as an athlete, he idled his days in bed and his nights at the tavern. His father, an honest thrall, was dead; his mother lived by splitting and drying the stock-fish for English traders. He was the foolish old woman's pride, and she kept him. Such was the man whom the daughter of the Governor had chosen before the Minister for Iceland.

At that Jorgen's hard face grew livid and white by turns. They were sitting at supper in Government House, and, with an oath, the Governor brought his fist down on the table. It was a lie; his daughter knew no more of the man than he did. The Count shrugged his shoulders and asked where she was then, that she was not with them. Jorgen answered, with an absent look, that she was forced to keep her room.

At that moment a message came for the Count. It was urgent and could not wait. The Count went to the door, and, returning presently, asked if Jorgen was sure that his daughter was in the house. Certain of it he was, for she was ill, and the days were deepening to winter. But for all his assurance, Jorgen sprang up from his seat and made for his daughter's chamber. She was not there, and the room was empty. The Count met him in the corridor. "Follow me," he whispered, and Jorgen followed, his proud, stern head bent low.

In the rear of the Government House at Reykjavik there is a small meadow. That night it was inches deep in the year's first fall of snow, but two persons stood together there, close locked in each other's arms— Stephen Orry and the daughter of Jorgen Jorgensen. With the tread of a cat a man crept up behind them. It was the brother of Patricksen. At his back came the Count and the Governor. The snow cloud lifted, and a white gush of moonlight showed all. With the cry of a wild beast Jorgen flung himself between his daughter and her lover, leapt at Stephen and struck him hard on the breast, and then, as the girl dropped to her knees at his feet, he cursed her.

"Bastard," he shrieked, "there's no blood of mine in your body. Go to your filthy offal, and may the devil damn you both."

She stopped her ears to shut out the torrent of a father's curse, but before the flood of it was spent she fell backward cold and senseless, and her upturned face was whiter than the snow. Then her giant lover lifted her in his arms as if she had been a child, and strode away in silence.

II: The Mother of a Man

The daughter of the Governor-General and the seaman of Stappen were made man and wife. The little Lutheran priest, who married them, Sigfus Thomson, a worthy man and a good Christian, had reason to remember the ceremony. Within a week he was removed from his chaplaincy at the capital to the rectory of Grimsey, the smallest cure of the Icelandic Church, on an island separated from the mainland by seven Danish miles of sea.

The days that followed brought Rachel no cheer of life. She had thought that her husband would take her away to his home under Snaefell, and so remove her from the scene of her humiliation. He excused himself, saying that Stappen was but a poor place, where the great ships never put in to trade, and that there was more chance of livelihood at Reykjavik. Rachel crushed down her shame, and they took a mean little house in the fishing quarter. But Stephen did no work. Once he went out four days with a company of Englishmen as guide to the geysers, and on his return he idled four weeks on the wharves, looking at the foreign seamen as they arrived by the boats. The fame of his exploit at Thingvellir had brought him a troop of admirers, and what he wanted for his pleasure he never lacked. But necessity began to touch him at home, and then he hinted to Rachel that her father was rich. She had borne his indifference to her degradation, she had not murmured at the idleness that pinched them, but at that word something in her heart seemed to break. She bent her head and said nothing. He went on to hint that she should go to her father, who seeing her need would surely forgive her. Then her proud spirit could brook no more. "Rather than darken my father's doors again," she said, "I will starve on a crust of bread and a drop of water."

Things did not mend, and Stephen began to cast down his eyes in shame when Rachel looked at him. Never a word of blame she spoke, but he reproached himself and talked of his old mother at Stappen. She was the only one who could do any good with him. She knew him and did not spare him. When she was near he worked sometimes, and did not drink too much. He must send for her.

Rachel raised no obstacle, and one day the old mother came, perched upon a bony, ragged-eared pony, and with all her belongings on the pack behind her. She was a little, hard featured woman; and at the first sight of her seamed and blotted face Rachel's spirit sank.

The old woman was active and restless. Two days after her arrival she was at work at her old trade of splitting and drying the stock-fish. All the difference that the change had made for her was that she was working on the beach at Reykjavik instead of the beach at Stappen, and living with her son and her son's wife instead of alone.

Her coming did not better the condition of Rachel. She had measured her new daughter-in-law from head to foot at their first meeting, and neither smiled nor kissed her. She was devoted to her son, and no woman was too good for him. Her son had loved her, and Rachel had come between them. The old woman made up her mind to hate the girl, because her fine manners and comely face were a daily rebuke to her own coarse habits and homely looks, and an hourly contrast always present to Stephen's eyes.

Stephen was as idle as ever, and less ashamed of his sloth now that there was someone to keep the wolf from the door. His mother accepted with cheerfulness the duty of bread-winner to her son, but Rachel's helplessness chafed her. For all her fine fingering the girl could finger nothing that would fill the pot. "A pretty wife you've brought me home to keep," she muttered morning and night.

But Rachel's abasement was not even yet at its worst. "Oh," she thought, "if I could but get back my husband to myself alone, he would see my humiliation and save me from it." She went a woman's way to work to have the old mother sent home to Stappen. But the trick that woman's wit can devise woman's wit can baulk, and the old mother held her ground. Then the girl bethought her of her old shame at living in a hovel close to her father's house, and asked to be taken away. Anywhere, anywhere, let it be to the world's end, and she would follow. Stephen answered that one place was like another in Iceland, where the people were few and all knew their history; and, as for foreign parts, though a seaman he was not a seagoing man, farther than the whale-fishing lay about their coasts, and that, go where they might to better their condition, yet other poor men were there already. At that, Rachel's heart sank, for she saw that the great body of her husband must cover a pigmy soul. Bound she was for all her weary days to the place of her disgrace, doomed she was to live to the last with the woman who hated her, and to eat that woman's bitter bread. She was heavy with child at this time, and her spirit was broken. So she sat herself down with her feet to the hearth, and wept.

There the old mother saw her as often as she bustled in and out of the house from the beach, and many a gibe she flung her way. But Stephen sat beside her one day with a shame-faced look, and cursed his luck, and said if he only had an open boat of his own what he would do for both of them. She asked how much a boat would cost him, and he answered sixty kroner; that a Scotch captain then in the harbor had such a one to sell at that price, and that it was a better boat than the fishermen of those parts ever owned, for it was of English build. Now it chanced that sitting alone that very day in her hopelessness, Rachel had overheard a group of noisy young girls in the street tell of a certain Jew, named Bernard Frank, who stood on the jetty by the stores buying hair of the young maidens who would sell to him, and of the great money he had paid to some of them, such as they had never handled before.

And now, at this mention of the boat, and at the flash of hope that came with it, Rachel remembered that she herself had a plentiful head of hair, and how often it had been commended for its color and texture, and length and abundance, in the days (now gone forever) when all things were good and beautiful that belonged to the daughter of the Governor. So, making some excuse to Stephen, she rose up, put off her little house cap with the tassel, put on her large linen head-dress, hurried out, and made for the wharf.

There in truth the Jew was standing with a group of girls about him. And some of these would sell outright to him, and then go straightway to the stores to buy filigree jewelry and rings, or bright-hued shawls, with the price of their golden locks shorn off. And some would hover about him between desire of so much artificial adornment and dread of so much natural disfigurement, until, like moths, they would fall before the light of the Jew's bright silver.

Rachel had reached the place at the first impulse of her thought, but being there her heart misgave her, and she paused on the outskirts of the crowd. To go in among these girls and sell her hair to the Jew was to make herself one with the lowest and meanest of the town, but that was not the fear that held her back. Suddenly the thought had come to her that what she had intended to do was meant to win her husband back to her, yet that she could not say what it was that had won him for her at the first. And seeing how sadly the girls were changed after the shears had passed over their heads, she could not help but ask herself what it would profit her, though she got the boat for her husband, if she lost him for herself? And thinking in this fashion she was turning away with a faltering step, when the Jew, seeing her, called to her, saying what lovely fair hair she had, and asking would she part with it. There was no going back on her purpose then, so facing it out as bravely as she could, she removed her head-dress, dropped her hair out of the plaits, until it fell in its sunny wavelets to her waist, and asked how much he would give for it. The Jew answered, "Fifty kroner."

"Make it sixty," she said, "and it is yours."

The Jew protested that he would lose by the transaction, but he paid the money into Rachel's hands, and she, lest she should repent of her bargain, prayed him to take her hair off instantly. He was nothing loth to do so, and the beautiful flaxen locks, cut close to the crown, fell in long tresses to his big shears. Rachel put back her linen head-dress, and, holding tightly the sixty silver pieces in her palm, hurried home.

Her cheeks were crimson, her eyes were wet, and her heart was beating high when she returned to her poor home in the fishing quarter. There in a shrill, tremulous voice of joy and fear, she told Stephen all, and counted out the glistening coins to the last of the sixty into his great hand.

"And now you can buy the English boat," she said, "and we shall be beholden to no one."

He answered her wild words with few of his own, and showed little pleasure; yet he closed his hand on the money, and, getting up, he went out of the house, saying he must see the Scotch captain there and then. Hardly had he gone when the old mother came in from her work on the beach, and, Rachel's hopes being high, she could not but share them with her, and so she told her all, little as was the commerce that passed between them. The mother only grunted as she listened and went on with her food.

Rachel longed for Stephen to return with the good news that all was settled and done, but the minutes passed and he did not come. The old woman sat by the hearth and smoked. Rachel waited with fear at her heart, but the hours went by and still Stephen did not appear. The old woman dozed before the fire and snored. At length, when the night had worn on towards midnight, an unsteady step came to the door, and Stephen reeled into the house drunk. The old woman awoke and laughed.

Rachel grew faint and sank to a seat. Stephen dropped to his knees on the ground before her, and in a maudling cry went on to tell of how he had thought to make one hundred kroner of her sixty by a wager, how he had lost fifty, and then in a fit of despair had spent the other ten.

16

"Then all is gone—all," cried Rachel. And thereupon the old woman shuffled to her feet and said bitterly, "And a good thing, too. I know you— trust me for seeing through your sly ways, my lady. You expected to take my son from me with the price of your ginger hair, you ugly baldpate."

Rachel's head grew light, and with the cry of a bated creature she turned upon the old mother in a torrent of hot words. "You low, mean, selfish soul," she cried, "I despise you more than the dirt under my feet."

Worse than this she said, and the old woman called on Stephen to hearken to her, for that was the wife he had brought home to revile his mother.

The old witch shed some crocodile tears, and Stephen lunged in between the women and with the back of his hand struck his wife across the face.

At that blow Rachel was silent for a moment, trembling like an affrighted beast, and then she turned upon her husband. "And so you have struck me—me—me," she cried. "Have you forgotten the death of Patricksen?"

The blow of her words was harder than the blow of her husband's hand. The man reeled before it, turned white, gasped for breath, then caught up his cap and fled out into the night.

III: The Lad Jason

Of Rachel in her dishonor there is now not much to tell, but the little that is left is the kernel of this history.

That night, amid the strain of strong emotions, she was brought to bed before her time was yet full. Her labor was hard, and long she lay between life and death, for the angel of hope did not pull with her. But as the sun shot its first yellow rays through the little skin-covered windows, a child was born to Rachel, and it was a boy. Little joy she found in it, and remembering its father's inhumanity, she turned her face from it to the wall, trying thereby to conquer the yearning that answered to its cry.

It was then for the first time since her lying-in that the old mother came to her. She had been out searching for Stephen, and had just come upon news of him.

"He has gone in an English ship," she cried. "He sailed last night, and I have lost him forever."

And at that she leaned her quivering white face over the bed, and raised her clenched hand over Rachel's face.

"Son for son," she cried again. "May you lose your son, even as you have made me to lose mine."

The child seemed likely to answer to the impious prayer, for its little strength waned visibly. And in those first hours of her shameful widowhood the evil thought came to Rachel to do with it as the baser sort among her people were allowed to do with the children they did not wish to rear—expose it to its death before it had yet touched food. But in the throes, as she thought, of its extremity, the love of the mother prevailed over the hate of the wife, and with a gush of tears she plucked the babe to her breast. Then the neighbor, who out of pity and charity had nursed her in her dark hour, ran for the priest, that with the blessing of baptism the child might die a Christian soul.

The good man came, and took the little, sleep-bound body from Rachel's arms, and asked her the name. She did not answer, and he asked again. Once more, having no reply, he turned to the neighbor to know what the father's name had been.

"Stephen Orry," said the good woman.

"Then Stephen Stephensen," he began, dipping his fingers into the water; but at the sound of that name Rachel cried, "No, no, no."

"He has not done well by her, poor soul," whispered the woman; "call it after her own father."

"Then Jorgen Jorgensen," the priest began again; and again Rachel cried, "No, no, no," and raised herself upon her arm.

"It has no father," she said, "and I have none. If it is to die, let it go to God's throne with the badge of no man's cruelty; and if it is to live, let it be known by no man's name save its own. Call it Jason—Jason only."

And in the name of Jason the child was baptised, and so it was that Rachel, little knowing what she was doing in her blind passion and pain, severed her son from kith and kin. But in what she did out of the bitterness of her heart God himself had his own great purposes.

From that hour the child increased in strength, and soon waxed strong, and three days after, as the babe lay cooing at Rachel's breast, and she in her own despite was tasting the first sweet joys of motherhood, the old mother of Stephen came to her again.

"This is my house," she said, "and I will keep shelter over your head no longer. You must pack and away—you and your brat, both of you."

That night the Bishop of the island—Bishop Petersen, once a friend of Rachel's mother, now much in fear of the Governor, her father—came to her in secret to say that there was a house for her at the extreme west of the fishing quarter, where a fisherman had lately died, leaving the little that he had to the Church. There she betook herself with her child as soon as the days of her lying-in were over. It was a little oblong shed, of lava blocks laid with peat for mortar, resembling on the outside two ancient seamen shoving shoulders together against the weather, and on the inside two tiny bird cages.

And having no one now to stand to her, or seem to stand, in the place of bread-winner, she set herself to such poor work as she could do and earn a scanty living by. This was cleaning the down of the eider duck, by passing it through a sieve made of yarn stretched over a hoop. By a deft hand, with extreme labor, something equal to sixpence a day could be made in this way from the English traders. With such earnings Rachel lived in content, and if Jorgen Jorgensen had any knowledge of his daughter's necessities he made no effort to relieve them.

Her child lived—a happy, sprightly, joyous bird in its little cage—and her broken heart danced to its delicious accents. It sweetened her labors, it softened her misfortunes, it made life more dear and death more dreadful; it was the strength of her arms and the courage of her soul, her summons to labor and her desire for rest. Call her wretched no longer, for now she had her child to love. Happy little dingy cabin in the fishing quarter, amid the vats for sharks' oil and the heaps of dried cod! It was filled with heaven's own light, that came not from above but radiated from the little cradle where her life, her hope, her joy, her solace lay swathed in the coverlet of all her love.

And as she worked through the long summer days on the beach, with the child playing among the pebbles at her feet, many a dream danced before her of the days to come, when her boy would sail in the ships that came to their coast, and perhaps take her with him to that island of the sea that had been her mother's English home, where men were good to women and women were true to men. Until then she must live where she was, a prisoner chained to a cruel rock; but she would not repine, she could wait, for the time of her deliverance was near. Her liberator was coming. He was at her feet; he was her child, her boy, her darling; and when he slumbered she saw him wax and grow, and when he awoke she saw her fetters break. Thus on the bridge of hope's own rainbow she spanned her little world of shame and pain.

The years went by, and Jason grew to be a strong-limbed, straight, stalwart lad, red-haired and passionate-hearted, reckless and improvident as far as improvidence was possible amid the conditions of his bringing up. He was a human waterfowl, and all his days were spent on the sea. Such work as was also play he was eager to do. He would clamber up the rocks of the island of Engy outside the harbor, to take the eggs of the eider duck from the steep places where she built her nest; and from the beginning of May to the end of June he found his mother in the eider down that she cleaned for the English traders. People whispered to Rachel that he favored his father, both in stature and character, but she turned a deaf ear to their gloomy forebodings. Her son was as fair as the day to look upon, and if he had his lazy huhumors, he had also one quality which overtopped them all—he loved his mother. People whispered again that in this regard also he resembled his father, who amid many vices had the same sole virtue.

Partly to shut him off from the scandal of the gossips, who might tell him too soon the story of his mother's wrecked and broken life, and partly out of the bitterness and selfishness of her bruised spirit, Rachel had brought up her boy to speak the tongue of her mother—the English tongue. Her purpose failed her, for Jason learned Icelandic on the beach as fast as English in the house; he heard the story of his mother's shame and of his father's baseness, and brought it back to her in the colors of a thrice-told tale. Vain effort of fear and pride! It was nevertheless to prepare the lad for the future that was before him.

And through all the days of her worse than widowhood, amid dark memories of the past and thoughts of the future wherein many passions struggled together, the hope lay low down in Rachel's mind that Stephen would return to her. Could he continue to stand in dread of the threat of his own wife? No, no, no. It had been only the hot word of a moment of anger, and it was gone. Stephen was staying away in fear of the brother of Patricksen. When that man was dead, or out of the way, he would return. Then he would see their boy, and remember his duty towards him, and if the lad ever again spoke bitterly of one whom he had never yet seen, she on her part would chide him, and the light of revenge that had sometimes flashed in his brilliant blue eyes would fade away and in uplooking and affection he would walk as a son with his father's hand.

Thus in the riot of her woman's heart hope fought with fear and love with hate. And at last the brother of Patricksen did indeed disappear. Rumor whispered that he had returned to the Westmann Islands, there to settle for the rest of his days and travel the sea no more.

"Now he will come," thought Rachel. "Wherever he is, he will learn that there is no longer anything to fear, and he will return."

And she waited with as firm a hope that the winds would carry the word as Noah waited for the settling of the waters after the dove had found the dry land.

But time went on and Stephen did not appear, and at length under the turmoil of a heart that fought with itself, Rachel's health began to sink.

Then Patricksen returned. He had a message for her. He knew where her husband was. Stephen Orry was on the little Island of Man, far away south, in the Irish Sea. He had married again, and he had another child. His wife was dead, but his son was living.

Rachel in her weakness went to bed and rose from it no more. The broad dazzle of the sun that had been so soon to rise on her wasted life was shot over with an inky pall of cloud. Not for her was to be the voyage to England. Her boy must go alone.

It was the winter season in that stern land of the north, when night and day so closely commingle that the darkness seems never to lift. And in the silence of that long night Rachel lay in her little hut, sinking rapidly and much alone. Jason came to her from time to time, in his great sea stockings and big gloves and with the odor of the brine in his long red hair. By her bedside he would stand half-an-hour in silence, with eyes full of wonderment; for life like that of an untamed colt was in his own warm limbs, and death was very strange to him. A sudden hemorrhage brought the end, and one day darker than the rest, when Jason hastened home from the boats, the pain and panting of death were there before him. His mother's pallid face lay on her arm, her great dark eyes were glazed already, she was breathing hard and every breath was a spasm. Jason ran for the priest—the same that had named him in his baptism. The good old man came hobbling along, book in hand, and seeing how life flickered he would have sent for the Governor, but Rachel forbade him. He read to her, he sang for her in his crazy cracked voice, he shrived her, and then all being over, as far as human efforts could avail, he sat himself down on a chest, spread his print handkerchief over his knee, took out his snuffbox and waited.

Jason stood with his back to the glow of the peat fire, and his hard set face in the gloom. Never a word came from him, never a sign, never a tear. Only with the strange light in his wild eyes he looked on and listened.

Rachel stirred, and called to him.

"Are you there, Jason?" she said, feebly, and he stepped to her side.

"Closer," she whispered; and he took her cold hand in both his hands, and then her dim eyes knew where to look for his face.

"Good-bye, my brave lad," she said. "I do not fear to leave you. You are strong, you are brave, and the world is kind to them that can fight it. Only to the weak it is cruel—only to the weak and the timid—only to women—only to helpless women sold into the slavery of heartless men."

And then she told him everything—her love, her loyalty, her life. In twenty little words she told the story.

"I gave him all—all. I took a father's curse for him. He struck me—he left me—he forgot me with another woman. Listen—listen—closer still—still closer," she whispered, eagerly, and then she spoke the words that lie at the heart of this history.

"You will be a sailor, and sail to many lands. If you should ever meet your father, remember what your mother has borne from him. If you should never meet him, but should meet his son, remember what your mother has suffered at the hands of his father. Can you hear me? Is my speech too thick? Have you understood me?"

Jason's parched throat was choking, and he did not answer.

"My brave boy, farewell," she said. "Good-bye," she murmured again, more faintly, and after that there was a lull, a pause, a sigh, a long-drawn breath, another sigh, and then over his big brown hands her pallid face fell forward, and the end was come.

For some minutes Jason stood there still in the same impassive silence. Never a tear yet in his great eyes, now wilder than they were; never a cry from his dry throat, now surging hot and athirst; never a sound in his ears, save a dull hum of words like the plash of a breaker that was coming— coming—coming from afar. She was gone who had been everything to him. She had sunk like a wave, and the waves of the ocean were pressing on behind her. She was lost, and the tides of life were flowing as before.

The old pastor shuffled to his feet, mopping his moist eyes with his red handkerchief. "Come away, my son," he said, and tapped Jason on the shoulder.

"Not yet," the lad answered hoarsely. And then he turned with a dazed look and said, like one who speaks in his sleep, "My father has killed my mother."

"No, no, don't say that," said the priest.

"Yes, yes," said the lad more loudly; "not in a day, or an hour, or a moment, but in twenty long years."

"Hush, hush, my son," the old priest murmured.

But Jason did not hear him. "Now listen," he cried, "and hear my vow." And still he held the cold hand in his hands, and still the ashy face rested on them.

"I will hunt the world over until I find that man, and when I have found him I will slay him."

"What are you saying?" cried the priest.

But Jason went on with an awful solemnity. "If he should die, and we should never meet, I will hunt the world over until I find his son, and when I have found him I will kill him for his father's sake."

"Silence, silence," cried the priest.

"So help me God!" said Jason.

"My son, my son, Vengeance is His. What are we that we should presume to it?"

Jason heard nothing, but the frost of life's first winter that had bound up his heart, deafening him, blinding him, choking him, seemed all at once to break. He pushed the cold face gently back on to the pillow, and fell over it with sobs that shook the bed.

They buried the daughter of the Governor in the acre allotted to the dead poor in the yard of the Cathedral of Reykjavik. The bells were ringing a choral peal between matins and morning service. Happy little girls in bright new gowns, with primroses on their breasts yellowing their round chins, went skipping in at the wide west doorway, chattering as they went like linnets in spring. It was Easter Day, nineteen years after Stephen Orry had fled from Iceland.

Next morning Jason signed articles on the wharf to sail as seaman before the mast on an Irish schooner homeward bound for Belfast, with liberty to call at Whitehaven in Cumberland, and Ramsey in the Isle of Man.

IV: An Angel in Homespun

The little island in the middle of the Irish Sea has through many centuries had its own language and laws, and its own judges and governors. Very, very long ago, it had also its own kings; and one of the greatest of them was the Icelandic seadog who bought it with blood in 1077. More recently it has had its own reigning lords, and one of the least of them was the Scottish nobleman who sold it for gold in 1765. After that act of truck and trade the English crown held the right of appointing the Governor-General. It chose the son of the Scottish nobleman. This was John, fourth Duke of Athol, and he held his office fifty-five bad years. In his day the island was not a scene of overmuch gaiety. If the memory of old men can be trusted, he contrived to keep a swashbuckler court there, but its festivities, like his own dignities, must have been maimed and lame. He did not care to see too much of it, and that he might be free to go where he would he appointed a deputy governor.

Now when he looked about him for this deputy he found just six and twenty persons ready to fall at his feet. He might have had either of the Deemsters, but he selected neither; he might have had any of the twenty-four Keys, but he selected none. It was then that he heard of a plain farmer in the north of the island, who was honored for his uprightness, beloved for his simplicity, and revered for his piety. "The very man for me," thought the lord of the swashbucklers, and he straightway set off to see him.

He found him living like a patriarch among his people, surrounded by his sons, and proud of them that they were many and strong. His name was Adam Fairbrother. In his youth he had run away to sea, been taken prisoner by the Algerines, kept twenty-eight months a slave in Barbary, had escaped and returned home captain of a Guineaman. This had been all his education and all his history. He had left the island a wild, headstrong, passionate lad; he had returned to it a sober, patient, gentle-hearted man.

Adam's house was Lague, a loose, straggling, featureless and irresolute old fabric, on five hundred hungry acres of the rocky headland of Maughold. When the Duke rode up to it Adam himself was ringing the bell above the door lintel that summoned his people to dinner. He was then in middle life, stout, yet flaccid and slack, with eyes and forehead of sweetest benevolence, mouth of softest tenderness, and hair already whitening over his ears and temples.

"The face of an angel in homespun," thought the Duke.

Adam received his visitor with the easy courtesy of an equal, first offering his hand. The Duke shook hands with him. He held the stirrup while the Duke alighted, took the horse to the stable, slackened its girths, and gave it a feed of oats, talking all the time. The Duke stepped after him and listened. Then he led the way to the house. The Duke followed. They went into the living room—an oblong kitchen with an oak table down the middle, and two rows of benches from end to end. The farming people were trooping in, bringing with them the odor of fresh peat and soil. Bowls of barley broth were being set in front of the big chair at the table end. Adam sat in this seat and motioned the Duke to the bench at his right. The Duke sat down. Then six words of grace and all were in their places—Adam himself, his wife, a shrewd-faced body, his six sons, big and shambling, his men, bare-armed and quiet, his maids, with skirts tucked up, plump and noisy, and the swashbuckler Duke, amused and silent, glancing down the long lines of the strangest company with whom he had ever yet been asked to sit at dinner. Suet pudding followed the broth, sheep's head and potatoes followed the pudding, then six words of thanks and all rose and trooped away except the Duke and Adam. That good man had not altered the habit of his life by so much as a plate of cheese for the fact that the "Lord of Mann" had sat at meat with him. "The manners of a prince," thought the Duke.

They took the armchairs at opposite sides of the ingle.

"You look cosy in your retreat, Mr. Fairbrother," said the Duke; "but since your days in Guinea have you never dreamt of a position of more power, and perhaps of more profit?"

"As for power," answered Adam, "I have observed that the name and the reality rarely go together."

"The experience of a statesman," thought the Duke.

"As for profit," he continued, "I have reflected that money has never yet since the world began tempted a happy man."

24

"The wisdom of a judge," thought the Duke.

"And as for myself I am a completely happy one."

"With more than a judge's integrity," thought the Duke.

At that the Duke told the purpose of his visit.

"And now," he said, with uplifted hands, "don't say I've gone far to fare worse. The post I offer requires but one qualification in the man who fills it, yet no one about me possesses the simple gift. It needs an honest man, and all the better if he's not a fool. Will you take it?"

"No," said Adam, short and blunt.

"The very man," thought the Duke.

Six months later the Duke had his way. Adam Fairbrother, of Lague, was made Governor of Mann (under the Duke himself as Governor-General) at a salary of five hundred pounds a year.

On the night of Midsummer Day, 1793, the town of Ramsey held high festival. The Royal George had dropped anchor in the bay, and the Prince of Wales, attended by the Duke of Athol, Captain Murray and Captain Cook, had come ashore to set the foot of an English Prince for the first time on Manx soil. Before dusk, the Royal ship had weighed anchor again, but when night fell in the festivities had only begun. Guns were fired, bands of music passed through the town, and bonfires were lighted on the top of the Sky Hill. The kitchens of the inns were crowded, and the streets were thronged with country people enveloped in dust. In the market place the girls were romping, the young men drinking, the children shouting at the top of their voices, the peddlers edging their barrows through the crowd and crying their wares. Over all the tumult of exuberant voices, the shouting, the laughter, the merry shrieks, the gay banter, the barking of sheep-dogs, the snarling of mongrel setters, the streaming and smoking of hawkers' torches across a thousand faces, there was the steady peal of the bell of Ballure.

In the midst of it all a strange man passed through the town. He was of colossal stature—stalwart, straight, and flaxen-haired, wearing a goatskin cap without brim, a gray woollen shirt open at the neck and belted with a leathern strap, breeches of untanned leather, long thick stockings, a second pair up to his ankles, and no shoes on his feet. His face was pale, his cheek bones stood high, and his eyes were like the eyes of a cormorant. The pretty girls stopped their chatter to look after him, but he strode on with long steps, and the people fell aside for him.

At the door of the Saddle Inn he stood a moment, but voices came from within and he passed on. Going by the Court House he came to the Plough Tavern, and there he stopped again, paused a moment, and then stepped in. After a time the children who had followed at his heels separated, and the girls who had looked after him began to dance with arms akimbo and skirts held up over their white ankles. He was forgotten.

An hour later, four men, armed with cutlasses, and carrying ship's irons, came hurrying from the harbor. They were blue-jackets from the revenue cutter lying in the bay, and they were in pursuit of a seaman who had escaped from the English brig at anchor outside. The runaway was a giant and a foreigner, and could not speak a word of English or Manx. Had anyone seen him? Yes, everyone. He had gone into the Plough. To the Plough the blue-jackets made their way. The good woman who kept it, Mother Beatty, had certainly seen such a man. "Aw, yes, the poor craythur, he came, so he did," but never a word could he speak to her, and never a word could she speak to him, so she gave him a bit of barley cake, and maybe a drop of something, and that was all. He was not in the house then? "Och, let them look for themselves." The blue-jackets searched the house, and came out as they had entered. Then they passed through every street, looked down every alley, peered into every archway, and went back to their ship empty-handed.

When they were gone Mother Beatty came to the door and looked out. At the next instant the big-limbed stranger stepped from behind her.

"That way," she whispered, and pointed to a dark alley opposite.

The man watched the direction of her finger in the darkness, doffed his cap, and strode away.

The alley led him by many a turn to the foot of a hill. It was Ballure. Behind him lay the town, with the throngs, the voices, and the bands of music. To his left was the fort, belching smoke and the roar of cannon. To his right were the bonfires on the hilltop, with little dark figures passing before them, and a glow above them embracing a third of the sky. In front of him was the gloom and silence of the country. He walked on; a fresh coolness came to him out of the darkness, and over him a dull murmur hovered in the air. He was going towards Kirk Maughold.

He passed two or three little houses by the wayside, but most of them were dark. He came by a tavern, but the door was shut, and no one answered when he knocked. At length, by the turn of a byroad, he saw a light through the trees, and making towards it he found a long shambling house under a clump of elms. He was at Lague.

The light he saw was from one window only, and he stepped up to it. A man was sitting alone by the hearth, with the glow of a gentle fire on his face—a beautiful face, soft and sweet and tender. It was Adam Fairbrother.

The stranger stood a moment in the darkness, looking into the quiet room. Then he tapped on the windowpane.

On this evening Governor Fairbrother was worn with toil and excitement. It had been Tynwald Day, and while sitting at St. John's he had been summoned to Ramsey to receive the Prince of Wales and the Duke of Athol. The royal party had already landed when he arrived, but not a word of apology had he offered for the delayed reception. He had taken the Prince to the top of the Sky Hill, talking as he went, answering many questions and asking not a few, naming the mountains, running through the island's history, explaining the three legs of its coat of arms, glancing at its ancient customs and giving a taste of its language. He had been simple, sincere, and natural from first to last, and when the time had come for the Prince to return to his ship he had presented his six sons to him with the quiet dignity of a patriarch, saying these were his gifts to his king that was to be. Then on the quay he had offered the Prince his hand, hoping he might see him again before long; for he was a great lover of a happy face, and the Prince, it was plain to see, was, like himself, a man of a cheerful spirit.

But when the Royal George had sailed out of the bay at the top of the tide, and the great folk who had held their breath in awe of so much majesty were preparing to celebrate the visit with the blazing of cannon and the beating of drums, Adam Fairbrother had silently slipped away. He lived at Government House, but had left his three elder boys at Lague, and thought this a happy chance of spending a night at home. Only his sons' housekeeper, a spinster aunt of his own, was there, and when she had given him a bite of supper he had sent her after the others to look at the sights of Ramsey. Then he had drawn up his chair before the fire, charged his long pipe, purred a song to himself, begun to smoke, to doze, and to dream.

His dreams that night had been woven with vision of his bad days in the slave factory at Barbary—of his wreck and capture, of his cruel tortures before his neck was yet bowed to the yoke of bondage, of the whip, before he knew the language of his masters to obey it quickly, of the fetters on his hands, the weights on his legs, the collar about his neck, of the raw flesh where the iron had torn the skin; and then of the dark wild night of his escape when he and three others, as luckless and as miserable, had run a raft into the sea, stripped off their shirts for a sail, and thrust their naked bodies together to keep them warm.

Such was the gray silt that came up to him that night from the deposits of his memory. The Tynwald, the Prince, the Duke, the guns, the music, the bonfires, were gone; bit by bit he pieced together the life he had lived in his youth, and at the thought of it, and that it was now over, he threw back his head and gave thanks where they were due.

At that moment he heard a tap at the windowpane, and turning about he saw a man's haggard face peering in at him from the darkness. Then he rose instantly, and threw open the door of the porch.

"Come in," he called.

The man entered.

He took one step into the house and stopped, seemed for a moment puzzled, dazed, sleepless, and then by a sudden impulse stepped quietly forward, pulled up the sleeve of his shirt and held out his arm. Around his wrist there was a circular abrasure where the loop of a fetter had worn away the skin, leaving the naked flesh raw and red.

He had been in irons.

With a word of welcome the Governor motioned the man to a seat. Some inarticulate sounds the man made and waved his hand.

He was a foreigner. What was his craft?

A tiny model of a full-rigged ship stood on the top of a corner cupboard. Adam pointed to it, and the man gave a quick nod of assent.

He was a seaman. Of what country?

"Shetlands?" asked the Governor.

The man shook his head.

"Sweden? Norway?—"

"Issland," said the man.

He was an Icelander.

Two rude portraits hung on the walls, one of a fair boy, the other of a woman in the early bloom of womanhood—Adam's young wife and first child. The Governor pointed to the boy, and the man shook his head.

He had no family.

The Governor pointed to the woman, and the man hesitated, seemed about to assent, and then, with the look of one who tries to banish an unwelcome thought, shook his head again.

He had no wife. What was his name?

The Governor took down from a shelf a Bible covered in green cloth, and opened at the writing on the fly-leaf between the Old and New Testaments. The writing ran:—"Adam Fairbrother, son of Jo: Fairbrother, and Mar: his wife, was born August the 11th, 1753, about 5 o'clock in the morning, half flood, wind at southwest, and christened August 18th." To this he pointed, then to himself, and finally to the stranger. An abrupt change came over the man's manner. He grew sullen and gave no sign. But his eyes wandered with a fierce eagerness to the table, where the remains of the Governor's supper were still lying.

Adam drew up a chair and motioned the stranger to sit and eat. The man ate with frightful voracity, the perspiration breaking out in beads over his face. Having eaten, he grew drowsy, fell to nodding where he sat, and in a moment of recovered consciousness pointed to the stuffed head of a horse that hung over the door. He wished to sleep in the stable.

The Governor lit a lantern and led the way to the stable loft. There the man stretched himself on the straw, and soon his long and measured breathing told that he slept.

Hardly had the Governor got back to the house when his boys, his men, and the maids returned from Ramsey. Very full they all were of the doings of the day, and Adam, who never asked that son or servant of his should abridge the flow of talk for his presence, sat with his face to the fire and smoked, dozed, dreamt or thought, and left his people to gossip on. What chance had brought the poor man to his door that night? An Icelander, dumb for all uses of speech, who had lain in the chains of some tyrant captain—a lone man, a seaman without wife or child in his own country, and a fugitive, a runaway, a hunted dog in this one! What angel of pleading had that very night been busy in his own memory with the story of his similar sufferings?

All at once his ear was arrested by what was being said behind him. The talk was of a sailor who had passed through the town, and of the blue-jackets who were in pursuit of him. He had stolen something. No, he had murdered somebody. Anyway there was a warrant for his arrest, for the High Bailiff had drawn it. An ill-looking fellow, but he would be caught yet, thank goodness, in God's good time.

The Governor twisted about, and asked what the sailor was like, and his boys answered him that he was a foreigneering sort of a man in a skin cap and long stockings, and bigger by half a head than Billy-by-Nite.

Just then there was the tramp of feet on the gravel outside and a loud rap at the door. Four men entered. They were the blue-jackets. The foreign seaman that they were in search of had been seen creeping up Ballure, and turning down towards Lague. Had he been there?

At that one of the boys, saying that his father had been at home all evening, turned to the Governor and repeated the question. But the good Adam had twisted back to the fire, and with the shank of his pipe hanging loosely from his lips, was now snoring heavily.

"His Excellency is asleep," said the blue-jacket.

No, no; that could not be, for he had been talking as they entered. "Father," cried the lad, and pushed him.

Then the Governor opened his eyes, and yawned heavily. The blue-jacket, cap in hand, told his story again, and the good Adam seemed to struggle hard in the effort to grasp it through the mists of sleep. At length he said, "What has the man done?"

"Deserted his ship, your Excellency."

"Nothing else—no crime?"

"Nothing else, your Excellency. Has he been here?"

"No;" said the Governor.

And at that the weary man shut his eyes again and began to breathe most audibly. But when the blue-jackets, taking counsel together, concluded that somewhere thereabouts the man must surely be, and decided to sleep the night in the stable loft, that they might scour the country in the morning, the Governor awoke suddenly, saying he had no beds to offer them, but they might sleep on the benches of the kitchen.

An hour later, when all Lague was asleep, Adam rose from his bed, took a dark lantern and went back to the stable loft, aroused the Icelander and motioned him to follow. They crossed the paved courtyard and came in front of the window. Adam pointed, and the man looked in. The four blue-jackets were lying on the benches drawn round the fire, and the dull glow of the slumbering peat was on their faces. They were asleep. At that sight the man's eyes flashed, his mouth set hard, the muscles of his cheeks contracted, and with a hoarse cry in his throat, he fumbled the haft of the seaman's knife that hung in his belt and made one step forward.

But Adam, laying hold of his arm, looked into his eyes steadfastly, and in the light of the lantern their wild glance fell before him. At the next instant the man was gone.

The night was now far spent. In the town the forts were silent, the streets quiet, the market place vacant, and on the hilltops the fires had smouldered down. By daybreak next morning the blue-jackets had gone back empty to Ramsey, and by sunrise the English brig had sailed out of the bay.

Two beautiful creeks lie to the south of Ramsey and north of Maughold Head. One is called Lague, the other Port-y-Vullin. On the shore of Port-y-Vullin there is a hut built of peat and thatched with broom—dark, damp, boggy and ruinous, a ditch where the tenant is allowed to sit rent free. The sun stood high when a woman, coming out of this place, found a man sleeping in a broken-ribbed boat that lay side down on the beach. She awakened him, and asked him into her hut. He rose to his feet and followed her. Last night he had been turned out of the best house in the island; this morning he was about to be received into the worst.

The woman was Liza Killey—the slut, the trollop, the trull, the slattern and drab of the island.

The man was Stephen Orry.

V: Little Sunlocks

One month only had then passed since the night of Stephen Orry's flight from Iceland, and the story of his fortunes in the meantime is quickly told. In shame of his brutal blow, as well as fear of his wife's threat, he had stowed away in the hold of an English ship that sailed the same night. Two days later famine had brought him out of his hiding place, and he had been compelled to work before the mast. In ten more days he had signed articles as able seaman at the first English port of call. Then had followed punishments for sloth, punishments for ignorance, and punishments for not knowing the high-flavored language of his boatswain. After that had come bickerings, threats, scowls, oaths, and open ruptures with this chief of petty tyrants, ending with the blow of a marlin-spike over the big Icelander's crown, and the little boatswain rolling headlong overboard. Then had followed twenty-eight days spent in irons, rivetted to the ship's side on the under deck, with bread and water diet every second day and nothing between. Finally, by the secret good fellowship of a shipmate with some bowels of compassion, escape had come after starvation, as starvation had come after slavery, and Stephen had swum ashore while his ship lay at anchor in Ramsey Bay.

What occurred thereafter at the house whereto he had drifted no one could rightly tell. He continued to live there with the trull who kept it. She had been the illegitimate child of an insolvent English debtor and the daughter of a neighboring vicar, had been ignored by her father, put out to nurse by her mother, bred in ignorance, reared in impurity, and had grown into a buxom hussy. By what arts, what hints, what appeals, what allurements, this trollop got possession of Stephen Orry it is not hard to guess. First, he was a hunted man, and only one who dare do anything dare open doors to him. Next, he was a foreigner, dumb for speech, and deaf for scandal, and therefore unable to learn more than his eyes could tell him of the woman who had given him shelter. Then the big Icelander was a handsome fellow; and the veriest drab that ever trailed a petticoat knows how to hide her slatternly habits while she is hankering after a fine-grown man. So the end of many conspiring circumstances was that after much gossip in corners, many jeers, and some tossings of female heads, the vicar of the parish, Parson Gell, called one day at the hut in Port-y-Vullin, and on the following Sunday morning, at church, little Robbie Christian, the clerk and sexton, read out the askings for the marriage of Liza Killey, spinster, of the parish of Maughold, and Stephen Orry, bachelor, out of Iceland.

What a wedding it was that came three weeks later! Liza wore a gay new gown that had been lent her by a neighbor, Bella Coobragh, a girl who had meant to be married in it herself the year before, but had not fully carried out her moral intention and had since borne a child. Wearing such borrowed plumes and a brazen smile of defiance, Liza strutted up to the Communion rail, looking impudently into the men's faces, and saucily into the women's—for the church was thronged with an odorous mob that kept up the jabbering of frogs at spawn—and Stephen Orry slouched after her in his blowzy garments with a downward, shame-faced, nervous look that his hulky manners could not conceal. Then what a wedding feast it was that followed! The little cabin in Port-y-Vullin reeked and smoked with men and women, and ran out on to the sand and pebbles of the beach, for the time of year was spring and the day was clear and warm. Liza's old lovers were there in troops. With a keg of rum over his shoulder Nary Crowe, the innkeeper, had come down from the "Hibernian" to give her joy, and Cleave Kinley, the butcher, had brought her up half a lamb from Ballaglass, and Matt Mylechreest, the net maker—a venal old skinflint—had charged his big snuff horn to the brim for the many noses of the guests. On the table, the form, the three-legged stool, the bed and the hearth, they sat together cheek by jowl their hats hung on the roof rafters, their plates perched on their knees.

And loud was their laughter and dubious their talk. Old Thurstan Coobragh led off on the advantages of marriage, saying it was middlin' plain that the gels nowadays must be wedded when they were babies in arms, for bye-childers were common, and a gel's father didn't care in a general way to look like a fool; but Nary Crowe saw no harm in a bit of sweetheartin', and Cleave Kinley said no, of course, not if a man wasn't puttin' notions into a gel's head, and Matt Mylechreest, for his part, thought the gels were amazin' like the ghosts, for they got into every skeleton closet about the house.

"But then," said Matt, "I'm an ould bachelor, as the sayin' is, and don't know nothin'."

"Ha, ha, ha! of course not," laughed the others; and then there was a taste of a toast to Liza's future in Nary's rum.

"Drop it," said Liza, as Nary, lifting his cup, leaned over to whisper.

"So I will, but it'll be into your ear, woman," said Nary. "So here's to the king that's comin'."

By this time Stephen had slipped out of the noisome place, and was rambling on the quiet shore alone, with head bent, cheeks ashy pale, eyes fixed, and his brawny hands thrust deep into his pockets. At last, through the dense fumes within the house, Bella Coobragh noted Stephen's absence, and "Where's your man?" she said to Liza, with a tantalizing light in her eyes.

"Maybe where yours is, Bella," said Liza, with a toss of the head; "near enough, perhaps, but not visible to the naked eye."

The effects of going to church on Liza Killey were what they often are of a woman of base nature. With a man to work for her she became more idle than before, and with nothing to fear from scandal more reckless and sluttish. Having hidden her nakedness in the gown of marriage, she lost the last rag of womanly shame.

The effects on Stephen Orry were the deepening of his sloth, his gloom and his helplessness. What purpose in life he ever had was paralyzed. On his first coming to the island he had sailed to the mackerel fishing in the boats of Kane Wade—a shrewd Manxman, who found the big, dumb Icelander a skilful fisherman. Now he neglected his work, lost self-reliance, and lay about for hours, neither thinking nor feeling, but with a look of sheer stupidity. And so the two sat together in their ditch, sinking day by day deeper and yet deeper into the mire of idleness, moroseness, and mutual loathing. Nevertheless, they had their cheerful hours together.

The "king" of Nary's toast soon came. A child was born —a bonny, sunny boy as ever yet drew breath; but Liza looked on it as a check to her freedom, a drain on her energy, something helpless and looking to her for succor. So the unnatural mother neglected it, and Stephen, who was reminded by its coming that Rachel had been about to give birth to a child, turned his heart from it and ignored it.

Thus three spirit-breaking years dragged on, and Stephen Orry grew woe-begone and stone-eyed. Of old he had been slothful and spiritless indeed, but not a base man. Now his whole nature was all but gone to the gutter. He had once been a truth-teller, but living with a woman who assumed that he must be a liar, he had ended by becoming one. He had no company save her company, for his slow wit had found it hard to learn the English tongue, and she alone could rightly follow him; he had no desires save the petty ones of daily food and drink; he had no purpose save the degrading purpose of defeating the nightly wanderings of his drunken wife. Thus without any human eye upon him in the dark way he was going, Stephen Orry had grown coarse and base.

But the end was not yet, of all this than was to be and know. One night, after spending the day on the sea with the lines for cod, the year deepening to winter, the air muggy and cold, he went away home, hungry, and wet and cold, leaving his mates at the door of the "Plough," where there was good company within and the cheer of a busy fire! Home! On reaching Port-y-Vullin he found the door open, the hearth cold, the floor in a puddle from the driving rain, not a bite or sup in the cupboard, and his wife lying drunk across the bed, with the child in its grimy blueness creeping and crying about her head.

It was the beginning of the end. Once again he fumbled the haft of his seaman's knife, and then by a quick impulse he plucked up the child in his arms.

"Now God be praised for your poor face," he said, and while he dried the child's pitiful eyes, the hot drops started to his own.

He lit the fire, he cooked a cod he had brought home with him, he ate himself and fed the little one. Then he sat before the hearth with the child at his breast, as any mother might do, for at length it had come to him to know that, if it was not to be lost and worse than orphaned, he must henceforth be father and mother both to it.

And when the little eyes, wet no longer, but laughing like sunshine into the big seared face above them struggled in vain with sleep, he wrapped the child in his ragged guernsey and put it to lie like a bundle where the fire could warm it. Then all being done he sat again, and leaning his elbows on his knees covered his ears with his hands, so that they might shut out the sound of the woman's heavy breathing.

It was on that night, for the first time since he fled from Iceland, that he saw the full depth of his offence. Offence? Crime it was, and that of the blackest; and in the terror of his loneliness he trembled at the thought that some day his horrible dumb secret would become known, that something would happen to tell it—that he was married already when he married the woman who lay behind him.

At that he saw how low he had fallen—from her who once had been so pure and true beside him, and had loved him and given up father, and home, and fame for him; to this trull, who now dragged him through the slush, and trod on him and hated him. Then the bitter thought came that what she had suffered for him who had given him everything, he could never repay by one kind word or look. Lost she was to him forever and ever, and parted from him by a yet wider gulf than eight hundred miles of sea. Such was the agony of his shame, and through it all the snore of the sleeping woman went like iron through his head, so that at last he wrapped his arms about it and sobbed out to the dead fire at his feet, "Rachel! Rachel! Rachel!"

All at once he became conscious that the heavy breathing had ceased, that the house was silent, that something had touched him on the shoulder, and that a gaunt shadow stood beside him. It was the woman, who at the sound of his voice had arisen from her drunken sleep, and now gasped,

"Who is Rachel?"

At that word his blood ran cold, and shivering in his clothes, he crouched lower at the hearth, neither answering her nor looking up.

Then with eyes of hate she cried again,

"Who is Rachel?"

But the only voice that answered her was the voice that rang within him—"I'm a lost man, God help me."

"Who is Rachel?" the woman cried once more, and the sound of that name from her lips, hardening it, brutalizing it, befouling it, was the most awful thing by which his soul had yet been shaken out of its stupor.

"Who is she, I say? Answer me," she cried in a raging voice; but he crouched there still, with his haggard face and misty eyes turned down.

Then she laid her hand on his shoulder and shook him, and cried bitterly.

"Who is she, this light o' love—this baggage?"

At that he stiffened himself up, shuddered from head to foot, flung her from him and answered in a terrible voice.

"Woman, she is my wife."

That word, like a thunderbolt, left a heavy silence behind it. Liza stood looking in terror at Stephen's face, unable to utter a cry.

But next day she went to Parson Gell and told him all. She got small comfort. Parson Gell had himself had two wives; the first had deserted him, and after an interval of six years, in which he had not heard from her, he had married the second. So to Liza he said,

"He may have sinned against the law, but what proof have you? None."

Then she went to the Deemster at Ramsey. It was Deemster Lace—a bachelor much given to secret gallantries.

She got as little cheer from this source, but yet she came away with one drop of solace fermenting in the bitterness of her heart.

"Tut, woman, it's more common than you think for. And where's the harm? Och! it's happened to some of the best that's going. Now, if he'd beaten you, or struck you"—and the good man raised both hands and shook his head.

Then the thought leapt to her mind that she herself could punish Stephen a hundredfold worse than any law of bishop or deemster. If she could she would not now put him away. He should live on with her, husband or no husband, and she with him, wife or no wife.

On her way home she called at the house of Kane Wade, sat down with old Bridget, shed some crocodile tears, vowed she daren't have tould it on no occount to no other morthal sowl, but would the heart of woman belave it? her man had a wife in his own counthry!

Bridget, who had herself had four husbands, lifted her hands in horror, and next day when Stephen Orry went down to the boats Kane Wade, who had newly turned Methodist, was there already, and told him—whittling a stick as he spoke—that the fishing was wonderful lean living gettin', and if he didn't shorten hands it would be goin' begging on the houses they'd all be, sarten sure.

Stephen took the hint in silence, and went off home. Liza saw him coming, watched him from the door, and studied his hard set face with a grim smile on her own.

Next day Stephen went off to Matt Mylechreest, the net maker, but Matt shook his head, saying the Manxmen had struck against foreign men all over the island, and would not work with them. The day after that Stephen tried Nary Crowe, the innkeeper, but Nary said of course it wasn't himself that was partic'lar, only his customers were gettin' nice extraordinary about a man's moral character.

As a last hope Stephen went up to Cleave Kinley, who had land, and asked for a croft of five acres that ran down to the beach of Port-y-Vullin.

"Nothing easier," said Kinley, "but I must have six pounds for it, beginning half-quarter day."

The rent was high, but Stephen agreed to it, and promised to go again the following day to seal his bargain. Stephen was prompt to his engagement, but Kinley had gone on the mountains after some sheep. Stephen waited, and four hours later Kinley returned, looking abashed but dogged and saying he must have good security or a year's rent down.

Stephen went back home with his head deep in his breast. Again the woman saw him coming, again she studied his face, and again she laughed in her heart.

"He will lift his hand to me," she thought, "and then we shall see."

But he seemed to read her purpose, and determined to defeat it. She might starve him, herself, and their child, but the revenge she had set her mind upon she should not have.

Yet to live with her and to contain himself at every brutal act or bestial word was more than he could trust himself to do, and he determined to fly away. Let it be anywhere—anywhere, if only out of the torture of her presence. One place was like another in Man, for go where he would to any corner of the island, there she would surely follow him.

Old Thurston Coobragh, of Ballacreggan, gave him work at draining a flooded meadow. It was slavery that no other Christian man would do, but for a month Stephen Orry worked up to his waist in water, and lived on barley bread and porridge. At the end of his job he had six and thirty shillings saved, and with this money in his pocket, and the child in his arms, he hurried down to the harbor at Ramsey, where an Irish packet lay ready to sail.

Could he have a passage to Ireland? Certainly he could, but where was his license?

Stephen Orry had never heard until then that before a man could leave the Isle of Man he must hold a license permitting him to do so.

"Go to the High Bailiff," said the captain of the packet; and to the High Bailiff Stephen Orry went.

"I come for a license to go away into Ireland," he said.

"Very good. But where is your wife?" said the High Bailiff. "Are you leaving her behind you to be a burden on the parish?"

At that Stephen's heart sank, for he saw that his toil had been wasted, and that his savings were worthless. Doomed he was for all his weary days to live with the woman who hated him. He was bound to her, he was leashed to her, and he must go begrimed and bedraggled to the dregs of life with her. So he went back home, and hid his money in a hole in the thatch of the roof, that the touch of it might vex his memory no more.

And then it flashed upon him that what he was now suffering from this woman was after all no more than the complement and counterpart of what Rachel had suffered from him in the years behind them. It was just—yes, it Was just—and because he was a man and Rachel a woman, it was less than he deserved. So thinking, he sat himself down in his misery with resignation if not content, vowing never to lift his hand to the woman, however tormented, and never to leave her, however tempted. And when one night after a storm an open boat came ashore, he took it and used it to fish with, and thus he lived, and thus he wore away his wretched days.

And yet he could never have borne his punishment but for the sweet solace of the child. It was the flower in his dungeon; the bird at its bars. Since that bad night, when his secret had burst from him, he had nursed it and cherished it, and done for it its many tender offices. Every day he had softened its oatcake in his broth; and lifted the barley out of his own bowl into the child's basin. In summer he had stripped off shoes and stockings to bathe the little one in the bay, and in winter he had wrapped the child in his jacket and gone bare-armed. It was now four years old and went everywhere with Stephen, astride on his broad back or perched on his high shoulders. He had christened it Michael, but because its long wavy hair grew to be of the color of the sun he called it, after the manner of his people, Sunlocks. And like the sun it was, in that hut in Port-y-Vullin, for when it awoke there was a glint of rosy light, and when it slept all was gloom.

He taught it to speak his native Icelandic tongue, and the woman, who found everything evil that Stephen did, found this a barrier between her and the child. It was only in his ignorance that he did it. But oh, strange destiny! that out of the father's ignorance was to shape the child's wisdom in the days that were to come!

And little Sunlocks was eyes and ears to Stephen, and hope to his crushed spirit and intelligence to his slow mind. At sight of the child the vacant look would die away from Stephen's face; at play with him Stephen's great hulking legs would run hither and thither in ready willingness; and at hearing his strange questions, his wondrous answers, his pretty clever sayings, Stephen's dense wit would seem to stand agape.

Oh, little Sunlocks—little Sunlocks—floating like the day-dawn into this lone man's prison house, how soon was your glad light to be overcast! For all at once it smote Stephen like a blow on the brain that though it was right that he should live with the woman, yet it was an awful thing that the child should continue to do so. Growing up in such an atmosphere, with such an example always present to his eyes, what would the child become? Soured, saddened, perhaps cunning, perhaps malicious; at least adopting himself, as his father had done before him, to the air he had to breathe. And thinking that little Sunlocks, now so sweet, so sunny, so artless, so innocent, must come to this, all the gall of Stephen Orry's fate rose to his throat again.

What could he do? Take little Sunlocks away? That was impossible, for he could not take himself away. Why had the child been born? Why had it not died? Would not the good God take it back to Himself even now, in all the sweetness of his childhood? No, no, no, not that either; and yet yes, yes, yes!

Stephen's poor slow brain struggled long with this thought, and at length a strange and solemn idea took hold of it: little Sunlocks must die, and he must kill him.

Stephen Orry did not wriggle with his conscience, or if he cozened it at all he made himself believe that it would not be sin but sacrifice to part with the thing he held dearest in all the world. Little Sunlocks was his life, but little Sunlocks must die! Better, better, better so!

And having thus determined, he went cautiously, and even cunningly, to work. When the little one had disappeared, he himself would never be suspected, for all the island would say he loved it too tenderly to do it a wrong, and he would tell everybody that he had taken it to some old body in the south who had wished to adopt a child. So, with Sunlocks laughing and crowing astride his shoulder, he called at Kane Wade's house on Ballure one day, and told Bridget how he should miss the little chap, for Sunlocks was going down to the Calf very soon, and would not come home again for a long time, perhaps not for many a year, perhaps not until he was a big slip of a lad, and, maybe—who can tell?—he would never come back at all.

Thus he laid his plans, but even when they were complete he could not bring himself to carry them through, until one day, going up from the beach to sell a basket of crabs and eels, he found Liza drinking at the "Hibernian."

How she came by the money was at first his surprise, for Nary Crowe had long abandoned her; and having bitter knowledge of the way she had once spent his earnings, he himself gave her nothing now. But suddenly a dark thought came, and he hurried home, thrust his hand into the thatch where he had hidden his savings, and found the place empty.

That was the day to do it, he thought; and he took little Sunlocks and washed his chubby face and combed his yellow hair, curling it over his own great undeft fingers, and put his best clothes on him—the white cotton pinafore and the red worsted cap, and the blue stockings freshly darned.

This he did that he might comfort the child for the last time, and also that he might remember him at his best.

And little Sunlocks, in high glee at such busy preparations, laughed much and chattered long, asking many questions.

"Where are we going, father? Out? Eh? Where?"

"We'll see, little Sunlocks; we'll see."

"But where? Church? What day is this?"

"The last, little Sunlocks; the last."

"Oh, I know—Sunday."

When all was ready, Stephen lifted the child to the old perch across his shoulders, and made for the shore. His boat was lying aground there; he pushed it adrift, lifted the child into it, and leapt after him. Then taking the oars, he pulled out for Maughold Head.

Little Sunlocks had never been out in the boat before, and everything was a wonder and delight to him.

"You said you would take me on the water some day. Didn't you, father?"

"Yes, little Sunlocks, yes."

It was evening, and the sun was sinking behind the land, very large and red in its setting.

"Do the sun fall down eve'y day, father?"

"It sets, little Sunlocks, it sets."

"What is sets?"

"Dies."

"Oh."

The waters lay asleep under the soft red glow, and over them the seafowl were sailing.

"Why are the white birds sc'eaming?"

"Maybe they're calling their young, little Sunlocks."

It was late spring, and on the headland the sheep were bleating.

"Look at the baby one—away, away up yonder. What's it doing there by itself on the 'ock, and c'ying, and c'ying, and c'ying?"

"Maybe it's lost, little Sunlocks."

"Then why doesn't somebody go and tell its father?"

And the innocent face was full of trouble.

The sun went down and the twilight deepened, the air grew chill, the waters black, and Stephen was still pulling round the head.

"Father, where does the night go when we are asleep?"

"To the other world, little Sunlocks."

"Oh, I know—heaven."

Stephen stripped off his guernsey and wrapped it about the child. His eyes shone brightly, his mouth was parched, but he did not flinch. All thoughts, save one thought, had faded from his view.

As he came by Port Mooar the moon rose, and about the same time the light appeared on Point of Ayre. A little later he saw the twinkle of lesser lights to the south. They were the lights of Laxey, where many happy children gladdened many happy firesides. He looked around. There was not a sail in sight, and not a sound came to his ears over the low murmur of the sea's gentle swell. "Now is the time," he thought. He put in his oars and the boat began to drift.

But no, he could not look into the child's eyes and do it. The little one would sleep soon and then it would be easier done. So he took him in his arms and wrapped him in a piece of sail-cloth.

"Shut your eyes and sleep, little Sunlocks."

"I'm not sleepy, I'm not."

Yet soon the little lids fell, opened again and fell once more, and then suddenly the child started up.

"But I haven't said my p'ayers."

"Say them now, little Sunlocks."

"Gentle Jesus, meek and mild, Look upon a little child, Guard me while in sleep I lie, Take me to Thy home on—on—"

"Would you like to go to heaven, little Sunlocks?"

"No."

"Why not?"

"I want to keep with—with—my fath——"

The little eyes were closed by this time, and the child was asleep on Stephen's knees. Now was the time—now—now. But no, it was harder now than ever.

The little face—so silent, so peaceful—how formidable it was! The little soft hand in his own big hard palm—how strong and terrible!

Stephen looked down at the child and his bowels yearned over it. It cost him a struggle not to kiss it; but no, that would only make the task harder.

Suddenly a new thought smote him. What had this child done that he should take its life? Who was he that he should rob it of what he could never give it again? By what right did he dare to come between this living soul and heaven? When did the Almighty God tell him what the after life of this babe was to be? Stephen trembled at the thought. It was like a voice from the skies calling on him to stop, and a hand reaching out of them to snatch the child from his grasp.

What he had intended to do was not to be! Heaven had set its face against it! Little Sunlocks was not to die! Little Sunlocks was to live! Thank God! Oh! Thank God!

But late that night a group of people standing at their doors on the beach at Port Lague saw a tall man in his shirt sleeves go by in the darkness, with a sleeping child in his arms. The man was Stephen Orry, and he was sobbing like a woman whose heart is broken. The child was little Sunlocks, and he was being carried back to his mother's home.

The people hailed Stephen and told him that a foreigner from a ship in the bay had been asking for him that evening. They had sent the man along to Port-y-Vullin.

Stephen hurried home with fear in his heart. In five minutes he was there, and then his life's blood ran cold. He found the house empty, except for his wife, and she lay outstretched on the floor. She was cold—she was dead; and in clay on the wall above her head, these words were written in the Icelandic tongue, "So is Patricksen avenged—signed S. Patricksen."

Avenged! Oh, powers of Heaven, that drive the petty passions of men like dust before you!

VI: The Little World of Boy and Girl

Three days later the bad lottery of Liza Killey's life and death was played out and done. On the morning of the fourth day, some time before the dawn, though the mists were rolling in front of it, Stephen Orry rose in his silent hut in Port-y-Vullin, lit a fire, cooked a hasty meal, wakened, washed, dressed and fed little Sunlocks, then nailed up the door from the outside, lifted the child to his shoulders, and turned his face towards the south. When he passed through Laxey the sun stood high, and the dust of the roads was being driven in their faces. It was long past noon when he came to Douglas, and at a little shop by the harbor-bridge he bought a penny worth of barley cake, gave half to Sunlocks, put the other half into his pocket, and pushed on with longer strides. The twilight was deepening when he reached Castletown, and there he inquired for the house of the Governor. It was pointed out to him, and through heavy iron gates, up a winding carriage-way lined with elms and bordered with daffodils, he made towards the only door he saw.

It was the main entrance to Government House, a low broad porch, with a bench on either side and a cross-barred door of knotted oak. Stephen

Orry paused before it, looked nervously around, and then knocked with his knuckles. He had walked six and twenty miles, carrying the child all the way. He was weary, footsore, hungry, and covered with dust. The child on his shoulder was begrimed and dirty, his little face smeared in streaks, his wavy hair loaded and unkempt. A footman in red and buff, powdered, starched, gartered and dainty, opened the door. Stephen Orry asked for the Governor. The footman looked out with surprise at the bedraggled man with the child, and asked who he was. Stephen told his name. The footman asked where he came from. Stephen answered. The footman asked what he came for. Stephen did not reply. Was it for meal? Stephen shook his head. Or money? Stephen said no. With another glance of surprise the footman shut the door, saying the Governor was at dinner.

Stephen Orry lowered the little one from his shoulder, sat on the bench in the porch, placed the child on his knee, and gave him the remainder of the barley cake. All the weary journey through he had been patient and cheerful, the brave little man, never once crying aloud at the pains of his long ride, never once whimpering at the dust that blinded him, or the heat that made him thirsty. Holding on at his father's cap, he had laughed and sung even with the channels still wet on his cheeks where the big drops had rolled from his eyes to his chin.

Little Sunlocks munched at his barley cake in silence, and in the gathering darkness Stephen watched him as he ate. All at once a silvery peal of child's laughter came from within the house, and little Sunlocks dropped the barley cake from his mouth to listen. Again it came; and the grimy face of little Sunlocks lightened to a smile, and that of Stephen Orry lowered and fell.

"Wouldn't you like to live in a house like this, little Sunlocks?"

"Yes—with my father."

Just then the dark door opened again, and the footman, with a taper in his hand, came out to light the lamp in the porch.

"What? Here still?" he said.

"I am; been waiting to see the Governor," Stephen Orry answered.

Then the footman went in, and told the Governor that a big man and a child were sitting in the porch, talking some foreign lingo together, and refusing to go away without seeing His Excellency.

"Bring them in," said the Governor.

Adam Fairbrother was at the dinner table, enveloped in tobacco clouds. His wife, Ruth, had drawn her chair aside that she might knit. Stephen Orry entered slowly with little Sunlocks by the hand.

"This is the person, your Excellency," said the footman.

"Come in, Stephen Orry," said the Governor.

Stephen Orry's face softened at that word of welcome. The footman's dropped and he disappeared.

Then Stephen told his errand. "I shall come to have give you something," he said, trying to speak in English.

Adam's wife raised her eyes and glanced over him. Adam himself laid down his pipe and held out his hand towards Sunlocks. But Stephen held the child back a moment and spoke again.

"It's all I shall have got to give," he said.

"What is it?" said Adam.

"The child," said Stephen, and passed little Sunlocks to Adam's outstretched hand.

At that Adam's wife dropped her knitting to her lap, but Stephen, seeing nothing of the amazement written in her face, went on in his broken words to tell them all—of his wife's life, her death, his own sore temptation, and the voice out of heaven that had called to him. And then with a moistened eye and a glance at Sunlocks, and in a lowered tone as if fearing the child might hear, he spoke of what he meant to do now—of how he would go back to the herrings, and maybe to sea, or perhaps down into the mines, but never again to Port-y-Vullin. And, because a lone man was no company for a child, and could not take a little one with him if he would, he had come to it at last that he must needs part with little Sunlocks, lending him, or maybe giving him, to someone he could trust.

"And so," he said, huskily, "I shall say to me often and often, 'The Governor is a good man and kind to me long, long ago, and I shall give little Sunlocks to him.'"

He had dropped his head into his breast as he spoke, and being now finished he stood fumbling his scraggy goatskin cap.

Then Adam's wife, who had listened in mute surprise, drew herself up, took a long breath, looked first at Stephen, then at Adam, then back at Stephen, and said in a bated whisper—

"Well! Did any living soul ever hear the like in this island before?"

Not rightly understanding what this might mean, poor Stephen looked back at her, in his weak, dazed way, but made her no answer.

"Children might be scarce," she said, and gave a little angry toss of her head.

Still the meaning of what she said had not worked its way through Stephen's slow wit, and he mumbled in his poor blundering fashion:

"He is all I have, ma'am."

"Lord-a-massy, man," she cried, sharply, "but we might have every child in the parish at your price."

Stephen's fingers now clutched at his cap, his parted lips quivered, and again he floundered out, stammering like an idiot:

"But I love him, ma'am, more nor all the world."

"Then I'll thank you to keep him," she answered, hotly; and after that there was dead silence for a moment.

In all Stephen's reckoning never once had he counted on this—that after he had brought himself to that sore pass, at which he could part with Sunlocks and turn his back on him, never more to be cheered by his sunny face and merry tongue, never again to be wakened by him in the morning, never to listen for his gentle breathing in the night, never to feed him and wash him, never to carry him shoulder high, any human creature could say no to him from thought of the little food he would eat or the little trouble he would ask.

Stephen stood a moment, with his poor, bewildered, stupefied face hung down and the great lumps surging hot in his throat, and then, without a word more, he stretched out his hand towards the child.

But all this time Adam had looked on with swimming eyes, and now he drew little Sunlocks yet closer between his knees, and said, quietly:

"Ruth, we are going to keep the little one. Two faggots will burn better than one, and this sweet boy will be company for our little Greeba."

"Adam," she cried, "haven't you children enough of your own, but you must needs take other folks'?"

"Ruth," he answered, "I have six sons, and if they had been twelve, perhaps, I should have been better pleased, so they had all been as strong and hearty; and I have one daughter, and if there had been two it would have suited me as well."

Now the rumor of Stephen Orry's former marriage, which Liza had so zealously set afoot, had reached Government House by way of Lague, and while Stephen had spoken Adam had remembered the story, and thinking of it he had smoothed the head of little Sunlocks with a yet tenderer hand. But Adam's wife, recalling it now, said warmly:

"Maybe you think it wise to bring up your daughter with the merry-begot of any ragabash that comes prowling along from goodness knows where."

"Ruth," said Adam, as quietly as before, "we are going to keep the little one," and at that his wife rose and walked out of the room.

The look of bewilderment had not yet been driven from Stephen Orry's face by the expression of joy that had followed it, and now he stood glancing from Adam to the door and from the door to Adam, as much as to say that if his coming had brought strife he was ready to go. But the Governor waved his hand, as though following his thought and dismissing it. Then lifting the child to his knee, he asked his name, whereupon the little man himself answered promptly that his name was Sunlocks.

"Michael," said Stephen Orry; "but I call him Sunlocks."

"Michael Sunlocks—a good name too. And what is his age?"

"Four years."

"Just the age of my own darling," said the Governor; and setting the child on his feet he rang the bell and said, "Bring little Greeba here."

A minute later a little brown-haired lassie with ruddy cheeks and laughing lips and sparkling brown eyes, came racing into the room. She was in her nightgown, ready for bed, her feet were bare, and under one arm she carried a doll.

"Come here, Greeba veg," said the Governor, and he brought the children face to face, and then stood aside to watch them.

They regarded each other for a moment with the solemn aloofness that only children know, twisting and curling aside, eyeing one another furtively, neither of them seeming so much as to see the other, yet neither seeing anything or anybody else. This little freak of child manners ran its course, and then Sunlocks, never heeding his dusty pinafore, or the little maiden's white nightgown, but glancing down at her bare feet, and seeming to remember that when his own were shoeless someone carried him, stepped up to her, put his arms about her, and with lordly, masculine superiority of strength proceeded to lift her bodily in his arms. The attempt was a disastrous failure, and in another moment the two were rolling over each other on the floor; a result that provoked the little maiden's direst wrath and the blank astonishment of little Sunlocks.

But before the tear-drop of vexation was yet dry on Greeba's face, or the silent bewilderment had gone from the face of Sunlocks, she was holding out her doll in a sidelong way in his direction, as much as to say he might look at it if he liked, only he must not think that she was asking him; and he, nothing loth for her fierce reception of his gallant tender, was devouring the strange sight with eyes full of awe.

Then followed some short inarticulate chirps, and the doll was passed to Sunlocks, who turned the strange thing—such as eyes of his had never beheld—over and over and over, while the little woman brought out from dark corners of the room, and from curious recesses unknown save to her own hands and knees, a slate with a pencil and sponge tied to it by a string, a picture-book whereof the binding hung loose, some bits of ribbon, red and blue, and finally three tiny cups and saucers with all the accompanying wonder of cream jug and teapot. In three minutes more two little bodies were sitting on their haunches, two little tongues were cackling and gobbling, the room was rippling over with a merry twitter, the strange serious air was gone from the little faces, the little man and the little maid were far away already in the little world of childhood, and all the universe beside was gone, and lost, and forgotten.

Stephen Orry had looked down from his great height at the encounter on the floor, and his dull, slow eyes had filled, for in some way that he could not follow there had come to him at that sweet sight the same deep yearning that had pained him in the boat. And seeing how little Sunlocks was rapt, Stephen struggled hard with himself and said, turning to the Governor:

"Now's the time for me to slip away."

Then they left the room, unnoticed of the busy people on the floor.

Two hours later, after little Sunlocks, having first missed his father, his life's friend and only companion, had cried a little, and soon ceased to cry out of joy of his new comradeship, and had then nestled down his sunny head on the pillow where little Greeba's curly poll also lay, with the doll between him and her, and some marbles in his hand to comfort his heart, Stephen Orry, unable to drag himself away, was tramping the dark roads about the house. He went off at length, and was seen no more at Castletown for many years thereafter.

Now this adoption of Little Sunlocks into the family of the Governor was an incident that produced many effects, and the first of them was the serious estrangement of Adam and his wife. Never had two persons of temperaments so opposed lived so long in outward harmony. Her face, like some mountain country, revealed its before and after. Its spring must have been keen and eager, its summer was overcast, and its winter would be cold and frozen. She was not a Manxwoman, but came of a family of French refugees, settled as advocates on the north of the island. Always vain of show, she had married in her early womanhood, when Adam Fairbrother was newly returned from Barbary, and his adventures abroad were the common gossip and speculation. But Adam had disappointed her ambition at the outset by dropping into the ruts of a homely life. Only once had she lifted him out of them, and that was after twenty years, when the whim and wisdom of the Duke had led him to visit Lague; and then her impatience, her importunity, her fuss and flurry, and appeals in the name of their children, had made him Governor. Meantime, she had borne him six sons in rapid succession during the first ten years of marriage, and after an interval of ten other years she had borne a daughter. Four and twenty years the good man had lived at peace with her, drained of his serenity by her restlessness, and of his unselfishness by her self-seeking. With a wise contempt of trifles, he had kept peace over little things, and the island had long amused itself about his pliant disposition, but now that for the first time he proved unyielding, the island said he was wrong. To adopt a child against the wish of his wife, to take into his family the waif of a drunken woman and an idle foreigner, was an act of stubborn injustice and folly. But Adam held to his purpose, and Michael Sunlocks remained at Government House.

A year passed, and Sunlocks was transformed. No one would have recognized him. The day his father brought him he had been pale under the dust that covered him; he had been timid and had trembled, and his eyes had looked startled, as though he had already been beaten and cuffed and scolded. A child, like a flower, takes the color of the air it breathes, and Sunlocks had not been too young to feel the grimy cold of the atmosphere in which he had been born. But now he had opened like a rose to the sun, and his cheeks were ruddy and his eyes were bright. He had become plump and round and sturdy, and his hair had curled around his head and grown yet warmer of hue, like the plumes of a bird in the love season. And, like a bird, he chirruped the long day through, skipping and tripping and laughing and singing all over the house, idolized by some, beloved by many, caressed by all, even winning upon Mrs. Fairbrother herself, who, whatever her objection to his presence, had not yet steeled herself against his sweetness.

Another year passed, and the children grew together—Sunlocks and Greeba, boy and girl, brother and sister—in the innocent communion of healthy childhood, with their little whims, their little ways, their little tiffs, and with the little sorrows that overcast existence. And Sunlocks picked up his English words as fast as he picked shells on the beach, gathering them on his tongue as he gathered the shells into his pinafore, dropping them and picking them up again.

Yet another year went by, and then over the luminous innocence of the children there crept the strange trail of sex, revealing already their little differences of character, and showing what they were to be in days to come— the little maid, quick, urgent, impulsive and vain; the little man, quiet, unselfish and patient, but liable to outbursts of temper.

A fourth year passed, and then the little people were parted. The Duchess came from London, where her nights had no repose and her days no freshness, to get back a little of the color of the sun into her pallid cheeks, and driving one day from Mount Murray to Government House she lit on Greeba in the road outside Castletown. It was summer, and the little maid of eight, bright as the sunlight that glistened on her head, her cheeks all pink and white, her eyes sparkling under her dark lashes, her brown hair rippling behind her, her frock tucked up in fishwife fashion, her legs bare, and her white linen sunbonnet swinging in her hand, was chasing a butterfly amid the yellow-tipped gorse that grew by the roadside. That vision of beauty and health awakened a memory of less charm and freshness. The Duchess remembered a little maiden of her own who was also eight years old, dainty and pretty, but pale and sickly, peaked up in a chill stone house in London, playing alone with bows and ribbons, talking to herself, and having no companion except a fidgety French governess, who was wrinkled and had lost some of her teeth.

A few days later the Duchess came again to Government House, bought a gay new hat for Greeba, and proposed that the little maid should go home with her as playfellow for her only child. Adam promptly said "No" to her proposal, with what emphasis his courtesy would permit, urging that Greeba, being so much younger than her brothers, was like an only child in the family, and that she was in any case an only daughter. But Adam's wife, thinking she saw her opportunity, found many reasons why Greeba should be allowed to go. For would it be right to cross the wish of so great a lady?—and one, too, who was in a sense their mistress also. And then who could say what the Duchess might do for the child some day?—and in any event wasn't it a chance for which any body else in the island would give both his ears to have his daughter brought up in London, and at the great house of the Duke of Athol?

The end of it was that Adam yielded to his wife now, as he had often yielded before. "But I'll sadly miss my little lassie," he said, "and I much misdoubt but I'll repent me of letting her go."

Yet, while Adam shook his head and looked troubled, the little maid herself was in an ecstasy of delight.

"And would you really like to go to London, Greeba ven?"

"But should I see the carriages, and the ladies on horseback, and the shops, and the little girls in velvet—should I, eh?"

"Maybe so, my ven, maybe so."

"Oh!"

The little maid gave one glance at the infinite splendor of her new bow and feather, and her dark eyes sparkled, while the eyes of her father filled.

"But not Michael Sunlocks, you know, Greeba ven; no, nor mother, nor father."

At that word there was a pretty downward curve of the little lip; but life had no real sorrow for one with such a hat and such a prospect, and the next instant the bright eyes leapt again to the leaping heart.

"Then run away, Greeba ven—run."

The little maiden took her father at his word, though it was but sadly spoken, and bounded off in chase of Michael Sunlocks, that she might tell him the great news. She found him by the old wooden bridge of the Silver Burn near the Malew Church.

Michael Sunlocks had lately struck up a fast friendship with the carrier, old crazy Chalse A'Killey, who sometimes lent him his donkey for a ride.

Bareheaded, barefooted, with breeches rolled up above the knees, his shoes and stockings swung about his neck, and his wavy yellow hair rough and tangled, Michael Sunlocks was now seated bareback on this donkey, tugging the rope that served it for curb and snaffle, and persuading it, by help of a blackthorn stick, to cross the river to the meadow opposite. And it was just when the donkey, a creature of becoming meekness and most venerable age, was reflecting on these arguments, and contemplating the water at his shoes with a pensive eye, that Greeba, radiant in the happiness of her marvellous hat, came skipping on to the bridge.

In a moment she blurted out her news between many gusts of breath, and Michael Sunlocks, pausing from his labors, sat on his docile beast and looked up at her with great wonder in his wide blue eyes.

"And I shall see the carriages, and the ladies on horseback, and the ships, and the waxworks, and the wild beasts."

The eyes of Sunlocks grew hazy and wet, but the little maiden rattled on, cocking her eye down as she spoke at her reflection in the smooth river, for it took a world of glances to grow familiar with the marvel that sat on her head.

"And I shall wear velvet frocks, and have new hats often and lots of goodies and things; and—and didn't I always say a good fairy would come for me some day?"

"What are you talking of, you silly?" said Michael Sunlocks.

"I'm not a silly, and I'm going away, and you are not; and I'll have girls to play with now, not boys—there!"

Michael Sunlocks could bear no more. His eyes overflowed, but his cheeks reddened, and he said—

"What do I care, you stupid? You can go if you like," and then down came his stick with a sounding thwack on the donkey's flank.

Now startled out of all composure by such sudden and summary address, the beast threw up his hinder legs and ducked down his head, and tumbled his rider into the water. Michael Sunlocks scrambled to his feet, all dripping wet, but with eyes aflame and his little lips set hard, and then laid hold of the rope bridle and tugged with one hand, while with the stick in the other he cudgelled the donkey until he had forced it to cross the river.

While this tough work was going forward, Greeba, who had shrieked at Michael's fall, stood trembling with clasped hands on the bridge, and, when all was over, the little man turned to her with high disdain, and said, after a mighty toss of his glistening wet head:

"Did you think I was drowned, you silly? Why don't you go, if you're going?"

Not all the splendor of bow and feather could help the little maiden to withstand indifference like this, so her lip fell, and she said:

"Well, you needn't say so, if you are glad I'm going."

And Sunlocks answered, "Who says I'm glad? Not that I say I'm not, neither," he added quickly, leaping astride his beast again.

Whereupon Greeba said, "If you had been going away I should have cried," and then, to save herself from bursting out in his very face, she turned about quickly and fled.

"But I'm not such a silly, I'm not," Michael Sunlocks shouted after her, and down came another thwack on the donkey, and away he sped across the meadow. But before he had ridden far he drew rein and twisted about, and now his blue eyes were swimming once more.

"Greeba," he called, and his little voice broke, but no answer came back to him.

"Greeba," he called again, more loudly, but Greeba did not stop.

"Greeba!" he shouted with all his strength. "Greeba! Greeba!"

But the little maid had gone, and there was no response. The bees were humming in the gold of the gorse, and the fireflies were buzzing about the donkey's ears, while the mountains were fading away into a dim wet haze.

Half an hour later the carriage of the Duchess drove out through the iron gates of Government House, and the little maiden seated in it by the side of the stately lady, was crying in a voice of childlike grief—

"Sunlocks! Sunlocks! Little Sunlocks!"

The advantage which the Governor's wife proposed to herself in parting with her daughter she never gained, and one of the secret ends of her life was thereby not only disappointed but defeated; for while the Duchess did nothing for Greeba, the girl's absence from home led Adam to do the more for Michael Sunlocks. Deprived of his immediate object of affection, his own little maiden, Adam lavished his love on the stranger whom chance had brought to his door; being first prompted thereto by the thought, which came only when it was too late, that in sending Greeba away to be company to some other child he had left poor little Sunlocks at home to be sole company to himself.

But Michael Sunlocks soon won for himself the caresses that were once due merely to pity of his loneliness, and Adam's heart went out to him with the strong affection of a father. He throve, he grew—a tall, lithe, round-limbed lad, with a smack of the man in his speech and ways, and all the strong beauty of a vigorous woman in his face. Year followed year, his school days came and went, he became more and yet more the Governor's quick right hand, his pen and his memory, even his judgment, and the staff he leaned on. It was "Michael Sunlocks" here, and "Michael Sunlocks" there, and "Michael Sunlocks will see to that," and "You may safely leave it to Michael Sunlocks;" and meantime the comely and winsome lad, with man's sturdy independence of spirit, but a woman's yearning for love, having long found where this account lay in the house of Governor Fairbrother, clung to that good man with more than the affection, because less than the confidence, of a son, and like a son he stood to him.

Now, for one who found this relation sweet and beautiful, there were many who found it false and unjust, implying an unnatural preference of a father for a stranger before his own children; and foremost among those who took this unfavorable view were Mrs. Fairbrother and her sons. She blamed her husband, and they blamed Michael Sunlocks.

The six sons of Adam Fairbrother had grown into six rude men, all big, lusty fellows, rough and hungry, seared and scarred like the land they lived on, but differing much at many points. Asher, the eldest, three-and-thirty when Sunlocks was fifteen, was fair, with gray eyes, flabby face, and no chin to speak of, good-hearted, but unstable as water. He was for letting the old man and the lad alone. "Aisy, man, aisy, what's the odds?" he would say, in his drawling way of speaking. But Ross, the second son, and Stean, the third, both cruel and hot-blooded men, reproached Asher with not objecting from the first, for "Och," they would say, "one of these fine days the ship will be wrecked and scuttled before yer very eyes, and not a pound of cargo left at her; and all along of that cursed young imp that's after sniffin' and sniffin' abaft of the ould man,"—a figure of speech which meant that Adam would will his belongings to Michael Sunlocks. And at that conjecture, Thurstan, the fourth son, a black-bearded fellow in top boots, always red-eyed with much drinking, but strong of will and the ruler of his brethren, would say, "Aw, well, let the little beachcomber keep his weather eye liftin';" and Jacob, the fifth son, sandy as a fox, and as sly and watchful, and John, the youngest, known as Gentleman Johnny, out of tribute to his love of dress, would shake their heads together, and hint that they would yet find a way to cook the goose of any smooth-faced hypocrite shamming Abraham.

Many a device they tried to get Michael Sunlocks turned away. They brought bad stories of his father, Stephen Orry, now a name of terror to good people from north to south of the island, a secret trader running between the revenue cutters in the ports and the smugglers outside, perhaps a wrecker haunting the rough channels of the Calf, an outlaw growing rich by crime, and, maybe, by blood. The evil rumors made no impression on old Adam, but they produced a powerful effect where no effect had been expected. Bit by it, as his heart went out to the Governor, there grew upon Michael Sunlocks a deep loathing of the very name and thought of his father. The memory of his father was now a thing of the mind, not the affections; and the chain of the two emotions, love for his foster father and dread of his natural one, slowly but surely tightened about him, so that his strongest hope was that he might never again set eyes on Stephen Orry. By this weakness he fell at length into the hands of the six Fairbrothers, and led the way to a total rupture of old Adam's family.

One day when Michael Sunlocks was eighteen years old a man came to him from Kirk Maughold with an air of wondrous mystery. It was Nary Crowe, the innkeeper, now bald, bottled-nosed, and in a bad state of preservation. His story, intended for Michael's ear alone, was that Stephen Orry, flying from the officers of the revenue cutters, was on the point of leaving the island forever, and must see his son before going. If the son would not go to the father, then the father must come to the son. The meeting place proposed was a schooner lying outside the Calf Sound, and the hour midnight of the day following.

It was as base a plot as the heart of an enemy ever concocted, for the schooner was a smuggler, and the men of the revenue cutter were in hiding under the Black Head to watch her movements. The lad, in fear of his father, fell into the trap, and was taken prisoner on suspicion in a gig making for the ship. He confessed all to the Governor, and Nary Crowe was arrested. To save his own carcase Nary gave up his employers. They were Ross and Stean Fairbrother, and Ross and Stean being questioned pointed to their brothers Jacob and Gentleman Johnny as the instigators of the scheme.

When the revelation was complete, and the Governor saw that all but his whole family was implicated, and that the stain on his house was so black that the island would ever remember it against him, his placid spirit forsook him and his wrath knew no bounds. But the evil was not ended there, for Mrs. Fairbrother took sides with her sons, and straightway vowed to live no longer under the same roof with an unnatural father, who found water thicker than blood.

At that Adam was shaken to his depths. The taunt passed him by, but the threat touched him sorely.

"It would be but a poor business," he said, "to part now after so many years of life together, with seven children that should be as bonds between us, in our age and looking to a longer parting."

But Mrs. Fairbrother was resolved to go with her sons, and never again to darken her husband's doors.

"You have been a true wife to me and led a good life," said Adam, "and have holpen me through many troubles, and we have had cheerful hours together despite some crosses."

But Mrs. Fairbrother was not to be pacified.

"Then let us not part in anger," said Adam, "and though I will not do your bidding, and send away the lad—no, nor let him go of himself, now that for sake of peace he asks it—yet to show you that I mean no wrong by my own flesh and blood, this is what I will do: I have my few hundreds for my office, but all I hold that I can call my own is Lague. Take it—it shall be yours for your lifetime, and our sons' and their sister's after you."

At these terms the bad bargain was concluded, and Mrs. Fairbrother went away to Lague, leaving Adam with Michael Sunlocks at Government House.

And the old man, being now alone with the lad, though his heart never wavered or rued the price he had paid for him, often turned yearningly towards thoughts of his daughter Greeba, so that at length he said, speaking of her as the child he had parted from, "I can live no longer without my little lass, and will go and fetch her."

Then he wrote to the Duchess at her house in London, and a few days afterwards he followed his letter.

He had been a week gone when Michael Sunlocks, having now the Governor's routine work to do, was sent for out of the north of the island to see to the light on the Point of Ayre, where there was then no lighthouse, but only a flase stuck out from a pole at the end of a sandstone jetty, a poor proxy, involving much risk to ships. Two days he was away, and returning home he slept a night at Douglas, rising at sunrise to make the last stage of his journey to Castletown. He was riding Goldie, the Governor's little roan; the season was spring, and the morning, fresh from its long draught of dew, was sweet and beautiful. But Michael Sunlocks rode heavily along, for he was troubled by many misgivings. He was asking himself for the hundredth time whether it was right of him, and a true man's part, to suffer himself to stand between Adam Fairbrother and his family. The sad breach being made, all that he could do to heal it was to take himself away, whether Adam favored that course or not. And he had concluded that, painful as the remedy would be, yet he must needs take it, and that very speedily, when he came up to the gate of Government House, and turned Goldie down the path to the left that led to the stables.

He had not gone far when over the lowing of the cattle in the byres, and the steady munching of the sheep on the other side of the hedge, and through the smell of the early grass there came to him the sweetest sounds he had ever heard, and some of the queerest and craziest. Without knowing what he did, or why he did it, but taking himself at his first impulse, he drew rein, and Goldie came to a stand on the mossgrown pathway. Then he knew that two were talking together a little in front of him, but partly hidden by a turn of the path and the thick trammon that bordered it. Rising in his stirrups he could see one of them, and it was his old friend, Chalse A'Killey, the carrier, a shambling figure in a guernsey and blue seaman's cap, with tousled hair and a simple vacant face, and lagging lower lip, but eyes of a strange brightness.

And "Aw, yes," Chalse was saying, "he's a big lump of a boy grown, and no pride at all, at all, and a fine English tongue at him, and clever extraordinary. Him and me's same as brothers, and he was mortal fond to ride my ould donkey when he was a slip of a lad. Aw, yes, him and me's middlin' well acquent."

Then some linnets that were hiding in the trammon began to twitter, and what was said next Michael Sunlocks did not catch, but only heard the voice that answered old Chalse, and that seemed to make the music of the birds sound harsh.

"'What like is he?' Is it like it is?" old Chalse said again. "Aw, straight as the backbone of a herrin' and tall and strong; and as for a face, maybe there's not a man in the island to hold a candle to him. Och, no, nor a woman neither—saving yourself, maybe. And aw, now, the sweet and tidy ye're looking this morning, anyway: as fresh as the dewdrop, my chree."

Goldie grew restless, began to paw the path, and twist his round flanks into the leaves of the trammon, and at the next instant Michael Sunlocks was aware that there was a flutter in front of him, and a soft tread on the silent moss, and before he could catch back the lost consciousness of that moment, a light and slender figure shot out with a rhythm of gentle movement, and stood in all its grace and lovely sweetness two paces beyond the head of his horse.

"Greeba!" thought Michael Sunlocks; and sure enough it was she, in the first bloom of her womanhood, with gleams of her child face haunting her still and making her woman's face luminous, with the dark eyes softened and the dimpled cheeks smoothed out. She was bareheaded, and the dark fall of her hair was broken over her ears by eddies of wavy curls. Her dress was very light and loose, and it left the proud lift of her throat bare, as well as the tower of her round neck, and a hint of the full swell of her bosom.

In a moment Michael Sunlocks dropped from the saddle, and held out his hand to Greeba, afraid to look into her face as yet, and she put out her hand to him and blushed: both frightened more than glad. He tried to speak, but never a word would come, and he felt his cheeks burn red. But her eyes were shy of his, and nothing she saw but the shadow of Michael's tall form above her and a glint of the uncovered shower of fair hair that had made him Sunlocks. She turned her eyes aside a moment, then quickly recovered herself and laughed a little, partly to hide her own confusion and partly in joy at the sight of his, and all this time he held her hand, arrested by a sudden gladness, such as comes with the first sunshine of spring and the scent of the year's first violet.

There was then the harsh scrape on the path of old Chalse A'Killey's heavy feet going off, and, the spell being broken, Greeba was the first to speak.

"You were glad when I went away—are you sorry that I have come back again?"

But his breath was gone and he could not answer, so he only laughed, and pulled the reins of the horse over its head and walked before it by Greeba's side as she turned towards the stable. In the cowhouse the kine were lowing, over the half-door a calf held out his red and white head and munched and munched, on the wall a peacock was strutting, and across the paved yard the two walked together, Greeba and Michael Sunlocks, softly, without words, with quick glances and quicker blushes.

Adam Fairbrother saw them from a window of the house, and he said within himself, "Now God grant that this may be the end of all partings between them and me." That chanced to be the day before Good Friday, and it was only three days afterwards that Adam sent for Michael Sunlocks to see him in his room.

Sunlocks obeyed, and found a strange man with the Governor. The stranger was of more than middle age, rough of dress, bearded, tanned, of long flaxen hair, an ungainly but colossal creature. When they came face to face, the face of Michael Sunlocks fell, and that of the man lightened visibly.

"This is your son, Stephen Orry," said old Adam, in a voice that trembled and broke. "And this is your father, Michael Sunlocks."

Then Stephen Orry, with a depth of languor in his slow gray eyes, made one step towards Michael Sunlocks, and half opened his arms as if to embrace him. But a pitiful look of shame crossed his face at that moment, and his arms fell again. At the same instant Michael Sunlocks, growing very pale and dizzy, drew slightly back, and they stood apart, with Adam between them.

"He has come for you to go away into his own country," Adam said, falteringly.

It was Easter Day, nineteen years after Stephen Orry had fled from Iceland.

VII: The Vow of Stephen Orry

Stephen Orry's story was soon told. He desired that his son, being now of an age that suited it, should go to the Latin school at Reykjavik, to study there under old Bishop Petersen, a good man whom all Icelanders venerated, and he himself had known from his childhood up. He could bear the expense of it, and saying so he hung his head a little. An Irish brig, hailing from Belfast, and bound for Reykjavik, was to put in at Ramsey on the Saturday following. By that brig he wished his son to sail. He should be back at the little house in Port-y-Vullin between this and then, and he desired to see his son there, having something of consequence to say to him. That was all. Fumbling his cap, the great creature shambled out, and was gone before the others were aware.

Then Michael Sunlocks declared stoutly that come what might he would not go. Why should he? Who was this man that he should command his obedience? His father? Then what, as a father, had he done for him? Abandoned him to the charity of others. What was he? One whom he had thought of with shame, hoping never to set eyes on his face. And now, this man, this father, this thing of shame, would have him sacrifice all that was near and dear to him, and leave behind the only one who had been, indeed, his father, and the only place that had been, in truth, his home. But no, that base thing he should not do. And, saying this, Michael Sunlocks tossed his head proudly, though there was a great gulp in his throat and his shrill voice had risen to a cry.

And to all this rush of protest old Adam, who had first stared out at the window with a look of sheer bewilderment, and then sat before the fire to smoke, trying to smile though his mouth would not bend, and to say something more though there seemed nothing to say, answered only in a thick under-breath, "He is your father, my lad, he is your father."

Hearing this again and again repeated, even after he had fenced it with many answers, Michael Sunlocks suddenly bethought himself of all that had so lately occurred, and the idea came to him in the whirl of his stunned senses that perhaps the Governor wished him to go, now that they could part without offence or reproach on either side. At that bad thought his face fell, and though little given to woman's ways he had almost flung himself at old Adam's feet to pray of him not to send him away whatever happened, when all at once he remembered his vow of the morning. What had come over him since he made that vow, that he was trying to draw back now? He thought of Greeba, of the Governor, and again of Greeba. Had the coming of Greeba altered all? Was it because Greeba was back home that he wished to stay? Was it for that the Governor wished him to go, needing him now no more? He did not know, he could not think; only the hot flames rose to his cheeks and the hot tears to his eyes, and he tossed his head again mighty proudly, and said as stoutly as ever, "Very well—very well—I'll go—since you wish it."

Now old Adam saw but too plainly what mad strife was in the lad's heart to be wroth with him for all the ingratitude of his thought, so, his wrinkled face working hard with many passions—sorrow and tenderness, yearning for the lad and desire to keep him, pity for the father robbed of the love of his son, who felt an open shame of him—the good man twisted about from the fire and said, "Listen, and you shall hear what your father has done for you."

And then, with a brave show of composure, though many a time his old face twitched and his voice faltered, and under his bleared spectacles his eyes blinked, he told Michael Sunlocks the story of his infancy—how his father, a rude man, little used to ways of tenderness, had nursed him when his mother, being drunken and without natural feelings, had neglected him; how his father had tried to carry him away and failed for want of the license allowing them to go; how at length, in dread of what might come to the child, yet loving him fondly, he had concluded to kill him, and had taken him out to sea in the boat to do it, but could not compass it from terror of the voice that seemed to speak within him, and from pity of the child's own art-less prattle; and, last of all, how his father had brought him there to that house, not abandoning him to the charity of others, but yielding him up re-luctantly, and as one who gave away in solemn trust the sole thing he held dear in all the world.

And pleading in this way for Stephen Orry, poor old Adam was tearing at his own heart woefully, little wishing that his words would prevail, yet urging them the more for the secret hope that, in spite of all, Michael Sun-locks, like the brave lad he was, would after all refuse to go. But Michael, who had listened impatiently at first, tramping the room to and fro, paused presently, and his eyes began to fill and his hands to tremble. So that when Adam, having ended, said, "Now, will you not go to Iceland?" thinking in his heart that the lad would fling his arms about him and cry, "No, no, never, never," and he himself would then answer, "My boy, my boy, you shall stay here, you shall stay here," Michael Sunlocks, his heart swelling and his eyes glistening with a great new pride and tenderness, said softly, "Yes, yes—for a father like that I would cross the world."

Adam Fairbrother said not a word more. He blew out the candle that shone on his face, sat down before the fire, and through three hours thereaf-ter smoked in silence.

The next day, being Monday, Greeba was sent on to Lague, that her mother and brothers might see her after her long absence from the island. She was to stay there until the Monday following, that she might be at Ram-sey to bid good-bye to Michael Sunlocks on the eve of his departure for Iceland.

Three days more Michael spent at Government House, and on the morning of Friday, being fully ready and his leather trunk gone on before in care of Chalse A'Killey, who would suffer no one else to carry it, he was mounted for his journey on the little roan Goldie when up came the Governor astride his cob.

"I'll just set you as far as Ballasalla," he said, jauntily, and they rode away together.

All the week through since their sad talk on Easter Day old Adam had affected a wondrous cheerfulness, and now he laughed mightily as they rode along, and winked his gray eyes knowingly like a happy child's, until sometimes from one cause or other the big drops came into them. The morning was fresh and sweet, with the earth full of gladness and the air of song, though Michael Sunlocks was little touched by its beauty and thought it the heaviest he had yet seen. But Adam told how the spring was toward, and the lambs in fold, and the heifers thriving, and how the April rain would bring potatoes down to sixpence a kishen, and fetch up the grass in such a crop that the old island would rise—why not? ha, ha, ha!—to the opulence and position of a State.

But, rattle on as he would, he could neither banish the heavy looks of Michael Sunlocks nor make light the weary heart he bore himself. So he began to rally the lad, and say how little he would have thought of a trip to Iceland in his old days at Guinea; that it was only a hop, skip and a jump after all, and, bless his old soul, if he wouldn't cut across some day to see him between Tynwald and Midsummer—and many a true word was said in jest.

Soon they came by Rushen Abbey at Ballasalla, and then old Adam could hold back no longer what he had come to say.

"You'll see your father before you sail," he said, "and I'm thinking he'll give you a better reason for going than he has given to me; but, if not, and Bishop Petersen and the Latin School is all his end and intention, remember our good Manx saying that 'learning is fine clothes to the rich man, and riches to the poor one.' And that minds me," he said, plunging deep into his pocket, "of another good Manx saying, that 'there are just two bad pays— pay beforehand and no pay at all;' so to save you from both, who have earned yourself neither, put you this old paper into your fob—and God bless ye!"

So saying, he thrust into the lad's hand a roll of fifty Manx pound notes, and then seemed about to whip away. But Michel Sunlocks had him by the sleeve before he could turn his horse's head.

"Bless me yourself," the lad said.

And then Adam Fairbrother, with all his poor bankrupt whimseys gone from his upturned face, now streaming wet, and with his white hair gently lifted by the soft morning breeze, rose in the saddle and laid his hand on Michael's drooping head and blessed him. And so they parted, not soon to meet again, or until many a strange chance had befallen both.

It was on the morning of the day following that Michael Sunlocks rode into Port-y-Vullin. If he could have remembered how he had left it, as an infant in his father's arms, perhaps the task he had set himself would have been an easier one. He was trying to crush down his shame, and it was very hard to do. He was thinking that go where he would he must henceforth bear his father's name.

Stephen Orry was waiting for him, having been there three days, not living in the little hut, but washing it, cleaning it, drying it, airing it, and kindling fires in it, that by such close labor of half a week it might be worthy that his son should cross its threshold for half an hour. He had never slept in it since he had nailed up the door after the death of Liza Killey, and as an unblessed place it had been safe from the intrusion of others.

He saw Michael Sunlocks riding up, and raised his cap to him as he alighted, saying, "Sir" to him, and bowing as he did so. There were deep scars on his face and head, his hands were scratched and discolored, his cheeks were furrowed with wrinkles, and about his whole person there was a strong odor as of tobacco, tar, and bilge water.

"I shall not have ought to ask you here, sir," he said, in his broken English.

"Call me Michael," the lad answered, and then they went into the hut.

The place was not much more cheerful than of old, but still dark, damp and ruinous; and Michael Sunlocks, at the thought that he himself had been born there, and that his mother had lived her shameful life and died her dishonored death there, found the gall again in his throat.

"I have something that I shall have to say to you," said Stephen Orry, "but I cannot well speak English. Not all the years through I never shall have learn it." And then, as if by a sudden thought, he spoke six words in his native Icelandic, and glanced quickly into the face of Michael Sunlocks.

At the next instant the great rude fellow was crying like a child. He had seen that Michael understood him. And Michael, on his part, seemed at the sound of those words to find something melt at his heart, something fall from his eyes, something rise to his throat.

"Call me Michael," he said once more. "I am your son;" and then they talked together, Stephen Orry in the Icelandic, Michael Sunlocks in English.

"I've not been a good father to you, Michael, never coming to see you all these years. But I wanted you to grow up a better man than your father before you. A man may be bad, but he doesn't like his son to feel ashamed of him. And I was afraid to see it in your face, Michael. That's why I stayed away. But many a time I felt hungry after my little lad, that I loved so dear and nursed so long, like any mother might. And hearing of him sometimes, and how well he looked, and how tall he grew, maybe I didn't think the less about him for not coming down upon him to shame him."

"Stop, father, stop," said Michael Sunlocks.

"My son," said Stephen Orry, "you are going back to your father's country. It's nineteen years since he left it, and he hadn't lived a good life there. You'll meet many a one your father knew, and, maybe, some your father did wrong by. He can't undo the bad work now. There's a sort of wrong-doing there's no mending once it's done, and that's the sort his was. It was against a woman. Some people seem to be sent into this world to be punished for the sins of others. Women are mostly that way, though there are those that are not; but she was one of them. It'll be made up to them in the other world; and if she has gone there she has taken some of my sins along with her own—if she had any, and I never heard tell of any. But if she is in this world still, perhaps it can be partly made up to her here. Only it is not for me to do it, seeing what has happened since. Michael, that's why you are going to my country now."

"Tell me everything," said Michael.

Then Stephen Orry, his deep voice breaking and his gray eyes burning with the slow fire that had lain nineteen years asleep at the bottom of them, told his son the story of his life—of Rachel and of her father and her father's curse, of what she had given up and suffered for him, and of how he had repaid her with neglect, with his mother's contempt, and with his own blow. Then of her threat and his flight and his coming to that island; of his meeting with Liza, of his base marriage with the woman and the evil days they spent together; of their child's birth and his own awful resolve in his wretchedness and despair; and then of the woman's death, wherein the Almighty God had surely turned to mercy what was meant for vengeance. All this he told and more than this, sparing himself not at all. And Michael listened with a bewildered sense of fear and shame, and love and sorrow, that may not be described, growing hot and cold by turns, rising from his seat and sinking back again, looking about the walls with a chill terror, as the scenes they had witnessed seemed to come back to them before his eyes, feeling at one moment a great horror of the man before him, and at the next a great pity, and then clutching his father's huge hands in his own nervous fingers.

"Now you know all," said Stephen Orry, "and why it is not for me to go back to her. There is another woman between us, God forgive me, and dead though she is, that woman will be there forever. But she, who is yonder, in my own country, if she is living, is my wife. And heaven pity her, she is where I left her—down, down, down among the dregs of life. She has no one to protect and none to help her. She is deserted for her father's sake, and despised for mine. Michael, will you go to her?"

The sudden question recalled the lad from a painful reverie. He had been thinking of his own position, and that even his father's name, which an hour ago he had been ashamed to bear, was not his own to claim. But Stephen Orry had never once thought of this, or that the dead woman who stood between him and Rachel also stood between Rachel and her son.

"Promise me, promise me," he cried, seeing one thing only—that Michael was his son, that his son was as himself, and that the woman who was dead had been as a curse to both of them.

But Michael Sunlocks made him no answer.

"I've gone from bad to worse—I know that, Michael. I've done in cold blood what I'd have trembled at when she was by me. Maybe I was thinking sometimes of my boy even then, and saying to myself how some day he'd go back for me to my own country, when I had made the money to send him."

Michael trembled visibly.

"And how he'd look for her, and find her, and save her, if she was alive. And if she wasn't—if she was dead, poor girl, with all her troubles over, how he'd look for the child that was to come when I left her—my child, and hers—and find it where it would surely be, in want and dirt and misery, and then save it for its mother's sake and mine. Michael, will you go?"

But still Michael Sunlocks made him no answer.

"It's fourteen years since God spared your life to me; just fourteen years to-night, Michael. I remembered it, and that's why we are here now. When I brought you back in my arms she was there at my feet, lying dead, who had been my rod and punishment. Then I vowed, as I should answer to the Lord at the last day, that if I could not go back, you should."

Michael covered his face with hands.

"My son, my son—Michael, my little Sunlocks, I want to keep my vow. Will you go?"

"Yes, yes," cried Michael, rising suddenly. His doubt and pride and shame were gone. He felt only a great tenderness now for the big rude man, who had sinned deeply and suffered much and found that all he could do alone would avail him nothing.

"Father, where is she?"

"I left her at Reykjavik, but I don't know where she is now."

"No matter, I will hunt the world over until I find her, and when I have found her I will be as a son to her, and she shall be as a mother to me."

"My boy, my boy," cried Stephen.

"If she should die, and we should never meet, I will hunt the world over until I find her child, and when I have found it I will be as a brother to it for my father's sake."

"My son, my son," cried Stephen. And in the exultation of that moment, when he tried to speak but no words would come, and only his rugged cheeks glistened and his red eyes shone, it seemed to Stephen Orry that the burden of twenty heavy years had been lifted away.

VIII: The Going of Sunlocks

It was then past noon. The Irish brig was in the harbor taking in Manx cloth and potatoes, a few cattle and a drove of sheep. At the flow of the tide it was to go out into the bay and anchor there, waiting for the mails, and at nine o'clock it was to sail. In the meantime Michael was to arrange for his passage, and at half-past eight he was to meet his father on the quay.

But he had also to see Greeba, and that was not easy to do. The family at Lague had heard the great news of his going, and had secretly rejoiced at it, but they refused to see him there, even for the shortest leave-taking at the longest parting. And at the bare mention of the bargain that Greeba had made with him, to bid him farewell on the eve of his departure, all the Fairbrothers were up in arms. So he had been sorely put to it to devise a means of meeting Greeba, if he could do so without drawing suspicion down on her; for come what might of risk or danger to himself he meant to see her again before ever he set foot on the ship. The expedient he could not hit on did not long elude a woman's wit, and Greeba found the way by which they were to meet.

A few of last year's heifers were grazing on Barrule and at nightfall somebody went up for them and brought them home. She would go that night, and return by the glen, so that at the bridge by the turn of the river and the low road to Lague, where it was quiet enough sometimes, she could meet anybody about dusk and nobody be the wiser. She contrived a means to tell Michael of this, and he was prompt to her appointment.

The day had been fair but close, with a sky that hung low, and with not a breath of wind, and in the evening when the mist came down from the mountain a fog came up from the sea, so that the air was empty and every noise went through it as if it had been a speaking-trumpet. Standing alone on the bridge under the quiet elms, Michael could hear the rattle of chains and the whistling of horns, and by that he knew that the brig had dropped anchor in the bay. But he strained his ears for other sounds, and they came at last; the thud of the many feet of the heifers, the flapping of their tails, the cattle-call in a girl's clear voice, and the swish of a twig that she carried in her hand.

Greeba came along behind the cattle, swinging her body to a jaunty gait, her whole person radiant with health and happiness, her long gown, close at the back and loose over her bosom, showing well her tall lithe form and firm bearing. She wore no bonnet, but a white silk handkerchief was tied about her head, half covering her mouth, and leaving visible in the twilight only the tip of her nose, a curl of her hair, and her bright dark eyes, with their long bright lashes. She was singing to herself as she came up to the bridge, with an unconcerned and unconscious air. At sight of Michael she made a start and a little nervous cry, so that he thought, poor lad, not knowing the ways of women, that for all the pains she had been at to fetch him she had somehow not expected him to be there.

She looked him over from head to foot, and her eyes gleamed from the white kerchief.

"So you are going, after all," she said, and her voice seemed to him the sweetest music he had ever heard. "I never believed you would," she added.

"Why not?" he asked.

"Oh, I don't know," she said, and laughed a little. "But I suppose there are girls enough in Iceland," and then she laughed outright. "Only they can't be of much account up there."

"But I've heard they are very fine girls," he answered; "and it's a fine country, too."

She tossed her head and laughed and swung her switch.

"Fine country! The idea! Fine company, fine people and a good time. That's what a girl wants if she's worth anything."

"Then I suppose you will go back to London some day," he said.

"That doesn't follow," she answered. "There's father, you see; and, oh, what a pity he can't live at Lague!"

"Do you like it so much?" he said.

"Like it?" she said, her eyes full of laughter. "Six big hungry brothers coming home three times a day and eating up everything in the house—it's delightful!"

She seemed to him magnificently beautiful.

"I dare say they'll spoil you before I come back," he said, "or somebody else will."

She gave him a deliberate glance from her dark eyes, and then threw back her head and laughed. He could see the heaving of her breast. She laughed again—a fresh, merry laugh—and then he tried to laugh too, thinking of the foolish thing he had said.

"But if there are plenty of girls up there," she said, slyly glancing under her long lashes, "and they're so very wonderful, maybe you'll be getting married before you come home again?"

"Maybe so," he said quietly, and looked vacantly aside.

There was a pause. Then a sharp snap or two broke the silence and recalled him to the maiden by his side. She was only breaking up the twig she had carried.

There was another pause, in which he could hear the rippling of the river and the leaping of a fish. The heifers were munching the grass by the roadside a little ahead.

"I must go now," she said, coldly, "or they'll be out seeking me."

"I'll walk with you as far as Lague—it's dark," he said.

"No, no, you must not!" she cried, and fumbling the loose fold about her throat she turned to go.

But he laid hold of her arm.

"Why not?" he asked.

"Only think of my brothers. Your very life would be in danger."

"If all six of them were ranged across the other end of this bridge, and you had to walk the rest of the road alone, I would go through them," he said.

She saw the high lift of his neck and she smiled proudly. Then they walked on some distance. He was gazing at her in silence. There was a conscious delight of her beauty in the swing of her step and the untamed glance of her eyes.

"Since the country is so fine I suppose you'll stay a long while there?" she said in her sweetest tone.

"No longer than I must," he answered.

"Why not?"

"I don't know."

"But why not?" she said again, looking at him sideways with a gleam of a smile.

He did not answer, and she laughed merrily.

"What a girl you are for laughing," he said. "It may be very laughable to you that I'm going away——"

"But isn't it to you? Eh?" she said, as fast as a flash of quicksilver.

He had no answer, so he tried to laugh also, and to take her hand at the same time. She was too quick for him, and swung half a pace aside. They were then at the gate of Lague, where long years before Stephen Orry first saw the light through the elms. A late rook was still cawing overhead; the heifers had gone on towards the courtyard.

"You must go now, so good-bye," she said, softly.

"Greeba," he said.

"Well? Only speak lower," she whispered, coming closer. He could feel the warm glow of her body.

"Do you think, now, if I should be a long time away—years it may be, perhaps many years—we should ever forget each other, we two?"

"Forget? No, not to say forget, you know," she answered.

"But should we remember?"

"Remember? You silly, silly boy, if we should not forget how ever could we fail to remember?"

"Don't laugh at me, Greeba; and promise me one thing," and then he whispered in her ear.

She sprang away and laughed once more, and started to run down the path. But in three strides he had her again.

"That will not do for me, Greeba," he said breathing fast. "Promise me that you will wait for me."

"Well," she said softly, her dark eyes full of merriment, "I'll promise that while you are away no one else shall spoil me. There! Good-bye!"

She was tearing herself out of his hands.

"First give me a token," he said.

Daffodils lined the path, though in the dusk he could not see them. But she knew they were there, and stopped and plucked two, blew upon both, gave one to him, and put the other into the folds at her bosom.

"Good-bye! Good-bye!" she said in an under-breath.

"Good-bye!" he answered.

She ran a few steps, but he could not let her go yet, and in an instant he sprang abreast of her. He threw one arm about her waist and the other about her neck, tipped up her chin, and kissed her on the lips. A gurgling laugh came up to him.

"Remember!" he whispered over the upturned face in the white kerchief.

At the next instant he was gone. Then, standing under the dark elms alone, she heard the porch door opening, a heavy foot treading on the gravel, and a deep voice saying: "Here are the heifers home, but where's the little lass?"

It was her eldest brother, Asher, and she walked up to him and said quite calmly:—

"Oh! what a bad hasp that gate has—it takes such a time to open and close."

Michael Sunlocks reached the harbor at the time appointed. As he crossed the quay some fishermen were lounging there with pipes between their teeth. A few of them came up to him to bid him Godspeed in their queer way.

Stephen Orry was standing apart by the head of the harbor steps, and at the bottom of them his boat, a yawl, was lying moored. They got into it and Stephen sculled out of the harbor. It was still very thick over the town, but they could see the lights of the Irish brig in the bay. Outside the pier the air was fresher, and there was something of a swell on the water.

"The fog is lifting," said Stephen Orry. "There'll be a taste of a breeze before long."

He seemed as if he had something to say but did not know how to begin. His eye caught the light on Point of Ayre.

"When are they to build the lighthouse?" he asked.

"After the spring tides," said Michael.

They were about midway between the pier and the brig when Stephen rested his scull under his arm and drew something from one of his pockets.

"This is the money," he said, and he held out a bag towards Michael Sunlocks.

"No," said Michael, and he drew quickly back.

There was a moment's silence, and then Michael added, more softly:—

"I mean, father, that I have enough already. Mr. Fairbrother gave me some. It was fifty pounds."

Stephen Orry turned his head aside and looked over the dark water. Then he said:—

"I suppose that was so that you wouldn't need to touch money same as mine."

Michael's heart smote him. "Father," he said, "how much is it?"

"A matter of two hundred pounds," said Stephen.

"How long has it taken you to earn—to get it?"

"Fourteen years."

"And have you been saving it up for me?"

"Ay."

"To take me to Iceland?"

"Ay."

"How much more have you?"

"Not a great deal."

"But how much?"

"I don't know—scarcely."

"Have you any more?"

Stephen made no answer.

"Have you any more, father?"

"No."

Michael Sunlocks felt his face flush deep in the darkness.

"Father," he said, and his voice broke, "we are parting, you and I, and we may not meet again soon; indeed, we may never meet again. I have made you a solemn promise. Will you not make me one?"

"What is it, sir?"

"That you will never, never try to get more by the same means."

"There'll be no occasion now."

"But will you promise me?"

"Ay."

"Then give me the money."

Stephen handed the bag to Michael.

"It's fourteen years of your life, is it not?"

"So to say."

"And now it's mine, isn't it, to do as I like with it?"

"No, sir, but to do as you ought with it."

"Then I ought to give it back to you. Come, take it. But wait! Remember your promise, father. Don't forget—I've bought every hour of your life that's left."

Father and son parted at the ship's side in silence, with throats too full for speech. Many small boats, pulled by men and boys, were lying about the ladder, and there was a good deal of shouting and swearing and noisy laughter there. Some of the boatmen recognized Michael Sunlocks and bellowed their farewells to him. "Dy banne Jee oo?"

"God bless you! God bless you!" they said, and then among themselves they seemed to discuss the reason of his going. "Well, what's it saying?" said one; "the crab that lies always in its hole is never fat."

The air had freshened, the swell of the sea had risen, and a sharp breeze was coming up from the east. Stephen Orry stepped to his mast, hoisted mainsail and mizzen, and stood out to sea. He had scarcely got clear away when he heard the brig weigh its anchor and beat down behind him. They were making towards the Point of Ayre, and when they came by the light Stephen Orry slackened off, and watched the ship go by him in the darkness.

He felt as if that were the last he was ever to see of his son in this world. And he loved him with all the strength of his great broken, bleeding heart. At that thought the outcast man laid his head in his hands, where he sat crouching at the tiller, and sobbed. There were none to hear him there; he was alone; and the low moan of the sea came up through the night from where his son was sailing away.

How long he sat there he did not know; he was thinking of his past, of his bad life in Iceland, and his long expiation in the Isle of Man. In the multitude of his sensations it seemed impossible to his dazed mind to know which of these two had been the worst, or the most foolish. Together they had left him a wreck. In the one he had thrown away the wife who loved him, in the other he had given up the son whom he loved. What was left to him? Nothing. He was a waif, despised and downtrodden. He thought of what might have happened to him if the chances of life had been different, and in that first hour of his last bereavement all the softening influences of nineteen years, the uplooking and upworking, and the struggle towards atonement, were as much gone from him as if they had never been. Then he thought of the money, and told himself that it was not now that he lost his son for the first time; he had lost him fourteen years ago, when he parted with him to the Governor. Since then their relations had been reversed. His little Sunlocks was his little Sunlocks no longer. He felt humiliated, he felt hardened, and by a strange impulse, whereof he understood but little, he cursed in his heart his sufferings more than his sins. They had been useless, they had been wasted, and he had been a fool not to live for himself. But in that moment, when the devil seemed to make havoc of good and evil together, God himself was not doing nothing.

Stephen Orry was drifting with the tide, when all at once he became conscious of the lapping of the water on stones near at hand, and of a bright light shed over the sea. Then he saw that he had drifted close to low ground off the Point of Ayre. He bore hard aport and beat out to sea again. Very soon the white water way was behind him; nothing was visible save the dark hull of the vessel going off towards the north, and nothing audible save the cry of a few gulls that were fishing by the light of the flare. It had been the work of three minutes only, but in that time one vivid impression had fixed itself on Stephen's preoccupied mind. The end of the old sandstone pier had been battered down by a recent storm; the box that once held the light had gone down with it, a pole had been thrust out at an angle from the overthrown stones, and from the end of this pole the light swung by a rope. No idea connected itself with this impression, which lay low down behind other thoughts.

The fog had lifted, but the night was still very dark. Not a star was shining and no moon appeared. Yet Stephen's eye—the eye of a sailor accustomed to the darkness of the sea at night—could descry something that lay to the north. The Irish brig had disappeared. Yes, her sails were now gone. But out at sea—far out, half a league away—what black thing was there? Oh, it must be a cloud, that was all; and no doubt a storm was brewing. Yet no, it was looming larger and larger, and coming nearer and nearer. It was a sail. Stephen could see it plainly enough now against the leaden sky. It was a schooner; he could make out its two masts, with fore and aft sails. It was an Irish schooner; he could recognize its heavy hull and hollowed cutwater. It was tacking against wind and tide from the northeast; it was a Dublin schooner and was homeward bound from Iceland, having called at Whitehaven and now putting in at Ramsey.

Stephen Orry had been in the act of putting about when this object caught his eye, but now a strange thing occurred. All at once his late troubles lay back in his mind, and by a sort of unconscious mechanical habit of intellect he began to put familiar ideas together. This schooner that was coming from Iceland would be heavy laden; it would have whalebone, and eider down, and tallow. If it ran ashore and was wrecked some of this cargo might be taken by some one and sold for something to a French smuggler that lay outside the Chicken Rocks. That flare on the Point of Ayre was the only sea-light on this north coast of the island, and it hung by a rope from a pole. The land lay low about it, there was not a house on that sandy headland for miles on miles, and the night was very dark. All this came up to Stephen Orry's mind by no effort of will; he looked out of his dull eyes on the dull stretch of sea and sky, and the thoughts were there of themselves.

What power outside himself was at work with him? Did anything tell him that this was the great moment of his life—that his destiny hung on it—that the ordeal he had just gone through was as nothing to the ordeal that was yet before him? As he sat in his boat, peering into the darkness at the black shadow on the horizon, did any voice whisper in his ear:—"Stephen Orry, on the ship that is yonder there is one who hates you and has sworn to slay you? He is coming, he is coming, and he is flesh of your flesh? He is your own son, and Rachel's!"

Stephen Orry fetched his boat away to leeward, and in two minutes more he had run down the light on the Point of Ayre. The light fell into the water, and then all was dark. Stephen Orry steered on over the freshening sea, and then slackened off to wait and watch. All this time he had been sitting at the tiller, never having risen from it since he stepped his mast by the side of the brig. Now he got on his feet to shorten sail, for the wind was rising and he meant to drift by the mizzen. As he rose something fell with a clank to the boat's bottom from his lap or his pocket. It was the bag of money, which Michael Sunlocks had returned to him.

Stephen Orry stooped down to pick it up; and having it in his hand he dropped back like a man who has been dealt a blow. Then, indeed, a voice rang in his ears; he could hear it over the wind that was rising, the plash of the white breakers on the beach, and the low boom of the deep sea outside. "Remember your promise, father. I have bought every hour of your life that's left."

His heart seemed to stand still. He looked around in the dull agony of a fear that was new to him, turning his eyes first to the headland that showed faintly against the heavy sky, then to the pier where no light now shone, and then to the black cloud of sail that grew larger every instant. One minute passed—two—three. Meantime the black cloud of sail was drawing closer. There were living men aboard of that ship, and they were running on to their death. Yes, they were men, living men—men with wives who loved them, and children who climbed to their knees. But perhaps they had seen the light when it went down. Merciful heaven, let it be so—let it be so!

The soul of Stephen Orry was awake at length. Another minute he waited, another and another, and the black shadow came yet nearer. At her next tack the ship would run on the land, and already Stephen seemed to hear the grating of her keel over the rocks below the beach. He could bear the suspense no longer, and hoisted sail to bear down on the schooner and warn her. But the wind was strong by this time, driving hard off the sea and the tide ran faster than before.

Stephen Orry was now some thirty fathoms space to the north of the broken pier, and at that point the current from across Maughold Head meets the current going across the Mull of Galloway. Laboring in the heavy sea he could barely fetch about, but when at last he got head out to sea he began to drive down on the schooner at a furious speed. He tried to run close along by her on the weather side, but before he came within a hundred fathoms he saw that he was in the full race of the north current, and strong seaman though he was, he could not get near. Then he shouted, but the wind carried away his voice. He shouted again, but the schooner gave no sign. In the darkness the dark vessel scudded past him.

He was now like a man possessed. Fetching about he ran in before the wind, thinking to pass the schooner on her tack. He passed her indeed: he was shot far beyond her, shouting as he went, but again his voice was drowned in the roar of the sea. He was almost atop of the breakers now, yet he fetched about once more, and shouted again and again and again. But the ship came on and on, and no one heard the wild voice, that rang out between the dark sea and sky like the cry of a strong swimmer in his last agony.

IX: The Coming of Jason

The schooner was the Peveril, homeward bound from Reykjavik to Dublin, with a hundred tons of tallow, fifty bales of eider down, and fifty casks of cods' and sharks' oil. Leaving the Icelandic capital on the morning after Easter Day, with a fair wind, for the outer Hebrides, she had run through the North Channel by the middle of the week, and put into Whitehaven on the Friday. Next day she had stood out over the Irish Sea for the Isle of Man, intending to lie off at Ramsey for contraband rum. Her skipper and mate were both Englishmen, and her crew were all Irish, except two, a Manxman and an Icelander.

The Manxman was a grizzled old sea dog, who had followed the Manx fisheries twenty years and smuggling twenty other years, and then turned seaman before the mast. His name was Davy Kerruish, and when folks asked if the Methodists had got hold of him that he had turned honest in his old age, he closed one rheumy yellow eye very knowingly, tipped one black thumb over his shoulder to where the Government cutters lay anchored outside, and said in a touching voice, "Aw, well, boy, I'm thinking Castle Rushen isn't no place for a poor man when he's gettin' anyways ould."

The Icelander was a brawny young fellow of about twenty, of great height and big muscles, and with long red hair. He had shipped at Reykjavik, in the room of an Irishman, who had died on the outward trip and been buried at sea off the Engy Island. He was not a favorite among the crew; he spoke English well, but was no good at a yarn in the forecastle; he was silent, gloomy, not too fond of work, and often the butt of his mates in many a lumbering jest that he did not seem to see. He had signed on the wharf on the morning the schooner sailed, and the only kit he had brought aboard was a rush cage with a canary. He hung the bird in the darkness above his bunk, and it was all but his sole companion. Now and again he spoke to old Kerruish, but hardly ever to the other men.

"Och, sollum and quiet lek," old Davy would say at the galley fire, "but none so simple at all. Aw no, no, no; and wonderful cur'ous about my own bit of an island yander."

The Icelander was Jason, son of Rachel and Stephen Orry.

There is not a more treacherous channel around the British Isles than that which lies between St. Bee's Head, the Mull of Galloway, and the Point of Ayre, for four strong currents meet and fight in that neck of the Irish Sea. With a stiff breeze on the port quarter, the Peveril had been driven due west from Whitehaven on the heavy current from the Solway Frith, until she had met the current from the North Channel and then she had tacked down towards the Isle of Man. It was dark by that time, and the skipper had leaned over the starboard gangway until he had sighted the light on the Point of Ayre. Even then he had been puzzled, for the light was feebler than he remembered it.

"Can you make it out, Davy?" he had said to old Kerruish.

"Aw, yes, though, and plain as plain," said Davy; and then the skipper had gone below.

The Manxman had been at the helm, and Jason, who was on the same watch, had sidled up to him at intervals and held a conversation with him in snatches, of which this is the sum and substance.

"Is it the Isle of Man on the starboard bow, Davy?"

"I darn' say no, boy."

"Lived there long, Davy?"

"Aw, thirty years afore you were born, maybe."

"Ever known any of my countrymen on the island?"

"Just one, boy; just one."

"What was he?"

"A big chap, six feet six, if an inch, and ter'ble strong; and a fist at him like a sledge; and a rough enough divil, too, and ye darn' spit afore him; but quiet for all—aw, yes, wonderful quiet."

"Who was he, Davy?"

"A widda man these teens of years."

"But what was his name?"

"Paul?—no! Peter?—no! Chut, bless ye, it's clane gone at me; but it's one of the lot in the ould Book, any way."

"Was it Stephen?"

"By gough, yes, and a middlin' good guess too."

"Stephen what?"

"Stephen—shoo! it's gone at me again! What's that they're callin' the ould King that's going buryin' down Laxey way?"

"Orry?"

"Stephen Orry it is, for sure. Then it's like you knew him, boy?"

"No—that is—no, no."

"No relations?"

"No. But is he still alive?"

"Aw, yes, though. It's unknownced to me that he's dead, anyway."

"Where is he living now?"

"Down Port Erin way, by the Sound, some place."

"Davy, do we put into the harbor at Ramsey?"

"Aw, divil a chance of that, boy, with sperrits comin' over the side quiet-like in the night, you know, eighteen-pence a gallon, and as much as you can drink for nothin'."

"How far do we lie outside?"

"Maybe a biscuit throw or two. We never useder lie farther, boy."

"That's nothing, Davy."

After that the watch had been changed, and then a strange thing had happened. The day had been heavy and cold, with a sky that hung low over the sea, and a mist that reduced the visible globe to a circle of fifty fathoms wide. As the night had closed in the mist had lifted, and the wind had risen and some sheets of water had come combing over the weather quarter. The men had been turned up to stow the yards and bring the schooner to the wind, and when they had gone below they had been wet and miserable, chewing doggedly at the tobacco in their cheeks, and growling at the darkness of the forecastle, for the slush-lamp had not yet been lighted. And just then, above the muttered curses, the tramping of heavy boots and the swish of oilskins that were being shaken to drain them, there arose the sweet song of a bird. It was Jason's canary, singing in the dark corner of his bunk a foot above his head, for on coming below the lad had thrown himself down in his wet clothes. The growling came to an end, the shuffling of feet stopped, and the men paused a moment to listen, and then burst into peals of laughter. But the bird gave no heed either to their silence or their noise, but sang on with a full throat. And the men listened, and then laughed again, and then suddenly ceased to laugh. A match was struck and the slush-lamp began to gleam out over mahogany faces that looked at each other with eyes of awe. The men shook out their coats and hung them over the stanchions. Still the bird sang on. It was uncanny, this strange singing in the darkness. The men charged their cuddies, fired up, and crouched together as they smoked. Still the bird sang on.

"Och, it's the divil in the craythur," said one; "you go bail there's a storm brewin'. It's just ould Harry hisself rej'icing."

"Then, by St. Patrick, I'll screw the neck of him," said another.

"Aisy, man, aisy," said old Davy; "it's the lad's."

"The lad be——" said the other, and up he jumped. Jason saw the man coming towards his bunk, and laid hold of the wrist of the arm that he stretched over it.

"Stop that," said Jason; but the lad was on his back, and in an instant the man had thrown his body on top of him, leaned over him and wrenched open the door of the cage. The song stopped; there was a short rustle of wings, a slight chirp-chirp, and then a moment's silence, followed by the man's light laugh as he drew back with the little yellow bird dangling by the neck from his black thumb and forefinger.

But before the great hulking fellow had twisted about to where his mates sat and smoked under the lamp, Jason had leapt from his bunk, stuck his fist into the ruffian's throat and pinned him against a beam.

"—— you," he cried, thrusting his face into the man's face, "shall I kill you after it?"

"Help! My God, help!" the man gurgled out, with Jason's knuckles ground hard into his windpipe.

The others were in no hurry to interfere, but they shambled up at length, and amid shouts and growls of "Let go," "Let go the hoult," and "God's sake, slack the grip," the two were parted. Then the man who had killed the bird went off, puffing and cursing between his chattering teeth, and his mates began to laugh at the big words that came from his weak stomach, while old Davy Kerruish went over to Jason to comfort him.

"Sarve him right, the craythur," said Davy. "He's half dead, but that's just half too much life in him yet, though. It's what I've tould them times on times. 'Lave him alone,' says I; 'the lad's quiet, but he'll be coorse enough if he's bothered. And my gough, boy, what a face at ye yander, when you were twissin' the handkercher at him! Aw, thinks I, he's the spittin picsher of the big widda man Orry—Stephen Orry—brimstone and vinegar, and gunpowder atop of a slow fire."

And it was just at that moment, as old Davy was laughing through his yellow eyes and broken teeth at young Jason, and the other men were laughing at Jason's adversary, and the dim forecastle under its spluttering slush-lamp echoed and rang with the uproar, that a wild voice came down from the deck—"Below there! All hands up! Breakers ahead!"

Now the moment when the watch had been changed had been the very moment when Stephen Orry had run down the lamp, so that neither by the Manxman who gave up the helm nor by the Irishman who took it had the light been missed when it fell into the sea. And the moment when Stephen Orry shouted to the schooner to warn it had been the moment when the muffled peals of laughter at the bird's strange song had come up from the watch below in the forecastle. The wind had whistled among the sheets, and the flying spray had smitten the men's faces, but though the mist had lifted, the sky had still hung low and dark, showing neither moon nor stars, nor any hint of the land that lay ahead. But straight for the land the vessel had been driving in the darkness, under the power of wind and tide. After a time the helmsman had sighted a solitary light close in on the lee bow. "Point of Ayre," he thought, and luffed off a little, intending to beat down the middle of the bay. It had been the light on the jetty at Ramsey; and the little town behind it, with its back to the sea, lay dark and asleep, for the night was then well worn towards midnight. After that the helmsman had sighted two stronger lights beyond. "Ramsey," he thought, and put his helm aport. But suddenly the man on the lookout had shouted, "Breakers ahead," and the cry had been sent down the forecastle.

In an instant all hands were on deck, amid the distraction and uproar, the shouting and blind groping of the cruel darkness. Against the dark sky the yet darker land could now be plainly seen, and a strong tide was driving the vessel on to it. The helm was put hard to starboard, and the schooner's head began to pay off towards the wind. Then all at once it was seen that right under the vessel's bow some black thing lay just above the level of the sea, with a fringe of white foam around it.

"Davy, what do you make of it?" shouted the skipper.

"Lord-a-massy, it's the Carick," screamed Davy.

"Let go the anchor," roared the skipper.

But it was too late even for that last refuge. At the next moment the schooner struck heavily; she was on the reef in Ramsey Bay, and pitching miserably with every heave of the sea.

The two bright lights that led the vessel to her ruin came from the two little bays that lie under Maughold Head. The light in Port-y-Vullin was in the hut of Stephen Orry, who had lit his lamp and placed it in the window when he went out to bid farewell to Michael Sunlocks, thinking no evil thereby to any man but only that it would guide him home again when he should return in the boat. The light in Port Lague was from the cottage of three old net weavers, who had lived there without woman or girl, or chick or child, through more than forty years. Two or three were brothers, Danny and Jemmy Kewley, both over seventy years old, and their housemate, who was ninety, and had been a companion of their father, was known as Juan McLady. Danny and Jemmy still worked at the looms year in and year out, every working hour of the day and night, and Juan, long past other labor, cooked and sewed and cleaned for them. All three had grown dim of sight, and now groped about like three old earthworms. Every year for five years past they had needed an extra candle to work by, so that eight tallow dips, made in their own iron mould, swung from the open roof rafters over the meshes on that night when the Peveril struck on the Carick.

It was supper-time, though old Danny and old Jemmy were still at the looms. Old Juan had washed out a bowl of potatoes, filled the pot with them, hung them on the chimney hook and stirred the peats. Then to make them boil the quicker he had gone out with the tongs to the side of the house for some dry gorse from the gorse heap. While there he had peered through the darkness of the bay for the light on the Point of Ayre, and had missed it, and on going back he had said:

"It's out again. That's the third time inside a month. I'll go bail something will happen yet."

He had got no answer, and so sat down on the three-legged stool to feed the fire with gorse lifted on the tongs. When the potatoes had boiled he had carried them to the door to drain them, and then, with the click-clack of the levers behind him, he had thought he heard, over the deep boom and plash of the sea in front, a voice like a cry. Going indoors he had said, "Plague on the water-bailiff and commissioners and kays and councils. I'll go bail there's smuggling going on under their very noses. I'd have the law on the lot of them, so I would."

Old Danny and old Jemmy knew the temper of their housemate—that he was never happy save when he had somebody to higgle with—so they paid no heed to his mutterings. But when Juan, having set the potatoes to steam with a rag spread over them, went out for the salt herrings, to where they hung to dry on a stick against the sunny side of the porch, he was sure that above the click of the levers, the boom and plash of the sea and the whistle of the wind, he could hear a clamorous shout of many voices, like a wild cry of distress. Then he hobbled back with a wizzened face of deadly pallor and told what he had heard, and the shuttles were stopped, and there was silence in the little house.

"It went by me same as the wind," said old Juan.

"Maybe it was the nightman," said old Danny.

At that old Jemmy nodded his head very gravely, and old Juan held on to the lever handles; and through those precious minutes when the crew of the schooner were fighting in the grip of death in the darkness, these three old men, their nearest fellow creatures, half dead, half blind, were held in the grip of superstitious fears.

"There again," cried old Juan; and through the door that he had left open the cry came in above roar of wind and sea.

"It's men that's yander," said old Jemmy.

"Ay," said old Danny.

"Maybe it's a ship on the Carick," said old Juan.

"Let's away and look," said old Jemmy.

And then the three helpless old men, trembling and affrighted, straining their dim eyes to see and their deaf ears to hear, and clinging to each other's hands like little children, groped their slow way to the beach. Down there the cries were louder than they had been on the brows above.

"Mercy me, let's away to Lague for the boys," said old Juan; and leaving behind them the voices that cried for help, the old men trudged and stumbled through the dark lanes.

Lague was asleep, but the old men knocked, and the windows were opened and night-capped heads thrust through. Very soon the house and courtyard echoed with many footsteps, and the bell over the porch rang out through the night, to call up the neighbors far and near.

Ross and Stean and Thurstan were the first to reach the shore, and there they found the crew of the Peveril landed—every man safe and sound, but drenching wet with the water they had passed through to save their lives. The schooner was still on the Carick, much injured already, plunging with every hurling sea on to the sharp teeth of the shoal beneath her, and going to pieces fast. And now that help seemed to be no more needed the people came flocking down in crowds—the Fairbrothers, with Greeba, and all their men and maids, Kane Wade the Methodist, with Chalse A'Killey, who had been sleeping the night at his house, Nary Crowe, and Matt Mylechreest and old Coobragh. And while Davy Kerruish shook the salt water from his sou'wester, and growled out to them with an oath that they had been a pla-guy long time coming, and the skipper bemoaned the loss of his ship, and the men of their kits, Chalse was down on his knees on the beach, lifting up his crazy, cracked voice in loud thanksgiving. At that the growling ended, and then Asher Fairbrother, who had been the last to come, invited the ship-broken men to Lague, and all together they turned to follow him.

Just at that moment a cry was heard above the tumult of the sea. It was a wild shriek that seemed to echo in the lowering dome of the sky. Greeba was the first to hear it.

"There was some one left on the ship!" she cried.

The men stopped and looked into each other's faces one by one.

"No," said the skipper, "we're all here."

The cry was heard once more; it was a voice of fearful agony.

"That's from Port-y-Vullin," said Asher Fairbrother: and to Port-y-Vullin they all hastened off, following the way of the beach. There it was easy to see from whence the cries had come. An open fishing boat was la-boring in the heavy sea, her stern half prancing like an unbroken horse, and her forepart jammed between two horns of the rock that forks out into the sea from Maughold Head. She had clearly been making for the little bay, when she had fallen foul of the shoal that lies to the north of it. Dark as the night was, the sea and sky were lighter than the black headland, and the fig-ure of a man in the boat could be seen very plainly. He was trying to unship the mast, that he might lighten the little craft and ease her off the horns that held her like a vice, but every fresh wave drove her head deeper into the cleft, and at each vain effort he shouted again and again in rage and fear.

A boat was lying high and dry on the shore. Two of the Fairbrothers, Stean and Thurstan, ran it into the water, jumped into it, and pushed off. But the tide was still making, the sea was running high, a low ground swell was scooping up the shingle and flinging it through the air like sleet, and in an instant the boat was cast back on the shore. "No use, man," shouted many voices.

But Greeba cried, "Help, help, help!" She seemed to be beside herself with suspense. Some vague fear, beyond the thought of a man's life in peril, seemed to possess her. Did she know what it was? She did not. She dared not fix her mind upon it. She was afraid of her own fear. But, low down within her, and ready at any moment to leap to her throat, was the dim ghost of a dread that he who was in the boat, and in danger of his life on the rock, might be very near and dear to her. With her hood fallen back from her head to her shoulders, she ran to and fro among the men on the beach, crying, "He will be lost. Will no one save him?"

But the other women clung to the men, and the men shook their heads and answered, "He's past saving," and "We've got wives and childers lookin' to us, miss—and what's the use of throwing your life away?"

Still the girl cried "Help," and then a young fellow pushed through to where she stood, and said, "He's too near for us to stand here and see him die."

"Oh, God bless and keep you forever and ever," cried Greeba; and, lifted completely out of all self-control, she threw her arms about the young man and kissed him fervently on the cheek. It was Jason. He had found a rope and coiled one end of it about his waist, and held the other end in his hand. The touch of Greeba's quivering lips had been as fire to him. "Lay hold," he cried, and threw the loose end of the rope to Thurstan Fairbrother. At the next moment he was breast-high in the sea. The man must have seen him coming, for the loud clamor ceased.

"Brave lad!" said Greeba, in a deep whisper.

"Brave, is it? It's mad, I'm calling it," said old Davy.

"Who is it?" said the skipper.

"The young Icelander," said Davy.

"Not the lad Jason?"——

"Aw, yes, though—Jason—the gawk, as they're saying. Poor lad there's a heart at him."

The people held their breath. Greeba covered her eyes with her hands, and felt an impulse to scream. Wading with strong strides, and swimming with yet stronger strokes, Jason reached the boat. A few minutes afterwards he was back on the shore, dragging the man after him.

The man lay insensible in Jason's arms, bleeding from a wound in the head. Greeba stooped quickly to peer into his face in the darkness, and then rose up and turned away with a sigh that was like a sigh of relief.

"He's done for," said Jason, putting him down.

"Who is he?" cried a score of voices.

"God knows; fetch a lantern," said Jason.

"See, there's a light in old Orry's hut yonder. Let's away there with him. It will be the nearest place," said Kane Wade.

Then shoulder-high they raised the insensible man and carried him to Stephen Orry's hut.

"What a weight he is!" said Kane Wade. "Slip along, somebody, and get the door opened."

Chalse A'Killey ran on ahead.

"Where's Stephen, to-night, that he's not out with us at work same as this?" said Matt Mylechreest.

"He's been down here all week," puffed Nary Crowe.

In another minute Chalse was knocking at the door, and calling loudly as he knocked:

"Stephen! Stephen! Stephen Orry!"

There came no answer, and he knocked again and called yet louder:

"Stephen, let us in. There's a man here dying."

But no one stirred within the house. "He's asleep," said one.

"Stephen—Stephen Orry—Stephen Orry—wake up, man—can't you hear us? Have you no bowels, that you'd keep the man out?"

"He's not at home—force the door," Kane Wade shouted.

One blow was enough. The door was fastened only by a hemp rope wound around a hasp on the outside, and it fell open with a crash. Then the men with the burden staggered into the house. They laid the insensible man on the floor, and there the light of the lamp that burned in the window fell upon his face.

"Lord-a-massy!" they cried, "it's Stephen Orry hisself."

X: The End of Orry

When the tumult was over, and all lives appeared to be saved, and nothing seemed lost save the two vessels—the schooner and the yawl, which still rose and fell on the Carick and the forked reef of the head—and the people separated, and the three old net weavers straggled back to their home, the crew of the Peveril went off with the Fairbrothers to Lague. Great preparations were already afoot there, for Asher had sent on a message ahead of them, and the maids were bustling about, the fire was rekindled in the kitchen, and the kettle was singing merrily. And first there was a mouthful of grog, steaming hot, for every drenched and dripping seaman, with a taste of toast to sweeten it. Then there was getting all the men into a change of dry clothes in order that they might wait for a bite of supper, and until beds were shuffled about and shakedowns fetched out. And high was the sport and great the laughter at the queer shifts the house was put to that it might find clean rigging for so many, on even so short a cruise. When the six Fairbrothers had lent all the change they had of breeches and shirts, the maids had to fish out from their trunks a few petticoats and some gowns, for the sailors still unfurnished. But the full kit was furnished out at length, and when the ship's company mustered down in the kitchen from the rooms above, all in their motley colors and queer mixture of garments, with their grizzled faces wiped dry, but their hair still wet and lank and glistening, no one could have guessed, from the loud laughter wherewith they looked each other over, that only an hour before Death itself had so nearly tricked them. Like noisy children let out of school they all were, now that they were snugly housed; for a seagoing man, however he may be kicked about on the sea, is not used to be downhearted on the land. And if two or three of the company continued to complain of their misfortunes, their growlings but lent zest to the merriment of the rest. So that they laughed loud when old Davy, cutting a most ridiculous figure in a linsey-wolsey petticoat and a linen bodice that would not meet over his hairy chest, began to grumble that he had followed the sea forty years and never been wrecked before, as if that were the best of all reasons why he should not come by such rough harm now, and a base advantage taken of him by Providence in his old age.

And louder still they laughed at the skipper himself when still sorely troubled by his evil luck, he wanted to know what all their thanking God was for, since his good ship lay a rotten hulk on a cruel reef; and if it was so very good of Providence to let them off that rock, it would have been better far not to let them on to it. And loudest of all they laughed, and laughed again, when an Irish sailor told them, with all his wealth of brogue, of a prayer that he had overheard old Davy pray while they hung helpless on the rock, thinking never to escape from it. "Oh, Lord, only save my life this once, and I'll smuggle no more," the Manxman had cried; "and it's not for myself but ould Betty I ax it, for Thou knowest she's ten years dead in Maughold churchyard with twenty rolls of good Scotch cloth in the grave atop of her. But I had nowhere else to put it, and, good Lord, only remember the last day, and save my life till I dig it up from off of her chest, for she was never a powerful woman."

And the danger being over, neither Davy nor the skipper took it ill that the men should make sport of their groanings, for they laughed with the rest, and together they waked a most reckless uproar.

All this while, though Mrs. Fairbrother had not left her bedroom, the girls' feet had been jigging about merrily over the white holy-stoned floor to get some supper spread, and Greeba, having tapped Jason, on the shoulder, had carried him off quietly to the door of the parlor, and pushed him in there while she ran to get a light, for the room was dark. It was also cool, with crocks of milk standing for cream, and basins of eggs and baskets of new-made cheese. And when she returned with the candle in one hand, shaded by the luminous fingers of the other, and its bright light on her comely face, she would have loaded him with every good thing the house contained— collared head, and beef, and binjeen and Manx jough, and the back of the day's pudding. Nothing he would have, however, save one thing, and that made great sport between them: for it was an egg, and he ate it raw, shell included, crunching it like an apple. At that sight she made pretence to shudder. And then she laughed like a bell, saying he was a wild man indeed, and she had thought so when she first set eyes on him on the shore, and already she was more than half afraid of him.

Then they laughed again, she very slyly, he very bashfully, and while her bright eyes shone upon him she told him how like he was, now that she saw him in the light, to some one else she knew of. He asked her who that was, and she answered warily, with something between a smile and a blush, that it was one who had left the island that very night.

By this time the clatter of dishes mingled with the laughter and merry voices that came from the other side of the hall, and the two went back to the kitchen.

Asher Fairbrother, who had been dozing like a sheep dog in the ingle, was then rising to his feet, and saying, "And now for supper; and let it be country fashion, girls, at this early hour of the morning."

Country fashion indeed it was, with the long oak table scrubbed white like a butcher's board, and three pyramids of potatoes, boiled in their jackets, tossed out at its head and foot and middle, three huge blocks of salt, each with its wooden spoon, laid down at the same spaces, and a plate with a boiled herring and a basin of last night's milk before every guest. And the seamen shambled into their places, any man anywhere, all growling or laughing, or both; and the maids flipped about very lightly, rueing nothing, amid so many fresh men's faces, of the strange chance that had fetched them out of their beds for work at double tides.

And seeing the two coming back together from the parlor, the banter of the seamen took another turn, leaving old Davy for young Jason, who was reminded of the kiss he had earned on the beach, and asked if ever before a sailor lad had got the like from a lady without look or longing. Such was the flow of their banter until Greeba, being abashed, and too hard set to control the rich color that mounted to her cheeks, fled laughing from the room to hide her confusion.

But no rudeness was intended by the rude sea dogs, and no offence was taken; for in that first hour, after they had all been face to face with death, the barrier of manners stood for nothing to master or man or mistress or maid.

But when the rough jest seemed to have gone far enough, and Jason, who had laughed at first, had begun to hang his head—sitting just where Stephen Orry had sat when, long years before, he took refuge in that house from the four blue-jackets in pursuit of him—Old Davy Kerruish got up and pulled his grizzled forelock, and shouted to him above the tumult of the rest:

"Never mind the loblolly-boys, lad," he cried, "it's just jealous they are, being so long out of practice; and there's one thing you can say, anyway, and that's this—the first thing you did on setting foot in the Isle of Man was to save the life of a Manxman."

"Then here's to his right good health," cried Asher Fairbrother, with his mouth in a basin of milk; and in that brave liquor, with three times three and the thud and thung of twenty hard fists on the table, the rough toast was called round.

And in the midst of it, when Greeba, having conquered her maiden shame, had crept back to the kitchen, and Mrs. Fairbrother, aroused at length by the lightsome hubbub, had come down to put an end to it, the door of the porch opened, and crazy old Chalse A'Killey stood upon the threshold, very pale, panting for breath, and with a ghastly light in his sunken eyes, and cried, "He's dying. Where's the young man that fetched him ashore? He's crying out for him, and I'm to fetch him along with me straight away."

Jason rose instantly. "I'll go," he said, and he snatched up a cap.

"And I'll go with you," said Greeba, and she caught up a shawl.

Not a word more was said, and at the next instant, before the others had recovered from their surprise, or the laughter and shouting were yet quite gone from their lips, the door had closed again and the three were gone.

Chalse, in his eagerness to be back, strode on some paces ahead in the darkness, and Jason and Greeba walked together.

"Who is it?" said Jason. "Do you know?"

"No," said Greeba. "Chalse!" she cried, but the old man, with his face down, trudged along as one who heard nothing. She tripped up to him, and Jason walking behind heard the sound of muttered words between them, but caught nothing of what passed. Dropping back to Jason's side, the girl said: "It's a man whom nobody holds of much account, poor soul."

"What is he?" said Jason.

"A smuggler, people say, or perhaps worse. His wife has been long years dead, and he has lived alone ever since, shunned by most folks, and by his own son among others. It was his son who sailed to Iceland to-night."

"Iceland? Did you say Iceland?"

"Yes, Iceland. It is your own country, is it not? But he hadn't lived with his father since he was a child. He was brought up by my own dear father. It was he who seemed to be so like to you."

Jason stopped suddenly in the dark lane.

"What's the name?" he asked, hoarsely.

"The son's name? Michael."

"Michael what?"

"Michael Sunlocks."

Jason drew a long breath, and strode on without a word more. Very soon they were outside the little house in Port-y-Vullin.

Chalse was there before them, and he stood with the door ajar.

"Whist!" the old man whispered. "He's ebbing fast. He's going out with the tide. Listen!"

They crept in on tiptoe, but there was small need for quiet. The place was a scene of direful uproar and most gruesome spectacle. It was all but as thronged of people as it had been nineteen years before, on the day of Liza Killey's wedding. On the table, the form, the three-legged stool, and in the chimney corner, they sat together cheek-by-jowl, with eyes full of awe, most of them silent or speaking low behind their hands. On the bed the injured man lay and tossed in a strong delirium. The wet clothes wherein he had passed through the sea had been torn off, his body wrapped in a gray blanket, and the wound on his head bandaged with a cloth. His lips were discolored, his cheeks were white, and his hair was damp with the sweat that ran in big drops to his face and neck. At his feet Nary Crowe stood, holding a horn cup of brandy, and by his head knelt Kane Wade, the Methodist, praying in a loud voice.

"God bring him to Thy repentance," cried Kane Wade; "restore him to the joy of Thy salvation. The pains of hell have gotten hold of him. Hark how the devil is tearing him. He is like to the man with the unclean spirit, who had his dwelling among the tombs. The devil is gotten into him. But out wi' thee, Satan, and no more two words about it! Thanks be unto God, we can wrestle with thee in prayer. Gloom at us, Satan, but never will we rise from our knees until God hath given us the victory over thee, lest our brother fall into the jaws of hell, and our own souls be not free from blood-guiltiness."

In this strain he prayed, shouting at the full pitch of the vast bellows of his lungs, and loudest of all when the delirium of the sick man was strongest, until his voice failed him from sheer exhaustion, and then his lips still moved, and he mumbled hoarsely beneath his breath.

Jason stood in the middle of the floor and looked on in his great stature over the heads of the people about him, while Greeba, with quiet grace and gentle manners, thinned the little hut of some of the many with whom the dense air smoked and reeked. After that she lifted the poor restless, tumbling, wet head from its hard pillow, and put it to rest on her own soft arm, with her cool palm to the throbbing brow, and then she damped the lips with the brandy from Nary Crowe's cup. This she did, and more than this, seeming to cast away from her in a moment all her lightness, her playfulness, her bounding happy spirits, and in the hour of need to find such tender offices come to her, as to all true women, like another sense.

And presently the delirium abated, the weary head lay still, the bleared eyes opened, the discolored lips parted, and the dying man tried to speak. But before ever a word could come, the change was seen by Kane Wade, who cried, "Thank God, he has found peace. Thank the Lord, who has given us the victory. Satan is driven out of him. Mercy there is for the vilest of sinners." And on the top of that wild shout old Chalse struck up, without warning, and in the craziest screech that ever came from human throat, a rugged hymn of triumph, wherein all the lines were one line and all the notes one note, but telling how the Lord was King over death and hell and all the devils.

Again and again he sang a verse of it, going faster at every repetition, and the others joined him, struggling to keep pace with him: and all but Greeba, who tried by vain motions to stop the tumult, and Jason, who looked down at the strange scene with eyes full of wonder. At last the mad chorus of praise came to an end, and the sick man said, casting his weak eyes into the faces about him, "Has he come?"

"He is here," whispered Greeba, and she motioned to Jason.

The lad pushed through to the bedside, and then for the first time he came face to face with Stephen Orry.

Did any voice, unheard of the others, cry in his ear at that moment, "Jason, Jason, this is he whom you have crossed the seas to slay, and he has sent for you to bless you, for the last sands of his life are running out?"

"Leave us alone together," said Stephen Orry; and Greeba, after beating out his pillow and settling his head on it, was about to move away, when he whispered, "Not you," and held her back.

Then with one accord the others called on to him not to tarry over carnal thoughts, for his soul was passing through dark waters, and he should never take rest until he had cast anchor after a troublous voyage.

"Get religion," cried Kane Wade. "Lay hoult of a free salvation," cried old Chalse. "All flesh is as grass," cried Matt Mylechreest. "Pray without ceasing," they all cried together, with much besides in the same wild strain.

"I cannot pray," the sick man muttered.

"Then we'll pray for you, mate," shouted Kane Wade.

"Ah, pray, pray, pray," mumbled Stephen Orry, "but it's no good; it's too late, too late."

"Now is the 'pointed time," shouted Kane Wade. "The Lord can save to the uttermost the worst sinner of us all."

"If I'm a sinner, let me not be a coward in my sins," said Stephen Orry. "Have pity on me and leave me."

But Kane Wade went on to tell the story of his own conversion:—It was on a Saturday night of the mackerel season down at Kinsale. The conviction had been borne in upon him that if he did not hear the pardoning voice before the clock struck twelve, he would be damned to all eternity. When the clock began to warn for midnight the hair of his flesh stood up, for he was still unsaved. But before it had finished striking the Saviour was his, and he was rejoicing in a blessed salvation.

"How can you torture a poor dying man?" muttered Stephen Orry.

"Call on the Lord, mate," shouted Kane Wade, "'Lord, I belave, help Thou my unbelafe.'"

"I've something to do, and the pains of death have hold of me," muttered Stephen Orry.

"He parthoned the thafe on the cross," cried old Chalse, "and he's gotten parthon left for you."

"Cruel, cruel! Have you no pity for a wretched dying man?" mumbled Stephen Orry.

"Ye've not lived a right life, brother," cried Kane Wade, "and ye've been ever wake in yer intellects, so never take rest till ye've read your title clear."

"You would scarce think they could have the heart, these people—you would scarce think it, would you?" said Stephen Orry, lifting his poor glassy eyes to Greeba's face.

Then with the same quiet grace as before, the girl got up, and gently pushed the men out of the house one by one. "Come back in an hour," she whispered.

It was a gruesome spectacle—the rude Methodists, with their loud voices and hot faces and eyes of flame, trying to do their duty by the soul of their fellow creature; the poor tortured sinner, who knew he had lived an evil life and saw no hope of pardon, and would not be so much a coward as to cry for mercy in his last hours; the young Icelander looking on in silence and surprise: and the girl moving hither and thither among them all, like a soft-voiced dove in a cage of hoarse jackdaws.

But when the little house was clear, and the Methodists, who started a hymn on the beach outside, had gone at last, and their singing had faded away, and there was only the low wail of the ebbing tide where there had been so loud a Babel of many tongues, Stephen Orry raised himself feebly on his elbow and asked for his coat. Jason found it on the hearth and lifted it up, still damp and stiff, from the puddle of water that lay under it. Then Stephen Orry told him to put his hand in the breast pocket and take out what he would find there. Jason did as he was bidden and drew forth the bag of money. "Here it is," he said; "what shall I do with it?"

"It is yours," said Stephen Orry.

"Mine?" said Jason.

"I meant it for my son," said Stephen Orry. He spoke in his broken English, but let us take the words out of his mouth. "It's yours now, my lad. Fourteen years I've been gathering it, meaning it for my son. Little I thought to part with it to a stranger, but it's yours, for you've earned it."

"No, no," said Jason. "I've earned nothing."

"You tried to save my life," said Stephen Orry.

"I couldn't help doing that," said Jason, "and I want no pay."

"But it's two hundred pounds, my lad."

"No matter."

"Then how much have you got?"

"Nothing."

"Has the wreck taken all?"

"Yes—no—that is, I never had anything."

"Take the money; for God's sake take it, and do what you like with it, or I'll die in torture," cried Stephen Orry, and with a groan he threw himself backward on the bed.

"I'll keep it for your son," said Jason. "His name is Michael Sunlocks, isn't it? And he has sailed for Iceland, hasn't he? That's my country, and I may meet him some day."

Then in a broken voice Stephen Orry said, "If you have a father he must be proud of you, my lad. Who is he?"

And Jason answered moodily, "I have no father—none I ever knew."

"Did he die in your childhood?"

"No."

"Before you were born?"

"No."

"Is he alive?"

"Ay, for aught I know."

Stephen Orry struggled to his elbow again. "Then he had wronged your mother?" he said with his breath coming quick.

"Ay, maybe so."

"The villain! Yet who am I to rail at him? Is your mother still alive?"

"No."

"Where is your father?"

"Don't speak of him," said Jason in an under-breath.

"But what's your name, my lad?"

"Jason."

With a long sigh of relief Stephen Orry dropped back and muttered to himself, "To think that such a father should never have known he had such a son."

The power of life ebbed fast in him, but after a pause he said,

"My lad."

"Well?" said Jason.

"I've done you a great wrong."

"When did you do me a wrong?"

"To-night."

"How?"

"No matter. There's no undoing it now; God forgive me. But let me be your father, though I'm a dying man, for that will give you the right to keep my poor savings for yourself."

"But they belong to your son," said Jason.

"He'll never touch them," said Stephen Orry.

"Why not?" said Jason.

"Don't ask me. Leave me alone. For mercy's sake don't torture a dying man," cried Stephen Orry.

"That's not what I meant to do," said Jason, giving way; "and, if you wish it, I will keep the money."

"Thank God," said Stephen Orry.

Some moments thereafter he lay quiet, breathing fast and loud, while Greeba hovered about him. Then in a feebler voice he said, "Do you think, my lad, you'll ever meet my son?"

"Maybe so," said Jason. "I'll go back when I've done what I came to do."

"What is that?" Greeba whispered, but he went on without answering her.

"Though our country is big, our people are few. Where will he be?"

"I scarce can say. He has gone to look for someone. He's a noble boy, I can tell you that. And it's something for a father to think of when his time comes, isn't it? He loves his father, too—that is, he did love me when he was a little chap. You must know he had no mother. Only think, I did everything for him, though I was a rough fellow. Yes, I nursed him and comforted him as any woman might. Ay, and the little man loved me then, for all he doesn't bear his father's name now."

Jason glanced up inquiringly, first at Stephen Orry and then at Greeba. Stephen saw nothing. His eyes were dim, but full of tenderness, and his deep voice was very gentle, and he rambled on with many a break and between many a groan, for the power of life was low in him.

"You see I called him Sunlocks. That was because it was kind and close-like. He used to ride on my shoulder. We played together then, having no one else, and I was everything to him and he was all the world to me. Ah, that was long ago, Sunlocks! Little Sunlocks! My little Sunlocks! My own little——"

At that point he laughed a little, and then seemed to weep like a child, though no tears came to his eyes, and the next moment, under the pain of joyful memories and the flow of blood upon the brain, his mind began to wander. It was very pitiful to look upon. His eyes were open, but it was clear that they did not see; his utterance grew thick and his words were confused and foolish; but his face was lit up with a surprising joy, and you knew that the years had rolled back, and the great rude fellow was alone with his boy, and doating on him. Sometimes he would seem to listen as if for the child's answer, and then he would laugh as if at its artless prattle. Again he would seem to sing the little one to sleep, crooning very low a broken stave that ran a bar and then stopped. Again he would say very slowly what sounded like the words of some baby prayer, and while he did so his chin would be twisted into his breast and his arms would struggle to cross it, as though the child itself were once more back in his bosom.

At all this Greeba cried behind her hands, unable to look or listen any longer, and Jason, though he shed no tears, said, in a husky voice, "He cannot be altogether bad who loved his son so."

The delirium grew stronger, the look of joy and the tender words gave place to glances of fear and some quick beseeching, and then Jason said in a tremulous whisper, "It must be something to know you have a father who loves you like that."

But hardly had the words been spoken when he threw back his head and asked in a firm voice how far it was to Port Erin.

"About thirty miles," said Greeba, looking up at the sudden question.

"Not more?" asked Jason.

"No. He has lived there," she answered, with a motion of her head downwards towards the bed.

"He?"

"Yes, ever since his wife died. Before that they lived in this place with Michael Sunlocks. His wife met with a terrible death."

"How?"

"She was murdered by some enemy of her husband. The man escaped, but left his name behind him. It was Patricksen."

"Patricksen?"

"Yes. That must be fourteen years ago, and since then he has lived alone at Port Erin. Do you wish to go there?"

"Ay—that is, so I intended."

"Why?"

"To look for someone."

"Who is it?"

"My father."

For a moment Greeba was silent, and then she said with her eyes down: "Why look for him if he wronged your mother?"

"That's why I meant to do so."

She looked up into his face, and stammered, "But why?"

He did not appear to hear her: his eyes were fixed on the man on the bed; and hardly had she asked the question when she covered her ears with her hands as though to shut out his answer.

"Was that why you came?" she asked.

"Yes," he answered. "If we had not been wrecked to-night I should have dropped overboard and deserted."

"Strange," she said. "It was just what he did, when he came to the island nineteen years ago."

"Yes, nineteen years ago," Jason repeated.

He spoke like a man in a sleep, and she began to tremble.

"What is the matter?" she said.

Within a few minutes his face had suddenly changed, and it was now awful to look upon. Not for an instant did he turn his eyes from the bed.

The delirium of the sick man had deepened by this time; the little, foolish, baby play-words in the poor broken English came from him no more, but he seemed to ask eager questions, in a tongue that Greeba did not understand.

"This man is an Icelander," said Jason.

"Didn't you know that before?" said Greeba.

"What is his name?" said Jason.

"Haven't you heard it yet?"

"What is his name?"

Then for one quick instant he turned his face towards her face, and she seemed to read his thought.

"Oh God!" she cried, and she staggered back.

Just then there was a sound of footsteps on the shingle outside, and at the next moment Stean and Thurstan Fairbrother and old Davy Kerruish pushed open the door. They had come to fetch Greeba.

"The Methodee man tould us," said Davy, standing by Jason's side, "and, my gough, but it's mortal cur'ous. What's it saying, 'Talk of the divil, and sure enough it was the big widda man hisself we were talking of, less nor a half hour afore we struck."

"Come, my lass," said Thurstan.

"No, no, I'll stay here," said Greeba.

"But your mother is fidgeting, and this is no place for a slip of a girl—come!"

"I'll stay with him alone," said Jason.

"No, no," cried Greeba.

"It's the lad's right, for all," said old Davy. "He fetched the poor chap out of the water. Come, let's take the road for it."

"Will no one stay instead of me?" said Greeba.

"Where's the use?" said Davy. "He's raelly past help. He's outward bound, poor chap. Poor Orry! Poor ould Stephen!"

Then they drew Greeba away, and with a look of fear fixed on Jason's face she passed out at the door.

Jason was now alone with Stephen Orry, and felt like a man who had stumbled into a hidden grave. He had set out over the seas to search for his father, and here, at his first setting foot on the land, his father lay at his feet. So this was Stephen Orry; this was he for whom his mother had given up all; this was he for whom she had taken a father's curse; this was he for whom she had endured poverty and shame; this was he who had neglected her, struck her, forgotten her with another woman; this was he who had killed her—the poor, loving, loyal, passionate heart—not in a day, or an hour, or a moment, but in twenty long years. Jason stood over the bed and looked down. Surely the Lord God had heard his great vow and delivered the man into his hands. He would have hunted the world over to find him, but here at a stride he had him. It was Heaven's own justice, and if he held back now the curse of his dead mother would follow him from the grave.

Yet a trembling shook his whole frame, and his heart beat as if it would break. Why did he wait? He remembered the tenderness that had crept upon him not many minutes ago, as he listened to the poor baby babble of the man's delirium, and at that the gall in his throat seemed to choke him. He hated himself for yielding to it, for now he knew for whom it had been meant. It had been meant for his own father doating over the memory of another son. That son had supplanted himself; that son's mother had supplanted his own mother; and yet he, in his ignorance, had all but wept for both of them. But no matter, he was now to be God's own right hand of justice on this evil-doer.

Dawn was breaking, and its woolly light crept lazily in at the little window, past the lamp that still burned on the window board. The wind had fallen, and the sea lay gloomy and dark, as if with its own heavy memories of last night's work. The gray light fell on the sick man's face, and under Jason's eyes it seemed to light up the poor, miserable, naked soul within. The delirium had now set in strong, and many were the wild words and frequent was the cry that rang through the little house.

"Not while he is like that," thought Jason. "I will wait for the lull."

He took up a pillow in both hands and stood by the bed and waited, never lifting his eyes off the face. But the lull did not come. Would it not come at all? What if the delirium were never to pass away? Could he still do the thing he intended? No, no, no! But Heaven had heard his vow and led him there. The delirium would yet pass; then he would accuse his father, face to face and eye to eye, and then—

The current of Jason's thoughts was suddenly arrested by a cry from the sick man. It was "Rachel! Rachel! Rachel!" spoken in a voice of deep entreaty, and there came after it in disjointed words of the Icelandic tongue a pitiful appeal for forgiveness. At that a great fear seized upon Jason, and the pillow dropped from his hands to the ground. "Rachel! Rachel!" It was the old cry of the years that were gone, but working with how great a difference—then, to stir up evil passions—now, to break down the spirit of revenge.

"Rachel! Rachel!" came again in the same pitiful voice of supplication; and at the sound of that name so spoken, the bitterness of Jason's heart went off like a wail of the wind. It was a cry of remorse; a cry for pardon; a cry for mercy. There could be no jugglery. In that hour of the mind's awful vanquishment a human soul stood naked behind him as before its Maker.

Jason's great resolve was shaken. Had it been only a blind tangle of passion and pain? If the Almighty had called him to be the instrument of His vengeance, would He have delivered his enemy into his hands like this— dying, delirious, with broken brain and broken heart?

Still his mother's name came from his father's lips, and then his mind went back to the words that had so lately passed between them. "Let me be your father, though I am a dying man." Ah! sweet, beautiful, blind fallacy— could he not let it be?

The end was very near; the delirium passed away, and Stephen Orry opened his eyes. The great creature was as quiet as a child now, and as soft and gentle as a child's was his deep hoarse voice. He knew that he had been wandering in his mind, and when he looked into Jason's face a pale smile crossed his own.

"I thought I had found her," he said, very simply, "my poor young wife that once was; it was she that I lost so long ago, and did such wrong by."

Jason's throat was choking him, but he stammered out, "Lie still, sir, lie still and rest."

But Stephen Orry talked on in the same simple way: "Ah, how silly I am! I forgot you didn't know."

"Lie still and rest," said Jason again.

"There was someone with her, too. I thought I was her son—her child and mine, that was to come when I left her. And, only think, I looked again, and it seemed to be you. Yes, you—for it was the face of him that fetched me out of the sea. I thought you were my son indeed."

Then Jason could bear up no longer. He flung himself down on his knees by the bedside, and buried his face in the dying man's breast.

"Father," he sobbed, "I am your son."

But Stephen Orry only smiled, and answered very quietly, "Ah, yes, I remember—that was part of our bargain, my good lad. Well, God bless you, my son. God bless and speed you."

And that was the end of Orry.

The Book of Michael Sunlocks by Hall Caine

I: Red Jason

Now the facts of this history must stride on some four years, and come to a great crisis in the lives of Greeba and Jason. Every event of that time seemed to draw these two together, and the first of the circumstances that bound them came very close on the death of Stephen Orry. Only a few minutes after Greeba, at the bidding of her two brothers, Stean and Thurstan, had left Jason alone with the dying man, she had parted from them without word or warning, and fled back to the little hut in Port-y-Vullin. With a wild laboring of heart, panting for breath and full of dread, she had burst the door open, fearing to see what she dare not think of; but, instead of the evil work she looked for, she had found Jason on his knees by the bedside, sobbing as if his heart would break, and Stephen Orry passing away with a tender light in his eyes and a word of blessing on his lips. At that sight she had stood on the threshold like one who is transfixed, and how long that moment had lasted she never knew. But the thing she remembered next was that Jason had taken her by the hand and drawn her up, with all the fire of her spirit gone, to where the man lay dead before them, and had made her swear to him there and then never to speak of what she had seen, and to put away from her mind forever the vague things she had but partly guessed. After that he had told her, with a world of pain, that Stephen Orry had been his father; that his father had killed his mother by base neglect and cruelty; that to wipe out his mother's wrongs he had vowed to slay his father; and that his father, not knowing him, save in the vision of his delirium, had died in the act of blessing him. Greeba had yielded to Jason, because she had been conquered by his stronger will, and was in fear of the passion which flashed in his face; but hearing all this, she remembered Michael Sunlocks, and how he must stand as the son of the other woman; and straightway she found her own reasons why she should be silent on all that she had that night seen and heard. This secret was the first of the bonds between them; and the second, though less obvious, was even more real.

Losing no time, Adam Fairbrother had written a letter to Michael Sunlocks, by that name, telling him of the death of his father, and how, so far as the facts were known, the poor man came by it in making the port in his boat after seeing his son away in the packet. This he had despatched to the only care known to him, that of the Lord Bishop Petersen, at his Latin School of Reykjavik; but after a time the letter had come back, with a note from the Bishop saying that no such name was known to him, and no such student was under his charge. Much afraid that the same storm that had led Stephen Orry to his end had overtaken Michael Sunlocks also, Adam Fairbrother had then promptly re-addressed his letter to the care of the Governor-General, who was also the Postmaster, and added a postscript asking if, after the sad event whereof he had thought it his task in love and duty to apprise him, there was the same necessity that his dear boy should remain in Iceland. "But, indite me a few lines without delay," he wrote, "giving me assurance of your safe arrival, for what has happened of late days has haunted me with many fears of mishap."

Then in due course an answer had come from Michael Sunlocks, saying he had landed safely, but there being no regular mails, he had been compelled to await the sailing of English ships to carry his letters; that by some error he had missed the first of these, and was now writing by the next; that many strange things had happened to him, and he was lodged in the house of the Governor-General; that his father's death had touched him very deeply; being brought about by a mischance that so nearly affected himself; that the sad fact, so far from leaving him free to return home, seemed to make it the more necessary that he should remain where he was until he had done what he had been sent to do: and, finally, that what that work was he could not tell in a letter, but only by word of mouth, whenever it pleased God that they should meet again. This, with many words of affection for Adam himself, in thanks for his fatherly anxiety, and some mention of Greeba in tender but guarded terms, was the sum of the only letter that had come from Michael Sunlocks in the four years after Stephen Orry's death to the first of the events that are now to be recorded.

And throughout these years Jason had lived at Lague, having been accepted as housemate by the six Fairbrothers, when the ship-broken men had gone their own ways on receiving from their Dublin owners the wages that were due to them. Though his relation to Stephen Orry had never become known, it had leaked out that he had come into Orry's money. He had done little work. His chief characteristics had been love of liberty and laziness. In the summer he had fished on the sea and in the rivers and he had shot and hunted in the winter. He had followed these pursuits out of sheer love of an idle life; but if he had a hobby it was the collecting of birds. Of every species on the island, of land or seafowl, he had found a specimen. He stuffed his birds with some skill, and kept them in the little hut in Port-y-Vullin.

The four years had developed his superb physique, and he had grown to be a yet more magnificent creature than Stephen Orry himself. He was rounder, though his youth might have pardoned more angularity; broader, and more upright, with a proud poise of head, long wavy red hair, smooth cheeks, solid white teeth, face of broad lines, an intelligent expression, and a deep voice that made the mountain ring. His dress suited well his face and figure. He wore a skin cap with a peak, a red woollen shirt belted about the waist, breeches of leather, leggings and seaman's boots. The cap was often awry, and a tuft of red hair tumbled over his bronzed forehead, his shirt was torn, his breeches were stained, and his leggings tied with rope; but rough, and even ragged, as his dress was, it sat upon him with a fine rude grace. With a knife in his sheath, a net or a decoy over his arm, a pouch for powder slung behind him, a fowling piece across his shoulder, and a dog at his heels, he would go away into the mountains as the evening fell. And in the early gleams of sunrise he would stride down again and into the "Hibernian," scenting up the old tavern with tobacco smoke, and carrying many dead birds at his belt, with the blood still dripping from their heads hung down. Folks called him Red Jason, or sometimes Jason the Red.

He began to visit Government House. Greeba was there, but at first he seemed not to see her. Simple greetings he exchanged with her, and that was all the commerce between them. With the Governor, when work was over, he sat and smoked, telling of his own country and its laws, and the ways of its people, talking of his hunting and fishing, calling the mountains Jokulls, and the Tynwald the Löberg, and giving names of his own to the glens, the Chasm of Ravens for the Dhoon, and Broad Shield for Ballaglass. And Adam loved to learn how close was the bond between his own dear isle and the land of the great sea kings of old time, but most of all he listened to what Jason said, that he might thereby know what kind of world it was wherein his dear lad Michael Sunlocks had to live away from him.

"A fine lad," Adam Fairbrother would say to Greeba; "a lad of fearless courage, and unflinching contempt of death, with a great horror of lying and treachery, and an inborn sense of justice. Not tender and gentle with his strength, as my own dear Sunlocks is, but of a high and serious nature, and having passions that may not be trifled with." And hearing this, and the more deliberate warning of her brothers at Lague, Greeba would remember that she had herself the best reason to know that the passions of Jason could be terrible.

But nothing she recked of it all, for her heart was as light as her manners in those days, and if she thought twice of her relations with Jason she remembered that she was the daughter of the Governor, and he was only a poor sailor lad who had been wrecked off their coast.

Jason was a great favorite with Mrs. Fairbrother, notwithstanding that he did no work. Rumor had magnified the fortune that Stephen Orry had left him, and the two hundred pounds stood at two thousand in her eyes. With a woman's quick instinct she saw how Jason stood towards Greeba, almost before he had himself become conscious of it, and she smiled on him and favored him. A whisper of this found its way from Lague to Government House, and old Adam shook his head. He had nothing against Jason, except that the lad was not fond of work, and whether Jason was poor or rich counted for very little, but he could not forget his boy Sunlocks.

Thus while Greeba remained with her father there was but little chance that she could wrong the promise she had made to Michael; but events seemed to force her into the arms of Jason. Her mother had never been of an unselfish spirit, and since parting from her husband she had shown a mean penuriousness. This affected her six sons chiefly, and they realized that when she had taken their side against their father she had taken the cream of their living also. Lague was now hers for her lifetime, and only theirs after she was done with it; and if they asked much more for their work than bed and board she reminded them of this, and bade them wait. Soon tiring of their Lenten entertainment, they trooped off, one after one, to their father, badly as they had dealt by him, and complained loudly of the great wrong he had done them when he made over the lands of Lague to their mother. What were they now, though sons of the Governor? No better than hinds on their mother's farm, expected to work for her from light to dusk, and getting nothing for their labor but the house she kept over their heads. Grown men they all were now, and the elder of them close on their prime, yet none were free to marry, for none had the right to a penny for the living he earned; and all this came of their father's unwise generosity.

Old Adam could not gainsay them, and he would not reproach them, so he did all that remained to him to do, and that was to exercise a little more of the same unwise generosity, and give them money. And finding this easy means of getting what they wanted, they came again and again, all six of them, from Asher to Gentleman Johnny, and as often as they came they went away satisfied, though old Adam shook his head when he saw how mean and small was the spirit of his sons. Greeba also shook her head, but from another cause, for though she grudged her brothers nothing she knew that her father was fast being impoverished. Once she hinted as much, but old Adam made light of her misgivings, saying that if the worst came to the worst he had still his salary, and what was the good of his money if he might not use it, and what was the virtue of charity if it must not begin at home?

But the evil was not ended there for the six lumbering men who objected to work without pay were nothing loth to take pay without work. Not long after the first of the visits to Government House, Lague began to be neglected.

Asher lay in the ingle and dozed; Thurstan lay about in the "Hibernian" and drank; Ross and Stean started a ring of gamecocks, Jacob formed a nest of private savings, and John developed his taste for dress and his appetite for gallantries. Mrs. Fairbrother soon discovered the source of the mischief, and railed at the name of her husband, who was ruining her boys and bringing herself to beggary.

Thus far had matters gone, during the four years following the death of Stephen Orry, and then a succession of untoward circumstances hastened a climax of grave consequence to all the persons concerned in this history. Two bad seasons had come, one on the end of the other. The herring fishing had failed, and the potato crop had suffered a blight. The fisher folk and the poor farming people were reduced to sore straits. The one class had to throw the meal bag across their shoulders and go round the houses begging, and the other class had to compound with their landlords or borrow from their neighbors.

Where few were rich and many were poor, the places of call for either class were not numerous. But two houses at least were always open to those who were in want—Lague and Government House; though their welcome at the one was very unlike their welcome at the other. Mrs. Fairbrother relieved their necessities by lending them money on mortgage on their lands or boats, and her interest was in proportion to their necessities. They had no choice but accept her terms, however rigid, and if in due course they could not meet them they had no resource but to yield up to her their little belongings. In less than half a year boat after boat, croft after croft, and even farm after farm had fallen into her hands. She grew rich, and the richer she grew the more penurious she became. There were no banks in the north of the island then, and the mistress of Lague was in effect the farmer's banker.

Government House, in the south of the island, had yet more applicants; but what the Governor had he gave, and when his money was gone he served out orders on the millers for meal and the weavers for cloth. It soon became known that he kept open house to the poor, and from north and south, east and west, the needy came to him in troops, and with them came the idle and the dissolute. He knew the one class from the other, yet railed at both in threatening words, reproaching their improvidence and predicting his own ruin, but he ended by giving to all alike. They found out his quarter-day and came in throngs to meet it, knowing that, bluster as he would, while the good man had money he was sure to give it to all who asked. The sorry troop, good and bad, worthy and unworthy, soon left him without a pound. He fumed at this when Greeba cast up his reckoning, but comforted himself with the thought that he had still his stipend of five hundred pounds a year coming in to him, however deeply it might be condemned beforehand.

At the first pinch of his necessity his footman deserted him and after the footman went the groom.

"They say the wind is tempered to the shorn sheep, Greeba," said he, and laughed.

He had always stood somewhat in awe of these great persons, and his spirits rose visibly at the loss of them, for he had never yet reconciled himself to the dignity of his state.

"It's wonderful how much a man may do for himself when he's put to it," he said, as he groomed his own horse next morning. His sons were not so easily appeased, and muttered hard words at his folly, for their own supplies had by this time suffered curtailment. He was ruining himself at a breakneck pace, and if he came to die in the gutter, who should say that it had not served him right? The man who threw away his substance with his eyes open deserved to know by bitter proof that it had gone. Jason heard all this at the fireside at Lague, and though he could not answer it, he felt his palms itch sorely, and his fists tighten like ribs of steel, and his whole body stiffen up and silently measure its weight against that of Thurstan Fairbrother, the biggest and heaviest and hardest-spoken of the brothers. Greeba heard it, too, but took it with a gay lightsomeness, knowing all yet fearing nothing.

"What matter?" she said, and laughed.

But strange and silly enough were some of the shifts that her father's open-handedness put her to in these bad days of the bitter need of the island's poor people.

It was the winter season, when things were at their worst, and on Christmas Eve Greeba had a goose killed for their Christmas dinner. The bird was hung in one of the out-houses, to drain and cool before being plucked, and while it was there Greeba went out, leaving her father at home. Then came three of the many who had never yet been turned empty from the Governor's door. Adam blustered at all of them, but he emptied his pockets to one, gave the goose to another, and smuggled something out of the pantry for the third.

The goose was missed by the maid whose work it was to pluck it, and its disappearance was made known to Greeba on her return. Guessing at the way it had gone, she went into the room where her father sat placidly smoking, and trying to look wondrous, serene and innocent.

"What do you think, father?" she said; "someone has stolen the goose."

"I'm afraid, my dear," he answered, meekly, "I gave it away to poor Kinrade, the parish clerk. Would you believe it, he and his good old wife hadn't a bit or a sup for their Christmas dinner?"

"Well," said Greeba, "you'll have to be content with bread and cheese for your own, for we have nothing else in the house now."

"I'm afraid, my dear," he stammered, "I gave away the cheese too. Poor daft Gelling, who lives on the mountains, had nothing to eat but a loaf of bread, poor fellow."

Now the rapid impoverishment of the Governor was forcing Greeba into the arms of Jason, though they had yet no idea that this was so; and when the crisis came that loosened the ties which held Greeba to her father, it came as a surprise to all three of them.

The one man in the island who had thus far shown a complete indifference to the sufferings of the poor in their hour of tribulation was the Bishop of Sodor and Man. This person was a fashionable ecclesiastic—not a Manxman—a Murray, and a near kinsman of the Lord of the Island, who had kept the See four years vacant that the sole place of profit in the island might thereby be retained for his own family. Many years the Bishop had drawn his stipend, tithe and glebe rents, which were very large in proportion to the diocese, and almost equal in amount to the emoluments of the whole body of the native clergy. He held small commerce with his people, and the bad seasons troubled him little until he felt the pinch of them himself. But when he found it hard to gather his tithe he began to realize that the island was passing through sore straits. Then he sold his tithe charges by auction in England, and they were knocked down to a Scotch factor—a hard man, untroubled by sentiment, and not too proud to get his own by means that might be thought to soil the cloth of a Bishop.

When news of this transfer reached the island the Manx clergy looked black, though they dared say nothing; but the poor people grumbled audibly, for they knew what was coming. It soon came, in the shape of writs from the Bishop's seneschal, served by the Bishop's sumner. Then the cry of the poor reached the Governor at Castletown. No powers had he to stay the seizure of goods and stock, for arrears that were forfeit to the Church Courts, but he wrote to the Bishop, asking him to stay execution at such a moment of the island's necessity. The Bishop answered him curtly that the matter was now outside his control. At that the Governor inquired into the legality of the sale, and found good reason to question it. He wrote again to the Bishop, hinting at his doubts, and then the Bishop told him to mind his own business. "My business is the welfare of the people," the Governor answered, "and be you Bishop or Lord, or both, be sure that while I am here I will see to it."

"Such is the penalty of setting a beggar on horseback," the Bishop rejoined.

Meantime the Scotch factor went on with his work, and notices were served that if arrears of tithe rent were not paid by a given date, cattle or crop to the value of them would then be seized in the Bishop's name. When the word came to Government House, the Governor announced to Greeba his intention to be present at the first seizure. She tried to restrain him, fearing trouble; but he was fully resolved. Then she sent word by old Chalse A'Killey to her brothers at Lague, begging them to go with their father and see him through, but one and all refused. There was mischief brewing, and if the Governor had a right to interfere, he had a right to have the civil forces at the back of him. If he had no right to the help of Castle Rushen he had no right to stop the execution. In any case, they had no wish to meddle.

When old Chalse brought back this answer, Red Jason chanced to be at Castletown. He had been at Government House oftener than usual since the clouds had begun to hang on it. Coming down from the mountains, with his pipe in his mouth, his fowling piece over his shoulder, and his birds hanging from his belt, he would sometimes contrive to get up into the yard at the back, fling down a brace of pheasants on to the kitchen floor, and go off again without speaking to anyone. Greeba had been too smart for him this time, and he was standing before her with a look of guilt when Chalse came up on his errand. Then Jason heard all, and straightway offered to go with the Governor, and never let wit of his intention.

"Oh, thank you, thank you!" said Greeba, and she looked up into his bronzed face and smiled proudly, and her long lashes blinked over her beautiful eyes. Her glance seemed to go through him. It seemed to go through all nature; and fill the whole world with a new, glad light.

The evil day came, and the Governor was as good as his word. He went away to Peel, where the first seizure was to be made. There a great crowd had already gathered, and at sight of Adam's face a great shout went up. The factor heard it, as he came on from Bishop's Court with a troop of his people about him. "I'll mak' short shrift of a' that, the noo," he said. When he came up he ordered that a cow house door should be opened and the cattle brought out for instant sale, for he had an auctioneer by his side. But the door was found to be locked, and he shouted to his men to leap on to the roof and strip off the thatch. Then the Governor cried "Stop," and called on the factor to desist, for though he might seize the cattle there would be no sale that day, since no man there present would take the bread out of the mouths of the poor.

"Then they shall try the milk," said the factor, with a hoarse laugh, and at the same moment the Bishop's seneschal, a briefless advocate, stepped out, pushed his hot face into Adam's, and said that, Governor as he was, if he encouraged the people to resist, the sumner should there and then summon him to appear before the Church Courts for contempt.

At that insult the crowd surged around, muttering deep oaths, and factor and seneschal were both much hustled. In another moment there was a general struggle; people were shouting, the Governor was on the ground and in danger of being trodden under foot, the factor had drawn a pistol, and some of his men were flourishing hangers.

By this time Red Jason had lounged up, as if by chance, to the outskirts of the crowd, and now he pushed through with great strides, lifted the Governor to his feet, laid the factor on the broad of his back, and clapped his pistol hand under one heavy heel. Then the hangers flashed round Jason's face, and he stretched his arms and laid out about him. In two minutes he had made a wide circle where he stood, and in two minutes more the factor and his men, with seneschal, sumner, auctioneer, and all the riffraff of the Church Courts, were going off up the road with best foot foremost, and a troop of the people, like a pack of hounds at full cry, behind.

Then the remnant of the crowd compared notes and bruises.

"Man alive, what a boy to fight," said one.

"Who was it?" said another.

"Och, Jason the Red, of coorse," said a third.

Jason was the only man badly injured. He had a deep cut over the right brow, and though the wound bled freely he made light of it. But Adam was much troubled at the sight.

"I much misdoubt me but we'll rue the day," he said.

Jason laughed at that, and they went back to Castletown together. Greeba saw them coming, and all but fainted at the white bandage that gleamed across Jason's forehead; but he bade her have no fear, for his wound was nothing. Nevertheless she must needs dress it afresh, though her deft fingers trembled woefully, and, seeing how near the knife had come to the eye, all her heart was in her mouth. But he only laughed at the bad gash, and thought with what cheer he would take such another just to have the same tender hands bathe it, and stitch it, and to see the troubled heaving of the round bosom that was before him while his head was held down.

"Aren't you very proud of yourself, Jason?" she whispered softly, as she finished.

"Why proud?" said he.

"It's the second time you have done as I have bidden you, and suffered for doing so," she said.

He knew not what reply to make, scarcely realizing which way her question tended. So, feeling very stupid, he said again,

"But why proud?"

"Aren't you, then?" she said. "Because I am proud of you."

They were alone, and he saw her breast heave and her great eyes gleam, and he felt dizzy. At the next instant their hands touched, and then his blood boiled, and before he knew what he was doing he had clasped the beautiful girl in his arms, and kissed her on the lips and cheek. She sprang away from him, blushing deeply, but he knew that she was not angry, for she smiled through her deep rich color, as she fled out of the room on tiptoe. From that hour he troubled his soul no more with fears that he was unworthy of Greeba's love, for he looked at his wound in the glass, and remembered her words, and laughed in his heart.

The Governor was right that there would be no sale for arrears of tithe charges. After a scene at Bishop's Court the factor went back to England, and no more was heard of the writs served by the sumner. But wise folks predicted a storm for Adam Fairbrother, and the great people were agreed that his conduct had been the maddest folly.

"He'll have to take the horns with the hide," said Deemster Lace.

"He's a fool that doesn't know which side his bread is buttered," said Mrs. Fairbrother.

The storm came quickly, but not from the quarter expected.

Since the father of the Duke of Athol had sold his fiscal rights to the English Crown the son had rued the bargain. All the interest in the island that remained to him lay in his title, his patronage of the Bishopric, and his Governor-Generalship. His title counted for little, for it was unknown at the English Court, and the salary of his Governor-Generalship counted for less, for, not being resident in the island, he had to pay a local Governor. The patronage of the Bishopric was the one tangible item of his interest, and when the profits of that office were imperilled he determined to part with his truncated honors. Straightway he sold them bag and baggage to the Crown, for nearly six times as much as his father had got for the insular revenues. When this neat act of truck and trade was complete he needed his deputy no more, and sent Adam Fairbrother an instant warning, with half-a-year's salary for smart money.

The blow came with a shock on Greeba and her father, but there was no leisure to sigh over it. Government House and its furniture belonged to the Government, and the new Governor might take possession of it at any moment. But the stock on its lands was Adam's and as it was necessary to dispose of it, he called a swift sale. Half the island came to it, and many a brave brag came then from many a vain stomach. Adam was rightly served! What was there to expect when jacks were set in office? With five hundred a year coming in for twenty years he was as poor as a church mouse? Aw, money in the hands of some men was like water in a sieve!

Adam's six sons were there, looking on with sneering lips, as much as to say, "Let nobody blame us for a mess like this." Red Jason was there, too, glooming as black as a thundercloud, and itching to do battle with somebody if only a fit case would offer.

Adam himself did not show his face. He was ashamed—he was crushed—he was humiliated—but not for the reason attributed to him by common report. Alone he sat, and smoked and smoked, in the room at the back, from whence he had seen Greeba and Michael Sunlocks that day when they walked side by side into the paved yard, and when he said within himself, "Now, God grant that this may be the end of all parting between them and me." He was thinking of that day now: that it was very, very far away. He heard the clatter of feet below, and the laughter of the bidders and the wondrous jests of the facetious auctioneer.

When the work was over, and the house felt quiet and so, so empty, Greeba came in to him, with eyes large and red, and kissed him without saying a word. Then he became mighty cheerful all at once, and bade her fetch out her account books, for they had their own reckoning yet to make, and now was the time to make it. She did as she was bidden, and counted up her father's debts, with many a tear dropping over them as if trying to blot them out forever. And meanwhile he counted up his half-year's smart money, and the pile of silver and gold that had come of the sale. When all was reckoned, they found they would be just fifteen pounds to the good, and that was now their whole fortune.

Next morning there came a great company of the poor, and stood in silence about the house. They knew that Adam had nothing to give, and they came for nothing; they on their part had nothing to offer, and they had nothing to say; but this was their way of showing sympathy with the good man in his dark hour.

The next morning after that old Adam said to Greeba,

"Come, girl, there is only one place in the island that we have a right to go to, and that's Lague. Let's away."

And towards Lague they set their faces, afoot, all but empty-handed, and with no one but crazy old Chalse A'Killey for company.

II: How Greeba was Left with Jason

It was early summer, and the day was hot; there had been three weeks of drought, and the roads were dusty. Adam walked with a stout blackthorn stick, his flaccid figure sometimes swaying for poise and balance, and his snow-white hair rising gently in the soft breeze over his tender old face, now ploughed so deep with labor and sorrow. Chalse was driving his carrier's cart, whereon lay all that was left of Adam's belongings, save only what the good man carried in his purse. And seeing how heavy the road was to one of Adam's years, though his own were hardly fewer, poor old Chalse, recking nothing of dignity lost thereby, would have had him to mount the shafts and perch on the box behind the pony's tail. But Adam, thinking as little of pride, said No, that every herring should hang by its own gills, and the pony had its full day's work before it; moreover, that it was his right to walk at his own expense now, having ridden twenty years at the expense of the island. So he kept the good blackthorn moving, and Greeba stepped along nimbly by his side. And when the Castletown coach overtook and passed them on its way to Douglas, and some of the farming folk who rode on it leaned over saucily and hailed Adam by his Christian name, he showed no shame or rancor, until, when the coach was gone, he caught a glimpse of the hot color that had mounted to Greeba's cheeks. Then, without a word, he turned his mellow old face to his feet, and strode along a good half mile in silence.

And meantime, Chalse, thinking to lighten the burden of the way with cheerful talk, rattled along in his crazy screech on many subjects, but found that all came round, by some strange twist, to the one subject that might not be discussed. Thus, looking at his pony, he told of the donkey he had before it, the same that Michael Sunlocks rode long years ago; how he himself had fallen sick and could not to keep it, and so gave it without a penny to a neighbor for feeding it; and how when he got better he wanted to borrow it, but the neighbor, in base ingratitude and selfishness, would not lend it without pay.

"Faith, it's alwis lek that," said Chalse. "Give a man yer shirt, and ye must cut yer lucky or he'll be after axing ye for yer skin."

When they came by Douglas, Chalse was for skirting round by the Spring Valley through Braddon, but old Adam, seeing his drift, would not pretend to be innocent of it, and said that if there were dregs in his cup he was in the way of draining them without making too many wry faces about it. And as for the people of the town, if they thought no shame to stare at him he thought no shame to be stared at, yet that what was good enough for himself might not be so for one who had less deserved it, and Greeba could go with Chalse by Braddon, and they would meet again on Onchan Hill.

To this Greeba would not consent; and as it chanced there was little need, for when they got into Douglas the town was all astir with many carriages and great troops of people making for the quay, so that no one seemed so much as to see the little company of three that came covered with dust out of the country roads.

"Aw, bad cess, what jeel is this?" said Chalse; and before they had crossed the little market place by the harbor, where the bells of old St. Matthew's rang out a merry peal, they learned for certain the cause of the joyful commotion; for there they were all but run down by the swaying and surging crowds, that came shouting and cheering by the side of an open carriage, wherein sat a very old gentleman in the uniform of a soldier. It was, as Adam had already divined, the new Governor-General, Colonel Cornelius Smelt, newly arrived that day in the island as the first direct representative of the English crown in succession to the Lords of Man. And at that brave sight poor old Chalse, who jumbled in his distraught brain the idea of Adam's late position with that of his master the Duke of Athol, and saw nothing but that this gentleman, in his fine rigging, was come in Adam's place, and was even now on his way to Castletown to take possession of Government House, and that the bellowing mob that not a month before had doffed their caps before Adam's face, now shoved him off the pavement without seeing him, stamped and raved and shook his fist over the people, as if he would brain them.

They slept at Onchan that night, and next day they reached Kirk Maughold. And coming on the straggling old house at Lague, after so long an absence, Adam was visibly moved, saying he had seen many a humiliation since the days when he lived in it, and might the Lord make them profitable to his soul; but only let it please God to grant him peace and content and daily bread, and there should be no more going hence in the years that were left to him.

At that Greeba felt a tingling on both sides her heart, for her fears were many of the welcome that awaited them.

It was nigh upon noon, and the men were out in the fields; but Mrs. Fairbrother was at home, and she saw the three when they opened the gate and came down under the elms.

"Now, I thought as much," she said within herself, "and I warrant I know their errand."

Adam entered the house with what cheer of face he could command, being hard set to keep back his tears, and hailed his wife in a jovial tone, although his voice threatened to break, and sat himself down in his old seat by the chimney corner, with his blackthorn stick between his knees and his hands resting upon it. But Mrs. Fairbrother made no answer to his greeting, and only glanced from him to Greeba who tripped softly behind him, and from Greeba to Chalse, who came shambling in after them, vacantly scratching his uncovered head. Then, drawing herself up, and holding back her skirts, she said very coldly, while her wrinkled face twitched—

"And pray what ill wind blows you here?"

"An ill wind indeed, Ruth," Adam answered, "for it is the wind of adversity. You must have heard of our misfortune since the whole island knows of it. Well, it is not for me to complain, for God shapes our ways, and He knows what is best. But I am an old man now, Ruth, little able to look to myself, still less to another, and——"

While he spoke, Mrs. Fairbrother tapped her foot impatiently, and then broke in with—

"Cut it short, sir. What do you want?"

Adam lifted his eyes with a stupefied look, and answered very quietly, "I want to come home, Ruth."

"Home!" cried Mrs. Fairbrother, sharply. "And what home if you please?"

Adam sat agape for a moment, and then said, speaking as calmly as before, "What home, Ruth? Why, what home but this?"

"This, indeed! This is not your home," said Mrs. Fairbrother.

"Not my home!" said Adam, slowly, dropping back in his seat like one who is dumbfounded.

"Not my home! Did you say that this was not my home?" he said, suddenly bracing up. "Why, woman, I was born here; so was my father before me, and my father's father before him. Five generations of my people have lived and died here, and the very roof rafters over your head must know us."

"Hoity-toity!" cried Mrs. Fairbrother, "and if you had lived here much longer not a rafter of them all would have been left to shelter us. No, sir. I've kept the roof on this house, and it is mine."

"It is yours, indeed," said Adam slowly, "for I gave it you."

"You gave it me!" cried Mrs. Fairbrother. "Say I took it as my right when all that you had was slipping through your fingers like sand, as everything does that ever touches them."

At that hard word old Adam drew himself up with a great dignity of bearing, and said—

"There is one thing that has indeed slipped through my fingers like sand, and that is the fidelity of the woman who swore before God forty and odd years ago to love and honor me."

"Crinkleum-crankum!" cried Mrs. Fairbrother. "A pretty thing, truly, that I should toil and moil at my age to keep house and home together ready and waiting for you, when your zany doings have shut every other door against you. Misfortunes, indeed! A fine name for your mistakes!"

"I may have made mistakes, madam," said Adam; "but true it is, as the wise man has said, that he who has never made mistakes has never made anything."

"Tush!" said Mrs. Fairbrother.

"Ruth, do you refuse to take me in?" said Adam.

"This house is mine," said she; "mine by law and deed, as tight as wax can make it."

"Do you refuse to take me in?" said Adam again, rising to his feet.

"You have brought ruin on yourself by your shilly-shally and vain folly," said she; "and now you think to pat your nose and say your prayers by my fireside."

"Ruth," said Adam once more, "do you refuse to take me in?"

"Yes, and that I do," said she. "You would beggar me as you have beggared yourself, but that I warrant you never shall."

Then there was a grim silence for a moment. Old Adam gripped convulsively the staff he leaned on, and all but as loud as the ticking of the clock was the beating of his heart.

"God give me patience," he said. "Yes, I'll bear it meekly. Ruth," he said, huskily, "I'll not trouble you. Make yourself sure of that. While there's a horse-wallet to hang on my old shoulders, and a bit of barley bread to put in it, I'll rove the country round, but I'll never come on my knees to you and say, 'I am your husband, I gave you all you had, and you are rich and I'm a beggar, and I am old—give me for charity my bed and board.'"

But, unable to support any longer the strife for mastery that was tearing at his heart, he gave way to his wrath, and cried out in a loud voice, "Out on you, woman! Out on you! God forgive me the evil day I set eyes on you! God forgive me the damned day I took you to my breast to rend it."

While this had been going forward Greeba had stood silent at the back of her father's chair, with eyelashes quivering and the fingers of both hands clenched together. But now she stepped forward and said, "Forgive him, mother. Do not be angry with him. He will be sorry for what he has said: I'm sure he will. But only think, dear mother: he is in great, great trouble, and he is past work, and if this is not his home, then he is homeless."

And at the sound of that pleading voice Adam's wrath turned in part to tenderness, and he dropped back to the chair and began to weep.

"I am ashamed of my tears, child," he said; "but they are not shed for myself. Nor did I come here for my own sake, though your mother thinks I did. No, child, no; say no more. I'll repent me of nothing I have said to her—no, not one word. She is a hard, a cruel woman; but, thank heaven, I have my sons left to me yet. She is not flesh of my flesh, though one with me in wedlock; but they are, they will never see their father turned from the door."

At that instant three of the six Fairbrothers, Asher, Ross and Thurstan, came in from the stackyard, with the smell of the furze-rick upon them that they had been trimming for the cattle. And Adam, without waiting to explain, cried in the fervor of his emotion, "This is not your will, Asher?"

Whereupon Asher, without any salutation, answered him, "I don't know what you mean, sir," and turned aside.

"He has damned your mother," said Mrs. Fairbrother, with her morning apron to her eyes, "and cursed the day he married her."

"But she is turning me out of the house," said Adam. "This house—my father's house."

"Ask her pardon, sir," Asher muttered, "and she will take you back."

"Her pardon! God in heaven!" Adam cried.

"You are an old man now, sir," said Thurstan.

"So I am; so I am," said Adam.

"And you are poor as well."

"That's true, Thurstan; that's true, though your brother forgets it."

"So you should not hold your head too high."

"What! Are you on her side, also? Asher, Thurstan, Ross, you are my sons—would you see me turned out of the house?"

The three men hung their heads. "What mother says he must agree to," muttered Asher.

"But I gave you all I had," said Adam. "If I am old I am your father, and if I am poor you know best who made me so."

"We are poor, too, sir; we have nothing, and we do not forget who is to blame for it," Thurstan growled.

"You gave everything away from us," grumbled Ross; "and, because your bargain is a rue bargain, you want us now to stand aback of you."

And Stean, and Jacob, and John coming in at that moment, Jacob said, very slyly, with something like a sneer—

"Ah, yes, and who took the side of a stranger against his own children? What of your good Michael Sunlocks now, sir? Is he longing for you? Or have you never had the scribe of a line from him since he turned his back on you, four years ago?"

Then Greeba's eyes flashed with anger. "For shame," she cried, "for shame! Oh, you mean, pitiful men, to bait and badger him like this."

Jacob threw up his head and laughed, and Mrs. Fairbrother said, "Chut, girl, you're waxing apace with your big words, considering you're a chit that has wasted her days in London and hasn't learned to muck a byre yet."

Adam did not hear her. He sat like a man who is stunned by a heavy blow. "Not for myself," he mumbled, "no, not for myself, though they all think it." Then he turned to his sons and said, "You think I came to beg for bed and board for myself, but you are wrong. I came to demand it for the girl. I may have no claim upon you, but she has, for she is one with you all and can ask for her own. She has no home with her father now, for it seems that he has none for himself; but her home is here, and here I mean to leave her."

"Not so fast, sir," said John. "All she can ever claim is what may one day be hers when we ourselves come into anything. Meantime, like her brothers, she has nothing but what she works for."

"Works for, you wagtail?" cried Adam; "she is a woman! Do you hear?—a woman?"

"Woman or man, where's the difference here?" said Gentleman John, and he snapped his fingers.

"Where's the difference, you jackanapes? Do you ask me where's the difference here? Here? In grace, in charity, in unselfishness, in faith in the good; in fidelity to the true, in filial love and duty! There's the difference, you jackanapes."

"You are too old to quarrel with, sir; I will spare you," said Gentleman John.

"Spare me, you whipper-snapper! You will spare me! But oh, let me have patience! If I have cursed the day I first saw my wife let me not also curse the hour when she first bore me children and my heart was glad. Asher, you are my firstborn, and heaven knows what you were to me. You will not stand by and listen to this. She is your sister, my son. Think of it—your only sister."

Asher twisted about, where he sat by the window nook, pretending to doze, and said, "The girl is nothing to me. She is nothing to any of us. She has been with you all the days of her life except such as you made her to spend with strangers. She is no sister of ours."

Then Adam turned to Ross, "And do you say the same?" he asked.

"What can she do here?" said Ross. "Nothing. This is no place for your great ladies. We work, here, every man and woman of us, from daylight to dark, in the fields and the dairy. Best send her back to her fine friends in London."

"Ay," said Jacob, glancing up with a brazen smile into Greeba's face, "or marry her straight off—that is the shortest way. I heard a little bird tell of someone who might have her. Don't look astonished, Miss, for I make no doubt you know who it is. He is away on the mountains now, but he'll be home before long."

Greeba's eyes glistened, but not a muscle of her countenance changed. Only she clutched at the back of her father's chair and clung to it. And Adam, struggling hard to master the emotion that made his whole body to sway and tremble in his seat, said slowly, "If she is not your sister, at least she is your mother's daughter, and a mother knows what that means." Then turning to Mrs. Fairbrother, who still stood apart with her housewife's apron to her eyes, he said, "Ruth, the child is your daughter, and by that deed you speak of she is entitled to her share of all that is here——"

"Yes," said Mrs. Fairbrother, sharply, "but only when I am done with it."

"Even so," said Adam, "would you see the child want before that, or drive her into any marriage, no matter what?"

"I will take her," said Mrs. Fairbrother deliberately, "on one condition."

"What is it, Ruth?" said Adam; "name it, that I may grant it."

"That you shall give up all control of her, and that she shall give up all thought of you."

"What?"

"That you shall never again expect to see her or hear from her, or hold commerce of any kind with her."

"But why? Why?"

"Because I may have certain plans for her future welfare that you might try to spoil."

"Do they concern Michael Sunlocks?"

"No, indeed," said Mrs. Fairbrother, with a toss of the head.

"Then they concern young Jason, the Icelander," said Adam.

"If so, it is my concernment," said Mrs. Fairbrother.

"And that is your condition?"

"Yes."

"And you ask me to part from her forever? Think of it, she is my only daughter. She has been the light of my eyes. You have never loved her as I have loved her. You know it is the truth. And you ask me to see her no more, and never more to hear from her. Now, God punish you for this, you cold-hearted woman!"

"Take care, sir. Fewer words, or mayhap I will recall my offer. If you are wise you will be calm for the girl's sake."

"You are right," he said, with his head down. "It is not for me to take the bread out of my child's mouth. She shall choose for herself."

Then he twisted about to where Greeba stood in silence behind his chair. "Greeba," he said, with a world of longing in his eyes, "my darling, you see how it is. I am old and very poor, and heaven pity my blind folly, I have no home to offer you, for I have none to shelter my own head. Don't fear for me, for I have no fear for myself. I will be looked to in the few days that remain to me, and, come what may, the sorry race of my foolish life will soon be over. But you have made no mistakes that merit my misfortunes. So choose, my child, choose. It is poverty with me or plenty with your mother. Choose, my child, choose; and let it be quickly, let it be quickly, for my old heart is bursting."

Then the brave girl drew herself proudly up, her brilliant eyes aflame, and her whole figure erect and quivering.

"Choose?" she cried, in a piercing voice; "there is no choice. I will go with my father, and follow him over the world, though we have no covering but the skies above us."

And then Adam leapt from his chair to his feet, and the infirmity of his years seemed gone in an instant, and his wet face shone with the radiance of a great joy. "Do you hear that, you people?" he cried. "There's grace, and charity, and unselfishness, and love left in the world still. Thank heaven, I have not yet to curse the day her body brought forth children. Come, Greeba, we will go our ways, and God's protection will go with us. 'I have been young and now am old, yet have I not seen the righteous forsaken, nor his seed begging bread.'"

He strode across to the door, then stopped and looked back to where his sons stood together with the looks of whipped dogs.

"And you, you unnatural sons," he cried, "I cast you out of my mind. I give you up to your laziness and drunkenness and vain pleasures. I am going to one who is not flesh of my flesh, and yet he is my son indeed."

Again he made for the door, and stopped on the threshold, and faced about towards his wife. "As for you, woman, your time will come. Remember that! Remember that!"

Greeba laid one hand softly on his shoulder and said, "Come, father, come," but again he looked back at his sons and said, "Farewell, all of you! Farewell! You will see me no more. May a day like this that has come to your father never, never come to you."

And then all his brave bearing, his grand strength broke down in a moment, and as the girl laid hold of his arm, lest he should reel and fall, he stumbled out at the threshold, sobbing beneath his breath, "Sunlocks, my boy; Sunlocks, I am coming to you—I am coming to you."

Chalse A'Killey followed them out, muttering in an under-breath some deep imprecations that no one heeded. "Strange," said he, "the near I was to crucifying the Lord afresh and swearing a mortal swear, only I remembered my catechism and the good John Wesley."

At the gate to the road they met Jason, who was coming down from Barrule with birds at his belt. With bewildered looks Jason stood and looked at them as they came up, a sorry spectacle, in the brightness of the midday sun. Old Adam himself strode heavily along, with his face turned down and his white hair falling over his cheeks. By his side Greeba walked bearing herself as proudly as she might, with her head thrown back and her wet eyes trying hard to smile. A pace or two behind came Chalse with his pony and cart grunting hoarsely in his husky throat. Not a word of greeting did they give to Jason, and he asked for no explanation, for he saw it all after a moment: they being now homeless had drifted back to their old home and had just been turned away from it. And not a word of pity did he on his part dare to offer them, but in the true sympathy of silence he stepped up to Adam and gave him his strong arm to lean upon, and then turned himself about to go their way.

They took the road to Ramsey, and little was said by any of them throughout the long two miles of the journey, save only by Chalse, who never ceased to mutter dark sayings to himself, whereof the chief were praises to God for delivering them without loss of life or limb or hand or even out of a den of lions, for, thanks be to the Lord! He had drawn their teeth.

Now though the world is hard enough on a good man in the hour of his trouble, there are ever more tender hearts to compassionate his distresses than bitter ones to triumph over his adversity, and when Adam Fairbrother came to Ramsey many a door was thrown open to him by such as were mindful of his former state and found nothing in his fall to merit their resentment. No hospitality would he accept, however, but took up his abode with Greeba in a little lodging in the market place, with its face to the cross and its back towards the sea. And being safely housed there, he thanked Jason at the door for the help of his strong arm, and bade him come again at ten o'clock that night, if so be that he was in the way of doing a last service for a poor soul who might never again have it in his power to repay. "I'll come back at ten," said Jason, simply, and so he left them for the present.

And when he was gone Adam said to Greeba as he turned indoors, "A fine lad that, and as simple as a child, but woe to the man who deceives him. Ay, or to the woman either. But you'll never do it, girl? Eh? Never? Never?"

"Why, father, what can you mean? Are we not going away together?" said Greeba.

"True, child, true," said Adam; and so without further answer to her question, twice repeated, he passed with her into the house.

But Adam had his meaning as well as his reason for hiding it. Through the silent walk from Lague he had revolved their position and come to a fixed resolution concerning it. In the heat of his emotion it had lifted up his heart that Greeba had chosen poverty with him before plenty with her mother and her brothers, but when his passion had cooled he rebuked himself for permitting her to do so. What right had he to drag her through the slough of his own necessities! He was for going away, not knowing the fate that was before him, but on what plea made to his conscience dare he take her with him? He was old, his life was behind him, and, save herself, he had no ties. What did it matter to him how his struggle should end? But she was young, she was beautiful, she might form new friendships, the world was before her, the world might yet be at her feet, and life, so sweet and so sad, and yet so good a thing withal, was ready and waiting for her.

Once he thought of Michael Sunlocks, and that the arms that would be open to himself in that distant land would not be closed to Greeba. And once he thought of Jason, and that to leave her behind was to help the schemes that would bring them together. But put it as he would, no farther could he get than this, that she must stay, and he must go away alone.

Yet, knowing the strength of her purpose, he concealed his intention, and his poor bewildered old head went about its work of preparation very artfully. It was Friday, and still not far past noon, when they reached their lodging by the cross. After a hasty meal he set out into the town, leaving Greeba to rest, for she had walked far since early morning. At the quay he inquired the date of a vessel that called there sometimes in summer on its passage from Ireland to Iceland, and to his surprise he found that she was even then in the harbor, and would go out with the first tide of the next day, which would flow at one o'clock in the morning.

Thereupon he engaged his berth, and paid for his passage. It cost six pounds, besides a daily charge of four shillings for rations. The trip was calculated to last one month with fair wind and weather, such as then promised. Adam counted the cost, and saw that with all present debts discharged, and future ones considered, he might have somewhat between six and seven pounds in his pocket when he set foot in Reykjavik. Being satisfied with this prospect, he went to the High Bailiff for his license to leave the island.

Greeba had heard nothing of this, and as soon as night fell in she went up to bed at her father's entreaty. Her room was at the back of the house and looked out over the sea, and there she saw the young moon rise over the waters as she undressed and laid down to sleep.

Prompt to his hour Jason came, and then Adam told him all.

"I am going away," he said, "far away, indeed into your own country. I go to-night, though my daughter, who is asleep, knows nothing of my intention. Will you do me a service?"

"Try me," said Jason.

And then Adam asked him to stay in Ramsey over night, that he might be there when Greeba came down in the morning, to break the news to her that her father had gone, and to take her back with him to Lague.

"They will not say no to her, seeing her father is not with her; and the time is coming when she will hold her right to a share of all they have, and none of them dare withhold it."

Jason who had been up to Lague, had heard of all that had passed there, and played his own part too, though he said nothing of that. He was now visibly agitated. His calm strength had left him. His eyes were afire, his face twitched, his hands trembled, and he was plainly struggling to say what his quivering lips refuse to utter.

"Is there no other way?" he asked. "Must she go back to Lague? Is there no help for it?"

"None," said Adam; "for she is penniless, God forgive me, and beggars may not be choosers."

At that word Jason was unable to support any longer the wild laboring of his heart.

"Yes, yes, but there is a way," he cried, "for there is one to whom she is rich enough though he is poor himself, for he would give his life's blood if so be that he could buy her. Many a day he has seen all and stood aside and been silent, because afraid to speak, but he must speak now, or never."

Hearing this, Adam's face looked troubled, and he answered—

"I will not misdoubt you, my good lad, or question whom you mean."

And Jason's tongue being loosed at last, the hot words came from him like a flood.

"I have been an idle fellow, sir, I know that; good for nothing in the world, any more than the beasts of the field, and maybe it's because I've had nobody but myself to work for; but give me the right to stand beside her and you shall see what I can do, for no brother shall return her cold looks for her sweetness, and never again shall she go back where she will only be despised."

"You are a brave lad, Jason," said Adam, as best he could for the tears that choked him; "and though I have long had other thoughts concerning her, yet could I trust her to your love and keeping and go my ways with content. But no, no, my lad, it is not for me to choose for her; and neither is for her to choose now."

Pacified by that answer Jason gave his promise freely, faithfully to do what Adam had asked of him. And the night being now well worn towards midnight, with the first bell of the vessel rung, and old Chalse fussing about in busy preparation, the time had come for Adam to part from Greeba. To bid her farewell was impossible, and to go away without doing so was well-nigh as hard. All he could do was to look upon her in her sleep and whisper his farewell in his heart. So he entered on tiptoe the room where she lay. Softly the moon shone through the window from across the white sea, and fell upon the bed. Pausing at the door he listened for her breathing, and at last he heard it, for the night was very still, and only by the sea's gentle plash on the beach was the silence broken. Treading softly he approached the bedside, and there she lay, and the quiet moonlight lay over her—the dear, dear girl, so brave and happy-hearted. Her lips seemed to smile; perhaps she was dreaming. He must take his last look now. Yet no, he must kiss her first. He reached across and lightly touched her pure forehead with his lips. Then she moved and moaned in her sleep, and then her peaceful breathing came again. "Now, peace be with her," Adam murmured, "and the good hand to guard her of the good Father of all."

So Adam Fairbrother went his way, leaving Greeba behind him, and early the next morning Jason took her back to Lague.

III: The Wooing of Jason

Now the one thing that Jason did not tell to Adam Fairbrother was that, on hearing from Jacob, as spokesman of his brothers, the story of their treatment of Greeba and their father, he had promised to break every bone in their six worthless bodies, and vowed never to darken their door again. His vow he could not keep if he was also to keep his word with Adam, and he deferred the fulfilment of his promise; but from that day he left Lague as a home, and pitched his tent with old Davy Kerruish in Maughold village, at a little cottage by the Sundial that stood by the gates of the church. Too old for the sea, and now too saintly for smuggling, Davy pottered about the churchyard as gravedigger—for Maughold had then no sexton—with a living of three and sixpence a service, and a marvellously healthy parish. So the coming of Jason to share bed and board with him was a wild whirl of the wheel of fortune, and straightway he engaged an ancient body at ninepence a week to cook and clean for them.

By this time Jason had spent nearly half his money, for he had earned nothing, but now he promptly laid his idle habits aside. No more did he go up to the mountains, and no longer out on to the sea. His nets were thrown over the lath of the ceiling, his decoy was put in a cage, his fowling piece stood in the corner, and few were the birds that hung at his belt. He was never seen at the "Hibernian," and he rarely scented up the house with tobacco smoke. On his first coming he lay two days and nights in bed without food or sleep, until Davy thought surely he was sick, and, willy-nilly, was for having his feet bathed in mustard and hot water, and likewise his stomach in rum and hot gruel. But he was only settling his plans for the future, and having hit on a scheme he leaped out of bed like a grayhound, plunged his head up to the neck in a bucket of cold water, came out of it with gleaming eyes, red cheeks and a vapor rising from his wet skin, and drying himself with a whir on a coarse towel, he laid hold with both hands of a chunk of the last hare he had snared, and munched it in vast mouthfuls.

"Davy," he cried, with the white teeth still going, "are there many corn mills this side of the island?"

"Och, no, boy," said Davy; "but scarce as fresh herrings at Christmas."

"Any mill nearer than old Moore's at Sulby, and Callow's wife's down at Laxey?"

"Aw, no, boy, the like of them isn't in."

"Any call for them nearer, Davy?"

"Aw 'deed, yes, boy, yes; and the farmer men alwis keen for one in Maughold, too. Ay, yes, keen, boy, keen; and if a man was after building one here they'd be thinking diamonds of him."

"Then why hasn't somebody set up a mill before now, Davy?"

"Well, boy, ye see a Manxman is just the cleverest of all the people goin' at takin' things aisy. Aw, clever at it, boy, clever!"

There is a full stream of water that tumbles into the sea over the brows of Port-y-Vullin, after singing its way down from the heights of Barrule. Jason had often marked it as he came and went from the hut of Stephen Orry that contained his stuffed birds, and told himself what a fine site it was for anybody that wanted to build a water mill. He remembered it now with a freshened interest, and bowling away to Mrs. Fairbrother at Lague for the purchase of a rod of the land that lay between the road and the beach, to the Bailiff for the right of water, and to old Coobragh for the hire of a cart to fetch stones from the screes where the mountains quarried them, he was soon in the thick of his enterprise.

He set the carpenter to work at his wheel, the smith at his axle, and the mason at his stones, but for the walls and roof of the mill itself he had no help but old Davy's. Early and late, from dawn to dusk, he worked at his delving and walling, and when night fell in he leaned over the hedge and smoked and measured out with his eye the work he meant to do next day. When his skill did not keep pace with his ardor he lay a day in bed thinking hard, and then got up and worked yet harder. In less than two months he had his first roof—timbers well and safely pitched, and if he went no farther it was because the big hope wherewith his simple heart had been buoyed up came down with a woeful crash.

"Aw, smart and quick, astonishin'," said old Davy of Jason to Mrs. Fairbrother at Lague. "Aw 'deed, yes, and clever to, and steady still. The way he works them walls is grand. I'll go bail the farming men will be thinking diamonds of him when he makes a start."

"And then I wouldn't doubt but he'll be in the way of making a fortune, too," said Mrs. Fairbrother.

"I wouldn' trust, I wouldn' trust," said Davy.

"And he'll be thinking of marrying, I suppose. Isn't he, Davy?" said Mrs. Fairbrother.

"Marrying, is it?" said Davy; "aw, divil a marry, ma'am. The boy's innocent. Aw, yes, innocent as a baby."

Mrs. Fairbrother had her own good reasons for thinking otherwise, though Jason came to Lague but rarely. So with hint and innuendo she set herself to see how Greeba stood towards the future she had planned for her. And Greeba was not slow to see her mother's serious drift under many a playful speech. She had spent cheerful hours at Lague since the sad surprise that brought her back. Little loth for the life of the farm, notwithstanding Ross's judgment, she had seemed to fall into its ways with content. Her mother's hints touched her not at all, for she only laughed at them with a little of her old gayety; but one day within the first weeks she met Jason, and then she felt troubled. He was very serious, and spoke only of what he was doing, but before his grave face her gay friendliness broke down in an instant.

Hurrying home she sat down and wrote a letter to Michael Sunlocks. Never a word had she heard from him since he left the island four years ago, so she made excuse of her father's going away to cover her unmaidenly act, and asked him to let her know if her father had arrived, and how he was and where, with some particulars of himself also, and whether he meant to come back to the Isle of Man, or had quite made his home in Iceland; with many a sly glance, too, at her own condition, such as her modesty could not forbear, but never a syllable about Jason, for a double danger held her silent on that head. This she despatched to him, realizing at length that she loved him, and that she must hear from him soon, or be lost to him forever.

And waiting for Michael's answer she avoided Jason. If she saw him on the road she cut across the fields, and if he came to the house she found something to take her out of the kitchen. He saw her purpose quickly, and his calm eyes saddened, and his strong face twitched, but he did not flinch; he went on with his work, steadily, earnestly, only with something less of heart, something less of cheer. Her mother saw it, too, and then the playful hints changed to angry threats.

"What has he done?" said Mrs. Fairbrother.

"Nothing," said Greeba.

"Have you anything against him?"

"No."

"Then why are you driving him from the house?"

Greeba could make no answer.

"Are you thinking of someone else?"

Again Greeba was silent.

"I'll beg of you to mend your manners," cried Mrs. Fairbrother. "It's full time you were wedded and gone."

"But perhaps I don't wish to leave home," said Greeba.

"Tush!" said Mrs. Fairbrother. "The lad is well enough, and if he hasn't land he has some money, and is like to have more. I'll give you a week to think of it, and if he ever comes and speaks for you I'll ask you to give him his civil answer. You will be three and twenty come Martinmas, and long before your mother was as old as that she had a couple of your brothers to fend for."

"Some of my brothers are nearly twice my age, and you don't ask them to marry," said Greeba.

"That's a different matter," said Mrs. Fairbrother.

It turned out that the week was more than enough to settle the difference between Greeba and her mother, for in less time than that Mrs. Fairbrother was stricken down by a mortal illness. It was only a month since she had turned Adam from her door, but her time was already at hand, and more than he predicted had come to pass. She had grown old without knowing a day's illness; her body, like a rocky headland that gives no sign of the seasons, had only grown harder every year, with a face more deeply seamed; but when she fell it was at one blow of life's ocean. Three little days she had lost appetite, on the morning of the fourth day she had found a fever in a neglected cattle trough that had drained into the well, and before night she had taken her death-warrant.

She knew the worst, and faced it, but her terror was abject. Sixty-five years she had scraped and scratched, but her time was come. She had thought of nothing save her treasure, and there it lay, yet it brought her no solace.

Two days she tossed in agony, remembering the past, and the price she had paid, and made others to pay, for all that she had held so dear and must leave so soon, for now it was nothing worth. Then she sent for the parson, Parson Gell, who was still living, but very old. The good man came, thinking his mission was spiritual comfort, but Mrs. Fairbrother would hear nothing of that. As she had lived without God in the world, even so did she intend to die. But some things that had gone amiss with her in her eager race after riches she was minded to set right before her time came to go. In lending she had charged too high an interest; in paying she had withheld too much for money; in seizing for mortgage she had given too little grace. So she would repay before it was too late, for Death was opening her hands.

"Send for them all," she cried; "there's Kinvig of Ballagawne, and Corlett's widow at Ballacreggan, and Quirk of Claughbane, and the children of Joughan the weaver at Sherragh Vane, and Tubman of Ginger Hall, and John-Billy-Bob at Cornah Glen, and that hard bargainer, old Kermode of Port-e-chee. You see, I remember them all, for I never forget anything. Send

118

for them, and be quick fetching them, or it'll be waste of time for them to come."

"I'll do it, Mistress Fairbrother," mumbled the old parson through his toothless gums, "for right is right, and justice justice."

"Chut!" said Mrs. Fairbrother.

But the parson's deaf ears did not hear. "And, ah!" he said, "the things of this world seem worthless, do they not, when we catch a glimpse into eternity?"

"Less cry and more wool," said Mrs. Fairbrother, dryly. "I wouldn't trust but old as you are you'd look with more love on a guinea than the Gospel calls for."

The people answered the parson's summons quickly enough, and came to Lague next morning, the men in their rough beavers, the old women in their long blue cloaks, and they followed the old parson into Mrs. Fairbrother's room, whispering among themselves, some in a doleful voice others in an eager one, some with a cringing air, and others with an arrogant expression. The chamber was darkened by a heavy curtain over the window, but they could see Mrs. Fairbrother propped up by pillows, whereon her thin, pinched, faded face showed very white. She had slept never a moment of the night; and through all the agony of her body her mind had been busy with its reckonings. These she had made Greeba to set down in writing, and now with the paper on the counterpane before her, and a linen bag of money in her hand, she sat ready to receive her people. When they entered there was deep silence for a moment, wherein her eyes glanced over them, as they stood in their strong odors of health around her.

"Where's your brother, Liza Joughan?" she said to a young woman at the foot of the bed.

"Gone off to 'Meriky ma'am," the girl faltered, "for he couldn't live after he lost the land."

"Where's Quirk of Claughbane?" asked Mrs. Fairbrother, turning to the parson.

"The poor man's gone, sister," said the parson, in a low tone. "He died only the week before last."

Mrs. Fairbrother's face assumed a darker shade, and she handed the paper to Greeba.

"Come, let's have it over," she said, and then, one by one, Greeba read out the names.

"Daniel Kinvig, twelve pounds," Greeba read, and thereupon an elderly man with a square head stepped forward.

"Kinvig," said Mrs. Fairbrother, fumbling the neck of the linen bag, "you borrowed a hundred pounds for two years, and I charged you twelve per cent. Six per cent. was enough, and here is the difference back to your hand."

So saying, she counted twelve pound notes and held them out in her wrinkled fingers, and the man took them without a word.

"Go on," she cried, sharply.

"Mrs. Corlett, two pounds," read Greeba, and a woman in a widow's cap and a long cloak came up, wiping her eyes.

"Bella Corlett," said Mrs. Fairbrother, "when I took over Ballacreggan for my unpaid debt, you begged for the feather bed your mother died on and the chair that had been your father's. I didn't give them, though I had enough besides, so here are two pounds to you, and God forgive me."

The woman took the money and began to cry.

"God reward you," she whimpered. "It's in Heaven you'll be rewarded, ma'am."

But Mrs. Fairbrother brushed her aside, with an angry word and a fretful gesture, and called on Greeba for the next name on the list.

"Peter Kermode, twenty-four pounds ten shillings," read Greeba, and a little old man, with a rough head and a grim, hard, ugly face, jostled through the people about him.

"Kermode," said Mrs. Fairbrother, "you always tried to cheat me, as you try to cheat everybody else, and when you sold me those seventy sheep for six shillings apiece last back end you thought they were all taking the rot, and you lost thirty pounds by them and brought yourself to beggary, and serve you right, too. But I sold them safe and sound for a pound apiece three days after; so here's half of the difference, and just try to be honest for the rest of your days. And it won't be a long task, either, for it's plain to see you're not far from death's door, and it isn't worth while to be a blood-sucker."

At that she paused for breath, and to press her lean hand over the place of the fire in her chest.

"Ye say true, ma'am, aw, true, true," said the man, in a lamentable voice. "And in the house of death it must be a great consolation to do right. Let's sing wi' ye, ma'am. I'm going in the straight way myself now, and plaze the Lord I'll backslide no more."

And while he counted out the money in his grimy palm, the old hypocrite was for striking up a Ranter hymn, beginning—

"Oh, this is the God we adore,
Our faithful, unchangeable friend."

But Mrs. Fairbrother cried on him to be silent, and then gathering strength she went on with the others until all were done. And passing to each his money, as the grasp of Death's own hand relaxed the hard grip of her tight fingers, she trembled visibly, held it out and drew it back again, and held it out again, as though she were reluctant to part with it even yet.

And when all was over she swept the people out of the room with a wave of her hand, and fell back to the bolster.

Then Greeba, thinking it a favorable moment to plead for her father, mentioned his name, and eyed her mother anxiously. Mrs. Fairbrother seemed not to hear at first, and, being pressed, she answered wrathfully, saying she had no pity for her husband, and that not a penny of her money should go to him.

But late the same day, after the doctor, who had been sent for from Douglas, had wagged his head and made a rueful face over her, she called for her sons, and they came and stood about her, and Greeba, who had nursed her from the beginning, was also by her side.

"Boys," she said, between fits of pain, "keep the land together, and don't separate; and mind you bring no women here or you'll fall to quarrelling, and if any of you must marry let him have his share and go. Don't forget the heifer that's near to calving, and see that you fodder her every night. Fetch the geese down from Barrule at Martinmas, and count the sheep on the mountains once a week, for the people of Maughold are the worst thieves in the island."

They gave her their promise duly to do and not to do what she had named, and, being little used to such scenes, they grew uneasy and began to shamble out.

"And, boys, another thing," she said, faintly, stretching her wrinkled hand across the counterpane, "give the girl her rights, and let her marry whom she will."

This, also, they promised her; and then she, thinking her duty done as an honest woman towards man and the world, but recking nothing of higher obligations, lay backward with a groan.

Now it did not need that the men should marry in order that they might quarrel, for hardly was the breath out of their mother's body when they set to squabbling, without any woman to help them. Asher grumbled that Thurstan was drunken, Thurstan grumbled that Asher was lazy, Asher retorted that, being the eldest son, if he had his rights he would have every foot of the land, and Ross and Stean arose in fury at the bare thought of either being hands on their brother's farm or else taking the go-by at his hands. So they quarrelled, until Jacob said that there was plainly but one way of peace between them, and that was to apportion the land into equal parts and let every man take his share, and then the idleness of Asher and the drunkenness of Thurstan would be to each man his own affair. At that they remembered that the lands of Lague, then the largest estate on the north of the island, had once been made up of six separate farms, with a house to each of them, though five of the six houses had long stood empty. And seeing that there were just six of themselves it seemed, as Jacob said, as if Providence had so appointed things to see them out of their difficulty. But the farms, though of pretty equal acreage, were of various quality of land, and therein the quarrelling set in afresh.

"I'll take Ballacraine," said Thurstan.

"No, but I'll take it," said Jacob, "for I've always worked the meadows."

In the end they cast lots, and then, each man having his farm assigned to him, all seemed to be settled when Asher cried.

"But what about the girl?"

At that they looked stupidly into each other's faces, for never once in all their bickering had they given a thought to Greeba. But Jacob's resource was not yet at an end, for he suggested that Asher should keep her at Lague, and at harvest the other five should give her something, and that her keep and their gifts together should be her share; and if she had all she needed what more could she wish?

They did not consult Greeba on this head, and before she had time to protest they were in the thick of a fresh dispute among themselves. The meadow lands of Ballacraine had fallen to Jacob after all, while Thurstan got the high and stony lands of Ballafayle, at the foot of Barrule. Thurstan was less than satisfied, and remembering that Jacob had drawn out the papers for the lottery, he suspected cheating. So he made himself well and thoroughly drunk at the "Hibernian," and set off for Ballacraine to argue the question out. He found Jacob in no mood for words of recrimination, and so he proceeded to thrash him, and to turn him off the fat lands and settle himself upon them.

Then there was great commotion among the Fairbrothers, and each of the other four took a side in the dispute. The end of it all was a trial for ejectment at Deemster's Court at Ramsey, and another for assault and battery. The ejectment came first and Thurstan was ousted, and then six men of Maughold got up in the juror's box to try the charge of assault. There was little proof but a multitude of witnesses, and before all were heard the Deemster adjourned the court for lunch and ventilation, for the old courthouse had become poisonous with the reeking breath of the people that crowded it.

And the jury being free to lunch where they pleased, each of the parties to the dispute laid hold of his man and walked him off by himself, to persuade him, also to treat him, and perhaps to bribe him. Thus Thurstan was at the Saddle Inn with a juryman on either hand, and Jacob was at the Plough with as many by his side, and Ross and Stean had one each at the tavern by the Cross. "You're right," said the jurymen to Thurstan. "Drink up," said Thurstan to the jurymen. "I'm your man," said the jurymen to Jacob. "Slip this in your fob," said Jacob to the jurymen. Then they reeled back to the courthouse arm-in-arm, and when the six good men of Maughold had clambered up to their places again, the juror's box contained several quarts more ale than before.

The jury did not agree on a verdict, and the Deemster dismissed them with hot reproaches. But some justice to Greeba seemed likely to come of this wild farce of law, for an advocate, who had learned what her brothers were doing for her, got up a case against them, for lack of a better brief, and so far prevailed on her behalf that the Deemster ordered that each of the six should pay her eight pounds yearly, as an equivalent for the share of land they had unlawfully withheld.

Now Red Jason had spent that day among the crowd at the courthouse, and his hot blood had shown as red as his hair through his tanned cheeks, while he looked on at the doings of Thurstan of the swollen eyes, and Jacob of the foxy face. He stood up for a time at the back like a statue of wrath with a dirty mist of blood dancing before it. Then his loathing and scorn getting the better of him he cursed beneath his breath in Icelandic and English, and his restless hands scraped in and out of his pockets as if they itched to fasten on somebody's throat, or pick up something as a dog picks up a rat. All he could do was to curl his lip in a terrible grin, like the grin of a mastiff, until he caught a side-long glimpse of Greeba's face with the traces of tears upon it, and then, being unable to control any longer the unsatisfied yearning of his soul to throttle Jacob, and smash the ribs of Thurstan, and give dandified John a backhanded facer, he turned tail and slunk out of the place, as if ashamed of himself that he was so useless. When all was over he stalked off to Port-y-Vullin, but, too nervous to settle to his work that day, he went away in the evening in the direction of Lague, not thinking to call there, yet powerless to keep away.

Greeba had returned from Ramsey alone, being little wishful for company, so heavy was her heart. She had seen how her brothers had tried to rob her, and how beggarly was the help the law could give her, for though the one might order the others might not obey. So she had sat herself down in her loneliness, thinking that she was indeed alone in all the world, with no one to look up to any more, and no strong hand to rest on. It was just then that Jason pushed open the door of the porch, and stood on the threshold, in all the quiet strength of his untainted young manhood, and the calm breadth of his simple manner.

"Greeba, may I come in?" he said, in a low tone.

"Yes," she answered, only just audibly, and then he entered.

She did not raise her eyes, and he did not offer his hand, but as he stood beside her she grew stronger, and as she sat before him he felt that a hard lump that had gathered at his heart was melting away.

"Listen to me, Greeba," he said. "I know all your troubles, and I'm very sorry for them. No, that's not what I meant to say, but I'm at a loss for words. Greeba!"

"Yes?"

"Doesn't it seem as if Fate meant us to come together—you and I? The world has dealt very ill with both of us thus far. But you are a woman and I am a man; and only give me the right to fight for you——"

As he spoke he saw the tears spring to her eyes, and he paused and his wandering fingers found the hand that hung by her side.

"Greeba!" he cried again, but she stopped the hot flow of the words that she saw were coming.

"Leave me now," she said. "Don't speak to me to-day; no, not to-day, Jason. Go—go!"

He obeyed her without a word, and picking up his cap from where it had fallen at his feet, he left her sitting there with her face covered by her hands.

She had suddenly bethought herself of Michael Sunlocks; that she had pledged her word to wait for him, that she had written to him and that his answer might come at any time. Next day she went down to the post-office at Ramsey to inquire for a letter. None had yet come for her, but a boat from the Shetlands that might fetch mails from Iceland would arrive within three days. Prompt to that time she went down to Ramsey again, but though the boat had put into harbor and discharged its mails there was still no letter for her. The ordinary Irish trader between Dublin and Reykjavik was expected on its homeward trip in a week or nine days more, and Greeba's heart lay low and waited. In due course the trader came, but no letter for her came with it. Then her hope broke down. Sunlocks had forgotten her; perhaps he cared for her no longer; it might even be that he loved some one else. And so with the fall of her hope her womanly pride arose, and she asked herself very haughtily, but with the great tears in her big dark eyes, what it mattered to her after all. Only she was very lonely, and so weary and heart-sick, and with no one to look to for the cheer of life.

She was still at Lague, where her eldest brother was now sole master, and he was very cold with her, for he had taken it with mighty high dudgeon that a sister of his should have used the law against him. So, feeling how bitter it was to eat the bread of another, she had even begun to pinch herself of food, and to sit at meals but rarely.

But Jason came again about a fortnight after the trial, and he found Greeba alone as before. She was sitting by the porch, in the cool of the summer evening, combing out the plaits of her long brown hair, and looking up at Barrule, that was heaving out large and black in the sundown, with a nightcap of silver vapor over its head in the clouds.

"I can stay away no longer," he said, with his eyes down. "I've tried to stay away and can't, and the days creep along. So think no ill of me if I come too soon."

Greeba made him no answer, but thought within herself that if he had stayed a day longer he must have stayed a day too long.

"It's a weary heart I've borne," he said, "since I saw you last, and you bade me leave you, and I obeyed, though it cost me dear. But let that go."

Still she did not speak, and looking up into her face he saw how pale she was, and weak and ill as he thought.

"Greeba," he cried, "what has happened?"

But she only smiled and gave him a look of kindness, and said that nothing was amiss with her.

"Yes, by the Lord, but something is amiss," he said, with his blood in his face in an instant. "What is it?" he cried. "What is it?"

"Only that I have not eaten much to-day," she said, "that's all."

"All!" he cried. "All!"

He seemed to understand everything at a glance, as if the great power of his love had taught him.

"Now, by God——" he said, and shook his fist at the house in front of him.

"Hush!" Greeba whispered, "it is my own doing. I am loth to be beholden to any one, least of all to such as forget me."

The sweet tenderness of her look softened him, and he cast down his eyes again, and said:

"Greeba, there is one who can never forget you; morning and night you are with him, for he loves you dearly; ay, Greeba, as never maiden was loved by any one since the world began. No, there isn't the man born, Greeba, who loves a woman as he loves you, for he has nothing else to love in all the wide world."

She looked up at him as he spoke and saw the courage in his eyes, and that he who loved her stood as a man beside her. At that her heart swelled and her eyes began to fill, and he saw her tears and knew that he had won her, and he plucked her to his breast with a wild cry of joy, and she lay there and wept, while he whispered to her through her hair.

"My love! my love! love of my life!" he whispered.

"I was so lonely," she murmured.

"You shall be lonely no more," he whispered; "no more, my love, no more," and his soft words stole over her drooping head.

He stayed an hour longer by her side, laughing much and talking greatly, and when he went off she heard him break into a song as he passed out at the gate.

Then, being once more alone, she sat and tried to compose herself, wondering if she should ever repent what she had done so hastily, and if she could love this man as he well deserved and would surely wish. Her meditations were broken by the sound of Jason's voice. He was coming back with his happy step, and singing as merrily as he went.

"What a blockhead I am," he said, cheerily, popping his head in at the door. "I forgot to deliver you a letter that the postmaster gave me when I was at Ramsey this morning. You see it's from Iceland. Good news from your father, I trust. God bless him!"

So saying he pushed the letter into Greeba's hand and went his way jauntily, singing as before a gay song of his native country.

The letter was from Michael Sunlocks.

IV: The Rise of Michael Sunlocks

"Dear Greeba," the letter ran, "I am sorely ashamed of my long silence, which is deeply ungrateful towards your father, and very ungracious towards you. Though something better than four years have passed away since I left the little green island, the time has seemed to fly more swiftly than a weaver's shuttle, and I have been immersed in many interests and beset by many anxieties. But I well know that nothing can quite excuse me, and I would wrong the truth if I were to say that among fresh scenes and fresh faces I have borne about me day and night the memory of all I left behind. So I shall not pretend to a loyalty whereof I have given you no assurance, but will just pray of you to take me for what I truly am—a rather thankless fellow—who has sometimes found himself in danger of forgetting old friends in the making of new ones, and been very heartily ashamed of himself. Nevertheless, the sweetest thoughts of these four years have been thoughts of the old home, and the dearest hope of my heart has been to return to it some day. That day has not yet come; but it is coming, and now I seem to see it very near. So, dear Greeba, forgive me if you can, or at least bear me no grudge, and let me tell you of some of the strange things that have befallen me since we parted.

"When I came to Iceland it was not to join the Latin school of the venerable Bishop Petersen (a worthy man and good Christian, whom it has become by happiness to call my friend), but on an errand of mercy, whereof

126

I may yet say much but can tell you little now. The first of my duties was to find a good woman and true wife who had suffered deeply by the great fault of another, and, having found her, to succor her in her distress. It says much for the depth of her misfortunes that, though she had been the daughter of the Governor-General, and the inhabitants of the capital of Iceland are fewer than two thousand in all, I was more than a week in Reykjavik before I came upon any real news of her. When I found her at last she was in her grave. The poor soul had died within two months of my landing on these shores, and the joiner of the cathedral was putting a little wooden peg, inscribed with the initials of her name, over her grave in the forgotten quarter of the cemetery where the dead poor of this place are buried. Such was the close of the first chapter of my quest.

"But I had still another duty, and, touched by the pathos of that timeless death, I set about it with new vigor. This was to learn if the unhappy soul had left a child behind her, and if she had done so to look for it as I had looked for its mother, and succor it as I would have succored her. I found that she had left a son, a lad of my own age or thereabouts, and therefore less than twenty at that time. Little seemed to be known about him, save that he had been his mother's sole stay and companion, that they had both lived apart from their neighbors, and much under the shadow of their distresses. At her death he had been with her, and he had stood by her grave, but never afterwards had he been seen by anyone who could make a guess as to what had become of him. But, whilst I was still in the midst of my search, the body of a young man came ashore on the island of Engy, and though the features were no longer to be recognized, yet there were many in the fishing quarter of this city who could swear, from evidences of stature and of clothing, to its identity with him I looked for; and thus the second chapter of my quest seemed to close at a tomb.

"I cannot say that I was fully satisfied, for nothing that I had heard of the boy's character seemed to agree with any thought of suicide, and I noticed that the good old Lutheran priest who had sat with the poor mother in her last hours shook his head at the mention of it, though he would give no reasons for his determined unbelief. But perhaps my zeal was flagging, for my search ceased from that hour, and as often since as my conscience has reproached me with a mission unfulfilled I have appeased it with the assurance that mother and son are both gone, and death itself has been my sure abridgment.

"Some day, dear Greeba, I will tell you who sent me (which you may partly guess) and who they were to whom I was sent. But it is like the way of the world itself, that, having set ourselves a task, we must follow it as regularly as the sun rises and sets, and the day comes and the night follows, or once letting it slip it will drop into a chaos. For a thing happened just at that moment of my wavering which altered the current of my life, so that my time here, which was to be devoted to an unselfish work, seems to have been given up to personal ambitions.

"I have mentioned that the good woman had been the daughter of the Governor-General. His name was Jorgen Jorgensen. He had turned her adrift because of her marriage, which was in defiance of his wish, and through all the years of her poverty he had either abandoned her to her necessities, or her pride had hidden them from his knowledge. But he had heard of her death when it came to pass, and by that time his stubborn spirit had begun to feel the lonesomeness of his years, and that life was slipping past him without the love and tenderness of a child to sweeten it. So partly out of remorse, but mainly out of selfishness, he had set out to find the son whom his daughter had left behind her, thinking to give the boy the rightful place of a grandson by his side. It was then that on the same search our paths converged, and Jorgen Jorgensen met with me, and I with Jorgen Jorgensen. And when the news reached Reykjavik of the body that had come out of the sea at Engy, the Governor was among the first to give credence to the rumor that the son of his daughter was dead. But meantime he had found something in me to interest him, and now he asked who I was, and what, and why I was come. His questions I answered plainly, without concealment or any disguise, and when he heard that I was the son of Stephen Orry, though he knew too well what my father had been to him and to his daughter (all of which, dear Greeba, you shall yet learn at length), he asked me to take that place in his house that he had intended for his daughter's son.

"How I came to agree to this while I distrusted him and almost feared him would take too long to tell. Only remember that I was in a country foreign to me, though it was my father's home, that I was trifling with my errand there, and had no solid business of life beside. Enough for the present that I did so agree, and that I became the housemate and daily companion of Jorgen Jorgensen. His treatment of me varied with his moods, which were many. Sometimes it was harsh, sometimes almost genial, and always selfish. I think I worked for him as a loyal servant should, taking no account of his promises, and never shutting my eyes to my true position or his real aims in having me. And often and again when I remembered all that we both knew of what had gone before, I thought the Fates themselves must shriek at the turn of fortune's wheel that had thrown this man and me together so.

"I say he was selfish; and truly he did all he could in the years I was with him to drain me of my best strength of heart and brain, but some of his selfish ends seemed to lie in the way of my own advancement. Thus he had set his mind on my succeeding him in the governorship, or at least becoming

Speaker, and to that end he had me elected to Althing, a legislative body very like to the House of Keys. Violating thereby more than one regulation touching my age, nationality and period of residence in Iceland. There he made his first great error in our relations, for while I was a servant in his house and office my mind and will were his, but when I became a delegate they became my own, in charge for the people who elected me.

"It would be a long story to tell you of all that occurred in the three years thereafter; how I saw many a doubtful scheme hatched under my eyes without having the power or right to protest while I kept the shelter of the Governor's roof; how I left his house and separated from him; how I pursued my way apart from him, supported by good men who gathered about me; how he slandered and maligned and injured me through my father, whom all had known, and my mother, of whom I myself had told him; how in the end he prompted the Danish Government to propose to Althing a new constitution for Iceland, curtailing her ancient liberties and violating her time-honored customs, and how I led the opposition to this unworthy project and defeated it. The end of all is that within these two months Iceland has risen against the rule of Denmark as administered by Jorgen Jorgensen, driving him away, and that I, who little thought to sit in his place even in the days when he himself was plotting to put me there, and would have fled from the danger of pushing from his stool the man whose bread I had eaten, am at this moment president of a new Icelandic republic.

"It will seem to you a strange climax that I am where I am after so short a life here, coming as a youth and a stranger only four years ago, without a livelihood and with little money (though more I might perhaps have had), on a vague errand, scarcely able to speak the language of the people, and understanding it merely from the uncertain memories of childhood. And if above the pleasures of a true patriotism—for I am an Icelander, too, proud of the old country and its all but thousand years—there is a secret joy in my cup of fortune, the sweetest part of it is that there are those—there is one— in dear little Ellan Vannin who will, I truly think, rejoice with me and be glad. But I am too closely beset by the anxieties that have come with my success to give much thought to its vanities. Thus in this first lull after the storm of our revolution, I have to be busy with many active preparations. Jorgen Jorgensen has gone to Copenhagen, where he will surely incite the Danish Government to reprisals, though a powerful State might well afford to leave to its freedom the ancient little nation that lives on a great rock of the frozen seas. In view of this certainty, I have to organize some native forces of defence, both on land and sea. One small colony of Danish colonists who took the side of the Danish powers has had to be put down by force, and I have removed the political prisoners from the jail of Reykjavik, where they did no good, to the sulphur mines at Krisuvik, where they are opening an industry that should enrich the State. So you see that my hands are full of anxious labor, and that my presence here seems necessary now. But if, as sanguine minds predict, all comes out well in the end, and Denmark leaves us to ourselves, or the powers of Europe rise against Denmark, and Iceland remains a free nation, I will not forget that my true home is in the dear island of the Irish Sea, and that good souls are there who remember me and would welcome me, and that one of them was my dear little playfellow long ago.

"And now, dear Greeba, you know what has happened to me since we parted on that sweet night at the gate of Lague, but I know nothing of all that has occurred to you. My neglect has been well punished by my ignorance and my many fears.

"How is your father? Is the dear man well, and happy and prosperous? He must be so, or surely there is no Providence dispensing justice in this world.

"Are you well? To me the years have sent a tawny beard and a woeful lantern jaw. Have they changed you greatly? Yet how can you answer such a question? Only say that you are well, and have been always well, and I will know the rest, dear Greeba—that the four years past have only done what the preceding eight years did, in ripening the bloom of the sweetest womanhood, in softening the dark light of the most glorious eyes, and in smoothing the dimples of the loveliest face that ever the sun of heaven shone upon.

"But, thinking of this, and trying to summon up a vision of you as you must be now, it serves me right that I am tortured by fears I dare not utter. What have you been doing all this time? Have you made any new friends? I have made many, yet none that seem to have got as close to me as the old ones are. One old friend, the oldest I can remember, though young enough yet for beauty and sweet grace, is still the closest to my heart. Do you know whom I mean? Greeba, do you remember your promise? You could hardly speak to make it. I had forgotten my manners so that I had left you little breath. Have you forgotten? To me it is a delicious memory, and if it is not a painful one to you, then all is well with both of us. But, oh, for the time to come, when many a similar promise, and many a like breach of manners, will wipe away the thought of this one! I am almost in love with myself to think it was I who stood with you by the bridge at Lague, and could find it in my heart, if it were only in my power, to kiss the lips that kissed you. I'll do better than that some day. What say you? But say nothing, for that's best, dearest. Ah, Greeba—"

At this point there was a break in the letter, and what came after was in a larger, looser, and more rapid handwriting.

"Your letter has this moment reached me. I am overwhelmed by the bad news you send me. Your father has not yet come. Did his ship sail for Reykjavik? Or was it for Hafnafiord? Certainly it may have put in at the Orkneys, or the Faroes. But if it sailed a fortnight before you wrote, it ought to be here now. I will make inquiries forthwith.

"I interrupted my letter to send a boat down the fiord to look. It is gone. I can see it now skirting the Smoky Harbor on its way to the Smoky Point. If your father comes back with it, he shall have a thousand, thousand welcomes. The dear good man—how well I remember that on the day I parted from him he rallied me on my fears, and said he would yet come here to see me! Little did he think to come like this. And the worst of his misfortunes have followed on his generosities! Such bighearted men should have a store like the widow's curse to draw from, that would grow no less, however often they dipped into it. God keep him till we meet again and I hold once more that hand of charity and blessing, or have it resting on my head.

"I am anxious on your account also, dearest Greeba, for I know too well what your condition must be in your mother's house. My dear girl, forgive me for what I send you with this letter. The day I left the island your father lent me fifty pounds, and now I repay it to his daughter. So it is not a gift, and, if it were, you should still take it from me, seeing there are no obligations among those who love.

"The duties that hold me here are now for the first time irksome, for I am longing for the chance of hastening to your side. But only say that I may do so with your consent and all that goes with it, and I will not lose a day more in sending a trustworthy person to you who shall bring you here to rejoin your father and me. Write by the first ship that will bring your letter. I shall not rest until I have heard from you; and having heard in such words as my heart could wish, I shall not sleep until you are with me, never, never to be parted from me again as long as life itself shall last. Write, dearest girl—write—write."

Here there was another break in the letter, and then came this postscript.

"It is part of the penalty of life in these northern lands that for nearly one-half of the year we are entirely cut off from intercourse with the rest of the world, and are at the mercy of wind and sea for that benefit during the other half. My letter has waited these seven days for the passing of a storm before the ship that is to carry it can sail. This interval has seen the return of the sloop that I sent down the fiord as far as Smoky Point, but no tidings has she brought back of the vessel your father sailed in, and no certain intelligence has yet reached me from any other quarter. So let me not alarm you when I add that a report has come to Reykjavik by a whaler on the seas under Snaefell that an Irish schooner has lately been wrecked near the mouth of some basaltic caves by Stappen, all hands being saved, but the vessel gone to pieces, and crew and passengers trying to make their way to the capital overland. I am afraid to fear, and as much afraid to hope, that this may have been the ship that brought your father; but I am fitting out an expedition to go along the coast to meet the poor ship-broken company, for whoever they are they can know little of the perils and privations of a long tramp across this desolate country. If more and better news should come my way you shall have it in its turn, but meantime bethink you earnestly whether it is not now for you to come and to join me, and your father also, if he should then be here, and, if not, to help me to search for him. But it is barely just to you to ask so much without making myself clear, though truly you must have guessed my meaning. Then, dear Greeba, when I say 'Come,' I mean Come to be my wife. It sounds cold to say it so, and such a plea is not the one my heart has cherished; for through all these years I have heard myself whisper that dear word through trembling lips, with a luminous vision of my own face in your beautiful eyes before me. But that is not to be, save in an aftermath of love, if you will only let the future bring it. So, dearest love, my darling—more to me than place and power and all the world can give—come to me—come—come—come."

V: Strong Knots of Love

Now never did a letter bring more contrary feelings to man or maid than this one of Michael Sunlocks brought to Greeba. It thrilled her with love, it terrified her with fear; it touched her with delight, it chilled her with despair; it made her laugh, it made her weep; she kissed it with quivering lips, she dropped it from trembling fingers. But in the end it swept her heart and soul away with it, as it must have swept away the heart and soul of any maiden who ever loved, and she leaped at the thought that she must go to Sunlocks and to her father at once, without delay—not waiting to write, or for the messenger that was to come.

Yet the cooler moment followed, when she remembered Jason. She was pledged to him; she had given him her promise; and if she broke her word she would break his heart. But Sunlocks—Sunlocks—Sunlocks! She could hear his low, passionate voice in the words of his letter. Jason she had loved for his love of her; but Sunlocks she had loved of her love alone.

What was she to do? Go to Sunlocks, and thereby break her word and the heart of Jason, or abide by Jason, and break her own heart and the hope of Sunlocks? "Oh," she thought, "if the letter had but come a day earlier— one little day—nay, one hour—one little, little hour!" Then, in her tortured mind, she reproached Jason for keeping it back from her by his forgetfulness, and at the next instant she reproached Sunlocks for his tardy despatch, and last of all she reproached herself for not waiting for it. "Oh," she thought, "was ever a girl born to bring such misery to those who love her!"

All the long night thereafter she tossed in restless doubt, never once closing her eyes in sleep; and at daydawn she rose and dressed, and threw open her window, and cool waves of morning air floated down upon her from the mountains, where the bald crown of Barrule was tipped with rosy light from the sun that was rising over the sea. Then, in the stillness of the morning, before the cattle in the meadows had begun to low, or the sheep on the hills to bleat, and there was yet no noise of work in the rickyard or the shippon, and all the moorland below lay asleep under its thin coverlet of mist, there came to her from across the fields the sound of a happy, cheery voice that was singing. She listened, and knew that it was Jason, chanting a song of Iceland after a night spent on the mountains; and she looked and saw that he was coming on towards the house, with his long, swinging stride and leap, over gorse and cushag and hedge and ditch.

It was more than she could bear after such night-long torment, to look upon the happiness she seemed about to wreck, so she turned her head away and covered her ears with her hands. But, recking nothing of this, Jason came on, singing in snatches and whistling by turns, until his firm tread echoed in the paved courtyard in the silence that was broken by nothing beside, except the wakening of the rooks in the elms.

"She must be awake, for she lies there, and her window is open," he thought to himself.

"Whisht!" he cried, tossing up a hand.

And then, without moving from where she stood, with her back resting against the window shutter, she turned her head about and her eyes aslant, and saw him beneath her casement. He looked buoyant and joyous, and full of laughter. A gun was over his shoulder, a fishing rod was in the other hand, at his belt hung a brace of birds, with the blood dripping on to his leggings, and across his back swung a little creel.

"Greeba, whisht!" he called again, in a loud whisper; and a third time he called her.

Then, though her heart smote her sore, she could not but step forward; and perhaps her very shame made her the more beautiful at that moment, for her cheeks were rosy red, and her round neck drooped, and her eyes were shy of the morning light, and very sweet she looked to the lad who loved her there.

"Ah!" he said almost inaudibly, and drew a long breath. Then he made pretence to kiss her, though so far out of reach, and laughed in his throat. After that he laid his gun against the porch, and untied the birds and threw them down at the foot of the closed door.

"I thought I would bring you these," he said. "I've just shot them."

"Then you've not been to bed," said Greeba nervously.

"Oh, that's nothing," he said, laughing. "Nothing for me. Besides, how could I sleep? Sleep? Why I should have been ready to kill myself this morning if I could have slept last night. Greeba!"

"Well!"

"You could never think what a glorious night it has been for me."

"So you've had good sport?" she said, feeling ashamed.

"Sport!" he cried, and laughed again. "Oh, yes, I've had sport enough," he said. "But what a night it was! The happiest night of all my life. Every star that shone seemed to shine for me; every wind that blew seemed to bring me a message; and every bird that sang, as the day was dawning, seemed to sing the song of all my happiness. Oh, it has been a triumphant night, Greeba."

She turned her head away from him, but he did not stop.

"And this morning, coming down from Barrule, everything seemed to speak to me of one thing, and that was the dearest thing in all the world. 'Dear little river,' I said, 'how happily you sing your way to the sea.' And then I remembered that before it got there it would turn the wheel for us at Port-y-Vullin some day, and so I said 'Dear little mill, how merrily you'll go when I listen to your plash and plunge, with her I love beside me."

She did not speak, and after a moment he laughed.

"That's very foolish, isn't it?" he said.

"Oh, no," she said. "Why foolish?"

"Well it sounds so; but, ah, last night the stars around me on the mountain top seemed like a sanctuary, and this morning the birds among the gorse were like a choir, and all sang together, and away to the roof their word rang out—Greeba! Greeba! Greeba!"

He could hear a faint sobbing.

"Greeba!"

"Yes?"

"You are crying."

"Am I? Oh, no! No, Jason, not that."

"I must go. What a fool I am," he muttered, and picked up his gun.

"Oh no; don't say that."

"Greeba!"

"Well, Jason?"

"I'm going now, but——"

"Why?"

"I'm not my own man this morning. I'm talking foolishly."

"Well, and do you think a girl doesn't like foolishness?"

He threw his head back and laughed at the blue sky. "But I'm coming back for you in the evening. I am to get the last of my rafters on to-day, and when a building is raised it's a time to make merry."

He laughed again with a joyous lightness, and turned to go, and she waved her hand to him as he passed out of the gate. Then, one, two, three, four, his strong rhythmic steps went off behind the elms, and then he was gone, and the early sun was gone with him, for its brightness seemed to have died out of the air.

And being alone Greeba knew why she had tried to keep Jason by her side, for while he was with her the temptation was not strong to break in upon his happiness, but when he was no longer there, do what she would, she could not but remember Michael Sunlocks.

"Oh, what have I done that two brave men should love me?" she thought; but none the less for that her heart clamored for Sunlocks. Sunlocks, Sunlocks, always Sunlocks—the Sunlocks of her childhood, her girlhood, her first womanhood—Sunlocks of the bright eyes and the smile like sunshine.

And thinking again of Jason, and his brave ways, and his simple, manly bearing, and his plain speech so strangely lifted out of itself that day into words with wings, she only told herself that she was about to break his heart, and that to see herself do it it would go far to break her own. So she decided that she would write to him, and then slip away as best she could, seeing him no more.

At that resolve she sat and wrote four pages of pleading and prayer and explanation. But having finished her letter, it smote her suddenly, as she folded and sealed it, that it would be a selfish thing to steal away without warning, and leave this poor paper behind her to crush Jason, for though written in pity for him, in truth it was fraught with pity only for herself. As mean of soul as that she could not be, and straightway she threw her letter aside, resolved to tell her story face to face. Then she remembered the night of Stephen Orry's death, and the white lips of Jason as he stood above the dying man—his father whom he had crossed the seas to slay—and, again, by a quick recoil, she recalled his laughter of that morning, and she said within herself, "If I tell him, he will kill me."

But that thought decided her, and she concluded that tell him she must, let happen what would. So partly in the strength of her resolve, and partly out of its womanly weakness, and the fear that she might return to her first plan at last, she took up her own letter to Jason, and locked it in a chest. Then taking from the folds at her breast the letter of Sunlocks to herself, she read it again, and yet again, for it was the only love letter she had ever received, and there was a dear delight in the very touch of it. But the thought of that sensuous joy smote her conscience when she remembered what she had still to do, and thinking that she could never speak to Jason eye to eye, with the letter of Sunlocks lying warm in her bosom, she took it out, and locked it also in the chest.

Jason came back at sundown to fetch her away that they might make some innocent sport together because his mill was roofed. Then with her eyes on her feet she spoke, and he listened in a dull, impassive silence, while all the laughter died off his face and a look of blank pallor came over it. And when she had finished, she waited for the blow of his anger, but it did not come.

"Then all is over between us," he said with an effort.

And looking up, she saw that he was a forlorn man in a moment, and fell to her knees before him with many pitiful prayers for forgiveness. But he only raised her and said gently,

"Mistress Greeba, maybe I haven't loved you enough."

"No, no," she cried.

"I'm only a rough and ignorant fellow, a sort of wild beast, I dare say, not fit to touch the hand of a lady, and maybe a lady could never stoop to me."

"No, no, there's not a lady in all the world would stoop if she were to marry you."

"Then maybe I vexed you by finding my own advantage in your hour of need."

"No, you have behaved bravely with me in my trouble."

"Then, Greeba, tell me what has happened since yesterday."

"Nothing—everything. Jason I have wronged you. It is no fault of yours, but now I know I do not love you."

He turned his face away from her, and when he spoke again his voice broke in his throat.

"You could never think how fast and close my love will grow. Let us wait," he said.

"It would be useless," she answered.

"Stay," he said stiffly, "do you love anyone else?"

But before she had time to speak, he said quickly,

"Wait! I've no right to ask that question, and I will not hear you answer it."

"You are very noble, Jason," she said.

"I was thinking of myself," he said.

"Jason," she cried, "I meant to ask you to release me, but you have put me to shame and now I ask you to choose for me. I have promised myself to you, and if you wish it I will keep my promise."

At that he stood, a sorrowful man, beside her for a moment's space before he answered her, and only the tones of his voice could tell how much his answer cost him.

"No—ah, no," he said; "no, Greeba, to keep your promise to me would be too cruel to you."

"Think of yourself now," she cried.

"There's no need to do that," he said, "for either way I am a broken man. But you shall not also be broken-hearted, and neither shall the man who parts us."

Saying this, a ghastly white hand seemed to sweep across his face, but at the next moment he smiled feebly and said, "God bless you both."

Then he turned to go, but Greeba caught him by both hands.

"Jason," she murmured, "It is true I cannot love you, but if there was another name for love that is not—"

He twisted back to her as she spoke, and his face was unutterably mournful to see. "Don't look at me like that," he said, and drew away.

She felt her face flush deep, for she was ashamed. Love was her polestar. What was Jason's? Only the blankness of despair.

"Oh, my heart will break," she cried. "Jason," she cried again, and again she grasped his hands, and again their eyes met, and then the brave girl put her quivering lips to his.

"Ah, no," he said, in a husky voice, and he broke from her embrace.

VI: Esau's Bitter Cry

Shrinking from every human face, Jason turned in his dumb despair towards the sea, for the moan of its long dead waves seemed to speak to him in a voice of comfort if not of cheer. The year had deepened to autumn, and the chill winds that scattered the salt spray, the white curves of the breakers, the mists, the dapple-gray clouds, the scream of the sea fowl, all suited with his mood, for at the fountains of his own being the great deeps were broken up.

It was Tuesday, and every day thereafter until Saturday he haunted the shore, the wild headland to seaward, and the lonesome rocks on the south. There, bit by bit, the strange and solemn idea of unrequited love was borne in upon him. It was very hard to understand. For one short day the image of a happy love had stood up before his mind, but already that day was dead.

That he should never again clasp her hand whom he loved, that all was over between them—it was painful, it was crushing.

And oh! it was very cruel. His life seemed as much ended as if he had taken his death-warrant, for life without hope was nothing worth. The future he had fondly built up for both of them lay broken at his own feet. Oh, the irony of it all! There were moments when evil passions arose in his mind and startled him. Standing at the foot of the lone crags of the sea he would break into wild peals of laughter, or shriek out in rebellion against his sentence. But he was ashamed of these impulses, and would sink away from the scene of them, though no human eye had there been on him like a dog that is disgraced.

Yet he felt that like a man among men he could fight anything but this relentless doom. Anything, anything—and he would not shrink. Life and love, life and love—only these, and all would be well. But no, ah! no, not for him was either; and creeping up in the dead of night towards Lague, just that his eyes might see, though sorrow dimmed them, the house where she lay asleep, the strong man would sob like a woman, and cry out: Greeba! Greeba! Greeba!

But with the coming of day his strength would return, and watching the big ships outside pass on to north and south, or listening to the merry song of the seamen who weighed anchor in the bay, he told himself sadly, but without pain, that his life in the island was ended, that he could not live where she lived, surrounded by the traces of her presence, that something called him away, and that he must go. And having thus concluded his spirits rose, and he decided to stay until after Sunday, thinking to see her then in church, and there take his last tender look of her and bid her farewell in silence, for he could not trust himself to speak.

So he passed what remained of his time until then without bitterness or gloom, saying within himself as often as he looked with bereaved eyes towards Lague, where it lay in the sunshine, "Live on, and be happy, for I wish you no ill. Live on, and the memory of all this will pass away."

But he did not in the meantime return to his work at the mill, which stood as he had left it on the Tuesday when the carpenter fixed the last of its roof timbers. This, with the general rupture of his habits of life, was the cause of sore worry and perplexity to his housemate.

"Aw, reglar bruk—bruk complete," old Davy said far and wide. "A while ago ye couldn' hould him for workin' at the mill, and now he's never puttin' a sight on it, and good goold waitin' for him; and showin' no pride—and what he's thinkin' of no one's knowin'."

Davy tried hard to sound the depth of Jason's trouble, but having no line to fathom it he had recourse to his excellent fancy.

"Aw, bless yer sowls, the thick as a haddick I was," he whispered one day, "and me wonderin' why, and wonderin' why, and the thing as plain as plain what's agate of the poor boy. It's divils that's took at him—divils in the head. Aw, yes, and two of them, for it's aisy to see there's fightin' goin' on inside of him. Aw, yes, same as they tell of in Revelations; and I've seen the like when I was sailin' forrin."

Having so concluded old Davy thought it his duty to consult an old body that lived in a dark tangle of birchwood at Ballaglass.

"It's fit to make a man cry to see the way he's goin'," said he, "and a few good words can't do no harm any way."

The old woman agreed with Davy as to the cause of trouble, and said that Jason must be somebody after all, since what he had was a malady the quality was much subject to; for to her own knowledge the "Clerk o' the Rowls" had suffered from it when a little dancing girl from France had left suddenly for England. Yet she made no question but she should cure him, if Davy could contrive to hang about his neck while he slept a piece of red ribbon which she would provide.

It was not easy for Davy to carry out his instructions, so little did Jason rest, but he succeeded at length, and thought he remarked that Jason became calmer and better straightway.

"But bless me, I was wrong," said he. "It was four divils the poor boy had in his head; and two of them are gone, but the other two are agate of him still."

When Sunday morning came Jason made himself ready for church, and then lounged at the doorway of old Davy's cottage by the dial, to watch the people go in at the gate. And many hailed him as they went by in the sweet sunshine, and some observed among themselves that in a few days his face had grown thin. In twos and threes they passed, while Davy rang the bell from the open porch, and though Jason seemed not to heed any of them, yet he watched them one by one. Matt Mylechreest he saw, and Nary Crowe, now toothless and saintly, and Kane Wade, who had trudged down from Ballure, and his wife Bridget, grown wrinkled and yellow, and some bright young maidens, too, who gave a side-long look his way, and John Fairbroth-er—Gentleman John—who tripped along with silken bows on the toes of his shoes. But one whom he looked for he did not see, and partly from fear that she might not come, and partly from dread lest she should pass him so close-ly by, he shambled into church with the rest before the bell had stopped.

He had not often been to church during the four years that he had lived on the island and the people made way for him as he pushed up into a dark corner under the gallery. There he sat and watched as before out of his slow eyes, never shifting their quiet gaze from the door of the porch. But the bell stopped, and Greeba had not come; and when Parson Gell hobbled up to the Communion-rail, still Greeba was not there. Then the service was begun, the door was closed, and Jason lay back and shut his eyes.

The prayers were said without Jason hearing them, but while the first lesson was being read, his wandering mind was suddenly arrested. It was the story of Jacob and Esau; how Isaac, their father, seeing the day of his death at hand, sent Esau for venison, that he might eat and bless him before he died; how Jacob under the person of Esau obtained the blessing, and how Esau vowed to slay his brother Jacob.

"And Isaac, his father, said unto him: Who art thou? And he said, I am thy son, thy first born Esau.

"And Isaac trembled very exceedingly, and said, Who? Where is he that hath taken venison, and brought it me, and I have eaten of all before thou camest, and have blessed him, yea, and he shall be blessed?

"And when Esau heard the words of his father, he cried with a great and exceeding bitter cry, and said unto his father, Bless me, even me also, O my father.

* * *

"And Isaac, his father, answered and said unto him, Behold, thy dwelling shall be the fatness of the earth, and the dew of heaven from above;

"And by thy sword shalt thou live, and shalt serve thy brother; and it shall come to pass when thou shalt have the dominion, that thou shalt break his yoke from off thy neck.

"And Esau hated Jacob because of the blessing wherewith his father blessed him. And Esau said in his heart, The days of mourning for my father are at hand; then will I slay my brother Jacob."

As Parson Gell at the reading-desk mumbled these words through his toothless gums, it seemed to Jason as though he were awakening from a long sleep—a sleep of four years, a sleep full of dreams, both sweet and sad—and that everything was coming back upon him in a dizzy whirl. He remembered his mother, her cruel life, her death, and his own vow, and so vivid did these recollections grow in a moment that he trembled with excitement.

A woman in a black crape bonnet, who sat next to him in the pew, saw his emotions, and put a Bible into his hands. He accepted it with a slight movement of the head, but when he tried to find the place he turned dizzy and his hands shook. Seeing this the good woman, with a look of pity and a thought of her runaway son who was far off, took the Bible back, and after opening it at the chapter in Genesis, returned it in silence. Even then he did not read, but sat with wandering eyes, while nervous twitches crossed his face.

He was thinking that he had forgotten his great vow of vengeance, lulled to sleep by his vain dream of love; he was telling himself that his vow must yet be fulfilled or his mother who had urged him to it, would follow him with her curse from her grave. For some minutes this feeling grew more and more powerful, and more and more his limbs and whole body quivered. The poor woman in the crape saw that he trembled, and leaned towards him and asked if he was ill. But he only shook his head and drew back in silence into the corner of the pew.

"I must be going mad," he thought, and to steady his mind he turned to the book, thinking to follow the old parson as he lisped along.

It was a reference Bible that the woman had lent him, and as his eyes rambled over the page, never resting until they alit on the words, then will I slay my brother Jacob, he shuddered and thought "How hideous!" All at once he marked the word slay in the margin with many references to it, and hardly knowing what he was doing he turned up the first of them. From that moment his senses were in a turmoil, and he knew nothing clearly of all that was being done about him. He thought he saw that through all ages God had made man the instrument of his vengeance on the wrongdoer. The stories of Moses, of Saul, of Samson, came back to him one by one, and as he read a chill terror filled his whole being.

He put the book down, trying to compose himself, and then he thought, "How childish? God is King of earth and heaven, and needs the help of no man." But his nervous fingers could not rest and he took up the Bible again, while the parson prosed through his short sermon. This time he turned away from the passages that haunted him, though "Esau, Esau, Esau," rang in his head. Rolling the leaves in his hand he read in one place how the Lord visits His vengeance upon the children for the sins of the fathers, and then in another place how the nearest of kin to him that is killed shall avenge the blood spilt, and then again in yet another place how if man keeps not his covenant with the Lord, the Lord will send a faintness upon him, and a great and woeful trembling, so that the sound of a shaken leaf shall chase him.

"Am I then afraid?" he asked himself, and shut the book once more. His head swam with vague thoughts. "I must keep my vow," he thought. "I am losing my senses," he thought again. "I am an Esau," he thought once more.

Then he looked around the church, and if he had seen Greeba at that moment the fire of his heart would have burnt itself out, and all thought of his vow would have gone from him as it had gone before. He did not see her, but he remembered her, and his soul dried away.

The service came to an end, and he strode off, turning from every face; but John Fairbrother tripped after him on the road, touched him on the arm, looked up at him with a smirk, and said:—

"Then you don't know where she is?"

"Who?" said Jason.

"Then you don't know, eh?" said John, with a meaning look.

"Who d'ye mean?—Greeba?"

"Just so. She's gone, though I warrant it's fetching coals to Newcastle to tell you so."

Hearing that, Jason pushed Gentleman John out of his way with a lunge that sent the dandy reeling, and bounded off towards Lague.

"Aw, well," muttered John, "you'd really think he didn't know."

The woman in crape who had followed Jason out of the church, thinking to speak to him, said: "Lave him alone. It's the spirit of the Lord that's strivin' with him."

And old Davy, who came up at the moment, said: "Divils ma'am—divils in the head."

When Jason got to Lague he found the other Fairbrothers assembled there. Asher had missed Greeba the night before, and on rising late that morning—Sunday morning—he had so far conquered his laziness as to walk round to his brothers' houses and inquire for her. All six, except John, had then trudged back to Lague, thinking in their slow way to start a search, and they began their quest by ransacking Greeba's room. There they found two letters in a chest, clearly forgotten in a hasty leave-taking. One of them was Greeba's abandoned letter to Red Jason, the other was the letter of Michael Sunlocks to Greeba. The Fairbrothers read both with grim wonderment, and Jacob put Greeba's letter in his pocket. They were discussing the letter of Sunlocks as Jason entered; and they fell back at sight of his ashy face and the big beads of sweat that dropped from it.

"What's this? Where is she?" he said, and his powerful voice shook.

Without a word they handed him the letter, and he glanced it over and turned it in his hands, like one who does not see or cannot read.

"Where's she gone?" he said again, lifting his helpless eyes to the faces about him.

"The devil knows," said Jacob; "but see—read—'Michael Sunlocks,'" running his finger along the signature.

At that a groan like the growl of a beast came from Jason's throat, and like a baited dog he looked around, not yet knowing on whom his wrath should fasten.

"It's very simple. It's plain to see that she has gone to him," said Jacob.

And then Jason's face was crossed by a ghastly smile.

"Oh, I'm a woman of a man," he muttered, looking stupidly down at the paper in his hand. "A poor-spirited fool," he muttered again. "I must be so, God knows." But at the next moment his white face grew blood-red, and he cried: "My curse upon him," and with that he tossed back the letter and swung out of the house.

He went on to Port-y-Vullin, mounted the new mill, threw down the roof rafters, and every wall that they had rested upon, until not one stone was left above another, and the house, so near completion, was only a heap of ruins. Then he went into the old hut, took up his treasures and flung them out to sea.

Meantime, the six Fairbrothers were putting their heads together.

"President!" said Thurstan; "that's as good as Governor-General."

"The deuce!" said John.

"She'll be rich," said Ross. "I always said she was fit for a lady."

"Hum! We've made a mess of it," said Stean.

"Well, you wouldn't take my advice," said Asher. "I was for treating the girl fair."

"Stay," said Jacob, "it's not yet too late."

"Well, what's to be done?" said the others together.

"Go after her," said Jacob.

"Ah!"

"Hum! Listen! This is what we had better do," said Jacob. "Sell Ballacraine and take her the money, and tell her we never meant to keep it from her."

"That's good," said John.

"A Governor-General has pickings, I can tell you," said Jacob.

"But who'll go?" said Asher.

"Go! Hum! What! The deuce! Well I mightn't refuse to go myself," said Jacob.

"And maybe I wouldn't mind going with you," said John.

And so it was settled. But the other four said to themselves: "What about the pickings?" And then each, of himself, concluded secretly that if Jacob and John went to Iceland, Jacob and John would get all that was to be got by going, and that to prevent such cheating it would be necessary to go with them.

VII: The Yoke of Jacob

Jason paid the last of his debts in the Isle of Man, and then set sail for Iceland with less money in his pocket than Adam Fairbrother had carried there. He knew nothing of the whereabouts or condition of the man he was going to seek, except that Michael Sunlocks was at Reykjavik; for so much, and no more, he had read of the letter that the Fairbrothers put into his hands at Lague. The ship he first sailed by was a trader between Copenhagen and the greater ports of Scotland, and Ireland, and at the Danish capital he secured a passage in a whaler bound for Reykjavik. His double voyage covered more than six weeks though there was a strong fair wind from the coast of Scotland to the coast of Denmark, and again from Denmark to Iceland. The delay fretted him, for his heart was afire; but there was no help for it, he had to submit. He did so with no cheer of spirit, or he might have learned something from the yarns of the seamen. All the gossip that came his way was a chance remark of the master, a Dane, who one day stopped in front of him as he lay by the hatches, and asked if he was an Icelander born. He answered that he was. Was he a seagoing man? Yes. Ship-broken, maybe, in some foreign country? That was so. How long had he been away from Iceland? Better than four years.

"You'll see many changes since that time," said the master, "Old Iceland is turned topsy-turvy."

Jason understood this to mean some political revolution, and turned a deaf ear to it, for such things seemed but sorry trifling to one with work like his before him.

They had then just sighted the Westmann Islands, through a white sea vapor, and an hour later they lay three miles off a rocky point, while an open boat came out to them over the rough water from the island called Home.

It was the post-boat of that desolate rock, fetching letters from the mainland, and ready to receive them from Denmark. The postman was little and old, and his name was Patricksen.

"Well, Patricksen, and what's the latest from the old country?" sang out the master, after two newspapers had been thrown down and one letter taken up.

"Why, and haven't you heard it?" shouted the postman.

"What's that?" cried the master.

"They've put up the young Manxman," shouted the postman. "I knew his father," he added, and laughed mockingly, as he bent to the oars and started back with his newspapers over his three miles of tumbling sea.

Jason's mind threw off its torpor at the sound of those words. While the boat lay alongside he leaned over the gunwale and listened eagerly. When it sheered off he watched it until it had faded into the fog. Then he turned to the master and was about to ask a question, but quickly recovered himself and was silent. "Better not," he thought. "It would be remembered when all should be over."

144

Late the same day they came for the first time in full view of the south-east coast of Iceland. The fog had lifted before a strong breeze from the west, where the red sun was dipping into the sea. They were then by the needles of Portland, side on to the vast arch which the heavy blow of the tides of ten thousand years has beaten out of the rock. At the sea's edge were a hundred jagged prongs of burnt crag, flecked with the white wings and echoing with the wild cry of countless sea birds; behind that was a plain of lava dust for seabeach; farther back the dome of a volcano, lying asleep under its coverlet of snow; still farther a gray glacier, glistening with silver spikes; and beyond all a black jokull, Wilderness-jokull, torn by many earthquakes, seamed and streaked with the unmelted ice of centuries and towering over a stony sea of desert, untrodden yet by the foot of man.

Desolate as the scene was, Jason melted at the sight of it; for this island, born of fire and frost, stood to him as the only place, in God's wide world that he could call his home, and little as it had done for him, less than nothing as he owed to it, yet it was his native land, and in coming back to its bleak and terrible shores he looked upon it with a thrill of the heart and saw it through his tears.

But he had little time and less desire to give way to tender feelings, and very soon he had small need to steel himself to the work before him, for everything served to spur him on to it. This was Iceland. This was the new home of Michael Sunlocks. This was where his mother had starved.

This was where she had fled to, who had wronged him sorely.

Early the next day they rounded the Smoky Point, leaving the Old Man crag under its shocks of foam to the right, and the rock called the Mealsack, under its white cloud of sea gulls, to the left, and began to beat down the fiord towards Reykjavik. It was not yet six o'clock—the Icelandic mid-evening—when they cast anchor inside the little island of Engy; but the year was far worn towards winter, and the night of the northern land had closed down.

And the time having come to leave the whaler, Jason remembered that he had been but a moody companion for his shipmates, though they had passed some perilous days and nights together. So he bade them good-bye with what cheer he could summon up at last, and the rough fellows kissed him after the manner of their people, showing no rancor at all, but only pity, and saying among themselves that it was plain to see he had known trouble and, though given to strange outbursts when alone, was as simple and as gentle as a child, and would never hurt a fly.

He had hailed a passing boat to run him ashore, and it was one of the light skiffs with the double prow that the boys of Iceland use when they hunt among the rocks for the eggs and down of the eider duck. Such, indeed though so late in the season, had that day been the work of the two lads whose boat he had chanced upon, and having dropped down to their side from the whaler with his few belongings—his long coat of Manx homespun over his arm, his seaman's boots across his shoulders, his English fowling piece in his hand and his pistol in his belt—he began to talk with them of their calling as one who knew it.

"Where have you been working, my lads?" said Jason.

"Out on Engy," said the elder of the boys.

"Found much?"

"Not to-day."

"Who cleans it?"

"Mother."

And at that a frown passed over Jason's face in the darkness. The boys were thinly clad, both were barelegged and barefooted. Plainly they were brothers, one of them being less than twelve years of age, and the other as young as nine.

"What's your father?"

"Father's dead," said the lad.

"Where do you live with your mother?"

"Down on the shore yonder, below the silversmith's."

"The little house behind the Missions, in front of the vats?"

"Yes, sir, do you know it?"

"I was born in it, my lad," said Jason sadly, and he thought to himself, "Then the old mother is dead."

But he also thought of his own mother, and her long years of worse than widowhood. "All that has yet to be paid for," he told himself with a cold shudder, and then he remembered that he had just revealed himself.

"See, my lads," he said, "here is a crown for you, and say nothing of who gave it you."

The little Icelandic capital twinkled low at the water's edge, and as they came near to it Jason saw that there was a flare of torchlights and open fires, with dark figures moving busily before the glow where he looked for the merchant stores that had faced the sea.

"What's this?" he asked.

"The fort that the new Governor is throwing up," said the boy.

Then through a number of smacks, some schooners, a brig, a coal hulk and many small boats, they ran in at the little wooden jetty that forked out over a reef of low rocks. And there some idlers who sat on casks under the lamp, with their hands in their pockets and their skin caps squashed down on their foreheads seemed to recognize Jason as he landed.

"Lord bless me," said one, with a look of terror, "it's the dead come to life again."

"God a-mercy me," said another, pausing with his snuff at his nose, "I could have sworn I fetched him a dead man out of the sea."

Jason knew them, but before they had so far regained their self-command as to hail to him, he had faced about, though eager to ask many questions, and walked away. "Better not," he thought, and hurried on.

He took the High Street towards the Inn, and then an irregular alley that led past the lake to a square in front of the Cathedral, and ended at a little house of basaltic blocks that nestled at its feet, for it was there he meant to lodge. It had been the home of a worthy couple whom he had known in the old days, caretakers of the Cathedral, and his mother's only friends in her last days. Old and feeble and very deaf they had both been then, and as he strode along in the darkness he wondered if he should find them still alive. He found them as he had left them: not otherwise changed than if the five years of his absence had been but five hours. The old man was still at the hearth chopping up some logs of driftwood, and the old woman was still at the table ironing her linen by the light of a rush candle. With uplifted hands and cries of wonderment they received him, and while he supped on the porridge and skyr that they set before him they talked and questioned.

"And where have you been this many a day?" said the old man.

"In England, Scotland, Denmark—many places," said Jason.

"Well they've buried you these four years and better," said the old man, with a grimace.

"Lord bless me, yes, love; and a cross over your grave too, and your name on it," said the old woman, with a look of awe.

"Who did that?" said Jason.

"Jorgen Jorgensen," said the old man, grinning.

"It's next to your mother's, love. He did that, too, for when he heard that she was gone he repented," said the old woman.

"It's no good folks repenting when their bad work's done and done with," said the old man.

"That's what I say. There's them above that won't call it repenting. And see what has come of it," said the old woman.

"What?" said Jason.

"Why, he has gone. Didn't you know, love?" said the old woman.

"How gone?" said Jason. "Dead?"

"Worse—disgraced—driven out of Iceland," said the old man.

Then an ugly smile crossed Jason's face. "It is the beginning," he thought.

"But the old mother is dead, is she not?" he said aloud.

"Your father's mother? Old Mother Orryson?" said the old woman.

"No such luck," the old man muttered. "Comes to service every morning, the old sinner."

"But there's another family living in her house," said Jason.

"Oh, that's because she's past her work, and the new Governor keeps her," said the old man. "No news of your father, though," he added, with a shrug, and then there was a silence for some minutes.

"Poor Rachel," said the old woman, presently. "Now there was a good creature. And, bless me, how she was wrapped up in her boy! I was just like that when I had my poor little Olaf. I never had but one child neither. Well, my lad," she said, dropping her flat iron and raising her apron, "you can say you had a good mother anyhow."

Jason finished his supper and went out into the town. All thoughts, save one thought, had been banished from his mind. Where was this Michael Sunlocks? What was he? How was he to be met with? "Better not ask," thought Jason. "Wait and watch." And so he walked on. Dark as was the night, he knew every step of the way. The streets looked smaller and meaner than he remembered them, and yet they showed an unwonted animation. Oil lamps hung over many stalls, the stores were still open and people passed to and fro in little busy throngs. Recalling that heavy quiet of that hour of night five years ago, Jason said to himself, "The town has awakened from a long sleep."

To avoid the glances of prying eyes, he turned down towards the bridge, passing the Deanery and the Bishop's Palace. There the streets were all but as quiet as of old, the windows showed few lights, and the monotonous chime of the sea came up through the silence from the iron-bound shore. Yet, even there, from two houses, there were sounds of work. These were the Latin school and the jail. In the school a company of students was being drilled by a sergeant, whose words of command rang out in the intervals of shuffling feet.

"What does this mean?" said Jason to a group of young girls, who, with shawls over their heads, were giggling together in the darkness by the gate.

"It's the regiment started by the new Governor," said one of the girls.

"The new Governor again," thought Jason, and turned away.

From the jail there came a noise as of carpenters hammering.

"What are they doing there?" said Jason to a little tailor, who passed him on the street at that moment with his black bag on his back.

"Turning the jail into a house for the new Governor," said the tailor.

"Again the new Governor," said Jason, and he strode on by the tailor's side. "A stirring fellow, whoever he may be."

"That's true, young as he is," said the tailor.

"Is he then so young?" said Jason, carelessly.

"Four or five and twenty, hardly more," said the tailor, "but with a headpiece fit for fifty. He has driven those Danish thieves out of the old country, with all their trick and truck. Why, you couldn't call your bread your own—no, nor your soul neither. Oh, a Daniel, sir—a young Daniel. He's to be married soon. She's staying with the old Bishop now. They say she's a foreigner."

"Who?" said Jason.

"Why, his wife that is to be," said the tailor. "Good-night, sir," he cried, and turned down an alley.

Then Jason remembered Greeba, and the hot blood tingled in his cheeks. Never yet for an instant had it come to him to think that Michael Sunlocks and the new Governor were the same man, and that Greeba and his bride were one. But, telling himself that she might even then be in that little town, with nothing but the darkness hiding him from her sight, he shuddered at the near chance of being discovered by her, and passed on by the river towards the sea. Yet, being alone there, with only the wash of the waves for company, he felt his great resolve begin to pall, as a hundred questions rose to torment him. Suppose she were here, and they were to meet, dare he after all do that? Though she loved this man, could he still do that? Oh, was it not horrible to think of—that he should cross the seas for that?

So, to put an end to the torture of such questionings, and escape from himself, he turned back from the shore to where the crowds looked thickest in the town. He went as he came, by the bank of the river, and when he was crossing the bridge some one shot past him on a horse. It was a man, and he drew up sharply at the Bishop's Palace, threw his reins over the pier of the gate, and bounded into the house with the light foot that goes with a light heart. "The new Governor," thought Jason, though he had seen him only as a shadow. "Who is he, I wonder?" he thought again, and with a sigh for his own condition within sight of this man's happiness he pushed heavily along.

Hardly had he got back into the town when he was seen and recognized, for with a whoop and a spring and a jovial oath a tipsy companion of former days came sweeping down upon him from the open door of a drinking-shop.

"What? Jason? Bless my soul! Come in," the fellow cried, embracing him; and to avoid the curious gaze of the throng that had gathered on the pavement Jason allowed himself to be led into the house.

"Well, God save us! So you're back! But I heard you had come. Old Jon Olafsson told us. He was down at the jetty. Boys," the fellow shouted to a little company of men who sat drinking in the hot parlor, "he's another Lazarus, come back from the dead."

"Here's to his goot healt, den," said a fat Dutch captain, who sat on the hearth, strumming a fiddle to tune it.

And while the others laughed and drank, a little deformed dwarf in a corner with an accordion between his twisted fingers began to play and sing.

"This is the last thing that should have happened," thought Jason, and with many excuses he tried to elbow his way out. But the tipsy comrade held him while he rattled on:

"Been away—foreign, eh? Married since? No? Then the girls of old Iceland are best, eh? What? Yes? And old Iceland's the fairest land the sun shines upon, eh? No? But, Lord bless me, what a mess you made of it by going away just when you did!"

At that Jason, while pushing his way through, turned about with a look of inquiry.

"Didn't know it? What? That after the mother died old Jorgen went about looking for you? No? Wanted? Why, to make a man of you, boy. Make you his son and the like of that, and not too soon either. And when he couldn't find you he took up with this Michael Sunlocks."

"Michael Sunlocks?" Jason repeated, in a distant sort of voice.

"Just so; this precious new Governor that wants to put down all the drinking."

"The new Governor?"

"Yes. Put your nose out, boy; for that was the start of his luck."

Jason felt dizzy, and under the hard tan of his skin his face grew white.

"You should know him, though. No? Well, after old Jorgen had quarrelled with him, everybody said he was a kind of bastard brother of yours."

The reeking place had got hotter and hotter. It was now stifling, and Jason stumbled out into the street.

Michael Sunlocks was the new Governor, and Michael Sunlocks was about to be married to Greeba. Thrice had this man robbed him of his blessing, standing in the place that ought to have been his; once with his father, once with Greeba, and once again with Jorgen Jorgensen.

He tried to reckon it all up, but do what he would he could not keep his mind from wandering. The truth had fallen upon him at a blow, and under his strong emotions his faculties seemed to be slain in a moment. He felt blind, and deaf, and unable to think. Presently, without knowing where he was going, but impelled by some blind force, and staggering along like a drunken man, he found himself approaching the Bishop's Palace.

"He is there," he thought: "the man who has stood in my place all his days: the man who has stripped me of every good thing in life. He is there, in honor, and wealth, and happiness; and I am here, a homeless outcast in the night. Oh, that I could do it now—now—now!"

But at that he remembered that he had never yet seen Michael Sun-locks, to know him from another man. "I must wait," he thought. "I must go to work cautiously. I must see him first, and watch him."

The night was then far spent towards midnight; the streets had grown quiet, the lights of the town no longer sent a yellow glare over the grass-clad housetops, and from a quiet sky the moon and stars shone out.

Jason was turning back towards his lodgings when he heard a voice that made him stand. It was a woman's voice singing, and it came with the un-dertones of some string instrument from the house in front of him. After a moment he pushed the gate open and walked across the little grass plat until he came beneath the only window from which a light still shone. There he stopped and listened, laying his hand on the sill to steady himself.

Ah! now he knew the voice too well. It was Greeba's. She was there; she was on the other side of that wall at that instant. And she was singing. It was a love-song that she sang. Her very heart seemed to speak in it, for her tones were the tones of love, and he must be beside her.

"It is for him she has left me," thought Jason, in the whirl of his dazed brain; "for him and his place, his station, and the pride of his success."

Then, remembering how his love of this woman had fooled him through five treacherous years, turning him aside from thoughts of his vow, giving him his father's money for his mother's wrongs, and how she who had been so damned dear to him had drawn him on in the days of her trouble, and cast him off when another beckoned to her, he cried in his tortured heart, "Oh, God in heaven, give me this man into my hands."

VIII: The Sword of Esau

Jason went back to his lodging by the Cathedral, found the old caretak-er sitting up for him, made some excuse for returning late, and turned in to bed. His room was the guest-chamber—a little, muggy, stifling box, with bed and bedding of eider down sewed into canvas sacks. He threw off his boots and lay down in his clothes. Hour followed hour and he did not sleep. He was nevertheless not wholly awake, but retained a sort of sluggish con-sciousness which his dazed brain could not govern. Twelve had chimed from the great clock of the turret overhead as he lay down, and he heard one, two, three, and four follow in their turn. By this time he was feeling a dull pain at the back of his head, and a heavy throbbing in his neck. Until then he had been ever a man of great bodily strength, with never an ache or ailment. "I am making myself ill before anything is done," he thought, "and if I fall sick nothing can come of my enterprise. That must not be." With an effort of will he composed himself to sleep. Still for a space he saw the weary night wear on; but the lapse, the broken thread, and the dazed sense stole over him at last, and he dropped into a deep slumber. When he awoke the white light of midday was coming in strong dancing bars through the rents of the dark blanket that covered the little window, the clock of the Cathedral was chiming twelve once again, and over the little cobble causeway of the street in front there was the light patter of many sealskin shoes. "How could I sleep away my time like this with so much to do?" he thought, and leapt up instantly.

His old landlady had more than once looked in upon him during the morning, and watched him with an air of pity. "Poor lad, he looks ill," she thought; and so left him to sleep on. While he ate his breakfast, of skyr and skate and coffee, the good soul busied herself about him, asking what work he had a mind to do now that he had come back, and where he meant to look for it, with other questions of a like kind. But he answered her many words with few of his own, merely saying that he intended to look about him before deciding on anything, and that he had something in his pocket to go on with in the meanwhile.

Some inquiries he made of her in his turn, and they were mainly about the new President, or Governor; what like he was to look upon, and what his movements were, and if he was much seen in the town. The good body could tell him very little, being old, very deaf, and feeble on her feet, and going about hardly at all farther than the floors of the Cathedral on cleaning days. But her deaf old husband, hobbling in from the street at that moment, said he had heard somebody say that a session of Althing was sitting then, and that under the Republic that had lately been proclaimed, Michael Sunlocks presided at the parliament-house daily about midday.

Hearing this, Jason rose from his unfinished breakfast, and went out on some pretended errand; but when he got to the wooden shed where Althing held its session he found the sitting over and the delegates dispersed. His only object had been to see Michael Sunlocks that he might know him, and having lost his first opportunity he returned the following day, coming earlier, before the sitting had begun or the delegates had yet gathered. But though he lounged within the door yard, while the members passed through, jesting and laughing together, he saw no one young enough to answer to Michael Sunlocks. He was too much in dread of attracting attention to inquire of the few idlers who looked on like himself, so he went away and came yet again the next day after and waited as before. Once more he felt that the man he looked for had not passed in with the rest, and, between fear of exciting suspicion and of throwing away further chances, he questioned the doorkeeper of the Chamber. This person stuttered before every word, but Jason learned at length that Michael Sunlocks had not been there for a week,

152

that by the rule of the new Constitution the Governor presided only at the sittings of the higher house, the Council, and that the present sittings were those of the lower house, the Senate.

That was Thursday, and Jason reflected that though four days were gone nothing was done. Vexed with himself for the caution that had wasted so much time, he boldly started inquiries on many sides. Then he learned that it was the daily practice of the Governor to go at twelve o'clock noon to the embankment in front of the merchant stores, where his gangs of masons were throwing up the new fort. At that hour that day Jason was there, but found that the Governor had already been and gone. Going earlier the next day, Friday, he learned that the Governor had not yet come, and so he lay about to wait for him. But the men whom he had questioned began to cast curious glances in his direction, and to mutter together in groups. Then he remembered that it was a time of revolution, that he might be mistaken for a Danish spy, and as such be forthwith seized and imprisoned. "That would stop everything," he thought, and moved away.

In a tavern of a by-street, a long lean youth, threadbare and tipsy, formerly a student and latterly expelled from the college for drunkenness, told him that the new Governor turned in at the Latin school every evening at dusk, to inspect the drill of the regiment he had enrolled. So to the Latin school at dusk Jason made his way, but the place was dark and silent when he came upon it, and from a lad who was running out at the moment he heard that the drill-sergeant had fallen ill, and the drill been discontinued.

On the wharf by the jetty the boatman who had recognized him on landing, old Jon Olafsson, told him that serving whiting and skate to the Bishop's Palace he found that the new Governor was ever coming and going there. Now of all houses Jason had most avoided that house, lest he should be seen of those eyes that would surely read his mission at a glance. Yet as night fell in, and he might approach the place with safety, he haunted the ways that led to it. But never again did he see Michael Sunlocks even in the uncertain darkness, and thinking how hard it was to set eyes on this man, whom he must know of a surety before ever his enterprise could be ripe, a secret dread took hold of him, and he all but renounced his design. "Why is it that I cannot see him?" he thought. "Why, of all men in the town, is he the only one whom I can never meet face to face? Why, of all men here, am I the only one whom he has never seen?" It was as if higher powers were keeping them apart.

By this time he realized that he was being observed, for in the dusk, on the Thingvellir road, that led past Government House, three men overtook him, and went on to talk with easy confidence in signs and broken words. He saw that they were Danes; that one was old and white-headed; another was young, sallow, and of a bitter spirit; and the third, who was elderly, was of a meek and quiet manner.

"How are they going on in the old country? Anything done yet? When are they coming?" said the young man.

"Ah, don't be afraid," said the old man. "We know you are watching him," he added, with a side-long motion of the head towards Government House. "But he will send no more of our sons and brothers to the sulphur mines, to slave like beasts of burden. His days are numbered."

Then the young man laughed bitterly.

"They say he is to be married. Let him make merry while he may," he said with a deep oath.

And at that Jason faced about to them.

"You have been mistaken, sirs," he said. "I am not a spy, and neither am I an assassin."

He walked away with what composure he could command, but he trembled like a leaf, for by this encounter three new thoughts possessed him; first, that when his attempt had been made and his work done, he who believed himself appointed by God as the instrument of His righteous retribution, would stand no otherwise before man than as a common midnight murderer; next, that unless he made haste with his design he would be forestalled by others with baser motives; and, again, that if his bearing had so nearly revealed his purpose to the Danes it might suggest it to others with more interest in defeating it.

In his former rashness he had gone everywhere, even where the throngs were thickest, and talked with everyone, even the six stalwart constables who had taken the place of the rheumatic watchmen whom he knew in earlier days. But from the hour of that meeting with the Danes he found himself going about as stealthily as a cat, watching everybody, thinking everybody was watching him, shrinking from every sight, and quaking at every sound. "They can do what they like with me after it is over," he thought, "but first let it be done."

He felt afraid, who had never before known the taste of fear; he felt weary, who had never until then known what it was to be tired. "Oh, what is this that is coming over me?" he thought. "If I am doing well, why do I tremble?" For even while he planned his daring attempt a great feebleness seemed to be in all his members.

Thus it chanced that on the next day thereafter, Saturday, he saw many busy preparations along the line of the High Street and its byways, such as the swinging of pulley ropes from house front to house front and the shaking out of bunting, without asking what festival they purported. But returning to his lodging in the evening he found his landlady busy with preparations of a like kind about the entrance to the yard of the Cathedral, and then he knew too well what new thing was coming. All the same he asked, and his landlady answered him:

"Lord bless me," she cried, "and haven't you heard that the young Governor is to be wedded?"

"When?" said Jason.

"To-morrow," said the old body.

"Where?"

"Why, in the Cathedral, surely. It will be a bonny sight, I promise you. You would like to see it, I make no doubt. Well, and so you shall, my son. I'll get you in. Only leave it to me. Only leave it to me."

Jason had expected this answer; like a horse that quivers under the lash, while it is yet hissing over his head, he had seen the blow coming, yet when it came it startled and stunned him. He got up, touching no food, and staggered back into the street.

It was now dark night. The stores were lit up by their open lamps, whose noisome smoke streamed out over the pathway, and mingled with the foul vapors that came from the drinking shops. The little town was very busy; throngs of people passed to and fro, and there was much shouting and noisy laughter.

To Jason all this was a mass of confusion, like a dream that is vague and broken and has no semblance of reality. His knees smote together as he walked, and his mind was clogged and numbed. At length he was conscious that some brawlers who were lounging at the door of a tavern were jeering as he went by them, and that a woman who was passing at the same moment was rating them roundly.

"Can't you see he's ill?" she was saying, and they were laughing lustily.

He turned towards the sea, and there, with only the black beach before his eyes and the monotonous beat of the waves in his ears, his faculties grew clearer. "Oh God!" he thought, "am I to strike him down before her face and at the very foot of the altar? It is terrible. It must be true that I am ill—or perhaps mad—or both."

But he wrestled with his irresolute spirit and overcame it. One by one he marshalled his reasons and bit by bit he justified himself. When his anger wavered against the man who had twice supplanted him, he recalled his vow to execute judgment, and when his vow seemed horrible he remembered that Greeba herself had wronged him.

Thus he had juggled with himself night after night, and if morning after morning peace had come with the coming of light, it was gone forever now. He rehearsed everything in his mind and saw it all as he meant it to be. To-morrow while the bells were ringing he would go into the Cathedral. His old landlady, the caretaker, would put him in the front seat before the altar-rail. The pews would already be thronged, and there would be whispering behind him, and little light fits of suppressed laughter. Presently the old Bishop would come, halting along in his surplice, holding the big book in his trembling hands. Then the bridegroom would step forward, and he should see him and mark him and know him. The bride herself would come next in a dazzling cloud of her bridesmaids, all dressed in white. Then as the two stood together—he and she, hand in hand, glancing softly at each other, and with all other eyes upon them, he himself would rise up—and do it. Suddenly there would be a wild cry, and she would turn towards him, and see him, and understand him, and fall fainting before him. Then while both lay at his feet he would turn to those about him and say, very calmly, "Take me. It was I." All being done, he would not shrink, and when his time came he would meet his fate without flinching, and in the awful hereafter he would stand before the white throne and say, "It would have been an evil thing if God's ways had not been justified before men: so I have executed on earth His judgment who has said in His Holy Writ that the wrongdoer shall surely suffer vengeance, even to the third and fourth generation of his children."

Thinking so, in the mad tangle of his poor, disordered brain, yet with a great awe upon him as of one laden with a mission from on high, Jason went back to his lodging, threw himself down, without undressing, upon the bed, and fell into a heavy sleep.

When he awoke next morning the bells in the turret overhead were jangling in his ears, and his deaf old landlady was leaning over him and calling to him.

"Get up, love, get up: it's late, love; you'll miss it all, love; it's time to go in, love," she was saying; and a little later she led him by a side door into the Cathedral.

He took a seat where he had decided to take it, in a corner of the pew before the altar-rail, and all seemed the same as he had pictured. The throngs of people were behind him, and he could hear their whispering and light laughter while they waited. There was the door at which the venerable Bishop would soon enter, carrying his big book, and there was the path, kept free and strewn with flowers, down which the bride and her train would pass on to the red form before him. Ah! the flowers—blood red and purple—how sweetly they trailed over altar-rail, and pulpit, and the tablet of the ten commandments! Following them with his eyes, while with his hands he fumbled his belt for that which he had concluded to carry there, suddenly he was smitten with an awful dread. One line of the printed words before him seemed to come floating through the air down to his face in a vapor of the same blood-red.

156

Thou shalt do no murder!

Jason started to his feet. Why was he there? What had he come to do? He must go. The place was stifling him. In another moment he was crushing his way out of the Cathedral. He felt like a man sentenced to death.

Being in the free air again he regained his self-control. "What madness! It is no murder," he thought. But he could not get back to his seat, and so he turned to where the crowd was thickest outside. That was down the line of the pathway to the wide west entrance. As he approached this point he saw that the people were in high commotion. He hurried up to them and inquired the cause. The bridal party had just passed through. At that moment the full swell of the organ came out through the open doors. The marriage service had begun.

After a while Jason had so far recovered his composure as to look about him. Deep as the year had sunk towards winter, the day was brilliant. The air was so bright that it seemed to ring. The sea in front of the town smiled under the sunlight; the broad stretch of lava behind it glistened, the glaciers in the distance sparkled, and the black jokulls far beyond showed their snowy domes against the blue sky. Oh, it was one of God's own mornings, when all His earth looks glad. And the Cathedral yard—for all it slept so full of dead men's bones—was that day a bright and busy place. Troops of happy girls were there in their jackets of gray, braided with gold or silver, and with belts of filigree; troops of young men, too, in their knee breeches, with bows of red ribbon, their dark-gray stockings and sealskin shoes; old men as well in their coats of homespun; and old women in their long blue cloaks; children in their plaited kirtles, and here and there a traveller with his leather wallet for his snuff and money. At the entrance gate there was a triumphal arch of ribbons and evergreens, and under its shadow there were six men with horns and guns, ready for a salute when the bride appeared; and in the street outside there was a stall laden with food and drink for all who should that day come and ask.

Only to Jason was the happy place a Gethsemane, and standing in the thick of the crowd, on a grave with a sunken roof, under the shadow of the Cathedral, he listened with a dull ear to the buzz of talk between two old gossips behind him. He noticed that they were women with prominent eyeballs, which produced a dreamy, serious, half-stupid, half-humorous look, like that of the dogs in the picture that sit in the judgment-seat.

"She's English," said one. "No, Irish. No, Manx—whatever that means. Anyway, she's foreign, and can't speak a word that anybody can understand. So Mother Helda says, and she's a worthy woman, you know, and cleans the floors at the Palace."

"But they say she's a sweet lady for all that," said the other; and just then a young student at their back pushed his laughing face between their shoulders and said,

"Who? Old Mother Helda?"

"Mother Helda be bothered. The lady. And her father has been wrecked in coming to her wedding, too! Poor old man, what a pity! The Governor sent my son Oscar with twenty of Loega's men to Stappen to look for me. That was a fortnight ago. I expect him back soon."

"They might have waited until he came. Why didn't they?"

"Oscar?" said the laughing face between them.

"The father, goose. Poor lady, how lonely she must feel! But then the old Bishop is so good to everybody."

"Well, he deserves a good wife."

"The old Bishop?" said the student, shaking his sides.

"The young Governor, I'm talking of; and don't be so quick in snapping folks up, Jon Arnason. He's the best Governor we ever had. And what a change from the last one. Why, he doesn't mind speaking to anyone. Just think, only yesterday he stopped me and said, 'Good morning;' he said, 'your son won't be long away now,' quite humble and homelike."

"Well, God bless him—and her too, foreign or not—and may they live long——"

"And have a good dozen," added the laughing voice behind them.

And then all three laughed together.

By this time the organ which had been silent for a little while, had burst forth afresh, and though its strains were loud and jubilant, yet to Jason they seemed to tell the story of his sorrow and all the trouble of his days. He tried not to listen, and to pass the moments in idly watching the swaying throng, whose heads beneath his own rose and fell like a broken sea. But his mind would be active, and the broad swell of the music floated into his soul and consumed it. "Can it be possible," he thought, "that I intend to smite him down when he comes through that doorway by her side? And yet I love her—and he is my brother."

Still the organ rang out over graveyard and people, and only by an effort of will could Jason hold back his tears. "Man! man!" he cried in his heart, "call it by its true name—not judgment, but murder. Yes, murder for jealous love, murder for love despised!"

A new and awful light had then illumined his gloomy mind, and his face betokened his sufferings, for, though no tears fell down his hard cheeks, his eyes were bloodshot. In complete self-forgetfulness he pressed forward, until his way was stopped by a little iron cross that stood at the head of a grave. "My mother's," he thought. "No, hers is next."

The organ broke into yet another strain at that moment—a proud, triumphant peal of song, which in the frenzy of Jason's mind seemed either to reach up to heaven's gate or to go down to the brink of hell. There was a movement among the people, a buzz of voices, a hush, and a whispered cry, "They are coming, they are coming!"

"God bless them," said one.

"Heaven protect them," said another.

And every blessing fell on Jason like a curse. "Murder let it be," he thought, and turned his eyes where other eyes were looking. Then passing under the broad arch, stepping out of the blue shadow into the white sunshine, all radiant in her grace and lovely sweetness, meek and tender, with tears in her soft brown eyes—it was she, it was she; it was Greeba—Greeba—Greeba.

Jason felt his strength exhausted. A strange dizziness seized him. He looked down to avoid the light. His eyes fell on the iron cross before him, and he read the name graven upon it. The name was his own.

Then everything seemed to whirl around him. He remembered no more, save a shuffling of feet, a dull hum over his head, like the noise of water in the ears of a drowning man, and a sense of being lifted and carried.

But another consciousness came to him, and it was very sweet, though uncertain. He was floating up—up—up to where the mountains were green, and the sea was tranquil, and the trees made music in the quiet air. And Greeba was there, and she was laying her cool hand on his hot forehead, and he was looking at the troubled heaving of her round bosom. "Aren't you very proud of yourself, Jason?" she was whispering softly, and then he was clasping the beautiful girl in his arms and kissing her, and she was springing away, blushing deeply, and he was holding down his head, and laughing in his heart.

"Lie still, love; lie you still," fell on his ear, and he opened his eyes. He was in his own room at the little cottage of the caretakers. The old woman was bending over him, and bathing his forehead with one hand, while with the other hand she was holding her apron to her eyes.

"He's coming round nicely, praise the Lord," she said, cheerily.

"I remember," said Jason, in a weak voice. "Did I faint?"

"Faint, love?" said the good soul, putting her deaf ear close to his lips. "Why, it's fever, love; brain fever."

"What time is it?" said Jason.

"Time, love? Lord help us, what does the boy want with the time? But it's just the way with all of them. Mid-evening, love."

"What day is it—Sunday?"

"Sunday, love? No, but Tuesday. It was on Sunday you fell senseless, poor boy."

"Where was that?"

"Where? Why, where but in the Cathedral yard, just at the very minute the weddiners were coming out at the door."

And hearing this Jason's face broke into a smile like sunshine, and he uttered a loud cry of relief. "Thank God. Oh, thank God."

But while an angel of hope seemed to bring him good tidings of a great peril averted, and even as a prayer gushed from his torn heart, he remembered the vision of his delirium, and knew that he was forever a bereaved and broken man. At that his face, which had been red as his hair, grew pale as ashes, and a low cunning came over him, and he wondered if he had betrayed himself in his unconsciousness.

"Have I been delirious?" he asked.

"Delirious, love? Oh, no, love, no; only distraught a little and cursing sometimes, the Saints preserve us," said the old landlady in her shrill treble.

Jason remembered that the old woman was deaf, and gathering that she alone had nursed him, and that no one else had seen him since his attack, except her deaf husband and a druggist from the High Street who had bled him, he smiled and was satisfied.

"Lord bless me, how he mends," said the hearty old woman, and she gave him the look of an affectionate dog.

"And now, good soul, I am hungry and must make up for all this fasting," said Jason.

"Ay, ay, and that you must, lad," said the old woman, and off she went to cook him something to eat.

But his talk of hunger had been no more than a device to get rid of her, for he knew that the kind creature would try to restrain him from rising. So when she was gone he stumbled to his feet, feeling very weak and dazed, and with infinite struggle and sweat tugged on his clothes—for they had been taken off—and staggered out into the streets.

It was night, and the clouds hung low as if snow might be coming, but the town seemed very light, as with bonfires round about it and rockets shot into the air, and very noisy, too, as with guns fired and music played, so that Jason's watery eyes felt dazzled, and his singing ears were stunned. But he walked on, hardly knowing which way he was going, and hearing only as sounds at sea the voices that called to him from the doors of the drinking-shops, until he came out at the bridge to the Thingvellir road. And there, in the sombre darkness, he was overtaken by the three Danes who had spoken to him before.

"So your courage failed you at the last moment—I watched you and saw how it was. Ah, don't be afraid, we are your friends, and you are one of us. Let us play at hide-and-seek no longer."

"They say he is going down the fiord in search of his wife's father. Take care he does not slip away. Old Jorgen is coming back. Good-night."

So saying, without once turning their faces towards Jason's face, they strode past him with an indifferent air. Then Jason became conscious that Government House was ablaze with lights, that some of its windows were half down, that sounds of music and dancing came from within, and that on the grass plat in front, which was lit by torches men and women in gay costumes were strolling to and fro, in pairs.

And turning from the bridge towards the house he saw a man go by on horseback in the direction of the sea, and remembered in a dull way that just there and at that hour he had seen Michael Sunlocks ride past him in the dusk.

What happened thereafter he never rightly knew, only that in a distempered dream he was standing with others outside the rails about Government House while the snow began to fall through the darkness, that he saw the dancers circling across the lighted windows and heard the music of the flutes and violins above the steady chime of the sea, that he knew this merry-making to be a festival of her marriage whom he loved with a love beyond that of his immortal soul, that the shame of his condition pained him, and the pain of it maddened him, the madness of it swept away his consciousness, and that when he came to himself he had forced his way into the house, thinking to meet his enemy face to face, and was in a room alone with Greeba, who was cowering before him with a white face of dismay.

"Jason," she was saying, "why are you here?"

"Why are you here?" he asked.

"Why have you followed me?" she cried.

"Why have you followed him?"

"What have you come for?"

"Is this what you have come for?"

"Jason," she cried again, "I wronged you, that is true, but you forgave me. I asked you to choose for me, and if you had said 'stay,' I should have stayed. But you released me, you know you did. You gave me up to him, and now he is my husband."

"But this man is Michael Sunlocks," said Jason.

"Didn't you know that before?" said Greeba. "Ah, then, I know what you have come for. You have recalled your forgiveness, and have come to punish me for deserting you. But spare me! Oh, spare me! Not for my own sake, but his; for I am his wife now and he loves me very dearly. No, no, not that, but only spare me, Jason," she cried, and crouched at his feet.

"I would not harm a hair of your head, Greeba," he said.

"Then what have you come for?" she said.

"This man is a son of Stephen Orry," he said.

"Then it is for him," she cried, and leaped to her feet. "Ah, now I understand. I have not forgotten the night in Port-y-Vullin."

"Does he know of that?" said Jason.

"No."

"Does he know I am here?"

"No."

"Does he know we have met?"

"No."

"Let me see him!"

"Why do you ask to see him?"

"Let me see him."

"But why?" she stammered. "Why see him? It is I who have wronged you."

"That's why I want to see him," said Jason.

She uttered a cry of terror and staggered back. There was an ominous silence, in which it passed through Greeba's mind that all that was happening then had happened before. She could hear Jason's labored breathing and the dull thud of the music through the walls.

"Jason," she cried, "What harm has he ever done you? I alone am guilty before you. If your vengeance must fall on anyone let it fall on me."

"Where is he?" said Jason.

"He is gone," said Greeba.

"Gone?"

"Yes, to find my poor father. The dear old man was wrecked in coming here, and my husband sent men to find him, but they blundered and came back empty-handed, and not a half an hour ago he went off himself."

"Was he riding?" said Jason; but without waiting for an answer he made towards the door.

"Wait! Where are you going?" cried Greeba.

Swift as lightning the thought had flashed though her mind, "What if he should follow him!"

Now the door to the room was a heavy, double-hung door of antique build, and at the next instant she had leaped to it and shot the heavy wooden bar that bolted it.

At that he laid one powerful hand on the bar itself, and wrenched it outward across the leverage of its iron loops, and it cracked and broke, and fell to the ground in splinters.

Then her strong excitement lent the brave girl strength, and her fear for her husband gave her courage, and crying, "Stop, for heaven's sake stop," she put her back to the door, tore up the sleeve of her dress, and thrust her bare right arm through the loops where the bar had been.

"Now," she cried, "you must break my arm after it."

"God forbid," said Jason, and he fell back for a moment at that sight. But, recovering himself, he said, "Greeba, I would not touch your beautiful arm to hurt it; no, not for all the wealth of the world. But I must go, so let me pass."

Still her terror was centred on the thought of Jason's vengeance.

"Jason," she cried, "he is my husband. Only think—my husband."

"Let me pass," said Jason.

"Jason," she cried again, "my husband is everything to me, and I am all in all to him."

"Let me pass," said Jason.

"You intend to follow him. You are seeking him to kill him."

"Let me pass."

"Deny it."

"Let me pass."

"Never," she cried. "Kill me if you will, but until you have done so you shall not pass this door. Kill me!"

"Not for my soul's salvation!" said Jason.

"Then give up your wicked purpose. Give it up, give it up."

"Only when he shall have given up his life."

"Then I warn you, I will show you no pity, for you have shown none to me."

At that she screamed for help, and presently the faint music ceased, and there was a noise of hurrying feet. Jason stood a moment listening; then he looked towards the window, and saw that it was of one frame, and had no sash that opened. At the next instant he had doubled his arms across his face and dashed through glass and bars.

A minute afterwards the room was full of men and women, and Jason was brought back into it, pale, sprinkled with snow and blood-stained.

"I charge that man with threatening the life of my husband," Greeba cried.

Then it seemed as if twenty strong hands laid hold of Jason at once. But no force was needed, for he stood quiet and silent, and looked like a man who had walked in his sleep, and been suddenly awakened by the sound of

Greeba's voice. One glance he gave her of great suffering and proud defiance, and then, guarded on either hand, passed out of the place like a captured lion.

IX: The Peace Oath

There was short shrift for Red Jason. He was tried by the court nearest the spot, and that was the criminal court over which the Bishop in his civil capacity presided, with nine of his neighbors on the bench beside him. From this court an appeal was possible to the Court of the Quarter, and again from the Quarter Court to the High Court of Althing; but appeal in this case there was none, for there was no defence. And because Icelandic law did not allow of the imprisonment of a criminal until after he had been sentenced, an inquest was called forthwith, lest Jason should escape or compass the crime he had attempted. So the Court of Inquiry sat the same night in the wooden shed that served both for Senate and House of Justice.

The snow was now falling heavily, and the hour was late, but the courthouse was thronged. It was a little place—a plain box, bare, featureless, and chill, with walls, roof and seats of wood, and floor of hard earth. Four short benches were raised, step above step, against the farthest side, and on the highest of these the Bishop sat, with three of his colleagues on each of the three rows beneath him. The prisoner stood on a broad stool to the right, and the witnesses on a like stool to the left. A wooden bar crossed the room about midway, and in the open space between that and the door the spectators were crowded together. The place was lighted by candles, and some were fixed to the walls, others were held by ushers on the end of long sticks, and a few were hung to the roof rafters by hemp ropes tied about their middle. The floor ran like a stream, and the atmosphere was full of the vapor of the snow that was melting on the people's clothes. Nothing could be ruder than the courthouse, but the Court that sat there observed a rule of procedure that was almost an idolatry of form.

The prisoner was called by the name of Jason, son of Stephen Orry, and having answered in a voice so hollow that it seemed to come out of the earth beneath him, he rose to his place. His attitude was dull and impassive, and he seemed hardly to see the restless crowd that murmured at sight of him. His tall figure stooped, there was a cloud on his strong brow, and a slow fire in his bloodshot eyes, and his red hair, long as a woman's, hung in disordered masses down his worn cheeks to his shoulders. The Bishop, a venerable prelate of great age, looked at him and thought, "That man's heart is dead within him."

The spokesman of the Court was a middle-aged man, who was short, had little piercing eyes, a square brush of iron-gray hair that stood erect across the top of his corded forehead, and a crisp, clear utterance, like the crackle of a horse's hoofs on the frost.

Jason was charged with an attempt to take the life of Michael Sunlocks, first President of the second Republic. He did not plead and had no defence, and the witnesses against him spoke only in answer to the leading questions of the judges.

The first of the witnesses was Greeba herself, and her evidence, given in English, was required to be interpreted. All her brave strength was now gone. She trembled visibly. Her eyes were down, her head was bent, her face was half-hidden by the hood of a cloak she wore, and her tones were barely audible. She had little to say. The prisoner had forced his way into Government House, and there, to her own face, had threatened to take the life of her husband. In plain words he had done so, and then made show of going in pursuit of her husband that he might carry out his design.

"Wait," said the Bishop, "your husband was not present?"

"No," said Greeba.

"There was, therefore, no direct violence?"

"None."

"And the whole sum of the prisoner's offence, so far as you know of it, lies in the use of the words that you have repeated?"

"Yes."

Then, turning to the spokesman of the Court, the old Bishop said—

"There has been no overt act. This is not an attempt, but a threat to take life. And this is not a crime by the law of this, or any other Christian country."

"Your pardon, my lord," said the little man, in his crisp tones. "I will show that the prisoner is guilty of the essential part of murder itself. Murder, my lord," he added, "is not merely to compass the destruction of a life, for there is homicide, by misadventure, there is justifiable homicide, and there are the rights, long recognized by Icelandic law, of the avengers of blood. Murder is to kill in secrecy and after long-harbored malice, and now my lord, I shall show that the prisoner has lain in wait to slay the President of the Republic."

At that Greeba stood down, and other witnesses followed her. Nearly everyone had been summoned with whom Jason had exchanged words since he landed eight days before. There was the lean student who had told him of the drill at the Latin school, the little tailor who had explained the work at the jail, the stuttering doorkeeper at the senate-house, and one of the masons at the fort. Much was made of the fainting in the Cathedral yard, on the

Sunday morning, and out of the deaf landlady, the Cathedral caretaker, some startling disclosures seemed to be drawn.

"Still," said the old Bishop, "I see no overt act."

"Good gracious, my lord," said the little spokesman, "are we to wait until the knife itself has been reddened?"

"God forbid!" said the old Bishop.

Then came two witnesses to prove motive. The first of them was the tipsy comrade of former days, who had drawn Jason into the drinking-shop. He could say of his own knowledge that Jason was jealous of the new Governor. The two were brothers in a sort of way. So people said, and so Jason had told him. They had the same father, but different mothers. Jason's mother had been the daughter of the old Governor, who turned his back on her at her marriage. At her death he relented, and tried to find Jason, but could not, and then took up with Michael Sunlocks. People said that was the beginning of the new President's fortune. At all events Jason thought he had been supplanted, was very wroth, and swore he would be revenged.

The second of the two witnesses pointed to a very different motive. He was one of the three Danes who had twice spoken to Jason—the elderly man with the meek and quiet manner. Though himself loyal to the Icelandic Republic he had been much thrown among its enemies. Jason was one of them; he came here as a spy direct from Copenhagen, and his constant associates were Thomsen, an old, white-headed man living in the High Street, and Polvesen, a young and sallow man, who kept one of the stores facing the sea. With these two Jason had been heard by him to plan the assassination of the President.

At this evidence there was a deep murmur among the people, and it was seen that Greeba had risen again to her feet. Her heart burned and stormed within her. She tried to speak but could not. At the same moment Jason turned his bloodshot eyes in her direction, and then her limbs gave way under her, and she sank back with a moan. The Court misread her emotion, and she was removed. Jason's red eyes followed her constantly.

"This is a case for the Warning, not for punishment," said the Bishop. "It is plainly written in our old Law Book that if a man threaten to slay another man he shall be warned of the gravity of the crime he contemplates and of the penalty attaching to it."

"Gracious heavens, my lord," cried the little spokesman, "what reason have we to assume that this prisoner is ignorant of either? With a life to guard that is prized by friends and precious to the State shall we let this man go free who had sworn before witnesses to destroy it?"

"God forefend!" said the Bishop.

It was lawful to question the prisoner, and so he was questioned.

"Is it true that you have been lying in wait to kill the President?" asked the spokesman.

But Jason made no answer.

"Is it true that you have done so from a desire for personal vengeance?"

No answer.

"Or from political motives?"

No answer.

"Or both?"

Still no answer.

Then the spokesman turned back to the Court. "The stubborn persistence of the prisoner is easy to understand," he said, and smiled.

"Wait," said the old Bishop, and he turned towards Jason.

"Have you any valid plea?"

But Jason gave no sign.

"Listen," said the Bishop. "Though the man who compasses the destruction of a single life is as though he had destroyed a world, for the posterity of him who is dead might have filled a world, yet have all laws of men since the Pentateuch recognized certain conditions that limit the gravity of the crime. If the man who is slain has himself slain the near kindred of his slayer, though the law of Iceland would no longer hold him guiltless, as in the ancient times when evil for evil was the rule and sentence, neither would it punish him as a murderer, who must eat the bread and drink the water of misery all his days. Now what is true of murder must be true of intent to murder, and though I am loth to believe it possible in this instance, honoring and loving as we all do that good man whom you are charged with lying in wait to kill, yet in my duty must I ask you the question—Has Michael Sunlocks spilled blood of your blood, and is it as a redeemer of blood that you go about to slay him?"

There was a dead hush in the little crowded courthouse as Jason lifted his heavy, bloodshot eyes to the Bishop's face and answered, in a weary voice, "I have nothing to say."

Then an aged Lutheran priest, who had sat within the rail, with a snuff-box in his hand and a red print handkerchief across his knee, hobbled up to the witness stool and tendered evidence. He could throw light on the prisoner's hatred of the President, if it was true that the President was a son of Stephen Orry. He knew the prisoner, and had named him in his baptism. He had known the prisoner's mother also, and had sat with her at her death. It was quite true that she was a daughter of the late Governor, and had been badly treated by her father. But she had been yet more badly treated by her husband, who married again while she was still alive, and had another son by the other wife. On her deathbed she had heard of this, and told the prisoner, who then and there, this witness being present, made an awful vow of vengeance upon his father and his father's son.

The old priest was heard in silence, and his words sent a quiver through the courthouse. Even Jason, who had shown no interest save when Greeba was removed, lifted up his bloodshot eyes again and listened.

And the Bishop, visibly moved, turned to the Court and said, "Let us put this prisoner back to be tried by the High Court and the Lagmann."

"What, my lord!" cried the little spokesman, with a lofty look, "and set him at liberty in the meantime, to carry out the crime he threatens?"

"Heaven forbid!" said the Bishop.

"Remember, until he has been condemned we have no power to hold him," said the spokesman.

The Bishop turned to an usher and said, "Bring me the Statute Book," and the great tome was brought. The Bishop opened it and again turned to the prisoner. "The Almighty," said he, "created one man at the beginning to teach us that all men are brethren, and the law of our old country provides that when two have had disputes and pursued each other on account of hatred, even as brethren they shall make peace before their neighbors. Now listen to the words I shall read to you, and be ready to say if you will swear to them."

Then a great silence fell upon the people, while in solemn tones the old Bishop read the Peace Oath.

"Ye two shall be set at one and live friendly together, at meat and at drink, in the Althing and at meetings, at kirk prayers and in King's palace; and in whatever place else men meet together, there shall ye be so set at one, as if this quarrel had never come between you. Ye shall share knife and meat together, and all things besides, as friends and not as enemies."

The Bishop paused and looked over his spectacles at Jason, who stood as before, with the cloud on his brow and the slow fire in his deep eyes, but with no sign of feeling or interest.

"Will you promise to swear to this, when he shall have returned who should swear to it with you?" said the Bishop.

Then all eyes turned towards Jason, and there came across his face at that moment the look of a bated dog.

"No," he growled.

The spokesman shifted in his seat and the people grew restless.

"Listen again," said the Bishop, and his long white beard shook and his solemn voice rose to a shrill cry as he twisted back to the book and read:—

"But if one of you be so mad that he breaks this truce thus made, and slays after pledges have been made and his blade has reddened, he shall be an outlaw, accursed and driven away, so far as men drive wolves farthest away. He shall be banished of God and all good Christian men, as far as Christian men seek churches, as mothers bring forth sons, son calls mother, flames blaze up, mankind kindle fire, earth is green, sun shines, and snow covers the ground; he shall flee from kirk and Christian men, God's house and mankind, and from every home save hell."

Then there was a pause and a great hush, and the Bishop lifted his eyes from the book, and said—

"Will you swear to it?"

Again all eyes turned towards Jason, and again his face, which had been impassive, took the look of a bated dog.

"No, no, no!" he cried in a loud voice, and then the great silence was broken by deep murmurs.

"It is useless," said the spokesman. "Warnings and peace oaths, though still valid, are the machinery of another age. This prisoner is not ignorant of the gravity of the crime he contemplates, nor yet of the penalty attaching to it."

There was an audible murmur of assent from the people.

"That's true," said one. "It's the truest word spoken to-night," said another. "The old man is all for mercy," said a third. "It isn't safe," said a fourth. And there was other whispering, and much nodding of heads and shuffling of feet.

Encouraged by these comments the little spokesman added—

"In any other country at this age of the world a man who tacitly admitted a design to take life would be promptly clapped into prison."

"Ay, ay," the people muttered, but the Bishop drew himself up and said, "In any other country a criminal who showed no fear of the death that hung over him would be straightway consigned to a madhouse."

"We have no madhouse in this island, my lord," said the little spokesman, "save the Sulpher Mines, and there he must go."

"Wait," said the Bishop, and once again he turned to the prisoner. "If this Court should agree to ship you out of Iceland will you promise never more to return to it?"

For the third time all eyes were turned on Jason, but he did not seem to hear the Bishop's question.

"Will you promise?" said the Bishop again.

"No," said Jason.

"Dangerous trifling," said the spokesman. "When you seize a mad dog you strangle it."

"Ay, ay," cried many voices at once, and great excitement prevailed.

The old Bishop drew back with a sigh of relief. He loved Michael Sunlocks and had been eager to save him. He pitied Greeba, and for her sake also had been anxious to protect her husband. But from the moment he saw Jason and thought, "That man's heart is dead within him," his love had struggled with his sense of duty. As the trial went on he had remembered Jason and recalled his bitter history, and seized with a strong sympathy he had strained every nerve to keep back his punishment. He had done all he could do, he had nothing to reproach himself with, and full of a deep and secret joy at the certainty of the safety of Sunlocks, he now fell back that the law might take its course.

The Court was counted out, and then the Bishop turned for the last time to Jason, and delivered judgment. "The sentence of this Court," he said "is that you be removed from here to the Sulpher Mines, and be kept there six months certain, and as long thereafter as you refuse to take the Oath of Peace pledging yourself forever, as long as you live or the world endures, to be at one with your enemy as brothers before all men living."

Now Greeba alone knew the truth about Jason. When she had fled from Mann without word or warning it had not been out of fear of him, but of her brothers. Her meeting with Michael Sunlocks, her short stay with the good old Bishop Petersen, her marriage and the festival that followed, had passed her by like a dream. Then came the first short parting with Sunlocks when he had said, "I must leave you for a fortnight, for the men I sent in search of your father have blundered and returned without him." She had cried a little at that, and he had kissed her, and made a brave show of his courage, though she could see the tears in his own big shining eyes. But it was all a dream, a sweet and happy dream, and only by the coming of Jason had the dream been broken.

Then followed her terror, her plea, her fear for her husband's life, her defiance of Jason, and the charge she made against him.

And the first burst of her passion over, she had thought to herself, "My husband is safe, but Jason will now tell all and I shall be a lost and ruined woman," for nothing had she yet said to Michael Sunlocks concerning the man who had wooed and won and released her during the long years of his silence and her trouble. "He will hear the story now," she thought, "and not from my lips but from Jason's."

Being then so far immersed she could not but go on, and so she had allowed herself to be led to the courthouse. No one there had thought to ask her if she had known anything of Jason before that day, and she on her part had said nothing of knowing him. But when Jason had looked at her with eyes of reproach that seemed to go through her soul, he seemed to be saying, "This is but half the truth. Dare you not tell the rest?"

Then listening to the lying of other witnesses, and looking up at Jason's face, so full of pain, and seeing how silent he was under cruel perjury, she remembered that this man's worst crime had been his love of her, and so she staggered to her feet to confess everything.

When she came to herself after that, she was back in her own home—her new home, the home of her happy dream, her husband's home and hers, and there her first fear returned to her. "He will tell all," she thought, "and evil tongues will make it worse, and shame will fall upon my husband, and I shall be lost, lost, lost."

She waited with feverish impatience for the coming of the Bishop to tell her the result of the trial, and at length he came.

"What have they done with him?" she cried; and he told her.

"What defence did he make?" she asked.

"None," said the Bishop.

"What did he say?" she asked again.

"Not a word but 'No,'" said the Bishop.

Then she drew a long breath of immense relief, and at the next instant she reproached herself. How little of soul she had been! And how great of heart had been Jason! He could have wrecked her life with a word, but he had held his peace. She had sent him to prison, and rather than smite he had suffered himself to be smitten. She felt herself small and mean.

And the Bishop, having, as he thought, banished Greeba's terror, hobbled to the door, for now the hour was very late, and the snow was still falling.

"The poor soul will do your good husband no mischief now. Poor lad! poor lad! After all, he is more fit for a madhouse than for a prison. Good-night, my child, good-night."

And so the good old man went his way.

It was intended that Jason should start for the Sulphur Mines on the following day, and he was lodged over night in a little house of detention that stood on the south of the High Street. But the snow continued to fall the whole night through, and in the morning the roads were impassable. Then it was decided to postpone the long journey until the storm should have passed, the frost set in, and the desolate white wastes to be crossed become hard and firm. It was now Wednesday of the second week in October—the Gore-month—and the people were already settling down to the long rest of the Icelandic winter. The merchants began to sleep the livelong day in their deserted stores in the cheapstead, and the bonders, who had come up with the last of their stock, to drink and doze in the taverns. All that day the snow fell in fine dust like flour, until, white as it was, the air grew dark with it. At the late dawn of the next day the snow was still falling, and a violent gale had then risen. Another and another and yet another day went by, and still the snow fell and the gale continued. For two days there was no daylight, and only at noon through the giddy air a fiery glow burned for an hour along the southern sky and then went out. Nothing could be seen of fell or fiord, and nothing could be heard save the baying of the hounds at night and the roar of the sea at all times, for the wind made no noise in the soft snow, but drove it along in sheets like silent ghosts.

Never before had Greeba seen anything so terrible; and still more fearful than the great snow itself was the anxiety it brought her. Where was Michael Sunlocks? Where was her father? There was only one other whose condition troubled her, and she knew too well where he was—he was lying in the dark cell of the dark house in the High Street.

While the storm lasted all Reykjavik lay asleep, and Greeba could do nothing. But one morning when she awoke and turned to the window, as was her wont, to learn if the weary snow was still falling, she could see nothing at first for the coating of ice and hoar frost that covered the glass. But the snow had ceased, the wind had fallen, the air was clear and the light was coming. The buildings of the town, from the Cathedral to the hovels of the fishing quarter, looked like snow mounds in the desert; the black waste of lava was gone; the black beach was gone; the black jokulls were gone; the black headland was gone that had stretched like a giant hand of many fingers into the black fiord; but height above height, and length beyond length, as far as from sea to sky, and from sea to sea, the world lay lifeless and silent and white around her.

Then, the town being once more awake, Greeba had news of Jason. It came through a little English maid, whom Sunlocks had found for her, from Oscar, the young man who had gone out in search of her father and returned without him. Jason was ill. Five days he had eaten nothing, and nothing had he drunk except water. He was in a fever—a brain fever—and it was now known for certain that he was the man who had fainted outside the Cathedral on the marriage morning, that he had been ill ever since then, and that the druggist of the High Street had bled him.

With these tidings Greeba hurried away to the Bishop.

"The poor man has brain fever," she said. "He was ill when he made the threat, and when he recovers he will regret it; I am sure he will—I know he will. Set him at liberty, for mercy's sake," she cried; and she trembled as she spoke, lest in the fervor of her plea the Bishop should read her secret.

But he only shook his head and looked tenderly down at her, and said very gently, though every word went to her heart like a stab—

"Ah, it is like a good woman to plead for one who has injured her. But no, my child, no; it may not be. Poor lad, no one now can do anything for him save the President himself; and he is not likely to liberate a man who lies in wait to kill him."

"He is likely," thought Greeba, and straightway she conceived of a plan. She would go to Jason in his prison. Yes, she herself would go to him, and prevail with him to put away all thoughts of vengeance and be at peace with her husband. Then she would wait for the return of Michael Sunlocks, and plead with that dear heart that could deny her nothing, to grant her Jason's pardon. Thus it would come about that she, who had stood between these two to separate them, would at length stand between them to bring them together.

So thinking, and crying a little, like a true woman, at the prospect of so much joy, she waited for Jason's recovery that she might carry her purpose into effect. Meantime she contrived to send him jellies and soups, such as might tempt the appetite of a sick man. She thought she sent them secretly, but with less than a woman's wit she employed a woman on her errand. This person was the little English maid, and she handed over the duty to Oscar, who was her sweetheart. Oscar talked openly of what he was doing, and thus all Reykjavik knew that the tender-hearted young wife of the Governor held communications of some sort with the man whom she had sent to jail.

Then one day, on hearing that Jason was better, though neither was he so well as to travel nor was the snow hard enough to walk upon, Greeba stole across to the prison in the dark of the afternoon, saying nothing to anyone of her mission or intention.

The stuttering doorkeeper of the Senate was the jailor, and he betrayed great concern when Greeba asked to see his prisoner, showing by his ghastly looks, for his words would not come, that it would be rash on her part, after helping so much towards Jason's imprisonment, to trust herself in his presence.

"But what have I to fear?" she thought; and with a brave smile, she pushed her way through.

She found Jason in a square box built of heavy piles, laid horizontally both for walls and roof, dark and damp and muggy, lighted in the day by a hole in the wood not larger than a man's hand, and in the night by a sputtering candle hung from the rafters. He sat on a stool; his face was worn, his head was close-cropped to relieve the heat of his brain, and on the table by his side lay all his red hair, as long as his mother's was when it fell to the shears of the Jew on the wharf.

He gave no sign when Greeba entered, though he knew she was there, but sat with his face down and one hand on the table.

"Jason," she said, "I am ashamed. It is I who have brought you to this. Forgive me! forgive me! But my husband's life was in danger, and what was I to do?"

Still he gave no sign.

"Jason," she said again, "you have heaped coals of fire on my head; for I have done nothing but injure you, and though you might have done as much for me you never have."

At that the fingers of his hand on the table grasped the edge of it convulsively.

"But, Jason," she said, "all is not lost yet. No, for I can save you still. Listen. You shall give me your promise to make peace with my husband, and when my husband returns he will grant me your pardon. Oh, yes, I know he will, for he is tender-hearted, and he will forgive you; yes, he will forgive you——"

"My curse on him and his forgiveness," cried Jason, rising suddenly and bringing down his fist on the table. "Who is he that he should forgive me? It has not been for his sake that I have been silent, with the devil at my side urging me to speak. And for all that you have made me to suffer he shall yet pay double. Let it go on; let him send me away; let him bury me at his mines. But I shall live to find him yet. Something tells me that I shall not die until I have met with that man face to face."

And Greeba went back home with these mad words ringing in her ears. "It is useless to try," she thought, "I have done all I can. My husband is before everything. I shall say nothing to him now."

None the less she cried very bitterly, and was still crying when at bedtime her little English maid came up to her and chattered of the news of the day. It seemed that some Danish store-keepers on the cheapstead had lately been arrested as spies, brought to trial, and condemned.

When Greeba awoke next morning, after a restless night, while the town still lay asleep, and only the croak of the ravens from the rocks above the fiord broke the silence of the late dawn, she heard the hollow tread of many footsteps on the frozen snow of the Thingvellir road, and peering out through the window, which was coated with hoar frost, she saw a melancholy procession. Three men, sparsely clad in thin tunics, snow stockings and skin caps, walked heavily in file, chained together hand to hand and leg to leg, with four armed warders, closely muffled to the ears, riding leisurely beside them. They were prisoners bound for the sulphur mines of Krisuvik. The first of them was Jason, and he swung along with his long stride and his shorn head thrown back and his pallid face held up. The other two were old Thomsen and young Polvesen, the Danish store-keepers.

It was more than Greeba could bear to look upon that sight, for it brought back the memory of that other sight on that other morning, when Jason came leaping down to her from the mountains, over gorse and cushag and hedge and ditch. So she turned her head away and covered her eyes with her hands. And then one—two—three—four—the heavy footsteps went on over the snow.

The next thing she knew was that her English maid was in her bedroom, saying, "Some strangers in the kitchen are asking for you. They are Englishmen, and have just come ashore, and they call themselves your brothers."

X: The Fairbrothers

Now when the Fairbrothers concluded that they could never give rest to their tender consciences until they had done right by their poor sister Greeba they set themselves straightway to consider the ways and means. Ballacraine they must sell in order that its proceeds might be taken to Greeba as her share and interest; but Ballacraine belonged to Jacob, and another provision would forthwith need to be made for him. So after much arguing and some nagging across the hearth of the kitchen at Lague it was decided that each of Jacob's five brothers should mortgage his farm to one-sixth its value, and that the gross sum of their five-sixths should be Jacob's for his share. This arrangement would have the disadvantage of leaving Jacob without land, but he showed a magnanimous spirit in that relation. "Don't trouble about me," said he, "it's sweet and nice to do a kindness to your own brothers."

And four of his brethren applauded that sentiment, but Thurstan curled up his red nose and thought, "Aw, yes, of coorse, a powerful big boiler of brotherly love the little miser keeps going under his weskit."

And having so decided they further concluded to see the crops off the ground, and then lose no time in carrying out their design. "Let's wait for the melya," said Asher, meaning the harvest-home, "and then off for Marky the Lord." The person who went by this name was one Mark Skillicorn, an advocate, of Ramsey, who combined the functions of pettifogger with those of money-lender and auctioneer. Marky the Lord was old, and plausible and facetious. He was a distant relative of the Fairbrothers by the side of their mother's French family; and it was a strange chain of circumstances that no big farmer ever got into trouble but he became a client of Marky the Lord's, that no client of Marky the Lord's did not in the end go altogether to the bad, and that poor Marky the Lord never had a client who did not die in his debt. Nevertheless Marky the Lord grew richer as his losses grew heavier, and more facetious as his years increased. Oh, he was a funny dog, was Marky the Lord; but there was just one dog on the island a shade or two funnier still, and that was Jacob Fairbrother. This thrifty soul had for many a year kept a nest of private savings, and even in the days when he and his brethren went down to make a poor mouth before their father at Castletown he had money secretly lent out on the conscientious interest of only three per cent. above the legal rate.

And thus it chanced that when Ballacraine was advertised in big letters on every barn door in the north of Mann, Jacob Fairbrother went down to Marky the Lord, and made a private bargain to buy it in again. So when the day of the sale came, and Marky the Lord strode over the fields with some thirty men—farmers, miners, advocates, and parsons—at his heels, and then drew up on the roadside by the "Hibernian," and there mounted the till-board of a cart for the final reckoning, little Jacob was too much moved to be present, though his brothers were there, all glooming around on the out-side of the group, with their hands in their breeches pockets.

Ballacraine was knocked down cheap to somebody that nobody knew, and then came the work of the mortgages; so once again Jacob went off to Marky the Lord, and bargained to be made mortgagor, though no one was to be a whit the wiser. And ten per cent. he was to get from each of his five brothers for the use of the money which next day came back to his own hands.

Thus far all was straight dealing, but with the approach of the time to go to Iceland the complications grew thick. Jacob had so husbanded his money that while seeming to spend he still possessed it, and now he was troubled to know where to lodge that portion of it which he should not want in Iceland and might find it unsafe to take there. And while he was in the throes of his uncertainty his brothers—all save John—were in the travail of their own big conception.

Now Asher, Stean, Ross and Thurstan, having each made up his mind that he would go to Iceland also, had to consider how to get there, for their late bargaining had left them all penniless. The proceeds of the sale of Bal-lacraine were lodged with Jacob for Greeba, and Jacob also held as his own what had come to each man from his mortgage. So thinking that Jacob must have more than he could want, they approached him one by one, confiden-tially and slyly. And wondrous were the lies they told him, for they dare not confess that their sole need of money was to go to Iceland after him, and watch him that he did not cheat them when Greeba sent them all their for-tunes in return for their brotherly love of her.

Thus Asher took Jacob aside and whispered, "I'm morthal hard pressed for a matter of five and thirty pound, boy—just five and thirty, for draining and fencing. I make bold to think you'll lend me the like of it, and six per cent. I'll be paying reg'lar."

"Ah, I can't do it, Asher," said Jacob, "for old Marky the Lord has stripped me."

Then came Stean, plucking a bit of ling and looking careless, and he said, "I've got a fine thing on now. I can buy a yoke of ploughing oxen for thirty pound. Only thirty, and a dead bargain. Can you lend me the brass? But whisht's the word, for Ross is sneaking after them."

"Very sorry, Stean," said Jacob, "but Ross has been here before you, and I've just lent him the money."

Ross himself came next, and said, "I borrowed five-and-twenty pound from Stean a bit back, and he's not above threatening to sell me up for a dirty little debt like that. Maybe ye'd tide me over the trouble and say nothing to Stean."

"Make your mind easy, Ross," said Jacob, "Stean told me himself, and I've paid him all you owe him."

So these two went their ways and thereafter eyed each other threateningly, but neither dare explode, for both had their secret fear. And last of all came Thurstan, made well drunk for the better support of his courage, and he maudled and cried, "What d'ye think? Poor Ballabeg is dead—him that used to play the fiddle at church—and the old parson wants me to take Ballabeg's place up in the gallery-loft. Says I'd be wonderful good at the viol-bass. I wouldn't mind doing it neither, only it costs such a power of money, a viol-bass does—twenty pound maybe."

"Well, what of that?" said Jacob, interrupting him, "the parson says he'll lend you the money. He told me so himself."

With such shrewd answers did Jacob escape from the danger of lending to his brothers, whom he could not trust. But he lost no time in going down to Marky the Lord and offering his money to be lent out on interest with good security. Knowing nothing of this, Asher, Stean, Ross, and Thurstan each in his turn stole down to Marky the Lord to borrow the sum he needed. And Marky the Lord kept his own worthy counsel, and showed no unwise eagerness. First he said to Jacob, "I can lend out your money on good security."

"Who to?" said Jacob.

"That I've given my word not to tell. What interest do you want?"

"Not less than twelve per cent." said the temperate Jacob.

"I'll get it," said Marky the Lord, and Jacob went away with a sly smile.

Then said Marky the Lord to each of the borrowers in turn, "I can find you the money."

"Whose is it?" asked Asher, who came the first.

"That I've sworn not to tell," said Marky the Lord.

"What interest?"

"Only four per cent. to my friend."

"Well, and that's reasonable, and he's a right honest, well-meaning man, whoever he is," said Asher.

"That he is, friend," said Marky the Lord, "but as he had not got the money himself he had to borrow it of an acquaintance, and pay ten per cent. for the convenience."

"So he wants fourteen per cent!" cried Asher. "Shoo! Lord save us! Oh, the grasping miser. It's outrageous. I'll not pay it—the Nightman fly away with me if I do."

"You need be under no uneasiness about that," said Marky the Lord, "for I've three other borrowers ready to take the money the moment you say you won't."

"Hand it out," said Asher, and away he went, fuming.

Then Stean, Ross, and Thurstan followed, one by one, and each behaved as Asher had done before him. When the transaction was complete, and the time had come to set sail for Iceland, many and wonderful were the shifts of the four who had formed the secret design to conceal their busy preparations. But when all was complete, and berths taken, all six in the same vessel, Jacob and Gentleman John rode round the farms of Lague to bid a touching farewell to their brethren.

"Good-bye, Thurstan," said Jacob, sitting on the cross-board of the cart. "We've had arguments in our time, and fallen on some rough harm in the course of them, but we'll meet for peace and quietness in heaven some day."

"We'll meet before that," thought Thurstan.

And when Jacob and John were gone on towards Ramsey, Thurstan mounted the till-board of his own cart, and followed. Meantime Asher, Stean, and Ross were on their journey, and because they did not cross on the road they came face to face for the first time, all six together, each lugging his kit of clothes behind him, on the deck of the ship that was to take them to Iceland. Then Jacob's pale face grew livid.

"What does this mean?" he cried.

"It means that we can't trust you," said Thurstan.

"None of you?" said Jacob.

"None of us, seemingly," said Thurstan, glancing round into the confused faces about him.

"What! Not your own brother?" said Jacob.

"'Near is my shirt, but nearer is my skin,' as the saying is," said Thurstan, with a sneer.

"'Poor once, poor forever,' as the saying is," mocked Jacob. "Last week you hadn't twenty pound to buy your viol-bass to play in the gallery loft."

Stean laughed at that, and Jacob turned hotly upon him. "And you hadn't thirty pound to buy your yoke of oxen that Ross was sneaking after."

178

Then Ross made a loud guffaw, and Jacob faced about to him. "And maybe you've paid back your dirty five-and-twenty pound that Stean threatened to sell you up for?"

Then Stean glowered hard at Ross, and Ross looked black at Stean, and Asher almost burst his sides with laughter.

"And you, too, my dear eldest brother," said Jacob, bitterly, "you have the advantage of me in years but not in wisdom. You thought, like the rest of them, to get the money out of me, to help you to follow me and watch me. So that was it, was it? But I was too much for you, my dear brother, and you had to go elsewhere for your draining and ditching."

"So I had, bad cess to you," said Asher; "and fourteen per cent. I had to pay for the shabby loan I got."

At that Stean and Ross and Thurstan pricked up their ears.

"And did you pay fourteen per cent.?" said Stean.

"I did, bad cess to Marky the Lord, and the grasping old miser behind him, whoever he is."

And now it was Jacob's turn to look amazed.

"Wait," he said; "I don't like the look of you."

"Then shut your eyes," said Thurstan.

"Did Marky the Lord lend you the money?" asked Jacob of Asher.

"Ay, he did," said Asher.

"And you, too, said Jacob?" turning stiffly to Stean.

"Ay," said Stean.

"And you?" said Jacob, facing towards Ross.

"I darn say no," said Ross.

"And you, as well?" said Jacob, confronting Thurstan.

"Why not?" said Thurstan.

"The blockhead!" cried Jacob, "The scoundrel! It was my money—mine—mine, I tell you, and he might as well have pitched it into the sea."

Then the four men began to double their fists.

"Wait!" said Asher. "Are you the grasping young miser that asked fourteen per cent.!"

"He is, clear enough," said Stean.

"Well," said Thurstan, "I really think—look you, boys, I really do think, but I speak under correction—I really think, all things considered, this Jacob is a damned rascal."

"I may have the advantage of him in years," said Asher, doubling up his sleeves, "but if I can't——"

"Go to the devil," said Jacob, and he went below, boiling hot with rage.

It was idle to keep up the quarrel, for very soon all six were out on the high seas, bound to each other's company at bed and board, and doomed to pass the better part of a fortnight together. So before they came to Iceland they were good friends, after their fashion, though that was perhaps the fashion of cat and mouse, and being landed at Reykjavik they were once more in their old relations, with Jacob as purse-bearer and spokesman.

"And now listen," said that thrifty person. "What's it saying? 'A bird in the hand is worth two in the bush.' We've got our bird in the hand, haven't we?"

"So we have," said Asher; "six hundred golden pounds that Ballacraine fetched at the sale."

"Just so," said Jacob; "and before we part with it let us make sure about the two in the bush."

With that intention they started inquiries, as best they could; touching the position of Michael Sunlocks, his salary and influence. And in spite of the difficulties of language they heard and saw enough to satisfy them. Old Iceland was awakening from a bad dream of three bad centuries and setting to work with a will to become a power among the States; the young President, Michael Sunlocks, was the restorer and protector of her liberties; fame and honor were before him, and before all who laid a hand to his plough. This was what they heard in many jargons on every side.

"It's all right," whispered Jacob, "and now for the girl."

They had landed late in the day of Greeba's visit to Red Jason at the little house of detention, and had heard of her marriage, of its festivities, and of the attempt on the life of the President. But though they knew that Jason was no longer in Mann they were too much immersed in their own vast schemes to put two and two together, until next morning they came upon the sad procession bound for the Sulphur Mines, and saw that Jason was one of the prisoners. They were then on their way to Government House, and Jacob said with a wink, "Boys, that's worth remembering. When did it do any harm to have two strings to your bow?"

The others laughed at that, and John nudged Thurstan and said, "Isn't he a boy!" And Thurstan grunted and trudged on.

When they arrived at the kitchen door of the house they asked for Greeba by her new name, and after some inarticulate fencing with a fat Icelandic cook, the little English maid was brought down to them.

"Leave her to me," whispered Jacob, and straightway he tackled her.

Could they see the mistress? What about? Well, it was a bit of a private matter, but no disrespect to herself, miss. Aw, yes, they were Englishmen—that's to say a sort of Englishmen—being Manxmen. Would the mistress know them? Ay, go bail on that. Eh, boys? Ha! ha! Fact was they were her brothers, miss. Yes, her brothers, all six of them, and longing mortal to clap eyes again on their sweet little sister.

And after that Master Jacob addressed himself adroitly to an important question, and got most gratifying replies. Oh, yes, the President loved his young wife beyond words; worshipped the very ground she walked on, as they say. And, oh, yes, she had great, great influence with him, and he would do anything in the wide world to please her.

"That'll do," whispered Jacob over his shoulder, as the little maid tripped away to inform her mistress. "I'll give that girl a shilling when she comes again," he added.

"And give her another for me," said Stean.

"And me," said Asher.

"Seeing that I've no land at home now I wouldn't mind staying here when you all go back," said Jacob.

"I'll sell you mine, Jacob," said Thurstan.

The maid returned to ask them to follow, and they went after her, stroking their lank hair smooth on their foreheads, and studying the remains of the snow on their boots. When they came to the door of the room where they were to meet with Greeba, Jacob whispered to the little maid, "I'll give you a crown when I come out again." Then he twisted his face over his shoulder and said: "Do as I do; d'ye hear?"

"Isn't he a boy?" chuckled Gentleman John.

Then into the room they passed, one by one, all six in file. Greeba was standing by a table, erect, quivering, with flashing eyes, and the old trembling on both sides her heart. Jacob and John instantly went down on one knee before her, and their four lumbering brethren behind made shift to do the same.

"So we have found you at last, thank God," said Jacob, in a mighty burst of fervor.

"Thank God, thank God," the others echoed.

"Ah, Greeba," said Jacob, in a tone of sorrowful reproach, "why ever did you go way without warning, and leave us all so racked with suspense? You little knew how you grieved us, seeming to slight our love and kindness towards you——"

"Stop," said Greeba. "I know too well what your love and kindness have been to me. Why have you come?"

"Don't say that," said Jacob, sadly, "for see what we have made free to fetch you—six hundred pound," he added, lugging a bag and a roll of paper out of his pocket.

"Six hundred golden pounds," repeated the others.

"It's your share of Lague—your full share, Greeba, woman," said Jacob, deliberately, "and every penny of it is yours. So take it, and may it bring you a blessing, Greeba. And don't think unkind of us because we have held it back until now, for we kept it from you for your own good, seeing plain there was someone harking after you for sake of what you had, and fearing your good money would thereby fall into evil hands, and you be made poor and penniless."

"Ay, ay," muttered the others; "that Jason—that Red Jason."

"But he's gone now, and serve him right," said Jacob, "and you're wedded to the right man, praise God."

So saying he shambled to his feet, and his brothers did likewise.

But Greeba stood without moving, and said through her compressed lips, "How did you know that I was here?"

"The letter, the letter," Asher blurted out, and Jacob gave him a sidelong look, and then said:

"Ye see, dear, it was this way. When you were gone, and we didn't know where to look for you, and were sore grieved to think you'd maybe left us in anger, not rightly seeing our drift towards you, we could do nothing but sit about and fret for you. And one day we were turning over some things in a box, just to bring back the memory of you, when what should we find but a letter writ to you by the good man himself."

"Ay, Sunlocks—Michael Sunlocks," said Stean.

"And a right good man he is, beyond gainsay; and he knows how to go through life, and I always said it," said Asher.

And Jacob continued, "So said I; 'Boys,' I said, 'now we know where she is, and that by this time she must have married the man she ought, let's do the right by her and sell Ballacraine, and take her the money and give her joy.'"

"So you did, so you did," said John.

"And we sold it dirt cheap, too," said Jacob, "but you're not the loser; no, for here is a full seventh of all Lague straight to your hand."

"Give me the money," said Greeba.

"And there it is, dear," said Jacob, fumbling the notes and the gold to count them, while his brethren, much gratified by this sign of Greeba's complacency, began to stretch their legs from the easy chairs about them.

"Ay, and a pretty penny it has cost us to fetch it," said John. "We've had to pinch ourselves to do it, I can tell you."

"How much has it cost you?" said Greeba.

"No matter of that," interrupted Jacob, with a lofty sweep of the hand.

"Let me pay you back what you have spent in coming," said Greeba.

"Not a pound of it," said Jacob. "What's a matter of forty or fifty pounds to any of us, compared to doing what's right by our own flesh and blood?"

"Let me pay you," said Greeba, turning to Asher, and Asher was for holding out his hand, but Jacob, coming behind him, tugged at his coat, and so he drew back and said,

"Aw, no, child, no; I couldn't touch it for my life."

"Then you," said Greeba to Thurstan, and Thurstan looked as hungry as a hungry gull at the bait that was offered him, but just then Jacob was coughing most lamentably. So with a wry face, that was all colors at once, Thurstan answered, "Aw, Greeba, woman, do you really think a poor man has got no feelings? Don't press it, woman. You'll hurt me."

Recking nothing of these refusals Greeba tried each of the others in turn, and getting the same answer from all, she wheeled about, saying, "Very well, be it so," and quickly locked the money in the drawer of a cabinet. This done, she said sharply, "Now, you can go."

"Go?" they cried, looking up from their seats in bewilderment.

"Yes," she said, "before my husband returns."

"Before he returns?" said Jacob. "Why, Greeba, we wish to see him."

"You had better not wait," said Greeba. "He might remember what you appear to forget."

"Why," said Jacob, with every accent of incredulity, "and isn't he our brother, so to say, brought up in the house of our own father?"

"And he knows what you did for our poor father, who wouldn't lie shipwrecked now but for your heartless cruelties," said Greeba.

"Greeba, lass, Greeba, lass," Jacob protested, "don't say he wouldn't take kind to the own brothers of his own wife."

"He also knows what you did for her," said Greeba, "and the sorry plight you brought her to."

"What!" cried Jacob, "you never mean to say you are going to show an ungrateful spirit, Greeba, after all we've brought you?"

"Small thanks to you for that, after defrauding me so long," said Greeba.

"What! Keeping you from marrying that cheating knave?" cried Jacob.

"You kept me from nothing but my just rights," said Greeba. "Now go—go."

Her words fell on them like swords that smote them hip and thigh, and like sheep they huddled together with looks of amazement and fear.

"Why, Greeba, you don't mean to turn us out of the house," said Jacob.

"And if I do," said Greeba, "it is no more than you did for our dear old father, but less; for that house was his, while this is mine, and you ought to be ashamed to show your wicked faces inside its doors."

"Oh, the outrageous little atomy," cried Asher.

"This is the thanks you get for crossing the seas to pay people what there was never no call to give them," said Stean.

"Oh, bad cess to it all," cried Ross, "I'll take what it cost me to come, and get away straight. Give it me, and I'm off."

"No," said Greeba, "I'll have no half measures. You refused what I offered you, and now you shall have nothing."

"Och, the sly slut—the crafty young minx," cried Ross, "to get a hold of the money first."

"Hush, boys, leave it to me," said Jacob. "Greeba," he said, in a voice of deep sorrow, "I never should have believed it of you—you that was always so kind and loving to strangers, not to speak of your own kith and kin——"

"Stop that," cried Greeba, lifting her head proudly, her eyes flashing, and the woman all over aflame. "Do you think I don't see through your paltry schemes? You defrauded me when I was poor and at your mercy, and now when you think I am rich, and could do you a service, you come to me on your knees. But I spurn you, you mean, grovelling men, you that impoverished my father and then turned your backs upon him, you that plotted against my husband and would now lick the dust under his feet. Get out of my house, and never darken my doors again. Come here no more, I tell you, or I will disown you. Go—go!"

And just as sheep they had huddled together, so as sheep she swept them out before her. They trooped away through the kitchen and past the little English maid, but their eyes were down and they did not see her.

"Did ye give her that crown piece?" asked Thurstan, looking into Jacob's eyes. But Jacob said nothing—he only swore a little.

"The numskull!" muttered Thurstan. "The tomfool! The booby! The mooncalf! The jobbernowl! I was a fool to join his crackbrained scheme."

"I always said it would come to nothing," said Asher, "and we've thrown away five and thirty pound apiece, and fourteen per cent. for the honor of doing it."

"It's his money, though—the grinding young miser—and may he whistle till he gets it," said Thurstan.

"Oh, yes, you're a pretty pack of wise asses, you are," said Jacob, bitterly. "Money thrown away, is it? You've never been so near to your fortune in your life."

"How is that?" asked the other five at once.

"How is it that Red Jason has gone to prison? For threatening Michael Sunlocks? Very likely," said Jacob, with a curl of the lip.

"What then?" said John.

"For threatening herself," said Jacob. "She has lied about it."

"And what if she has? Where's our account in that?" said Asher.

"Where? Why, with her husband," said Jacob, and four distinct whistles answered him.

"You go bail Michael Sunlocks knows less than we know," Jacob added, "and maybe we might tell him something that would be worth a trifle."

"What's that?" asked John.

"That she loved Red Jason, and ought to have married him," said Jacob; "but threw him up after they had been sweethearting together, because he was poor, and then came to Iceland and married Michael Sunlocks because he was rich."

"Chut! Numskull again! He'd never believe you," said Thurstan.

"Would he not?" said Jacob, "then maybe he would believe his own eyes. Look there," and he drew a letter out of his pocket.

It was the abandoned letter that Greeba wrote to Jason.

"Isn't he a boy!" chuckled Gentleman John.

Two days longer they stayed at Reykjavik, and rambled idly about the town, much observed by the Icelanders and Danes for their monkey jackets of blue Manx cloth, and great sea boots up to their thighs. Early on the afternoon of the second day they sighted, from the new embankment where they stood and watched the masons, a ship coming up the fiord from the Smoky Point. It was a brig, with square sails set, and as she neared the port she ran up a flag to the masthead. The flag was the Icelandic flag, the banner of the Vikings, the white falcon on the blue ground, and the Fairbrothers noticed that at the next moment it was answered by a like flag on the flagstaff of Government House.

"He's coming, he's yonder," said Jacob, flapping his hands under his armpits to warm them.

In a few minutes they saw that there was a flutter over the smooth surface of the life of the town, and that small groups of people were trooping down to the jetty. Half an hour later the brig ran into harbor, dropped anchor below the lava reef, and sent its small boat ashore. Three men sat in the boat; the two sailors who rowed, and a gentleman who sat on the seat between them. The gentleman was young, flaxen-haired, tall, slight, with a strong yet winsome face, and clad in a squirrel-skin coat and close-fitting squirrel-skin cap. When the boat grounded by the jetty he leapt ashore with a light spring, smiled and nodded to the many who touched their hats to him, hailed others with a hearty word, and then swung into the saddle of a horse that stood waiting for him, and rode away at an eager trot in the direction of Government House.

It was Michael Sunlocks.

XI: The Pardon

When the men whom Michael Sunlocks sent into the interior after Adam Fairbrother and his shipwrecked company returned to him empty-handed, he perceived that they had gone astray by crossing a great fiord lying far east of Hekla when they should have followed the course of it down to the sea. So, counting the time that had been wasted, he concluded to take ship to a point of the southern coast in the latitude of the Westmann Islands, thinking to meet old Adam somewhere by the fiord's mouth. The storm delayed him, and he reached the fiord too late; but he came upon some good news of Adam there: that, all well, though sore beset by the hard weather, and enfeebled by the misfortunes that had befallen them, the little band of ship-broken men had, three days before his own coming, passed up the western bank of the fiord on foot, going slowly and heavily laden, but under the safe charge of a guide from Stappen.

Greatly cheered in heart at these good tidings Michael Sunlocks had ordered a quick return, for it was unsafe, and perhaps impossible, to follow up through the narrow chasms of the fiord in a ship under sail. On getting back to Reykjavik he intended to take ponies across country in the direction of Thingvellir, hoping to come upon old Adam and his people before they reached the lake or the great chasm on the western side of the valley, known as the Chasm of All Men.

And thinking, amid the flutter of joyful emotions, that on the overland journey he would surely take Greeba with him, for he could never bear to be so long parted from her again, all his heart went back to her in sweet visions as his ship sped over the sea. Her beauty, her gentleness, her boldness, her playful spirits, and all her simple loving ways came flowing over him wave after wave, and then in one great swelling flood. And in the night watches, looking over the dark waters, and hearing nothing but their deep moan, he could scarce believe his fortune, being so far away from the sight of her light figure, and from the hearing of her sweet voice, that she was his—his love, his wife, his darling. A hundred tender names he would call her then, having no ear to hear him but the melancholy waves, no tongue to echo him but the wailing wind, and no eye to look upon him but the eye of night.

And many a time on that homeward voyage, while the sails bellowed out to the fair breeze that was carrying him to her, he asked himself however he had been able to live so long without her, and whether he could live without her now if evil chance plunged his great happiness into greater grief. Thinking so, he recalled the day of her coming, and the message he got from the ship in the harbor saying she had come before her time, and how he had hastened down, and into the boat, and across the bay, and aboard, with a secret trembling lest the years might have so changed her as to take something from her beauty, or her sweetness, or her goodness, or yet the bounding playfulness that was half the true girl's charm. But, oh, the delicious undeceiving of that day, when, coming face to face with her again, he saw the rosy tint in her cheek and the little delicate dimple sucked into it when she smiled, and the light footstep, and the grace of motion, and the swelling throat, and the heaving bosom and the quivering lids over the most glorious eyes that ever shone upon this earth! So, at least, it had seemed to him then, and still it seemed so as his ship sailed home.

At Smoky Point they lay off an hour or two to take in letters for the capital, and there intelligence had come aboard of the arrest, trial, and condemnation of Jason for his design and attempt upon the life of the President. Michael Sunlocks had been greatly startled and deeply moved by the news, and called on the master to weigh the anchor without more delay than was necessary, because he had now a double reason for wishing to be back in Reykjavik.

And being at length landed there he galloped up to Government House, bounded indoors with the thought of his soul speaking out of his eyes, and found Greeba there and every one of his sweetest visions realized. All his hundred tender, foolish, delicious names he called her over again, but with better ears to hear them, while he enfolded her in his arms, with both her own about his neck, and her beautiful head nestling close over his heart, and her fluttering breast against his breast.

"Dearest," he whispered, "my darling, love of my life, however could I leave you so long?"

"Michael," she whispered back, "if you say any more I shall be crying."

But the words were half smothered by sobs, for she was crying already. Seeing this, he sheered off on another tack, telling her of his mission in search of her father, and that if he had not brought the good man back, at least he had brought good news of him, and saying that they were both to start to-morrow for Thingvellir with the certainty of meeting him and bringing him home with great rejoicings.

"And now, my love, I have a world of things to attend to before I can go," said Michael Sunlocks, "and you have to prepare for two days in the saddle over the snow."

Greeba had been smiling through the big drops that floated in her eyes, but she grew solemn again, and said—

"Ah, Michael, you cannot think what trouble we have all had while you have been away."

"I know it—I know all," said Michael Sunlocks, "so say no more about it, but away to your room, my darling."

With that he rang a hand-bell that stood on the table, and Oscar, his servant, answered the call.

"Go across to the jail," he said, "and tell Jon that his prisoner is not to be removed until he has had orders from me."

"What prisoner, your Excellency?" said Oscar.

"The prisoner known as Jason," said Michael Sunlocks.

"He's gone, your Excellency," cried Oscar.

"Gone?"

"I mean to the Sulphur Mines, your Excellency."

"When was he sent?"

"Yesterday morning, at daybreak, your Excellency."

Michael Sunlocks sat at a table and wrote a few lines, and handed them to his man, saying, "Then take this to the Lagmann, and say I shall wait here until he comes."

While this was going forward Greeba had been standing by the door with a troubled look, and when Oscar was gone from the room she returned to her husband's side, and said, with great gravity, "Michael, what are you going to do with that man?"

But Michael Sunlocks only waved his hand, and said, "Nay, now, darling, you shall not trouble about this matter any more. It is my affair, and it is for me to see to it."

"But he has threatened your life," cried Greeba.

"Now, love, what did I say?" said Michael Sunlocks, with uplifted finger and a pretence at reproof. "You've fretted over this foolish thing too long; so think no more about it, and go to your room."

She turned to obey.

"And, darling," he cried in another voice, as she was slowly going, "that I may seem to have you with me all the same, just sing something, and I shall hear you while I work. Will you? There!" he cried, and laughed before she had time to answer. "See what a goose you have made of me!"

She came back, and for reply she kissed his forehead, and he put his lips to her lovely hand. Then, with a great lump in her throat, and the big drops rolling from her eyes to her cheeks, she left him to the work she sorely feared.

And being alone, and the candles lighted and the blinds drawn down, for night had now fallen in, he sat at the table to read the mass of letters that had gathered in his absence. There was no communication of any kind from the Government at Copenhagen, and satisfying himself on this point, and thinking for the fiftieth time that surely Denmark intended, as she ought, to leave the people of world-old Iceland to govern themselves, he turned with a sigh of relief to the strange, bewildering, humorous, pathetic hodge-podge of petitions, complaints, requests, demands and threats that came from every quarter of the island itself. And while he laughed and looked grave, and muttered, and made louder exclamations over these, as one by one they passed under his eye, suddenly the notes of a harpsichord, followed shortly by the sweeter notes of a sweet voice, came to him from another room, and with the tip of his pen to his lips, he dropped back in his chair to listen.

"My own song," he thought, and his eyelids quivered.
"Drink to me only with thine eyes,
And I will pledge with mine.
Oh, leave a kiss within the cup,
And I'll not ask for wine;
The thirst that from the soul doth rise
Doth ask a drink divine;
But might I of Jove's nectar sup
I would not change for thine."

It was Greeba singing to him as he had bidden her.
"God bless her," he thought again in the silence that followed.
Ah, little did he think as he listened to her song that the eyes of the singer were wet, and that her heart was eating itself out with fears.
"What have I done to deserve such happiness?" he asked himself. But just as it happens that at the moment when our passionate joy becomes conscious of itself we find some dark misgivings creep over us of evil about to befall, so the bounding gladsomeness of Michael Sunlocks was followed by a chill dread that he tried to put aside and could not.
It was at that moment that the Lagmann entered the room. He was very tall and slight, and had a large head that drooped like daffodil. His dress was poor, he was short-sighted, growing elderly, and silent of manner. Nothing in his appearance or bearing would have suggested that he had any pride of his place as Judge of the island. He was a bookworm, a student, a scholar, and learned in the old sagas and eddas.
"Lagmann," said Michael Sunlocks, with simple deference. "I have sent for you on a subject of some moment to myself."
"Name it!" said the Judge.
"During my absence a man has been tried and condemned by the Bishop's court for threatening my life," said Michael Sunlocks.
"Jason, the son of Stephen Orry and Rachel, daughter of the late Governor-General Jorgensen," said the Judge.
"That is he, and I want you to give me an opinion respecting him," said Michael Sunlocks.

"Gladly," said the Judge.

"He was sent to the Sulphur Mines," said Michael Sunlocks.

"For six months, certain," said the Judge.

"Can we recall him, and have him tried afresh by the Court of the Quarter or the High Court of Justice?" said Michael Sunlocks.

"Too late for that," said the Judge. "A higher court, if it had condemned at all, might certainly have given him a longer punishment, but his sentence of six months is coupled with a condition that he shall hereafter take an oath of peace towards you. So have no fear of him."

"I have none at all," said Michael Sunlocks, "as my next question will show."

"What is it?" said the Judge.

"Can I pardon him?" said Michael Sunlocks.

For a moment the Lagmann was startled out of his placid manner, but recovering his composure he answered, "Yes, a President has sovereign powers of pardon."

"Then, Lagmann," said Michael Sunlocks, "will you see the needful papers drawn for my signature?"

"Surely," said the Judge. "But, first, will you pardon me?" he added, with a shadow of a smile.

"Say what you please, Lagmann," said Michael Sunlocks.

"It is possible that you do not yet know the nature of the evidence given at the trial," said the Judge.

"I think I do," said Michael Sunlocks.

"That this man claims to be your half-brother?"

"He is my brother."

"That he thinks you have stood in his place?"

"I have stood in his place."

"That he is jealous of you, and in his madness has vowed to slay you?"

"His jealousy is natural, and his vow I do not dread."

The cold-mannered Lagmann paused a moment, wiped his short-sighted eyes with his red print handkerchief, and then said in a husky voice, "This is very noble of you. I'll go at once for the document."

He had only just gone from the room when Greeba returned to it. She had tried too long to conquer her agitation and could not, and now with wide eyes and a look of fear in them she hastened back to her husband the moment the Lagmann had left him.

"Michael," she cried, "what has the Lagmann gone for?"

"For a form of pardon," he answered.

"Pardon for that man?" she asked.

"Even so," he said, "and I have promised to sign it."

"Oh, Michael, my love—my dear, kind Michael!" she cried, in a pitiful voice of entreaty, "don't do it, don't I pray of you—don't bring that man back."

"Why, Greeba, what is this?" said Michael Sunlocks. "What is it troubles my little woman?"

"Dear Michael," she cried once more, "for your own sake think again before you sign that pardon."

"Ah, I see," said he, "my darling has been all unstrung by this ugly business. Yes, and now I remember what they told me down at Smoky Point. It was my love herself that gave the poor lad up to justice. That was very brave of my darling; for her husband, bless her dear heart, was before all the world to her. Ah, yes, I know that all her love is mine, her love is first and last with her as with all warm natures. But she must not fear for me. No, she must not worry, but go back, like a dear soul, and leave this matter to me."

"Michael, my dear, noble Michael, I have something to say; will you not hear me?"

"No, no, no," he answered.

"Not for a moment? I have set my heart on telling you."

"Not for one little moment. But if you have set your heart on anything else, then, my darling, just think of it double, whatever it is, and it is yours already."

"But why may I not speak of this pardon?"

"Because, though I have never yet set eyes upon this poor man I know more about him than my darling can ever know, and because it is natural that her sweet little heart, that is as brave as a lion for herself but as timid as a fawn for me, should exaggerate my peril. So now, no more words about it, but go, go."

She was about to obey when the maid came to say that dinner was ready. And then with a little shout of joy Michael Sunlocks threw down his papers, encircled his arm about Greeba's waist, and drew her along laughing, with her smiles fighting their way through her tears.

During the dinner he talked constantly of the dangers and trials and amusing mischances of his voyage, laughing at them all now they were over, and laughing at Greeba, too, for the woeful face with which she heard of them. And when they rose from the table he called on her for another song, and she sat at the harpsichord and sang, though something was swelling in her throat and often her heart was in her mouth. But he recked nothing of this, and only laughed when her sweet voice failed her, and filled up the breaks with his own rich tones.

In the midst of the singing the maid came in and said something which Michael Sunlocks did not catch, for it was drowned to his ear by the gladsome uproar that he himself was making; but Greeba heard it and stopped playing, and presently the Lagmann entered the room.

"A good thing is no worse for being done betimes," said the Judge, "so here is the pardon ready to your hand for signature."

And with that he handed a paper to Michael Sunlocks, who said with cheer, "You're right, Lagmann, you're right; and my wife will give you a glass of wine while I write you my name."

"A cup of coffee, if you are taking it," said the Judge, with a bow to Greeba, who saw nothing of it, for her eyes were following her husband.

"Michael," she said, "I beseech you not to sign that paper. Only give way to me this once; I have never asked you before, and I will never ask you again. I am in earnest, Michael dear, and if you will not yield to me for your own sake, yield to me for mine."

"How is this? How grave we are!" said Michael Sunlocks, pausing with pen in hand.

"I know I have no right to meddle in such matters, but, dear Michael, don't sign that pardon—don't bring that man back. I beseech you, I beg of you."

"This is very strange," said Michael Sunlocks.

"It is also very simple," said the Judge, bringing his red handkerchief up to his dim eyes again.

"What!" said Michael Sunlocks. "Greeba, you do not know this man— this Jason?"

Greeba hesitated a moment, and glanced at the Lagmann.

"You don't know him?" repeated Michael Sunlocks.

She was sorely tempted, and she fell. "For my husband's sake," she thought, and then with a prayer for pardon she lifted her head and said falteringly, "No, no—why no, of course not."

Michael Sunlocks was satisfied. "'Why no, of course not,'" he echoed, laughing a little, and then he dipped his quill in the ink-horn.

"But I beseech you again, do not bring that man back," she cried.

There was a painful pause, and, to cover it, the Lagmann said, "Your husband is a brave-hearted man, who does not know the name of fear."

And then Michael Sunlocks said, "I will ask your pardon, Lagmann, while I step into the next room with my wife. I have something to tell her. Come, Greeba, come. I'll leave the document with you for the present, Lagmann," he added over his shoulder as he passed out. Greeba walked beside him with downcast eyes, like a guilty thing condemned.

"Now, love," he said, when they were alone, "it is sweet and beautiful of you to think so much of me, but there is something that you do not know, and I ought to tell you. Maybe I hinted at it in my letter, but there has never been a chance to explain. Have you heard that this Jason is my brother?"

"Yes," said Greeba, faintly.

"It is true," said Michael Sunlocks. "And you know that when I first came to Iceland it was not to join the Latin school, but on an errand of mercy?"

"Yes," said Greeba.

"Well, the first of my duties was to find Jason's mother, and the next, was to find Jason himself."

"Jason!" cried Greeba.

"Yes, it was my father who sent me, for they had suffered much through his great fault, God forgive him! and I was to succor them in their distress. You know what followed?"

"Yes," said Greeba, softly.

"I came too late for the mother; the good woman was in her grave. I could not light upon her son, and lent an ear to the idle story that he was dead also. My search ceased, my zeal flagged, and, putting aside the solemn promise I made my father, I went on with my own affairs. But I never believed that he was dead, and I felt I should live to meet with him yet."

"Oh! oh!" cried Greeba.

"And many a time since my conscience has reproached me with a mission unfulfilled; and, awakening from many a dream of the hour and the place wherein I pledged my word to him that died trusting me, loving me, doting on me—heaven pity him, bad man though he was—as never a son was loved by a father before, it has not appeased me to say to myself, 'Michael, while you are here, given up to your ambitions, he is there amid the perils and hardships of the sea, and he is your brother, and the only kinsman left to you in the wide world.'"

Greeba was sobbing by this time.

"And now, my darling, you know all, and why I wish to sign this pardon. Could I ever know a moment's happiness with my brother slaving like a beast at yonder mines? What if he is jealous of me, and if his jealousy had driven him to madness! There is a sense in which he is right. But, whether right or wrong, mad or sane, he shall not be punished for my sake. So, dearest love, my darling, dry your beautiful eyes, and let me ease my conscience the only way I may, for I have no fear, and my wife must have none."

"Sunlocks," said Greeba, "you have made me ashamed. I am no fit wife for a man like you. I am too little-hearted. Oh, why did I ever come? Why?

Why?" And she wept as if her heart would break. He comforted her with tender protests, enfolding her in his arms and caressing her lovely head.

"Tell me," he whispered, "nay, there, hide your face in my breast. There, there, tell me now—tell me all."

"Sunlocks," she said, drawing back, "I have lied to you."

"Lied?"

"When I told you I had not known Jason I told you what was false."

"Then you have known him?"

"Yes, I knew him in the Isle of Man."

"The Isle of Man?"

"He lived there nearly five years."

"All the time he was away?"

"Yes, he landed the night you sailed. You crossed him on the sea."

"Greeba, why did he go there? Yet how should you know?"

"I do know, Michael—it was to fulfil his vow—his vow that the old priest spoke of in court—his wicked vow of vengeance."

"On my father?"

"On your father and on you."

"God in heaven!" cried Michael Sunlocks, with great awe. "And that very night my father was saved from his own son by death."

"It was he who saved your father from the sea."

"Wait," said Michael Sunlocks; "did you know of this vow before you accused him of an attempt upon me?"

Greeba caught her breath, and answered, "Yes."

"Did you know of it while you were still in the Isle of Man?"

"Yes," she answered again, more faintly.

"Did he tell you?"

"Yes, and he bound me by a promise never to speak of it, but I could not keep it from my own husband."

"That's strange," said Michael Sunlocks, with a look of pain. "To share a secret like that with you was very strange," he added.

Greeba was flurried, and said again, too bewildered to see which way her words were tending, "And he gave me his promise in return to put aside his sinful purpose."

"That's still stranger," said Michael Sunlocks. "Greeba," he added, in another tone, "why should you say you did not know Jason?"

"Because the Lagmann was with us."

"But why, my girl? Why?"

"Lest evil rumors might dishonor my husband."

"But where was the dishonor to me in my wife knowing this poor lad, Greeba?"

At that she hesitated a moment, and then in a tone of gentle reproof she said, nestling close to him and caressing his sleeve, "Michael, why do you ask such questions?"

But he did not turn aside for that, but looked searchingly into her face, and said, "He was nothing to you, was he?"

She hesitated again, and then tried to laugh, "Why, what should he be to me?" she said.

He did not flinch, but repeated, "He was nothing to you then?"

"Nobody save my husband has ever been anything to me," she said, with a caress.

"He was nothing to you—no?"

"No," she answered, throwing back her head.

Just then the English maid came to say that the six big Englishmen who had been there before were in the kitchen again, and asking to see her master, not her mistress, this time. In an instant Greeba's little burst of disdain was spent, and she was all humility and entreaty.

"Don't go to them," she cried. "Don't listen to them."

"Who are they?" he asked.

"My brothers. I have not had time to tell you, but I will tell you now."

She put her arms about his neck as if to hold him.

"What have they come for?"

"To tell you some falsehood, and so revenge themselves on me. I know it, I feel it. Ah, a woman's instinct is sure. But, dear Michael, you will not receive them. Refuse, and I will tell you such a story. And you will laugh——"

"Let me go, Greeba," he said, unloosing the grip of her tightening arms, and the next moment he was gone from the room. Then all the spirit of the woman arose in Greeba, and, throwing aside her vague fears, she resolved, as only a woman could, in the cruel hour when a dear heart seemed to be slipping away from her, that, come what would, she should hold to her husband at all hazards, and that whatever her brothers might say against her, let it be true or false, if it threatened to separate her from him, she must deny it. What matter about the truth? Her love was before everything. And who was to disprove her word? Jason alone could do so, and his tongue was sealed forever in a silence as deep as the grave's.

Michael Sunlocks went out of the room like a man in a dream: an ugly dream, a dream of darkening terrors undefined. He came back to it like one who has awakened to find that his dream has come true. Within one hour his face seemed to have grown old. He stooped, he stumbled on the floor, his limbs shook under him, he was a broken and sorrowful man. At sight of him

Greeba could scarcely restrain an impulse to scream. She ran to him, and cried, "Michael, husband, what have they told you?"

At first he looked stupidly into her quivering face, and then glancing down at a paper he held in one hand he made an effort to conceal it behind him. She was too quick for him, and cried, "What is it? Show it me."

"It's nothing," he said; "nothing, love, nothing——"

"What have they told you?" she said again, "tell me—tell me."

"They say that you loved Jason," he answered with a great effort.

"It's a lie," she cried stoutly.

"They say that you were to marry him."

She tried to answer as stoutly as before, "And that's a lie, too," but the words stuck in her throat.

"Oh! God," he cried, and turned away from her.

There was a stove in the room, and he stepped up to it, opened the iron door, and thrust the paper into the crackling fire.

"What is that you are burning?" she cried. And in another moment, before he knew what she was doing, she had run to the stove, pulled back with her bare hands the hot door that he was closing with the tongs, thrust her arm into the fire, and brought out the paper. It was in flames, and she rolled it in her palms until little but its charred remains lay in her scorched fingers. But she saw what it had been—her own abandoned letter to Red Jason. Then, slowly looking up, she turned back to her husband, pale, a fearful chill creeping over her, and he had thrown himself down on a chair by the table and hidden his face in his arms.

It was a pitiful and moving sight. To see that man, so full of hope and love and simple happy trust a little hour ago, lie there with bent head and buried eyes, and hands clasped together convulsively, because the idol he had set up for himself lay broken before him, because the love wherein he lived lay dead; and to see that woman, so beautiful, and in heart so true, though dogged by the malice of evil chance, though weak as a true woman may be, stand over him with whitening lips and not a word to utter—to see this was to say, "What devil of hell weaves the web of circumstance in this world of God?"

Then, with a cry of love and pain in one, she flung herself on her knees beside him, and enfolded him in her arms. "Michael," she said, "my love, my darling, my dear kind husband, forgive me, and let me confess everything. It is true that I was to have married Jason, but it is not true that I loved him. I esteemed him, for he is of a manly, noble soul, and after the departure of my father and the death of my mother, and amid the cruelties of my brothers and your own long, long silence, I thought to reward him for his great fidelity. But I loved you, you only, only you, dear Michael, and when

196

your letter reached me at last I asked him to release me that I might come to you, and he did so, and I came. This is the truth, dear Michael, as sure as we shall meet before God some day."

Michael Sunlocks lifted his face and said, "Why did you not tell me this long ago, Greeba, and not now when it is dragged from you?"

She did not answer him, for to be met with such a question after a plea so abject, stung her to the quick. "Do you not believe I've told you the truth?" she asked.

"God knows; I know not what to believe," he answered.

"Do you rather trust my brothers, who have deceived you?" she said.

"So, heaven help me! has my wife, whom I have loved so dear."

At that she drew herself up. "Michael," she said, "what lie have these men told you? Don't keep it from me. What have I done?"

"Married me, while loving him," he answered. "That's enough for me, God pity me!"

"Do you believe that?" she said.

"Your concealments, your deceptions, your subterfuges all prove it," he said. "Oh, it is killing me, for it is the truth."

"So you believe that?" she said.

"If I had not written you would now be Jason's wife," he said. "And by this light I see his imprisonment. It was you who accused him of a design upon my life. Why? Because you knew what he had confessed to you. For your own ends you used his oath against him, knowing he could not deny it. And what was your purpose? To put him away. Why? Because he was pursuing you for deserting him. But you made his vow your excuse, and the brave lad said nothing. No, not a word; and yet he might have dishonored you before them all. And when I wished to sign his pardon you tried to prevent me. Was that for my sake? No, but yours. Was it my life you thought to protect? No, but your own secret."

Thus, in the agony of his tortured heart, the hot hard words came from him in a torrent, but before the flood of them was spent, Greeba stepped up to him with flashing eyes, and all the wrath in her heart that comes of outraged love, and cried,

"It is false. It is false, I say. Send for him and he himself will deny it. I can trust him, for he is of a noble soul. Yes, he is a man indeed. I challenge you to send for him. Let him come here. Bring him before me, and he shall judge between us."

"No," said Michael Sunlocks, "I will not send for him. For what you have done he shall suffer."

Then there was a knock at the door, and after a pause the Lagmann entered, with his stoop and uncertain glance. "Excuse me," he said, "will you sign the pardon now, or leave it until the morning?"

"I will not sign it at all," said Michael Sunlocks. But at the next moment he cried: "Wait! after all it is not the man's fault, and he shall not suffer." With that he took the paper out of the law-man's hand and signed it hurriedly. "Here," he said, "see that the man is set free immediately."

The Lagmann looked at both of them out of his nearsighted eyes, coughed slightly, and left the room without a word more.

XII: The President or the Man

I.

When the Fairbrothers left Government House after their dirty work was done, Jacob was well content with himself, but his brothers were still grumbling.

"He didn't seem any ways keen to believe it," Thurstan muttered.

"Leave him alone for that," said Jacob. "Did ye see when I gave him the letter?"

"Shoo! I wouldn't trust but she will persuade him she never writ it," said Thurstan.

"He's got it anyways, and we have nothing to show for it," said Stean.

"And noways powerful grateful either. And where's the fortune that was coming straight to our hand?" said Ross.

"Chut, man, there's nothing for us in his mighty schame," said Thurstan.

"I always said so," said Asher; "and five and thirty pounds of good money thrown into the sea."

"Go on," said Jacob, with a lofty smile, "go on, don't save your breath for your porridge," and he trudged along ahead of his brethren. Presently he stopped, faced about to them, and said, "Boys, you're mighty sure that nothing is coming of this mighty schame," with a look of high disdain at Thurstan.

"Sure as death and the taxman," sneered Thurstan.

"Then there's a boat sailing for Dublin at high water, and I'll give five and thirty pounds apiece to every man of you that likes to go home with her."

At that there was an uneasy scraping of five pairs of feet, and much hum-ing and ha-ing and snuffling.

"Quick, which of you is it to be? Speak out, and don't all speak at once," said Jacob.

Then Asher, with a look of outraged reason, said, "What! and all our time go for nothing, and the land lying fallow for months, and the winter cabbage not down, and the men's wages going on?"

"You won't take it?" said Jacob.

"A paltry five and thirty, why, no," said Asher.

"Then let's have no more of your badgering," said Jacob.

"But, Jacob, tell us where's our account in all this jeel with the girl and the Governor," said Gentleman John.

"Find it out," said Jacob, with a flip of finger and thumb, as he strode on again before his brothers.

"Aw, lave him alone," said Stean. "He's got his schame."

II.

Next morning, before the light was yet good, and while the warm vapor was still rising into the chill air from the waters of the fiord, Michael Sunlocks sat at work in the room that served him for office and study. His cheeks were pale, his eyes were heavy, and his whole countenance was haggard. But there was a quiet strength in his slow glance and languid step that seemed to say that in spite of the tired look of age about his young face and lissome figure he was a man of immense energy, power of mind and purpose.

His man Oscar was bustling in and out of the room on many errands. Oscar was a curly-headed youth of twenty, with a happy upward turn of the corners of the mouth, and little twinkling eyes full of a bright fire.

The lad knew that there was something amiss with his master by some queer twist of nature that gave a fillip to his natural cheerfulness.

Michael Sunlocks would send Oscar across the arg to the house of the Speaker, and at the next moment forget that he had done so, touch the bell, walk over to the stove, stir the fire, and when the door opened behind him deliver his order a second time without turning round. It would be the maid who had answered the bell, and she would say, "If you please, your Excellency, Oscar has gone out. You sent him across to the Speaker." And then Michael Sunlocks would bethink himself and say, "True, true; you are quite right."

He would write his letters twice, and sometimes fold them without sealing them; he would read a letter again and again and not grasp its contents.

His coffee and toast that had been brought in on a tray lay untouched until both were cold, though they had been set to stand on the top of the stove. He would drop his pen to look vacantly out at the window, and cross the room without an object, and stand abruptly and seem to listen.

The twinkling eyes of young Oscar saw something of this, and when the little English maid stopped the lad in the long passage and questioned him of his master's doings, he said with a mighty knowing smirk that the President was showing no more sense and feeling and gumption that morning than a tortoise within its shell.

Towards noon the Fairbrothers asked for Michael Sunlocks, and were shown into his room. They entered with many bows and scrapes, and much stroking of their forelocks. Michael Sunlocks received them gravely, with an inclination of the head, but no words.

"We make so bold as to come to see you again," said Jacob, "for we've got lands at us lying fallow—the lot of us, bar myself, maybe—and we must be getting back and putting a sight on them."

Michael Sunlocks bowed slightly.

"We've lost a good crop by coming," said Jacob, "and made no charge neither, though it's small thanks you get in this world for doing what's fair and honest."

"Well?" said Michael Sunlocks.

"She never was good to them that was good to her," said Jacob, "and we're taking sorrow to see that we're not the only ones that suffer from her ingratitude."

"Not another word on that head," said Michael Sunlocks. "What do you want?"

"Want? Well, it isn't so mortal kind to say want," said Jacob, with the look of one whose self-respect had been wounded.

"A man may be poor, but a poor man has got feelings," said Asher.

"Poor or rich, I say again, 'What do you want?'" said Michael Sunlocks.

"Only to say that we're going to keep this little thing quiet," said Jacob.

"Aw, quiet, quiet," said the others.

"I must leave that to you," said Michael Sunlocks.

"Aw, and safe, too," said Jacob, "for what for should we be going disgracing our own sister? It isn't natural, and her the wife of the President, too."

"Aw, no, no," said the brethren.

"He won't hear a word against her for all," whispered John to Jacob.

"A girl may be a bit wild, and doing sweethearting before she was married," said Jacob, "but that is no reason why all the world should be agate of her, poor thing; and what's it saying, 'The first slip is always forgotten?'"

200

"Silence," said Michael Sunlocks, sternly. "If this is what you have come to say, we can cut this meeting short."

"Lord-a-massy," cried Asher. "Is he for showing us the door, too?"

"Who says so?" said Jacob, changing his tone. Then facing about to Michael Sunlocks, he said, "It wouldn't do to be known that the President of Iceland had married a bad woman—would it?"

Michael Sunlocks did not reply, and Jacob answered himself: "No, of course not. So perhaps you'll give me back that letter I lent you yesterday."

"I haven't got it. It is destroyed," said Michael Sunlocks.

"Destroyed!" cried Jacob.

"Make yourself easy about it," said Michael Sunlocks. "It will do no more mischief. It's burnt. I burnt it myself."

"Burnt it?" Jacob exclaimed. "Why, do you know, I set great store by that letter? I wouldn't have lost it for a matter of five hundred pounds."

Michael Sunlocks could bear no more. In an instant the weary look had gone from his face. His eyes flashed with anger; he straightened himself up, and brought his fist down on the table. "Come," he cried, "let us have done with this fencing. You want me to pay you five hundred pounds. Is that it?"

"For the letter—that's it," said Jacob.

"And if I refuse to do so you mean to publish it abroad that I have married a wicked woman?"

"Aw, when did we say so?" said Jacob.

"No matter what you say. You want five hundred pounds?"

"For the letter."

"Answer. You want five hundred pounds?"

"For the letter."

"Then you shall not have one sixpence. Do you think I would pay you for a thing like that? Listen to me. I would give you all the wealth of the world, if I had it, never to have heard your evil news."

"That won't pass, master," said Jacob. "It's easy said now the letter's gone, and no danger left. But five hundred pounds I'll have or I'll not leave Iceland till Iceland knows something more than she knows to-day."

"Say what you like, do what you like," cried Michael Sunlocks; "but if ever you set foot in this house again, I'll clap every man of you in jail for blackmailing."

III.

Out again in the chilly dusky air, with the hard snow under foot, the Fairbrothers trudged along. Jacob gloomed as dark as any pitch, and Thurstan's red eyes, like fire of ice, probed him with a burning delight.

"I always said so," Asher whimpered; and then over Jacob's stooping shoulder he whispered, "I'll take half of what you offered me, and leave you to it."

Hearing that Thurstan laughed fiercely, and repeated his hot christenings of two days before—"Numskull! tomfool! blatherskite!" and yet choicer names beside. Jacob bore all and showed no rancor, but trampled along ahead of the others, crestfallen, crushed, and dumb. And, left to themselves for conversation and comfort, his brethren behind compared notes together.

"Strange! He doesn't seem to care what is thought of his wife," said John.

"Aw, what's disgrace to a craythur same as that? Like mother like son," said Ross.

"She had better have married the other one," said Asher, "and I always said so."

"It's self, self, self, with a man like yonder," said Stean.

"Curse him for a selfish brute," said John.

"Aw, an unfeeling monster," said Ross.

And with such heat of anger these generous souls relieved themselves on the name of Michael Sunlocks.

"Boys," said Thurstan, "maybe he has no feeling for the girl, but I'll go bail he has some for himself, and I wouldn't trust but he'd be feeling it mortal keen if he was after getting pulled down from his berth."

"What d'ye mean?" asked all four at once.

"Leave that to myself," said Thurstan, "and maybe since I set foot ashore I've heard tell of schames that's going."

IV.

Greeba sat in her room, trying to cheat time of its weary hours by virtue of much questioning of her little English maid, who from time to time brought news of Michael Sunlocks. He had risen very early, as early as midmorning (six o'clock), and ever since then he had been writing in his office. Oscar had been running here and there for him, first to the Senate, then to the Speaker's, and then to the Bishop's. The tall doorkeeper, stammering Jon, had seen him, being sent for, and the feckless busybody had told him ever such needless stories of the jellies and the soups and the mistress's visit to the poor man in the prison, and however people got wind of things was just puzzling beyond words.

With such cackle and poor company Greeba passed her time, thinking no ill of the pert little maid who dressed up her hair and dressed down her pride as well, for a woman will have any confidante rather than none, and the sweetest and best of women, being estranged from her husband, her true stay and support, will lay hold of the very sorriest staff to lean on. And the strange twist of little natures, that made Oscar perky while his master was melancholy, made the maid jubilant while her mistress wept. She was a dark-haired mite with eyes of the shallow brightness of burnished steel. Her name was Elizabeth. She meant no harm to anyone.

Towards noon the little woman burst into the room with great eagerness, and cried, in a hushed whisper, "The Speaker has come. I am sure that something is going to happen; Oscar says so, too. What is it? What can it be?"

Greeba listened, and carried herself bravely while the maid was near, but when the door had closed upon the chatterer she leaned against the window and cried, hearing nothing but her own weeping and the grief of the half-frozen river that flowed beneath. Then, drying her eyes and summoning what remained of her pride, she left her own room to go to the room of her husband.

V.

In his little silk skullcap and spectacles the Lagmann came back, for he was Judge and Speaker in one, and found Michael Sunlocks alone. At a glance he saw that the trouble of the night before had deepened, and that something of great moment was afoot.

"Lagmann," said Michael Sunlocks, "I wish you to summon both Chambers to meet at the Senate House to-morrow night."

"It will be inconvenient," said the Speaker, "for the Committee of Althing has risen, and the members are preparing to go back home."

"That is why I wish them to be summoned at once," said Michael Sunlocks.

"Is the matter of such pressing importance?" asked the Speaker.

"It is; and it admits of no delay," answered Michael Sunlocks.

"May I mention its purport?" said the Speaker.

"Say only that the President has a message for Althing," said Michael Sunlocks.

"At what hour to-morrow night?" asked the Speaker.

"At mid-evening," answered Michael Sunlocks, and then, with the sigh of a weary man, he turned towards the stove.

The Speaker glanced at him with his dim eyes screwed up, pushed back his little skullcap, and ran his forefinger along his bald crown, then shook his head gravely and left the room, saying within himself, "Why this haste?

And why the message? Ah, these impetuous souls that rise so high and so fast sometimes go down headlong to the abyss!"

VI.

Michael Sunlocks was turning round from the stove when Greeba entered, and for all the womanly courage with which she tried to carry herself before him, he could see that she looked frightened, and that her eyes sought his eyes for mercy and cheer.

"Michael," she cried, "what is it that you are about to do? Tell me. I cannot bear this suspense any longer."

He made her no answer, but sat at his desk and lifted his pen. At that she stamped her foot and cried again—

"Tell me, tell me. I cannot, and I will not bear it."

But he knew, without lifting his head, that with all her brave challenge, and the spark of her defiant eyes, behind her dark lashes a great tear-drop lay somewhere veiled. So he showed no anger, and neither did he reply to her appeal, but made some show of going on with his writing.

And being now so far recovered from her first fear as to look upon his face with eyes that could see it, Greeba realized all that she had but partly guessed from the chatter of her maid, of the sad havoc the night had made with him. At that she could bear up no longer, for before her warm woman's feeling all her little stubborn spirit went down as with a flood, and she flung herself at his feet and cried, "Michael, forgive me; I don't know what I am saying."

But getting no answer to her passionate agony any more than her hot disdain, her pride got the better of her again, and she tried to defend herself with many a simple plea, saying between a sob and a burst of wrath that if she had deceived him, and said what was barely true, it was only from thinking to defend his happiness.

"And why," she cried, "why should I marry you while loving him?"

Then, for the first time, he raised his head and answered her—

"Because of your pride, Greeba—your fatal pride," he said; "your pride that has been your bane since you were a child and you went to London and came back the prouder of your time there. I thought it was gone; but the old leaven works as potently as before, and rises up to choke me. I ought to have known it, Greeba, that your old lightness would lead you to some false dealing yet, and I have none but myself to blame."

Now if he had said this with any heat of anger, or with any rush of tears, she would have known by the sure instinct of womanhood that he loved her still, and was only fighting against love in vain. Then she would have flung herself into his arms with a burst of joy and a cry of "My darling, you are mine, you are mine." But instead of that he spoke the hard words calmly, coldly, and without so much as a sigh, and by that she knew that the heart of his love had been killed within him, and now lay dead before her. So, stung to the quick, she said, "You mean that I deserted Jason because he was poor, and came here to you because you are rich. It is false—cruelly, basely false. You know it is false; or, if you don't, you ought."

"I am far from rich, Greeba," he said, "although to your pride I may seem so, seeing that he whom you left for the sake of the poor glory of my place here was but a friendless sailor lad."

"I tell you it is false," she cried. "I could have loved my husband if he had never had a roof over his head. And yet you tell me that? You that should know me so well! How dare you?" she cried, and by the sudden impulse of her agony, with love struggling against anger, and fire and tears in her eyes together, she lifted up her hand and struck him on the breast.

That blow did more than any tearful plea to melt the icy mistrust that had all night been freezing up his heart, but before he had time to reply Greeba was on her knees before him, praying of him to forgive her, because she did not know what she was doing.

"But, Michael," she said again, "it isn't true. Indeed, indeed, it is not, and it is very, very cruel. Yes, I am proud, very proud, but I am proudest of all of my husband. Proud of him, proud for him—proud that he should be the bravest and noblest gentleman in the world. That is the worst of my pride, Michael—that I want to be proud of him I love. But if that might not have been, and he had been the lowliest man on earth, I could have shared his lot though it had been never so poor and humble, so that I could have had him beside me always."

As he listened to her passionate words there was a fluttering at his throat. "Are you sure of that, Greeba?" he said.

"Only let me prove it to you," she cried, with the challenge of beauty in her beautiful eyes.

"So you shall, Greeba," he said, "for we leave this house to-morrow."

"What?" she cried, rising to her feet.

"Yes," he said, "from to-morrow our condition will be different. So get yourself ready to go away from here."

Then her courageous challenge sank away in an instant.

"Whatever do you mean?" she cried, in great terror.

"If you have married the President you shall live with the man," he answered.

"Oh, Michael, Michael, what are you going to do?" she cried. "To degrade yourself?"

"Even so," he said calmly.

"To punish me?" she cried, "To prove me? To test me?"

"If you can go through with it I shall be happy and content," he answered.

"Are you then to be nothing in Iceland?" she said.

"And what of that?" he asked. "Think of what you have just been saying."

"Then I have come into your life to wreck it," she cried. "Yes, I, I! Michael," she added, more quietly, "I will go away. I would not bring shame and humiliation upon you for all that the world can give. I will leave you."

"That you never shall," said Michael Sunlocks. "We are man and wife now, and as man and wife we shall live together."

"I tell you I will not stay," she cried.

"And I tell you," he replied, "that I am your husband, and you shall give me a wife's obedience."

"Michael, dear Michael," she said, "it is for your own good that I want to leave you, so that the great promise of your life may not be wasted. It is I who am breaking in upon it. And I am nothing. Let me go."

"It is too late, Greeba. As poor man and poor woman we must pass the rest of our life together."

At that she burst into sobs again, blaming her brothers, and telling of their mean mission, and how she resented it, and what revenge of wicked slander they had wreaked upon her.

"You see it is all an error," she cried: "a cruel, cruel error."

"No, Greeba, it is not all an error," he answered. "It is not an error that you deceived me—and lied to me."

At that word her tears fell back, and the fire of her heart was in her eyes in an instant. "You say that, do you?" she cried. "Ah, then, perhaps there has been yet another error than you think of—the error of throwing him away for sake of you. He is noble, and simple, and true. His brave heart is above all suspicion. God pity him, and forgive me!"

Then for the first time that day since the six Fairbrothers had left the house, the calmness of Michael Sunlocks forsook him, and in a stern voice, with a look of fierce passion in his face, he cried, "Let me never, never meet that man. Five years ago I came here to save him, but now if we ever come face to face it will be the hour of his death or mine."

XIII: The Fall of Michael Sunlocks

When the Fairbrothers, in the first days after their coming to Iceland, started inquiries touching the position and influence of Michael Sunlocks, thinking thereby to make sure of their birds in the bush before parting with their bird in the hand, they frequented a little drinking-shop in the Cheapstead where sailors of many nations congregated, Danes, Icelanders, Norwegians, English, and Irish. Hearing there what satisfied their expectations, their pride began to swell, and as often as Michael Sunlocks was named with honor they blew up their breasts like bantams and said he was their brother, so to speak, and had been brought up in the same house with them since he was a slip of a brat of two or three. And if any who heard them glanced them over with doubtful eyes they straightway broke into facetious stories concerning the boyhood of Sunlocks, showing all their wondrous kindness to him as big brothers towards a little one.

Now these trifling events were of grave consequence to the fortunes of the Fairbrothers, and the fate of Michael Sunlocks, at two great moments. The first of the two was when Thurstan broke into open rebellion against Jacob. Then, with a sense of his wise brother's pitiable blunderheadedness, the astute Thurstan went off to the same drinking-shop to console himself with drink, and there he was addressed, when he was well and comfortably drunk, by a plausible person who spoke an unknown tongue. The end of that conference was nevertheless an idea firmly settled in Thurstan's mind that if he could not get money out of Michael Sunlocks he could at least get satisfaction.

This was the matter that Thurstan darkly hinted at when Jacob, being utterly discomfited, had to leave all further schemes to his brethren. So that day he returned to his rendezvous, met the plausible person again, and later in the evening sought out his brothers and said, "Didn't I tell ye to leave to me?"

"What's going doing?" said four voices at once.

"Plucking him down, the upstart, that's what's going doing," said Thurstan.

Then to five pairs of eager ears it slowly leaked out that a Danish ship lay in the harbor with a mysterious cargo of great casks, supposed to contain tallow; that after discharging their contents these casks were to be filled with shark's oil; that waiting the time to fill them they were to be stored (as all other warehouses were full of bonder's stock) in the little cell of detention under the senate-house; and, finally and most opportunely, that a meeting of Althing had been summoned on special business for the next night following, and that Michael Sunlocks was to be present.

The Fairbrothers heard all this with eyes that showed how well they understood it and keenly gloated over it. And late the same night the cargo of great casks was unshipped at the jetty, wheeled up to the senate-house and lodged there, carefully, silently, one by one. Thurstan helping, a few stragglers looking on, the stammering doorkeeper, long Jon, not anywhere visible, and no one else in the little sleepy town a whit the wiser. This being done, Thurstan went back to his lodging with the content of a soul at ease, saying to himself, "As I say, if we don't get anything else, we'll get satisfaction; and if we get what's promised I've a safe place to put it until the trouble's over and we can clear away, and that's the little crib under the turret of the cathedral church."

Then the worthy man lay down to sleep.

* * *

Before Thurstan was awake next morning Reykjavik was all astir. It had become known that a special sitting of Althing had been summoned for that night, and because nothing was known much was said concerning the business afoot. People gathered in groups where the snow of the heavy drifts had been banked up at the street corners, and gossiped and guessed. Such little work as the great winter left to any man was done in haste or not at all, that men might meet in the stores, the drinking-shops, and on the Cheapstead and ask, "Why?" "Wherefore?" and "What does it mean?" That some event of great moment was pending seemed to be the common opinion everywhere, though what ground it rested on no one knew, for no one knew anything. Only on one point was the feeling more general, or nearer right; that the President himself was at the root and centre of whatever was coming.

Before nightfall this vague sentiment, which ever hovers, like a dark cloud over a nation when a storm is near to breaking upon it, had filled every house in the capital, so that when the hour was come for the gathering of Althing the streets were thronged. Tow-headed children in goatskin caps ran here and there, women stood at the doors of houses, young girls leaned out of windows in spite of the cold, sailors and fishermen with pipes between their lips and their hands deep in their pockets lounged in grave silence outside the taverns, and old men stood under the open lamps by the street corners and chewed and snuffed to keep themselves warm.

In the neighborhood of the wooden senate-house on the High Street the throng was densest, and such of the members as came afoot had to crush their ways to the door. All the space within that had been allotted to the public was filled as soon as stammering Jon opened the side door. When no more room was left the side door was closed again and locked, and it was afterwards remembered, when people had time to put their heads together, that long Jon was there and then seen to pass the key of this side door to one of the six English strangers who had lately come to the town. That stranger was Thurstan Fairbrother.

The time of waiting before the proceedings commenced was passed by those within the Senate House in snuff-taking and sneezing and coughing, and a low buzz of conversation, full of solemn conjecture.

The members came in twos and threes, and every fresh comer was quizzed for a hint of the secret of the night. But grave and silent, when taken together, with the gravity and solemnity of so many oxen, and some of the oxen's sullen stupidity, were the faces both of members and spectators. Yet among both were faces that told of amused unbelief; calculating spirits that seemed to say that all this excitement was a bubble and would presently burst like one; sapient souls who, when the world is dead, will believe in no judgment until they hear the last trump.

There were two parties in the Senate—the Church party, that wanted religion to be the basis of the reformed government; and the Levellers, who wished the distinctions of clergy and laity to be abolished so far as secular power could go. The Church party was led by the Bishop, who was a member of the higher chamber, the Council, by virtue of his office; the Levellers were led by the little man with piercing eyes and the square brush of iron-gray hair who had acted as spokesman to the Court at the trial of Red Jason. As each of these arrived there was a faint commotion through the house.

Presently the Speaker came shuffling in, wiping his brow with his red handkerchief, and at the same moment the thud of a horse's hoofs on the hard snow outside, followed by a deep buzz as of many voices—not cheering nor yet groaning—told of the coming of the President.

Then, amid suppressed excitement, Michael Sunlocks entered the house, looking weary, pale, much older, and stooping slightly under his flaxen hair, as if conscious of the gaze of many eyes fixed steadfastly upon him.

After the Speaker had taken his chair, Michael Sunlocks rose in his place amid dead stillness.

"Sir, and gentlemen," he said in a tense voice, speaking slowly, calmly and well, "you are met here at my instance to receive a message of some gravity. It is scarcely more than half a year since it was declared and enacted by this present Council of Althing that the people of Iceland were and should be constituted, established and confirmed to be a Republic or Free State, governed by the Supreme Authority of the Nation, the people's representatives. You were then pleased to do me the honor of electing me to be your first President, and though I well knew that no man had less cause to put himself forward in the cause of his country than I, being the youngest among you, the least experienced, and, by birth, an Englishman, yet I undertook the place I am now in because I had taken a chief hand in pulling down the old order, and ought, therefore, to lend the best help I could towards putting up the new. Other reasons influenced me, such as the desire to keep the nation from falling amid many internal dissensions into extreme disorder and becoming open to the common enemy. I will not say that I had no personal motives, no private aims, no selfish ambitions in stepping in where your confidence opened the way, but you will bear me witness that in the employment to which the nation called me, though there may have been passion and mistakes, I have endeavored to discharge the duty of an honest man."

There was a low murmur of assent, then a pause, then a hush, and then Michael Sunlocks continued:

"But, gentlemen, I have come to see that I am not able for such a trust as the burden of this government, and I now beg to be dismissed of my charge."

Then the silence was broken by many exclamations of surprise. They fell on the ear of Michael Sunlocks like the ground-swell of a distant sea. His white face quivered, but his eye was bright, and he did not flinch.

"It is no doubt your concernment to know what events and what convictions have so suddenly influenced me, and I can only claim your indulgence in withholding that part of both that touches the interests of others. For myself, I can but say that I have made mistakes and lost self-confidence; that being unable to manage my own affairs I am unwilling to undertake the affairs of the nation; that I am convinced I am unfit for the great place I hold; that any name were fitter than mine for my post, any person fitter than I am for its work; and I say this from my heart, God knows."

He was listened to in silence but amid a tumult of unheard emotion, and as he went on his voice, though still low, was so charged with suppressed feeling that it seemed in that dead stillness to rise to a cry.

"Gentlemen," he said, "though this may come on you with surprise do not think it has been lightly resolved upon, or that it is to me a little thing to renounce the honor with the burden of government; I will deal plainly and faithfully with you and say that all my heart was in the work you gave me, and though I held my life in my hand, I was willing to adventure it in that high place where the judgment of Althing placed me. So if I beg of you to release me I sacrifice more by my resignation than you by your dismissal. If I had pride, heaven has humbled it, and that is a righteous judgment of God. Young and once hopeful, I am withdrawing from all sight of hope. I am giving up my cherished ambitions and the chances of success. When I leave this place you will see me no more. I am to be as nothing henceforward, for the pole-star of my life is gone out. So not without feeling, not without pain, I ask you to dismiss me and let me go my ways."

He sat down upon these words amid the stunned stupefaction of those who heard him, and when he had ceased to speak it seemed as if he were still speaking. Presently the people recovered their breath and there was the harsh grating of feet, and a murmur like a low sough of wind.

Then rose the little man with the brush hair, the leader of the Levellers, and the chief opponent of Michael Sunlocks in the Presidency. His name was Grimmsson. Clearing his throat, raspily, he began to speak in short, jerky sentences. This was indeed a surprise that moved the house to great astonishment. There was a suspicion of mock heroics about it that he, for his part, could not shake off, for they all knew the President for a dreamer of dreams. The President had said that it was within the concernment of Althing to know how it stood that he had so suddenly and surprisingly become convinced of his unfitness. Truly he was right there. Also the President had said that he had undertaken his post not so much out of hope of doing any good as out of a desire to prevent mischief and evil. Yet what was he now doing? Running them headlong into confusion and disorder.

The leader of the Levellers sat down, and a dark-browed fellow from among his followers rose in his place. What did this hubbub mean? If the President had been crazy in his health they might have understood it; but the Lord was pleased to preserve him. Perhaps they had to look deeper. Whispers were abroad among some who had been near to the President's person that the time had come to settle the order and prosperity of Iceland on a new basis. He made no doubt such whispers implied a Protectorate, perhaps even a Monarchy. Did the President think to hasten the crisis that would lead to that change? Did he hope to alter the name of President for Protector, or for something yet higher? Was he throwing his sprat to catch a mackerel? Let them look to it.

The dark-browed man sat down, with a grin of triumph, and his place was taken by a pert little beardless person, with a smirk on his face. They had all read the parable of how a certain man made a feast, and did his friends the honor to invite them; but first one friend for one halting reason, and then another for a reason yet more lame, excused himself from sitting at the good man's table. Well, one of these excuses was from a man who had married a wife, and therefore could not come. Now the President had married a wife——

The little man got no further, for Michael Sunlocks, whose features had flushed up, leaped to his feet again, against all order and precedent in that rude chamber so reverent of law.

"I knew," he said, amid the silence of the wide-eyed people, "when I came to this house to-day, that the censure of Iceland might follow me when I left it, but its shame shall not pursue me. I also knew that there were persons not well content with the present order of things who might show their discontent as they had opportunity; but before the insinuations of base motives that have just been made I take you to witness that all that go with them are malicious figments. My capacity any man may impeach, but my honest name none shall question without challenge, for the sole pride I shall carry away with me when I leave this place shall be the pride of an upright life."

With that he put on his hat where he stood, and the people, thrilled to their hearts by his ringing voice, and his eyes full of splendid courage, broke into a great clamor of cheers.

"Peace, peace," cried a deep voice over the tumult. The old Bishop had risen to speak.

"This is a quarrelsome age," he said, "an age when there seems to be a strange itching in the spirits of men, when near every man seems to seek his brother's disquiet all he may, when wretched jealousies and the spirit of calumny turn everything to gall and wormwood. But can we not take the President's message for what it claims to be, asking him for no reasons that concern us not? When has he betrayed us? His life since his coming here has been marked by strict integrity. When has pride been his bane? His humility has ever been his praise. He has been modest with the highest power and shown how little he valued those distances he was bound to keep up. When has mammon been his god? If he leaves us now he leaves us a poor man, as Althing may well assure itself. But let us pray that this may not come to pass. When he was elected to the employment he holds, being so young a man, many trembled—and I among them—for the nation that had intrusted its goods and its lives to his management, but now we know that only in his merit and virtue can it find its safety and repose. Let me not be prodigal of praise before his face, but honor and honesty require this, that we say that so true a man is not to be found this day in Iceland."

The Bishop's words had quickened the pulse of the people, and cheer followed cheer again. "It is written," continued the Bishop, "that whosoever exalteth himself shall be abased, and he that humbleth himself shall be exalted. Our young President has this day sat down in the lowest room; and if he must needs leave us, having his own reasons that are none of ours, may the Lord cause His face to shine upon him, and comfort him in all his adversities."

Then there was but one voice in that assembly, the voice of a loud Amen. And Michael Sunlocks had risen again with a white face and dim eyes, to return his thanks, and say his last word before the vote for his release should be taken, when there was a sudden commotion, a sound of hurrying feet, a rush, a startled cry, and at the next moment a company of soldiers had entered the house from the cell below, and stood with drawn swords on the floor.

Before anyone had recovered from his surprise one of the soldiers had spoken. "Gentlemen," he said, "the door is locked—you are prisoners of the King of Denmark."

"Betrayed!" shouted fifty voices at once, and then there was wild confusion.

"So this mysterious mummery is over at last," said the leader of the Levellers, rising up with rigid limbs, and a scared and whitened face. "Now we know why we have all been brought here to-night. Betrayed indeed,—and there stands the betrayer."

So saying he pointed scornfully at Michael Sunlocks, who stood where he had risen, with the look of deep emotion hardly yet banished from his face by the look of bewilderment that followed it.

"False," Michael Sunlocks cried. "It is false as hell."

But in that quick instant the people looked at him with changed eyes, and received his words with a groan of rage that silenced him.

That night Jorgen Jorgensen sailed up the fiord, and, landing at Reykjavik, took possession of it, and the second Republic of Iceland was at an end.

That night, too, when the Fairbrothers, headed by Thurstan, trudged through the streets on their way to Government House, looking to receive the reward that had been promised them, they were elbowed by a drunken company of the Danes who frequented the drinking-shops on the Cheapstead.

"Why, here are his brothers," shouted one of the roysterers, pointing at the Fairbrothers.

"His brothers! His brothers!" shouted twenty more.

Thurstan tried to protest and Jacob to fraternize, but all was useless. The brethren were attacked for the relation they had claimed with the traitor who had fallen, and thus the six worthy and unselfish souls who had come to Iceland for gain and lost everything, and waited for revenge and only won suspicion, were driven off in peril of their necks, with a drunken mob at full cry behind them.

They took refuge in a coasting schooner, setting sail for the eastern fiords. Six days afterwards the schooner was caught in the ice at the mouth of Seydis fiord, imprisoned there four months, out of reach of help from land or sea, and every soul aboard died miserably.

Short as had been the shrift of Red Jason, the shrift of Michael Sunlocks was yet shorter. On the order of Jorgen Jorgensen, the "late usurper of the Government of Iceland" was sent for the term of his natural life to the Sulphur Mines that he had himself established as a penal settlement.

And such was the fall of Michael Sunlocks.

The Book of Red Jason by Hall Caine

I: What Befell Old Adam

Now it would be a long task to follow closely all that befell the dear old Adam Fairbrother, from the time when the ship wherein he sailed for Iceland weighed anchor in Ramsey bay. Yet not to know what strange risks he ran, and how in the end he overcame all dangers, by God's grace and his own extreme labor, is not to know this story of how two good men with a good woman between them pursued each other over the earth with vows of vengeance, and came together at length in heaven's good time and way. So not to weary the spirit with much speaking, yet to leave nothing unsaid that shall carry us onward to that great hour when Red Jason and Michael Sunlocks stood face to face, let us begin where Adam's peril began, and hasten forward to where it ended.

Fourteen days out of Ramsey, in latitude of 64 degrees, distant about five leagues north of the Faroes, and in the course of west northwest, hoping to make the western shores of Iceland, Adam with his shipmates was overtaken by foul weather, with high seas and strong wind opposing them stoutly from the northwest. Thus they were driven well into the latitude of sixty-six off the eastern coast of Iceland, and there, though the seas still ran as high as to the poop, they were much beset by extraordinary pieces of ice which appeared to come down from Greenland. Then the wind abated, and an unsearchable and noisome fog followed; so dense that not an acre of sea could be seen from the top-mast head, and so foul that the compasses would not work in it. After that, though they wrought night and day with poles and spikes, they were beaten among the ice as scarce any ship ever was before, and so terrible were the blows they suffered that many a time they thought the planks must be wrenched from the vessel's sides. Nevertheless they let fall sail, thinking to force their way through the ice before they were stowed to pieces, and, though the wind was low, yet the ship felt the canvas and cleared the shoals that encompassed her. The wind then fell to a calm, but still the fog hung heavily over the sea, which was black and smelt horribly. And when they thought to try their soundings, knowing that somewhere thereabouts the land must surely be, they heard a noise that seemed at first like the tract of the shore. It was worse than that, for it was the rut of a great bank of ice, two hundred miles deep, breaking away from the far shores of

Greenland, and coming with its steady sweep, such as no human power could resist, towards the coasts of Iceland. Between that vast ice floe and the land they lay, with its hollow and terrible voice in their ears, and with no power to fly from it, for their sail hung loose and idle in the dead stillness of the air.

Oh! it is an awful thing to know that death is swooping down on you hour by hour; to hear it coming with its hideous thunder, like the groans of damned souls, and yet to see nothing of your danger for the day darkness that blinds you. But the shipmaster was a stout-hearted fellow, and while the fog continued and he was without the help of wind or compass, he let go a raven that he had aboard to see if it could discover land. The raven flew to the northeast, and did not return to the ship, and by that token the master knew that the land of Iceland lay somewhere near on their starboard bow. So he was for lowering the long boat, to stand in with the coast and learn what part of Iceland it was, when suddenly the wind larged again, and before long it blew with violence.

At this their peril was much increased, for the night before had been bitterly cold, and the sails had been frozen where they hung outspread, and some of the cables were as stiff as icicles and half as thick as a man's body. Thus under wind that in a short space rose to a great storm, with canvas that could not be reefed, an ocean of ice coming down behind, and seas beneath of an untouchable depth, they were driven on and on towards an unknown shore.

From the like danger may God save all Christian men, even as he saved old Adam and his fellowship, for they had begun to prepare themselves to make a good end of their hopeless lives, when in the lift of the fog the master saw an opening in the coast, and got into it, and his ship rode safely on a quick tide down the fiord called Seydis fiord.

There the same night they dropped anchor in a good sound, and went instantly to prayer, to praise God for His delivery of them, and Adam called the haven where they moored, "The Harbor of Good Providence." So with cheerful spirits, thinking themselves indifferently safe, they sought their births, and so ended the first part of their peril in God's mercy and salvation.

But the storm that had driven them into their place of refuge drove their dread enemy after them, and in the night, while they lay in the first sleep of four days, the ice encompassed them and crushed them against the rocks. The blow struck Adam out of a tranquil rest, and he thought nothing better than that he was awakening for another world. All hands were called to the pumps, for the master still thought the ship was staunch and might be pushed along the coast by the shoulders with crows of iron, and thus ride out to sea. But though they worked until the pumps sucked, it was clear that the poor vessel was stuck fast in the ice, and that she must soon get her death-wound. So, at break of day, the master and crew, with Adam Fairbrother, took what they could carry of provisions and clothes, and clambered ashore, leaving the ship to her fate.

It was a bleak and desolate coast they had landed upon, with never a house in sight, never a cave that they might shelter in, or a stone that would cover them against the wind; with nothing around save the bare face of a broad fell, black and lifeless, strewn over with small light stones sucked full of holes like the honeycomb, but without trees, or bush, or grass, or green moss. And there they suffered more privations than it is needful to tell, waiting for the ice to break, looking on at its many colors of blue, and purple, and emerald green, and yellow, and its many strange and wonderful shapes, resembling churches, and castles, and spires, and turrets, and cities, all ablaze in the noonday sun.

They built themselves a rude hut of the stones like pumice, and, expecting the dissolution of the ice, they kept watch on their ship, which itself looked like an iceberg frozen into a ship's shape. And meantime some of their company suffered very sorely. Though the year was not yet far advanced towards winter, some of the men swooned of the cold that came up from the ice of the fiord; the teeth of others became loose and the flesh of their gums fell away, and on the soles of the feet of a few the frost of the nights raised blisters as big as walnuts.

Partly from these privations and partly from loss of heart when at last one evil day he saw his good ship crushed to splinters against the rocks, the master fell sick, and was brought so low that in less than a week he lay expecting his good hour. And feeling his extremity he appointed Adam to succeed him as director of the company, to guide them to safety over the land, since Providence forbade that they should sail on the seas. Then, all being done, so far as his help could avail, he stretched himself out for his end, only praying in his last hours that he might be allowed to drink as much ale as he liked from the ship's stores that had been saved. This Adam ordered that he should, and as long as he lived the ale was brought to him in the hut where he lay, and he drank it until, between draught and draught, it froze in the jug at his side. After that he died—an honest, a worthy, and strong-hearted man.

And Adam, being now by choice of the late master and consent of his crew the leader of the company, began to make a review of all men and clothes and victuals, and found that there were eleven of them in all, with little more than they stood up in, and provisions to last them, with sparing, three weeks at utmost. And seeing that they were cut off from all hope of a passage by sea, he set himself to count the chances of a journey by land, and by help of the ship's charts and much beating of the wings of memory to recover what he had learned of Iceland in the days when his dear lad Sunlocks had left him for these shores, he reckoned that by following the sea line under the feet of the great Vatna-Jokull, they might hope, if they could hold out so long, to reach Reykjavik at last. Long and weary the journey must be, with no town and scarce a village to break it, and no prospect of shelter by the way, save what a few farms might give them. So Adam ordered the carpenter to recover what he could of the ship's sails to make a tent, and of its broken timbers to make a cart to carry victuals, and when this was done they set off along the fell side on the first stage of their journey.

The same day, towards nightfall, they came upon a little group of grass-covered houses at the top of the fiord, and saw the people of Iceland for the first time. They were a little colony cut off by impassable mountains from their fellows within the island, and having no ships in which they dare venture to their kind on the seas without; tall and strong-limbed in their persons, commonly of yellow hair, but sometimes of red, of which neither sex was ashamed; living on bread that was scarce eatable, being made of fish that had been dried and powdered; lazy and unclean; squalid and mean-spirited, and with the appearance of being depressed and kept under. It was a cheerless life they lived at the feet of the great ice-bound jokull and the margin of the frozen sea, so that looking around on the desolate place and the dumb wilderness of things before and behind, Adam asked himself why and how any living souls had ever ventured there.

But for all that the little colony were poor and wretched, the hearts of the shipwrecked company leapt up at sight of them, and in the joyful gabble of unintelligible speech between them old Adam found that he could understand some of the words. And when the islanders saw that in some sort Adam understood them they singled him out from the rest of his company, falling on his neck and kissing him after the way of their nation, and concluding among themselves that he was one of their own people who had gone away in his youth and never been heard of after. And Adam, though he looked shy at their musty kisses, was nothing loth to allow that they might be Manxmen strayed and lost.

For Adam and his followers two things came of this encounter, and the one was to forward and the other to retard their journey. The first was that the islanders sold them twelve ponies, of the small breed that abound in that latitude, and gave them a guide to lead them the nearest way to the capital. The ponies cost them forty kroner, or more than two pounds apiece, and the guide was to stand to them in two kroner, or two shillings, a day. This took half of all they had in money, and many were the heavy groans of the men at parting with it; but Adam argued that their money was of no other value there than as a help out of their extremity, and that all the gold in the banks, if he had it, would be less to him then than the little beast he was bestriding.

The second of the two things that followed on that meeting with the islanders was that, just as they had started afresh on their way, now twelve in all, each man on his horse, and a horse in the shafts of the cart that held the victuals, a woman came running after them with a child in her arms, and besought them to take her with them. That anyone could wish to share their outcast state was their first surprise, but the woman's terrified looks, her tears and passionate pleadings, seemed to say that to be homeless and houseless on the face of that trackless land was not so awful a fate but that other miseries could conquer the fear of it. So, failing to learn more of her condition, than that she was friendless and alone, Adam ordered that, with her child, she should be lifted into the cart that was driven ahead of them.

But within an hour they were overtaken by a man, who came galloping after them, and said the woman had stolen the child—that it was his child, and that he had come to carry it back with him. At that Adam called on the woman to answer through the guide, and she said that the man was indeed the child's father, but that she was its mother; that he was a farmer, and had married her only that he might have a son to leave his farm to; that having given him this child he had turned her out of doors, and that in love and yearning for her little one, from whom she had been so cruelly parted, she had stolen into her old home, plucked up the babe and run away with it. Hearing this story, which the woman told through her tears, Adam answered the man that if the law of his country allowed a father to deal so with the mother of his child it was a base and unnatural law, and merited the obedience of no man; so he meant to protect the woman against both it and him, and carry her along with their company. With that answer the man turned tail, but Adam's victory over him was dearly bought, at the cost of much vexation afterwards and sore delay on the hard journey.

And now it would be long to tell of the trials of that passage over those gaunt solitudes, where there was no fingerpost or mark of other human travellers. The men bore up bravely, loving most to comfort the woman and do her any tender office, or carry her child before them on their saddles. And many a time, at sight of the little one, and at hearing its simple prattle in a tongue they did not understand, the poor fellows would burst into tears, as if remembering, with a double pang, that they were exiles from that country far away, where other mothers held their own children to their breasts. Two of them sickened of the cold, and had to be left behind at a farm, where the people were kind and gentle and promised to nurse them until their companions could return for them. But the heaviest blow to all that company was the sickness and death of the child. Tenderly the rude sailor men nursed the little fellow one by one, and when nothing availed to keep his sweet face among them they mourned his loss as the worst disaster that had yet befallen them. The mother herself was distraught, and in the madness of her agony turned on Adam and reproached him, saying he had brought her child into this wilderness to kill it. Adam understood her misery too well to rebuke her ingratitude, and the same night that her babe was laid in his rest with a cross of willow wood to mark the place of it, she disappeared from their company, and where she went or what became of her no one knew, for she was seen by them no more.

But next morning they were overtaken by a number of men riding hard, and one of them was the woman's husband, and another the High Sheriff of the Quarter. These two called on Adam to deliver up the child, and when he told them that it was dead, and the mother gone, the husband would have fallen upon him with his knife, but for the Sheriff, who, keeping the peace, said that, as accessory after the fact of theft, Adam himself must go to prison.

Now, at this the crew of the ship began to set up a woeful wail, and to double their fists and measure the strength of nine sturdy British seamen against that of ten lanky Icelanders. But Adam restrained them from violence, and indeed there was need for none, for the Sheriff was in no mood to carry his prisoner away with him. All he did was to take out his papers, and fill them up with the name and description that Adam gave him, and then hand them over to Adam himself, saying they were the warrant for his imprisonment, and that he was to go on his way until he came to the next district, where there was a house of detention, which the guide would find for him, and there deliver up the documents to the Sheriff in charge.

With such instructions, and never doubting but they would be followed, the good man and his people wheeled about, and returned as they came.

And being so easily rid of them the sailors began to laugh at their simpleness, and, with many satisfied grunts, to advise the speedy destruction of the silly warrant that was the sole witness against Adam. But Adam himself said, no—that he was touched by the simplicity of a people that could trust a man to take himself to prison, and he would not wrong that confidence by any cheating. So he ordered the guide to lead on where he had been directed.

They reached the prison towards nightfall, and there old Adam bade a touching farewell of his people, urging them not to wait for him, but to push on to Reykjavik where alone they could find ships to take them home to England. And some of the good fellows wept at this parting, though they all thought it foolish, but one old salt named Chalse shed no tears, and only looked crazier than ever, and chuckled within himself from some dark cause.

And indeed there was small reason to weep, because, simple as the first Sheriff's conduct had been, that of the second Sheriff was yet simpler, for when Adam presented himself as a prisoner the Sheriff asked for his papers, and then diving into his pocket to find them, the good man found that they were gone—lost, dropped by the way or destroyed by accident—and no search sufficed to recover them. So failing of his warrant the Sheriff shook his head at Adam's story and declined to imprison him, and the prisoner had no choice but to go free. Thus Adam returned to his company, who heard with laughter and delight of the close of his adventure, all save Chalse, who looked sheepish and edged away whenever Adam glanced at him. Thus ended in merriment an incident that threatened many evil consequences, and was attended by two luckless mischances.

The first of these two was that, by going to the prison, which lay three Danish miles out of the direct track to the capital, Adam and his company had missed young Oscar and Zoega's men, whom Michael Sunlocks had sent out from Reykjavik in search of them. The second was that their guide had disappeared and left them, within an hour of bringing them to the door of the Sheriff. His name was Jonas; he had been an idle and a selfish fellow; he had demanded his wages day by day; and seeing Adam part from the rest, he had concluded that with the purse-bearer the purse of the company had gone. But he alone had known the course, and, worthless as he had been to them in other ways, the men began to rail at him when they found that he had abandoned them and left them to struggle on without help.

"The sweep!" "the thief!" "the wastrel!" "the gomerstang!" they called him, with wilder names beside. But old Adam rebuked them and said, "Good friends, I would persuade myself that urgent reasons alone can have induced this poor man to leave us. Were we not ourselves constrained to forsake two of our number several days back, though with the full design of returning to them to aid them when it should lie in our power? Thus I cannot blame the Icelander without more knowledge of his intent, and so let us push on still and trust in God to deliver us, as he surely will."

And, sure enough, the next day after they came upon a man who undertook the place of the guide who had forsaken them. He was a priest and a very learned man, but poor as the poorest farmer. He spoke in Latin, and in imperfect Latin Adam made shift to answer him. His clothes were all but worn to rags, and he was shoeing his horse in the little garth before his door. His house, which stood alone save for the wooden church beside it, looked on the outside like a line of grass cones, hardly higher to their peaks than the head of a tall man, and in the inside it was low, dark, noisome, and noisy. In one room to which Chalse and the seamen were taken, three or four young children were playing, an old woman was spinning, and a younger woman, the priest's wife, was washing clothes. This was the living room and sleeping room, the birth room and death room of the whole family. In another room, to which Adam was led by the priest himself, the floor was strewn with saddles, nails, hammers, horseshoes, whips, and spades, and the walls were covered with bookshelves, whereon stood many precious old black-letter volumes. This was the workshop and study, wherein the good priest spent his long, dark days of winter.

And, being once more fully equipped for the journey, Adam ordered that they should lose no time in setting out afresh, with the priest on his own pony in front of them. Two days then passed without misadventure of any kind, and in that time they had come to a village, at which they should have forsaken the coast line and made for the interior, in order that they might cross to Reykjavik by way of Thingvellir, and so cut off the peninsula ending in the Smoky Point. But a heavy fall of snow coming down suddenly, they were compelled to seek shelter at a farm, the only one for more than a hundred miles to east or west of them. There they rested while the snow-storm lasted, and it was the same weary downfall that kept Greeba to her house while Red Jason lay in his brain fever in the cell in the High Street, and Michael Sunlocks was out on the sea in search of themselves.

And when the snow had ceased to fall, and the frost that followed had hardened it, and the country, now white instead of black, was again fit to travel upon, it was found that the priest was unwilling to start. Then it appeared that downright drinking had been his sole recreation and his only bane; that the most serious affairs of night and day had always submitted to this great business; that in the interval of waiting for the passing of the snow, finding himself with a few kroner at command, he had begun on his favorite occupation, and that he now was too deeply immersed therein to be disturbed in less than a week.

Once again the seamen railed at their guide, as well as at the whole race of Icelanders, but Adam was all for lenity towards the priest and hope for themselves.

"My faithful companions," he said, "be not dismayed by any of these disasters, but let us put our whole trust in God. If it be our fortune to end our days in this desolate land, we are as near heaven here as at home. Yet let us use all honest efforts to save our natural lives, and we are not yet so far past hope of doing so but that I see a fair way by which we may effect it."

With that they set out again alone, and within an hour they had fallen on the second mischance of their journey, for failing to find the pass that would have led them across country through Thingvellir, they kept close by the sea line in the direction of the Smoky Point.

Now these misadventures, first with the mother and child, next with the Sheriffs, and then with the guides, though they kept back Adam and his company from that quick deliverance which they would have found in meeting with the messengers of Michael Sunlocks or with Michael Sunlocks himself, yet brought them in the end in the way of the only persons who are important to this story. For pursuing their mistaken way by the line of sea they came upon the place called Krisuvik. It was a grim wilderness of awful things, not cold and dead and dumb like the rest of that haggard land, but hot and alive with inhuman fire and clamorous with devilish noises. A wide ashen plain within a circle of hills whereon little snow could rest for the furnace that raged beneath the surface; shooting with shrill whistles its shafts of hot steam from a hundred fumeroles; bubbling up in a thousand jets of boiling water; hissing from a score of green cauldrons; grumbling low with mournful sounds underneath like the voice of subterranean wind, and sending up a noxious stench through heavy whorls of vapor that rolled in a fetid atmosphere overhead. Oh, it was a fearsome place, like nothing on God's earth but a mouldering wreck of human body, vast and shapeless, and pierced deep with foulest ulcers; a leper spot on earth's face; a seething vat full of broth of hell's own brewing. And all around was the peaceful snow, and beyond the lines of the southern hills was the tranquil sea, and within the northern mountains was a quiet lake of water as green as the grass of spring.

Coming upon the ghastly place, printed deep with Satan's own features on the face of it, Adam thought that surely no human footstep was ever meant by God to echo among bodeful noises. But there he found two wooden sheds busy with troops of men coming and going about them, and a third house of the same kind in an early stage of building. Then asking questions as well as he was able he learned that the boiling pits were the Sulphur Mines that the new Governor, the President of the Republic, had lately turned to account as a penal settlement, that the two completed sheds were the workshops and sleeping places of the prisoners, and that the unfinished house was intended for their hospital.

And it so chanced that while with his poor broken company Adam rested on his horse, to look on at this sight with eyes of wonder and fear, a gang of four prisoners passed on to their work in charge of as many warders, and one of the four men was Red Jason. His long red hair was gone, his face was thin and pale instead of full and tawny, and his eyes, once so bright, were heavy and slow. He walked in file, and about his neck was a collar of iron, with a bow coming over his head and ending on the forehead in a bell that rang as he went along. The wild vitality of his strong figure seemed lost, he bent forward as he walked, and looked steadfastly on the ground.

Yet, changed as he was, Adam knew him at a glance, and between surprise and terror, called on him by his name. But Jason heard nothing, and strode on like a man who had suddenly become deaf and blind under the shock of some evil day.

"Jason! Jason!" Adam cried again, and he dropped from the saddle to run towards him. But the warders raised their hands to warn the old man off, and Jason went on between them, without ever lifting his eyes or making sign or signal.

"Now, God save us! what can this mean?" cried Adam; and though with the lame help of his "old Manx" he questioned as well as he was able the men who were at work at the building of the hospital, nothing could he learn but one thing, and that was the strange and wondrous chance that his own eyes revealed to him: namely, that the last face he saw as he was leaving Mann, on that bad night when he stole away from Greeba while she slept, was the first face he had seen to know it since he set foot on Iceland.

Nor was this surprise the only one that lay waiting for him in that gaunt place. Pushing on towards Reykjavik, the quicker for this sight of Red Jason, and with many troubled thoughts of Michael Sunlocks, Adam came with his company to the foot of the mountain that has to be crossed before the lava plain is reached which leads to the capital. And there the narrow pass was blocked to them for half-an-hour of precious time by a long train of men and ponies coming down the bridle path. They were Danes, to the number of fifty at least, mounted on as many horses, and with a score of tired horses driven on ahead of them. What their work and mission was in that grim waste Adam could not learn until he saw that the foremost of the troop had drawn up at one of the two wooden sheds, and then he gathered from many signs that they were there as warders to take charge of the settlement in place of the Icelandic officers who had hitherto held possession of it.

Little time he had, however, to learn the riddle of these strange doings, or get knowledge of the double rupture of state of affairs that had caused them, for presently old Chalse came hurrying back to him from some distance ahead, with a scared face and stammering tongue, and one nervous hand pointing upwards to where the last of the men and horses were coming down the bridle path.

"Lord-a-massy, who's this," cried Chalse; and following the direction of his hand Adam saw what the old fellow pointed at, and the sight seemed to freeze the blood at his heart.

It was Michael Sunlocks riding between two of the Danish warders as their prisoner, silent, fettered and bound.

Then Adam felt as if he had somewhere fallen into a long sleep, and was now awakening to a new life in a new world, where the people were the same as in the old one but everything about them was strange and terrible. But he recovered from his terror as Michael Sunlocks came on, and he called to him, and Sunlocks heard him, and turned towards him with a look of joy and pain in one quick glance of a moment.

"My son! my boy!" cried Adam.

"Father! Father!" cried Michael Sunlocks.

But in an instant the warders had closed about Sunlocks, and hurried him on in the midst of them, while their loud shouts drowned all other voices.

And when the troop had passed him, Adam sat a moment silent on his little beast, and then he turned to his company and said:

"My good friends and faithful companions, my journey is at an end, and you must go on without me. I came to this land of Iceland only to find one who is my son indeed, though not flesh of my flesh, thinking to rest my old arm on his young shoulder. I have found him now, but he is in trouble, from some cause that I have yet to learn, and it is my old shoulder that his young arm must rest upon. And this that you have witnessed is not the meeting I looked for, and built my hopes on, and buoyed up my failing spirits with, through all the trouble of our many weary days. But God's will be done! So go your ways and leave me where His wisdom has brought me, and may His mercy fetch you in safety to your native country, and to the good souls waiting for you there."

But the rough fellows protested that come what might, leave him they never would, and old Chalse without more ado began to make ready to pitch their tent on the thin patch of grass where they stood.

And that evening, while Adam wandered over the valley, trying to get better knowledge of the strange events which he had read as if by flashes of lightning, and hearing in broken echoes of the rise and fall of the Republic, of the rise and fall of Michael Sunlocks, of the fall and return of Jorgen Jorgensen, a more wondrous chance than any that had yet befallen him was fast coming his way.

For late that night, when he sat in his grief, with his companions busied about him, comforting him with what tender offices and soft words their courageous minds could think of, a young Icelander came to the gap of the tent and asked, in broken English, if they would give a night's shelter to a lady who could find no other lodging, and was alone save for himself, who had been her guide from Reykjavik.

At that word Adam's own troubles were gone from him in an instant, and, though his people would have demurred, he called on the Icelander to fetch the lady in, and presently she came, and then all together stood dumb-founded, for the lady was Greeba herself.

It would be hard to tell how at first every other feeling was lost in one of surprise at the strange meeting of father and daughter, how surprise gave place to joy, and joy to pain, as bit by bit the history of their several adventures was unfolded each to the other. And while Greeba heard of the mischances that had overtaken old Adam, he, on his part, heard of the death of her mother and her brother's ill-usage, of the message that came from Michael Sunlocks and her flight from home, of how she came to Iceland and was married, and of how Sunlocks went in pursuit of himself, and, returning to the capital, was betrayed into the hands of his enemies. All the long story of plot and passion he heard in the wild tangle of her hot and broken words, save only that part of it which concerned her quarrel with her husband; but when he mentioned Red Jason, saying that he had seen him, he heard that sad passage of her story also, told with fear and many bitter tears.

Adam comforted Greeba with what words of cheer he could command, in an hour when his own heart was dark and hopeless, and then amid the turmoil of so many emotions, the night being worn to midnight, they composed themselves to sleep.

Next morning, rising anxious and unrested, Adam saw the Icelandic warders, who had been supplanted in their employment by the Danes, start away from the settlement for their homes, and after them went a group of the Danish prisoners as free men, who had been imprisoned by the Republic as spies of the Government of Denmark. By this time Adam had decided on his course.

"Greeba," he said, "this imprisonment of Michael Sunlocks is unjust, and I see a way to put an end to it. No governor shall sentence him without judge or jury. But I will go on to Reykjavik and appeal to this Jorgen Jorgensen. If he will not hear me, I will appeal to his master, the King of Denmark. If Denmark will not listen, I will appeal to England, for Michael Sunlocks is a British subject, and may claim the rights of an Englishman. And if England turns a deaf ear to me, I will address my prayer to God, who has never yet failed to right the wronged, or humble the arrogance of the mighty. Thank Heaven, that has brought me here. I thought I was coming to end my days in peace by his side who would shelter my poor foolish gray head, that had forgotten to protect itself. But strange are the ways of Providence. God has had his own purposes in bringing me here thus blindfolded, and, thanks to His mercy! I am not yet so old but I may yet do something. So come, girl, come, make ready, and we will go on our great errand together."

But Greeba had her own ends from the first in following Michael Sunlocks to the place of his imprisonment, and she answered and said,

"No, father, no. You may go on to Reykjavik, and do all this if you can, but my place is here, at my husband's side. He lost faith in my affection, and said I had married him for the glory that his place would bring me; but he shall see what a woman can go through for sake of the man she loves. I have my own plan of life in this place, and the power to carry it out. Therefore do not fear to leave me, but go, and God prosper you!"

"Let it be so," said Adam, and with that, after some words of explanation with the brave fellows who had followed him from the hour when, as ship-broken men, they set out on foot from the eastern fiord, he started on his journey afresh, leaving the tent and the last of their ship's victuals behind with Greeba, for Reykjavik was no more than a day's ride from Krisuvik.

When he was gone, Greeba went down to the tents at the mouth of the mines, and asked for the Captain. A Danish gentleman who did not know her, and whom she did not know, answered to that title, and then she said that hearing that a hospital was being built she had come out from Reykjavik to offer herself as a nurse if a nurse was wanted.

"A nurse is wanted," said the Captain, "and though we had no thought of a woman you have come in the nick of time."

So Greeba, under some assumed name, unknown to the contingent of Danish officers fresh from Denmark, who had that day taken the places of the Icelandic warders, and recognizable in her true character by two men only in Krisuvik, Michael Sunlocks and Red Jason, if ever they should see her, took up her employment as hospital nurse to the sick prisoners of the Sulphur Mines.

But having attained her end, or the first part of it, her heart was torn by many conflicting feelings. Would she meet with her husband? Would he come to be in her own charge? Oh, God forbid that it should ever come to pass. Yet God grant it, too, for that might help him to a swifter release than her dear old father could compass. Would she see Red Jason? Would Michael Sunlocks ever see him? Oh! God forbid that also. And yet, and yet, God grant it, after all.

Such were her hopes and fears, when the hospital shed was finished, and she took her place within it. And now let us see how heaven fulfilled them.

II: The Sulphur Mines

Red Jason and Michael Sunlocks were together at last, within the narrow stockade of a penal settlement. These two, who had followed each other from land to land, the one on his errand of vengeance, the other on his mission of mercy, both now nourishing hatred and lust of blood, were thrown as prisoners into the Sulphur Mines of Krisuvik. There they met, they spoke, they lived and worked side by side yet neither knew the other for the man he had sought so long and never found. This is the strange and wondrous chance that has now to be recorded, and only to think of it, whether as accident or God's ordinance, makes the blood to tingle in every vein. Poor and petty are the passions of man, and God's hand is over all.

The only work of Michael Sunlocks which Jorgen Jorgensen did not undo in the swift reprisals which followed on the restoration of his power was the use of the Sulphur Mines as a convict settlement. All he did was to substitute Danish for Icelandic guards, but this change was the beginning and end of the great event that followed. The Icelandic guards knew Red Jason, and if Michael Sunlocks had been sent out to them they would have known him also, and thus the two men must have soon known each other. But the Danish warders knew nothing of Jason, and when they brought out Michael Sunlocks they sent the Icelandic guards home. Thus Jason never heard that Michael Sunlocks was at the Sulphur Mines, and though in the whirl of many vague impressions, the distant hum of a world far off, there floated into his mind the news of the fall of the Republic he could never suspect, and there was no one to tell him, that the man whom he had pursued and never yet seen, the man he hated and sought to slay, was a convict like himself, working daily and hourly within sight and sound of him.

Michael Sunlocks, on his part, knew well that Red Jason had been sent to the Sulphur Mines; but he also knew that he had signed Jason's pardon and ordered his release. More than this, he had learned that Jorgen Jorgensen had liberated all who had been condemned by the Republic, and so he concluded that Jason had become a free man when he himself became a prisoner. But there had been a delay in the despatch of Jason's pardon, and when the Republic had fallen and the Danish officers had taken the place of the Icelanders, the captain of the mines had released the political prisoners only, and Jason, as a felon, had been retained. The other prisoners at the mines, some fifty in all, knew neither Michael Sunlocks nor Red Jason. They were old criminals from remote districts, sentenced to the jail at Reykjavik, during the first rule of Jorgen Jorgensen, and sent out to Krisuvik in the early days of the Republic.

Thus it chanced from the first that though together within a narrow space of ground Jason and Sunlocks were cut off from all knowledge of each other such as might have been gleaned from those about them. And the discipline of the settlement kept them back from that knowledge by keeping them for many months apart.

The two houses used as workshops and sleeping places were at opposite sides of the stockade, one at the north, the other at the south; one overlooking a broad waste of sea, the other at the margin of a dark lake of gloomy shore. Red Jason was assigned to the house near the sea, Michael Sunlocks to the house by the lake. These houses were built of squared logs with earthen floors, and wooden benches for beds. The prisoners entered them at eight o'clock in the evening, and left them at five in the morning, their hours of labor in summer being from five a. m. to eight p. m. They brought two tin cans, one tin containing their food, their second meal of the day, a pound of stock fish, and four ounces of bread; the other tin intended for their refuse of slops and victuals and dirt of other kinds. Each house contained some twenty-five men and boys, and so peopled and used they had quickly become grimy and pestilential, the walls blotched with vermin stains, the floors encrusted with hard trodden filth that was wet and slippery to the feet, and the atmosphere damp and foul to the nostrils from the sickening odors of decayed food.

It had been a regulation from the beginning that the latest comer at each of these houses should serve three months as housekeeper, with the duty of cleansing the horrible place every morning after his housemates had left it for their work. During this time he wore the collar of iron and the bell over his forehead, for it was his period of probation and of special degradation. Thus Red Jason served as housekeeper in the house by the sea, while Michael Sunlocks did the same duty in the house by the lake. Jason went through his work listlessly, slowly, hopelessly, but without a murmur. Michael Sunlocks rebelled against its horrible necessities, for every morning his gorge rose at the exhalations of five-and-twenty unwashed human bodies, and the insupportable odor that came of their filthy habits.

This state of things went on for some two months, during which the two men had never met, and then an accident led to a change in the condition of both.

The sulphur dug up from the banks of the hot springs was packed in sacks and strapped upon ponies, one sack at each side of a pony and one on its back, to be taken to Hafnafiord, the nearest port for shipment to Denmark. Now the sulphur was heavy, the sacks were large, the ponies small, and the road down from the solfataras to the valley was rough with soft clay and great basaltic boulders. And one day as a line of the ponies so burdened came down the breast of the mountain, driven on by a carrier who lashed them at every step with his long whip of leather thongs, one little piebald mare, hardly bigger than a donkey, stumbled into a deep rut and fell. At that the inhuman fellow behind it flogged it again, and showered curses on it at every blow.

"Get up, get up, or I'll skin you alive," he cried, with many a hideous oath beside.

And at every fresh blow the little piebald struggled to rise but she could not, while its terrified eyeballs stood out from the sockets and its wide nostrils quivered.

"Get up, you little lazy devil, get up," cried the brute with the whip, and still his blows fell like raindrops, first on the mare's flanks, then on its upturned belly, then on its head, its mouth, and last of all on its eyes.

But the poor creature's load held it down, and, struggle as it would, it could not rise. The gang of prisoners on the hillside who had just before burdened the ponies and sent them off, heard this lashing and swearing, and stopped their work to look down. But they thought more of the carrier than of the fallen pony, and laughed aloud at his vain efforts to bring it to its feet.

"Send him a hand up, Jonas," shouted one of the fellows.

"Pick him up in your arms, old boy," shouted another, and at every silly sally they all roared together.

The jeering incensed the carrier, and he brought down his whip the fiercer and quicker at every fresh blow, until the whizzing of the lash sang in the air, and the hills echoed with the thuds on the pony's body. Then the little creature made one final, frantic effort, and plunging with its utmost strength it had half risen to its forelegs when one of the sacks slid from its place and got under its hind legs, whereupon the canvas gave way, the sulphur fell out, and the poor little brute slipped afresh and fell again, flat, full length, and with awful force and weight, dashing its head against a stone. At sight of this misadventure the prisoners above laughed once more, and the carrier leaped from his own saddle and kicked the fallen piebald in the mouth.

Now this had occurred within the space of a stone's-throw from the house which Red Jason lived in and cleaned, and hearing the commotion as he worked within he had come out to learn the cause of it. Seeing everything in one quick glance, he pushed along as fast as he could for the leg-fetters that bound him, and came upon the carrier as he was stamping the life out of the pony with kicks on its palpitating sides. At the next moment he had laid the fellow on his back, and then, stepping up to the piebald, he put his arms about it to lift it to its feet. Meantime the prisoners above had stopped their laughing, and were looking on with eyes of wonder at Jason's mighty strength.

"God! Is it possible he is trying to lift a horse to its feet?" cried one.

"What? and three sacks of sulphur as well?" cried another.

"Never," cried a third; and all held their breath.

Jason did not stop to remove the sacks. He wound his great arms first under the little beast's neck, and raised it to its forefeet, and then squaring his broad flanks above his legs that held the ground like the hoofs of an ox, he made one silent, slow, tremendous upward movement, and in an instant the piebald was on its feet, affrighted, trembling, with startled eyeballs and panting nostrils, but secure and safe, and with its load squared and righted on her back.

"Lord bless us!" cried the convicts, "the man has the strength of Samson."

And at that moment one of the warders came hurrying up to the place.

"What's this?" said the warder, looking at the carrier on the ground, who was groaning in some little blood that was flowing from the back of his head.

At that question the carrier only moaned the louder, thinking to excite the more commiseration, and Jason said not a word. But the prisoners on the hillside very eagerly shouted an explanation; whereupon the carrier, a prisoner who had been indulged, straightway lost his privileges as punishment for his ill use of the property of the Government; and Jason, as a man whose great muscles were thrown away on the paltry work of prison-cleaning, was set to delving sulphur on the banks of the hot springs.

Now this change for the better in the condition of Red Jason led to a change for the worse in that of Michael Sunlocks, for when Jason was relieved of his housekeeping and of the iron collar and bell that had been the badge of it, Sunlocks, as a malcontent, was ordered to clean Jason's house as well as his own. But so bad a change led to the great event in the lives of both, the meeting of these men face to face, and the way of it was this:

One day, the winter being then fully come, the mornings dark, and some new fallen snow lying deep over the warm ground of the stockade, Michael Sunlocks had been set to clearing away from the front of the log house on the south before Jason and his housemates had come out of it. His bodily strength had failed him greatly by this time, his face was pale, his large eyes were swollen and bloodshot, and under the heavy labor of that day his tall, slight figure stooped. But a warder stood over him leaning on a musket and urging him on with words that were harder to him than his hard work. His bell rang as he stooped, and rang again as he rose, and at every thrust of the spade it rang, so that when Jason and his gang came out of the sickening house, he heard it. And hearing the bell, he remembered that he himself had worn it, and, wondering who had succeeded him in the vile office whereof he had been relieved, he turned to look upon the man who was clearing the snow.

There are moments when the sense of our destiny is strong upon us, and this was such a moment to Red Jason. He saw Michael Sunlocks for the first time, but without knowing him, and yet at that sight every pulse beat and every nerve quivered. A great sorrow and a great pity took hold of him. The face he looked upon moved him, the voice he heard thrilled him, and by an impulse that he could not resist he stopped and turned to the warder leaning on the musket and said:

"Let me do this man's work. It would be nothing to me. He is ill. Send him up to the hospital."

"March!" shouted his own warders, and they hustled him along, and at the next minute he was gone. Then the bell stopped for an instant, for Michael Sunlocks had raised his head to look upon the man who had spoken. He did not see Jason's face, but his own face softened at the words he had heard and his bloodshot eyes grew dim.

"Go on!" cried the warder with the musket, and the bell began again.

All that day the face of Michael Sunlocks haunted the memory of Red Jason.

"Who was that man?" he asked of the prisoner who worked by his side.

"How should I know?" the other fellow answered sulkily.

In a space of rest Jason leaned on his shovel, wiped his brow, and said to his warder, "What was that man's name?"

"A 25," the warder answered moodily.

"I asked for his name," said Jason.

"What's that to you?" replied the warder.

A week went by, and the face of Sunlocks still haunted Jason's memory. It was with him early and late, the last thing that stood up before his inward eye when he lay down to sleep, the first thing that came to him when he awoke; sometimes it moved him to strange laughter when the sun was shining, and sometimes it touched him to tears when he thought of it in the night. Why was this? He did not know, he could not think, he did not try to find out. But there it was, a living face burnt into his memory—a face so strangely new to him, yet so strangely familiar, so unlike to anything he had ever yet seen, and yet so like to everything that was near and dear to himself, that he could have fancied there had never been a time when he had not had it by his side. When he put the matter to himself so he laughed and thought "How foolish." But no self-mockery banished the mystery of the power upon him of the man's face that he saw for a moment one morning in the snow.

He threw off his former listlessness and began to look keenly about him. But one week, two weeks, three weeks passed, and he could nowhere see the same face again. He asked questions but learned nothing. His fellow-prisoners began to jeer at him. Upon their souls, the big red fellow had tumbled into love with the young chap with the long flaxen hair, and maybe he thought it was a woman in disguise.

Jason knocked their chattering heads together and so stopped their ribald banter, but his warders began to watch him with suspicion, and he fell back on silence.

A month passed, and then the chain that was slowly drawing the two men together suddenly tightened. One morning the order came down from the office of the Captain that the prisoners' straw beds were to be taken out into the stockyard and burnt. The beds were not old, but dirty and damp and full of foul odors. The officers of the settlement said this was due to the filthy habits of the prisoners. The prisoners on their part said it came of the pestilential hovels they were compelled to live in, where the ground was a bog, the walls and roof were a rotten coffin, and the air was heavy and lifeless. Since the change of warders, there had been a gradual decline in the humanity with which they had been treated, and to burn up their old beds without giving them new ones was to deprive them of the last comfort that separated the condition of human beings from that of beasts of the field.

But the Captain of the Mines was in no humor to bandy parts with his prisoners, and in ordering that the beds should be burnt to prevent an outbreak of disease, he appointed that the prisoner B 25, should be told off to do the work. Now B 25 was the prison name of Red Jason, and he was selected by reason of his great bodily strength, not so much because the beds required it, as from fear of the rebellion of the poor souls who were to lose them.

So at the point of a musket Red Jason was driven on to his bad work, and sullenly he went through it, muttering deep oaths from between his grinding teeth, until he came to the log hut where Michael Sunlocks slept, and there he saw again the face that had haunted his memory.

"This bed is dry and sound," said Michael Sunlocks, "and you shall not take it."

"Away with it," shouted the warder to Jason, who had seemed to hesitate.

"It is good and wholesome, let him keep it," said Jason.

"Go on with your work," cried the warder, and the lock of his musket clicked.

"Civilized men give straw to their dogs to lie on," said Michael Sunlocks.

"It depends what dogs they are," sneered the warder.

"If you take our beds, this place will be worse than an empty kennel," said Michael Sunlocks.

"Better that than the mange," said the warder. "Get along, I tell you," he cried again, handling his musket and turning to Jason.

Then, with a glance of loathing, Jason picked up the bed in his fingers, that itched to pick up the warder by the throat, and swept out of the place.

"Slave!" cried Michael Sunlocks after him. "Pitiful, miserable, little-hearted slave!"

Jason heard the hot words that pursued him, and his face grew as red as his hair, and his head dropped into his breast. He finished his task in less than half an hour more, working like a demented man at piling up the dirty mattresses, into a vast heap, and setting light to the damp straw. And while the huge bonfire burned, and he poked long poles into it to give it air to blaze by, he made excuse of the great heat to strip of the long rough overcoat that had been given him to wear through the hard months of the winter. By this time the warder had fallen back from the scorching flames, and Jason, watching his chance, stole away under cover of deep whorls of smoke, and got back into the log cabin unobserved.

He found the place empty; the man known to him as A 25 was not anywhere to be seen. But finding his sleeping bunk—a bare slab resembling a butcher's board—he stretched his coat over it where the bed had been, and then fled away like a guilty thing.

When the great fire had burned low the warder returned, and said, "Quick there; put on your coat and let's be off."

At that Jason pretended to look about him in dismay.

"It's gone," he said, in a tone of astonishment.

"Gone? What? Have you burnt it up with the beds?" cried the warder.

"Maybe so," said Jason, meekly.

"Fool," cried the warder; "but it's your loss. Now you'll have to go in your sheepskin jacket, snow or shine."

With a cold smile about the corners of his mouth, Jason bent his head and went on ahead of his warder.

If the Captain of the Mines had been left to himself he might have been a just and even a merciful man, but he was badgered by inhuman orders from Jorgen Jorgensen at Reykjavik, and one by one the common privileges of his prisoners were withdrawn. As a result of his treatment, the prisoners besieged him with petitions as often as he crossed their path. The loudest to complain and the most rebellious against petty tyranny was Michael Sunlocks; the humblest, the meekest, the most silent under cruel persecution was Red Jason. The one seemed aflame with indignation; the other appeared destitute of all manly spirit.

"That man might be dangerous to the Government yet," thought the Captain, after one of his stormy scenes with Michael Sunlocks. "That man's

234

heart is dead within him," he thought again, as he watched Red Jason working as he always worked, slowly, listlessly, and as if tired out and longing for the night.

The Captain's humanity at length prevailed over his Governor's rigor, and he developed a form of penal servitude among the prisoners which he called the Free Command. This was a plan whereby the men whose behavior had been good were allowed the partial liberty of living outside the stockade in huts which they built for themselves. Ten hours a day they wrought at the mines, the rest of the day and night was under their own control; and in return for their labor they were supplied with rations from the settlement.

Now Red Jason, as a docile prisoner, was almost the first to get promotion to the Free Command. He did not ask for it, he did not wish for it, and when it came he looked askance at it.

"Send somebody else," he said to his warders, but they laughed and turned him adrift.

He began to build his house of the lava stones on the mountain side, not far from the hospital, and near to a house being built by an elderly man much disfigured about the cheeks, who had been a priest, imprisoned long ago by Jorgen Jorgensen out of spite and yet baser motives. And as he worked at raising the walls of his hut, he remembered with a pang the mill he built in Port-y-Vullin, and what a whirlwind of outraged passion brought every stone of it to the ground again. With this occupation, and occasional gossip with his neighbor, he passed the evenings of his Free Command. And looking towards the hospital as often as he saw the little groups of men go up to it that told of another prisoner injured in the perilous labor of the sulphur mines, he sometimes saw a woman come out at the door to receive them.

"Who is she?" he asked of the priest.

"The foreign nurse," said the priest. "And a right good woman, too, as I have reason to say, for she nursed me back to life after that spurt of hot water had scalded these holes into my face."

That made Jason think of other scenes, and of tender passages in his broken life that were gone from him forever. He had no wish to recall them; their pleasure was too painful, their sweets too bitter; they were lost, and God grant that they could be forgotten. Yet every night as he worked at his walls he looked longingly across the shoulder of the hill in the direction of the hospital, half fancying he knew the sweet grace of the figure he sometimes saw there, and pretending with himself that he remembered the light rhythm of its movement. After a while he missed what he looked for, and then he asked his neighbor if the nurse were ill that he had not seen her lately.

"Ill? Well, yes," said the old priest. "She has been turned away from the hospital."

"What!" cried Jason; "you thought her a good nurse."

"She was too good, my lad," said the priest, "and a blackguard warder who had tried to corrupt her, and could not, announced that somebody else had done so."

"It's a lie," cried Jason.

"It was plain enough," said the priest, "that she was about to give birth to a child, and as she would make no explanation she was turned adrift."

"Where is she now?" asked Jason.

"Lying in at the farmhouse on the edge of the snow yonder," said the priest. "I saw her last night. She trusted me with her story, and it was straight and simple. Her husband had been sent out to the mines by the old scoundrel at Reykjavik. She had followed him, only to be near him and breathe the air he breathed. Perhaps with some wild hope of helping his escape she had hidden her true name and character and taken the place of a menial, being a lady born."

"Then her husband is still at the mines?" said Jason.

"Yes," said the priest.

"Does he know of her disgrace?"

"No."

"What's his name?"

"The poor soul would give me no name, but she knew her husband's number. It was A 25."

"I know him," said Jason.

Next day, his hut being built and roofed after some fashion, Jason went down to the office of the Captain of the Mines and said, "I don't like the Free Command, sir. May I give it up in favor of another man?"

"And what man, pray?" asked the Captain.

"A 25," said Jason.

"No," said the Captain.

"I've built my house, sir," said Jason, "and if you won't give it to A 25, let the poor woman from the hospital live in it, and take me back among the men."

"That won't do, my lad. Go along to your work," said the Captain.

And when Jason was gone the Captain thought within himself, "What does this mean? Is the lad planning the man's escape? And who is this English woman that she should be the next thought in his head?"

So the only result of Jason's appeal was that Michael Sunlocks was watched the closer, worked the harder, persecuted the more by petty tyrannies, and that an order was sent up to the farmhouse where Greeba lay in the

236

dear dishonor of her early motherhood, requiring her to leave the neighborhood of Krisuvik as speedily as her condition allowed.

This was when the long dark days of winter were beginning to fall back before the sweet light of spring. And when the snow died off the mountains, and the cold garment of the jokulls was sucked full of holes like the honeycomb, and the world that had been white grew black, and the flowers began to show in the corries, and the sweet summer was coming, coming, coming, then Jason went down to the Captain of the Mines again.

"I've come, sir," he said, "to ask you to lock me up."

"Why?" said the Captain, "what have you been doing?"

"Nothing," said Jason, "but if you don't prevent me, I'll run away. This Free Command was bad enough to fear when the snow cut us off from all the world. But now that it is gone and the world is free, and the cuckoo is calling, he seems to be calling me, and I must go after him."

"Go," said the Captain, "and after you've tramped the deserts and swam the rivers, and slept on the ground, and starved on roots, we'll fetch you back, for you can never escape us, and lash you as we have lashed the others who have done likewise."

"If I go," said Jason, defiantly, "you shall never fetch me back, and if you catch me you shall never punish me."

"What? Do you threaten me?" cried the Captain.

Something in the prisoner's face terrified him, though he would have scorned to acknowledge his fear, and he straightway directed that Jason should be degraded, for insolence and insubordination, from the Free Command to the gangs.

Now this was exactly what Jason wanted, for his heart had grown sick with longing for another sight of that face which stood up before his inward eye in the darkness of the night. But remembering Jason's appeal on behalf of Michael Sunlocks, and his old suspicion regarding both, the Captain ordered that the two men should be kept apart.

So with Jason in the house by the sea, and Sunlocks in the house by the lake, the weeks went by; and the summer that was coming came, and like a bird of passage the darkness of night fled quite away, and the sun shone that shines at midnight.

And nothing did Jason see of the face that followed him in visions, and nothing did he hear of the man known to him as A 25, except reports of brutal treatment and fierce rebellion. But on a day—a month after he had returned to the stockade—he was going in his tired and listless way between warders from one solfatara at the foot of the hill to another on the breast of it, when he came upon a horror that made his blood run cold.

It was a man nailed by his right hand to a great socket of iron in a log of driftwood, with food and drink within sight but out of reach of him, and a huge knife lying close by his side. The man was A 25.

Jason saw everything and the meaning of everything in an instant, that to get at the food for which he starved that man must cut off his own right hand. And there, like a devil, at his left lay the weapon that was to tempt him.

Nothing so inhuman, so barbarous, so fiendish, so hellish, had Jason yet seen, and with a cry like the growl of an untamed beast, he broke from his warders, took the nail in his fingers like a vice, tore it up out of the bleeding hand, and set Michael Sunlocks free.

At the next instant his wrath was gone, and he had fallen back to his listless mood. Then the warders hurried up, laid hold of both men, and hustled them away with a brave show of strength and courage to the office of the Captain.

Jorgen Jorgensen himself was there, and it was he who had ordered the ruthless punishment. The warders told their tale, and he listened to them with a grin on his cruel face.

"Strap them up together," he cried, "leg to leg and arm to arm."

And when this was done he said, bitterly—

"So you two men are fond of one another's company! Well, you shall have enough of it and to spare. Day after day, week after week, month after month, like as you are now, you shall live together, until you abhor and detest and loathe the sight of each other. Now go!"

III: The Valley of the Shadow of Death

Red Jason and Michael Sunlocks, now lashed together, were driven back to their work like beasts of the field. They knew well what their punishment meant to them—that in every hour of life henceforward, in every act, through every thought, each man should drag a human carcase by his side. The barbarity of their doom was hideous; but strangely different were the ways they accepted it. Michael Sunlocks was aflame with indignation; Jason was crushed with shame. The upturned face of Sunlocks was pale, his flaxen hair was dishevelled, his bloodshot eyes were afire. But Jason's eyes, full of confusion, were bent on the ground, his tanned face trembled visibly, and his red hair, grown long as of old, fell over his drooping shoulders like a mantle of blood.

And as they trudged along, side by side, in the first hours of their unnatural partnership, Sunlocks struggled hard to keep his eyes from the man with whom he was condemned to live and die, lest the gorge of his very soul should rise at the sight of him. So he never once looked at Jason through many hours of that day. And Jason, on his part, laboring with the thought that it was he who by his rash act had brought both of them to this sore pass, never once lifted his eyes to the face of Sunlocks.

Yet each man knew the other's thought before ever a word had passed between them. Jason felt that Sunlocks already abhorred him, and Sunlocks knew that Jason was ashamed. This brought them after a time into sympathy of some sort, and Jason tried to speak and Sunlocks to listen.

"I did not mean to bring you to this," said Jason, humbly. And Sunlocks, with head aside, answered as well as he could for the disgust that choked him, "You did it for the best."

"But you will hate me for it," said Jason.

And once again, with what composure he could command, Sunlocks answered, "How could I hate you for saving me from such brutal treatment."

"Then you don't regret it?" said Jason, pleadingly.

"It is for you, not me, to regret it," said Sunlocks.

"Me?" said Jason.

Through all the shameful hours the sense of his own loss had never yet come to him. From first to last he had thought only of Sunlocks.

"My liberty was gone already," said Sunlocks. "But you were free—free as anyone can be in this hell on earth. Now you are bound—you are here like this—and I am the cause of it."

Then Jason's rugged face was suddenly lit up with a surprising joy. "That's nothing," he said.

"Nothing?" said Sunlocks.

"I mean that I care nothing, if you don't," said Jason.

It was the turn of Sunlocks to feel surprise. He half turned towards Jason. "Then you don't regret it?" he asked.

"No," said Jason firmly. "And you?"

Sunlocks felt that tears, not disgust, were choking him now.

"No," he answered, shamefacedly, turning his head away.

"March!" shouted the warders, who had been drinking their smuggled sneps while their prisoners had been talking.

That day, Jorgen Jorgensen went back to Reykjavik, for the time of Althing was near, and he had to prepare for his fourteen days at Thingvellir. And the Governor being gone, the Captain of the Mines made bold so far to relax the inhumanity of his sentence as to order that the two men who were bound together during the hours of work should be separated for the hours of sleep. But never forgetting his own suspicion that Red Jason was an ally of Michael Sunlocks, planning his escape, he ordered also that no speech should be allowed to pass between them. To prevent all communion of this kind he directed that the men should work and sleep apart from the other prisoners, and that their two warders should attend them night and day.

But though the rigor of discipline kept them back from free intercourse, no watchfulness could check the stolen words of comfort that helped the weary men to bear their degrading lot.

That night, the first of their life together, Michael Sunlocks looked into Jason's face and said, "I have seen you before somewhere. Where was it?"

But Jason remembered the hot words that had pursued him on the day of the burning of the beds, and so he made no answer.

After awhile, Michael Sunlocks looked closely into Jason's face again, and said, "What is your name?"

"Don't ask it," said Jason.

"Why not," said Sunlocks.

"You might remember it."

"Even so, what then?"

"Then you might also remember what I did, or tried to do, and you would hate me for it," said Jason.

"Was your crime so inhuman?" said Sunlocks.

"It would seem so," said Jason.

"Who sent you here?"

"The Republic."

"You won't tell me your name?"

"I've got none, so to speak, having had no father to give me one. I'm alone in the world."

Michael Sunlocks did not sleep much that night, for the wound in his hand was very painful, and next morning, while Jason dressed it, he looked into his face once more and said, "You say you are alone in the world."

"Yes," said Jason.

"What of your mother?"

"She's dead, poor soul."

"Have you no sister?"

"No."

"Nor brother?"

"No—that's to say—no, no."

"No one belonging to you?"

"No."

"Are you quite alone?"

"Ay, quite," said Jason. "No one to think twice what becomes of me. Nobody to trouble whether I am here or in a better place. Nobody to care whether I live or die."

He tried to laugh as he said this, but in spite of his brave show of unconcern his deep voice broke and his strong face quivered.

"But what's your own name?" he said abruptly.

"Call me—brother," said Michael Sunlocks.

"To your work," cried the warders, and they were hustled out.

Their work for the day was delving sulphur from the banks of the solfataras and loading it on the backs of the ponies. And while their warders dozed in the heat of the noonday sun, they wiped their brows and rested.

At that moment Jason's eyes turned towards the hospital on the opposite side of the hill, and he remembered what he had heard of the good woman who had been nurse there. This much at least he knew of her, that she was the wife of his yoke-fellow, and he was about to speak of her trouble and dishonor when Michael Sunlocks said,

"After all, you are luckiest to be alone in the world. To have ties of affection is only to be the more unhappy."

"That's true," said Jason.

"Say you love somebody, and all your heart is full of her? You lose her, and then where are you?"

"But that's not your own case," said Jason. "Your wife is alive, is she not?"

"Yes."

"Then you have not lost her?"

"There is a worse loss than that of death," said Sunlocks.

Jason glanced quickly into his face, and said tenderly, "I know—I understand. There was another man?"

"Yes."

"And he robbed you of her love?" said Jason, eagerly.

"Yes."

"And you killed him?" cried Jason, with panting breath.

"No. But God keep that man out of my hands."

"Where is he now?"

"Heaven knows. He was here, but he is gone; for when the Republic fell I was imprisoned, and two days before that he was liberated."

"Silence!" shouted the warders, awakening suddenly and hearing voices.

Jason's eyes had begun to fill, and down his rugged cheeks the big drops were rolling one by one. After that he checked the impulse to speak of the nurse. The wife of his yoke-fellow must be an evil woman. The prisoner-priest must have been taken in by her. For once the warders must have been right.

And late that night, while Jason was dressing the wounded hand of Michael Sunlocks with wool torn from his own sheepskin jerkin, he said, with his eyes down,

"I scarce thought there was anything in common between us two. You're a gentleman, and I'm only a rough fellow. You have been brought up tenderly, and I have been kicked about the world since I was a lad in my poor mother's home, God rest her! But my life has been like yours in one thing."

"What's that?" said Michael Sunlocks.

"That another man has wrecked it," said Jason. "I never had but one glint of sunshine in my life, and that man wiped it out forever. It was a woman, and she was all the world to me. But she was proud and I was poor. And he was rich, and he came between us. He had everything, and the world was at his feet. I had nothing but that woman's love, and he took it from me. It was too cruel, and I could not bear it—God knows I could not."

"Wait," cried Michael Sunlocks. "Is that why you are here! Did you——you did not——no——"

"No, I know what you mean; but I did not kill him. No, no, I have never seen him. I could never meet with him, try how I would."

"Where is he now?"

"With her—in happiness and freedom and content, while I am here in misery and bondage and these ropes. But there will be a reckoning between us yet. I know there will. I swear there will. As sure as there is a God in Heaven, that man and I will one day stand together face to face."

Then Michael Sunlocks took both Jason's hands.

"My brother," he cried fervently. "Brother now more than ever; brother in suffering, brother in weakness, brother in strength."

"Silence there!" shouted the warders, and the two men were separated for the night.

The wound in the hand of Michael Sunlocks grew yet more painful, and he slept even less than before. Next day the power of life was low in him, and seeing this, Jason said, when the warders stepped up to lash them together, "He is ill, and not fit to go out. Let me work alone to-day. I'll do enough for both of us."

But no heed was paid to Jason's warning, and Michael Sunlocks was driven out by his side. All that day, the third of their life together, they worked with difficulty, for the wound in the hand of Sunlocks was not only a trouble to himself but an impediment to Jason also. Yet Jason gave no hint of that, but kept the good spade going constantly, with a smile on his face through the sweat that stood on it, and little stolen words of comfort and cheer. And when the heat was strongest, and Sunlocks would have stumbled and fallen, Jason contrived a means to use both their spades together, only requiring that Sunlocks should stoop when he stooped, that the warders might think he was still working. But their artifice was discovered, and all that came of it was that they were watched the closer and driven the harder during the hours that remained of that day.

Next day, the fourth of their direful punishment, Sunlocks rose weak and trembling, and scarce able to stand erect. And with what spirit he could summon up he called upon the warders to look upon him and see how feeble he was, and say if it was fair to his yoke-fellow that they should compel him to do the work of two men and drag a human body after him. But the warders only laughed at his protest, and once again he was driven out by Jason's side.

Long and heavy were the hours that followed, but Sunlocks, being once started on his way, bore up under it very bravely, murmuring as little as he might, out of thought for Jason. And Jason helped along his stumbling footsteps as well as he could for the arm that was bound to him. And seeing how well they worked by this double power of human kindness, the warders laughed again, and made a mock at Sunlocks for his former cry of weakness. And so, amid tender words between themselves, and jeers cast in upon them by the warders, they made shift to cheat time of another weary day.

The fifth day went by like the fourth, with heavy toil and pain to make it hard, and cruel taunts to make it bitter. And many a time, as they delved the yellow sulphur bank, a dark chill crossed the hearts of both, and they thought in their misery how cheerfully they would dig for death itself, if only it lay in the hot clay beneath them.

That night when they had returned to the hut wherein they slept, or tried to sleep, they found that some well-meaning stranger had been there in their absence and nailed up on the grimy walls above their beds, a card bearing the text, "Come unto Me all ye that labor and are heavy laden, and I will give you rest." And so ghastly seemed the irony of those words in that place that Jason muttered an oath between his teeth as he read them, and Sunlocks threw himself down, being unbound for the night, with a peal of noisy laughter, and a soul full of strange bitterness.

The next day after that, the sixth of their life together, rose darker than any day that had gone before it, for the wounded hand of Michael Sunlocks was then purple and black, and swollen to the size of two hands, and his bodily strength was so low that, try as bravely as he might to stand erect, whenever he struggled to his feet he fell to the ground again. Thinking nothing of this, the warders were for strapping him up to Jason as before, but while they were in the act of doing so he fainted in their hands. Then Jason swept them from him, and vowed that the first man that touched Sunlocks again should lie dead at his feet.

"Send for the Captain," he cried, "and if the man has any bowels of compassion let him come and see what you have done."

The warders took Jason at his word, and sent a message to the office saying that one of their prisoners was mutinous, and the other pretending to be ill. After a time the Captain despatched two other warders to the help of the first two and these words along with them for his answer: "If one rebels, punish both."

Nothing loth for such exercise, the four warders set themselves to decide what the punishment should be, and while they laid their heads together, Jason was bending over Sunlocks, who was now recovered to consciousness, asking his pardon in advance for the cruel penalty that his rash act was to bring on both of them.

"Forgive me," he said. "I couldn't help it. I didn't know what I was doing."

"There is nothing to forgive, brother," whispered Michael Sunlocks.

And thus with stammering tongues they comforted one another, and with hands clasped together they waited for the punishment that had to come.

At length the warders concluded that for refusing to work, for obstinate disobedience, and for threatening, nothing would serve but that their prisoners should straightway do the most perilous work to be found that day at the sulphur mines.

Now this was the beginning of the end for Red Jason and Michael Sunlocks, and if the evil chance had not befallen them, God alone can say how long they might have lived together at Krisuvik, or how soon or how late they would have become known to one another by their true names and characters. But heaven itself had its purposes, even in the barbarity of base-hearted men, as a means towards the great end that was near at hand. And this was the way of its coming.

A strange change that no one could rightly understand had lately come upon the natural condition of the sulphur mines. The steam that rose from the solfataras had grown less and less week by week and day by day, until in some places it had altogether subsided. This was a grave sign, for in the steam lay the essence of the sulphur, and if it ceased to rise from the pits the sulphur would cease to grow.

Other changes came with this, such as that deep subterranean noises arose from parts of the plain where no fissures had yet been seen, and that footsteps on the earth around these places produced a hollow sound.

From these signs, taken together, the Captain had concluded that the life of the mines, the great infernal fire that raged beneath the surface, was changing ground, leaving the valley, where it had lived for ages, for the mountain heights, where the low grumblings were now heard to come from beneath the earth's crust of lava and basaltic rock.

So, taking counsel of his people, he decided to bore the ground in these new places in the hope of lighting on living solfataras that would stand to him against the loss of the dead ones. And it chanced that he was in the midst of many busy preparations for this work when the report of the warders reached him, and the boring was still uppermost in his mind when he sent back his answer as he came upon the flogging and stopped it.

Thus it happened that the first thought that came to the warders was to send their prisoners to one of the spots that had been marked on the hillside for the test of bore and spade.

So, in less than half-an-hour more, Jason and Sunlocks, lashed together, arm to arm and leg to leg, were being driven up the mountain to the place assigned to them. They found it a hideous and awesome spot. Within a circle of two yards across, the ground was white and yellow and scaly, like a scab on evil flesh. It was hot, so that the hand could not rest upon it, and hollow, so that the foot made it shake, and from unseen depths beneath it a dull thud came up at intervals like nothing else but the knocking of a man buried alive at the sealed door of his tomb.

Beneath this spot the heart of the solfatara was expected to lie, and Jason and Sunlocks were commanded to open it. Obeying gloomily, they took the bore first and pierced the scaly surface, and instantly a sizzling and bubbling sound came up from below. Then they followed with the spades, but scarcely had they lifted the top crust when twenty great fissures seemed to open under their feet, and they could see lurid flames rushing in wild confusion, like rivers of fire in the bowels of the earth.

It was a sight at which the stoutest heart might have quailed, and Jason leapt back to the bank and dragged Sunlocks after him.

"This is not safe," he said.

"In with you," shouted the warders from their own safe footing of four yards away. With a growl from between his clenched teeth, Jason stepped back into the hole, and Sunlocks followed him. But hardly had they got down to the fearsome spot again, when a layer of clay fell in from it, leaving a deep wide gully, and then scarcely a yard of secure footing remained.

"Let us stop while we are safe," Jason cried.

"Dig away," shouted the warders.

"If we do, we shall be digging our own graves," said Jason.

"Begin," shouted the warders.

"Listen to me," said Jason. "If we are to open this pit of fire and brimstone, at least let us be free of these ropes. That's but fair, that each man may have a chance of his life."

"Go on," shouted the warders.

"If we go on like this we shall be burnt and boiled alive," said Jason.

"Get along," shouted the warders with one voice, and then an awful light flashed in Jason's eyes, for he saw that out of revenge for their paltry fines they had resolved to drive two living men to their death.

"Now, listen again," said Jason, "and mark my words. We will do as you command us, and work in this pit of hell. I will not die in it—that I know. But this man beside me is weak and ill, heaven curse your inhumanity; and if anything happens to him, and I am alive to see it, as sure as there is strength left in my arms, and blood in my body, I will tear you limb from limb."

So saying, he plunged his spade into the ground beneath him, with an oath to drive it, and at the next instant there was a flash of blue flame, an avalanche of smoke, a hurricane of unearthly noises, a cry like that of a dying man, and then an awful silence.

When the air had cleared, Jason stood uninjured, but Michael Sunlocks hung by his side inert and quiet, and blinded by a jet of steam.

What happened to Jason thereafter no tongue of man could tell. All the fire of his spirit, and all the strength of all his days seemed to flow back upon him in that great moment. He parted the ropes that bound him as if they had been green withes that he snapped asunder. He took Sunlocks in his arms and lifted him up to his shoulder, and hung him across it, as if he had been a child that he placed there. He stepped out of the deadly pit, and strode along over the lava mountain as if he were the sole creature of the everlasting hills. His glance was terrific, his voice was the voice of a wounded beast. The warders dropped their muskets and fled before him like affrighted sheep.

IV: Through the Chasm of All Men

It was still early morning; a soft gray mist lay over the moorlands, but the sun that had never set in that northern land was rising through clouds of pink and white over the bald crown of a mountain to the northeast. And towards the rising sun Jason made his way, striding on with the red glow on his own tanned and blackened face, and its ghastly mockery of the hues of life on the pallid cheeks and whitened lips of Sunlocks. From his right ankle and right wrist hung the rings of his broken fetters, and from the left ankle and left wrist of Sunlocks trailed the ropes that had bound them both. Never a moment did he pause to breathe or think or question himself. On and on he went, over lava blocks and lava dust, basaltic rock and heavy clay, and hot blue earth and scorched and withered moss. And still Sunlocks lay over his right side and shoulder, motionless and unconscious, hardly breathing, but alive, with his waist encircled by Jason's great right arm, and his waist-belt grasped tight as with the grip of a talon by Jason's hard right hand.

Before long, Sunlocks recovered some partial consciousness and cried in a faint voice for water. Jason glanced around on the arid plain as if his eyes would pierce the ground for a spring, but no water could he see on any side of him, and so without a word of answer he strode along.

"Water, water," cried Sunlocks again, and just then Jason caught the side-long glint of a river that ran like a pearl chain down the black breast of a mountain.

"Water," cried Sunlocks again and yet again, in a voice of pain and deep pleading, not rightly knowing yet where he was or what bad chance had befallen him.

"Yes, yes, one moment more, only a moment, there—there—there!" whispered Jason.

And muttering such words of comfort and cheer, he quickened his pace towards the river. But when he got near to it he stopped short with a cry of dismay. The river bubbled and smoked.

"Hot! It is hot," cried Jason. "And the land is accursed."

At that word, Sunlocks uttered a low groan, and his head, which had been partly lifted, fell heavily backwards, and his hair hung over Jason's shoulder. He was again unconscious.

Then more than ever like a wild beast ranging the hills with its prey, Jason strode along. And presently he saw a lake of blue water far away. He knew it for cold water, blessed, ice-cold water, water to bathe the hot forehead with, water to drink. With a cry of joy, which there was no human ear to hear, he turned and made towards it; but just as he did so, softening as he went, and muttering from his own parched throat words of hope and comfort to the unconscious man he carried, a gunshot echoed through the mountains above his head.

He knew what the shot was; it was the signal of his escape. And looking down to the valley, he saw that the guards of the settlement were gathering on their ponies in the very line of the plain that he must traverse to reach the water for which Sunlocks thirsted.

Then "Water, water," came again in the same faint voice as before, and whether with his actual ear he heard that cry, or in the torment of his distraught sense it only rang out in his empty heart, no man shall say. But all the same he answered it from his choking throat, "Patience, patience."

And then, with another look downward, the look of a human stag, at the cool water which he might not reach and live, he turned himself back to the mountains.

What happened to him then, and for many weary hours thereafter, it would weary the spirit to tell: what plains he crossed, what hills he climbed, and in what desolate wilderness he walked alone, with no one for company save the unconscious man across his shoulder, and no eye to look upon him save the eye of God.

And first he crossed a wide sea of lava dust, black as the ravens that flew in the air above it, and bounded by hills as dark as the earth that were themselves vast sand drifts blown up into strange and terrible shapes by mighty tempests. Then he came upon a plain strewn over with cinders, having a grim crag frowning upon it, like the bank of a smelting-house, with its screes of refuse rolling down. By this time the sun had risen high and grown hot, and the black ground under his feet began to send up the reflection of the sun's rays into his face to scorch it.

And still the cry of "water, water," rang in his ears, and his eyes ranged the desolate land to find it, but never a sign of it could he see, and his strong heart sank. Once, when he had mounted with great toil to the top of a hill, where all behind him had been black and burnt and blistered, he saw a wide valley stretching in front of him that was as green as the grass of spring. And he thought that where there was grass there would surely be water, streams of water, rivers of water, pools of water, sunny stretches of sweet water lying clear and quiet over amber pebbles and between soft brown banks of turf.

So at this sight his heart was lifted up, and bounding down the hillside, over the lava blocks, as fast as he could go for his burden, he began to sing from his cracked throat in his hoarse and quavery voice. But when he reached the valley his song stopped, and his heart sank afresh, for it was not grass, but moss that grew there, and it lay only on big blocks of lava, with never a drop of moisture or a handful of earth between them.

He was crushed, but he was strong of heart and would not despair. So he pushed on over this green plain, through a hundred thousand mossy mounds that looked like the graves of a world of dead men.

But when he came out of it his case seemed yet more forlorn, for leaving the soft valley behind he had come upon a lava stream, a sea of stones, not dust or cinders, but a bleached cake of lava rock, with never a soft place for the foot, and never a green spot for the eye. Not a leaf to rustle in the breeze, not a blade of grass to whisper to it, not a bird's sweet voice, or the song of running water. Nothing lived there but dead silence on earth and in air. Nothing but that, or in other hours the roar of wind, the rattle of rain, and the crash of thunder.

All this time Jason had walked on under the sweltering sun, never resting, never pausing, buoyed up with the hope of water—water for the fainting man that he might not die. But in the desolation of that moment he dropped Sunlocks from his shoulder, and threw himself down beside him.

And sitting there, with the head of his unconscious comrade upon his knees, he put it himself to say what had been the good of all that he had done, and if it would not have been better for both of them if he had submitted to base tyranny and remained at the Mines. Had he not brought this man out to his death? What else was before him in this waste wilderness, where there was no drop of water to cool his hot forehead or moisten his parched tongue? And thinking that his yoke-fellow might die, and die at his hands, and that he would then be alone, with the only man's face gone from him that had ever brightened life for him, his heart began to waver and to say, "Rise up, Jason, rise up and go back."

But just then he was conscious of the click-clack of horses' hoofs on the echoing face of the stony sea about him, and he shaded his eyes and looked around, and saw in the distance a line of men on ponies coming on in his direction. And though he thought of the guards that had been signalled to pursue him, he made no effort to escape. He did not stir or try to hide himself, but sat as before with the head of his comrade on his knees.

The men on the ponies came up and passed him closely by without seeing him. But he saw them clearly and heard their talk. They were not the guard from the settlement, but Thing-men bound for Thingvellir and the meeting of Althing there. And while they were going on before him in their laughter and high spirits, Jason could scarce resist the impulse to cry out on them to stop and take him along with them as their prisoner, for that he was an outlaw who had broken his outlawry, and carried away with him this fainting man at his knees.

But before the words would form themselves, and while his blistering lips were shaping to speak them, a great thought came to him, and struck him back to silence.

Why had he torn away from the Sulphur Mines? Only from a gloomy love of life, life for his comrade, and life for himself. And what life was there in this trackless waste, this mouldering dumb wilderness? None, none. Nothing but death lay here; death in these gaunt solitudes; death in these dry deserts; death amid these ghastly, haggard wrecks of inhuman things. What chance could there be of escape from Iceland? None, none, none.

But there was one hope yet. Who were these men that had passed him? They were Thing-men; they were the lawmakers. Where were they going?

They were going to the Mount of Laws. Why were they going there? To hold their meeting of Althing. What was Althing? The highest power of the State; the supreme Court of legislature and law.

What did all this mean? It meant that Jason as an Icelander knew the laws of his country, and that one great law above all other laws he remembered at that instant. It concerned outlaws. And what were they but outlaws, both of them? It ordered that the condemned could appeal at Althing against the injustice of his sentence. If the ranks of the judges opened for his escape, then he was saved.

Jason leaped to his feet at the thought of it. That was what he would do for his comrade and for himself. He would push on to Thingvellir. It was five and thirty heavy miles away; but no matter for that. The angel of hope would walk with him. He would reach the Mount of Laws, carrying his comrade all the way. And when he got there, he would plead the cause of both of them. Then the judges would rise, and part, and make way for them, and they would be free men thereafter.

Life, life, life! There was life left for both of them, and very sweet it seemed after the shadow of death that had so nearly encompassed them. Only to live! Only to live! They were young yet and loved one another as brothers.

And while thinking so, in the whirl of his senses as he strode to and fro over the lava blocks, Jason heard what his ear had hitherto been too heavy to catch, the thin music of falling water near at hand. And, looking up, he saw a tiny rivulet like a lock of silken hair dropping over a round face of rock, and thanking God for it, he ran to it, and filled both hands with it, and brought it to Sunlocks and bathed his forehead with it, and his poor blinded eyes, and moistened his withered lips, whispering meantime words of hope and simple tender nothings, such as any woman might croon over her sick boy.

"Come, boy, come then, come, boy, come," he whispered, and clapped his moist hands together over the placid face to call it back to itself.

And while he did so, sure enough Sunlocks moved, his lips parted, his cheeks quivered, and he sighed. And seeing these signs of consciousness, Jason began to cry, for the great rude fellow who had not flinched before death was touched at the sight of life in that deep place where the strongest man is as a child.

But just then he heard once more the sound of horses' hoofs on the lava ground, and, looking up, he saw that there could be no error this time, and that the guards were surely coming. Ten or twelve of them there seemed to be, mounted on as many ponies, and they were driving on at a furious gallop over the stones. There was a dog racing in front of them, another dog was running at their heels, and with the barking of the dogs, the loud whoops of the men to urge the ponies along, and to the clatter of the ponies' hoofs, the plain rang and echoed.

Jason saw that the guards were coming on in their direction. In three minutes more they would be upon them. They were taking the line followed by the Thing-men. Would they pass them by unseen as the Thing-men had passed them? That was not to be expected, for they were there to look for them. What was to be done? Jason looked behind him. Nothing was there but an implacable wall of stone, rising sheer up into the sky, with never a bough, or tussock of grass to cling to that a man might climb. He looked around. The ground was covered with cracked domes like the arches of buried cities, but the caverns that lay beneath them were guarded by spiked jaws which only a man's foot could slip through. Not a gap, not a hole to creep into; not a stone to crouch under; not a bush to hide behind; nothing in sight on any side but the bare, hard face of the wide sea of stone.

There was not a moment to lose. Jason lifted Sunlocks to his shoulder and crept along, bent nearly double, as silently and swiftly as he could go. And still behind him was the whoop of the men, the barking of the dogs and the clatter of hoofs.

On and on he went, minute after precious minute. The ground became heavier at every stride with huge stones that tore his stockinged legs and mangled his feet in his thin skin shoes. But he recked nothing of this, or rejoiced in it, for the way was as rough for the guards behind him, and he could hear that the horses had been drawn up from their gallop to a slow-paced walk. At each step he scoured the bleak plain for shelter, and at length he saw among piles of vitreous snags a hummock of great slabs clashed together, with one side rent open. It was like nothing else on earth but a tomb in an old burial ground, where the vaults have fallen in and wrecked the monuments above them. Through the cankered lips of this hummock into its gaping throat, Jason pushed the unconscious body of Sunlocks, and crept in after it. And lying there in the gloom he waited for the guards to come on, and as they came he strained his ear to catch the sound of the words that passed between them.

"No, no, we're on the right course," said one voice. How hollow and far away it sounded! "You saw his footmarks on the moss that we've just crossed over, and you'll see them again on the clay we're coming to."

"You're wrong," said another voice, "we saw one man's footsteps only, and we are following two."

"Don't I tell you the red man is carrying the other."

"All these miles? Impossible! Anyhow that's their course, not this."

"Why so?"

"Because they're bound for Hafnafiord."

"Why Hafnafiord?"

"To take ship and clear away."

"Tut, man, they've got bigger game than that. They're going to Reykjavik."

"What! To run into the lion's mouth?"

"Yes, and to draw his teeth, too. What has the Captain always said? Why, that the red man has all along been spy for the fair one, and we know who he is. Let him once set foot in Reykjavik and he'll do over again what he did before."

Crouching over Sunlocks in the darkness of that grim vault, Jason heard these words as the guards rode past him in the glare of the hot sun, and not until they were gone did he draw his breath. But just as he lay back with a sigh of relief, thinking all danger over, suddenly he heard a sound that startled him. It was the sniffing of a dog outside his hiding place, and at the next instant two glittering eyes looked in upon him from the gap whereby he had entered.

The dog growled, and Jason tried to pacify it. It barked, and then Jason laid hold of it, and gripped it about the throat to silence it. It fumed and fought, but Jason held it like a vice, until there came a whistle and a call, and then it struggled afresh.

"Erik!" shouted a voice without. "Erik, Erik!" and then whistle followed whistle.

Thinking the creature would now follow its master, Jason was for releasing it, but before he had yet fully done so the dog growled and barked again.

"Erik! Erik!" shouted the voice outside, and from the click-clack of hoofs Jason judged that one of the men was returning.

Then Jason saw that there was nothing left to him but to quiet the dog, or it would betray them to their death; so, while the brute writhed in his great hands, struggling to tear the flesh from them, he laid hold of its gaping jaws and rived them apart and broke them. In a moment more the dog was dead.

In the silence that followed, a faint voice came from a distance, crying, "Sigurd, Sigurd, why are you waiting!"

And then another voice shouted back from near at hand—very near, so near as to seem to be on top of the hummock, "I've lost the dog; and I could swear I heard him growling somewhere hereabouts not a minute since."

Jason was holding his breath again, when suddenly a deep sigh came from Sunlocks; then another, and another, and then some rambling words that had no meaning, but made a dull hum in that hollow place. The man outside must have heard something, for he called his dog again.

At that Jason's heart fell low, and all he could do he did—he reached over the outstretched form of his comrade, and put his lips to the lips of Sunlocks, just that he might smother their deadly babble with noiseless kisses.

This must have served, for when the voice that was far away shouted again "Sigurd! Sigurd!" the voice that was near at hand answered, "Coming." And a moment later, Jason heard the sounds of hoofs going off from him as before.

Then Michael Sunlocks awoke to full consciousness, and realized his state, and what had befallen him, and where he was, and who was with him. And first he was overwhelmed by a tempest of agony at feeling that he was a lost and forlorn man, blind and maimed, as it seemed at that time, for all the rest of his life to come. After that he cried for water, saying that his throat was baked and his tongue cracked, and Jason replied that all the water they had found that day they had been forced to leave behind them where they could never return to it. Then he poured out a torrent of hot reproaches, calling on Jason to say why he had been brought out there to go mad of thirst; and Jason listened to all and made no answer, but stood with bent head, and quivering lips, and great tear-drops on his rugged cheeks.

The spasm of agony and anger soon passed, as Jason knew it must, and then, full of remorse, Sunlocks saw everything in a new light.

"What time of day is it?" he asked.

"Evening," said Jason.

"How many hours since we left Krisuvik?"

"Ten."

"How many miles from there!"

"Twenty."

"Have you carried me all the way?"

"Yes."

There was a moment's pause, then an audible sob, and then Sunlocks felt for Jason's hand and drew it down to his lips. That kiss was more than Jason could bear, though he bore the hot words well enough; so he made a brave show of unconcern, and rattled on with hopeful talk, saying where they were to go, and what he was to do for both of them, and how they would be free men to-morrow.

And as he talked of the great task that was before them, his heart grew strong again, and Sunlocks caught the contagion of his spirit and cried, "Yes, yes, let us set off. I can walk alone now. Come, let us go."

At that Jason drew Sunlocks out of the hummock, and helped him to his feet.

"You are weak still," he said. "Let me carry you again."

"No, no, I am strong. Give me your hand. That's enough," said Sunlocks.

"Come, then," said Jason, "the guards have gone that way to Reykjavik. It's this way to Thingvellir—over the hill yonder, and through the chasm of All Men, and down by the lake to the Mount of Laws."

Then Jason wound his right arm about the waist of Sunlocks, and Sunlocks rested his left hand on the shoulder of Jason, and so they started out again over that gaunt wilderness that was once a sea of living fire. Bravely they struggled along, with words of courage and good cheer passing between them, and Sunlocks tried to be strong for Jason's sake, and Jason tried to be blind for sake of Sunlocks. If Sunlocks stumbled, Jason pretended not to know it, though his strong arm bore him up, and when Jason spoke of water and said they would soon come to a whole lake of it, Sunlocks pretended that he was no longer thirsty. Thus, like little children playing at make-believe, they tottered on, side by side, arm through arm, yoked together by a bond far tighter than ever bound them before, for the love that was their weakness was God's own strength.

But no power of spirit could take the place of power of body, and Sunlocks grew faint and very feeble.

"Is the sun still shining?" he asked at one time.

"Yes," said Jason.

Whereupon Sunlocks added, sadly, "And I am blind—blind—blind."

"Courage," whispered Jason, "the lake is yonder. I can see it plainly. We'll have water soon."

"It's not that," said Sunlocks, "but something else that troubles me."

"What else?" said Jason.

"That I'm blind, and sick, and have a broken hand, a broken heart, and a broken brain, and am not worth saving."

"Lean heavier on my shoulder, and wind your arm about my neck," whispered Jason.

Sunlocks struggled on a little longer, and then the power of life fell low in him, and he could walk no farther. "Let me go," he said, "I will lie down here a while."

And when Jason had dropped him gently to the ground, thinking he meant to rest a little and then continue his journey, Sunlocks said, very gently:

"Now, save yourself. I am only a burden to you. Escape, or you will be captured and taken back."

"What?" cried Jason, "and leave you here to die?"

"That may be my fate in any case," said Sunlocks faintly, "so go, brother—go—farewell—and God bless you!"

"Courage," whispered Jason again. "I know a farm not far away, and the good man that keeps it. He will give us milk and bread; and we'll sleep under his roof to-night, and start afresh in the morning."

But the passionate voice fell on a deaf ear, for Sunlocks was unconscious before half the words were spoken. Then Jason lifted him to his shoulder once more, and set out for the third time over the rocky waste.

It would be a weary task to tell of the adventures that afterwards befell him. In the fading sunlight of that day he crossed trackless places, void of any sound or sight of life; silent, save for the hoarse croak of the raven; without sign of human foregoer, except some pyramidal heaps of stones, that once served as mournful sentinels to point the human scapegoat to the cities of refuge.

He came up to the lake and saw that it was poisonous, for the plovers that flew over it fell dead from its fumes; and when he reached the farm he found it a ruin, the good farmer gone, and his hearth cold. He toiled through mud and boggy places, and crossed narrow bridle paths along perpendicular sides of precipices. The night came on as he walked, the short night of that northern summer, where the sun never sets in blessed darkness that weary eyes may close in sleep, but a blood-red glow burns an hour in the northern sky at midnight, and then the bright light rises again over the unrested world. He was faint for bread, and athirst for water, but still he struggled on—on—on—on—over the dismal chaos.

Sometimes when the pang of thirst was strongest he remembered what he had heard of the madness that comes of it—that the afflicted man walks round in a narrow circle, round and round over the self-same place (as if the devil's bridle bound him like an unbroken horse) until nature fails and he faints and falls. Yet thinking of himself so, in that weary spot, with Sunlocks over him, he shuddered, but took heart of strength and struggled on.

And all this time Sunlocks lay inert and lifeless on his shoulder, in a deep unconsciousness that was broken by two moments only of complete sensibility. In the first of these he said:

"I must have been dreaming, for I thought I had found my brother."

"Your brother?" said Jason.

"Yes, my brother; for I have got one, though I have never seen him," said Sunlocks. "We were not together in childhood, as other brothers are, but when we grew to be men I set out in search of him. I thought I had found him at last—but it was in hell."

"God-a-mercy!" cried Jason.

"And when I looked at him," said Sunlocks, "it seemed to me that he was you. Yes, you; for he had the face of my yoke-fellow at the Mines. I thought you were my brother indeed."

"Lie still, brother," whispered Jason; "lie still and rest."

In the second moment of his consciousness Sunlocks said, "Do you think the judges will listen to us?"

"They must—they shall," said Jason.

"But the Governor himself may be one of them," said Sunlocks.

"What matter?" said Jason.

"He is a hard man—do you know who he is?"

"No," said Jason; but he added, quickly, "Wait! Ah, now I remember. Will he be there?"

"Yes."

"So much the better."

"Why?" said Sunlocks.

And Jason answered, with heat and flame of voice, "Because I hate and loathe him."

"Has he wronged you also?" said Sunlocks.

"Yes," said Jason, "and I have waited and watched five years to requite him."

"Have you never yet met with him?"

"Never! But I'll see him now. And if he denies me this justice, I'll——"

"What?"

At that he paused, and then said quickly, "No matter."

But Sunlocks understood and said, "God forbid it."

Half an hour later, Red Jason, still carrying Michael Sunlocks, was passing through the chasm of All Men, a grand, gloomy diabolical fissure opening into the valley of Thingvellir. It was morning of the day following his escape from the Sulphur Mines of Krisuvik. The air was clear, the sun was bright, and a dull sound, such as the sea makes when far away, came up from the plain below. It was a deep multitudinous hum of many voices. Jason heard it, and his heavy face lightened with the vividness of a grim joy.

V: The Mount of Laws

I.

And now, that we may stride on the faster, we must step back a pace or two. What happened to Greeba after she parted from her father at Krisuvik, and took up her employment as nurse to the sick prisoners, we partly know already from the history of Red Jason and Michael Sunlocks. Accused of unchastity, she was turned away from the hospital; and suspected of collusion to effect the escape of some prisoner unrecognized, she was ordered to leave the neighborhood of the Sulphur Mines. But where her affections are at stake a woman's wit is more than a match for a man's cunning, and Greeba contrived to remain at Krisuvik. For her material needs she still had the larger part of the money that her brothers, in their scheming selfishness, had brought her, and she had her child to cheer her solitude. It was a boy, unchristened as yet, save in the secret place of her heart, where it bore a name that she dare not speak. And if its life was her shame in the eyes of the good folk who gave her shelter, it was a dear and sweet dishonor, for well she knew and loved to remember that one word from her would turn it to glory and to joy.

"If only I dare tell," she would whisper into her babe's ear again and again. "If I only dare!"

But its father's name she never uttered, and so with pride for her secret, and honor for her disgrace, she clung the closer to both, though they were sometimes hard to bear, and she thought a thousand times they were a loving and true revenge on him that had doubted her love and told her she had married him for the poor glory of his place.

Not daring to let herself be seen within range of the Sulphur Mines, she sought out the prisoner-priest from time to time, where he lived in the partial liberty of the Free Command, and learned from him such tidings of her husband as came his way. The good man knew nothing of the identity of Michael Sunlocks in that world of bondage where all identity was lost, save that A 25 was the husband of the woman who waited without. But that was Greeba's sole secret, and the true soul kept it.

And so the long winter passed, and the summer came, and Greeba was content to live by the side of Sunlocks, content to breathe the air he breathed, to have the same sky above her, to share the same sunshine and the same rain, only repining when she remembered that while she was looking for love into the eyes of their child, he was slaving like a beast of burden; but waiting, waiting, waiting, withal for the chance—she knew not what—that must release him yet, she knew not when.

Her great hour came at length, but an awful blow came with it. One day the prisoner-priest hurried up to the farm where she lived, and said, "I have sad news for you; forgive me; prisoner A25 has met with an accident."

She did not stay to hear more, but with her child in her arms she hurried away to the Mines, and there in the tempest of her trouble the secret of months went to the winds in an instant.

"Where is he?" she cried. "Let me see him. He is my husband."

"Your husband!" said the warders, and without more ado they laid hands upon her and carried her off to their Captain.

"This woman," they said, "turns out to be the wife of A25."

"As I suspected," the Captain answered.

"Where is my husband?" Greeba cried. "What accident has befallen him? Take me to him."

"First tell me why you came to this place," said the Captain.

"To be near my husband," said Greeba.

"Nothing else?"

"Nothing."

"Who is this other man?" asked the Captain.

"What man?" said Greeba.

Then they told her that her husband was gone, having been carried off by a fellow-prisoner who had effected the escape of both of them.

"Escaped!" cried Greeba, with a look of bewilderment, glancing from face to face of the men about her. "Then it is not true that he has met with an accident. Thank God, oh! thank God!" And she clutched her child closer to her breast, and kissed it.

"We know nothing of that either way," said the Captain. "But tell us who and what is this other man? His number here was B25. His name is Jason."

At that, Greeba gazed up again with a terrified look of inquiry.

"Jason?" she cried.

"Yes, who is he?" the Captain asked.

And Greeba answered, after a pause, "His own brother."

"We might have thought as much," said the Captain.

There was another pause, and then Greeba said, "Yes, his own brother, who has followed him all his life to kill him."

The Captain smiled upon his warders and said, "It didn't look like it, madam."

"But it is true," said Greeba.

"He has been your husband's best friend," said the Captain.

"He is my husband's worst enemy," said Greeba.

"He has carried him off, I tell you," said the Captain.

"Then it is only that he may have his wicked will of him," said Greeba. "Ah, sir, you will tell me I don't know what I'm saying. But I know too well. It was for attempting my husband's life that Jason was sent to this place. That was before your time; but look and see if I speak the truth. Now I know it is false that my husband is only injured. Would he were! Would he were! Yet, what am I saying? Mercy me, what am I saying? But, only think, he has been carried off to his death. I know he has—I am sure he has; and better, a thousand thousand times better, that he should be here, however injured, with me to nurse him! But what am I saying again? Indeed, I don't know what I am saying. Oh, sir, forgive me; and heaven forgive me, also. But send after that man. Send instantly. Don't lose an hour more. Oh, believe me, sir, trust me, sir, for I am a broken-hearted woman; and why should I not speak the truth?"

"All this is very strange," said the Captain. "But set your mind at ease about the man Jason. The guards have already gone in pursuit of him, and he cannot escape. It is not for me to say your story is not true, though the facts, as we know them, discredit it. But, true or not, you shall tell it to the Governor as you have told it to me, so prepare to leave Krisuvik immediately."

And in less than an hour more Greeba was riding between two of the guards towards the valley of Thingvellir.

II.

Jorgen Jorgensen had thrice hardened his heart against Michael Sunlocks: first, when he pushed Sunlocks into Althing, and found his selfish ends were not thereby in the way of advancement; next, when he fell from his place and Sunlocks took possession of it; again, when he regained his stool and Sunlocks was condemned to the Sulphur Mines. But most of all he hated Sunlocks when old Adam Fairbrother came to Reykjavik and demanded for him, as an English subject, the benefit of judge and jury.

"We know of no jury here," said Jorgen; "and English subject or not English subject, this man has offended against the laws of Denmark."

"Then the laws of Denmark shall condemn him," said Adam, bravely, "and not the caprice of a tyrant governor."

"Keep a civil tongue in your old head, sir," said Jorgen, "or you may learn to your cost how far that caprice can go."

"I care nothing for your threats, sir," said Adam, "and I mean to accuse you before your master."

"Do your worst," said Jorgen, "and take care how you do it."

And at first Adam's worst seemed likely to be little, for hardly had he set foot in Reykjavik when he was brought front to front with the material difficulty that the few pounds with which he had set out were spent. Money was justice, and justice money, on that rock of the sea, as elsewhere, and on the horns of his dilemma, Adam bethought him to write to his late master, the Duke of Athol, explaining his position, and asking for the loan of fifty pounds. A long month passed before he got back his answer. The old Duke sent forty pounds as a remonstrance against Adam's improvidence, and stern counsel to him to return forthwith to the homes of his children. In the meantime the old Bishop, out of love of Michael Sunlocks and sympathy with Greeba, had taken Adam into his house at Reykjavik. From there old Adam had sent petitions to the Minister at Copenhagen, petitions to the Danish Rigsdag, and finally petitions to the Danish King. His reward had been small, for no justice, or promise of justice, could he get.

But Jorgen Jorgensen had sat no easier on his seat for Adam's zealous efforts. He had been hurried out of his peace by Government inquiries, and terrified by Government threats. But he had wriggled, he had lied, he had used subterfuge after subterfuge, and so pushed on the evil day of final reckoning.

And while his hoary head lay ill at ease because of the troubles that came from Copenhagen, the gorge of his stomach rose at the bitter waters he was made to drink at Reykjavik. He heard the name of Michael Sunlocks on every lip, as a name of honor, a name of affection, a name to conjure with whenever and wherever men talked of high talents, justice, honor and truth.

Jorgen perceived that the people of Iceland had recovered from the first surprise and suspicion that followed on the fall of their Republic, and no longer saw Michael Sunlocks as their betrayer, but had begun to regard him as their martyr. They loved him still. If their hour ever came they would restore him. On the other hand, Jorgen realized that he himself was hated where he was not despised, jeered at where he was not feared, and that the men whom he had counted upon because he had bought them with the places in his gift, smiled loftily upon him as upon one who had fallen on his second childhood. And so Jorgen Jorgensen hardened his heart against Michael Sunlocks, and vowed that the Sulphur Mines of Krisuvik should see the worst and last of him.

He heard of Jason, too, that he was not dead, as they had supposed, but alive, and that he had been sent to the Mines for attempting the life of Sunlocks. That attempt seemed to him to come of a natural passion, and as often as he spoke of it he warmed up visibly, not out of any human tenderness towards Jason, but with a sense of wild triumph over Sunlocks. And the more he thought of Jason, the firmer grew his resolve to take him out of the Sulphur Mines and place him by his side, not that his old age needed a stay, not that he was a lonely old man, and Jason was his daughter's son, but only because Jason hated Sunlocks and would crush him if by chance he rose again.

With such thoughts uppermost he went down to Krisuvik, and there his bitter purpose met with a shock. He found Jason the sole ally of Michael Sunlocks, his friend, his defender and champion against tyranny. It was then that he ordered the ruthless punishment of Sunlocks, that he should be nailed by his right hand to a log of driftwood, with meat and drink within sight but out of reach of him, and a huge knife by his side. And when Jason had liberated Sunlocks from this inhuman cruelty, and the two men, dearest foes and deadliest friends, were brought before him for their punishment, the gall of Jorgen's fate seemed to suffocate him. "Strap them up together," he cried, "leg to leg and arm to arm." Thus he thought to turn their love to hate; but he kept his own counsel, and left the Sulphur Mines without saying what evil dream had brought him there, or confessing to his Danish officers the relation wherein this other prisoner stood to him, for secrecy is the chain-armor of the tyrant.

Back in Reykjavik he comforted himself with the assurance that Michael Sunlocks must die. "There was death in his face," he thought, "and he cannot last a month longer. Besides, he will fall to fighting with the other, and the other will surely kill him. Blind fools, both of them!"

In this mood he made ready for Thingvellir, and set out with all his people. Since the revolution, he had kept a bodyguard of five and twenty men, and with this following he was crossing the slope of the Basket Hill, behind the capital, when he saw half a score of the guards from Krisuvik riding at a gallop from the direction of Hafnafiord. They were the men who had been sent in pursuit of Red Jason and Michael Sunlocks, the same that had passed them in the hummock, where the carcase of the dog still lay.

Then Jorgen Jorgensen received news that terrified him.

Michael Sunlocks had escaped, and Red Jason had escaped with him. They had not been seen at Hafnafiord, and no ship had set sail from there since yesterday. Never a trace of them had been found on any of the paths from Krisuvik, and it was certain that they must be in the interior still. Would his Excellency lend them ten men more to scour the country?

Such was the message of the guards, and at hearing it Jorgen's anger and fear overmastered him.

"Fools! Blockheads! Asses!" he cried. "The man is making for Reykjavik. He knows what he is doing if you do not. Is not this the time of Althing, and must I not leave Reykjavik for Thingvellir? He is making for Reykjavik now! Once let him set foot there, and these damned Icelanders will rise at the sight of him. Then you may scour the country till you fall dead and turn black, and he will only laugh at the sight of you. Back, you blockheads, back! Back to Reykjavik, every man of you! And I am going back with you."

Thus driven by his frantic terror, Jorgen Jorgensen returned to the capital and searched every house and hovel, every hole and sty, for the two fugitives; and when he had satisfied himself that they were not anywhere within range of Reykjavik, his fears remembered Thingvellir, and what mischief might be going forward in his absence. So next day he left his bodyguard with the guard from Krisuvik to watch the capital, and set out alone for the Mount of Laws.

III.

The lonely valley of Thingvellir was alive that morning with a great throng of people. They came from the west by the Chasm of All Men, from the east by the Chasm of Ravens, and from the south by the lake. Troop after troop flowed into the vast amphitheatre that lies between dark hills and great jokulls tipped with snow. They pitched their tents on the green patch, under the fells to the north, and tying their ponies together, head to tail, they turned them loose to graze. Hundreds of tents were there by early morning, gleaming white in the sunlight, and tens of hundreds of ponies, shaggy and unkempt, grubbed among the short grass that grew between.

Near the middle of the plain stood the Mount of Laws, a lava island of oval shape, surrounded by a narrow stream, and bounded by overhanging walls cut deep with fissures. Around this mount the people gathered. There friend met friend, foe met foe, rival met rival, northmen met southmen, the Westmann islander met the Grimsey islander, and the man from Seydisfiord met the man from Patriksfiord. And because Althing gathered only every other year, many musty kisses went round, with snuffboxes after them, among those who had not met before for two long years.

It was a vast assembly, chiefly of men, in their homespun and sheepskins and woollen stockings, cross-gartered with hemp from ankle to knee. Women, too, and young girls and children were there, all wearing their Sunday best. And in those first minutes of their meeting, before Althing began, the talk was of crops and stock, of the weather, and of what sheep had been lost in the last two hard winters. The day had opened brightly, with clear air and bright sunshine, but the blue sky had soon become overcast with threatening clouds, and this lead to stories of strange signs in the heavens, and unaccustomed noises on the earth and under it.

A man from the south spoke of rain of black dust as having fallen three nights before until the ground was covered deep with it. Another man, from the foot of Hekla, told of a shock of earthquake that had lately been felt there, travelling northeast to southwest. A third man spoke of grazing his horse on the wild oats of a glen that he had passed through, with a line of some twenty columns of smoke burst suddenly upon his view. All this seemed to pass from lip to lip in the twinkling of an eye, and when young men asked what the signs might mean, old men lifted both hands and shook their heads, and prayed that the visitations which their island had seen before might never come to it again.

Such was the talk, and such the mood of the people when the hour arrived for the business of Althing to begin, and then all eyes turned to the little wooden Thing House by the side of the church, wherein the Thing-men were wont to gather for their procession to the Mount of Laws. And when the hour passed, and the procession had not yet appeared, the whisper went around that the Governor had not arrived, and that the delay was meant to humor him. At that the people began to mutter among themselves, for the slumbering fire of their national spirit had been stirred. By his tardy coming the Governor meant to humiliate them! But, Governor or no Governor, let Althing begin its sitting. Who was the Governor that Althing should wait for him? What was Althing that it should submit to the whim or the will of any Governor?

Within the Thing House, as well as outside of it, such hot protests must have had sway, for presently the door of the little place was thrown open and the six and thirty Thing-men came out.

Then followed the solemn ceremonies that had been observed on the spot for nigh a thousand years. First walked the Chief Judge, carrying the sword of justice, and behind him walked his magistrates and Thing-men. They ascended to the Mount by a flight of steps cut out of its overhanging walls. At the same moment another procession, that of the old Bishop and his clergy, came out of the church and ascended to the Mount by a similar flight of steps cut out of the opposite side of it. The two companies parted, the Thing-men to the north and the clergy to the south, leaving the line of this natural causeway open and free, save for the Judge, who stood at the head of it, with the Bishop to the right of him and the Governor's empty place to the left.

And first the Bishop offered prayer for the sitting of Althing that was then to begin.

"Thou Judge of Israel," he prayed, in the terrible words which had descended to him through centuries, "Thou that sittest upon the cherubims, come down and help Thy people. O, most mighty God, who art more pleased with the sacrifice of thanksgiving than with the burnt offerings of bullocks and goats, keep now our mouths from guile and deceit, from slander and from obloquy. O Lord God most holy, O Lord most mighty, endue Thy ministers with righteousness. Give them wisdom that they may judge wisely. Give them mercy that they may judge mercifully. Let them judge this nation as Thou wilt judge Thy people. Let them remember that he who takes the name of justice for his own profit or hatred or revenge is worse than the vulture that watches for the carcase. Let them not forget that howsoever high they stand or proudly they bear themselves, nothing shall they take from hence but the oak for their coffin. Let them be sure that when

Thou shalt appear with a consuming fire before Thee and a tempest round about Thee, calling the heaven and the earth together, no portion can they have in that day like to the portion of thine inheritance."

The fierce prayer came to an end, and then the Judge, holding his sword erect, read his charge and repeated his oath, to deal justly between man and man, even as the sword stood upright before him. And the vast assembly of rude men in sheepskins and in homespun looked on and listened, all silent and solemn, all worshipful of law and reverent of its forms.

The oath being taken, the Judge had laid the sword aside and begun to promulgate the new laws, reading them clause by clause, first in Icelandic and then in Danish, when there was an uneasy movement at the outskirts of the crowd to the west of the Mount.

"The Governor," whispered one. "It's himself," muttered another. "He's here at last," murmured a third, and dark were the faces turned round to see. It was the Governor, indeed, and he pushed his way through the closely-packed people, who saw him coming, but stood together like a wall until riven apart by his pony's feet. At the causeway he dismounted and stepped up to the top of the Mount. He looked old and feeble and torn by evil passions; his straight gray hair hung like a blasted sheaf on to his shoulders, his forehead was blistered with blue veins, his cheeks were guttered with wrinkles, his little eyes were cruel, his jaw was broad and heavy, and his mouth was hard and square.

The Judge made him no obeisance, but went on with his reading. The Bishop seemed not to see him, but gazed steadfastly forward. The Thing-men gave no sign.

He stood a moment, and looked around, and the people below could see his wrath rising like a white hand across his haggard face. Then he interrupted and said, "Chief Justice, I have something to say."

All heard the words, and the Speaker stopped, and, amid the breathless silence of the people, he answered quietly, "There will be a time and a place for that, your Excellency."

"The time is now, and the place is here," cried Jorgen Jorgensen, in a tense voice, and quivering with anger. "Listen to me. The rebel and traitor who once usurped the government of this island has escaped."

"Escaped!" cried a hundred voices.

"Michael Sunlocks!" cried as many more.

And a wave of excitement passed over the vast assembly.

"Yes, Michael Sunlocks has escaped," cried Jorgen Jorgensen. "That scoundrel is at liberty. He is free to do his wicked work again. Men of Iceland, I call on you to help me. I call on you to help the Crown of Denmark. The traitor must be taken. I call on you to take him."

A deep murmur ran through the closely-pressed people.

"You've got your guards," shouted a voice from below. "Why do you come to us?"

"Because," cried Jorgen Jorgensen, "my guards are protecting Reykjavik, and because they might scour your island a hundred years and never find what they looked for."

"Thank God!" muttered another voice from below.

"But you know it, every fell and fiord," cried Jorgen Jorgensen, "and never a toad could skulk under a stone but you would root him out of it. Chief Justice," he added, sweeping about, "I have a request to make of you."

"What is it, your Excellency?" said the Judge.

"That you should adjourn this Althing so that every man here present may go out in search of the traitor."

Then a loud involuntary murmur of dissent rose from the people, and at the same moment the Judge said in bewilderment, "What can your Excellency mean?"

"I mean," cried Jorgen Jorgensen, "that if you adjourn this Althing for three days, the traitor will be taken. If not, he will be at liberty as many years. Will you do it?"

"Your Excellency," said the Judge, "Althing has lived nigh upon a thousand years, and every other year for that thousand years it has met on this ancient ground, but never once since it began has the thing you ask been done."

"Let it be done now," cried Jorgen Jorgensen. "Will you do it?"

"We will do our duty by your Excellency," said the Judge, "and we will expect your Excellency to do your duty by us."

"But this man is a traitor," cried Jorgen Jorgensen, "and it is your duty to help me to capture him. Will you do it?"

"And this day is ours by ancient right and custom," said the Judge, "and it is your duty to stand aside."

"I am here for the King of Denmark," cried Jorgen Jorgensen, "and I ask you to adjourn this Althing. Will you do it?"

"And we are here for the people of Iceland," said the Judge, "and we ask you to step back and let us go on."

Then Jorgen Jorgensen's anger knew no bounds.

"You are subjects of the King of Denmark," he cried.

"Before ever Denmark was, we were," answered the Judge, proudly.

"And in his name I demand that you adjourn. Will you do it now?" cried Jorgen Jorgensen, with a grin of triumph.

"No," cried the Judge, lifting an undaunted face to the face of Jorgen Jorgensen.

The people held their breath through this clash of words, but at the Judge's brave answer a murmur of approval passed over them. Jorgen Jorgensen heard it, and flinched, but turned back to the Judge and said,

"Take care. If you do not help me, you hinder me; if you are not with me, you are against me. Is that man a traitor? Answer me—yes or no."

But the Judge made no answer, and there was dead silence among the people, for they knew well in what way the cruel question tended.

"Answer me—yes or no," Jorgen Jorgensen cried again.

Then the Bishop broke silence and said,

"Whatever our hearts may be, your Excellency, our tongues must be silent."

At that, Jorgen Jorgensen faced about to the crowd.

"I put a price on his head," he cried. "Two thousand kroner to anyone who takes him, alive or dead. Who will earn it?"

"No Icelander earns money with blood," said the Bishop. "If this thing is our duty, we will do it without pay. If not, no bribe will tempt us."

"Ay, ay," shouted a hundred voices.

Jorgen Jorgensen flinched again, and his face whitened as he grew darker within.

"So, I see how it is," he said, looking steadfastly at the Bishop, the Judge, and the Thing-men. "You are aiding this traitor's escape. You are his allies, every man of you. And you are seducing and deceiving the people."

Then he faced about towards the crowd more and more, and cried in a loud voice:

"Men of Iceland, you know the man who has escaped. You know what he is, and where he came from; you know he is not one of yourselves, but a bastard Englishman. Then drive him back home. Listen to me. What price did I put on his head? Two thousand kroner! I will give ten thousand! Ten thousand kroner for the man who takes him alive, and twenty thousand kroner—do you hear me?—twenty thousand for the man who takes him dead."

"Silence!" cried the Bishop. "Who are you, sir, that you dare tempt men to murder?"

"Murder!" cried Jorgen Jorgensen. "See how simple are the wise? Men of Iceland, listen to me again. The traitor is an outlaw. You know what that means. His blood is on his own head. Any man may shoot him down. No man may be called to account for doing so. Do you hear me? It is the law of Iceland, the law of Denmark, the law of the world. He is an outlaw, and killing him is no murder. Follow him up! Twenty thousand kroner to the man who lays him at my feet."

He would have said more, for he was heaving with passion, and his white face had grown purple, but his tongue seemed suddenly paralyzed, and his wide eyes fixed themselves on something at the outskirts of the crowd. One thin and wrinkled hand he lifted up and pointed tremblingly over the heads of the people. "There!" he said in a smothered cry, and after that he was silent.

The crowd shifted and looked round, amid a deep murmur of surprise and expectation. Then by one of the involuntary impulses that move great assemblies, the solid wall of human beings seemed to part of itself, and make a way for someone.

It was Red Jason, carrying Michael Sunlocks across his breast and shoulder. His bronzed cheeks were worn, his sunken eyes burned with a dull fire. He strode on, erect and strong, through the riven way of men and women. A breathless silence seemed to follow him. When he came to the foot of the Mount, he stopped, and let Sunlocks drop gently to the ground. Sunlocks was insensible, and his piteous white face looked up at the heavy dome of the sky. A sensation of awe held the vast crowd spellbound. It was as if the Almighty God had heard the blasphemy of that miserable old man, and given him on the instant his impious wish.

IV.

Then, in that breathless silence, Jason stood erect and said, in a firm, clear, sonorous voice, "You know who I am. Some of you hate me. Some of you fear me. All of you think me a sort of wild beast among men. That is why you caged me. But I have broken my bars, and brought this man along with me."

The men on the Mount had not time to breathe under the light and fire that flashed upon them when Jason lifted his clenched hand and said, "O, you that dwell in peace; you that go to your beds at night; you that eat when you are hungry and drink when you are athirst, and rest when you are weary: would to God you could know by bitter proof what this poor man has suffered. But I know it, and I can tell you what it has been. Where is your Michael Sunlocks, that I may tell it to him? Which is he? Point him out to me."

Then the people drew a deep breath, for they saw in an instant what had befallen these two men in the dread shaping of their fate.

"Where is he?" cried Jason, again.

And in a voice quivering with emotion, the Judge said:

"Don't you know the man you've brought here?"

"No—yes—yes," cried Jason. "My brother—my brother in suffering—my brother in misery—that's all I know or care. But where is your Michael Sunlocks? I have something to say to him. Where is he?"

Jorgen Jorgensen had recovered himself by this time, and pressing forward, he said with a cruel smile,

"You fool; shall I tell you where he is?"

"Heaven forbid it!" said the Bishop, stepping out and lifting both hands before the Governor's face. But in that instant Jason had recognized Jorgen Jorgensen.

"I know this old man," he said. "What is he doing here? Ah, God pity me, I had forgotten. I saw him at the mines. Then he is back. And, now I remember, he is Governor again."

Saying this, an agony of bewilderment quivered in his face. He looked around.

"Then where is Michael Sunlocks?" he cried in a loud voice. "Where is he? Which is he? Who is he? Will no one tell me? Speak! For the merciful Christ's sake let some one speak."

There was a moment of silence, in which the vast crowd trembled as one man with wonder and dismay. The Bishop and Judge stood motionless. Jorgen Jorgensen smiled bitterly and shook his head, and Jason raised his right hand to cover his face from the face of the insensible man at his feet, as if some dark foreshadowing of the truth had swept over him in an instant.

What happened thereafter Jason never knew, only that there was a shrill cry and a rustle like a swirl of wind, only that someone was coming up behind him through the walls of human beings, that still stood apart like riven rocks, only that in a moment a woman had flung herself over the prostrate body of his comrade, embracing it, raising it in her arms, kissing its pale cheeks, and sobbing over it, "My husband! my husband."

It was Greeba. When the dark mist had cleared away from before his eyes, Jason saw her and knew her. At the same instant he saw and knew his destiny, that his yoke-fellow had been Michael Sunlocks, that his lifelong enemy had been his life's sole friend.

It was a terrible discovery, and Jason reeled under the shock of it like a beast that is smitten to its death. And while he stood there, half-blind, half-deaf, swaying to and fro as if the earth rocked beneath him, across his shoulders, over his cheeks and his mouth and his eyes fell the lash of the tongue of Jorgen Jorgensen.

"Yes, fool that you are and have been," he cried in his husky voice, "that's where your Michael Sunlocks is."

"Shame! Shame!" cried the people.

But Jorgen Jorgensen showed no pity or ruth.

"You have brought him here to your confusion," he cried again, "and it's not the first time you've taken this part to your own loss."

More he would have said in the merciless cruelty of his heart, only that a deep growl came up from the crowd and silenced him.

But Jason heard nothing, saw nothing, felt nothing, knew nothing, save that Michael Sunlocks lay at his feet, that Greeba knelt beside him, and that she was coaxing him, caressing him, and kissing him back to life.

"Michael," she whispered, "Michael! My poor Michael!" she murmured, while she moistened his lips and parched tongue with the brenni-vin from the horn of some good man standing near.

Jason saw this and heard this, though he had eyes and ears for nothing besides. And thinking, in the wild tumult of his distempered brain, that such tenderness might have been his, should have been his, must have been his, but for this man who had robbed him of this woman, all the bitterness of his poisoned heart rose up to choke him.

He remembered his weary life with this man, his sufferings with him, his love for him, and he hated himself for it all. What devil of hell had made sport of him, to give him his enemy for his friend? How Satan himself must shriek aloud to see it, that he who had been thrice robbed by this man—robbed of a father, robbed of a mother, robbed of a wife—should in his blindness tend him, and nurse him, and carry him with sweat of blood over trackless wastes that he might save him alive for her who waited to claim him!

Then he remembered what he had come for, and that all was not yet done. Should he do it after all? Should he give this man back to this woman? Should he renounce his love and his hate together—his love of this woman, his hate of this man? Love? Hate? Which was love? Which was hate? Ah, God! They were one; they were the same. Heaven pity him, what was he to do?

Thus the powers of good and the powers of evil wrestled together in Jason's heart for mastery. But the moment of their struggle was short. One look at the piteous blind face lying on Greeba's bosom, one glance at the more piteous wet face that hung over it, and love had conquered hate in that big heart forever and forever.

Jason was recalled to himself by a dull hum of words that seemed to be spoken from the Mount. Someone was asking why he had come there, and brought Michael Sunlocks along with him. So he lifted his hand, partly to call attention, partly to steady himself, and in a broken voice he said these words:—

"Men and women, if you could only know what it means that you have just witnessed, I think it would be enough to move any man. You know what I am—a sort of bastard who has never been a man among men, but has walked alone all the days of his life. My father killed my mother, and so I vowed to kill my father. I did not do it, for I saved him out of the sea, and he died in my arms, as you might say, doating on the memory of another son. That son's mother had supplanted my mother and that son himself had supplanted me, so I vowed to kill him for his father's sake. I did not do that nei-neither. I had never once set eyes on my enemy, I had done nothing but say what I meant to do, when you took me and tried me and condemned me. Perhaps that was injustice, such as could have been met with nowhere save here in Iceland, yet I thank God for it now. By what chance I do not know, but in that hell to which you sent me, where all names are lost and no man may know his yoke-fellow, except by his face if he has seen it, I met with one who became my friend, my brother, my second self. I loved him, as one might love a little child. And he loved me—yes, me,—I could swear it. You had thought me a beast, and shut me out from the light of day and the company of Christian men. But he made me a man, and lit up the darkness of my night."

His deep strong voice faltered, and he stopped, and nothing was audible save the excited breathing of the people. Greeba was looking up into his haggard face with amazement written upon her own.

"Must I go on," he cried, in a voice rent with agony. "I have brought him here, and he is Michael Sunlocks. My brother in suffering is my brother in blood. The man I have vowed to slay is the man I have tried to save."

Some of the people could not restrain their tears, and the white faces of the others quivered visibly.

"Why have you brought him here?" asked the Judge.

At that moment Michael Sunlocks began to move and to moan, as if consciousness were coming back to him. Jorgen Jorgensen saw this, and the proud composure with which he had looked on and listened while Sunlocks lay like a man dead left him in an instant.

"Why have you brought Michael Sunlocks here?" said the Judge again.

"Why has he brought him here?" said Jorgen Jorgensen bitterly. "To be arrested. That's why he has brought him here. See, the man is coming to. He will do more mischief yet, unless he is prevented. Take him," he shouted to two of the guards from Krisuvik, who had come with Greeba, and now stood behind her.

"Wait!" cried the Judge, lifting his hand.

There was no gainsaying his voice, and the guards who had stepped forward dropped back.

Then he turned to Jason again and repeated his question, "Why have you brought Michael Sunlocks here?"

At that, Jorgen Jorgensen lost all self-control and shouted, "Take him, I say!" And facing about to the Judge he said, "I will have you know, sir, that I am here for Denmark and must be obeyed."

The guards stepped forward again, but the crowd closed around them and pushed them back.

Seeing this, Jorgen Jorgensen grew purple with rage, and turning to the people, he shouted at the full pitch of his voice, "Listen to me. Some minutes past, I put a price on that man's head. I said I would give you twenty thousand kroner. I was wrong. I will give you nothing but your lives and liberty. You know what that means. You have bent your necks under the yoke already, and you may have to do it again. Arrest that man—arrest both men!"

"Stop!" cried the Judge.

"Those men are escaped prisoners," said Jorgen Jorgensen.

"And this is the Mount of Laws, and here is Althing," said the Judge; "and prisoners or no prisoners, if they have anything to say, by the ancient law of Iceland they may say it now."

"Pshaw! your law of Iceland is nothing to me," said Jorgen Jorgensen, and turning to the crowd he cried, "In the name of the King of Denmark I command you to arrest those men."

"And in the name of the King of Kings," said the Judge, turning after him, "I command you to let them alone."

There was a dead hush for a moment, and then the Judge looked down at Jason and said once more, "Why have you brought Michael Sunlocks here! Speak!"

But before Jason could make answer, Jorgen Jorgensen had broken in again:

"My guards are at Reykjavik," he cried, "and I am here alone. You are traitors, all of you, and if there is no one else to arrest that enemy of my country, I will do it myself. He shall go no further. Step back from him."

So saying, he opened his cloak, drew a pistol from his belt and cocked it. A shrill cry arouse from the crowd. The men on the Mount stood quaking with fear, and Greeba flung herself over the restless body of Michael Sunlocks.

But Jason did not move a feature.

"Old man," he said, looking up with eyes as steadfast as the sun into Jorgensen's face, and pointing towards Sunlocks, "if you touch one hair of this head, these hands will tear you to pieces."

Then one of the men who had stood near, a rough fellow with a big tear-drop rolling down his tanned cheeks, stepped up to Jason's side, and without speaking a word offered him his musket; but Jason calmly pushed it back. There was dead silence once more. Jorgen Jorgensen's uplifted hand fell to his side, and he was speechless.

"Speak now," said the Judge. "Why have you brought Michael Sunlocks here?"

Jason stood silent for a moment as if to brace himself up, and then he said, "I have laid my soul bare to your gaze already, and you know what I am and where I come from."

A low moan seemed to echo him.

"But I, too, am an Icelander, and this is our ancient Mount of Laws, the sacred ground of our fathers and our fathers' fathers for a thousand years."

A deep murmur rose from the vast company.

"And I have heard that if any one is wronged and oppressed and unjustly punished, let him but find his way to this place, and though he be the meanest slave that wipes his forehead, yet he will be a man among you all."

There were loud cries of assent.

"I have also heard that this Mount, on this day, is as the gate of the city in old time, when the judges sat to judge the people; and that he who is permitted to set foot on it, and cross it, though he were as guilty as the outlaws that hide in the desert, is innocent and free forever after. Answer me—is it true? Yes or no?"

"Yes! yes!" came from a thousand throats.

"Then, judges of Iceland, fellow-men and brothers, do you ask why I have brought this man to this place? Look at this bleeding hand." He lifted the right hand of Sunlocks. "It has been pierced with a nail." A deep groan came from the people. He let the hand fall back. "Look at these poor eyes. They are blind. Do you know what that means? It means hellish barbarity and damned tyranny."

His voice swelled until it seemed to shake the very ground on which he stood. "What this man's crime may be I do not know, and I do not care. Let it be what it will, let the man be what he may—a felon like myself, a malefactor, a miscreant, a monster—yet what crime and what condition deserves punishment that is worse than death and hell?"

"None, none," shouted a thousand voices.

"Then, judges of Iceland, fellow-men and brothers, I call on you to save this man from that doom. Save him for his sake—save him for your own, for He that dwells above is looking down on you."

He paused a moment and then cried, "Listen!"

There was a low rumble as of thunder. It came not from the clouds, but from the bowels of the earth. The people turned pallid with dismay, but Jason's face was lit up with a wild frenzy.

"Do you hear it? It is the voice that was heard when these old hills were formed, and the valleys ran like fire. It is the voice of the Almighty God calling on you."

The word was like a war cry. The people answered it with a shout. And still Jason's voice pealed over their heads.

"Vengeance is God's but mercy belongs to man."

He stooped to Michael Sunlocks, where Greeba held him at her bosom, picked him up in his arms as if he had been a child, turned his face towards the Mount and cried, "Let me pass."

Then at one impulse, in one instant, the Judge and the Bishop parted and made a way, and Jason, carrying Sunlocks, strode up the causeway and swept through.

There was but one voice then in all that great assembly, and it was a mighty shout that seemed to rend the dome of the heavy sky. "Free! Free! Free!"

V.

But the end was not yet. More, and more terrible, is to follow, though the spirit is not fain to tell of it, and the hand that sets it down is trembling. Let him who thinks that this world of time is founded in justice, wait long and watch patiently, for up to the eleventh hour he may see the good man sit in misery, and the evil man carried in honor. And let him who thinks that Nature is sweet and benignant and that she leaps to the aid of the just, learn from what is to come that she is all things to all men and nothing to any man.

Now when Jason had crossed the Mount of Laws with Sunlocks, thinking that by virtue of old custom he had thereby set him free of tyranny, Jorgen Jorgensen did what a man of shallow soul must always do when he sees the outward signs of the holy things that move the deeper souls of other men. He smiled with bitterness and laughed with contempt.

"A pretty thing, truly," he sneered, "out of some forgotten age of musty laws and old barbarians. But there is something else that is forgotten. It is forgotten that between these two men, Jason and Michael Sunlocks, there is this difference, that the one is a prisoner of Iceland, and the other of Denmark. Jason is a prisoner of Iceland, a felon of Iceland, therefore Iceland may pardon him, and if this brave mummery has made him free, then so be it, and God pity you! But Michael Sunlocks is a prisoner of Denmark, a traitor against the crown of Denmark, therefore Denmark alone may pardon him—and he is still unpardoned."

The clamorous crowd that had gathered about Michael Sunlocks looked up in silence and bewilderment at this fresh blow. And Jorgen Jorgensen saw his advantage and went on.

"Ask your Lagmann and let him answer you. Is it as I say or is it not? Ask him."

The people looked from face to face of the men on the Mount, from Jorgen Jorgensen to the Judge and from the Judge to the Bishop.

"Is this true?" shouted a voice from the crowd.

But the Judge made no answer, and the Bishop said, "Why all this wrangling over the body of a dying man?"

"Dying indeed!" said Jorgen Jorgensen, and he laughed. "Look at him." Michael Sunlocks, again lying in the arms of Greeba, was showing signs of life. "He will recover fast enough when all is over."

"Is it true?" shouted the same voice from the crowd.

"Yes," said the Judge.

Then the look of bewilderment in the faces of the people deepened to consternation. At that moment Michael Sunlocks was raised to his feet. And Jorgen Jorgensen, standing like an old snuffy tiger on the watch, laughed again, and turning to Jason he pointed at Sunlocks and said, "What did I say? A pretty farce truly, this pretence at unconsciousness. Small good it has done him. And he has little to thank you for. You have brought him here to his death."

What answer Jason would have made him, no man may say, for at that moment the same terrestrial thunder that had been heard before was heard again, and the earth became violently agitated as with a deep pulsation. The people looked into each other's faces with dismay, and scarcely had they realized the horror that waited to pour itself out on the world, when a man came galloping from the south and crying, "The mountains are coming down at Skaptar. Fly! fly!"

They stopped the man and questioned him, and he answered, with terror in his eyes, that the ice-mountain itself was sweeping down into the plain. Then he put his heels to his horse and broke away.

Hardly had the people heard this dread word when another man came galloping from the southwest, and crying, "The sea is throwing up new islands at Reykianess, and all the rivers are dry."

They stopped this man also, and questioned him, and he answered that the sky at the coast was raining red-hot stones, so that the sea hissed with them, and all the land was afire. Then he, too, put his heels to his horse and broke away.

Scarcely had he gone, when a third man came galloping from the southeast, and crying, "The land around Hekla is washed away, and not a green place is left on the face of the earth."

This man also they stopped and questioned, and he answered that a torrent of boiling water was rolling down from the Kotlugia yakul, hurling ice-blocks before it, and sweeping farms, churches, cattle, horses, and men, women, and children into the sea. Then this man also put his heels to his horse and broke away, like one pursued by death itself.

For some moments thereafter the people stood where the men had left them, silent, helpless, unable to think or feel. Then there rose from them all, as from one man, such a shriek of mortal agony as never before came from human breasts. In their terror they ran hither and thither, without thought or intention. They took to their tents, they took to their ponies, they galloped north, they galloped south, they galloped east, they galloped west, and then came scurrying back to the Mount from which they had started. A great danger was about to burst upon them, but they could not tell from what direction it would come. Some remembered their homes and the wives and children they had left there. Others thought only of themselves and of the fire and water that were dealing out death.

In two minutes the Mount was a barren waste, the fissures on its sides were empty, and the seats on the crags were bare. The Thing-men and the clergy were rushing to and fro in the throng, and the old Bishop and the Judge were seeking their horses.

Greeba stood, with fear on her face, by the side of Michael Sunlocks, who, blind and maimed, unable to see what was going on about him, not knowing yet where he was and what new evil threatened him, looked like a man who might have been dead and was awakening to consciousness in a world of the damned.

Two men, and two only, of all that vast multitude, kept their heads and were cool through this mad panic. One of these was Jorgen Jorgensen; the other was Red Jason. They watched each other constantly, the one with the eyes of the lynx, the other with the eyes of a lion.

A troop of men came riding through the throng from the direction of the Chasm of Ravens. Twenty of them were the bodyguard of the Governor, and they pushed their way to the feet of Jorgen Jorgensen.

"Your Excellency," said one of them, "we had news of you that you would want us; so we made bold to come."

"You have come in time," said Jorgen Jorgensen, and his cruel eyes flashed with the light of triumph.

"There has been a great eruption of Skaptar," said the man, "and the people of the south are flocking into Reykjavik."

"Leave old Skaptar to take care of itself," said Jorgen Jorgensen, "and do you take charge of that man there, and the woman beside him."

So saying, he pointed towards Michael Sunlocks, who, amid the whirl of the crowd around, had stood still in his helpless blindness.

Jason saw and heard all, and he shouted to the people to come to his help, for he was one man against twenty. But the people paid no heed to his calling, for every man was thinking of himself. Then Jason fell on the guards with his bare hands only. And his mighty muscles would have made havoc of many of them, but that Jorgen Jorgensen drew his pistol again and fired at him, and wounded him. Jason knew nothing of his injury until his right arm fell to his side, bleeding and useless. After that, he was seized from behind and from before, and held to the ground while Michael Sunlocks and Greeba were hurried away.

Then the air began to be filled with smoke, a wind that was like a solid wall of black sand swept up from the south, and sudden darkness covered everything.

"It is the lava!" shouted one.

"It's the fiery flood!" shouted another.

"It's the end of the world!" shouted a third.

And at one impulse the people rushed hither, thither—north, south, east, west—some weeping, some shrieking, some swearing, some laughing like demons—all wild with frenzy and mad with terror.

Jorgen Jorgensen found his little piebald pony where he had left it, for the docile beast, with the reins over its head, was munching the grass at the foot of the causeway. He mounted, and rode past Jason as the men were loosening their hold of him, and peering into his face he said with a sneer, "If this is the end of the world, as they say, make the best of what is left of it, and fly."

With that, he thrust spurs into his horse's sides, and went off at utmost speed.

Then Jason was alone on the plain. Not another human soul was left. The crowd was gone; the Mount of Laws was silent, and a flock of young sheep ran past it bleating. Over the mountains to the south a red glow burned along the black sky, and lurid flames shot through it.

Such was the beginning of the eruption of Skaptar. And Jason staggered along in the day-darkness, alone, abandoned, shouting like a maniac, swearing like a man accursed, crying out to the desolate waste and the black wind sweeping over it, that if this were the end of the world, he had a question to ask of Him who made it: Why He had broken His word, which said that the wages of sin was death—why the avenger that was promised had not come to smite down the wicked and save the just?

VI.

In this valley of the Loberg there is a long peninsula of rock stretching between the western bank of the lake and the river called the Oxara. It begins in a narrow neck where is a pass for one horse only, and ends in a deep pool over a jagged precipice, with a mighty gorge of water falling from the opposite ravine. It is said that this awful place was used in ancient days for the execution of women who had killed their children, and of men who had robbed the widow and the orphan.

Near the narrowest part of the peninsula a man was plunging along in the darkness, trusting solely to the sight of his pony, for his own eyes could see nothing. Two long hours he had been groping his way from the Mount of Laws, and he was still within one short mile of it. But at last he saw help at hand in his extremity, for a man on foot approached him out of the gloom. He took him for a farmer of those parts, and hailed him with hearty cheer.

"Good man," he said, "put me on the right path for Reykjavik, and you shall have five kroner, and welcome."

But scarcely had he spoken when he recognized the man he had met, and the man recognized him. The one was Jason, and the other Jorgen Jorgensen.

Jorgen Jorgensen thought his hour had come, for, putting his hand to his weapon, he remembered that he had not reloaded it since he had shot at Jason, and so he flung it away. But the old tiger was not to be subdued. "Come," he said, out of the black depths of his heart, "let us have done. What is it to be?"

Then Jason stepped back, and said, "That is the way to Reykjavik—over the stream and through the first chasm on the left."

At this, Jorgen Jorgensen seemed to catch his breath. He tried to speak and could not.

"No," said Jason. "It may be weakness, it may be folly, it may be madness, but you were my mother's father, God pity her and forgive you, and not even at the price of my brother's life will I have your blood on my hands. Go!"

Jorgen Jorgensen touched his horse and rode on, with his gray, dishonored head deep in his breast. And, evil man as he was, surely his cold heart was smitten with shame.

VI: The Gospel of Love

No Althing was held in Iceland in that year of the great eruption of Skaptar. The dread visitation lasted six long months, from the end of June to the beginning of January of the year following. During that time the people of the South and Southeast, who had been made homeless and penniless, were constantly trooping into Reykjavik in hundreds and tens of hundreds. The population of the capital rose from less than two thousand to more than twenty thousand. Where so many were housed no man ever knew, and how they lived none can say. Every hut, every hovel, every hole was full of human beings. Men, women, and children crawled like vermin in every quarter. For food, they had what fish came out of the sea, and when the frost covered the fiord a foot deep with ice, they starved on fish bones and and moss and seaweed.

By this time a cry for help had gone up throughout Europe, and Denmark and England had each sent a shipload of provisions, corn and meal and potatoes. The relief came late, the ships were caught in the ice, and held icebound a long month off Reykianess, and when at length the food for which the people famished was brought into Reykjavik harbor, the potatoes were like slabs of leather and the corn and meal like blocks of stone.

But even in this land of fire and frost, the Universal Mother is good to her children, and the people lived through their distresses. By the end of February they were trooping back to the scenes of their former homes, for, desolate as those places were, they loved them and clung to them still.

In the days of this awful calamity there were few that remembered Michael Sunlocks. Jorgen Jorgensen might have had his will of him then, and scarce anybody the wiser. That he held his hand was due first to fear and then to contempt; fear of Copenhagen, contempt of the man who had lost his influence over the people of Iceland. He was wrong on both counts. Copenhagen cared nothing for the life of Michael Sunlocks, and laughed at the revolution whereof he had been the head and centre. But when the people of Iceland recovered from the deadly visitation, their hearts turned back to the man who had suffered for their sakes.

Then it appeared that through these weary months Michael Sunlocks had been lying in the little house of detention at Reykjavik, with no man save one man, and that was old Adam Fairbrother, to raise a voice on his behalf, and no woman save one woman, and that was Greeba, to cling to him in his extremity. Neither of these had been allowed to come near to him, but both had been with him always. Again and again old Adam had forced his way to the Governor, and protested that Michael Sunlocks was not being treated as a prisoner, but as a condemned criminal and galley-slave; and again and again Greeba had come and gone between her lodgings at the house of the Bishop and her heart's home at the prison, with food and drink for him who lay in darkness and solitude. Little he knew to whom he was thus beholden, for she took pains to keep her secret, but all Reykjavik saw what she was doing. And the heart of Reykjavik was touched when she brought her child from Krisuvik, thinking no shame of her altered state, content to exist in simple poverty where she had once lived in wealth, if so be that she might but touch the walls that contained her husband.

Seeing how the sympathy was going, Jorgen Jorgensen set himself to consider what step to take, and finally concluded to remove Michael Sunlocks as far as possible from the place where his power was still great, and his temptation to use it was powerful. The remotest spot under his rule was Grimsey, an island lying on the Arctic circle, thirty-five miles from the mainland. It was small, it was sparsely populated, its inhabitants were fishermen with no craft but open row boats; it had no trade; no vessels touched at it, and the sea that separated it from Iceland was frozen during many months of the year. And to this island Jorgensen decided that Michael Sunlocks should go.

When the word was brought to Michael Sunlocks, he asked what he was expected to do on that little rock at the end of the world, and said that Grimsey would be his sentence of Jorgen death.

"I prefer to die, for I have no great reason to wish for life," he said; "but if I must live, let me live here. I am blind, I do not know the darkness of this place, and all I ask of you is air and water."

Old Adam, too, protested loudly, whereupon Jorgen Jorgensen answered with a smile that he had supposed that all he intended to do was for the benefit of the prisoner himself, who would surely prefer a whole island to live upon to being confined in a cell at Reykjavik.

"He will there have liberty to move about," said Jorgen, "and he will live under the protection of the Danish laws."

"Then that will be more than he has done here," said Adam, boldly, "where he has existed at the caprice of a Danish tyrant."

The people of Reykjavik heard of the banishment with surprise and anger, but nothing availed to prevent it. When the appointed day came, Michael Sunlocks was marched out of his prison and taken off towards the Bursting-sand desert between a line of guards. There was a great throng to bid adieu to him, and to groan at the power that sent him. His face was pale, but his bodily strength was good. His step was firm and steady, and gave hardly a hint of his blindness. His farewell of those who crowded upon him was simple and manly.

"Good-bye," he said, "and though with my eyes I cannot see you, I can see you with my heart, and that is the better sight whereof death alone can rob me. No doubt you have much to forgive to me; so forgive it to me now, for we shall meet no more."

There was many a sob at that word, but the two who would have been most touched by it were not there to hear it, for Greeba and old Adam were busy with their own enterprise, as we shall learn hereafter.

When Michael Sunlocks was landed at Grimsey, he was offered first as bondman for life, or prisoner-slave to the largest bonder there, a grasping old miser named Jonsson, who, like Jorgen himself, had never allowed his bad conscience to get the better of him. But Jonsson looked at Sunlocks with a curl of the lip and said, "What's the use of a blind man?" So the end of all was that Sunlocks was put in charge of the priest of the island. The priest was to take him into his house, to feed, clothe and attend to him, and report his condition twice a year to the Governor at Reykjavik. For such service to the State, the good man was to receive an annual stipend of one hundred kroner. And all arrangements being made, the escort that had brought Michael Sunlocks the ten days' journey over the desert, set their faces back towards the capital.

Michael Sunlocks was then on the edge of the habitable world. There was no attempt to confine him, for his home was an island bound by a rocky coast; he was blind and, therefore, helpless; and he could not step out a thousand yards alone without the danger of walking over a precipice into the sea. So that with all his brave show of liberty, he was as much in fetters as if his feet had been enchained to the earth beneath them.

The priest, who was in truth his jailer, was one who has already been heard of in this history, being no other than the Sigfus Thomsson (titled Sir from his cure of souls) who was banished from his chaplaincy at Reykjavik six and twenty years before for marrying Stephen Orry to Rachael, the daughter of the Governor-General Jorgensen. He had been young then, and since his life had been cut in twain he had fallen into some excesses. Thus it had often happened that when his people came to church over miles of their trackless country he had been too drunk to go through with it, and sometimes when they wished to make sure of him for a wedding or a christening, they had been compelled to decoy him into his house over night and lock him up until morning. Now he was elderly and lived alone, save for a fractious old man-servant, in a straggling old moss-covered house, or group of houses. He was weak of will, timid as a deer, and infirm of purpose, yet he was beloved by all men and pitied by all women for his sweet simplicity, whereof anyone might take advantage, and for the tenderness that could never resist a story of distress.

The coming of Michael Sunlocks startled him out of his tipsy sleep of a quarter of a century, and his whole household was put into a wild turmoil. In the midst of it, when he was at his wit's end to know what to do for his prisoner-guest, a woman, a stranger to Grimsey, carrying a child in her arms, presented herself at his door. She was young and comely, poorly but not meanly clad, and she offered herself to the priest as his servant. Her story was simple, touching, and plausible. She had lately lost her husband, an Icelander, though she herself was a foreigner, as her speech might tell. And hearing at Husavik that the priest of Grimsey was a lone old gentleman without kith or kin or belongings, she had bethought herself to come and say that she would be glad to take service from him for the sake of the home he might offer her.

It was Greeba, and simple old Sir Sigfus fell an easy prey to her woman's wit. He wiped his rheumy eyes while she told her story, and straightway sent her into the kitchen. Only one condition he made with her, and that was that she was to bear herself in his house as Iceland women bear themselves in the houses of Iceland masters. No more than that and no less. She was to keep to her own apartments and never allow herself to be seen or heard by a guest that was henceforth to live with him. That good man was blind, and would trouble her but little, for he had seen sorrow, poor soul, and was very silent.

Greeba consented to this with all earnestness, for it fell straight in the way of her own designs. But with a true woman's innocent duplicity she showed modesty and said "He shall never know that I'm in your house, sir, unless you tell him so yourself."

Thus did Greeba place herself under the same roof with Michael Sunlocks, and baffle discovery by the cunning of love. Two purposes were to be served by her artifice. First she was to be constantly by the side of her husband, to nurse him and tend him, to succor him, and to watch over him. Next, she was to be near him for her own sake, and for love's sake, to win him back to her some day by means more dear than those that had won him for her at the first. She had decided not to reveal herself to him in the meantime, for he had lost faith in her affection. He had charged her with marrying him for pride's sake, but he should see that she had married him for himself alone. The heart of his love was dead, but day by day, unknown, unseen, unheard, she would breathe upon it, until the fire in its ashes lived again. Such was the design with which Greeba took the place of a menial in the house where her husband lived as a prisoner, and little did she count the cost of it.

Six months passed, and she kept her promise to the priest to live as an Iceland servant in the house of an Iceland master. She was never seen, and never heard, and what personal service was called for was done by the snappish old man-servant. But she filled the old house, once so muggy and dark, with all the cheer and comfort of life. She knew that Michael Sunlocks felt the change, for one day she heard him say to the priest, as he lifted his blind face and seemed to look around, "One would think that this place must be full of sunshine."

"Why, and so it is," said the priest, "and that's my good housekeeper's doing."

"I have heard her step," said Michael Sunlocks. "Who is she?"

"A poor young woman that has lately lost her husband," said the priest.

"Young, you say?" said Sunlocks.

"Why, yes, young as I go," said the priest.

"Poor soul!" said Sunlocks.

It cost Greeba many a pang not to fling herself at her husband's feet at hearing that word so sadly spoken. But she remembered her promise and was silent. Not long afterwards she heard Michael Sunlocks ask the priest if he had never thought of marriage. And the priest answered yes, that he was to have married at Reykjavik about the time he was sent to Grimsey, but the lady had looked shy at his banishment and declined to share it.

"So I have never looked at a woman again," said the priest.

"And I daresay you have your tender thoughts of her, though so badly treated," said Sunlocks.

"Well, yes," said the priest, "yes."

"You were chaplain at Reykjavik, but looking to be priest or dean, and perhaps bishop some day?" said Sunlocks.

"Well, maybe so; such dreams come in one's youth," said the priest.

"And when you were sent to Grimsey there was nothing before you but a cure of less than a hundred souls?" said Sunlocks.

"That is so," said the priest.

"The old story," said Sunlocks, and he drew a deep breath.

But deeper far was the breath that Greeba drew, for it seemed to be the last gasp of her heart.

A year passed, and never once had Greeba spoken that her husband might hear her. But if she did not speak, she listened always, and the silence of her tongue seemed to make her ears the more keen. Thus she found a way to meet all his wishes, and before he had asked he was answered. If the day was cold he found gloves to his hand; if he thought to wash there was water beside him; if he wished to write the pen lay near his fingers. Meantime he never heard more than a light footfall and the rustle of a dress about him, but as these sounds awoke painful memories he listened and said nothing.

The summer had come and gone in which he could walk out by the priest's arm, or lie by the hour within sound of a stream, and the winter had fallen in with its short days and long nights. And once, when the snow lay thick on the ground, Greeba heard him say how cheerfully he might cheat time of many a weary hour of days like that if only he had a fiddle to beguile them. At that she remembered that it was not want of money that had placed her where she was, and before the spring of that year a little church organ came from Reykjavik, addressed to the priest, as a present from someone whose name was unknown to him.

"Some guardian angel seems to hover around us," said Michael Sunlocks, "to give us everything that we can wish for."

The joy in his blind face brought smiles into the face of Greeba, but her heart was heavy for all that. To live within hourly sight of love, yet never to share it, was to sit at a feast and eat nothing. To hear his voice, yet never to answer it, to see his face, yet never to touch it with the lips that hungered to kiss it, was an ordeal more terrible than any woman's heart could bear. Should she not speak? Might she not reveal herself? Not yet, not yet! But how long, oh, how long?

In the heat of her impatience she could not quite restrain herself, and though she dare not speak, she sang. It was on the Sunday after the organ came, when all the people at Grimsey were at church, in their strong odor of fish and sea fowl, to hear the strange new music. Michael Sunlocks played it, and when the people sang Greeba also joined them. Her voice was low at first, but she soon lost herself and then it rose above the other voices. Suddenly the organ stopped, and she was startled to see the blind face of her husband turning in her direction.

Later the same day she heard Sunlocks say to the priest, "Who was the lady who sang?"

"Why, that was my good housekeeper," said the priest.

"And did you say that she had lost her husband?" said Sunlocks.

"Yes, poor thing, and she is a foreigner, too," said the priest.

"Did you say a foreigner?" said Sunlocks.

"Yes, and she has a child left with her also," said the priest.

"A child?" said Sunlocks. And then after a pause he added, with more indifference, "Poor girl! poor girl!"

Hearing this, Greeba fluttered on the verge of discovering herself. "If only I could be sure," she thought, but she could not; and the more closely for the chance that had so nearly revealed her, she hid herself henceforward in the solitude of an Iceland servant.

Two years passed and then Greeba had to share her secret with another. That other was her own child. The little man was nearly three years old by this time, walking a little and talking a great deal, and not to be withheld by any care from going over every corner of the house. He found Michael Sunlocks sitting alone in his darkness, and the two struck up a fast friendship. They talked in baby fashion, and played on the floor for hours. With a wild thrill of the heart, Greeba saw those twain together, and it cost her all she had of patience and self-command not to break in upon them with a shower of rapturous kisses. But she held back her heart like a dog on the leash and listened, while her eyes rained tears and her lips smiled, to the words that passed between them.

"And what's your name, my sweet one?" said Sunlocks in English.

"Michael," lisped the little man.

"So? And an Englishman, too. That's brave."

"Ot's the name of your 'ickle boy?"

"Ah, I've got none, sweetheart."

"Oh."

"But if I had one perhaps his name would be Michael also."

"Oh."

The little eyes looked up into the blind face, and the little lip began to fall. Then, by a sudden impulse, the little legs clambered up to the knee of Sunlocks, and the little head nestled close against his breast.

"I'll be your 'ickle boy."

"So you shall, my sweet one, and you shall come again and sit with me, and sing to me, for I am very lonely sometimes, and your dear voice will cheer me."

But the little man had forgotten his trouble by this time, and scrambled back to the floor. There he sat on his haunches like a frog, and cried, "Look! look! look!" as he held up a white pebble in his dumpy hand.

"I cannot look, little one, for I am blind."

"Ot's blind?"

"Having eyes that cannot see, sweetheart."

"Oh."

"But your eyes can see, and if you are to be my little boy, my little Michael, your eyes shall see for my eyes also, and you shall come to me every day, and tell me when the sun is shining, and the sky is blue, and then we will go out together and listen for the birds that will be singing."

"Dat's nice," said the little fellow, looking down at the pebble in his palm, and just then the priest came into the house out of the snow.

"How comes it that this sweet little man and I have never met before?" said Sunlocks.

"You might live ten years in an Iceland house and never see the children of its servants," said the priest.

"I've heard his silvery voice, though," said Sunlocks. "What is the color of his eyes?"

"Blue," said the priest.

"Then his hair—this long curly hair—it must be of the color of the sun?" said Sunlocks.

"Flaxen," said the priest.

"Run along to your mother, sweetheart, run," said Sunlocks, and, dropping back in his seat, he murmured, "How easily he might have been my son indeed."

Kneeling on both knees, her hot face turned down and her parted lips quivering, Greeba had listened to all this with the old delicious trembling at both sides her heart. And going back to her own room, she caught sight of herself in the glass, and saw that her eyes were dancing like diamonds and all her cheeks a rosy red. Life, and a gleam of sunshine, seemed to have shot into her face in an instant, and while she looked there came over her a creeping thrill of delight, for she knew that she was beautiful. And because he loved beauty whose love was everything to her, she cried for joy, and picked up her boy, where he stood tugging at her gown, and kissed him rapturously.

The little man, with proper manly indifference to such endearments, wriggled back to the ground, and then Greeba remembered, with a flash that fell on her brain like a sword, that her husband was blind now, and all the beauty of the world was nothing to him. Smitten by this thought, she stood a moment, while the sunshine died out of her eyes and the rosy red out of her cheeks. But presently it came to her to ask herself if Sunlocks was blind forever, and if nothing could be done for him. This brought back, with pangs of remorse for such long forgetfulness, the memory of some man, an apothecary in Husavik, who had the credit of curing many of blindness after accidents in the northern mines where free men worked for wage. So, thinking of this apothecary throughout that day and the next, she found at last a crooked way to send money to him, out of the store that still remained to her, and to ask him to come to Grimsey.

But, waiting for the coming of the apothecary, a new dread, that was also a new hope, stole over her.

Since that first day on which her boy and her husband talked together, and every day thereafter when Sunlocks had called out "Little Michael! little Michael!" and she had sent the child in, with his little flaxen curls combed out, his little chubby face rubbed to a shiny red, and all his little body smelling sweet with the soft odors of childhood, she had noticed—she could not help it—that Sunlocks listened for the sound of her own footstep whenever by chance (which might have been rare) she passed his way.

And at first this was a cause of fear to her, lest he should discover her before her time came to reveal herself; and then of hope that he might even do so, and save her against her will from the sickening pains of hungry waiting; and finally of horror, that perhaps after all he was thinking of her as another woman. This last thought sent all the blood of her body tingling into her face, and on the day it flashed upon her, do what she would she could not but hate him for it as for an infidelity that might not be forgiven.

"He never speaks of me," she thought, "never thinks of me; I am dead to him; quite, quite dead and swept out of his mind."

It was a cruel conflict of love and hate, and if it had come to a man he would have said within himself, "By this token I know that she whom I love has forgotten me, and may be happy with another some day. Well, I am nothing—let me go my ways." But that is not the gospel of a woman's love, with all its sweet, delicious selfishness. So after Greeba had told herself once or twice that her husband had forgotten her, she told herself a score of times that do what he would he should yet be hers, hers only, and no other woman's in all the wide world. Then she thought, "How foolish! Who is there to take him from me? Why, no one."

About the same time she heard Sunlocks question the priest concerning her, asking what the mother of little Michael was like to look upon. And the priest answered that if the eyes of an old curmudgeon like himself could see straight, she was comely beyond her grade in life, and young, too, though her brown hair had sometimes a shade of gray, and gentle and silent, and of a soft and touching voice.

"I've heard her voice once," said Sunlocks. "And her husband was an Icelander, and he is dead, you say?"

"Yes," said the priest; "and she's like myself in one thing."

"And what is that?" said Sunlocks.

"That she has never been able to look at anybody else," said the priest. "And that's why she is here, you must know, burying herself alive on old Grimsey."

"Oh," said Sunlocks, in the low murmur of the blind, "if God had but given me this woman, so sweet, so true, so simple, instead of her—of her—and yet—and yet——"

"Gracious heavens!" thought Greeba, "he is falling in love with me."

At that, the hot flush overspread her cheeks again, and her dark eyes danced, and all her loveliness flowed back upon her in an instant. And then a subtle fancy, a daring scheme, a wild adventure broke on her heart and head, and made every nerve in her body quiver. She would let him go on; he should think she was the other woman; she would draw him on to love her, and one day when she held him fast and sure, and he was hers, hers, hers only forever and ever, she would open her arms and cry, "Sunlocks, Sunlocks, I am Greeba, Greeba!"

It was while she was in the first hot flush of this wild thought, never doubting but the frantic thing was possible, for love knows no impediments, that the apothecary came from Husavik, saying he was sent by some unknown correspondent named Adam Fairbrother, who had written from London. He examined the eyes of Michael Sunlocks by the daylight first, but the season being the winter season, and the daylight heavy with fog from off the sea, he asked for a candle, and Greeba was called to hold it while he examined the eyes again. Never before had she been so near to her husband throughout the two years that she had lived under the same roof with him, and now that she stood face to face with him, within sound of his very breathing, with nothing between them but the thin gray film that lay over his dear eyes, she could not persuade herself but that he was looking at her and seeing her. Then she began to tremble, and presently a voice said,

"Steadily, young woman, steadily, or your candle may fall on the good master's face."

She tried to compose herself, but could not, and when she had recovered from her first foolish dread, there came a fear that was not foolish—a fear of the verdict of the apothecary. Waiting for this in those minutes that seemed to be hours, she knew that she was on the verge of betraying herself, and however she held her breath she could see that her bosom was heaving.

"Yes," said the apothecary, calmly, "yes, I see no reason why you should not recover your sight."

"Thank God!" said Michael Sunlocks.

"Thank God again," said the priest.

And Greeba, who had dropped the candle to the floor at length, had to run from the room on the instant, lest the cry of her heart should straightway be the cry of her lips as well, "Thank God, again and again, forever and forever."

And, being back in her own apartment, she plucked up her child into her arms, and cried over him, and laughed over him, and whispered strange words of delight into his ear, mad words of love, wild words of hope.

"Yes, yes," she whispered, "he will recover his sight, and see his little son, and know him for his own, his own, his own. Oh, yes, yes, yes, he will know him, he will know him, for he will see his own face, his own dear face, in little Michael's."

But next day, when the apothecary had gone, leaving lotions and drops for use throughout a month, and promising to return at the end of it, Greeba's new joy made way for a new terror, as she reflected that just as Sunlocks would see little Michael if he recovered his sight, so he would see herself. At that thought all her heart was in her mouth again, for she told herself that if Sunlocks saw her he would also see what deception she had practiced in that house, and would hate her for it, and tell her, as he had told her once before, that it came of the leaven of her old lightness that had led her on from false-dealing to false-dealing, and so he would turn his back upon her or drive her from him.

Then in the cruel war of her feelings she hardly knew whether to hope that Sunlocks should recover his sight, or remain as he was. Her pity cried out for the one, and her love for the other. If he recovered, at least there would be light for him in his dungeon, though she might not be near to share it. But if he remained as he was, she would be beside him always, his second sight, his silent guardian spirit, eating her heart out with hungry love, but content and thanking God.

"Why couldn't I leave things as they were?" she asked herself, but she was startled out of the selfishness of her love by a great crisis that came soon afterwards.

Now Michael Sunlocks had been allowed but little intercourse with the world during the two and a half years of his imprisonment since the day of his recapture at the Mount of Laws. While in the prison at Reykjavik he had heard the pitiful story of that day; who his old yoke-fellow had been, what he had done and said, and how at last, when his brave scheme had tottered to ruin, he had gone out of the ken and knowledge of all men. Since Sunlocks came to Grimsey he had written once to Adam Fairbrother, asking tenderly after the old man's own condition, earnestly after Greeba's material welfare, and with deep affectionate solicitude for the last tidings of Jason. His letter never reached its destination, for the Governor of Iceland was the postmaster as well. And Adam on his part had written twice to Michael Sunlocks, once from Copenhagen where (when Greeba had left for Grimsey) he had gone by help of her money from Reykjavik, thinking to see the King of Denmark in his own person; and once from London, whereto he had followed on when that bold design had failed him. But Adam's letters shared the fate of the letter of Sunlocks, and thus through two long years no news of the world without had broken the silence of that lonely home on the rock of the Arctic seas.

But during that time there had been three unwritten communications from Jorgen Jorgensen. The first came after some six months in the shape of a Danish sloop of war, which took up its moorings in the roadstead outside; the second after a year, in the shape of a flagstaff and flag which were to be used twice a day for signalling to the ship that the prisoner was still in safe custody; the third after two years, in the shape of a huge lock and key, to be placed on some room in which the prisoner was henceforward to be confined. These three communications, marking in their contrary way the progress of old Adam's persistent suit, first in Denmark and then in England, were followed after a while by a fourth. This was a message from the Governor at Reykjavik to the old priest at Grimsey, that, as he valued his livelihood and life he was to keep close guard and watch over his prisoner, and, if need be, to warn him that a worse fate might come to him at any time.

Now, the evil hour when this final message came was just upon the good time when the apothecary from Husavik brought the joyful tidings that Sunlocks might recover his sight, and the blow was the heavier for the hope that had gone before it. All Grimsey shared both, for the fisherfolk had grown to like the pale stranger who, though so simple in speech and manner, had been a great man in some way that they scarcely knew—having no one to tell them, being so far out of the world—but had fallen upon humiliation and deep dishonor. Michael Sunlocks himself took the blow with composure, saying it was plainly his destiny and of a piece with the rest of his fate, wherein no good thing had ever come to him without an evil one coming on the back of it. The tender heart of the old priest was thrown into wild commotion, for Sunlocks had become, during the two years of their life together, as a son to him, a son that was as a father also, a stay and guardian, before whom his weakness—that of intemperance—stood rebuked.

But the trouble of old Sir Sigfus was as nothing to that of Greeba. In the message of the Governor she saw death, instant death, death without word or warning, and every hour of her life thereafter was beset with terrors. It was the month of February; and if the snow fell from the mossy eaves in heavy thuds, she thought it was the muffled tread of the guards who were to come for her husband; and if the ice-floes that swept down from Greenland cracked on the coast of Grimsey, she heard the shot that was to end his life. When Sunlocks talked of destiny she cried, and when the priest railed at Jorgen Jorgensen (having his own reason to hate him) she cursed the name of the tyrant. But all the while she had to cry without tears and curse only in the dark silence of her heart, though she was near to betraying herself a hundred times a day.

"Oh, it is cruel," she thought, "very, very cruel. Is this what I have waited for all this weary, weary time?"

And though so lately her love had fought with her pity to prove that it was best for both of them that Sunlocks should remain blind, she found it another disaster now, in the dear inconsistency of womanhood, that he should die on the eve of regaining his sight.

"He will never see his boy," she thought, "never, never, never now."

Yet she could hardly believe it true that the cruel chance could befall. What good would the death of Sunlocks do to anyone? What evil did it bring to any creature that he was alive on that rock at the farthest ends of the earth and sea? Blind, too, and helpless, degraded from his high place, his young life wrecked, and his noble gifts wasted! There must have been some mistake. She would go out to the ship and ask if it was not so.

And with such wild thoughts she hurried off to the little village at the edge of the bay. There she stood a long hour by the fisherman's jetty, looking wistfully out to where the sloop of war lay, like a big wooden tub, be-between gloomy sea and gloomy sky, and her spirit failed her, and though she had borrowed a boat she could go no further.

"They might laugh at me, and make a jest of me," she thought, "for I cannot tell them that I am his wife."

With that, she went her way back as she came, crying on the good powers above to tell her what to do next, and where to look for help. And entering in at the porch of her own apartments, which stood aside from the body of the house, she heard voices within, and stopped to listen. At first she thought they were the voices of her child and her husband; but though one of them was that of little Michael, the other was too deep, too strong, too sad for the voice of Sunlocks.

"And so your name is Michael, my brave boy. Michael! Michael!" said the voice, and it was strange and yet familiar. "And how like you are to your mother, too! How like! How very like!" And the voice seemed to break in the speaker's throat.

Greeba grew dizzy, and stumbled forward. And, as she entered the house, a man rose from the settle, put little Michael to the ground, and faced about to her. The man was Jason.

VII: The Gospel of Renunciation

I.

What had happened in the great world during the two years in which Michael Sunlocks had been out of it is very simple and easily told. Old Adam Fairbrother had failed at London as he had failed at Copenhagen, and all the good that had come of his efforts had ended in evil. It was then that accident helped him in his despair.

The relations of England and Denmark had long been doubtful, for France seemed to be stepping between them. Napoleon was getting together a combination of powers against England, and in order to coerce Denmark into using her navy—a small but efficient one—on the side of the alliance, he threatened to send a force overland. He counted without the resources of Nelson, who, with no more ado than setting sail, got across to Copenhagen, took possession of every ship of war that lay in Danish waters, and brought them home to England in a troop.

When Adam heard of this he saw his opportunity in a moment, and hurrying away to Nelson at Spithead he asked if among the Danish ships that had been captured there was a sloop of war that had lain near two years off the island of Grimsey. Nelson answered, No, but that if there was such a vessel still at liberty he was not of a mind to leave it to harass him. So Adam told why the sloop was there, and Nelson, waiting for no further instructions, despatched an English man-of-war, with Adam aboard of her, to do for the last of the Danish fleet what had been done for the body of it, and at the same time to recover the English prisoner whom she had been sent to watch.

Before anything was known of this final step of Nelson, his former proceeding had made a great noise throughout Europe, where it was loudly condemned as against the law of nations, by the rascals who found themselves outwitted. When the report reached Reykjavik, Jorgen Jorgensen saw nothing that could come of it but instant war between Denmark and England, and nothing that could come of war with England but disaster to Denmark, for he knew the English navy of old. So to make doubly sure of his own position in a tumult wherein little things would of a certainty be seized up with great ones, he conceived the idea of putting Michael Sunlocks out of the way, and thus settling one harassing complication. Then losing no time he made ready a despatch to the officer in command of the sloop of war off Grimsey, ordering him to send a company of men ashore immediately to execute the prisoner lying in charge of the priest of the island.

Now this despatch, whereof the contents became known throughout Reykjavik in less time than Jorgen took to write and seal it, had to be carried to Grimsey by two of his bodyguard. But the men were Danes, and as they did not know the way across the Bursting-sand desert, an Iceland guide had to be found for them. To this end the two taverns of the town were beaten up for a man, who at that season—it was winter, and the snow lay thick over the lava streams and the sand—would adventure so far from home.

And now it was just at this time, after two-and-a-half years in which no man had seen him or heard of him, that Jason returned to Reykjavik. Scarce anyone knew him. He was the wreck of himself, a worn, torn, pitiful, broken ruin of a man. People lifted both hands at sight of him, but he showed no self-pity. Day after day, night after night, he frequented the taverns. He drank as he had never before been known to drink; he laughed as he had never been heard to laugh; he sang as he had never been heard to sing, and to all outward appearance he was nothing now but a shameless, graceless, disorderly, abandoned profligate.

Jorgen Jorgensen heard that Jason had returned, and ordered his people to fetch him to Government House. They did so, and Jorgen and Jason stood face to face. Jorgen looked at Jason as one who would say, "Dare you forget the two men whose lives you have taken?" And Jason looked back at Jorgen as one who would answer, "Dare you remember that I spared your own life?" Then, without a word to Jason, old Jorgen turned to his people and said, "Take him away." So Jason went back to his dissipations, and thereafter no man said yea or nay to him.

But when he heard of the despatch, he was sobered by it in a moment, and when the guards came on their search for a guide to the tavern where he was, he leapt to his feet and said, "I'll go."

"You won't pass, my lad," said one of the Danes, "for you would be dead drunk before you crossed the Basket Slope Hill."

"Would I?" said Jason, moodily, "who knows?" And with that he shambled out. But in his heart he cried, "The hour has come at last! Thank God! Thank God!"

Before he was missed he had gone from Reykjavik, and made his way to the desert with his face towards Grimsey.

The next day the guards found their guide and set out on their journey.

The day after that a Danish captain arrived at Reykjavik from Copenhagen, and reported to Jorgen Jorgensen that off the Westmann Islands he had sighted a British man-of-war, making for the northern shores of Iceland. This news put Jorgen into extreme agitation, for he guessed at its meaning in an instant. As surely as the war ship was afloat she was bound for Grimsey, to capture the sloop that lay there, and as surely as England knew of the sloop, she also knew of the prisoner whom it was sent to watch. British sea-captains, from Drake downwards, had been a race of pirates and cut-throats, and if the captain of this ship, on landing at Grimsey, found Michael Sunlocks dead, he would follow on to Reykjavik and never take rest until he had strung up the Governor and his people to the nearest yardarm.

So thinking in the wild turmoil of his hot old head, wherein everything he had thought before was turned topsy-turvy, Jorgen Jorgensen decided to countermand his order for the execution of Sunlocks. But his despatch was then a day gone on its way. Iceland guides were a tribe of lazy vagabonds, not a man or boy about his person was to be trusted, and so Jorgen concluded that nothing would serve but that he should set out after the guards himself. Perhaps he would find them at Thingvellir, perhaps he would cross them on the desert, but at least he would overtake them before they took boat at Husavik. Twelve hours a day he would ride, old as he was, if only these skulking Iceland giants could be made to ride after him.

Thus were four several companies at the same time on their way to Grimsey: the English man-of-war from Spithead to take possession of the Danish sloop; the guards of the Governor to order the execution of Michael Sunlocks; Jorgen Jorgensen to countermand the order; and Red Jason on his own errand known to no man.

The first to reach was Jason.

II.

When Jason set little Michael from his knee to the floor, and rose to his feet as Greeba entered, he was dirty, bedraggled, and unkempt; his face was jaded and old-looking, his skin shoes were splashed with snow, and torn, and his feet were bleeding; his neck was bare, and his sheepskin coat was hanging to his back only by the woollen scarf that was tied about his waist. Partly from shock at this change, and partly from a confused memory of other scenes—the marriage festival at Government House, the night trial in the little chamber of the Senate, the jail, the mines, and the Mount of Laws—Greeba staggered at sight of Jason and would have cried aloud and fallen. But he caught her in his arms in a moment, and whispered her in a low voice at her ear to be silent, for that he had something to say that must be heard by no one beside herself.

She recovered herself instantly, drew back as if his touch had stung her, and asked with a look of dread if he had known she was there.

"Yes," he answered.

"Where have you come from?"

"Reykjavik."

She glanced down at his bleeding feet, and said, "on foot?"

"On foot," he answered.

"When did you leave?"

"Five days ago."

"Then you have walked night and day across the desert?"

"Night and day."

"Alone?"

"Yes, alone."

She had become more eager at every question, and now she cried, "What has happened? What is going to happen? Do not keep it from me. I can bear it, for I have borne many things. Tell me why have you come?"

"To save your husband," said Jason. "Hush! Listen!"

And then he told her, with many gentle protests against her ghastly looks of fear, of the guards that were coming with the order for the execution of Michael Sunlocks. Hearing that, she waited for no more, but fell to a great outburst of weeping. And until her bout was spent he stood silent and helpless beside her, with a strong man's pains at sight of a woman's tears.

"How she loves him!" he thought, and again and again the word rang in the empty place of his heart.

But when she had recovered herself he smiled as well as he was able for the great drops that still rolled down his own haggard face, and protested once more that there was nothing to fear, for he himself had come to forestall the danger, and things were not yet so far past help but there was still a way to compass it.

"What way?" she asked.

"The way of escape," he answered.

"Impossible," she said. "There is a war ship outside, and every path to the shore is watched."

He laughed at that, and said that if every goat track were guarded, yet would he make his way to the sea. And as for the war ship outside, there was a boat within the harbor, the same that he had come by, a Shetland smack that had made pretence to put in for haddock, and would sail at any moment that he gave it warning.

She listened eagerly, and, though she saw but little likelihood of escape, she clutched at the chance of it.

"When will you make the attempt?" she asked.

"Two hours before dawn to-morrow," he answered.

"Why so late?"

"Because the nights are moonlight."

"I'll be ready," she whispered.

"Make the child ready, also," he said.

"Indeed, yes," she whispered.

"Say nothing to anyone, and if anyone questions you, answer as little as you may. Whatever you hear, whatever you see, whatever I may do or pretend to do, speak not a word, give not a sign, change not a feature. Do you promise?"

"Yes," she whispered, "yes, yes."

And then suddenly a new thought smote her.

"But, Jason," she said, with her eyes aside, and her fingers running through the hair of little Michael, "but, Jason," she faltered, "you will not betray me?"

"Betray you?" he said, and laughed a little.

"Because," she added quietly, "though I am here, my husband does not know me for his wife. He is blind, and cannot see me, and for my own reasons I have never spoken to him since I came."

"You have never spoken to him?" said Jason.

294

"Never."

"And how long have you lived in this house?"

"Two years."

Then Jason remembered what Sunlocks had told him at the mines, and in another moment he had read Greeba's secret by the light of his own.

"I understand," he said, sadly, "I think I understand."

She caught the look of sorrow in his eyes, and said, "But, Jason, what of yourself?"

At that he laughed again, and tried to carry himself off with a brave gayety.

"Where have you been?" she asked.

"At Akureyri, Husavik, Reykjavik, the desert—everywhere, nowhere," he answered.

"What have you been doing?"

"Drinking, gaming, going to the devil—everything, nothing."

And at that he laughed once more, loudly and noisily, forgetting his own warning.

"Jason," said Greeba, "I wronged you once, and you have done nothing since but heap coals of fire on my head."

"No, no; you never wronged me," he said. "I was a fool—that was all. I made myself think that I cared for you. But it's all over now."

"Jason," she said again, "it was not altogether my fault. My husband was everything to me; but another woman might have loved you and made you happy."

"Ay, ay," he said, "another woman, another woman."

"Somewhere or other she waits for you," said Greeba. "Depend on that."

"Ay, somewhere or other," he said.

"So don't lose heart, Jason," she said; "don't lose heart."

"I don't," he said, "not I;" and yet again he laughed. But, growing serious in a moment, he said, "And did you leave home and kindred and come out to this desolate place only that you might live under the same roof with your husband?"

"My home was his home," said Greeba, "my kindred his kindred, and where he was there had I to be."

"And have you waited through these two long years," he said, "for the day and the hour when you might reveal yourself to him?"

"I could have waited for my husband," said Greeba, "through twice the seven long years that Jacob waited for Rachel."

He paused a moment, and then said, "No, no, I don't lose heart. Somewhere or other, somewhere or other—that's the way of it." Then he laughed louder than ever, and every hollow note of his voice went through Greeba like a knife. But in the empty chamber of his heart he was crying in his despair, "My God! how she loves him! How she loves him!"

III.

Half-an-hour later, when the winter's day was done, and the candles had been lighted, Greeba went in to the priest, where he sat in his room alone, to say that a stranger was asking to see him.

"Bring the stranger in," said the priest, putting down his spectacles on his open book, and then Jason entered.

"Sir Sigfus," said Jason, "your good name has been known to me ever since the days when my poor mother mentioned it with gratitude and tears."

"Your mother?" said the priest; "who was she?"

"Rachel Jorgen's daughter, wife of Stephen Orry."

"Then you must be Jason."

"Yes, your reverence."

"My lad, my good lad," cried the priest, and with a look of joy he rose and laid hold of both Jason's hands. "I have heard of you. I hear of you every day, for your brother is with me. Come, let us go to him. Let us go to him. Come!"

"Wait," said Jason. "First let me deliver you a message concerning him."

The old priest's radiant face fell instantly to a deep sadness. "A message?" he said. "You have never come from Jorgen Jorgensen?"

"No."

"From whom, then?"

"My brother's wife," said Jason.

"His wife?"

"Has he never spoken of her?"

"Yes, but as one who had injured him, and bitterly and cruelly wronged and betrayed him."

"That may be so, your reverence," said Jason, "but who can be hard on the penitent and the dying?"

"Is she dying?" said the priest.

Jason dropped his head. "She sends for his forgiveness," he said. "She cannot die without it."

"Poor soul, poor soul!" said the priest.

"Whatever her faults, he cannot deny her that little mercy," said Jason.

"God forbid it!" said the priest.

"She is alone in her misery, with none to help and none to pity her," said Jason.

"Where is she?" said the priest.

"At Husavik," said Jason.

"But what is her message to me?"

"That you should allow her husband to come to her."

The old priest lifted his hands in helpless bewilderment, but Jason gave him no time to speak.

"Only for a day," said Jason, quickly, "only for one day, an hour, one little hour. Wait, your reverence, do not say no. Think, only think! The poor woman is alone. Let her sins be what they may, she is penitent. She is calling for her husband. She is calling on you to send him. It is her last request—her last prayer. Grant it, and heaven will bless you."

The poor old priest was cruelly distressed.

"My good lad," he cried, "it is impossible. There is a ship outside to watch us. Twice a day I have to signal with the flag that the prisoner is safe, and twice a day the bell of the vessel answers me. It is impossible, I say, impossible, impossible! It cannot be done. There is no way."

"Leave it to me, and I will find a way," said Jason.

But the old priest only wrung his hands, and cried, "I dare not; I must not; it is more than my place is worth."

"He will come back," said Jason.

"Only last week," said the priest, "I had a message from Reykjavik which foreshadowed his death. He knows it, we all know it."

"But he will come back," said Jason, again.

"My good lad, how can you say so? Where have you lived to think it possible? Once free of the place where the shadow of death hangs over him, what man alive would return to it."

"He will come back," said Jason, firmly; "I know he will, I swear he will."

"No, no," said the old man. "I'm only a simple old priest, buried alive these thirty years, or nearly, on this lonely island of the frozen seas, but I know better than that. It isn't in human nature, my good lad, and no man that breathes can do it. Then think of me, think of me!"

"I do think of you," said Jason, "and to show you how sure I am that he will come back, I will make you an offer."

"What is it?" said the priest.

"To stand as your bondman while he is away," said Jason.

"What! Do you know what you are saying?" cried the priest.

"Yes," said Jason, "for I came to say it."

"Do you know," said the priest, "that any day, at any hour, the sailors from yonder ship may come to execute my poor prisoner?"

"I do. But what of that?" said Jason. "Have they ever been here before?"

"Never," said the priest.

"Do they know your prisoner from another man?"

"No."

"Then where is your risk?" said Jason.

"My risk? Mine?" cried the priest, with the great drops bursting from his eyes, "I was thinking of yours. My lad, my good lad, you have made me ashamed. If you dare risk your life, I dare risk my place, and I'll do it; I'll do it."

"God bless you!" said Jason.

"And now let us go to him," said the priest. "He is in yonder room, poor soul. When the order came from Reykjavik that I was to keep close guard and watch on him, nothing would satisfy him but that I should turn the key on him. That was out of fear for me. He is as brave as a lion, and as gentle as a lamb. Come, the sooner he hears his wife's message the better for all of us. It will be a sad blow to him, badly as she treated him. But come!"

So saying, the old priest was fumbling his deep pockets for a key, and shuffling along, candle in hand, towards a door at the end of a low passage, when Jason laid hold of his arm and said in a whisper, "Wait! It isn't fair that I should let you go farther in this matter. You should be ignorant of what we are doing until it is done."

"As you will," said the priest.

"Can you trust me?" said Jason.

"That I can."

"Then give me the key."

The old man gave it.

"When do you make your next signal?"

"At daybreak to-morrow."

"And when does the bell on the ship answer it?"

"Immediately."

"Go to your room, your reverence," said Jason, "and never stir out of it until you hear the ship's bell in the morning. Then come here, and you will find me waiting on this spot to return this key to you. But first answer me again, Do you trust me?"

"I do," said the old priest.

"You believe I will keep to my bargain, come what may?"

"I believe you will keep to it."

"And so I will, as sure as God's above me."

IV.

Jason opened the door and entered the room. It was quite dark, save for a dull red fire of dry moss that burned on the hearth in one corner. By this little fire Michael Sunlocks sat, with only his sad face visible in the gloom. His long thin hands were clasped about one knee which was half-raised; his noble head was held down, and his flaxen hair fell across his cheeks to his shoulders.

He had heard the key turn in the lock, and said quietly, "Is that you, Sir Sigfus?"

"No," said Jason.

"Who is it?" said Sunlocks.

"A friend," said Jason.

Sunlocks twisted about as though his blind eyes could see. "Whose voice was that?" he said, with a tremor in his own.

"A brother's," said Jason.

Sunlocks rose to his feet. "Jason?" he cried,

"Yes, Jason."

"Come to me! Come! Where are you? Let me touch you," cried Sunlocks, stretching out both his hands.

Then they fell into each other's arms, and laughed and wept for joy. After a while Jason said,—

"Sunlocks, I have brought you a message."

"Not from her, Jason?—no."

"No, not from her—from dear old Adam Fairbrother," said Jason.

"Were is he?"

"At Husavik."

"Why did you not bring him with you?"

"He could not come."

"Jason, is he ill?"

"He has crossed the desert to see you, but he can go no further."

"Jason, tell me, is he dying?"

"The good old man is calling on you night and day, 'Sunlocks!' he is crying. 'Sunlocks! my boy, my son. Sunlocks! Sunlocks!'"

"My dear father, my other father, God bless him!"

"He says he has crossed the seas to find you, and cannot die without seeing you again. And though he knows you are here, yet in his pain and trouble he forgets it, and cries, 'Come to me, my son, my Sunlocks.'"

"Now, this is the hardest lot of all," said Sunlocks, and he cast himself down on his chair. "Oh, these blind eyes! Oh, this cruel prison! Oh, for one day of freedom! Only one day, one poor simple day!"

And so he wept, and bemoaned his bitter fate.

Jason stood over him with many pains and misgivings at sight of the distress he had created. And if the eye of heaven saw Jason there, surely the suffering in his face atoned for the lie on his tongue.

"Hush, Sunlocks, hush!" he said, in a tremulous whisper. "You can have the day you wish for; and if you cannot see, there are others to lead you. Yes, it is true, it is true, for I have settled it. It is all arranged, and you are to leave this place to-morrow."

Hearing this, Michael Sunlocks made first a cry of delight, and then said after a moment, "But what of this poor old priest?"

"He is a good man, and willing to let you go," said Jason.

"But he has had warning that I may be wanted at any time," said Sunlocks, "and though his house is a prison, he has made it a home, and I would not do him a wrong to save my life."

"He knows that," said Jason, "and he says that you will come back to him though death itself should be waiting to receive you."

"He is right," said Sunlocks; "and no disaster save this one could take me from him to his peril. The good old soul! Come, let me thank him." And with that he was making for the door.

But Jason stepped between, and said, "Nay, it isn't fair to the good priest that we should make him a party to our enterprise. I have told him all that he need know, and he is content. Now, let him be ignorant of what we are doing until it is done. Then if anything happens it will appear that you have escaped."

"But I am coming back," said Sunlocks.

"Yes, yes," said Jason, "but listen. To-morrow morning, two hours before daybreak, you will go down to the bay. There is a small boat lying by the little jetty, and a fishing smack at anchor about a biscuit-throw farther out. The good woman who is housekeeper here will lead you——"

"Why she?" interrupted Sunlocks.

Jason paused, and said, "Have you anything against her?"

"No indeed," said Sunlocks. "A good, true woman. One who lately lost her husband, and at the same time all the cheer and hope of life. Simple and sweet, and silent, and with a voice that recalls another who was once very near and dear to me."

"Is she not so still?" said Jason.

"God knows. I scarce can tell. Sometimes I think she is dearer to me than ever, and now that I am blind I seem to see her near me always. It is only a dream, a foolish dream."

"But what if the dream came true?" said Jason.

"That cannot be," said Sunlocks. "Yet where is she? What has become of her? Is she with her father? What is she doing?"

"You shall soon know now," said Jason. "Only ask to-morrow and this good woman will take you to her."

"But why not you yourself, Jason?" said Sunlocks.

"Because I am to stay here until you return," said Jason.

"What?" cried Sunlocks. "You are to stay here?"

"Yes," said Jason.

"As bondman to the law instead of me? Is that it? Speak!" cried Sunlocks.

"And why not?" said Jason, calmly.

There was silence for a moment. Sunlocks felt about with his helpless hands until he touched Jason and then he fell sobbing upon his neck.

"Jason, Jason," he cried, "this is more than a brother's love. Ah, you do not know the risk you would run; but I know it, and I must not keep it from you. Any day, any hour, a despatch may come to the ship outside to order that I should be shot. Suppose I were to go to the dear soul who calls for me, and the despatch came in my absence—where would you be then?"

"I should be here," said Jason, simply.

"My lad, my brave lad," cried Sunlocks, "what are you saying? If you cannot think for yourself, then think for me. If what I have said were to occur, should I ever know another moment's happiness? No, never, never, though I regained my sight, as they say I may, and my place and my friends—all save one—and lived a hundred years."

Jason started at that thought, but there was no one to look upon his face under the force of it, and he wriggled with it and threw it off.

"But you will come back," he said. "If the despatch comes while you are away, I will say that you are coming, and you will come."

"I may never come back," said Sunlocks. "Only think, my lad. This is winter, and we are on the verge of the Arctic seas, with five and thirty miles of water dividing us from the mainland. He would be a bold man who would count for a day on whether in which a little fishing smack could live. And a storm might come up and keep me back."

"The same storm that would keep you back," said Jason, "would keep back the despatch. But why hunt after these chances? Have you any reason to fear that the despatch will come to-day, or to-morrow, or the next day? No, you have none. Then go, and for form's sake—just that, no more, no less—let me wait here until you return."

There was another moment's silence, and then Sunlocks said, "Is that the condition of my going?"

"Yes," said Jason.

"Did this old priest impose it?" asked Sunlocks.

Jason hesitated a moment, and answered, "Yes."

"Then I won't go," said Sunlocks, stoutly.

"If you don't," said Jason, "you will break poor old Adam's heart, for I myself will tell him that you might have come to him, and would not."

"Will you tell him why I would not?" said Sunlocks.

"No," said Jason.

There was a pause, and then Jason said, very tenderly, "Will you go, Sunlocks?"

And Sunlocks answered, "Yes."

V.

Jason slept on the form over against the narrow wooden bed of Michael Sunlocks. He lay down at midnight, and awoke four hours later. Then he stepped to the door and looked out. The night was calm and beautiful; the moon was shining, and the little world of Grimsey slept white and quiet under its coverlet of snow. Snow on the roof, snow in the valley, snow on the mountains so clear against the sky and the stars; no wind, no breeze, no sound on earth and in air save the steady chime of the sea below.

It was too early yet, and Jason went back into the house. He did not lie down again lest he should oversleep himself, but sat on his form and waited. All was silent in the home of the priest. Jason could hear nothing but the steady breathing of Sunlocks as he slept.

After awhile it began to snow, and then the moon went out, and the night became very dark.

"Now is the time," thought Jason, and after hanging a sheepskin over the little skin-covered window, he lit a candle and awakened Sunlocks.

Sunlocks rose and dressed himself without much speaking, and sometimes he sighed like a down-hearted man. But Jason rattled on with idle talk, and kindled a fire and made some coffee. And when this was done he stumbled his way through the long passages of the Iceland house until he came upon Greeba's room, and there he knocked softly, and she answered him.

She was ready, for she had not been to bed, and about her shoulders and across her breast was a sling of sheepskin, wherein she meant to carry her little Michael as he slept.

"All is ready," he whispered. "He says he may recover his sight. Can it be true?"

"Yes, the apothecary from Husavik said so," she answered.

"Then have no fear. Tell him who you are, for he loves you still."

And, hearing that, Greeba began to cry for joy, and to thank God that the days of her waiting were over at last.

"Two years I have lived alone," she said, "in the solitude of a loveless life and the death of a heartless home. My love has been silent all this weary, weary time, but it is to be silent no longer. At last! At last! My hour has come at last! My husband will forgive me for the deception I have practiced upon him. How can he hate me for loving him to all lengths and ends of love? Oh, that the blessed spirit that counts the throbbings of the heart would but count my life from to-day—to-day, to-day, to-day—wiping out all that is past, and leaving only the white page of what is to come."

Then from crying she fell to laughing, as softly and as gently, as if her heart grudged her voice the joy of it. She was like a child who is to wear a new feather on the morrow, and is counting the minutes until that morrow comes, too impatient to rest, and afraid to sleep lest she should awake too late. And Jason stood aside and heard both her weeping and her laughter.

He went back to Sunlocks, and found him yet more sad than before.

"Only to think," said Sunlocks, "that you, whom I thought my worst enemy, you that once followed me to slay me, should be the man of all men to risk your life for me."

"Yes, life is a fine lottery, isn't it?" said Jason, and he laughed.

"How the Almighty God tears our little passions to tatters," said Sunlocks, "and works His own ends in spite of them."

When all was ready, Jason blew out the candle, and led Sunlocks to the porch. Greeba was there, with little Michael breathing softly from the sling at her breast.

Jason opened the door. "It's very dark," he whispered, "and it is still two hours before the dawn. Sunlocks, if you had your sight already, you could not see one step before you. So give your hand to this good woman, and whatever happens hereafter never, never let it go."

And with that he joined their hands.

"Does she know my way?" said Sunlocks.

"She knows the way for both of you," said Jason. "And now go. Down at the jetty you will find two men waiting for you. Stop! Have you any money?"

"Yes," said Greeba.

"Give some to the men," said Jason. "Good-bye. I promised them a hundred kroner. Good-bye! Tell them to drop down the bay as silently as they can. Good-bye!"

"Good-bye!"

"Come," said Greeba, and she drew at the hand of Sunlocks.

"Good-bye! Good-bye!" said Jason.

But Sunlocks held back a moment, and then in a voice that faltered and broke he said, "Jason—kiss me."

At the next moment they were gone into the darkness and the falling snow—Sunlocks and Greeba, hand in hand, and their child asleep at its mother's bosom.

Jason stood a long hour at the open door, and listened. He heard the footsteps die away; he heard the creak of the crazy wooden jetty; he heard the light plash of the oars as the boat moved off; he heard the clank of the chain as the anchor was lifted; he heard the oars again as the little smack moved down the bay, and not another sound came to his ear through the silence of the night.

He looked across the headland to where the sloop of war lay outside, and he saw her lights, and their two white waterways, like pillars of silver, over the sea. All was quiet about her.

Still he stood and listened until the last faint sound of the oars had gone. By this time a woolly light had begun to creep over the mountain tops, and a light breeze came down from them.

"It is the dawn," thought Jason. "They are safe."

He went back into the house, pulled down the sheepskin from the window, and lit the candle again. After a search he found paper and pens and wax in a cupboard and sat down to write. His hand was hard, he had never been to school, and he could barely form the letters and spell the words. This was what he wrote:

"Whatever you hear, fear not for me. I have escaped, and am safe. But don't expect to see me. I can never rejoin you, for I dare not be seen. And you are going back to your beautiful island, but dear old Iceland is the only place for me. Greeba, good-bye; I shall never lose heart. Sunlocks, she has loved you, you only, all the days of her life. Good-bye. I am well and happy. God bless you both."

Having written and sealed this letter, he marked it with a cross for superscription, touched it with his lips, laid it back on the table and put a key on top of it. Then he rested his head on his hands, and for some minutes afterwards he was lost to himself in thought. "They would tell him to lie down," he thought, "and now he must be asleep. When he awakes he will be out at sea, far out, and all sail set. Before long he will find that he has been betrayed, and demand to be brought back. But they will not heed his anger, for she will have talked with them. Next week or the week after they will put in at Shetlands, and there he will get my letter. Then his face will brighten with joy, and he will cry, 'To home! To Home!' And then—even then— why not?—his sight will come back to him, and he will open his eyes and find his dream come true, and her own dear face looking up at him. At that he will cry, 'Greeba, Greeba, my Greeba,' and she will fall into his arms and he will pluck her to his breast. Then the wind will come sweeping down from the North Sea, and belly out the sail until it sings and the ropes crack and the blocks creak. And the good ship will fly along the waters like a bird to the home of the sun. Home! Home! England! England, and the little green island of her sea!"

"God bless them both," he said aloud, in a voice like a sob, but he leapt to his feet, unable to bear the flow of his thoughts. He put back the paper and pens into the cupboard, and while he was doing so he came upon a bottle of brenni-vin. He took it out and laughed, and drew the cork to take a draught. But he put it down on the table untouched. "Not yet," he said to himself, and then he stepped to the door and opened it.

The snow had ceased to fall and the day was breaking. Great shivering waifs of vapor crept along the mountain sides, and the valley was veiled in mist. But the sea was clear and peaceful, and the sloop of war lay on its dark bosom as before.

"Now for the signal," thought Jason.

In less than a minute afterwards the flag was floating from the flagstaff, and Jason stood waiting for the ship's answer. It came in due course, a clear-toned bell that rang out over the quiet waters and echoed across the land.

"It's done," thought Jason, and he went back into the house. Lifting up the brenni-vin, he took a long draught of it, and laughed as he did so. Then a longer draught, and laughed yet louder. Still another draught, and another, and another, until the bottle was emptied, and he flung it on the floor.

After that he picked up the key and the letter, and shambled out into the passage, laughing as he went.

"Where are you now, old mole?" he shouted, and again he shouted, until the little house rang with his thick voice and his peals of wild laughter.

The old priest came out of his room in his nightshirt with a lighted candle in his hand.

"God bless me, what's this?" said the old man.

"What's this? Why, your bondman, your bondman, and the key, the key," shouted Jason, and he laughed once more. "Did you think you would never see it again? Did you think I would run away and leave you? Not I, old mole, not I."

"Has he gone?" said the priest, glancing fearfully into the room.

"Gone? Why, yes, of course he has gone," laughed Jason. "They have both gone."

"Both!" said the priest, looking up inquiringly, and at sight of his face Jason laughed louder than ever.

"So you didn't see it, old mole?"

"See what?"

"That she was his wife?"

"His wife? Who?"

"Why, your housekeeper, as you called her."

"God bless my soul! And when are they coming back?"

"They are never coming back."

"Never?"

"I have taken care that they never can."

"Dear me! dear me! What does it all mean?"

"It means that the despatch is on its way from Reykjavik, and will be here to-day. Ha! ha! ha!"

"To-day? God save us! And do you intend—no, it cannot be—and yet—do you intend to die instead of him?"

"Well, and what of that? It's nothing to you, is it? And as for myself, there are old scores against me, and if death had not come to me soon, I should have gone to it."

"I'll not stand by and witness it."

"You will, you shall, you must. And listen—here is a letter. It is for him. Address it to her by the first ship to the Shetlands. The Thora, Shetlands—that will do. And now bring me some more of your brenni-vin, you good old soul, for I am going to take a sleep at last—a long sleep—a long, long sleep at last."

"God pity you! God help you! God bless you!"

"Ay, ay, pray to your God. But I'll not pray to him. He doesn't make His world for wretches like me. I'm a pagan, am I? So be it! Good-night, you dear old mole! Good-night! I'll keep to my bargain, never fear. Good-night. Never mind your brenni-vin, I'll sleep without it. Good-night! Good-night!"

Saying this, amid broken peals of unearthly laughter, Jason reeled back into the room, and clashed the door after him. The old priest, left alone in the passage, dropped the foolish candle, and wrung his hands. Then he listened at the door a moment. The unearthly laughter ceased and a burst of weeping followed it.

VI.

It was on the day after that the evil work was done. The despatch had arrived, a day's warning had been given, and four sailors, armed with muskets, had come ashore.

It was early morning, and not a soul in Grimsey who had known Michael Sunlocks was there to see. Only Sir Sigfus knew the secret, and he dare not speak. To save Jason from the death that waited for him would be to put himself in Jason's place.

The sailors drew up in a line on a piece of flat ground in front of the house whereon the snow was trodden hard. Jason came out looking strong and content. His step was firm, and his face was defiant. Fate had dogged him all his days. Only in one place, only in one hour, could he meet and beat it. This was that place, and this was that hour. He was solemn enough at last.

By his side the old priest walked, with his white head bent and his nervous hands clasped together. He was mumbling the prayers for the dying in a voice that trembled and broke. The morning was clear and cold, and all the world around was white and peaceful.

Jason took up his stand, and folded his arms behind him. As he did so the sun broke through the clouds and lit up his uplifted face and his long red hair like blood.

The sailors fired and he fell. He took their shots into his heart, the biggest heart for good or ill that ever beat in the breast of man.

VII.

Within an hour there was a great commotion on that quiet spot. Jorgen Jorgensen had come, but come too late. One glance told him everything. His order had been executed, but Sunlocks was gone and Jason was dead. Where were his miserable fears now? Where was his petty hate? Both his enemies had escaped him, and his little soul shrivelled up at sight of the wreck of their mighty passions.

"What does this mean?" he asked, looking stupidly around him.

And the old priest, transformed in one instant from the poor, timid thing he had been, turned upon him with the courage of a lion.

"It means," he said, face to face with him, "that I am a wretched coward and you are a damned tyrant."

While they stood together so, the report of a cannon came from the bay. It was a loud detonation, that seemed to heave the sea and shake the island. Jorgen knew what it meant. It meant that the English man-of-war had come.

The Danish sloop struck her colors, and Adam Fairbrother came ashore. He heard what had happened, and gathered with the others where Jason lay with his calm face towards the sky. And going down on his knees he whispered into the deaf ear, "My brave lad, your troubled life is over, your stormy soul is in its rest. Sleep on, sleep well, sleep in peace. God will not forget you."

Then rising to his feet he looked around and said, "If any man thinks that this world is not founded in justice, let him come here and see: There stands the man who is called the Governor of Iceland, and here lies his only kinsman in all the wide wilderness of men. The one is alive, the other is dead; the one is living in power and plenty, the other died like a hunted beast. But which do you choose to be: The man who has the world at his feet or the man who lies at the feet of the world?"

Jorgen Jorgensen only dropped his head while old Adam's lash fell over him. And turning upon him with heat of voice, old Adam cried, "Away with you! Go back to the place of your power. There is no one now to take it from you. But carry this word with you for your warning: Heap up your gold like the mire of the streets, grown mighty and powerful beyond any man living, and when all is done you shall be an execration and a curse and a reproach, and the poorest outcast on life's highway shall cry with me, 'Any fate, oh, merciful heaven, but not that! not that!' Away with you, away! Take your wicked feet away, for this is holy ground!"

And Jorgen Jorgensen turned about on the instant and went off hurriedly, with his face to the earth, like a whipped dog.

VIII.

They buried Jason in a piece of untouched ground over against the little wooden church. Sir Sigfus dug the grave with his own hands. It was a bed of solid lava, and in that pit of old fire they laid that young heart of flame. The sky was blue, and the sun shone on the snow so white and beautiful. It had been a dark midnight when Jason came into the world, but it was a glorious morning when he went out of it.

The good priest learning the truth from old Adam, that Jason had loved Greeba, bethought him of a way to remember the dead man's life secret at the last. He got twelve Iceland maidens and taught them an English hymn. They could not understand the words of it, but they learned to sing them to an English tune. And, clad in white, they stood round the grave of Jason, and sang these words in the tongue he loved the best:

Time, like an ever rolling stream
Bears all its sons away;
They fly forgotten, as a dream
Dies at the opening day.

On the island rock of old Grimsey, close to the margin of the Arctic seas, there is a pyramid of lava blocks, now honey-combed and moss-covered, over Jason's rest. And to this day the place of it is called "The place of Red Jason."

THE END

The Waif Woman A Cue From a Saga by Robert Louis Stevenson

This is a tale of Iceland, the isle of stories, and of a thing that befell in the year of the coming there of Christianity.

In the spring of that year a ship sailed from the South Isles to traffic, and fell becalmed inside Snowfellness. The winds had speeded her; she was the first comer of the year; and the fishers drew alongside to hear the news of the south, and eager folk put out in boats to see the merchandise and make prices. From the doors of the hall on Frodis Water, the house folk saw the ship becalmed and the boats about her, coming and going; and the merchants from the ship could see the smoke go up and the men and women trooping to their meals in the hall.

The goodman of that house was called Finnward Keelfarer, and his wife Aud the Light-Minded; and they had a son Eyolf, a likely boy, and a daughter Asdis, a slip of a maid. Finnward was well-to-do in his affairs, he kept open house and had good friends. But Aud his wife was not so much considered: her mind was set on trifles, on bright clothing, and the admiration of men, and the envy of women; and it was thought she was not always so circumspect in her bearing as she might have been, but nothing to hurt.

On the evening of the second day men came to the house from sea. They told of the merchandise in the ship, which was well enough and to be had at easy rates, and of a waif woman that sailed in her, no one could tell why, and had chests of clothes beyond comparison, fine coloured stuffs, finely woven, the best that ever came into that island, and gewgaws for a queen. At the hearing of that Aud's eyes began to glisten. She went early to bed; and the day was not yet red before she was on the beach, had a boat launched, and was pulling to the ship. By the way she looked closely at all boats, but there was no woman in any; and at that she was better pleased, for she had no fear of the men.

When they came to the ship, boats were there already, and the merchants and the shore folk sat and jested and chaffered in the stern. But in the fore part of the ship, the woman sat alone, and looked before her sourly at the sea. They called her Thorgunna. She was as tall as a man and high in flesh, a buxom wife to look at. Her hair was of the dark red, time had not changed it. Her face was dark, the cheeks full, and the brow smooth. Some of the merchants told that she was sixty years of age and others laughed and said she was but forty; but they spoke of her in whispers, for they seemed to think that she was ill to deal with and not more than ordinary canny.

Aud went to where she sat and made her welcome to Iceland. Thorgunna did the honours of the ship. So for a while they carried it on, praising and watching each other, in the way of women. But Aud was a little vessel to contain a great longing, and presently the cry of her heart came out of her.

"The folk say," says she, "you have the finest women's things that ever came to Iceland?" and as she spoke her eyes grew big.

"It would be strange if I had not," quoth Thorgunna. "Queens have no finer."

So Aud begged that she might see them.

Thorgunna looked on her askance. "Truly," said she, "the things are for no use but to be shown." So she fetched a chest and opened it. Here was a cloak of the rare scarlet laid upon with silver, beautiful beyond belief; hard by was a silver brooch of basket work that was wrought as fine as any shell and was as broad as the face of the full moon; and Aud saw the clothes lying folded in the chest, of all the colours of the day, and fire, and precious gems; and her heart burned with envy. So, because she had so huge a mind to buy, she began to make light of the merchandise.

"They are good enough things," says she, "though I have better in my chest at home. It is a good enough cloak, and I am in need of a new cloak." At that she fingered the scarlet, and the touch of the fine stuff went to her mind like singing. "Come," says she, "if it were only for your civility in showing it, what will you have for your cloak?"

"Woman," said Thorgunna, "I am no merchant." And she closed the chest and locked it, like one angry.

Then Aud fell to protesting and caressing her. That was Aud's practice; for she thought if she hugged and kissed a person none could say her nay. Next she went to flattery, said she knew the things were too noble for the like of her—they were made for a stately, beautiful woman like Thorgunna; and at that she kissed her again, and Thorgunna seemed a little pleased. And now Aud pled poverty and begged for the cloak in a gift; and now she vaunted the wealth of her goodman and offered ounces and ounces of fine silver, the price of three men's lives. Thorgunna smiled, but it was a grim smile, and still she shook her head. At last Aud wrought herself into extremity and wept.

"I would give my soul for it," she cried.

"Fool!" said Thorgunna. "But there have been fools before you!" And a little after, she said this: "Let us be done with beseeching. The things are mine. I was a fool to show you them; but where is their use, unless we show them? Mine they are and mine they shall be till I die. I have paid for them dear enough," said she.

Aud saw it was of no avail; so she dried her tears, and asked Thorgunna about her voyage, and made believe to listen while she plotted in her little mind. "Thorgunna," she asked presently, "do you count kin with any folk in Iceland?"

"I count kin with none," replied Thorgunna. "My kin is of the greatest, but I have not been always lucky, so I say the less."

"So that you have no house to pass the time in till the ship return?" cries Aud. "Dear Thorgunna, you must come and live with us. My goodman is rich, his hand and his house are open, and I will cherish you like a daughter."

At that Thorgunna smiled on the one side; but her soul laughed within her at the woman's shallowness. "I will pay her for that word daughter," she thought, and she smiled again.

"I will live with you gladly," says she, "for your house has a good name, and I have seen the smoke of your kitchen from the ship. But one thing you shall understand. I make no presents, I give nothing where I go— not a rag and not an ounce. Where I stay, I work for my upkeep; and as I am strong as a man and hardy as an ox, they that have had the keeping of me were the better pleased."

It was a hard job for Aud to keep her countenance, for she was like to have wept. And yet she felt it would be unseemly to eat her invitation; and like a shallow woman and one that had always led her husband by the nose, she told herself she would find some means to cajole Thorgunna and come by her purpose after all. So she put a good face on the thing, had Thorgunna into the boat, her and her two great chests, and brought her home with her to the hall by the beach.

All the way in she made much of the wife; and when they were arrived gave her a locked bed-place in the hall, where was a bed, a table, and a stool, and space for the two chests.

"This shall be yours while you stay here," said Aud. And she attended on her guest.

Now Thorgunna opened the second chest and took out her bedding— sheets of English linen, the like of it never seen, a cover of quilted silk, and curtains of purple wrought with silver. At the sight of these Aud was like one distracted, greed blinded her mind; the cry rose strong in her throat, it must out.

"What will you sell your bedding for?" she cried, and her cheeks were hot.

Thorgunna looked upon her with a dusky countenance. "Truly you are a courteous hostess," said she, "but I will not sleep on straw for your amusement."

At that Aud's two ears grew hot as her cheeks; and she took Thorgunna at her word; and left her from that time in peace.

The woman was as good as her spoken word. Inside the house and out she wrought like three, and all that she put her hand to was well done. When she milked, the cows yielded beyond custom; when she made hay, it was always dry weather; when she took her turn at the cooking, the folk licked their spoons. Her manners when she pleased were outside imitation, like one that had sat with kings in their high buildings. It seemed she was pious too, and the day never passed but she was in the church there praying. The rest was not so well. She was of few words, and never one about her kin and fortunes. Gloom sat on her brow, and she was ill to cross. Behind her back they gave her the name of the Waif Woman or the Wind Wife; to her face it must always be Thorgunna. And if any of the young men called her mother, she would speak no more that day, but sit apart in the hall and mutter with her lips.

"This is a queer piece of goods that we have gotten," says Finnward Keelfarer, "I wish we get no harm by her! But the good wife's pleasure must be done," said he, which was his common word.

When she was at work, Thorgunna wore the rudest of plain clothes, though ever clean as a cat; but at night in the hall she was more dainty, for she loved to be admired. No doubt she made herself look well, and many thought she was a comely woman still, and to those she was always favourable and full of pleasant speech. But the more that some pleased her, it was thought by good judges that they pleased Aud the less.

When midsummer was past, a company of young men upon a journey came to the house by Frodis Water. That was always a great day for Aud, when there were gallants at table; and what made this day the greater, Alf of the Fells was in the company, and she thought Alf fancied her. So be sure Aud wore her best. But when Thorgunna came from the bed-place, she was arrayed like any queen and the broad brooch was in her bosom. All night in the hall these women strove with each other; and the little maid, Asdis, looked on, and was ashamed and knew not why. But Thorgunna pleased beyond all; she told of strange things that had befallen in the world; when she pleased she had the cue to laughter; she sang, and her voice was full and her songs new in that island; and whenever she turned, the eyes shone in her face and the brooch glittered at her bosom. So that the young men forgot the word of the merchants as to the woman's age, and their looks followed her all night.

Aud was sick with envy. Sleep fled her; her husband slept, but she sat upright beside him in the bed, and gnawed her fingers. Now she began to hate Thorgunna, and the glittering of the great brooch stood before her in the dark. "Sure," she thought, "it must be the glamour of that brooch! She is not so fair as I; she is as old as the dead in the hillside; and as for her wit and her songs, it is little I think of them!" Up she got at that, took a light from the embers, and came to her guest's bed-place. The door was locked, but Aud had a master-key and could go in. Inside, the chests were open, and in the top of one the light of her taper shone upon the glittering of the brooch. As a dog snatches food she snatched it, and turned to the bed. Thorgunna lay on her side; it was to be thought she slept, but she talked the while to herself, and her lips moved. It seemed her years returned to her in slumber, for her face was grey and her brow knotted; and the open eyes of her stared in the eyes of Aud. The heart of the foolish woman died in her bosom; but her greed was the stronger, and she fled with that which she had stolen.

When she was back in bed, the word of Thorgunna came to her mind, that these things were for no use but to be shown. Here she had the brooch and the shame of it, and might not wear it. So all night she quaked with the fear of discovery, and wept tears of rage that she should have sinned in vain. Day came, and Aud must rise; but she went about the house like a crazy woman. She saw the eyes of Asdis rest on her strangely, and at that she beat the maid. She scolded the house folk, and, by her way of it, nothing was done aright. First she was loving to her husband and made much of him, thinking to be on his good side when trouble came. Then she took a better way, picked a feud with him, and railed on the poor man till his ears rang, so that he might be in the wrong beforehand. The brooch she hid without, in the side of a hayrick. All this while Thorgunna lay in the bed-place, which was not her way, for by custom she was early astir. At last she came forth, and there was that in her face that made all the house look one at the other and the heart of Aud to be straitened. Never a word the guest spoke, not a bite she swallowed, and they saw the strong shudderings take and shake her in her place. Yet a little, and still without speech, back she went into her bad-place, and the door was shut.

"That is a sick wife," said Finnward, "Her weird has come on her."

And at that the heart of Aud was lifted up with hope.

All day Thorgunna lay on her bed, and the next day sent for Finnward.

"Finnward Keelfarer," said she, "my trouble is come upon me, and I am at the end of my days."

He made the customary talk.

"I have had my good things; now my hour is come; and let suffice," quoth she. "I did not send for you to hear your prating."

314

Finnward knew not what to answer, for he saw her soul was dark.

"I sent for you on needful matters," she began again. "I die here—I!—in this black house, in a bleak island, far from all decency and proper ways of man; and now my treasure must be left. Small pleasure have I had of it, and leave it with the less!" cried she.

"Good woman, as the saying is, needs must," says Finnward, for he was nettled with that speech.

"For that I called you," quoth Thorgunna. "In these two chests are much wealth and things greatly to be desired. I wish my body to be laid in Skalaholt in the new church, where I trust to hear the mass-priests singing over my head so long as time endures. To that church I will you to give what is sufficient, leaving your conscience judge of it. My scarlet cloak with the silver, I will to that poor fool your wife. She longed for it so bitterly, I may not even now deny her. Give her the brooch as well. I warn you of her; I was such as she, only wiser; I warn you, the ground she stands upon is water, and whoso trusts her leans on rottenness. I hate her and I pity her. When she comes to lie where I lie—" There she broke off. "The rest of my goods I leave to your black-eyed maid, young Asdis, for her slim body and clean mind. Only the things of my bed, you shall see burned."

"It is well," said Finnward.

"It may be well," quoth she, "if you obey. My life has been a wonder to all and a fear to many. While I lived none thwarted me and prospered. See to it that none thwart me after I am dead. It stands upon your safety."

"It stands upon my honour," quoth Finnward, "and I have the name of an honourable man."

"You have the name of a weak one," says Thorgunna. "Look to it, look to it, Finnward. Your house shall rue it else."

"The rooftree of my house is my word," said Finnward.

"And that is a true saying," says the woman. "See to it, then. The speech of Thorgunna is ended."

With that she turned her face against the wall and Finnward left her.

The same night, in the small hours of the clock, Thorgunna passed. It was a wild night for summer, and the wind sang about the eaves and clouds covered the moon, when the dark woman wended. From that day to this no man has learned her story or her people's name; but be sure the one was stormy and the other great. She had come to that isle, a waif woman, on a ship; thence she flitted, and no more remained of her but her heavy chests and her big body.

In the morning the house women streaked and dressed the corpse. Then came Finnward, and carried the sheets and curtains from the house, and caused build a fire upon the sands. But Aud had an eye on her man's doings.

"And what is this that you are at?" said she.

So he told her.

"Burn the good sheets!" she cried. "And where would I be with my two hands? No, troth," said Aud, "not so long as your wife is above ground!"

"Good wife," said Finnward, "this is beyond your province. Here is my word pledged and the woman dead I pledged it to. So much the more am I bound. Let me be doing as I must, goodwife."

"Tilly-valley!" says she, "and a fiddlestick's end, goodman! You may know well about fishing and be good at shearing sheep for what I know; but you are little of a judge of damask sheets. And the best word I can say is just this," she says, laying hold of one end of the goods, "that if ye are made up to burn the plenishing, you must burn your wife along with it."

"I trust it will not go so hard," says Finnward, "and I beg you not to speak so loud and let the house folk hear you."

"Let them speak low that are ashamed!" cries Aud. "I speak only in reason."

"You are to consider that the woman died in my house," says Finnward, "and this was her last behest. In truth, goodwife, if I were to fail, it is a thing that would stick long in my throat, and would give us an ill name with the neighbours."

"And you are to consider," says she, "that I am your true wife and worth all the witches ever burnt, and loving her old husband"—here she put her arms about his neck. "And you are to consider that what you wish to do is to destroy fine stuff, such as we have no means of replacing; and that she bade you do it singly to spite me, for I sought to buy this bedding from her while she was alive at her own price; and that she hated me because I was young and handsome."

"That is a true word that she hated you, for she said so herself before she wended," says Finnward.

"So that here is an old faggot that hated me, and she dead as a bucket," says Aud; "and here is a young wife that loves you dear, and is alive for-by"—and at that she kissed him—"and the point is, which are you to do the will of?"

The man's weakness caught him hard, and he faltered. "I fear some hurt will come of it," said he.

There she cut in, and bade the lads tread out the fire, and the lasses roll the bed-stuff up and carry it within.

"My dear," says he, "my honour—this is against my honour."

But she took his arm under hers, and caressed his hand, and kissed his knuckles, and led him down the bay. "Bubble-bubble-bubble!" says she, imitating him like a baby, though she was none so young. "Bubble-bubble,

316

and a silly old man! We must bury the troll wife, and here is trouble enough, and a vengeance! Horses will sweat for it before she comes to Skalaholt; 'tis my belief she was a man in a woman's habit. And so now, have done, good man, and let us get her waked and buried, which is more than she deserves, or her old duds are like to pay for. And when that is ended, we can consult upon the rest."

So Finnward was but too well pleased to put it off.

The next day they set forth early for Skalaholt across the heaths. It was heavy weather, and grey overhead; the horses sweated and neighed, and the men went silent, for it was nowhere in their minds that the dead wife was canny. Only Aud talked by the way, like a silly sea-gull piping on a cliff, and the rest held their peace. The sun went down before they were across Whitewater; and the black night fell on them this side of Netherness. At Netherness they beat upon the door. The goodman was not abed nor any of his folk, but sat in the hall talking; and to them Finnward made clear his business.

"I will never deny you a roof," said the goodman of Netherness. "But I have no food ready, and if you cannot be doing without meat, you must e'en fare farther."

They laid the body in a shed, made fast their horses, and came into the house, and the door was closed again. So there they sat about the lights, and there was little said, for they were none so well pleased with their reception. Presently, in the place where the food was kept, began a clattering of dishes; and it fell to a bondman of the house to go and see what made the clatter. He was no sooner gone than he was back again; and told it was a big, buxom woman, high in flesh and naked as she was born, setting meats upon a dresser. Finnward grew pale as the dawn; he got to his feet, and the rest rose with him, and all the party of the funeral came to the buttery-door. And the dead Thorgunna took no heed of their coming, but went on setting forth meats, and seemed to talk with herself as she did so; and she was naked to the buff.

Great fear fell upon them; the marrow of their back grew cold. Not one word they spoke, neither good nor bad; but back into the hall, and down upon their bended knees, and to their prayers.

"Now, in the name of God, what ails you?" cried the goodman of Netherness.

And when they had told him, shame fell upon him for his churlishness.

"The dead wife reproves me," said the honest man.

And he blessed himself and his house, and caused spread the tables, and they all ate of the meats that the dead wife laid out.

This was the first walking of Thorgunna, and it is thought by good judges it would have been the last as well, if men had been more wise.

The next day they came to Skalaholt, and there was the body buried, and the next after they set out for home. Finnward's heart was heavy, and his mind divided. He feared the dead wife and the living; he feared dishonour and he feared dispeace; and his will was like a sea-gull in the wind. Now he cleared his throat and made as if to speak; and at that Aud cocked her eye and looked at the goodman mocking, and his voice died unborn. At the last, shame gave him courage.

"Aud," said he, "yon was a most uncanny thing at Netherness."

"No doubt," said Aud.

"I have never had it in my mind," said he, "that yon woman was the thing she should be."

"I dare say not," said Aud. "I never thought so either."

"It stands beyond question she was more than canny," says Finnward, shaking his head. "No manner of doubt but what she was ancient of mind."

"She was getting pretty old in body, too," says Aud.

"Wife," says he, "it comes in upon me strongly this is no kind of woman to disobey; above all, being dead and her walking. I think, wife, we must even do as she commanded."

"Now what is ever your word?" says she, riding up close and setting her hand upon his shoulder. "'The goodwife's pleasure must be done'; is not that my Finnward?"

"The good God knows I grudge you nothing," cried Finnward. "But my blood runs cold upon this business. Worse will come of it! he cried, "worse will flow from it!"

"What is this todo?" cries Aud. "Here is an old brimstone hag that should have been stoned with stones, and hated me besides. Vainly she tried to frighten me when she was living; shall she frighten me now when she is dead and rotten? I trow not. Think shame to your beard, goodman! Are these a man's shoes I see you shaking in, when your wife rides by your bridle-hand, as bold as nails?"

"Ay, ay," quoth Finnward. "But there goes a byword in the country: Little wit, little fear."

At this Aud began to be concerned, for he was usually easier to lead. So now she tried the other method on the man.

"Is that your word?" cried she. "I kiss the hands of ye! If I have not wit enough, I can rid you of my company. Wit is it he seeks?" she cried. "The old broomstick that we buried yesterday had wit for you."

So she rode on ahead and looked not the road that he was on.

Poor Finnward followed on his horse, but the light of the day was gone out, for his wife was like his life to him. He went six miles and was true to his heart; but the seventh was not half through when he rode up to her.

"Is it to be the goodwife's pleasure?" she asked.

"Aud, you shall have your way," says he; "God grant there come no ill of it!"

So she made much of him, and his heart was comforted.

When they came to the house, Aud had the two chests to her own bed-place, and gloated all night on what she found. Finnward looked on, and trouble darkened his mind.

"Wife," says he at last, "you will not forget these things belong to Asdis?"

At that she barked upon him like a dog.

"Am I a thief?" she cried. "The brat shall have them in her turn when she grows up. Would you have me give her them now to turn her minx's head with?"

So the weak man went his way out of the house in sorrow and fell to his affairs. Those that wrought with him that day observed that now he would labour and toil like a man furious, and now would sit and stare like one stupid; for in truth he judged the business would end ill.

For a while there was no more done and no more said. Aud cherished her treasures by herself, and none was the wiser except Finnward. Only the cloak she sometimes wore, for that was hers by the will of the dead wife; but the others she let lie, because she knew she had them foully, and she feared Finnward somewhat and Thorgunna much.

At last husband and wife were bound to bed one night, and he was the first stripped and got in. "What sheets are these?" he screamed, as his legs touched them, for these were smooth as water, but the sheets of Iceland were like sacking.

"Clean sheets, I suppose," says Aud, but her hand quavered as she wound her hair.

"Woman!" cried Finnward, "these are the bed-sheets of Thorgunna—these are the sheets she died in! do not lie to me!"

At that Aud turned and looked at him. "Well?" says she, "they have been washed."

Finnward lay down again in the bed between Thorgunna's sheets, and groaned; never a word more he said, for now he knew he was a coward and a man dishonoured. Presently his wife came beside him, and they lay still, but neither slept.

It might be twelve in the night when Aud felt Finnward shudder so strong that the bed shook.

"What ails you?" said she.

"I know not," he said. "It is a chill like the chill of death. My soul is sick with it." His voice fell low. "It was so Thorgunna sickened," said he. And he arose and walked in the hall in the dark till it came morning.

Early in the morning he went forth to the sea-fishing with four lads. Aud was troubled at heart and watched him from the door, and even as he went down the beach she saw him shaken with Thorgunna's shudder. It was a rough day, the sea was wild, the boat laboured exceedingly, and it may be that Finnward's mind was troubled with his sickness. Certain it is that they struck, and their boat was burst, upon a skerry under Snowfellness. The four lads were spilled into the sea, and the sea broke and buried them, but Finnward was cast upon the skerry, and clambered up, and sat there all day long: God knows his thoughts. The sun was half-way down, when a shepherd went by on the cliffs about his business, and spied a man in the midst of the breach of the loud seas, upon a pinnacle of reef. He hailed him, and the man turned and hailed again. There was in that cove so great a clashing of the seas and so shrill a cry of sea-fowl that the herd might hear the voice and nor the words. But the name Thorgunna came to him, and he saw the face of Finnward Keelfarer like the face of an old man. Lively ran the herd to Finnward's house; and when his tale was told there, Eyolf the boy was lively to out a boat and hasten to his father's aid. By the strength of hands they drove the keel against the seas, and with skill and courage Eyolf won upon the skerry and climbed up, There sat his father dead; and this was the first vengeance of Thorgunna against broken faith.

It was a sore job to get the corpse on board, and a sorer yet to bring it home before the rolling seas. But the lad Eyolf was a lad of promise, and the lads that pulled for him were sturdy men. So the break-faith's body was got home, and waked, and buried on the hill. Aud was a good widow and wept much, for she liked Finnward well enough. Yet a bird sang in her ears that now she might marry a young man. Little fear that she might have her choice of them, she thought, with all Thorgunna's fine things; and her heart was cheered.

Now, when the corpse was laid in the hill, Asdis came where Aud sat solitary in hall, and stood by her awhile without speech.

"Well, child?" says Aud; and again "Well?" and then "Keep us holy, if you have anything to say, out with it!"

So the maid came so much nearer, "Mother," says she, "I wish you would not wear these things that were Thorgunna's."

"Aha," cries Aud. "This is what it is? You begin early, brat! And who has been poisoning your mind? Your fool of a father, I suppose." And then she stopped and went all scarlet. "Who told you they were yours?" she asked again, taking it all the higher for her stumble. "When you are grown, then you shall have your share and not a day before. These things are not for babies."

The child looked at her and was amazed. "I do not wish them," she said. "I wish they might be burned."

"Upon my word, what next?" cried Aud. "And why should they be burned?"

"I know my father tried to burn these things," said Asdis, "and he named Thorgunna's name upon the skerry ere he died. And, O mother, I doubt they have brought ill luck."

But the more Aud was terrified, the more she would make light of it.

Then the girl put her hand upon her mother's. "I fear they are ill come by," said she.

The blood sprang in Aud's face. "And who made you a judge upon your mother that bore you?" cried she.

"Kinswoman," said Asdis, looking down, "I saw you with the brooch."

"What do you mean? When? Where did you see me?" cried the mother.

"Here in the hall," said Asdis, looking on the floor, "the night you stole it."

At that Aud let out a cry. Then she heaved up her hand to strike the child. "You little spy!" she cried. Then she covered her face, and wept, and rocked herself. "What can you know?" she cried. "How can you understand, that are a baby, not so long weaned? He could—your father could, the dear good man, dead and gone! He could understand and pity, he was good to me. Now he has left me alone with heartless children! Asdis," she cried, "have you no nature in your blood? You do not know what I have done and suffered for them. I have done—oh, and I could have done anything! And there is your father dead. And after all, you ask me not to use them? No woman in Iceland has the like. And you wish me to destroy them? Not if the dead should rise!" she cried. "No, no," and she stopped her ears, "not if the dead should rise, and let that end it!"

So she ran into her bed-place, and clapped at the door, and left the child amazed.

But for all Aud spoke with so much passion, it was noticed that for long she left the things unused. Only she would be locked somewhile daily in her bed-place, where she pored on them and secretly wore them for her pleasure.

Now winter was at hand; the days grew short and the nights long; and under the golden face of morning the isle would stand silver with frost. Word came from Holyfell to Frodis Water of a company of young men upon a journey; that night they supped at Holyfell, the next it would be at Frodis

Water; and Alf of the Fells was there, and Thongbrand Ketilson, and Hall the Fair. Aud went early to her bed-place, and there she pored upon these fineries till her heart was melted with self-love. There was a kirtle of a mingled colour, and the blue shot into the green, and the green lightened from the blue, as the colours play in the ocean between deeps and shallows: she thought she could endure to live no longer and not wear it. There was a bracelet of an ell long, wrought like a serpent and with fiery jewels for the eyes; she saw it shine on her white arm and her head grew dizzy with desire. "Ah!" she thought, "never were fine lendings better met with a fair wearer." And she closed her eyelids, and she thought she saw herself among the company and the men's eyes go after her admiring. With that she considered that she must soon marry one of them and wondered which; and she thought Alf was perhaps the best, or Hall the Fair, but was not certain, and then she remembered Finnward Keelfarer in his cairn upon the hill, and was concerned. "Well, he was a good husband to me," she thought, "and I was a good wife to him. But that is an old song now." So she turned again to handling the stuffs and jewels. At last she got to bed in the smooth sheets, and lay, and fancied how she would look, and admired herself, and saw others admire her, and told herself stories, till her heart grew warm and she chuckled to herself between the sheets. So she shook awhile with laughter; and then the mirth abated but not the shaking; and a grue took hold upon her flesh, and the cold of the grave upon her belly, and the terror of death upon her soul. With that a voice was in her ear: "It was so Thorgunna sickened." Thrice in the night the chill and the terror took her, and thrice it passed away; and when she rose on the morrow, death had breathed upon her countenance.

She saw the house folk and her children gaze upon her; well she knew why! She knew her day was come, and the last of her days, and her last hour was at her back; and it was so in her soul that she scarce minded. All was lost, all was past mending, she would carry on until she fell. So she went as usual, and hurried the feast for the young men, and railed upon her house folk, but her feet stumbled, and her voice was strange in her own ears, and the eyes of the folk fled before her. At times, too, the chill took her and the fear along with it; and she must sit down, and the teeth beat together in her head, and the stool tottered on the floor. At these times, she thought she was passing, and the voice of Thorgunna sounded in her ear: "The things are for no use but to be shown," it said. "Aud, Aud, have you shown them once? No, not once!"

And at the sting of the thought her courage and strength would revive, and she would rise again and move about her business.

Now the hour drew near, and Aud went to her bed-place, and did on the bravest of her finery, and came forth to greet her guests. Was never woman in Iceland robed as she was. The words of greeting were yet between her lips, when the shuddering fell upon her strong as labour, and a horror as deep as hell. Her face was changed amidst her finery, and the faces of her guests were changed as they beheld her: fear puckered their brows, fear drew back their feet; and she took her doom from the looks of them, and fled to her bed-place. There she flung herself on the wife's coverlet, and turned her face against the wall.

That was the end of all the words of Aud; and in the small hours on the clock her spirit wended. Asdis had come to and fro, seeing if she might help, where was no help possible of man or woman. It was light in the bed-place when the maid returned, for a taper stood upon a chest. There lay Aud in her fine clothes, and there by her side on the bed the big dead wife Thorgunna squatted on her hams. No sound was heard, but it seemed by the movement of her mouth as if Thorgunna sang, and she waved her arms as if to singing.

"God be good to us!" cried Asdis, "she is dead."

"Dead," said the dead wife.

"Is the weird passed?" cried Asdis.

"When the sin is done the weird is dreed," said Thorgunna, and with that she was not.

But the next day Eyolf and Asdis caused build a fire on the shore betwixt tide-marks. There they burned the bed-clothes, and the clothes, and the jewels, and the very boards of the waif woman's chests; and when the tide returned it washed away their ashes. So the weird of Thorgunna was lifted from the house on Frodis Water.

THE END

Grettir the Outlaw A Story of Iceland by Sabine Baring-Gould

I: WINTER TALES

It was night—drawing on to midnight—in summer, that I who write this book arrived at the little lonely farm of Biarg, on the Middle River, in the north of Iceland. It was night, near on midnight, and yet I could hardly call it night, for the sky overhead was full of light of the clearest amethyst, and every stock and stone was distinctly visible. Across the valley rose a rugged moor, and above its shoulder a snow-clad mountain, turned to rosy gold by the night sun. As I stood there watching the mist form on the cold river in the vale below, all at once I heard a strange sound like horns blowing far away in the sky, and looking up, I saw a train of swans flying from west to east, bathed in sunlight, their wings of silver, and their feathers as gold.

I had come all the way from England to see Biarg, for there was born, about the year A.D. 997, a man called Grettir, whose history I had read, and which interested me so much that I was resolved to see his native home, and the principal scenes where his stormy life was passed.

The landscape was the same as that on which Grettir's childish eyes had looked more than eight hundred and fifty years ago. The same outline of dreary moor, the same snowy ridge of mountain standing above it, catching the midnight summer sun, the same mist forming over the river; but the house was altogether different. Now there stood only a poor heap of farm-buildings, erected of turf and wood, where had once been a noble hall of wood, with carved gable-ends, surrounded by many out-houses.

Before we begin on the story of Grettir, it will be well to say a few words about its claim to be history.

Iceland never was, and it is not now, a much-peopled island. The farm-houses are for the most part far apart, and the farms are of very considerable extent, because, owing to the severity of the climate, very little pasturage is obtained over a wide extent of country for the sheep and cattle. The population lives round the coast, on the fiords or creeks of the sea, or on the rivers that flow into these fiords. The centre of the island is occupied by a vast waste of ice-covered mountain, and desert black as ink strewn with volcanic ash and sand, or else with a region of erupted lava that is impassable, because in cooling it has exploded, and forms a country of bristling spikes and gulfs and sharp edges, very much like the wreck of a huge ginger-beer bottle factory.

What are now farmhouses were the halls and mansions of families of noble descent. Indeed, the original settlers in Iceland were the nobles of Norway who left their native land to avoid the tyranny of Harold Fairhair, who tried to crush their power so as to make himself a despotic king in the land.

These Norse nobles came in their boats to Iceland, bringing with them their wives, children, their thralls or slaves, and their cattle; and they settled all round the coast. The present Icelanders are descended from these first colonists.

Now, the history of Iceland for a few hundred years consists of nothing but the history of the quarrels of these great families. Iceland was without any political organization, but it had an elected lawman or judge, and every year the heads of the families rode to Thingvalla, a plain in the south-west, where they brought their complaints, carried on their lawsuits, and had them settled by the judge. There was no army, no navy, no government in Iceland for a long time; also no foreign wars, and no internal revolutions.

These noble families settled in the valleys and upon the fiords thought a good deal of themselves, and they carefully preserved, at first orally then in writing, the record of their pedigrees, and also the tradition of the famous deeds of their great men.

In summer there is no night; in winter, no day. In winter there is little or nothing to be done but sit over the fire, sing songs, and tell yarns. Now, in winter the Icelanders told the tales of the brave men of old in their families, and so the tradition was handed on from father to son, the same stories told every winter, till all the particulars became well known. At the same time there can be no doubt that little embellishments were added, some exaggerations were indulged in, and here and there the grand deed of some other man was grafted into the story of the family hero. About two hundred or two hundred and fifty years after the death of Grettir, his history was committed to writing, and then it became fixed—nothing further was added to it, and we have his story after having travelled down over two hundred years as a tradition. That was plenty of time for additions and emendations, and the hobgoblin and ghost stories that come into his life are some of these embellishments. But the main facts of his life are true history. We are able to decide this by comparing his story with those of other families in the same part of the island, and to see whether they agree as to dates, and as to the circumstances narrated in them.

In the north-west of Iceland is an immense bay called the Huna-floi, which branches off into several creeks, the largest of which is called the

Ramsfirth, and the next to that is the Middlefiord. Into this flows a river that has its rise in the central desert, in a perfect tangle of lakes. Three rivers issuing from these lakes unite just above Biarg, and pour their waters a short morning's ride lower through sands into the Middlefirth.

The valley is not cheerful, running from north to south. Biarg lies on the east side, and faces the western sun. The moor which lies behind it, and forms the hill on the other side of the river, is not broken and picturesque, and if it were not for the peak of Burfell, covered with snow a good part of the year, the view from Biarg would be as uninteresting as any to be found in the land. But then, when one rides down to the coast, or ascends the moor, what a splendid view bursts on the sight! The great Polar Sea is before one, intensely blue, not with the deep ultramarine of the Mediterranean, but with the blue of the nemophyla or forget-me-not, rolling in from the mysterious North; and across the mighty bay of the Huna-floi can be seen the snowy mountains of that extraordinary peninsula which runs out to the north-west of Iceland, and is only just not converted into an island because connected with Iceland by a narrow strip of land. That great projection is like a hand with fiords between the fingers of land, and glacier-mountains where are the knuckles; but the wrist is very narrow indeed, only about one English mile across, and there lies a trough along this junction, with a little stream and a lake in it. Now, at this wrist, as we may call it, lies the farm of Eyre, where, somewhat later, lived the sister of Grettir, who married a man that farmed there, named Glum.

Looking away across the great blue bay, the mountains of the hand may be seen rising out of the sea, and looking like icebergs.

Grettir the Strong was the son of a well-to-do bonder, or yeoman, who lived at Biarg, and was descended from some of the great nobles of Norway. His father's name was Asmund with the Grey-head, and his mother's name was Asdis.

He had a brother called Atli, a gentle, kindly young fellow, who never wittingly quarrelled with anyone, and was liked by all with whom he had to do. He had also two sisters—one was called Thordis, and she was married to Glum of Eyre—but neither come into the story; and he had another sister called Rannveig, who was married to Gamli of Melar, at the head of Ramsfirth. He had also a little brother called Illugi, of whom more hereafter. Grettir was not a good-looking boy; he had reddish hair, a pale face full of freckles, and light blue eyes. He was broad-built, not tall as a boy, though in the end he grew to be a very big man.

He was not considered a good-tempered or sociable boy. He seemed lazy and sullen; he liked to sit by the fire without speaking to anyone, listening to what was said, and brooding over what he had heard.

If his father set him a task, he did it so unwillingly, and so badly that Asmund Greyhead regretted having set him to do anything.

Now, during the winter, as we have already seen, when there is but a very little daylight, and the nights are vastly long, when, moreover, the whole land is deep in snow, so that there is no farm-work that can be done, and no travelling about to visit neighbours, it was, and is still, usual in Iceland for those in the house to tell tales, or sagas, as they are called. Some of these sagas relate to the old gods of the Norsemen, some are fabulous stories of old heroes who never existed, or, if they did exist, have had all sorts of fantastic legends tacked on to their histories; but other sagas are the tales of the doings of ancestors of the family.

Now, among the sagas that Grettir used to hearken to with greatest delight was that of old Onund Treefoot, his great-grandfather, who first settled in Iceland. And this was the tale:

Onund, the son of Ufeigh Clubfoot, son of Ivar the Smiter, was a mighty Viking in Norway; that is, he went about every summer harrying the coasts of England, Ireland, and Scotland. He joined with three friends, and they had five ships together, and one summer they sailed to the Hebrides—which were then called the Sudereys, or southern isles. The Bishop of the Isle of Man is still called Bishop of Sodor and Man, because his diocese originally included the Sudereys. Then out against them came Kiarval, king of the Hebrides, with five ships, and they gave him battle, and there was a hard fray. But the men of Onund were the mightiest warriors. On each side many fell, but the end of the battle was that the king fled with only one ship. So Onund took the four vessels and great spoil, and he wrought great havoc on the coast, plundering and burning, and so in the fall of the year returned to Norway. In the history of England, and in that of Scotland and of Ireland, we read of the terrible annoyance given to the natives of Great Britain and Ireland by the northern pirates; and, indeed, they conquered Dublin, and established a kingdom there, and also took to themselves Orkney. Well, when Onund returned to Norway he did not find that matters were pleasant there; for King Harald the Unshorn had begun to establish himself sole king in Norway. Hitherto there had been many small kings and earls; but Harald had taken an oath that he would not cut or trim his hair till he had subdued all under his power, and made himself supreme throughout the land.

A great many bonders and all the little kings united against him, and there was a great battle fought at Hafrsfiord—the greatest battle that had as yet been fought in Norway. Onund was in the battle along with his friend, King Thorir Longchin, and he set his ship alongside of that of King Longchin. King Harald ran his ship up alongside of that of Longchin, grappled it, and boarded it. There was a furious fight, and Harald sent on board his Bearsarks, a set of half-mad ruffians, who wore not bear but wolf skins, and who were said to lead charmed lives, so that no weapon would wound them. Thorir Longchin and all his men were killed; and then King Harald cut away the ship and ran up against that of Onund. Onund was in the fore part, and he fought manfully. As the grappling-irons of Harald caught his ship, Onund made a sweep with his longsword at the man who threw the irons, and in so doing he put his leg over the bulwark. Then one on the king's ship threw a spear at Onund. He saw it flung, and leaned his head back to let it fly over him, and as he did so one on the king's ship smote at him with a battle-axe, and the axe fell on his leg below the knee and shore his leg off. Then Onund fell back on board his own vessel, and his men carried him across into that of a friend named Thrand, who lay alongside of him on the other board. And Thrand had a great cauldron there of pitch boiled, and Onund set his knee in the boiling pitch, and never blinked nor uttered a cry. That staunched the blood. If he had not done this he would have bled to death.

Now, Thrand saw that King Harald was gaining the mastery everywhere, so he fled away with his ship and sailed west.

Onund was healed of his wound, but ever after he walked with a wooden leg, and that is why he got the name of Onund Treefoot.

After the battle of Hafrsfiord, Onund could only return to Norway by stealth, and he could not recover his lands there, so he deemed it wisest for him to sail away and seek a home elsewhere. That is how he left Norway and settled in Iceland.

And when King Harald saw himself lord and master through all the land, then he had his hair trimmed and combed, and it was so long and so beautiful, that ever after he who had been called "The Unshorn" went by the name of "Fairhair," and in history he is known as King Harald Fairhair.

II: HOW GRETTIR PLAYED ON THE ICE

There are several tales told of Grettir when he was a boy, which show that he was a rough and unkindly lad. He was set by his father to keep geese on the moors, and this made him angry, so he threw stones at the geese and killed or wounded them all.

The old man suffered from lumbago, and in winter when unwell asked his wife and the boys to rub his back by the fire; but when Grettir was required to do this, he lost his temper, and on one occasion he snatched up a wool-carding comb and dug it into his old father's back.

Many other things he did which made those at home not like him, and there was not much love lost between him and his father. The fact was that

Grettir was a headstrong, wilful fellow, and bitterly had he to pay in after life for this youthful wilfulness and obstinacy. It was these qualities, untamed in him, that wrecked his whole life, and it may be said brought ruin and extinction on his family. There were great and good qualities in Grettir's nature, but they did not show when he was young; only much suffering and cruel privations brought out in the end the higher and nobler elements that were in him.

It is so with all who have any good in them, if by early discipline it is not manifested, then it is brought out by the rough usage of misfortune in after life.

And now I will give one incident of Grettir's boyhood. It was a favourite amusement for young fellows at that time to play golf on the ice, and in winter, when the Middlefirth was frozen over, large parties assembled there for the sport.

One winter a party was arranged for a match on the ice, and a good many lads came to Middlefirth from Willowdale, a valley only separated from the Middlefirth by a long shoulder of ugly moor. The Willowdalesmen had a much better sheet of water, a very large lake called Hop, into which their river flowed, before discharging itself into the sea; and the return match was to be played on Hop.

Among the young fellows who came from Willowdale was Audun, a fine, strapping fellow; frank, well-built, good-looking, and amiable.

When the parties were assembled at the place, there they were paired off according to age and strength; and on this occasion I am speaking of, Grettir, who was fourteen, was set to play with Audun, who was two years older than he, and a head taller.

Audun struck the ball and it flew over Grettir's head, and he missed it, and it went skimming away over the ice to a great distance, and Grettir had to run after it. Some of those who were looking on laughed. Then Grettir's anger was roused. He got the ball and came back carrying it, till he was within a few yards of Audun, and then, instead of dropping the ball, and striking it with his golfing-stick, he suddenly threw it with all his force against his adversary, and struck him between his eyes, so that it half-stunned him, and cut the skin. Audun whirled his golfing-bat round, and struck at Grettir, who dodged under and escaped the blow. Then Audun and Grettir grappled each other, and wrestled on the ice.

Every one thought that Audun would have the stumpy, thick-set boy down in a trice, but it was not so; Grettir held his ground;—they swung this way, that way; now one seemed about to be cast, and then the other, and although Audun was almost come to a man's strength, he could not for a long time throw Grettir. At last Grettir slipped on a piece of ice where some had been sliding, and went down. His blood was up, so was that of Audun; and the fight would have been continued with their sticks, had not Grettir's brother Atli thrown himself between the combatants and separated them. Atli held his brother back, and tried to patch up the quarrel.

"You need not hold me like a mad dog," said Grettir. "Thralls wreak their vengeance at once, cowards never."

Audun and Grettir were distant cousins. They were not allowed to play against each other any more, and the rest went on with their game.

III: OF THE RIDE TO THINGVALLA

There lived in Waterdale, a day's journey from Biarg, an old bonder, named Thorkel Krafla. He was the first Icelander who became a Christian.

In heathen times, among the Northmen as among the Romans, it was allowable for parents to expose their children to death, if they did not want to have the trouble of rearing them. Now Thorkel had been so exposed, with a napkin over his face. It so happened that a great chief called Thorkel Mani was riding along one day, thinking about the gods that he had been taught to believe in, who drank and got drunk, and fought each other, and, being a grave, meditative man, he could not make out what these rollicking, fighting gods could have had to do with the world,—with the creation of sun, moon, and stars, and the earth with its yield. He thought to himself, "There must be some God above these tipsy, quarrelsome deities; and this higher God must love men, and be good and kind to men."

As he thought this, he heard a little whimpering noise from behind a stone; he got off his horse, and went to see what produced this noise, and found there a poor little baby, that with its tiny hands had rumpled up the kerchief which had been spread over its nose and mouth. Thorkel Mani took up the deserted babe in his arms, and looking up to heaven, to the sun, said, "If the good God, who is high over all, called this little being into life, gave it eyes and mouth and ears and hands and feet, He surely never intended His handiwork to be cast out as a thing of no value, to die. For the love of Him I will take this child."

Then Thorkel Mani rode home, carrying the baby in his arms; and he called it by his own name, Thorkel; but to distinguish it from himself, it was given the nickname Krafla, which means to rumple, because the babe had rumpled up the kerchief, so as to let its cries be heard. So the child grew up, and kept the name through life of Thorkel Rumple. This Thorkel became a very great man, and Godi, or magistrate, of the Waterdale; and, as I have said, he was the first man to become a Christian, when missionaries of the gospel came to Iceland.

330

Very soon after Grettir's birth Christianity became general, and in the year 1000 was sanctioned by law; but there were few Christian priests in the land, so that the knowledge of the truth had not spread much, and taken hold and transformed men's lives. Thorkel Rumple was now very old. He was the bosom friend of Asmund, and every year when in the spring he rode to the great assizes at Thingvalla, he always halted at least one night at Biarg. Not only were Asmund and he men of like minds, and friends, but they were also connected. In the spring of the year 1011, Thorkel arrived as usual at Biarg, attended by a great many men, and he was most warmly received by Asmund and his wife. He remained with them three nights, and he and they fell a-talking about the prospects of the two young men, Atli and Grettir. Asmund told his kinsman that Atli was a quiet, amiable fellow, now at man's estate, and likely to prove a good farmer; a man who would worthily succeed him at Biarg when he died, and keep the honour of the family untarnished, and would enlarge the estate.

"Ah! I see," said Thorkel. "A useful man, good and respectable, like yourself. But what about Grettir?"

Asmund hesitated a moment before answering; but presently he said, "I hardly know what to say of him. He is unruly, sullen, makes no friends, and he has been a constant cause of vexation to me."

Thorkel answered, "That is a bad prospect; however, let him come with me to Thingvalla, and I shall be able to see on the journey of what stuff he is made."

To this Asmund agreed; and right glad was Grettir to think he was to go to the great law-gathering.

Thorkel had sixty men with him, and he rode in some state; for, as already said, he was a great man. The way led over the great desolate waste, called the Two-days-ride; but as on this expanse there were few halting-places, the grass most scanty, and not sufficient to allow of a stay, the party rode across it down to the settled lands nearer the coast as quickly as they could, and reached Fleet-tongue in time to sleep; so they took the bridles off their horses, and let them graze with their saddles on. Their road had lain among the lakes, from which issued the rivers that united above Biarg. In each lake floated a pair of swans. Often they heard the loud hoarse cry of the great northern diver; but there was hardly any grass, for the moor lies high, is swept by the icy blasts from the glacier mountains to the south, and is made up of black sand. Before them all day had stood towering into the sky the Eyreksjokull, a mountain with perfectly precipitous sides of black basalt, domed over with glittering ice. It resembles an immense bridecake. At one place this mountain in former times had gaped, and poured forth a fiery stream of lava that ran to the lakes, and for a while converted them to steam.

One can still see whence this great fiery river issued from the mountain. Little did Grettir think then as he passed under it, a boy of fourteen, that, for the three most lonely, wretched years of his life, that great glacier-crowned mountain was to be the one object on which his eye would rest.

The men were all very tired after their long ride, and they slept till late next morning, lying about on the scant herbage, around a fire made of the roots of trailing willows that they had dug out of the sand.

When they awoke many of the horses had strayed, and some had rolled in the sand, burst their girths and shaken off their saddles. But they could not have gone any great distance, for they were all hobbled. In Iceland thick woollen ropes are put round the legs of the horses, below the hocks, and twisted together into a knot with a knuckle-bone. This serves as a secure hobble, and the wool being soft does not gall the skin.

It was customary in those days for every one to take his own provisions with him, and most of those who went to the great assize carried meal-bags athwart their saddles. Grettir found his horse at last, but not his meal-bag, which had come off, and was lost; for the saddle was turned under the belly of his cob.

The horses could not have strayed far, not only because they were hobbled, but also because the Tongue where they had been turned loose was a narrow strip of land between two rivers; but then the slope was considerable in places, and the meal-bag might have rolled down into the water.

As Grettir was running about hunting for his bag, he saw another man in the same predicament. What is more, he saw that the rest of the party, impatient to get on their way, would tarry no longer for them, and were defiling down the hill to cross the river.

Grettir was in great distress. Just then he saw the man run very directly in one course, and at the same moment Grettir saw something white lying under a mass of lava. It was towards this that the fellow was running. Grettir ran towards it also. It was a meal-sack. The man reached it first, and threw it over his shoulder.

"What have you got there?" asked Grettir, coming up panting.

"My meal-sack," answered the fellow.

"Let me look at it," said Grettir. "It may be mine, not yours. Let me look before you appropriate it."

This the man refused to do.

Grettir's suspicion was confirmed, and he made a catch at the sack, and tried to drag it away from the fellow.

"Oh, yes!" sneered the man—who was a servant at a farm called The Ridge, in Waterdale, and his name Skeggi,—"Oh, yes! you Middlefirthers think you will have everything your own way."

"That is not it," answered Grettir. "Let each man take his own. If the sack be yours, keep it; if mine, I will have it."

"It is a pity Audun is not here," scoffed the serving-man, "or he would trip up your heels and throttle you, as he did on the ice when golfing."

"But as he is not here," retorted Grettir, "you are not like to get the better of me."

Skeggi suddenly took his axe by the haft and hewed at Grettir's head. Grettir saw what he was at, and instantly put up his left hand and caught the handle below where Skeggi's hand held it; wrenched it out of his grasp, and struck him with it, so that his skull was cleft. The thing was done in a moment, and Grettir had done it in self-preservation and without premeditation. He was but a boy of fourteen, and this was a full-grown stout churl.

Grettir at once seized the meal-bag, saw it was his own, and threw it across his saddle. Then he rode after the company. Thorkel Krafla rode at the head of his party, and he had no misgiving that anything untoward had taken place.

But, when Grettir came riding up with his meal-bag, the men asked him if he had left Skeggi still in search of his. Grettir answered in song:

"A rock Troll did her burden throw
Down on Skeggi's skull, I trow.
O'er the battle-ogress saw I flow
Ruby rivers all aglow.
She her iron mouth a-gape
Did the life of Skeggi take."

This sounds like nonsense; to understand it one must have a notion of what constituted poetry in the minds of Icelanders and Northmen. With them the charm of poetry consisted in never calling anything by its right name, but using instead of it some far-fetched similitude or periphrasis. Thus—the burden of the rock Troll is iron. The Troll is the spirit of the mountain, and the heaviest thing found in the mountain is iron. The battle-ogress is the axe which bites in battle. The verses that the Norse poets sang were a series of conundrums, and the hearers puzzled their brains to make out the sense. This time they soon understood what Grettir meant, and the men turned and went back to the Tongue, and there found Skeggi dead.

Grettir went on to Thorkel, and in few words, and to the point, told how things had fallen out. He was not the aggressor. He had merely defended himself.

Thorkel was much troubled, and he told Grettir that he might either come on to the assize or go home; that this act of man-slaughter would be investigated at the law-gathering, and judgment given upon it.

Grettir agreed to go on, and see how matters would turn out for him.

IV: THE DOOM-DAY

That evening they arrived at Thingvalla.

The great plain of Thingvalla is entirely composed of lava. At some remote period before Iceland was colonized a beautiful snowy cone of mountain, called "The Broad Shield," poured forth a deluge of molten rock, which ran in a fiery river down a valley for some miles, half-choking it up, and then spread out over a wide plain where anciently there had been a great lake. Then all cooled, but after the cooling, or whilst it was in process, there came a great crack, crack. The great mass of lava must have been poured over some subterranean caverns; at any rate the whole plain snapped and sank down a good many feet, the lava becoming cracked and starred like glass. Nowadays, one cannot cross the plain because it is all traversed with these fearful cracks, chasms the bottom of which is filled with black water. Where the plain sank deepest there water settled and formed the beautiful Thingvalla Lake.

At the side of one of the cracks where the plain broke off and sank is a very curious pinnacle of black rock, and this was called the Hanging Rock, as criminals were hung from it over the chasm.

In one place two of the cracks unite, and there is a high mound of blistered lava covered with turf and flowers between them. That is called the Law Hill, because the judge and his assessors sat there, and no one could get to them, nor could the accused get away across the chasms.

Now it was the law at this time in Iceland that when any man had been killed his nearest relatives came to the assize, and the slayer appeared by proxy and offered blood-money—that is to say, to pay a fine to the relations, and so patch up the quarrel. But if they refused the money then they were at liberty to pursue and kill him. There were no police then. If the relations wanted to have the criminal punished they must punish him themselves.

Upon this occasion the case was discussed in the court on the finger of rock between the two chasms, the people standing on the further sides of these gulfs, listening, but unable to come a step nearer; and Thorkel appeared for Grettir and offered to pay the blood-money. The relations of the dead Skeggi, after a little fuss, agreed to accept a certain sum, and Thorkel at once paid it. But the court ordered that, as Grettir had acted with undue violence, and as there was no evidence except his word that Skeggi had made the first attack, he should be outlawed, and leave Iceland for three winters. If he set his foot in Iceland till three winters had passed, his life was forfeit. He was allowed a moderate and reasonable time for finding a ship that would take him out of the country.

When the assize was over all rode home, and the way that Thorkel and Grettir went was up the valley that had been half-choked with the lava that rolled down from Broad Shield. They came to a small grassy plain with a gently-sloping hill rising out of it, a place where games took place, the women sitting up the slope and watching the men below. Here Grettir is said to have heaved an enormous stone. The stone is still shown, and I have seen it. I also know that Grettir never lifted it; for it has clearly been brought there by a glacier. But this is an instance of the way in which stories get magnified in telling. No doubt that Grettir did "put" there some big stone, and as it happened that at this spot there was a great rock standing by itself balanced on one point, in after days folks concluded that this must have been the stone thrown by Grettir.

V: THE VOYAGE

Grettir, then, was doomed by the court to leave his native land whilst only a boy, and remain in banishment for three years—that is to say, till he was eighteen. He was not over sorry for this, as he was tired of being at home, and he wanted to see the world.

There was a man called Haflid who had a ship in which he intended to sail that autumn to Norway, and Asmund sent to him to ask him to take Grettir out with him.

Haflid answered that he had not heard a good account of the boy, and did not particularly wish to have him in his boat; but he would stretch a point, because of the regard he had for old Asmund, and he would take him.

Grettir got ready to start; but Asmund would not give him much wherewith to trade when abroad, except some rolls of home-made wadmall, a coarse felty cloth, and a stock of victuals for his voyage. Grettir asked his father to give him some weapon; but the old man answered that he did not trust him with swords and axes, he might put them to a bad use, and it would be better he went without till he had learned to control his temper and keep a check on his hand.

So Grettir parted from his father without much love on either side; and it was noticed when he left home that, though there were plenty of folks ready to bid him farewell, hardly anyone said that he hoped to see him come home again—a certain token that he was not liked by those who had seen most of him. But indeed he had taken no pains to oblige anyone and obtain the regard and love of anyone.

His mother was an exception. She went along the road down the valley with him, wearing a long cloak; and when they were alone, at some distance from the house, she halted and drew out a sword from under her cloak, and handing it to Grettir, said: "This sword belonged to grandfather, and many a hard fight has it been in, and much good work has it done. I give it to you, and hope it may stand you in good stead."

Grettir was highly pleased, and told his mother that he would rather have the sword than anything else that could be given him.

Haflid received Grettir in a friendly manner, and he went at once on board; the ship's anchor was heaved, and forth they went to sea.

Now, directly Grettir got on board he looked about for a place where he could be comfortable, and chose to make a berth for himself under a boat that was slung on deck; then he put up his wadmall, making a sort of felt lining or wall round against the wind and spray, leaving open only the side inwards, and inside he piled his provisions and whatever he had; then he lay down there and did not stir from his snuggery. Now, it was the custom in those days for every man who went in a ship to help in the navigation; but Grettir would not only do nothing, but from his den he shouted or sang lampoons—that is, spiteful songs, making fun of every man on board. They were not good-natured jokes, but bitter, stinging ones.

Naturally enough the other men were annoyed, and they were not slow to tell Grettir what they thought of him. He made no other reply than a lampoon.

After the ship had lost sight of land a heavy sea was encountered, and unfortunately the vessel was rather leaky and hardly seaworthy in dirty weather. The weather was squally and very cold, so that the men suffered much. Moreover, they had to bale out the water from the hold, and this was laborious work. They had not pumps in those days.

The gale increased, and the crew and passengers had been engaged for several days and nights in baling without intermission, but Grettir would not help. He lay coiled up in his wadmall under the boat, peering out at the men and throwing irritating snatches of song at them. This exasperated them to such an extent that they determined to take him and throw him overboard. Haflid heard what they said, and he went to Grettir and reproached him, and told him what was menaced.

"Let them try to use force if they will," said Grettir. "All I can say is that I sha'n't go overboard alone as long as my sword will bite."

"How can you behave as you do?" said Haflid. "Keep silence at least, and do not madden the men with your mockery and sneers."

"I cannot hold my tongue from stabbing," said Grettir.

"Very well, then, stab on, but stab me."

"No; you have not hurt me."

"I say, stab me. Then, if the fellows hear you sing or say something spiteful of me, and I disregard it, they will not mind so much the ill-natured things you say of them."

Grettir considered a moment, and then, remembering that he had heard of something ridiculous that had once occurred to Haflid, he composed a verse about it and shouted it derisively at Haflid as he walked away.

"Just listen to him," said Haflid to the men. "Now he is slandering and insulting me. He is an ill-conditioned cur, so ill-conditioned that I will not stoop to take notice of his insolence. And if you take my advice you will disregard him as I do."

"Well," said the men, "if you shrug your shoulders and pay no regard to his bark, why should we?"

So Haflid, by his tact, smoothed over this difficulty, and averted a danger from Grettir's head.

The weather slowly began to mend, and the sun shone out between the clouds; but the wind was still strong, and the leak gained on the ship, for her bottom was rotten. Now that the sun shone, the poor women who had been aboard and under cover during the gale, crawled forth and came to the side where the boat was, and where was a little shelter, and there sat sewing; whilst Grettir still lay, like a dog in his hutch, within. Then the men began to laugh, and say that Grettir had found suitable company at last—he was not a man among men, but a milksop among women. This was turning the tables on him, and this roused him. Out he came crawling from his den, and ran aft to where the men were baling, and asked to be given the buckets. The way in which it was done was for one to go down into the hold into the water, and fill a tub or cask and hoist it over his head to another man, who carried it up on deck and poured it over the bulwarks. Grettir swung himself down into the hold, and filled and heaved so fast that there had to be two men set to carry up the baling casks, and then two more, four in all attending to him. At one time he even kept eight going, so vigorously did he work;—but then he was fresh, and they exhausted.

When the men saw what a strong, active fellow Grettir was, they praised him greatly, and Grettir, unaccustomed to praise, was delighted and worked on vigorously, and thenceforth was of the utmost assistance in the ship.

They still had bad weather, thick mist, in which they drifted and lost their bearings, and one night unawares they ran suddenly on a rock, and the rotten bottom of the ship was crushed in. They had the utmost difficulty in rescuing their goods and getting the boat ready; but fortunately they were able to put all the women and the loose goods into the boat, man her, and row off before the ship went to pieces. They came to a sandy island, ran the boat ashore, and disembarked in the cold and wet and darkness.

VI: THE RED ROVERS

One morning, after a night of storm on the coast of Norway, the servants ran into the hall of a wealthy bonder, named Thorfin, to tell him that during the night a ship had been wrecked off the coast, and that the crew and passengers were crowded on a little sandy holm, and were signalling for help.

The bonder sprang up and ran down to the shore. He ordered out a great punt from his boat-house, and jumping in with his thralls, rowed to the holm to rescue those who were there.

These were, I need not tell you, the crew and passengers of Haflid's merchant vessel. Thorfin took the half-frozen wretches on board his boat and rowed them to his farm, after which he returned to the islet and brought away the wares. In the meantime his good housewife had been lighting fires, preparing beds, brewing hot ale with honey to sweeten it, and making every preparation she could think of for the sufferers.

Haflid and the rest of the merchants or chapmen who had sailed with him remained at the farm a week, whilst the women were recovering from the cold and exposure and their goods were being dried and sorted. Then they departed, with many thanks for the hospitality shown them, on their way to Drontheim.

Grettir, however, remained. Thorfin, the master of the house, did not much like him. He did not ask him to stay; but then he had not the lack of hospitality to bid him depart. In the farm Grettir never offered to lend a hand in any of the work; he never joined in conversation, he sat over the fire warming himself, and ate and drank heartily.

Thorfin was much abroad, hunting or seeing after the wood-cutting, and he often asked Grettir to come with him. But he was granted no other answer than a shake of the head and a growl. Now the bonder was a merry, kindly-hearted fellow, and he liked to have all about him cheerful. It is no wonder, then, that Grettir, morose and indolent, found no favour with him.

Yule drew near, and Thorfin busked him to depart, with a number of his attendants, to keep the festival at one of his farms distant a good day's journey. His wife was unable to accompany him, as his eldest daughter was ill and needed careful nursing. Grettir he did not invite, as his sullenness would have acted as a damper on the joviality of the banquet.

338

The farmer started for his house where he was going to spend Yule some days before. A large company of guests were invited to meet him, so he took thirty serving-men to attend on him and them.

Norway was at this time being brought into order by Earl Erik, who was putting down with a high hand the bands of rovers who had been the terror of the country. He had outlawed all these men, and that meant that whoever killed them could not be fined or punished in any way for the slaying. Now Thorfin, the farmer with whom Grettir was staying, had been very active against these rovers, and they bore him a grudge. Among the worst of them were two brothers, Thorir wi' the Paunch and Bad Ogmund. They had not yet been caught, and they defied the power of the Earl. They robbed wherever they went, burned farms over the heads of the sleeping inmates, and with the points of their spears drove the shrieking victims back into the flames when they attempted to escape.

Christmas Eve was bright and sunny, and the sick girl was sufficiently recovered to be brought out to take the air on the sunny side of the great hall, leaning on her mother's arm.

Grettir spent the whole day out of doors, not in the most amiable mood at being shut out from the merry-makings, and left to keep house with the women and eight dunderheaded churls. He fed his discontent by sitting on a headland watching the boats glide by, as parties went to convivial gatherings at the houses of their friends. The deep blue sea was speckled with sails, as though gulls were plunging in the waters. Now a stately dragon-ship rolled past, her fearful carved head glittering with golden scales, her sails spread like wings before the breeze, and her banks of oars dipping into the sea and flashing as they rose. Now a wherry was rowed by laden with cakes and ale, and the boatmen's song rang merrily through the crisp air.

The day began to decline, and Grettir was on the point of returning to the farm, when the strange proceedings of a craft at no great distance attracted his attention. He noticed that she stole along in the shadows of the islets, keeping out of sight as much as possible. Grettir could make out of her just this much, that she was floating low in the water, and was built for speed. As she stranded the rowers jumped on the beach. Grettir counted them, and found they were twelve, all armed men. They burst into Thorfin's boathouse, thrust out his punt, and in its place drew in their own vessel, and pulled her up on the rollers.

Mischief was a-brewing—that was clear. So Grettir went down the hill, and sauntered up to the strangers, with his hands in his pockets, kicking the pebbles before him.

"Who is your leader?" he asked curtly.

"I am. What do you want with me?" answered a stout coarse man—
"Thorir, whom they nickname 'wi' the Paunch.' Here is my brother Ogmund.
I reckon that Thorfin knows our names well enough. Don't you think so,
brother? We have come here to settle a little outstanding reckoning. Is he at
home?"

"You are lucky fellows," laughed Grettir, "coming here in the very nick
of time. The bonder is away with all his able-bodied and fighting men, and
won't be back for a couple of days. His wife and daughter are, however, at
the farm. Now is your time if you have old scores to wipe off; for he has left
all his things that he values unprotected, silver, clothing, ale, and food in
abundance."

Thorir listened, then turning to Ogmund he said, "This is as I had expected. But what a chatterbox this fellow is, he lets out everything without
being asked questions."

"Every man knows the use of his tongue," said Grettir. "Now, follow
me, and I will do what I can for you."

The rovers at once followed. Then Grettir took fat Thorir by the hand
and led him to the farm, talking all the way as hard as his tongue could wag.
Now the housewife happened at the time to be in the hall, and hearing Grettir thus talking, she was filled with surprise, and called out to know whom
he had with him.

"I have brought you guests for Yule," said Grettir. "We shall not keep it
in as dull a fashion as we feared. Here come visitors uninvited, but merry,
uncommon merry."

"Who are they?" asked the housewife.

"Thorir wi' the Paunch and Ogmund the Bad, and ten of their com-
rades."

Then she cried out: "What have you done? These are the worst ruffians
in all Norway. Is this the way you repay the kindness Thorfin has shown you
in housing and keeping you here, without it's costing you anything?"

"Stay your woman's tongue!" growled Grettir. "Now bestir yourself and
bring out dry clothes for the guests."

Then the housewife ran away crying, and her sick daughter, who saw
the house invaded by ill-looking men all armed, hid herself.

"Well," said Grettir, "as the women are too scared to attend on you, I
will do what is necessary; so give me your wet clothes, and let me wipe your
weapons and set them by the fire lest they get rusted."

"You are a different fellow from all the rest in the house."

"I do not belong to the house. I am a stranger, an Icelander."

"Then I don't mind taking you along with us when we go away."

"As you will," answered the young fellow; "only mind, I don't behave like this to every one."

Then the freebooters gave him their weapons, and he wiped the salt water from them, and laid them aside in a warm spot. Next he removed their wet garments, and brought them dry suits which he routed out of the clothes-chests belonging to Thorfin and his men.

By this time it was night. Grettir brought in logs and faggots of fir branches, and made a roaring fire that filled the great hall with ruddy light and warmth. In those days the halls were long buildings with a set of hearths running down the middle, and benches beside the fires.

"Now, then, my men," said Grettir, "come to the table and drink, for I doubt not you are thirsty with long rowing."

"We are ready," said they. "But where are the cellars?"

"Oh, if you please, I will bring you ale."

"Certainly, you shall attend on us," said Thorir.

Then Grettir went and fetched the best and strongest ale in Thorfin's cellars, and poured it out for the men. They were very tired and thirsty, and they drank eagerly. Grettir did not stint them in meat or drink, and at last he took his place by them, and recited many tales that made them laugh, he also sang them songs; but they were becoming fast too tipsy to rack their brains to find out the meaning in the poetry.

Not one of the house-churls showed his face in the hall that evening; they slunk about the farm, in the stables and sheds, frightened and trembling.

Then said Thorir: "I'll tell you what, my men. I like this young chap, and I doubt our finding another so handy and willing. What say you all to our taking him into our band?"

The pirates banged their drinking-horns on the table in token of approval. Then Grettir stood up and said:

"I thank you for the offer, and if you are in the same mind to-morrow morning when the ale is no longer in your heads, I will strike hands and go with you."

"Let us drink brotherhood at once," shouted the rovers.

"Not so," said Grettir calmly. "I will not have it said that I took advantage of you when you were not sober. It is said that when the wine is in the wit is out."

They all protested that they would be of the same mind next morning, but Grettir stuck to his decision. They were now becoming so tipsy that he proposed they should go to bed.

"But first of all," said he, "I think you will like to run your eyes over Thorfin's storehouse where he keeps all his treasures."

"That we shall!" roared Thorir, staggering to his feet.

Then Grettir took a blazing firebrand from the hearth, and led the way out of the hall into the night.

The storehouse was detached from the main buildings. It was very strongly built of massive logs, firmly mortised together. The door also was very solid, and the whole stood on a strong stone basement, and a flight of stone steps led up to the door. Adjoining the storehouse was a lean-to building divided off from it by a partition of planks.

The sharp frosty air of night striking on the faces of the revellers increased their intoxication, and they became very riotous, staggering against each other, uttering howls and attempting to sing.

Drawing back the bolt Grettir flung the door open, and showed the twelve rovers into the treasury; and he held the flaming torch above his head and showed the silver-mounted drinking-horns, the embroidered garments, the rich fur mantles, gold bracelets, and bags filled with silver coins obtained from England. The drunken men dashed upon the spoil, knocking each other over and quarrelling for the goods they wanted.

In the midst of this noise and tumult Grettir quietly extinguished the torch, stepped outside and ran the bolt into its place; he had shut them all— all twelve, into the strong-room, and not one of them had his weapons about him.

Then Grettir ran to the farm door and shouted for the housewife. But she would not answer, as she mistrusted him; and no wonder, for he had seemed to be hand and glove with the pirates.

"Come, come!" shouted Grettir, "I have caught all twelve, and all I need now are weapons. Call up the thralls and arm them. Quick! not a moment must be lost."

"There are plenty of weapons here," answered the poor woman, emerging from her place of concealment. "But, Grettir, I mistrust you."

"Trust or no trust," said Grettir, "I must have weapons. Where are the serving-men? Here, Kolbein! Swein! Gamli! Rolf! Confound the rascals, where are they skulking?"

"Over Thorfin's bed hangs a great barbed spear," said the housewife. "You will also find a sword and helmet and cuirass. No lack of weapons, only pluck to wield them is needed."

Grettir seized the casque and spear, girded on the sword and dashed into the yard, begging the woman to send the churls after him. She called the eight men, and they came up timidly—that is to say, four appeared and took the weapons, but the other four, after showing their faces, ran and hid themselves again, they were afraid to measure swords with the terrible rovers.

In the meantime the pirates had been trying the door, but it was too massive for them to break through, so they tore down the partitions of boards between the store and the lean-to room at the side. They were mad with drink and fury. They broke down the door of the side-room easily enough, and came out on the platform at the head of the stone steps just as Grettir reached the bottom.

Thorir and Ogmund were together. In the fitful gleams of the moon they seemed like demons as they scrambled out, armed with splinters of deal they had broken from the planks and turned into weapons. The brothers plunged down the narrow stairs with a howl that rang through the snow-clad forest for miles. Grettir planted the boar-spear in the ground and caught Thorir on its point. The sharp double-edged blade, three feet in length, sliced into him and came out between his shoulders, then tore into Ogmund's breast a span deep. The yew shaft bent like a bow, and flipped from the ground the stone against which the butt-end had been planted. The wretched men crashed over the stair, tried to rise, staggered, and fell again. Grettir trod on Thorir, wrenched the spear out of him, and then running up the steps cut down another rover as he came through the door. Then the rest came out stumbling over each other, some armed with bits of broken stick, others unarmed, and as they came forth Grettir hewed at them with the sword, or thrust at them with the spear.

In the meantime the churls had come up, armed indeed, but not knowing how to use the weapons, and in a condition of too great terror to use them to any purpose. The pirates saw that they were being worsted, and their danger sobered them. They went back into the room and ripped the planks till they had obtained serviceable pieces, and then came two together down the stair, warding off Grettir's blows with their sticks, and not attempting to strike. Then they forced him back and allowed space and time for those behind to leap down to the ground. If then they had combined they might have recovered the mastery, but they did not believe that they were assailed by a single enemy, they thought that there must have been many; consequently those who had leaped from the platform, instead of attacking Grettir from behind, ran away across the farmyard, and those who were warding off his blows, finding themselves unsupported, lost heart, and leaped down as well and attempted to escape. The yard was full of flying frightened wretches, too blinded by their fear to find the gate, and in the wildness of their terror they climbed or leaped over the yard wall and ran towards the boat-house. Grettir went after them. They plunged into the dark boat-shed, and possessed themselves of the oars, whilst some tried to run their boat down into the water. Grettir followed them in the gloom, smiting to right and left. The bewildered wretches in the darkness hit each other, stumbled and fell in the boat, and some wounded went into the water.

The thralls, content that the pirates had cleared out of the yard, did not trouble themselves to pursue them, but went into the farmhouse. The good woman in vain urged them to go after and succour Grettir. They thought they had done quite enough. It is true, they had neither killed nor wounded anyone, but they had seen some men killed. So Grettir got no help from them. He was still in the boat-house, and he had this advantage: the boat-house was open to the air on the side that faced the sea, whilst the further side was closed with a door, consequently Grettir was himself in shadow. But the moon shone on the water, and he could see the black figures of the rovers cut sharply against this silver background. So he could see where to strike, whilst he himself was unseen.

One stroke from an oar reached him on the shoulder, and for the moment numbed his arm; but he speedily recovered sensation, and killed two more of the ruffians; then the remaining four made a dash together, past him, through the door, and separating into pairs, fled in opposite directions. Grettir went after one of the couples and tracked them to a neighbouring farm, where they dashed into a granary and hid among the straw. Unfortunately for them most of the wheat had been thrashed out, so that only a few bundles remained. Grettir shut and bolted the door behind him, then chased the poor wretches like rats from corner to corner, till he had cut them both down. Then he opened the door, and cast the corpses outside.

In the meanwhile the weather was changing, the sky had become overcast with a thick snow fog that rolled up from the sea, so that Grettir, on coming out, saw that he must abandon the pursuit of the remaining two. Moreover, his arm pained him, his strength was failing him, and a sense of overpowering fatigue stole over him.

The housewife had placed a lamp in a window of a loft as a guide to Grettir in the fog; the stupid house-thralls could not be induced by her to go out in search of him, and she was becoming uneasy at his protracted absence. The fog turned into small snow, thick and blinding, and Grettir struggled through it with difficulty, as the weariness he felt became almost overpowering. At last he reached the farm and staggered in through the door. He could hardly speak. He went to the table, took a horn of mead, drank some, and then threw himself down among the rushes on the floor by the fire, full armed grasping the sword, and in a moment was asleep.

He did not wake for twelve hours; but the cautious and prudent housewife had sent out the carles in search of the pirates. The dead bodies were found, some in the yard, some in the boat-house; then Grettir woke and came to them and pointed out in what direction the only remaining two had run. The snow had fallen so thick that their traces could not be followed, but before nightfall they were discovered, dead, under a rock where they had taken refuge; they had died of cold and loss of blood. All the bodies were collected and a great cairn of stones was piled over them.

When they had been buried, then the housewife made Grettir take the high seat in the hall, and she treated him with the utmost respect, as he deserved.

Time passed, and Thorfin prepared to return home; he dismissed his guests, and he and his men got into their boat to return home. No tidings had reached him of the events that had happened whilst he had been away. The first thing he saw as he came rowing to his harbour was his punt lying stranded. This surprised and alarmed him, and he bade his men row harder. They ran to the boat-house, and then saw it occupied by a vessel, on the rollers, which there was no mistaking; he knew it well, it belonged to those redoubted pirates Thorir and Ogmund. For a moment he was silent with the terror and grief that came on him. "The Red Rovers!" he said, when he recovered the stunning sense of alarm. "The Red Rovers are here—they are on my farm. God grant they have not hurt my wife and daughter!"

Then he considered what was to be done, whether it was best to go at once to the farm, or to make a secret approach to it from different quarters, and surprise the enemy.

Grettir was to blame. He ought not to have allowed Thorfin to be thus thrown into uncertainty and distress. He had seen the master's boat round the headland and enter the bay, but he would neither go himself to meet him on the strand, nor suffer anyone else to go.

"I do not care even if the bonder be a bit disturbed at what he sees," said the young man.

"Then let me go," urged the wife.

"You are mistress, do as you like," said Grettir bluntly.

So the housewife and her daughter went down towards the boat-house, and when Thorfin saw them he ran to meet them, greatly relieved but much perplexed, and he clasped his wife to his heart and said, "God be praised that you and my child are safe! But tell me how matters have stood whilst I have been away, for I cannot understand the boat being where I found it."

"We have been in grievous peril," answered his wife. "But the ship-wrecked boy whom you sheltered has been our protector, better than a dozen men."

Then he said, "Sit down on this rock by me and tell me all."

They took each other by the hand and sat on a stone; and the attendants gathered round, and the housewife told them the whole story from beginning to end. When she spoke of the way in which the young Icelander had led the tipsy rovers into the storehouse and fastened them in, without their swords, the men burst into a shout of joy; and when her tale was concluded, their exultant cries rang so loud that Grettir heard them in the farmhouse.

Thorfin said nothing to interrupt the thread of his wife's story; and after she had done he remained silent, rapt in thought. No one ventured to disturb him. Presently he looked up, and said quietly, "That is a good proverb which says, 'Never despair of anyone.' Now I must speak a word with Grettir."

Thorfin walked with his wife to the farm, and when he saw Grettir he held out both his hands to him, and thanked him.

"This I say to you," said Thorfin, "which few would say to their best of friends—that I hope some day you may need my help, and then I will prove to you how thankful I am for what you have done. I can say no more."

Grettir thanked him, and spent the rest of the winter at his house. The story of what he had done spread through all the country, and was much praised, especially by such as had suffered from the violence of the Ked Rovers. But Thorfin made to Grettir a present, in acknowledgment of what he had done; and that present was the sword that had hung above his bed, with which Grettir had killed so many of the rovers. Now, concerning this sword a tale has to be told.

VII: THE STORY OF THE SWORD

Some little while before the slaying of the Red Rovers, a strange event had taken place.

Grettir had made the acquaintance of a man called Audun, who lived at a little farm at some distance from the house of Thorfin, and he walked over there occasionally to sit and talk with his friend. As he returned late at night he noticed that a strange light used to dance at the end of a cliff that over-hung the sea, at the end of a headland; a lonely desolate headland it was, without house or stall near it. Grettir had never been there, and as it was so bare, he knew that no one lived on that headland, so he could not account for the light. One day he said to Audun that he had seen this strange light, which was not steady but flickered; and he asked him what it meant.

Audun at once became very grave, and after a moment's hesitation said, "You are right. No one lives on that ness, but there is a great mound there, under which is buried Karr the Old, the forefather of your host Thorfin; and it is said that much treasure was buried with him. That is why the ghostly light burns above the mound, for—you must know that flames dance over hidden treasure."

"If treasure be hidden there, I will dig it up," said Grettir.

"Attempt nothing of the kind," said Audun, "or Thorfin will be angry. Besides, Karr the Old is a dangerous fellow to have to deal with. He walks at night, and haunts all that headland and has scared away the dwellers in the nearest farms. No one dare live there because of him. That is why the Ness is all desolate without houses."

"I will stay the night here," said Grettir, "and to-morrow we will go together to the Ness, and take spade and pick and a rope, and I will see what can be found."

Audun did not relish the proposal, but he did not like to seem behindhand with Grettir, and he reluctantly agreed to go with him.

So next day the two went out on the Ness together. They passed two ruined farmhouses, the buildings rotting, the roofs fallen in. Those who had lived in them had been driven away by the dweller in the old burial mound, or barrow. The Norse name for these sepulchral mounds is Haug, pronounced almost like How; and where in England we have places with the names ending in hoe, there undoubtedly in former times were such mounds. Thus, in Essex are Langenhoe and Fingringhoe, that is to say the Long Barrow and Fingar's How. Also, the Hoe, the great walk at Plymouth above the sea, derives its name from some old burial mound now long ago destroyed.

The Ness was a finger of land running out into the sea, and on it grew no trees, only a little coarse grass; at the end rose a great circular bell-shaped mound, with a ring of stones set round it, to mark its circumference. Grettir began to dig at the summit, and he worked hard. The day was short, and the sun was touching the sea as his pickaxe went through an oak plank, into a hollow space beneath, and he knew at once that he had struck into the chamber of the dead. He worked with redoubled energy, and tore away the planks, leaving a black hole beneath of unknown depth, but which to his thinking could not be more than seven feet beneath him. Then he called to Audun for the rope. The end he fastened round his waist, and bade his friend secure the other end to a pole thrown across the pit mouth. When this was done, Audun cautiously let Grettir down into the chamber of the dead.

Now, you must know that in heathen times what was often done with old warriors was to draw up a boat on the shore, and to seat the dead man in the cabin, with his horse slain beside him, sometimes some of his slaves or thralls were also killed and put in with him, and his choicest treasures were heaped about him. This men did because they thought that the dead man would want his weapons, his raiment, his ornaments, his horse and his servants in the spirit world. Of late years such a mound has been opened in Norway, and a great ship found in it, well preserved, with the old dead chief's bones in it. When a ship was not buried, then a chamber of strong planks was built, and he was put in that, and the earth heaped over him. Into such a chamber had Grettir now dug.

He soon reached the bottom, and was in darkness, only a little light came in from above, through the hole he had broken in the roof of the cabin or chamber. His feet were among bones, and these he was quite sure were horse bones. Then he groped about.

As his eyes became more accustomed to the darkness, he discerned a figure seated in a throne. It was the long-dead Karr the Old. He was in full harness, with a helmet on his head with bull's horns sticking out, one on each side; his hands were on his knees, and his feet on a great chest. Round his neck was a gold torque or necklet, made of bars of twisted gold, hooked together behind the head. Grettir in the dark could only just make out the glimmer of the gold, but it seemed to him that a phosphorescent light played about the face of the dead chief.

So little light was left, that Grettir hasted to collect what he could. There stood a brazen vessel near the chair, in which were various articles, probably of worth, but it was too dark for Grettir to see what they were. He brought the vessel to the rope and fastened the end of the cord to its handle. Then he went back to the old dead man and drew away a short sword that lay on his lap, and this he placed in the brass vessel. Next he began to un-hook the gold torque from his neck, and as he did this the phosphorescent flame glared strangely about the dead man's face.

Then, all at once, as both his hands were engaged undoing the hook be-hind Karr's neck, he was clipped. The dead man's arms had clutched him, and with a roar like a bull Karr the Old stood up, holding him fast, and now all the light that had played over his features gathered into and glared out of his eyes.

When Audun heard the roar, he was so frightened that he ran from the barrow, and did not stay his feet till he reached home, feeling convinced that the ghost or whatever it was that lived in the tomb had torn Grettir to pieces.

Then began in the chamber of the dead a fearful wrestle. Grettir was at times nigh on smothered by the gray beard of the dead chief, that had been growing, growing, in the vault, ever since he had been buried.

How long that terrible struggle continued no one can tell. Grettir had to use his utmost force to stand against Karr the Old. The two wrestled up and down in the chamber, kicking the horse bones about from side to side, stum-bling over the coffer, and the brass vessel, and the horse's skull, striking against the sides, and when they did this then masses of earth and portions of broken plank fell in from above.

At last Karr's feet gave way under him and he fell, and Grettir fell over him. Then instantly he laid hold of his sword, and smote off Old Karr's head and laid it beside his thigh.

This, according to Norse belief, was the only way in which to prevent a dead man from walking, who had haunted the neighbourhood of his tomb, and in the Icelandic sagas we hear of other cases where the same proceeding was gone through. The Norsemen held to something more dreadful than ghosts walking; they thought that some evil spirit entered into the bodies of the dead, that when this happened the dead no longer decayed, but walked, and ate, and drank, and fought, very much like living ruffians, but with redoubled strength. Then, when this happened, nothing was of any avail save the digging up of the dead man, cutting off his head and laying it at his thigh.

When Grettir had done this, he despoiled Karr the Old of his helm, his breast-plate, his torque, and he took the box on which the feet had rested. He fastened all together to the rope, and called to Audun to haul up. He received no answer, so he swarmed up himself, and finding that his friend had run away he pulled up what he had tied together, and carried the whole lot in his arms to the house of Thorfin. Thorfin and his party were at supper; and when Grettir came in, the bonder looked up, and asked why he did not keep regular hours, and be at the table when the meal began. Grettir made no other answer than to throw all he carried down on the supper-table before the master. Thorfin raised his eyebrows when he saw so much treasure.

"Where did you get all this?" he asked.

Then Grettir answered in one of his enigmatical songs:

"Thou who dost the wave-shine shorten,
My attempt has been to find

In the barrow what was hidden,
Deep in darkness black and blind.

Nothing of the dragon's treasure
With the dead is left behind."

By the wave-shine shortener he meant Thorfin; the dragon's treasure meant gold, because dragons were thought to line their lairs with that metal.

Thorfin saw that Grettir's eye looked longingly at the short sword that had lain on the knees of Karr. He said: "It was a heathen custom in old times to bury very much that was precious along with the dead. I do not blame you for what you have done; but this I will say, that there is no one else about this place who would have ventured to attempt what you have done. As for that sword on which you cast your eyes so longingly, it has ever been in our family, and I cannot part with it till you have shown that you are worthy to wear it."

Then that sword was hung up over Thorfin's bed. You have heard how Grettir did show that he was worthy to wear it, and also how Thorfin gave it him.

Now, this tale about the sword will very well illustrate what was said at the beginning, that the history of Grettir contains, in the main, truth; but that this substance of truth has been embroidered over by fancy. What is true is, that during the winter in which he was with Thorfin he did dig into the mound in which Karr was buried, and did take thence his treasures and his sword. But all the story of his fight with the dead man was added. The same story occurs in a good many other sagas, as in that of Hromund Greip's son, who also got a sword by digging into a barrow for it. When the history of Grettir was told, and this adventure of his was related, those who told the story imported into it the legend of the fight of Hromund in the grave with the dead man, so as to make the history of Grettir more amusing. As you will see by the tale, no one else was present when it happened, for Audun had run away, and it was not like Grettir to boast of what he had done. This was an embellishment added by the story-teller, and from the storyteller the incident passed into the volume of the story-writer.

Grettir had now two good swords; one long, which he called Jokull's Gift, that he had received from his mother, and this short one that he wore at his girdle, which he had taken out of the grave of Karr the Old, and which he had won fairly by his bravery in the defence of the house and family of Thorfin.

VIII: OF THE BEAR

When spring came, then Grettir left his friend Thorfin, and went north along the Norwegian coast, and was everywhere well received, because the story of how he had killed twelve rovers, he being as yet but a boy, was noised through all the country, and every one who had anything to lose felt safer because that wicked gang was broken up. Nothing of consequence is told about him during that summer. For the winter he did not return to Thorfin as asked, but accepted the invitation of another bonder, named Thorgils.

Thorgils was a merry, pleasant man, and he had a great company in his house that winter. Among his visitors was a certain Biorn, a distant cousin, a man whom Thorgils did not like, as he was a slanderous-tongued fellow, and moreover he was a braggart. He was one of those persons we meet with not infrequently who cannot endure to hear another praised; who, the moment a good word is spoken of someone, immediately puts in a nasty, spiteful word, and tells an unkind story, so as to drag that person down in the general opinion. At the same time, concerning himself he had only praiseworthy and wonderful feats to relate about his wit, his wisdom, his craft, his knowledge of the world, about his strength and courage.

Thorgils knew how much, or rather how little, to believe of what Biorn said, and he did not pay much regard to his talk. But now Grettir had an opportunity of seeing and of feeling how mistaken had been his conduct on board the ship upon which he had come to Norway, when he made lampoons on the sailors and chapmen, and stung them with sharp words. He saw how disagreeable a fellow Biorn was, how much he was disliked, and by some despised; and he kept very greatly to himself and out of Biorn's way. He did not wish to quarrel with him, because he was the relative of his host, and he was afraid that his anger would get the better of him if he did come to words with the braggart.

Grettir had grown a great deal since he left Iceland, and he was now a strapping fellow, broad built but not short. He was not handsome, but his face was intelligent.

It fell out that a bear gave much trouble that winter to Thorgils and the neighbouring farmers. It was so strong and so daring that no folds were secure against it, and Thorgils and the other farmers endured severe losses through the depredations of Bruin.

Before Yule, a party was formed to go in search of and kill the bear, but all that was done was to find the lair.

The bear had taken up his abode in the face of a tremendous cliff that overhung the sea. There was but one path up to the cave, and that was so narrow that only one man could creep along it at a time. Moreover, if his foot slipped he would be flung over the edge upon the rocks or skerries below against which the waves dashed.

"When the den of the bear had been discovered," Biorn said, "That is the main thing. Now I know where the rogue lies, I'll settle with him, trust me. I've been the death of scores of bears. My only dread is lest he be afraid of me, and will not come on."

And, actually, Biorn went out on several moonlit nights to watch for the bear. He saw that the only way to deal with him would be to stop the track from the den, and fight him as he attempted to come away. He took his short sword and great shield with him covered with ox-hide, and one night he laid himself down on the path of the bear, and put his shield over him. He thought that Bruin would come smelling at the great hide-covered shield, and then all at once he (Biorn) would spring up and drive his sword into the heart of the bear. That was his plan—and not a bad plan—only, unfortunately for Biorn, the bear did not come out for a long time. He had got an inkling that a man was watching for him, so he was shy, and whilst he waited before venturing forth, Biorn, who had been drinking pretty freely that evening, went to sleep.

Presently the bear came out, crept cautiously down the narrow track, snuffing about, and when he came to Biorn, he plucked with his claws at the shield, and with one wrench had it off and tumbled it down the cliff.

Biorn woke with a start, rose to his knees, saw the huge bear before him, and in a moment turned tail, and ran as hard as he could run to Thorgils' house, and was too scared to be able to boast that he had killed or wounded the bear.

Next morning his shield was found where the bear had thrown it, and much fun did this adventure of the braggart occasion. This made him very irritable and more spiteful than ever.

Thorgils now said that really something must be done to rid the neighbourhood of the bear, so a party of eight set out well armed with spears; of this party were Biorn and Grettir. They reached the point where the track to the den ran up the cliff to the lair, and one man after another tried it. But there was no getting at the bear; for as soon as a man came near the beast put his great forepaws forth and caught and snapped the spear-heads or beat them down. As already said, only one could crawl up at a time.

Grettir had gone out that day in a fur coat that his friend Thorfin had given him, and which he greatly valued. When the onslaught against the bear began, he took off his fur coat, and folded it, and put it on a stone. Biorn saw this, and, when none observed, he took the fur coat and threw it into the cave of the bear. Grettir did not see what had been done till the party, disappointed with their want of success, made ready to depart, when he missed it, and then some suspicion entered his head as to what had been done with it, and by whom, but he said nothing.

As they walked home, Biorn began to taunt Grettir with having done nothing all day. He could kill robbers who were unarmed and were drunk, perhaps asleep, but a bear was too serious an adversary for him.

Grettir said nothing, but as his gaiter thong became broken, he stopped and stooped to mend it. Thorgils asked if they should wait for him. Grettir declined.

"Oh," said Biorn, "it is all nonsense. It is a pretence. He means to have all the glory of fighting the bear alone when we have gone on."

He said the truth, but he had no idea when he spoke that it was the truth.

Grettir tarried till the party had crossed a hill and was out of sight, then he turned and went back to the bear's den. He slipped his hand through the loop at the end of the handle of his short sword that he had taken from the grave of Karr the Old, and let it hang on his wrist, but he held the long sword, Jokull's gift, by the pommel. His plan was to use the long sword if needed, but if the bear came to close quarters he would throw it down and grasp the short one without having to put his hand to his girdle for it. Very cautiously he crept along the path. Bruin saw him, and was now angry and hungry, and came down to meet him. The bear was somewhat above him; Grettir halted, and the bear stood up growling on his hind-legs.

At once the long sword was whirled and fell on the right wrist above the paw, and cut it off. The bear immediately fell down on all-fours; but the amputated paw was on the side away from the wall of rock, and when he went down on the stump he was overbalanced, and came down with his whole weight on Grettir.

Grettir let fall his long sword at once, and with both hands grasped the brute's ears, and held his head off lest he should get a bite at him. Grettir, in after years, was wont to say that this was the hardest tussle he had in his life—it was even worse than anything he had to do with the rovers. For if the beast had but been able to nip him on the breast, or shoulder, or face with his great fangs, all would have been up with him. Moreover, the ears were so smooth that he had to do his utmost not to let them slip. Grettir had the wit to drag back the brute's head to the rock, and by so doing the bear could not use his only uninjured fore-leg, armed with terrible claws, which would have ripped Grettir's clothes and flesh.

In the struggle the two went over the edge, and for a moment Grettir thought, as they spun in the air, that he was lost. But the bear was heavier than the lad, consequently he fell crash on the rocks at the bottom first, and Grettir on him, breaking Grettir's fall by his great body. The bear's back was broken.

Then Grettir got up, shook himself, left the bear, went up the path and found his fur coat torn to tatters, and he put it about him, recovered also his long sword, and took the cut-off paw of the bear.

He now went back to Thorgils' house, and when he came into the hall where the fires were blazing, every one laughed to see him in his tattered coat; but when he gave the paw of the bear to Thorgils the general merriment exchanged to surprise. Biorn, however, could not contain himself for vexation, and launched forth some coarse jest that made Grettir's blood tingle in his veins.

"Do not listen to him," said Thorgils. "You are a brave fellow, and there are not many your like." Then turning to Biorn, he said, "Kinsman, I advise and warn you to keep a civil tongue in your head, or you will come to rue it, and have to be taught better manners."

"Oh, if I am to learn manners from Grettir, that is sending me to a cub indeed!"

"I want to know," said Grettir, "whether you threw my fur coat into the den?"

"I am not afraid of saying that I did."

"Will you give me another in its place?"

"I have not the smallest intention of doing charity to beggars."

The braggart knew that Grettir was restraining himself because he did not wish to quarrel with his host's kinsman, and he took advantage of his knowledge. But Thorgils was greatly distressed and ashamed, and he said to Grettir:

"Pay no attention to his words. He has insulted you, and I will pay you a fine in compensation for his insult, that it may be buried and forgotten."

That was customary then. When one had hurt another in body or in honour by blow or foul word, he was bound to pay a sum of money; if he did not then the man injured was required by the laws of honour to revenge the injury.

But when Biorn heard this proposal, he shouted out that he would not suffer the matter to be so compromised; he was not ashamed of his words. Thorgils drew Grettir aside, and said to him that his kinsman was a badly-behaved, brutal fellow, but that he hoped Grettir would not take up the quarrel in his house; and Grettir promised him solemnly that he would not attempt to take revenge for the rudeness of Biorn so long as they were both inmates of his house.

"As for what may happen between you later," said Thorgils, "I wash my hands of responsibility. If Biorn is offensive to those who have never hurt him, he must take the consequences."

So matters remained; only that Biorn, presuming on his position, became daily more arrogant, intolerable, and abusive, so that Grettir had to exercise daily self-restraint to keep his hands off him. And glad he was when spring came, that he might get away to another part of Norway.

As for Biorn, he went in the summer to England in a ship that belonged to Thorgils, trading there for Thorgils and for himself. Consequently, all that summer he and Grettir did not meet.

IX: THE SLAYING OF BIORN

Grettir left Thorgils very good friends, and he went with some merchants to the north, but when the summer was over he came back south, and arrived at a little island in the entrance of the Drontheim firth. His intention was to see Earl Sweyn, and perhaps take service under him; but if so, things fell out other than he had reckoned. For, as he was in this island, there came in a large merchant vessel from England, and Grettir and those with him at once went to see the shipmen, and among them was Biorn. The ship was, in fact, that of Thorgils, and it was laden with commodities bought in England, or obtained by exchange for the wool, and furs, and women's embroidery sent out in the spring by Thorgils.

Directly Biorn saw Grettir he turned red, and pretended not to recognize him; but Grettir went to him at once and said:

"Now has come the time when we two can settle our differences."

"Oh," said Biorn, "that is soon done. I don't object to paying a trifle."

"The time for paying is over," said Grettir. "Thorgils offered an indemnity for your insolence, and you refused to consent to it."

Then Biorn saw that there was no help for him but that he must fight. So he girded him for the conflict, and he and Grettir went down on the sand, and they fought.

The fight did not last long. Grettir's sword cut him that he fell and died.

When the news reached Thorgils, he got ready, and came by boat as fast as he could to see the earl at Drontheim. He found the earl very angry, but he said to him:

"I am a kinsman of the fallen man, and I know that he treated Grettir with intolerable insolence, and that he refused every compromise. Then remember what a benefit has been done to the country by Grettir, who ridded it of the Red Rovers, Thorir wi' the Paunch and Ogmund the Bad."

Thorfin also came to Drontheim when he heard of the straits into which Grettir had come through killing Biorn. The earl called a council on the matter, and said he would not come to a decision till he had heard what Biorn's brother Hiarandi had to say on the matter. Hiarandi was a violent man, and he was very wroth. He would hear of no patching up of the matter, and he vowed he would not, as he expressed it, "bring his brother into his purse." As already said, it was customary when a man had been killed to offer a sum of money to the next of kin, and if he accepted the money the quarrel was at an end. When we now speak of "pocketing an injury," reference is made to this same ancient usage, by which every offence was estimated at so much money, and if the wronged man took money for the offence committed against him, he was said to pocket it. When the earl went into the matter, and heard how Grettir had been wronged and outraged by Biorn, he gave his decision that Grettir had not acted contrary to law, and that Biorn had justly forfeited his life. Thorfin offered the sum of money which the earl considered was sufficient to atone to the relations for the death of Biorn, but Hiarandi refused absolutely to touch it.

Then Thorfin knew that Grettir's life was in danger, for Hiarandi would certainly try to take it; so he begged his kinsman Arinbiorn to go about with Grettir, and keep on the look-out against the mischief that threatened.

Now it fell out one day that Grettir and Arinbiorn were walking down a street in Drontheim when their way led before a narrow lane opening into it. They did not see any danger in the way, and were unaware of this lane. But just as they had passed it a man jumped out from behind, in the shadow, swinging an axe, and he struck at Grettir between the shoulder-blades. Fortunately, Arinbiorn had looked round at the lane, and he saw the man leap out, so he suddenly dragged Grettir forward with such a jerk that Grettir fell on his knee. This saved his life, for the axe came on his shoulder-blade, made a gash that cut to his armpit, and then the axe buried itself in the roadway. Instantly Grettir started to his feet, turned round, and with his short sword smote in the very nick of time as the man, who was Hiarandi, was pulling up his axe to cut at Grettir again. Grettir's sword fell on his upper arm near the shoulder, and cut it off. Then out rushed some servants of Hiarandi on Arinbiorn and Grettir, who set their backs against a house-wall and defended themselves with such valour that they killed or put to flight all who had assailed them.

Now, this had been a base and cowardly attempt on the life of Grettir, and Hiarandi richly deserved his fate. But the earl was exceedingly angry when he heard the news, and he called a council together. Thorfin and Grettir attended, and the earl angrily charged Grettir with having committed great violence, and being the cause of the death of Hiarandi and some of his servants.

Grettir acknowledged this; but showed his wound, and stated how he had been attacked from behind; how his life had been saved by the promptitude of Arinbiorn, and how he had but defended himself against enemies who sought his life.

"I wish you had been killed," said the earl, "and then there would have been an end to these disorders."

"You would not have a man not raise his hands to save his head?" said Grettir.

"I see one thing," exclaimed the earl. "Ill luck attends you, and you are doomed to commit violences wherever you are."

The end of it was that Earl Sweyn said he would not have Grettir to live in Norway any longer, lest he should be the cause of fresh troubles. But he remained over the third winter, and next spring sailed for Iceland, the time of his outlawing being ended.

X: OF GRETTIR'S RETURN

When Grettir came back to Biarg, he found his father so old and infirm as to be no more able to stir abroad, and Atli managed the farm for him along with Illugi, Grettir's youngest brother, now grown up to be a big boy. Grettir was now aged eighteen, but he looked and was a man. Illugi was about fifteen, a gentle, pleasant boy. He and the kindly, careful Atli were as unlike Grettir as well could be; they avoided quarrels, they had a civil word for every one, and took pains to make themselves agreeable, whether to guests in their house, or when staying anywhere, to their hosts. Grettir never troubled himself to be courteous or to be obliging to anyone. Now that he was back from Norway he was rather disposed to think much of himself as a man more brave and audacious than his fellows, for, had he not killed twelve rovers, broken into a barrow, slain a bear, and been the death of one man in a duel, and another who had attempted to assassinate him? Atli did not much like his manner, and cautioned him not to be overbearing whilst at home, lest he should involve himself in fresh troubles. But words were wasted on Grettir. He was not the fellow to listen to advice, but one of those men who must learn the bitter lessons of life by personal experience. It is so with men always. Some, who are thoughtful, see what God's law is which is impressed on all society, and listen to what others have found out as the lessons taught them by their lives, so they are able to go out equipped against the trials and difficulties of life. But others will neither look nor listen, and such have to go through every sort of adversity, till they have learned the great truths of social life, and perhaps they only acquire them when it is too late to put them in practice.

It is with laws and courtesies of life as with the three R's. A man will fare badly who cannot read, write, and cipher. If he learns these accomplishments as a child, he does well; he is furnished for the struggle of life, and starts on the same footing as other men; but if as a child he is morose and indifferent, and refuses to learn, then all through his life he is met with difficulties, owing to his ignorance, and he finds that he must learn to read, write, and do sums; and he has to acquire these in after years with much less ease than he might have learnt as a child, and after he has lost many chances of getting on which might have been seized, had he known these things before.

Grettir's temper on his return may be judged by one incident that happened almost directly. He had not forgotten his struggle on the ice with his cousin Audun, and he was resolved to have another trial of strength with him. So he had not been home many days before he rode over the hill to Audunstead in his best harness, and with a beautiful saddle on his horse that had been given him by Thorfin. The time was that of hay, and he saw the field round Audun's farm full of rich grass, ready to be cut. He took the bridle off his horse and turned it into Audun's meadow. This was not out of thoughtlessness, but out of insolence, and was intended to exasperate Audun. In Iceland grass grows very little, and only fit to be cut for hay round the farms in what is called the tun, where it is richly dressed with stable-dung. Consequently hay is very scarce and very precious. The grass never grows much longer than one's fingers, and so even in the tun it is not plentiful. He knocked at the door of the farm and asked for his cousin, and was told that Audun had gone to the highland sel to fetch curds, and would be back later. The sel was a farm on the highland, only occupied in summer, when the cattle were driven to the moors and hills to feed on the grass there, and to save that in the lowlands against winter.

Here a word or two must be said about Icelandic names of places and people. When Iceland was colonized, those who first settled in the land and built farms, called the places after their own names in a great many cases; they called them so-and-so's stead, or so-and-so's by or farm. A by is the Scotch byre, and in Icelandic is bœr, pronounced exactly like the Scotch word. Wherever, in the north and east of England, Norse settlers came, there we find names of places ending in the same way, and we know that these were farms and dwellings of old Norse settlers. Thus in Northumberland, Yorkshire, and Lincolnshire, are plenty of Norse place-names. Near Thirsk is Thirkelby or Thorkel's-byre, near Ripon is Enderby or Andrew's-byre. Not only so, but where there are high hills there we find also sels, that is summer-farms, like the Alps to which the cattle are driven in Switzerland. Next as to the names of people. What is a little puzzling to remember is the number of persons whose names begin with Thor. Thor, the god of thunder, was regarded with the highest reverence by the Icelanders; they thought of him even more than they did of Odin, the chief god of all, who had one eye, and his one fiery eye was the sun. Thor was called the Redbeard, and the aurora borealis was thought to be his waving red-beard in the sky. The thunderbolt they regarded as his hammer. To show their respect for him, children were named after him: Thor-grim means Thor's wrath; Thor-kel, Thor's kettle, in which the sacrificial meat was cooked in offering to Thor; Thor-gil was Thor's boy or servant; Thor-hall was Thor's flint spear-head, and so on. The Northumbrian king, St. Osmund, takes his name from the Hand of God, and the name is the same as Asmund, the father of Grettir. Oswald means the elect of the god; in Icelandic the name would be Aswald.

When Grettir found that Audun was from home, he went into the hall and lay down on the bench nearest the door. The hall was dark.

The halls of the Icelandic chiefs were like bodies of churches, and were divided into a nave with side aisles; and were lighted by windows in a clerestory that were covered with the skin of the lining of a sheep's stomach, to let in light and keep out cold, because they had no glass. In the side aisles were the beds of those who lived in the house, some with doors and shutters, which could be fastened from within; and a man in danger of his life would so sleep. He would go to bed, and then close himself in and lock the shutters, that no one could get at him when he was asleep. The fires and benches and tables were in the nave, or middle of the great hall. Over the partitions for the beds were hung shields and swords and spears, and on grand occasions hangings were put up all along the sides, hiding the beds and berths in the side aisles. The arrangement in an Icelandic house at the present day is much the same, only on a very much reduced scale. The people live and eat and sleep in the same room, like the saloon-cabin of a ship, with the berths round the walls.

Audun arrived in the afternoon with a horse that carried curds in skins on its back; that is to say, skins were made into bottles, as is still common in Palestine. When he saw that a horse with a saddle on it was wandering about in his meadow, trampling down the grass and eating it, he was very vexed; and throwing one bottle of curd over his back, and hanging another in front on his breast to counterbalance it, he ran into the house to ask who had done this.

The hall was dusky, and Audun's eyes were accustomed to the bright summer-light. As he entered Grettir put out his foot; Audun did not see it, and stumbled over it, fell on the skin of curds and burst it. Then he jumped up, very angry, and asked who had played him this scurvy trick. Grettir named himself, and said he had come over about that matter of the wrestle on the ice. Audun, still very irate, all at once stooped, picked up the burst skin, and dashed it in Grettir's face, smothering him with curds. Then he threw down the other curd-bottle, and began to wrestle with Grettir. They swung up and down the hall, kicking over the benches, now upon the floor, then on the stone-paved fire-hearth in the midst; then they crashed against the walls and pillars of the bed-chambers, and as they did so the shields and weapons hung over them clashed like bells. Some frightened servant-maids came in, and ran out again in alarm, calling for aid.

Audun felt now that Grettir had outgrown him in strength, but he would not give in; then they slipped on the curd and both fell, parted for a moment, rose, and flew at each other once more. Again, up and down, banging, stumbling, writhing in each other's arms, twisting legs round each other, to try to trip each other up, and ever Grettir bearing Audun backwards, but never wholly mastering him. Audun could not trust his cousin, for though they were akin, and though he had not really done him an injury, there was no telling to what a pitch Grettir's blood might mount and blind him; so as they wrestled, Audun took care to twist the short sword out of Grettir's belt and throw it away. As, to do this, he had to disengage his hand from Grettir's shoulder, he lost an advantage. Grettir managed to trip him, and throw him flat on his back.

At that moment, fortunately, a man, big, wearing a red kirtle, and in full harness, entered the hall and asked what was the meaning of the noise and fight? As he did not receive an immediate answer, he came to the rescue of Audun, and drew Grettir from him.

"We are only in play with each other," said Grettir.

"Rather rough play," said the man, "and likely to end in tears rather than laughter."

"Who are you that interfere?" asked Grettir.

"My name is Bard."

Then Audun scrambled to his feet.

"What is the reason of this rough play?" asked Bard.

Then Grettir answered, by singing:

"Prithee, Audun, will you say
How, upon the ice one day,
You to throttle did essay?
Now, for that I this have done,
On Audun honour I have won;
Curds and wrestle make good fun."

"Oh, I see," said Bard; "fighting out an old grudge. I have nothing to say against that. Now, shake hands, and be loving cousins again."

Audun held out his hand, and Grettir agreed to let the matter end thus. But he was dissatisfied, and ever after bore Bard a grudge. However, he never again wrestled with Audun, and remained on good terms with him.

XI: THE HORSE-FIGHT

One of the rude and cruel sports that amused the Icelanders in summer time was horse-fighting. A smooth piece of turf was chosen, and was staked round. Into this inclosure two or sometimes more horses were introduced, and a man attended each, who urged on his own horse, armed with a goad. By means of these goads the horses were stung to madness, and attacked each other, biting each other savagely. Now, Atli had a beautiful roan, with a black mane, which he and his old father were very proud of. Lower down the valley, near the sea, was a farm called Mais, in which lived a bonder named Kormak, and his brother; they had in their house a man called Odd the Foundling, a sly, captious fellow, who, like Grettir, made verses; but his verses were not generally thought to be so good as those of Grettir. On the opposite side of the river is a hot-spring; it is still hot, but not so hot as it was in those days, when it boiled up and poured forth a cloud of steam, and ran in a scalding rill down to the river. There was a convenient level place near the river for a horse-fight, and it stood above the water on one side rather steeply, so that it needed only fencing on three sides. Kormak had a brown horse that fought well, and it was resolved that autumn to have a fight between the horse of Kormak and the roan of Atli. Odd was to goad on Kormak's brown, and Grettir offered himself to his brother to run with the roan. Atli did not much like the proposal, as he feared Grettir's temper; but he could not well decline his offer, so he said, "I will consent, brother; only I pray you, be peaceable, for we have to do with overbearing men, and it will be very unfortunate if a broil should come of this."

"If they begin, I shall not run away," said Grettir.

"Not if they begin; but be very careful not to provoke a quarrel."

"Quarrels come and are not made," said Grettir.

"That I do not hold," answered Atli.

The day of the horse-fight arrived, and the horses were led to the place of contest. They had been fed up and groomed for the occasion, and each had a band round his middle of colour, by which he who went with the horse could hold, and the goad of each was tied with a tuft of feathers at the head, stained the same colour as the belt about the horse.

The two horses were introduced within the inclosure, and were soon goaded into anger, and began to plunge, and snort, and snap at each other. The by-standers outside the railing cheered and shouted, and the horses seemed to understand that they were to do their best; so they pranced about each other, struck at each other, and tried to get round each other so as to bite the flank. At one moment the roan bit the side of the brown, and held. Odd ran his goad into the horse of Grettir to make it let go;—this was against the rules; he did it to save his own horse from a terrible wound. Grettir saw what he did, but he said nothing. Now the horses bore towards the river, and were rearing and plunging close to the edge, and the two men had much ado to hold on. Then Odd took the opportunity when Grettir's back was turned to drive at him with his goad between the shoulders, where was the great scar still red, and only just fully healed, that he had received from the axe of Hiarandi. It was a cruel blow, and this also was against all rule of fair play.

At that moment the roan reared, and instantly Grettir ran under him, and struck Odd with such a blow that he reeled back towards the water edge, and in so doing dragged the brown horse he was holding over the edge, and both went down into the water together. The river was very full with the melted snows, and Odd was brought ashore with difficulty. It was found that three of his ribs were broken; but whether with the blow dealt by Grettir, or by his fall on the rock, or by the hoof of the horse as it fell and struggled in the river, cannot be said; but the party of Kormak, of course, charged Grettir with having broken Odd's ribs with his stick, and they flew to arms, and threatened the party from Biarg. However, the people of the nearest vales and firths interfered, and no bloodshed ensued. But the men of Mais and of Biarg separated bearing each other much ill-will, each charging the other with having broken the laws of the sport.

Atli did not say what he felt, he was greatly annoyed; but Grettir was less careful of his words, he said that the matter was by no means ended, and that he hoped there would be a meeting between the men of Mais and the men of Biarg, and then—it would not be a fight of horses, but of men; not a biting of horses, but of sharp blades.

XII: OF THE FIGHT AT THE NECK

The next fiord on the west of that into which the river that flowed past Biarg poured was called the Ramsfirth, and at the head of it lived Grettir's married sister.

In the following summer, that is in 1014, Grettir paid his sister a visit; he had with him two servant-men from Biarg, and he spent three days and nights at his sister's. Whilst there, news reached him that Kormak, who had been away from Mais for a week or two, was on his road home, and who was now staying at a house called Tongue. Grettir at once made ready to depart, and his brother-in-law sent two men with him, for it was not safe that Grettir should have only two churls with him, as there was ill blood between him and Kormak about that affair of the horse-fight.

A high, long shoulder of desolate moor lies between the Ramsfirth and the Westriver-dale, in which is a confluent of the river that flows past Biarg. This shoulder rises to the north into a great hump, called Burfell, and on the saddle is a little lake. A very fine view is obtained from this shoulder of moor over the northern immense bay of Hunafloi, towards the glaciers and mountains of that curious excrescence of land that lies on the north-west of Iceland. I know exactly the road taken by Grettir on this occasion, for I have ridden over it. Along the top of this shoulder the rocks are scraped by glaciers, that must at one time have occupied the whole centre of the island, and have slowly slidden down into the firths on all sides. Here, what is curious is, that the rocks are furrowed, just as if carved with a graving tool, in lines from south to north, showing the direction from which the glaciers slipped down. Now, on the slope of this bit of upland is a great stone poised on a point, which I have seen. Grettir came to this stone, and spent a long time in trying to upset it. It is called Grettir's-heave to this day. The men who were with him rather wondered at him why he wasted time over this, instead of pushing on. But his sharp eye had noticed the party of Kormak leaving Tongue, and he was bent on an encounter. He thought that if Odd had seen him going over the hill he would make a lampoon about him running away from his sister's house the moment he heard that danger was threatening. So he determined to tarry till Kormak came up and fight him. He had not long to wait, for presently over the top of the hill came Kormak with Odd and some others. Grettir at once rode to meet them, and said, "Now we have our weapons on both sides, let us fight like men of good birth, and not with sticks as churls."

Then Kormak turned to his men and bade them accept the challenge and fight.

Accordingly they ran at one another and fought. Grettir bade his two serving-men stand behind his back and defend that, and he, sweeping his longsword from left to right, went forward against Kormak. Thus they fought for a while, and some were wounded on both sides.

Now it so happened that at a rich farm in the Ramsfirth-dale lived a well-to-do, and very strong man, called Thorbiorn—that is, Thor's Bear—nicknamed Oxmain. He had ridden that day over Burfell-heath, with a party, and was now returning. As he came along he heard shouts and the clashing of arms, so he quickened his pace, and presently came in sight of the fighters. He at once ordered his men to dash in between the combatants. But by this time the passions of those engaged were so furious that they would not be separated. Grettir sweeping his long-sword about him strode forward, and the men of Kormak fell back before him. Down went two of those who were with Kormak, and one servant of Atli, Grettir's brother, was killed.

Then Thorbiorn Oxmain raised his great voice and roared out, that he and his party would take sides against the first man who dealt another blow. Grettir saw that it would hardly do if Thorbiorn Oxmain brought all his force against him, so he gave up the battle; but they did not part till every one of those engaged was wounded, and two were killed on one side, and one on the other. Grettir was ill pleased that the affray had ended in this manner, and he felt resentment against Oxmain for his interference. Unfortunately, Oxmain's brother, who went by the name of the Slow-coach, made fun of the matter, and laughed about Grettir sneaking away from the fight directly he saw that he was getting the worst of it. Whatever he said was reported at Biarg, and, as may well be imagined, did not improve Grettir's temper, or liking for Oxmain and Slow-coach. Nothing further occurred between him and Kormak, probably he and Kormak were content with the trial of strength that had taken place, and were disinclined to renew a profitless contest.

Atli took no notice of the loss of his house-churl; he desired peace, and not a stirring afresh of the fires of discord. To his peaceable behaviour it was doubtless due that the quarrel with Kormak came to an end. But the vexation felt by Grettir against Oxmain for his meddlesomeness, and against Slow-coach for his gibes, rankled in his breast.

XIII: HOW GRETTIR AND AUDUN MADE FRIENDS

Grettir remained through the autumn at Biarg, after the skirmish at the Neck, till September, and then he thought he would ride away east and see Audun again, with whom he had had that little ruffle that was almost a quarrel, and which was fortunately interrupted by the entrance of Bard. Audun was a cousin, though not a near one, and Grettir had no desire that any bad blood should exist between kinsfolk. Audun belonged to what was called the Madpate family; for it had had in it at least two who had been so odd in their ways that folk said they were not quite right in their minds. The relationship will easily be understood by a look at the pedigree. It will be remembered that old Onund Treefoot, who had settled in Iceland, had to wife secondly Thordis, an Icelandic woman, and his son by her was Thorgrim Grizzlepate, and this Thorgrim bought the estate and house of Biarg about the year 935. Onund Treefoot died in or about 920, and then his widow Thordis married again a man called Audun Skokull, and they had a son who was called Asgeir, who settled in Willowdale, and either went off his head or proved so queer in his ways that folks called him Madpate. This Madpate married and had a son Audun, and a daughter Thurid who married away west into a very good family; and she had a son called Thorstein Kuggson, of whom we shall hear more presently. Audun of Willowdale's son was Madpate the Second, and the lad Audun who wrestled with Grettir and burst the bottle of curds was the son of this Madpate the Second. Consequently the relationship to Grettir was through Grettir's great-grandmother, and Audun belonged to a generation younger than that of Grettir, because Grettir was the son of Asmund's old age. Moreover, Asmund's father Thorgrim had married somewhat late in life, whereas all the Madpate family had dashed into marriage at a very early age. Thus it came about that Grettir's great-grandmother was Audun's great-great-grandmother, and that, nevertheless, Audun was somewhat older than Grettir.

Grettir rode straight up over the hill behind his house. Now this hill like the Neck, already described, is rather curious, for on it are a number of rocks that have been deposited by glaciers, and not only so, but they have been dragged along by ice, scratching the rocks over which they were driven forward, and so these beds of rock are rubbed and scored with lines made by the stones forced over them by ice. Above Biarg there is one large stone that has scratched a deep furrow in the bed of rock and then has stopped at the end of the furrow it had itself scored. This remarkable phenomenon tells us of a time when the whole of the centre of Iceland was covered with glaciers, like the centre of Greenland now. These glaciers slided down the slopes of the hills, and were thrust along to the sea, where they broke off and floated away as icebergs.

Nowadays folk in Iceland do not understand these odd stones perched in queer places, which were deposited by the ancient glaciers, and they call them Grettir-taks or Grettir's-heaves. So the farmer at Biarg told me that the curious stone at the end of the furrow in the bed of rock on top of the hill was a Grettir-tak; it had been rubbed along the rock and left where it stands by Grettir. But I knew better. I knew that it was put there by an ancient glacier ages before Grettir was born, and before Iceland was discovered by the Norsemen. I have no doubt that in Grettir's time this stone was said to have been put there by some troll. Afterwards, when people ceased to believe in trolls, they said it was put there by Grettir.

Grettir's ride led him by a pretty little blue lake that lies folded in between high hills and has a stream flowing from it into a very large lake near Hop. But he did not follow the stream down; he crossed another hill, not very steep and high, and reached his cousin's house at Audun stead in Willowdale. Now this valley took its name from the woods of willows that grew in it when first settled, but at the present day none remain; all have in course of time been burnt for fuel, and except for scanty grass the Willowdale is very dreary-looking. We may be sure that Iceland presented a much more smiling and green appearance eight hundred or a thousand years ago than it does at present.

When Grettir came to Willowdale, Audun received him in a friendly manner, and Grettir made him a present of a handsome axe he had. He remained with him some little while, and they talked over old tales of Onund Treefoot and his doings, and every shadow of rivalry and anger disappeared, so that they parted at length in the best of tempers and as true and affectionate cousins.

Audun would have desired to keep Grettir there longer, but Grettir would not stay. He desired to get on to the head of Waterdale, where lived an uncle of his called Jokull, his mother's brother, at a place called Tongue.

So he rode away over the moor, and reached Tongue. Here a stream comes rushing through a gorge in a series of waterfalls, and meets another stream that comes down a valley called the Valley of Shadows further east.

Tongue is so called because it lies on a grassy slope exactly in the tongue of land between these two streams. There is now a good farm there and a church, and there I stayed a few days. At the back of Tongue the hill rises rapidly to a fell called Tongue-heath. This hill was covered with snow when Grettir arrived. This uncle Jokull was glad to see him.

He was a rough and violent man, very big and strong; and it was clear to everyone that his nephew took after his mother's family more than his father's, for there was a strong likeness both in build and face and in character between Jokull and Grettir.

He received Grettir heartily in his rough, blunt way, and bade him stay there as long as he liked. Jokull had been a seafaring man, and had made much by his merchant trips. He would probably have been a richer and more respected man had he not been so violent and overbearing and ready to pick quarrels.

Now Grettir had not been at Tongue three days before he heard a very strange tale. Jokull's mouth was full of it, and with good reason, for the events had taken place not an hour's ride distant. It was a tale about the nearest farm in the Valley of Shadows, a farm called Thorhall's-stead, which was reported to be haunted; and so serious had affairs become there that no servants would remain, and the farmer and his family had been driven from house and home by the hauntings last winter, and had come and lodged with Jokull at Tongue, and he had entertained them for some two or three months. Now this was not a case of mere fancy and fantastic fear. It was something very real and very marvellous. But it is a long story, and must be consigned to another chapter.

XIV: THE VALE OF SHADOWS

We have come now to an incident which formed a turning-point in Grettir's life. It is a very mysterious and inexplicable story, not one that can be put aside as we have that of his fight in the tomb with Karr the Old. This is a story even more gruesome. It relates to an event that so shook Grettir's nerves that he never after could endure to be alone in the dark, and would risk all kinds of dangers to escape solitude. How much of truth lies under this strange narrative we cannot now say, but that something really did take place is certain from the effect it had on Grettir ever after.

The richest valley for grass in all this quarter of Iceland, and the most peopled, is the Waterdale. On the east rises a mountain ridge of precipitous basaltic cliffs, down which leap waterfalls from the snows above. The river that flows through this valley is fed by two main streams that unite at the farm called Tongue. The stream on the east rises a long way inland in a mass of lava, and flows through a valley so narrow and so gloomy that it goes by the name of the Valley of Shadows. The high ranges of moor and waste to the south shut off the southern sun, and the lofty banks of mountain to east and west so close it in that it gets no sun morning or evening.

A little way up this valley—not far, and not where it is most gloomy—are now the scanty ruins of a farm called Thorhall's-stead. Above this the valley so contracts and the hills are so steep that it is only with great difficulty that a horse can be led along. This I know very well; for in crossing an avalanche slide my horse and I were almost precipitated into the torrent below. Further up the valley stands a tongue of high land with a waterfall on one side and the ravine on the other, and here at one time some robbers had their fortress who were the terror of the neighbourhood. No trace of their fortress remains at present, but it was to find this place that I explored the valley.

In the farm that is now but a heap of ruins lived a bonder named Thorhall and his wife. He was not a man of much consideration in the district, for he was planted on cold, poor land, and his wealth was but small. Moreover, he had no servants; and the reason was that his sheep-walks were haunted.

Not a herdsman would remain with him. He offered high wages, he threatened, he entreated, all in vain. One shepherd after another left his service, and things came to such a pass that he determined to have the advice of the law-man or chief judge at the next annual assize.

He saddled his horses and rode to Thingvalla. Skapti was the name of the judge then, a man with a long head, and deemed the best of men for giving counsel. Thorhall told him his trouble.

"I can help you," said Skapti. "There is a shepherd who has been with me, a rude, strange man, but afraid of neither man nor hobgoblin, and strong as a bull; but he is not very clear in his intellect."

"That does not matter," said Thorhall, "so long as he can mind sheep."

"You may trust him for that," said Skapti. "He is a Swede, and his name is Glam."

Towards the end of the assize two gray horses belonging to Thorhall slipped their hobbles and strayed; so, as he had no serving-man, he went after them himself, and on his way met a strange-looking fellow, driving before him an ass laden with faggots. The man was tall and stalwart; his face attracted Torhall's attention, for the eyes were ashen gray and staring. The powerful jaw was furnished with white protruding teeth, and about his low brow hung bunches of coarse wolf-gray hair.

"Pray, what are you called?" asked Thorhall, for he suspected that this was the man Skapti had spoken about.

"Glam, at your service."

"Do you like your present duties—wood-cutting?" asked the farmer.

"No, I do not. I am properly a shepherd."

"Then, will you come with me? Skapti has spoken of you and offered you to me."

"What are the drawbacks to your service?" asked Glam cautiously.

"None, save that my sheep-walks are haunted."

"Oh! is that all? Ghosts won't scare me. Here is my hand. I will come to you before winter."

They separated, and soon after the farmer found his horses; they had got into a little wood, and were nibbling the willow tops. He went home, having thanked Skapti.

Summer passed, then autumn, and nothing further was heard of Glam. The winter storms began to bluster up the valley from the cold Polar Sea, driving the flying snowflakes and heaping them in drifts at every turn of the vale. Ice formed in the shallows of the river, and the streams which in summer trickled down the sides were now turned to icicles. I was there the very end of June, and then the whole of the mountain flank to the west was covered with frozen streams spread like a net of icicle over the black and red striped bare rock.

One gusty night a violent blow at the door startled all in the farm. In another moment Glam, tall and wild, stood in the hall glowering out of his gray staring eyes, his hair matted with frost, his teeth rattling and snapping with cold, his face blood-red in the glare of the fire that glowed in the centre of the hall.

He was well received by Thorhall, but the housewife did not like the man's looks, and did not welcome him with much heartiness. Time passed, and the shepherd was on the moors every day with the flock; his loud and deep-toned voice was often borne down on the wind as he shouted to the sheep, driving them to fold. His presence always produced a chill in the house, and when he spoke it sent a thrill through the women, who did not like him.

Christmas-eve was raw and windy; masses of gray vapour rolled up from the Arctic Ocean, and hung in piles about the mountain tops. Now and then a scud of frozen fog, covering bar and beam with feathery hoar-frost, swept up the glen. As the day declined snow began to fall in large flakes.

When the wind lulled there could be heard the shout of Glam high up on the hillside. Darkness closed in, and with the darkness the snow fell thicker. There was a church then at Thorhall's farm; there is none there now, since the valley has been abandoned from its cold and ill name.

The lights were kindled in the church, and every snowflake as it sailed down past the open door burned like a golden feather in the light.

When the service was over, and the farmer and his party returned to the house, Glam had not come home. This was strange; as he could not live abroad in the cold, and the sheep would also require shelter. Thorhall was uneasy and proposed a search, but no one would go with him; and no wonder, it was not a night for a dog to be out in, and the tracks would all be buried in snow. So the family sat up all night listening, trembling and anxious.

Day broke at last faintly in the south over the great white masses of mountains. Now a party was formed to search for the missing man. A sharp climb brought them to the top of the moor above Tongue. Here and there a sheep was found shivering under a rock or half buried in a snowdrift, but of Glam—not a sign.

Presently the whole party was called together about a spot on the hilltop where the snow was trampled and kicked about, and it was clear that some desperate struggle had taken place there. There the snow was also dabbled with frozen blood. A red track led further up the mountain side, and the searchers were following it when a boy uttered a shriek of fear. In looking behind a rock he had come on the corpse of the shepherd lying on its back with the arms extended. The body was taken up and carried to the edge of the gorge, and was there buried under a pile of stones, heaped over it to the height of about six feet. How Glam had died, by whom killed, no one knew, nor could they make a guess.

Two nights after this one of the thralls who had gone for the cows burst into the hall with a face blank from terror; he staggered to a seat and fainted. On recovering his senses, in a broken voice he assured those who were round him that he had seen Glam walking past him, with huge strides, as he left the stable door. The shepherd had turned his head and looked at him fixedly from his great gray staring eyes. On the following day a stable lad was found in a fit under a wall, and he never after recovered his senses. It was thought he must have seen something that had scared him. Next, some of the women, declared that they had seen Glam looking in on them through a window of the dairy. In the dusk Thorhall himself met the dead man, who stood and glowered at him, but made no attempt to injure his master, and uttered not a word. The haunting did not end thus. Nightly a heavy tread was heard round the house, and a hand groping along the walls, and sometimes a hand came in at the windows, a great coarse hand, that in the red light from the fire seemed as though steeped in blood.

When the spring came round the disturbances lessened, and as the sun obtained full power, ceased altogether.

During the course of the summer a Norwegian vessel came into the fiord; Thorhall went on board and found there a man named Thorgaut, who had come out in search of work. Thorhall engaged him as a shepherd, but not without honestly telling him his trouble, and what there was uncanny about his sheep-walks, and how Glam had fared. The man did not regard this, he laughed, and promised to be with Thorhall at the appointed season.

Accordingly he arrived in autumn, and he soon established himself as a favourite in the house; he romped with the children, helped his fellow-servants, and was as much liked as his predecessor had been detested. He was such a merry careless fellow that he did not think anything of the risks that lay before him, and joked about them.

When winter set in strange sights and sounds began to alarm the folk at the farm, but Thorgaut was not troubled; he slept too soundly at night to be disturbed by the heavy tread round the house.

On the day before Yule, as was his wont, Thorgaut drove out the sheep to pasture. Thorhall was uneasy. He said to him: "I pray you be careful, and do not go near the barrow under which Glam was laid."

"Don't fear for me," laughed Thorgaut, "I shall be back in time for supper, and shall attend you to church."

Night settled in, but no Thorgaut arrived. There was little mirth at table when the supper was brought in. All were anxious and fearful.

The wind was cold and wetting. Blocks of ice were driving about in the bay, grinding against each other, and the sound could be heard far up the valley. Aloft, the aurora flames were lighting up the heavens with an arch of fire. Again this Christmas night the dwellers in the farm sat up and did not go to bed, waiting for the return of Thorgaut, but he did not arrive.

Next morning he was sought, and was found lying dead across the barrow of Glam, with his spine and one leg and one arm broken. He was brought home and laid in the churchyard.

Matters now rapidly became worse. Outbuildings were broken into of a night, and their woodwork was rent and shattered; the house door was violently shaken, and great pieces of it were torn away; the gables of the house were also pulled furiously to and fro.

Now it fell out that one morning the only man who remained in the service of the family went out early. Not another servant dared to remain in the place, and this man remained because he had been with Thorhall and with his father, and he could not make up his mind to desert his master in his need. About an hour after he had gone out Thorhall's wife took her milking cans and went to the cow-house that she might milk the cows, as she had now not a maid in the house, and had to do everything herself. On reaching the door of the cow-house she heard a terrible sound from within, the bellowing of the cattle, and the deep bell-notes of an unearthly voice. She was so frightened that she dropped her pails and ran back to the house and called her husband. Thorhall was in bed, but he rose instantly, caught up a weapon, and hastened to the cow-house.

On opening the door he found all the cattle loose and goring each other. Slung across the stone that separated their stalls was the old serving-man, perfectly dead, with his back broken. He had, apparently, been tossed by the cows, and had fallen on this stone backwards.

Neither Thorhall nor his wife explained his death in this way; they thought that Glam must have been there, have driven the cattle wild, and that just as he had broken the back of Thorgaut, so had he now broken that of the poor old serving-man.

It was impossible for the bonder to remain longer in that place; he and his wife therefore removed down to Tongue, which lies at the junction of the two rivers, and there things were quiet. There he was hospitably received by Jokull. Thorhall was able to persuade some of his runaway servants to come back to him, but no man all that winter would go near the moor where was the barrow of the shepherd Glam.

Not till the summer returned, and the sun had dispelled the darkness, did Thorhall venture back to the Vale of Shadows. In the meanwhile his daughter's health had given way under the repeated alarms of the winter; she became paler every day; with the autumn flowers she faded, and was laid in the churchyard before the first snowflakes fell. What was Thorhall to do through the winter? He knew that it was not possible for him to secure servants if he remained on his own farm; besides, he did not know what loss might come to his stock. Then, he could not spend the whole winter at Tongue, for that was another bonder's house, and though the farmer there had kindly received him and entertained him for three months the winter before, he could not ask him to give him houseroom to himself, his cattle, and servants for a whole long winter.

So he was in the greatest possible perplexity what to do. Help came to him from an unexpected quarter.

Grettir had heard the story of the hauntings, and he rode to Thorhall's farm and asked if he might be accommodated there for the night. He said that it was his great desire to encounter Glam.

Thorhall was surprised, but not exactly pleased, for he thought that the family at Biarg would attribute the wrong to him were anything to happen to Grettir.

Grettir put his horse into the stable, and retired for the night to one of the beds in the hall and slept soundly.

XV: HOW GRETTIR FOUGHT WITH GLAM

Next morning Grettir went with Thorhall to the stable for his horse. The strong wooden door was shivered and driven in. They stepped across it; Grettir called to his horse, but there was no responsive whinny. Grettir dashed into the stall and found his horse dead; its neck was broken.

"Now," said Thorhall, "I will give you a horse in exchange for that you have lost. You had better ride home to Biarg at once."

"Not at all. My horse has been killed, and I must avenge it." So Grettir remained.

Night set in. Grettir ate a hearty supper, and was right merry. But not so Thorhall, who had his misgivings. At bed-time the latter crept into a locked bedstead beside the hall; but Grettir said he would not go into a bed, he would lie by the fire in the hall. So he wrapped himself up in a long fur cloak and flung himself on a bench, with his feet against the posts of the high seat. The fur cloak was over his head, and he kept an opening through which he could look out.

There was a fire burning on the hearth, a smouldering heap of glowing embers, and by the red light Grettir looked up at the rafters of the blackened roof. The smoke escaped by a louvre in the middle. The wind whistled mournfully. The windows high up were covered with parchment, and admitted now and then a sickly yellow glare from the full moon, which, however, shone in through the smoke hole, silvering the rising smoke. A dog began to bark, then bay at the moon. Then the cat, which had been sitting demurely watching the fire, stood up with raised back and bristling tail, and darted behind some chests. The hall-door was in a sad plight. It had been so torn by Glam that it had to be patched up with wattles. Soothingly the river prattled over its shingly bed as it swept round the knoll on which stood the farm. Grettir heard the breathing of the sleeping women in the adjoining chamber, and the sigh of the housewife as she turned in her bed.

Then suddenly he heard something that shook all the sleep out of him, had any been stealing over his eyes. He heard a heavy tread, beneath which the snow crackled. Every footfall went straight to Grettir's heart. A crash on the turf overhead. The strange visitant had scrambled on the roof, and was walking over that. The roofs of the houses in Iceland are of turf. For a moment the chimney gap was completely darkened—the monster was looking down it—the flash of the red fire illumined the horrible face with its lacklustre eyes. Then the moon shone in again, and the heavy tramp of Glam was heard as he walked to the other end of the hall. A thud—he had leaped down.

Then Grettir heard his steps passing to the back of the house, then the snapping of wood showed that Glam was destroying some of the outhouse doors. Presently the tread was heard again approaching the house, and this time the main entrance. Grettir thought he could distinguish a pair of great hands thrust in over the broken door. In another moment he heard a loud snap—a long plank had been torn out of place, and the light of the moon shone in where the gap had been made. Then Glam began to unrip the wattles.

There was a cross-beam to the door, acting as bolt. Against the gray light Grettir saw a huge black arm thrust in trying to remove the bar. It was done, and then all the broken door was driven in and went down on the floor in shivers. Now Grettir could see a tall dark figure, almost naked, with wild locks of hair about the head standing in the doorway. That was but for a minute, and then Glam came in stealthily; he entered the hall and was illumined by the firelight. The figure Grettir now saw was unlike anything he had seen before. A few rags hung from the shoulders and waist, the long wolf-gray hair was matted. The eyes were staring and strange. Grettir could hear Thorhall within his locked bed trembling and breathing fast.

Presently Glam's eyes rested on the shaggy bundle by the high seat. He stepped towards it, and Grettir felt him groping about him. Then Glam laid hold of one end of the fur cloak and began to pull at it. The cloak did not come away. Another jerk. Grettir kept his feet firmly pressed against the posts, so that the fur was not pulled away. Glam seemed puzzled; he went to the other end of the bundle and began to pull at that. Grettir held to the bench, so that he was not moved himself, but the fur cloak was torn in half, and the strange visitant staggered back holding the portion in his hand wonderingly before his eyes. Before he could recover from his surprise, Grettir started to his feet, bent his body, flung his arms round Glam, and driving his head into the breast of the visitor, tried to bend him backward and so snap his spine. This was in vain, the cold hands grasped Grettir's arms and tore them from their hold. Grettir clasped them again about his body, and then Glam threw his also round Grettir, and they began to wrestle. Grettir saw that Glam was trying to drag him to the door, and he was sure that if he were got outside he would be at a disadvantage, and Glam would break his back. He therefore made a desperate effort not to be drawn forth. He clung to benches and posts, but the posts gave way, and the benches were torn from their places.

At each moment he was being dragged nearer to the door. Sharply twisting himself loose, Grettir flung his arms round a beam of the roof, for the hall was low. He was dragged off his feet at once. Glam clenched him about the waist, and tore at him to get him loose. Every tendon in Grettir's breast was strained; still he held on. The nails of Glam cut into his side like knives, then his hands gave way. He could endure the strain no longer, and Glam drew him towards the doorway, in so doing trampling over the broken fragments of the door, and the wattles that lay about. Grettir knew that the last chance was come for saving himself. Here, in the hall, he could hold to posts and beams, and so make some resistance; but outside he would have nothing to cling to, and strong though he was, his strength did not equal that of his opponent.

Now the door-posts were of stone, and the beam that had served as bolt went across the door, slid into a hollow on one side cut in the door-post, and was pulled across and fitted into another hollow in the other post. As the wrestlers neared the opening, Grettir planted both his feet against the stone posts, one against each, and put his arms round Glam. He had the enemy now at an advantage; but then, he merely held him, and could not hold him so for ever. He called to Thorhall, but Thorhall was too greatly frightened to leave his place of refuge.

"Now," thought Grettir, "if I can but break his back!" Then drawing Glam to him by the middle, he put his head beneath the chin of his opponent and forced back the head. If he could only drive the head far enough back he would break his neck.

At that moment one or both of the door-posts gave way; down crashed the gable-trees, ripping beams and rafters from their places, frozen clods of turf rattled from the roof and thumped into the snow.

Glam fell on his back outside the door, and Grettir on top of him. The moon was, as I said before, at her full; large white clouds chased each other across the sky. Grettir's strength was failing him, his hands quivered in the snow, and he knew that he could not support himself from dropping flat on the mysterious and dreadful visitant, eye to eye, lip to lip.

Then Glam said: "You have done ill matching yourself with me; now know that never shall you be stronger than you are to-day, and that, to your dying day, whenever you are in the dark you will see my eyes staring at you, so that for very horror you will not dare to be alone."

At this moment Grettir saw his short sword in the snow, it had slipped from his belt as he fell. He put out his hand at once, clutched the handle, and with a blow cut off Glam's head, and at once laid it beside his thigh.

Thorhall came out at this juncture, his face blanched; but when he saw how the fray had ended, he joyfully assisted Grettir to roll the dead man to the top of a pile of faggots that had been collected for winter fuel. Fire was applied, and soon far down the Waterdale the flames of the pyre startled folks, and made them wonder what new horror was being enacted in the Vale of Shadows.

Next day the charred bones were conveyed a long way—some hours' ride—into the great desert in the interior, and in one of the most lonely spots there a cairn or pile of stones was heaped over them. I have seen this mound, which is still pointed out as that under which the redoubted Glam lies.

And now we may well ask, what truth is there in the story? That there is a basis of truth can hardly be denied. The facts have been embellished, worked up, but not invented. The only probable explanation of the story is this.

As already said, further up the valley, in a spot difficult to be reached, stood the old fortress of some robbers, with many caves in the sandstone about it very convenient for shelter. Now, it is not improbable that some madman may have taken refuge in this safe retreat, and may have come out at night in search of food, and carried off the sheep of Thorhall. It may be that Glam caught him attempting to steal a sheep, and fought with him, and was killed, and that in like manner Thorgaut was killed. Then when people saw a great wild man wandering about they thought it was Glam, whereas it was the man who had haunted the region before Glam came there, and had killed Glam. This is the simplest and easiest explanation of this wild and fearful tale.

XVI: HOW GRETTIR SAILED TO NORWAY

Early in the spring of the year 1015, news reached Iceland of a change of rulers in Norway. Olaf Harald's son, commonly known as Olaf the Saint, had come to be King of Norway; Earl Sweyn had been defeated in battle and driven out of the country. Now Grettir was remotely connected with the king, that is to say, his father's grandfather was brother to the grandfather of Asta, Olaf's mother. The cousinship was somewhat distant; but in those days folk held to their kin more than they do now. Grettir thought that a good chance had opened to him for doing well in Norway, so he resolved to leave Iceland, and enter the service of his relative, the king. There was a ship bound for Norway lying in Eyjafiord, and Grettir engaged a berth in her, and made ready for the voyage.

Now his father Asmund was very old and feeble, and was well nigh bedridden. He had given over the entire management of the farm to his eldest son Atli, and to young Illugi, who was a few years younger than Grettir. Atli was everywhere liked, he was such a prudent, peaceable, and kindly man.

Grettir's ill-luck still followed him; for, as it chanced, Thorbiorn, the Slowcoach, the relation of Thorbiorn Oxmain, had resolved to go to Norway also, and in the same ship. Now the Slowcoach may have been overslow in his movements, but he was overnimble with his tongue, and he was strongly advised either not to go in the same boat with Grettir, or, if he did, to mind his words.

Such advice was thrown away on the Slowcoach, who, instead of practising caution, in order to show himself off, began to brag of his strength, and to say scurvy things of Grettir, which were duly reported by tale-bearers to Grettir. Consequently, when Grettir arrived in the Eyjafiord with his goods, he was not very amiably disposed towards the Slowcoach. However Atli had impressed on him the necessity of controlling himself, and Grettir was resolved not to quarrel with the man unless he could not help it.

At the side of the shore, those who were about to sail had run up booths and cabins for themselves and their stores. Many of those going in the boat were chapmen, and they took with them goods with which to traffic in Norway.

Just as the vessel was ready, and about to sail next day, Slowcoach arrived, slow as usual, and after every one else was ready, and their goods on board. As it was the last evening on shore, all the merchants and seamen were sitting about their booths, when Thorbiorn Slowcoach arrived, and rode along the lane between the wooden cabins. The men shouted to him to know if he had any news to tell them.

Thorbiorn's eye caught that of Grettir, who was sitting on a bench, and he answered, "I don't hear any news, except that the old idiot Asmund of Biarg is dead."

This was not true; the old man was not dead, but very ill. Some of those who heard him said, "That is sad news indeed, for he was a worthy and honourable old man, and he could ill be spared."

"I don't know that," said Thorbiorn with a scornful laugh.

"But how did he die? What did he die of?"

"Die of?" repeated the Slowcoach loud enough to be heard by Grettir. "Smothered like a dog in the poky little kennel they call their hall at Biarg. As for any loss in him, it is news to me that the world is not well rid of dotards."

"These are ill words," said those who heard him. "No good man will speak slightingly of old and blameless chiefs. Besides, such words as these Grettir will not endure."

"Grettir!" scoffed Thorbiorn. "Before I face him I must see him use his weapons better than he did last summer, when engaged with Kormak. Then I put my elbow between them, and Grettir was but too ready to accept the interference. I never saw a man before so shake in his shoes."

Thereat Grettir stood up, and controlling himself, said, "If I have any faculty of foresight, Slowcoach, I see that you will not be smothered with smoke like a dog. You should have done other than speak foul words of very aged men. Gray hairs deserve respect."

"I don't think more of your foresight than I do of the wisdom of your old fool of a father," said Thorbiorn.

The end was that they fought. The insult was too gross to be endured, and Grettir felt it incumbent on him to strike for his father's honour. The fight did not last long; the Slowcoach was slow in his fighting, slow of hand, only not slow of tongue, and Grettir's sharp sword wounded him to death.

Slowcoach was buried in the nearest churchyard; and the chapmen gave Grettir credit for having restrained himself as long as possible, and allowed that, according to the ideas of the time, he was justified in fighting and killing the Slowcoach for his spiteful and strife-provoking words. But Grettir was not pleased, he regretted the contest, because he knew that it left occasion of strife behind, which might occasion Atli trouble. Thorbiorn Oxmain would, lie feared, be sure to take up the quarrel, and then Atli would have to pay a heavy fine in silver to atone for the death.

The vessel set sail, and reached the south of Norway. There Grettir took ship in a trading keel, to go north to Drontheim, because he heard that the king was there, and his heart beat high with hopes that Olaf would acknowledge him as a cousin, and would take him into his body-guard, and treat him with honour; and that so, though he had had ill-luck in Iceland, good luck might attend him in Norway.

XVII: THE HOSTEL BURNING

There lived a man named Thorir at Garth in Iceland who had spent the summer in Norway when Olaf returned from England, and he had stood in great favour with the king. He had two sons, and at this time both were well-grown men.

Thorir left Norway for Iceland, where he broke up his ship, not intending again to go a seafaring. But when he heard the tidings that Olaf was king over the whole of Norway, then he deemed it would be well for his sons to go there and pay their respects to the king, and remind him of his old friendship for their father.

On reaching Norway much about the same time as had Grettir, they took a long rowing-boat, and skirted the coast on their way north to Drontheim. They preceded Grettir by a few days. On reaching a fine fiord, in which there was shelter from the gales that began to bluster violently with the approach of winter, the sons of Thorir ran in their boat, and as there was a large wooden hostelry there built for the shelter of weather-bound travellers, they took refuge in it, and spent their days in hunting and their nights in revelry.

Now it so fell out that Grettir's merchant ship came into this same fiord one evening and ran aground on the opposite shore to that on which was the hostel. The night was bitterly cold; storms of snow drove over the country, whitening the mountains. The men from the ship were worn out and numbed with cold, and they had no means of kindling a fire. Then, all at once, they saw a light spring up on the opposite side of the firth, twinkling cheerfully between the trees. This was a sight to make them more eager for a fire, and they began to wish that some one of their number would swim across and bring over a light.

"In the good old times there must have been men who would have thought nothing of swimming across the streak of water at night," said Grettir.

"No comfort to us to know that," said one of the crew. "It does not concern us what may have been in the past, we are shivering in the present. Why do you not get us fire?"

Grettir hesitated. The night was very like that on which he had fought with Glam: the same full moon, with snow-laden clouds rolling over its face for a while obscuring it, and then the full glare falling over the face of earth again; and, unaccountably, a sense of doubt and depression had come over him, as though that evil adversary were now about to revenge his downfall upon him. He looked round suddenly, for he thought that the fearful eyes were staring at him from out of the black shadows of the fir-wood.

The rest of the crew united in urging him, and at length, reluctantly, Grettir yielded. He flung his clothes off, and prepared himself to swim. He had on him a fur cape, and a pair of wadmal breeches. He took up an iron pot, and jumped into the sea and swam safely across.

On reaching the further shore, he shook the water off him, but before long his trousers froze like boards, and the water formed in icicles about the cape. Grettir ascended through the pine-wood towards the light, and on reaching the hostel from which it proceeded, walked in without speaking to anyone, and striding up to the fire, stooped and began to scrape the red-hot embers into his iron pot. The hall was full of revellers, and these revellers were the sons of Thorir and their boat's crew. They were already more than half intoxicated, and when they saw a wild-looking man enter the hall, half naked and hung with icicles, they thought he must be a troll or mountain-spirit.

At once every one caught up the first weapon to hand, and rushed to the attack. Grettir defended himself with a fire-brand plucked from the hearth; the sons of Thorir stumbled over the fire, and the embers were strewn about over the floor that was covered with fresh straw.

In a few moments the hall was filled with flame and smoke, and Grettir took advantage of the confusion to effect his escape. He ran down to the shore, plunged into the sea and swam across.

He found his companions waiting for him behind a rock, with a pile of dry wood which they had collected during his absence. The cinders were blown upon, and twigs applied, till a blaze was produced, and before long the whole party sat rubbing their almost frozen hands over a cheerful fire.

Next morning the merchants recognized the fiord, and, remembering that a hostel stood on the further side, they crossed the water to see it, when—what was their dismay to find of it only a heap of smoking embers! From under some of the charred timber were thrust scorched human limbs. The chapmen, in alarm and horror, turned upon Grettir and charged him with having maliciously burned the house with all its inmates.

"See, now," said Grettir, "I had a thought that this expedition would not bring luck. I would I had not taken the trouble to get fire for such a set of thankless churls."

The ship's crew raked out the embers, pulled aside the smoking rafters, in their search for the bodies. Some of these were not so disfigured but that they could recognize them. Moreover, they knew the ship that lay at anchor under the lee, hard by, and they saw that Grettir had brought the sons of Thorir to an untimely end. The indignation of the merchants became so vehement, and their fear so great that they might be implicated in the matter, that they drove Grettir from their company, and refused to receive him into their vessel for the remainder of their voyage. Grettir, in sullen wrath, would say no word of self-defence; he had to make his way on foot to Drontheim, where he resolved to lay the whole matter before the king.

The vessel reached Drontheim before him, and the news of the hostel burning roused universal indignation against Grettir.

XVIII: THE ORDEAL BY FIRE

One day, as King Olaf sat in audience in his great hall, Grettir strode in, and going before his seat, greeted the king. Olaf looked at him and said:
"Are you Grettir the Strong?"

He answered: "That is my name, and I have come hither, kinsman, to get a fair hearing, and to clear myself of the charge of having burned men maliciously. Of that I am guiltless."

King Olaf replied: "I heartily trust that what you say is true, and that you will be able to rid yourself of a charge so bad."

Grettir replied that he was ready to do whatsoever the king desired, in order to prove his innocence.

Then said the king to him, "Tell me the whole story, that I may be able to judge."

Grettir answered by relating the circumstances. He had simply taken fire from the hearth, when he was fallen upon by those who were drinking, and who were too tipsy to understand his explanation. He went away with the red-hot embers, and did not set fire to anything, but the drunken men kicked the glowing coals about amidst the straw.

The king remained silent some moments, and then he said: "There are no witnesses either on your behalf or against you. No man was by who is not dead. God and his angels alone know whether you speak the truth or not, therefore I must refer you to the judgment of God."

"What must I do?" asked Grettir.

"You will have to go through the ordeal of fire," said the king.

"What is that?" asked the young man.

"You must lift bars of red-hot iron, and walk with bare feet on plough-shares heated red in a furnace."

"And what if I am burnt?"

"Then will you be adjudged guilty."

Grettir shrugged his shoulders: "If it must be so, let it be at once; but whether I be burnt or not, I declare that I am clear of all intent to hurt those men."

"You cannot undergo the ordeal now," said the king. "You would be burned to a certainty. You must go through preparation first."

"What preparation?"

"A week of fasting and prayer," was the reply.

Then Grettir was taken away and put in ward, and fed with bread and water for a week, and the bishop visited him and taught him to pray that if he were innocent, God would reveal his innocence by enabling him to pass unscathed through the ordeal.

The day came, and Drontheim was thronged with people from all the country round, to see the Icelander of whom such tales were told. A procession was formed; first went the king's body-guard followed by the king himself, wearing his crown, then came the bishop, the choir, and the clergy, and last of all Grettir, his wild red hair flying loose in the breeze, his arms folded, and his eyes wandering over the sea of heads that filled the square before the cathedral doors. The crowd pressed in closer and closer. Opinions differed as to whether he were guilty or not. Among the mob was a young man of dark complexion, who made a great noise, shouldering his way to the front, and shouting.

"Look at the fellow!" he exclaimed. "This is the man who, in cold blood, burnt down a house over helpless men, and now he is to be given u chance of escape."

"But he says he is guiltless," argued one in the crowd.

"Guiltless!" exclaimed the youth. "If one of us had done the deed, should we have been trifled with? The king wants him for his body-guard, because he is so strong."

"He should be given a chance of clearing himself," said one who stood near.

"Yes—of course—because he is a kinsman of the king. So the irons have been painted red, to look as if hot. I know how the trick is done. But he shall not escape me."

Thereupon the young man sprang at Grettir and drove his nails into his face so that they drew blood; at the same time he poured forth against him a stream of insulting names.

This was more than the Icelander could bear; he caught the young man, as a cat catches a mouse, held him aloft, shook him, and then threw him away, when he fell on the ground and was stunned. It was feared he might be killed. This act gave occasion to a general uproar; the mob wanted to lay hands on Grettir; some threw stones, others assaulted him with sticks; but he, planting his back against the church wall, turned up his sleeves, guarded off the blows, shouting to his assailants to come on. Not a man came within his reach but was sent reeling back or was felled to the ground. In the meantime the king and the bishop were in the choir waiting. The red-hot ploughshares which had been laid on the pavement were gradually cooling, but no Grettir appeared.

At last the sounds of the uproar reached the king's ear, and he sent out to know the occasion. His messenger returned a moment after to report that the Icelander was fighting the whole town and had knocked down and well nigh killed several persons. The king thereupon sprang from his throne, hastened down the nave, and came out of the great western door when the conflict was at its height.

"Oh, sire," exclaimed Grettir, "see how I can fight the rascals!" and at the word he knocked a man over at the king's feet.

With difficulty the tumult was arrested, and Grettir separated from the combatants; and then he wanted to go with the king and try the ordeal of fire.

"Not so," answered Olaf, "you have already incurred sin. It is possible that some of those you have knocked down may never recover, so that their blood will lie at your door."

"What is to be done?" asked Grettir.

The king considered.

"I see you are a very wicked or at all events a very unlucky man. When you were here before you were the occasion of several deaths. I do not desire to keep you in Norway, but as winter has set in you may tarry here till next spring, and then you shall be outlawed and return to Iceland."

XIX: THE WINTER IN NORWAY

King Olaf had decided that Grettir must leave Norway and return to Iceland. If he was not a guilty man he was a most unfortunate one. Now, the Norse race, whether in Denmark, Norway, Sweden, or Iceland, believed in luck. They said that certain men were born to ill-luck, and such men they avoided, because they feared lest the ill-luck that clung to them might attach itself to, and involve those who came in contact with them.

It was not possible for Grettir to return that year to Iceland, for all the ships bound for his native land had sailed before winter set in, so King Olaf agreed to allow him to remain in the kingdom through the winter, but bound him to depart on the first opportunity next year.

Somewhat sad at heart with disappointment, and with the impression that perhaps Olaf the king was right, and that ill-luck really did weigh on him, Grettir left the court, and went at Yule to the house of a bonder or yeoman called Einar, and remained with him awhile. The farm was in a lonely place in a fiord opening back to the snowy mountains. Einar was a kindly man, hospitable, and he did his best to make Grettir's stay with him pleasant. He had a daughter, a fair, beautiful girl, with blue eyes, and hair like amber silk, and her name was Gyrid. Perhaps the beautiful Gyrid was one attraction to Grettir, but if so he never spoke what was on his heart, because he knew it would be useless. He was an unlucky man; he had made himself a name, indeed, as one of great daring, but he had won for himself neither home, nor riches, nor favour.

Now it fell out that at this time there were some savage ruffians in the country who were called Bearsarks. They were outlaws in most cases, and they lived in secret dens in the dense forests, whence they issued and swooped down on the farms, and there challenged the bonders to fight with them, or to give up to them whatever they needed. These ruffians wore bear-skins drawn over their bodies, and they thrust their heads through the jaws of the beasts, so that they presented a hideous and frightening appearance. Then they worked themselves into paroxysms of rage, when they were like madmen; they rolled their eyes, they roared and howled like wild beasts, and foam formed on their mouths and dropped on the ground. They were wont also, when these fits came on them, to bite the edges of their shields, and with their fangs they were known to have dinted the metal quite deep. Some folks even said they had bitten pieces out of solid shields. It was usually supposed that these Bearsarks were possessed by evil spirits, and it is proba-ble that in many cases they were really mad—mad through having given way to their violent passions, till they knew no law, and thought to carry everything before them by their violence. It was even at one time thought by the superstitious that they could change their shapes, and run about at will in the forms of bears or wolves; but this idea grew out of the fact of their cloth-ing themselves in bear or wolf skins, and drawing the skull of the beast over their heads as a rude helmet, and looking out through the open jaws that thus formed a visor.

One day, just after Yule, to the terror and dismay of Einar, one of the most redoubtable of these Bearsarks, a fellow called Snœkoll, came thunder-ing up to his door on a huge black horse, followed by three or four others on foot, all clothed in skins; but Snœkoll, instead of wearing the bear's skin over his head, had on a helmet with great tusks of a boar protruding from it, and a boar's head drawn over the metal.

It is worth remark that the crests worn later by knights, and which we have still on our plate and on harness, are derived from similar adornments to helmets. Some warriors put wings of eagles on their head-pieces, others put the paws of bears or representations of lions. These were badges of their prowess, or marks whereby they might be known.

Snœkoll struck the door of the farmhouse with his spear, and roared to the owner to come forth. At once Einar and Grettir issued from the hall, and Einar in great trepidation asked the Bearsark what he wanted.

"What do I want?" shouted Snœkoll. "I want one of two things. Either that you give me up your beautiful daughter to be my wife, and with her five-score bags of silver, or else that you fight me here. If you kill me, then luck is yours. If I kill you, then I shall carry off your daughter and all that you possess."

Einar turned to Grettir and asked him in a whisper what he was to do. He himself was an old man whose fighting days were over, and he had no chance against this savage.

Grettir answered that he had better consult his honour and the happiness of Gyrid, and not give way to a bully. The Bearsark sat on his horse rolling his eyes from one to another. He had a great iron-rimmed shield before him.

Then he bellowed forth: "Come! I am not going to wait here whilst you consider matters. Make your selection of the two alternatives at once. What is that great lout at your side whispering? Does he want to play a little game of who is master along with me?"

"For my part," said Grettir, "the farmer and I are about in equal predicament; he is too old to fight, and I am unskilled in arms."

"I see! I see!" roared Snœkoll. "You are both trembling in your shoes. Wait till my fit is on me, and then you will shake indeed."

"Let us see how you look in your Bearsark fit," said Grettir.

Then Snœkoll waxed wroth, and worked himself up into one of the fits of madness. There can be no doubt that in some cases this was all bluster and sham. But in many cases these fellows really roused themselves into perfect frenzies of madness in which they did not know what they did.

Now Snœkoll began to bellow like a bull, and to roll his eyes, and he put the edge of the great shield in his mouth and bit at it, and blew foam from his lips that rolled down the face of the shield. Grettir fixed his eyes steadily on him, and put his hands into his pockets. Snœkoll rocked himself on his horse, and his companions began also to bellow, and stir themselves up into madness. Grettir, with his eye fixed steadily on the ruffian, drew little by little nearer to him; but as he had no weapon, and held his hands confined, Snœkoll, if he did observe him, disregarded him. When Grettir stood close beside him and looked up at the red glaring eyes, the foaming lips of Snœkoll, and heard his howls and the crunching of his great teeth against the strong oak and iron of the shield, he suddenly laughed, lifted his foot, caught the bottom of the shield a sudden kick upwards, and the shield with the violence of the upward shock broke Snœkoll's jaw. Instantly the Bearsark stopped his bellows, let fall the shield, and before he could draw his sword Grettir caught his helmet by the great boar tusks, gave them a twist, and rolled Snœkoll down off his horse on the ground, knelt on him, and with the ruffian's own sword dealt him his death-blow.

When the others saw the fall of their chief they ceased their antics, turned and ran away to hide in the woods.

The bonder, Einar, thanked Grettir for his assistance, and the lovely Gyrid gave him also her grateful acknowledgments and a sweet smile; but Grettir knew that a portionless unlucky man like himself could not aspire to her hand, and feeling that he was daily becoming more attached to her, he deemed it right at once to leave, and he went away to a place called Tunsberg, where lived his half-brother, Thorstein Dromund.

Now, to understand the relationship of Dromund to Grettir, you must know that his father, Asmund, had been twice married. He had been in Norway when a young man with a merchant ship, and he had also gone with his wares to England and France, and had gained great wealth; and as he had many relations in Norway he was well received there in winter, when he came back from his merchant trips. On one of these occasions he had met a damsel called Ranveig, whose father and mother were dead. She was of good birth, and was wealthy. Asmund asked for her hand and married her, and settled on the lands that belonged to her in Norway. They had a son called Thorstein, who, because he was rather slow of speech and manner, was nicknamed Dromund; but as we meet with other Thorsteins in this story, to prevent confusion we will speak of him as Dromund.

After a while Asmund's wife Ranveig died, and then her relatives insisted on taking away all her lands and possessions and keeping them in trust for little Dromund. Asmund did not care to quarrel with them, so he left Dromund with his late wife's relatives and went home to Iceland, where, after a few years, he married Asdis, and by her became the father of Atli, Grettir, and Illugi, and of two daughters, one of whom he named after his first wife.

Dromund grew up in Norway on his estates at Tunsberg, and became a man of wealth and renown, a quiet man, but one who held his own, and was generally respected.

Now Grettir went to him, and his half-brother received him very affectionately, and insisted on his remaining with him all the rest of the winter till it was time for him to sail to Iceland.

One little incident is mentioned concerning that time that deserves to be recorded.

Grettir slept in the same apartment as did his brother.

One morning Dromund awoke early, and he saw how that Grettir's arms were out of bed, and he wondered at their size.

Presently Grettir awoke, and then Dromund said to him: "Grettir, I have been amused with looking at your bare arms. What muscles you have got! I never saw the like."

"I need strong muscles to do what I have to do."

"True enough, brother," said Dromund. "But I could wish there were a little more luck as well as muscle attached to those bones."

"Let me look at your arms," said Grettir.

Then Dromund put his arms out of bed, and when he saw them Grettir burst out laughing, for they were so thin and scraggy.

"Upon my word, brother, I never saw such a wretched pair of tongs in my life," he said.

"They may be a pair of tongs, old boy," answered Dromund, "but they are tongs that shall ever be extended to help you when in need. And," added Dromund in a lower tone, "if it should ever befall you that your ill-luck should overmaster you, and you not die in your bed; then, Grettir, I promise you, if I am alive, that I shall not let this pair of tongs rest till, with them, I have avenged you."

No more is related of their talk together. The spring wore on, and in summer Grettir took ship.

The brothers parted with much affection, and they never again saw each other's face.

XX: OF WHAT BEFELL AT BIARG

Whilst Grettir was in Norway, that ill-luck which pursued him did not fail to touch and trouble his Icelandic home as well.

It will be remembered that Grettir had been forced to fight the Slow-coach, and had killed him. Now the cousin of this man was Thorbiorn Oxmain, who lived in the Ramsfirth. This Thorbiorn had got a serving-man named Ali, a somewhat lazy man, strong, but unruly. As he did his work badly, and was slow about it, his master rebuked him, and when rebukes failed, he threatened him. Threats also proved unavailing, so Thorbiorn one day took the stick to his back, and beat him till he danced. After this Ali would remain no longer in his service; he ran away, crossed the ridge to the Midfiord, and came to Biarg, where he presented himself before Atli, who asked him what he wanted.

The fellow said that he was in quest of service.

"But," said Atli, "you are, I understand, one of Thorbiorn's workmen."

"I was so, but I have left his service because I was badly treated. He beat me till I was black and blue; no one can remain with him, he is so rough with his men, and he exacts of them too much work. I have come here because I hear that you treat your servants well."

Atli replied: "I have hands enough, you had better go back to Thorbiorn, for I do not want you."

"I will never go back to him, that I declare," said the churl. "If you turn me away, I have nowhere to which I can go."

So he remained for a few nights at Biarg; and Atli did not like to turn him out of the house. Then one day he went to work with Atli's men, and worked hard and well, for he was a powerful man. So time passed. Atli did not agree to pay him any wage, and he did not send him away. He did not feel best pleased at having the man there, but he was too kind-hearted to drive him away.

Not only did he remain there and work well, but he showed himself ready to turn his hand to anything, and was the most useful man about the place.

Now Thorbiorn heard that his churl was at Biarg. The death of Slowcoach had rankled in his breast. He had felt that it was his duty to take up the case and demand recompense, yet he had not done so; now he was angered that Atli had opened his doors to his runaway servant. He had covenanted with the man for a year, but the fellow was so disagreeable that he would have gladly dispensed with his service; but that Atli should have received him, and that the man should be making himself useful at Biarg,— that made him very angry indeed.

So he mounted his horse and rode to Biarg, attended by two men, and called out Atli to talk with him.

Atli came forth and welcomed him.

Then Thorbiorn said: "You are determined to pick up fresh occasion of quarrel, and stir ill-will between us. Why have you enticed away my servant? You had no right to behave thus to me."

Atli replied quietly: "You are mistaken. I did not entice him away. The fellow came to me. I did not know for certain that he was your servant, nor did I know for how long he was engaged to you. Show me that I have done wrong and I will make reparation. If he is yours, reclaim him, I will not keep him. At the same time I do not like to shut him out of my house."

"I claim the man," said Thorbiorn; "I forbid him to do a stroke of work here. I expect him returned to me."

"Nay," said Atli, "take the man, you are welcome to him; but I cannot bind him hand and foot and convey him to your house. If you can get him to go with you, well and good, I will not detain him."

Atli had answered fairly, but this did not satisfy Thorbiorn; he knew that he could not drag the man back to his farm, nor could he persuade him to follow, so he rode home in a mighty bad temper, his heart boiling with anger against Atli. And now he thought that he would at one and the same time punish Atli for taking away his servant, and wipe out the wrong of the slaying of the Slowcoach.

In the evening when the men came in from work, Atli said that Thorbiorn had been there and had reclaimed his churl, and Atli bade the fellow depart and go back to his master.

Then the man said: "That's a true proverb, He who is most praised is found most faulty at the test. I came to you because I heard so much good of you, and now that I have toiled for you without wages all the early summer, as I have worked for none else, you want to kick me out of doors as winter draws on. I will not go. You will have to beat me as Thorbiorn beat me to make me leave this house, and then, even, I am not sure but that I shall remain in spite of being beaten."

Atli did not know exactly what to do. He did not wish to ill-treat the fellow, and yet without ill-treatment there was no getting rid of him. So he let him remain on.

One day a warm wet rainy mist covered the land, the hills were enveloped in cloud; Atli sent out some of his men to mow at a distance where there was some grass, and others he sent out fishing. He remained at home himself with only two or three men.

That day Thorbiorn rode over the ridge that divided the dales, with a helmet on his head, a sword at his side, and a barbed spear in his hand. He came to Biarg, and no one noticed his approach. He went to the main door, and knocked at it. Then he drew back behind the buildings, so that no one might see him from the door. In Iceland the walls of a house between the gables are buttressed with turf—thick walls or buttresses that project several feet, and are about six or nine feet thick. Such buttresses stood one on each side of the hall door at Biarg, and behind one of these Thorbiorn concealed himself.

When he had knocked at the door, a woman came to it, unbarred and looked up and down the terrace or platform on which the house was built, but saw no one. Thorbiorn peeped from behind the wall of turf and caught a glimpse of her, and then backed again into his hiding-place. The woman then returned into the house, and told Atli that there was no one outside.

She had hardly spoken before Thorbiorn knocked again. Then Atli jumped up and said: "There must be someone there, and I will go and see myself who it is."

Then he went forth and looked out of the door, but saw no one, as Thorbiorn had again retreated behind the bank of turf. The water was streaming down, so Atli did not go from under cover, but laid a hand on each of the door-posts, and looked up and down the valley.

Just as he was looking away from where Thorbiorn was concealed, that man suddenly swung himself round the bank of turf, and with all his might drove the spear against Atli, using both his hands. The spear entered him below the ribs, and ran right through him. Atli uttered no cry, and fell forward over the threshold. At that the women rushed forth, and they took Atli up, but he was dead.

Then Thorbiorn, who had run to his horse, which was tied up behind the house, rode out on the terrace, and halting before the door proclaimed that he had done this deed.

Now this was a formality which, according to Icelandic law, made his act to be not regarded as a murder. A murder by law was the slaying of a man by one who concealed his name.

Then Thorbiorn rode home.

The goodwife, Asdis, sent for her men, and Atli's body was laid out, and he was buried beside his father, old Asmund, who had died during the winter. There was a church in those days at Biarg, but there is none there now. When I was there I asked of the farmer now living in Biarg where was the old churchyard, but its site was lost; so I could not tell where were the graves of Atli the kind-hearted, honourable man, and the rest of the family.

Great was the lamentation through the district at the death of one so loved and respected, and hard things were said of Thorbiorn for what he had done.

XXI: THE RETURN OF GRETTIR

That same summer news reached Iceland of the burning of the hostel by Grettir. When Thorir of Garth heard of the death of his sons he was furious. He rode to the great annual assize at Thingvalla, with a large retinue, and charged Grettir with having killed his boys maliciously; and he demanded that for this offence Grettir should be outlawed.

Then Skapti the judge said: "If things are as reported, then surely Grettir has committed an evil deed; but we have only heard one side of the story, and we only know of what has happened at third hand, by report; there are two ways of telling every story. Let us wait till Grettir returns to Iceland. There will be time enough for this action to be taken. I will not give my word that Grettir is guilty till we have heard what he has to say for himself."

But Thorir was such a powerful chieftain that he overbore all resistance. It was said that he could not lawfully take action against a man in his absence; but this was overridden by Thorir, who by packing the court was able to carry out what he wanted. Moreover, owing to the death of Atli there was no one to oppose him vigorously.

He pushed on matters so hard that nought could avail to acquit Grettir, and he was proclaimed an outlaw throughout the whole of Iceland, and Thorir also put a price on his head of many ounces of silver, which he said he would pay to that man who would kill him in Norway or Iceland, or wherever he might find him.

Towards the close of the summer Grettir arrived in a vessel off the mouth of the White-river, an exile from Norway.

It was a still summer night when the ship dropped anchor. A boat came from the shore, and was rowed to the ship. Grettir stood watching it from the bows, leaning on his sword. As it touched the side of the ship, he called, "What news do you bring?"

"Are you Grettir, Asmund's son?" asked a man rising in the boat.

"I am," replied Grettir.

"Then we bear you ill news: your father is dead."

Another man stood up in the boat, and said: "Grettir, he was an old man, and you can hardly have expected to hear that he was still alive. But what I have to say concerns you as closely, and is unexpected. Your brother Atli has been slain by Thorbiorn Oxmain."

Then a third man rose and said: "But these tidings concern others first and you secondly. What I have to say concerns you mainly. You have been made an outlaw throughout the length and breadth of the land, and a price is set on your head."

It is said that Grettir did not change colour, nor did a muscle in his whole body quiver; but he lifted up his voice and sang this strain—

"All at once are showered
Round me, the Rhymer,
Tidings sad—my exile,
Father's loss and brother's,
Branching boughs of battle!
Many a blue-blade-breaker
Shall suffer for my sorrow."

The branching bough of battle is a periphrasis for a man, so also is a blue-blade-breaker; and it is the use of such periphrases that constituted poetry to Icelandic ideas. One night Grettir swam ashore. He thought that his enemies would be awaiting him, and should he venture to land in a boat would fall on him in overwhelming numbers; so he took to the water and swam to a point at some distance. Then he took a horse that he found in a farm near where he came ashore, and he rode across country to the Middle-firth, and reached home in two days. He reached Biarg during the night when all were asleep; so instead of disturbing the household, he opened a private door, stepped into the hall, stole up to his mother's bed, and threw his arms round her neck.

She started up, and asked who was there. When he told her, she clasped him to her heart, and laid her head, sobbing, on his breast, saying. "Oh, my son! I am bereaved of my children! Atli, my eldest, has been foully murdered, and you are outlawed; only Illugi remains."

Grettir remained at home a few days in close concealment. Even the men of the farm were not suffered to know that he was there. He heard the story of how Thorbiorn Oxmain had basely and in cowardly manner slain his brother, when Atli was unarmed; and Grettir considered that it was his duty to avenge his death.

XXII: THE SLAYING OF OXMAIN

One fine day, soon after his return, Grettir mounted a horse, and without an attendant rode over the hill to the Ramsfirth, and came down to Thorod's-stead. This is still a good farm, the best on the fiord, and it is by far the best built pile of buildings thereabouts. It faces the south and is banked up with turf to the north, to shelter it against the cold and furious gales from the Polar Sea. The soil is comparatively rich there, and there are tracts of good grass land on the slope of the hill by the side of the inlet of sea. The farm buildings consists at present of a set of wooden gable ends painted red, and the roofs are all of turf, where the buttercups grow and shine luxuriantly.

Grettir rode up to the farmhouse, about noon, and knocked at the door. Some women came out and welcomed him; they did not know who he was, or they would have been more sparing in their welcome. He asked after Thorbiorn, and was told that he was gone to the meadow, a little way further down the firth, where he had gone to bind hay, and that he had taken with him his son, called Arnor, who was a boy of sixteen.

When Grettir heard this, he said farewell to the women, and turned his horse's head to ride down the fiord towards a boiling spring that bubbles up out of the rock, throwing up a cloud of steam, and running in a scalding rill into the sea. Now the rock is perhaps warm there, or the warm water helps vegetation; certain it is that thereabouts the grass grows thickly, and there it was that Thorbiorn was making his bundles of hay. As Grettir rode along near the water, below the field, Thorbiorn saw him. He had just made up one bundle of hay, and he was engaged on another. He had set his shield and sword against the load, and his lad Arnor had a hand-axe beside him.

Thorbiorn looked hard at Grettir as he came along, and he said to the boy: "There is a fellow riding this way. I wonder who he is, and whether he wants us. Leave tying up the hay, and let us find out what his errand is."

Then Grettir leaped off his horse; he had a helmet on his head, and was girt with the short sword, and he bore a great spear in his hand that had a long sharp blade but no barbs. The socket was inlaid with silver, and a nail went through the socket fastening it on to the staff of the spear. He sat down on a stone, and knocked the nail out. His reason was that he intended to throw the spear at Thorbiorn, and if he missed him, he thought the spear-head and the haft would come apart, and would be of no use to Thorbiorn to fling back at him.

Oxmain said to his son: "I verily believe that is Grettir, Asmund's son, he is so big; I know no one else so big. He has got occasion enough against us, and if he is come here it is not with peaceable intentions. Now we must manage cunningly. I do not know that he has seen you; so you hide behind the bundle of hay, and lie hid till you see him engaged with me. Then you steal up noiselessly behind with your axe, and strike him one blow with all your might between the shoulder-blades. When I see you coming up, I will fight the more furiously so as to draw off his attention, that he may not be able to look round. Have no fear, he cannot hurt you, as his back will be turned to you. Get close enough to make sure, and you will kill him with one blow."

Now Grettir came uphill into the field, and when he came within a spear-throw of them, he cast his spear at Thorbiorn; but the head was looser on the shaft than he had expected it would be, and it became detached in its flight, and fell off and dropped into a marshy place and sank, and the shaft flew on but a little way and then fell harmlessly to the ground.

Then Thorbiorn took his shield, put it before him, drew his sword and ran against Grettir and engaged him. Grettir had, as already said, the short sword that he had taken out of the barrow, and with that he warded off the blows of Thorbiorn and smote at him. Oxmain was a very strong man, and his shield was covered with well-tanned hide stretched over oak, and the blade of Grettir fell on it, hacked into it, and sometimes caught so that he could not at once withdraw it. Thorbiorn now began to deal more furious blows. Now just as Grettir was wrenching his sword away from the shield, into which it had bitten deep, he saw someone close behind him with an axe raised. Instantly he tore out his sword and smote back over his head to protect his back from his assailant behind, and the blow came on Arnor just as he was on the point of driving his axe in between the shoulders of Grettir, so that he staggered back, mortally wounded. Thorbiorn, whose eye was on his son, retreated a step, lost his presence of mind for a moment, and thereupon down came Grettir's sword on his shield and split it in half. Grettir pursued his advantage, pressed on him, and struck him down at his feet, dead at a blow.

Then he went in search of his silver-inlaid spear-head, but could not find it. So he mounted his horse again, rode on to the nearest farmhouse, and there told what he had done. Many, many years after, about 1250, the spear-head was found in the marsh. When I was in Iceland I also obtained a very similar spear-head, only not silver-inlaid, that was found in the volcanic sand; it had probably been lost in a very similar manner.

It seems to us in these civilized times very horrible this continual slaying that took place in Iceland; but we must remember that, as already said, there were in those days not a single policeman, soldier, or officer of justice in the island. When a trial took place, the prosecutor was the person aggrieved, or the nearest akin. The court pronounced sentence, and then the prosecutor was required to carry out what the law had ordered. He was to be constable and executioner. Now the law, or custom which was the same as law, for there was no written code, was that when one man had been killed, the next of kin was bound to prosecute the slayer and obtain from him money compensation, or outlawry, or else he might kill the slayer himself, or one of his kin. This latter provision seems to us outrageous, that because A kills B, therefore that C, who is B's brother, may kill D, who is brother to A. But so the law or custom stood and was recognized as binding, and not to carry out the law or custom was regarded as dishonourable. It must be remembered that Iceland was colonized about A.D. 900, and that Grettir was born only about 97 years after, and that Christianity was adopted in 1000; that is to say, it was sanctioned by law, but no one was forced to become a Christian unless he liked. Also, that there was no government in the island, no central authority, and that the colonists lived much as do the first settlers now in a new colony which is not under the crown, or like the diggers at the gold mines.

When Grettir had slain Thorbiorn Oxmain, he went home to Biarg and told his mother, who said it was well that Atli's blood was wiped out by the death of the man who had so basely and in such cowardly fashion slain him; but she said she foresaw more trouble coming like a rising black cloud, and that this would make it more difficult for Grettir to get relief from his outlawry.

XXIII: AT LEARWOOD

After the slaying of Thorbiorn Oxmain, Grettir would not remain at home, lest trouble should come on his mother; so he rode across the Neck first of all to his brother-in-law, at Melar, at the head of the Ramsfirth, to ask his advice. His brother-in-law there was called Gamli; he was not very rich or powerful, and he represented to Grettir that it would never do for him to remain in such near proximity to Thorod's-stead, in the same valley, at the head of the same firth. This Grettir acknowledged, so he stayed there but a few days, and then rode over the high table-land to the Lax, or Salmon-dale, where was the watershed, and the river of the salmon ran west into Hvamsfiord. One of the most interesting and best written of the Icelandic sagas relates to the history of this valley. The Hvamsfiord is by nature wonderfully protected against western storms, for the entrance is almost blocked to the west by a countless multitude of islands, of which only one is moderately large, and to the north-west is not only a grassy promontory, but also a natural breakwater of three long narrow islands.

Outside the cluster of islands are eddies and whirlpools, and the passage between them is not always safe; but when a vessel has passed through between the islets it enters as into a wide beautiful inland lake, the shape of which is that of a boot, with the sole to the east and the toe turned up north. Moreover, along the north side of this sheltered firth are high and steep hills that screen from the water all gales sweeping from the Pole; and in the glens and under the crags of these hills exposed to the south are beautiful woods of birch.

Formerly in Iceland the woods were much more extensive than they are now; for the old settlers found in them plenty of fuel, and the birch-trees grew to a fair size. Now, alas, with fatal want of consideration, the trees have been so cut down that the woods are rare and the trees are small. There is hardly a birch-tree whose top one cannot touch when riding through a wood on a little pony no bigger than a Shetlander.

Exactly at the toe of the boot is a rich grassy basin, where two streams flow into the fiord, and here is a beautiful view from the water. One sees in front the green basin, and above it rise the mountains to Skeggoxl, a cone covered with eternal snows and with glaciers streaming down its flanks. Here, in a sweet sheltered nook, basking in the sun, in spring with the riverside and the marshes blazing with immense marigolds, and with the short grass slopes speckled with blue tiny gentianella, is the farm, and near it the wooden church of Hvam. In another part of the basin is a settlement called Asgard, the "Home of the gods;" for those who settled there first thought the spot so delightful, so warm, that they named it after the sunny land of fable, where it was said that their ancestors, the hero-gods of the northern race, had lived in the east before ever they crossed Russia and settled in Norway. Asgard to their minds was Paradise.

Paradise in Iceland is not a paradise elsewhere; nevertheless, to one who has travelled over barren hills and between glaciers, this warm nook with its green grass and woods of glistening birch was a place of inexpressible charm. Now, just to the east, where would come the ball of the toe, looking across the end of this still blue lake-like fiord, up the valleys to the snows of Skeggoxl, is the farm of Learwood, in a grassy flat by the water, backed by birchwood and hills, and screened from the east as well as from the north winds. Here lived Thorstein Kuggson. Kuggson's mother was the daughter of Asgeir, the father of Audun of Willowdale, with whom Grettir had a tussle on the ice, and whom he afterwards upset with his foot when he was carrying curds. Kuggson through his father was related to the influential and wealthy family in the Laxdale, whose history is well known through the noble saga that relates the story of that valley.

Grettir spent the autumn with his relative Kuggson. Now, whilst he was there he fell to talking one day with Kuggson about his trial of strength with Audun, and Grettir said how glad he was that nothing had come of it. It was said that he was a man of ill-luck; yet luck had befriended him on that occasion in sending Bard to interrupt the struggle before both lost their tempers and the quarrel became serious.

Then said Kuggson: "You remind me of the story of Bottle-back, which, of course, you know."

"It is many years since I have heard the tale," answered Grettir; "for, indeed, I can be little at home now, and am out of the way of hearing stories of one's forefathers. Tell me the tale."

Then Kuggson told Grettir

The Story of Bottle-Back

"You know very surely, Grettir, that your great-grandfather was Onund Treefoot. He was so called because in the great battle of Haf's fiord, fought against King Harald, he had one of his legs cut off below the knee. You have been told how that Onund had first to wife Asa, and that he settled at Cold-back; and he had by his first wife two sons, Thorgeir and Ufeig, who was also called Grettir, and it is after him that you are named. Onund's second wife was the mother of Thorgrim Grizzlepate, your grandfather.

"The story I am going to tell you relates to Thorgeir, the eldest son of Onund, and how he got the name of Bottle-back. You might think he acquired the designation from a rounded back. It was not so, he had a back as straight as yours.

"But to understand the story of how he got the name, I must go back to the time when Onund, your great-grandfather, came to Iceland. That was in the year of Christ 900; he was unable to remain any longer in Norway, because the king, Harald, was in such enmity with him. So he resolved that he would come to Iceland and seek there a new home. Now this was somewhat late, for the colonization of this island had begun some five or six and twenty years before, and there had come out great numbers of Norwegian chiefs, who fled from the rapacity and the vengeance of King Harald Fairhair, who outlawed every man who took up arms against him."

But the story shall be told not in Kuggson's words, but in mine.

Onund sailed to Iceland from Norway in the summer of A.D. 900, and he had a hard voyage and baffling winds from the south that drove him far away to the north into the Polar Sea, till he came near the pack-ice; and then there came a change, and he made south, and after much beating about, for he had lost his reckoning, he made land, and found that he had come upon the north coast of Iceland, and those who knew the looks of the land said he was off the Strand Bay. To the west rose the rocks and glaciers of the Drang Jokull, and to the east the long promontory that separated the Hunafloi from Skagafiord.

Presently a ten-oared boat put off from shore, rowed by six men, and approached Onund's vessel, and the men in the boat hailed the vessel and asked whose it was. Onund gave his name and inquired to whom the men belonged. They said they were servant men belonging to a farm at Drangar, just under the mighty field of glacier of Drang Jokull. Onund asked if all the land was taken up by settlers, and the men answered that along the north coast all such land as was worth anything was taken already, and that most was also settled to the south.

Then Onund consulted with his shipmates what was to be done, whether coast along the north protuberance of Iceland in search of uninhabited land, or go into the great bay and see whether any chance opened for them there. They had arrived so late in Iceland after the main rush of settlers that they could not expect to get any really favourable quarters. The men advised against exploring the north, exposed to the cold gales from the Polar Sea, where the fiords would be blocked with ice half the year; and thought there would be no harm trying what they could find further south.

So Onund turned his vessel in towards the head of the splendid bay Hunafloi; but seeing a creek that seemed fairly sheltered, having on the north some quaint spikes of rock, and a great mountain to the south like a horn, and finding that this fiord gave a turn northwards under the shelter of the mountains, the men with Onund's consent ran in there, and having anchored the vessel, entered a boat and rowed ashore. On reaching the strand they were met by men who asked them who they were and what they did there. Onund said he had come with peaceable intentions, and then he was told that all that fiord was occupied, and that the owner of the land was Eric Trap, a wealthy man. Eric came to the beach and hospitably invited Onund and his ship's crew to his house. There Onund told him his difficulty. He had come to Iceland too late, and he feared that he would be able nowhere to find unclaimed lands.

Eric considered a while, and then said there was more land that he had claimed than he could well keep in hand, and that he would be pleased to accommodate a man of such noble family and character as was Onund. Onund pressed him to receive payment for the land, but this Eric generously refused. When he had come there, said Eric, the country had been unpeopled, and he had just claimed what he liked, and had claimed more than he wanted. Now he desired to have neighbours, and if Onund would be friendly none would be better pleased than himself to have him near.

This gratifying offer satisfied Onund, but, as the saying is, 'Don't look a gift-horse in the mouth,' he did not at once close with the offer, but asked to be allowed to see the land Eric was so ready to part with.

Accordingly he rode with Eric along the coast, passed the headland where was the horn-shaped mountain, and came upon a fiord where some boiling springs poured up in the sea out of its depths; the mountains on the north came down so abruptly to the water's edge that the only habitable ground lay at the head of the firth and on the south side, having a northern aspect. Moreover there was a lofty range to the south, so that in winter the sun would never light up this firth. Onund did not much like it, he thought that Eric had offered him the place because he did not care for it himself; so he went across the mountain range and down into the little bay south of it. As they rode it was over snow, a long descent of wintry mountain, till they reached a valley in which was a hot spring, a little lake, and some grass. The situation was somewhat more inviting than that Onund had already seen, but it was not very attractive, and looking back on the long dreary slope of snow he said, "A cold back! a cold back! I would like to have had one warmer." "That is not easily acquired," answered Eric. "Further south there is no fiord for many miles till you come to one occupied by a man called Biarni. That I can tell you is a fertile settlement, there are woods and pastures, and hot springs and good anchorage; but that is not my land to give you."

Then Onund sang a stave:

"All across life's strands do run,
I who many war-wagers won,
Meadows green and pastures fair
Once were mine, and woods to spare.
Left behind, I rid the steed
That o'er wave, with wind doth speed.
Cold—cold, icy back behind,
This is what alone I find,
Hard the lot that fate doth yield
To the bearer of the shield."

Eric answered, "Many men have lost everything in Norway, and have got nothing in exchange. Cold may be the back against which to lean; but better cold back than none at all."

This was true. Onund had not received Eric's offer graciously; but he now accepted it, and he called the second bay he saw—that into which he had descended over snow—Coldback, and that remains the name to this day.

Eric behaved very nobly; he gave up to Onund the whole tract of land from the Horn-headland to the limit where Biarni's land began. He received the whole of Reykjafiord, Fishless Creek, and Coldback Bay.

Then Onund built himself a house at Coldback; and there was no difficulty about wood, for the Gulfstream flowed up past the great north-west promontory of Iceland, curled round into Hunafloi, and deposited a quantity of American timber as drift all along that coast. Indeed, the drift was so abundant that neither Eric nor Onund made any agreement about it. Now, as it happened in the sequel, this was an oversight.

Onund prospered at Coldback, and even set up for himself a second farm at the head of the firth to the north, called Reykja-firth, from the boiling springs that puffed and bubbled up in the sea at the entrance; and a hot spring is in Icelandic—Reykr.

Now, a few years after Onund had settled in Iceland, his good wife Asa died. He had by her two sons—the elder was called Thorgeir, and the younger Ufeig Grettir. After a while Onund went courting a woman called Thordis, in Middle-firth, and he married her, and by her had a son called Thorgrim; he grew to be a big man, very strong, wise, and a capital man at husbandry. When he was twenty-five years old his hair grew gray, and so he went by the name of Thorgrim Grizzle-pate, and he was the grandfather of Grettir. After the death of Onund, his widow married, as already said, Audun of Willowdale, and their son was Asgeir, the father of Grettir's cousin Audun, with whom he had that affray on the ice, and then with the bottle of curds.

When Onund was a very old man, then he died in his bed, and he was buried under a great mound, which you may see at Coldback if you go there. It is called Old Treefoot's cairn. When he was dead, then Thorgrim Grizzlepate and his half-brothers, Thorgeir and Ufeig Grettir, lived together on the best of terms at Coldback, and managed the property between them.

In time Eric Trap of Arness died also, and left his lands to his son Flossi. He had remained in friendship with Onund all his life; but Flossi, his son, was a grasping man, and he was often heard to grumble about the Coldback family, and say that they were squatters on his father's land, and had no title to show for the land they held. Thorgrim Grizzlepate and his half-brothers did not wish to quarrel with Flossi, so they kept out of his company; and when there were sports of hurling, and wrestling, and horse-fighting, strayed away, so as not to be involved in a quarrel with him.

Now, Thorgeir was the eldest of the three brothers at Coldback, and he was mightily fond of fishing. This was known to Flossi, and he made a plot for slaying him; for he was envious of the brothers, and wanted to get back all their lands into his own possession. He had got a house-churl called Finn, and he and Finn had some talk together. The end of this talk was that Finn started secretly for Coldback armed with a hatchet, and he hid himself in the boat-house at Coldback.

Early in the morning Thorgeir got ready to go out fishing, for the weather was good, the sea calm and was alive with fish. His nets were in the boat, and before sunrise he left his bed and dressed, and went to the boat-house to start on his excursion. He had not the smallest suspicion of mischief, and as he was like to be on the water for a long time, he flung a great leather bottle of curds over his back. As already said, these leather bottles were no other than the hides of goats or sheep, sewn up and converted into receptacles for liquid.

So Thorgeir went to the boat-house with the bottle of curd over his back, opened the door, and went in. He did not look round, he had no suspicion of evil, and he did not see Finn lurking in the dark corner. It was, moreover, very dark in the boat-house. Thorgeir stooped to get hold of the boat and thrust her out, when all at once out from the dark corner leaped the churl, and brought the axe down on Thorgeir's back. The blow made the bottle squeak, and all the curds gushed out. That was enough for Finn. He made sure he had killed Thorgeir, so he ran away as fast as he could back to Arness, burst into the house, and shouted to his master "I have killed him! I have killed him! And he squeaked! he squeaked!"

"Let me look at the axe," said Flossi. Then, when he had the axe in his hand he turned it about and laughed, and said, "Verily, I did not think that Thorgeir had milk in his veins instead of blood. That accounts for it, that you have been able to slay him."

This affair was a subject of much comment, and much laughter did it provoke. Thorgeir had not received the smallest wound, only his bottle was split, and ever after he went by the name of Bottle-back.

But a song was made about this event which was never forgotten. It runs thus:—

"Of the days of old
Great tales are told

How heroes went forth to fight,
Their shields, for show
Were whitened as snow,

And their weapons were burnished bright
The battle began,
In the weapon-clang,

The red blood flowed apace
In rivers shed
It dyed red

The shields o'er all their face.
But nowaday
We tune our lay

To tell a different story.
The churls who fight
Bring axes white,

With curds and whey made gory."

When Kuggson ceased, Grettir laughed heartily. "Ah!" said he, "that cannot be said now, for indeed there flows much blood."

"You speak the truth," answered Kuggson; "and I wish that this red stream flowed less abundantly."

"That may be," said Grettir; "but I would fain hear the rest of the story. I have not heard it told me for a long time; and, indeed, to speak the truth, much of it I have clean forgotten, though I did hear it when I was a boy at home."

"If you will hear what follows, it must be as a new story," said Kuggson. Again I will tell it in my own words.

The Story of the Stranded Whale

Hard times came to Iceland, such as had not been known since it was settled, for the timber that had been thrown up by the sea came to an end, or very nearly so. There had been great accumulations, and these were exhausted, and for some reason or other that cannot now be explained the Gulf-stream ceased to carry on its current the amount of timber it had formerly, the wreckage of the forests on the Mississippi, swept down into the great Mexican Gulf, and thence washed out over the vast Atlantic, borne on the warm stream to the north, to give fuel to those lands which were by nature unprovided with trees. At this time the axe was laid against the largest and finest birch that grew in the forests in Iceland. But none of that timber was big and good enough for building purposes.

This deficiency in drift-wood continued for many seasons, and if men required building timber they were constrained to send to Norway for it. Now, it happened that about this time a great merchant vessel was wrecked in the fiord in the lap of which was Arness, where lived Flossi, and he took four or five of the chapmen to his house, and lodged them there well and hospitably, and the other wrecked men were quartered in other farmhouses near. All winter the men were engaged in building a new ship out of the wreck and what other timber they could get; but they were not skilful over their work, and they built a badly-proportioned vessel, over small at the stem and stern and over big amidships; and this vessel was much laughed at, and men called it the Wooden-tub, and that bay where Flossi lived was ever after called Wooden-tub Bay, because this broad-beamed, comical vessel was built there.[#]

[#] It is still so called, Trèkyllis-víc.

Now, it fell out that at the spring equinox there was a great storm from the north, and it lasted a week. The waves came in huge rollers against the cliffs, and spouted like geysers into the air, and all the air was in a haze with spray, and was full of the noise of the sea. Those who lived on the coast were not sorry for the storm, because they hoped it would blow in drift-wood and other spoils of the deep upon the shores; and sure enough, when it abated, a man who lived out on Reykja-ness came and told Flossi that there was a great whale washed ashore there. Then Flossi sent word to all the farms round to the north. But hard-by where the whale had come ashore lived a farmer named Einar, who was a tenant under the brothers at Cold-back, so he took a boat and rowed off to Coldback, and told them about the monster that was stranded.

When Thorgrim and his brothers Thorgeir and Ufeig heard this, they got ready at once, and were twelve in a ten-oared boat, with axes and knives for cutting up the whale. Another boat put off from another of their farms, with six men in it, and others were sure to come as soon as they could get ready.

In the meantime, Flossi and all his company, his kindred, servants, and tenants, had hurried to the spot, and were already engaged in cutting up the whale, when round the ness came the boat of the brothers. Now, the shore where the whale was cast up belonged to the brothers, and they called out to Flossi to assert their right to whatever was found on the strand. Flossi answered that if they had any right to the drift they must show their claim. They had, he said, been allowed by his father to squat on his land, but his father had never given over to them all his rights, certainly not the lordship over the strand, and claim to flotsam and jetsam. Whilst the dispute continued, up came other boats of the Coldback party, and then a long boat, that contained a fellow called Swan, who lived in Biornfiord, to the south of Coldback, a very warm friend of the brothers, and a plucky, resolute man.

Thorgrim was hesitating what to do, when Swan told him it would be mean to allow himself to be robbed. Moreover, this assault on his rights, if not resisted would establish a precedent, and Flossi would claim everything found on their strand, even at their very doors.

So a fight began. The Coldback men came ashore, and Thorgeir Bottle-back mounted the carcase of the whale, to drive off the servants of Flossi. Among these was Finn; he was near the head of the whale, and stood in a foothold he had cut for himself. Then Thorgeir Bottle-back said, "Ah! I owe you a stroke of the axe, which has not been repaid as yet," and he smote at him, and felled him.

Flossi egged on his men, and a desperate fight ensued; some fought on the body of the whale, some about it. There were hardly any present who had other weapons save choppers and axes, and they hewed at each other with these. But some had no other weapons than the ribs of the whale, and it is even said that some of the churls flourished great strips of blubber, with which they banged each other about, nearly smothering each other in oil, but not doing much harm.

The battle was going ill with Flossi, when there arrived a contingent of men from Drangar, with many boats, and gave help to Flossi, and then those of Coldback were borne back overpowered; but they did not retreat till they had loaded their boats. Swan shouted to the Coldbackers to get on board as quickly as they could, for he saw more men coming against them from the north. Flossi received a wound, but Ufeig, one of the three brothers, was dealt his death-wound before he could get into the boat, and he fell on the strand. Thorgeir Bottle-back at once leaped out of the vessel, ran to his brother, heaved him up in his arms and plunged back through the surf with him, and lifted him into the boat, where he died. It is told that in this battle one man was beaten to death by the rib of a whale, and that was one of the chapmen of the wrecked vessel.

After this, the matter was brought before the assize, for the question of the right to the shore had to be decided one way or the other. And it was decided in this manner: Flossi was condemned to outlawry for his high-handed proceeding, and because of the death of Ufeig Grettir; but the question of the rights was thus settled by the judge, Thorkel Moon. He said, "I cannot see that the claim made by the Coldback men is established, for no money passed between Onund and Eric. I know this about the land that was possessed by my grandfather Ingolf, and which is now my own. He received it from Steinver the Old; but then he gave her a mottled cloak, and that was a pledge of sale; and this has never been contested. In the matter of the lands inhabited by the Coldback men, as far as I can learn, not even a straw was given in exchange. However, it is proved that they have held the land, and have taken the drift for a long time; and that the original owner, Eric, did not dispute their doing so. I therefore decide that a compromise shall hold good. The Coldback brothers must surrender all the Reykja-firth, and content themselves with the land south of that. And I also decide that they shall exercise full and undisputed rights to the land, to all that grows on it, to the sea and what it throws up, along that bit of strand that remains to them."

Now when Kuggson had finished this story, then Grettir said, "You have not told how my grandfather and great-uncle parted."

"No," said Kuggson. "There is not much to tell about that. The two brothers agreed to separate, as your grandfather wanted to marry in the Middlefirth. Bottle-back remained at Coldback."

"Now that you have spoken so much about Coldback," said Grettir, "I will tell you something, though it is to my discredit."

"Say on," answered Kuggson. "Men are generally more ready to boast than to discredit themselves."

"When I was a little boy," said Grettir, "my father suffered from a cold back and great pains in it, in winter, and he only got ease when it was rubbed with a hot flannel. I was a bad, idle boy, and I was set in winter to rub his cold back. This I resented. I thought it was a work fit only for servants, and one day when my father had made me rub his old back till I was tired, then he said to me, 'You are growing slack; rub harder, that I may feel your hand.' 'Do you so want to feel my hand, father,' I said. Then I saw a wool-comb hard by that the women had used for carding wool, and I caught it and rubbed down my father's back with that—so that he shrieked with pain, and I made the blood flow. It was a wicked act. I think of it now the old man is dead, and I am sorry."

"Yes," said Kuggson, "it was an evil act. Men say that you are an unlucky man. Now, I do not wonder at your ill-luck, for none ever raised his hand against his father but there followed him ill in consequence of so doing all his days."

XXIV: THE FOSTER-BROTHERS

Now, the kinsmen of Oxmain heard where Grettir was, so they resolved to form a party, and fall upon him at Learwood. But Grettir's brother-in-law was aware of this and forewarned Grettir, so he went away to the north, and he followed Gilsfiord till he reached Reyk-knolls, where was a pleasant farm near the sea, where also were a great number of ever-boiling springs, that poured and squirted and fizzed out of mounds of red-clay. Here lived a man called Thorgils Arison, and he asked this man if he would give him shelter through the winter.

Arison said that he would. "But," said he, "there is only plain fare in my house."

"I am not choice as to my food, so long as I have a roof over my head," answered Grettir.

"There is one matter further," said Arison. "Somehow or other I get men come to me and offer to become my guests who cannot settle else-where, and I get a rough lot at times. That comes of being too good-hearted to bid them pack. Even now I have two such good-for-naughts guesting with me, two foster-brothers, Thorgeir and Thormod; rough, unkempt men, of bad tempers both, and I wot not how you will agree together. You may come and put your head within my doors if you will, but on one condition, that there be no fighting and knocking about of my other guests."

Grettir answered that he would not be the first to raise strife, and that if the foster-brothers provoked him beyond endurance he would go elsewhere, and not give his host annoyance by a brawl in his house.

With this promise Arison was content.

Thorgils Arison was a firm man, and he told the foster-brothers that he would have no disturbance whilst they were with him, and they also prom-ised to be orderly. Thorgeir did not like Grettir. He scowled at him and contradicted him, but did not pursue his rudeness beyond bounds; and when Grettir was ruffled, a word from the master of the house served to appease the rising blood.

So the early winter wore away.

Now, the good man, Thorgils Arison, owned a cluster of islands in the firth that are called Olaf's Isles; they lie a good sea-mile and a half beyond the ness. On them grass grows, and there the bonder kept his cattle to fatten in autumn. Now, there was an ox on one of these isles that Arison said he must have home before the snows and storms of winter came on, as he in-tended to kill the beast for the feastings of Yule. So the foster-brothers and Grettir volunteered to go out to the island, and fetch the ox home.

They went down to the sea and got out a ten-oared boat, and there were but these three to man it. The weather was cold, and the wind was shifting from the north and not settled. They rowed hard, and reached the island; but the sea was running and foaming over the shore, and they saw it would be no easy matter to get the ox on board with such a surf. So the brothers told Grettir he must hold the boat, whilst they got the ox in. He agreed, and went into the water, and stood amidships on the side out to sea, and thrust the boat towards the shore, whilst the brothers laboured to get the ox in. Thorgeir took up the ox by the hind legs, and Thormod by the fore legs, as the beast refused to be driven on board, and so they carried the animal into the boat; but Grettir, who held the craft, had the sea up to his shoulder-blades, and he held her perfectly fast.

When the ox was hove in, Grettir let go and got into the boat. Thormod took oar in the bows, Thorgeir amidships, and Grettir aft, and so they made out into the open bay. As they came out from the lee of the island the squall caught them, the waves leaped and foamed, and Thorgeir shouted "Now then, stern! Have you gone to sleep? Why are you lagging?"

Grettir answered, "The stern will not lag when the rowing afore is good."

Thereupon Thorgeir fell to rowing so furiously that both the tholes were broken. So he called to Grettir, "Row on steadily whilst I mend the thole-pins."

Then Grettir rowed so mightily, whilst Thorgeir was engaged mending the pins, that he wore through the oars, and when Thorgeir was ready they snapped like matches.

"Better row with less haste and more caution," growled Thormod.

Then Grettir stooped and picked out of the bottom of the boat two un-shapen oar-beams that lay there; but as they were too big to go between the thole-pins, he bored large holes in the gunwales, and thrust the oars through, and rowed thus so mightily that every rib and plank of the boat creaked, and the foster-brothers were in fear lest with his rowing he would tear the craft to pieces. However, they reached the shore in safety.

Then Grettir asked whether the brothers would rather haul up the boat, or go home with the ox. They preferred to haul the boat ashore, and found that it was hung with icicles, for the water had frozen on the sides; but Grettir led home the ox, which was very fat, and very unwilling to be dragged along, so that Grettir became impatient.

When the foster-brothers had finished bailing out the boat, and had put her under cover, they went up to the house, and on reaching it Thorgeir inquired after Grettir, but Arisen the bonder said he had not seen him or the ox. Then he sent out men in quest of him, for he supposed something must have befallen him; and when they came to where the land dipped towards the sea they saw a strange object indeed coming towards them, and did not know at first whether what they saw was a human being or a troll. On approaching nearer they saw that this strange object was Grettir, who was carrying the ox on his back, and striding up the hill with the beast, which had the head hanging over his shoulder, the tongue out, and was lowing plaintively. The sight was infinitely comical, and the men who saw it burst out laughing, and this made Grettir also laugh, so that he dropped the ox.

Now, it must be known that this story is not manifestly absurd, for the Icelandic cattle are very small, like Brittany cows, and bear the same relation to a good English ox that a pony does to a horse. Nevertheless the feat was only such as a strong man could have accomplished. It had taken the two brothers to carry the ox down into the boat, and here was Grettir alone carrying him up hill.

This deed of Grettir was much talked of, and this made Thorgeir, the elder of the foster-brothers, very jealous of Grettir, and he hated him, and sought to do him an injury. One day after Yule, Grettir went down to the bath that was made by turning a stream of hot water from one of the natural boiling springs into a walled basin into which also cold water could be turned from a rill. In former times the Icelanders were very particular about bathing, and were a clean people. At the present day they never bathe at all, and such of the old baths as remain are out of order and full of grass and mud.

Thorgeir said to his brother, "Let us go now and try how Grettir will start, if I set upon him as he comes away from his bath."

"I do not like this," answered Thormod; "you will vex our host, and get no advantage over Grettir."

"I will try what I can do," said the elder; and he took his axe, hid it under his cloak, and went down towards the bathing-place.

When he had reached it he said, "Grettir, there is a talk that you have boasted that no man could make you take to your heels."

"I never said that," answered Grettir, "but anyhow you are not the man to make me run."

Then Thorgier swung up his axe and would have cut at Grettir; but Grettir suspected that the man meant mischief, and he was ready, so that the instant he drew out the axe and swung it, Grettir clashed forward at him, struck him in the chest and sent him staggering back, so that he sprawled his length on the ground.

Then Thorgeir shouted to his brother, "Why do you stand by and let this savage kill me?"

Thormod then laid hold of Grettir, and endeavoured to drag him away, but his strength was not sufficient to effect this.

At that moment up came Arison, the bonder, and he bade them be quiet and have nought to do with Grettir.

So the brothers stood up, and Thorgeir pretended it was all sport, that he had only proposed giving Grettir a fright; but the bonder hardly believed him. As for the younger of the brothers, it was well seen that he had been drawn into the matter against his will. So the winter passed, and peace was kept. This little struggle with Grettir had shown Thorgeir that it would be ill for him to have dealings with a man so prompt and strong as Grettir, and he controlled himself and did not seek to pick a quarrel with him any more. At the same time he did not like him any better. Thorgils Arison got great credit, when it was reported that throughout an entire winter he had maintained such turbulent men as the foster-brothers and Grettir under his roof without their having fought.

But when spring came then they went away, all of them, away over the heaths and moors of the interior.

When we say that Grettir was on the heaths and moors, it must not be supposed that the region so called was at all like the moors of Scotland or England. The heaths and moors of Iceland are upland desert regions with only here and there a scanty growth of vegetation, a little whortleberry, no heath at all, but vast tracts of broken stone and mud and black sand, with perhaps here and there an occasional hill of yellow sandstone. Most of the rock is perfectly black, and breaks into pieces with sharp angles. What is called Icelandic moss is a black lichen that grows on the stones, and there is a very little gray moss to be seen. Where there is a burn or a stream a little grass may grow, but the amount is small indeed.

XXV: HOW GRETTIR WAS WELL-NIGH HUNG

Now, after the slaying of Thorbiorn Oxmain, his kinsman Thorod took the matter up, and rode to the great assize with a large train of men.

The relatives of Grettir also appeared at the assize, and they took advice of Skapti, the law-man; and he said that Atli was slain a week before the sentence of outlawry was pronounced against Grettir, that Thorbiorn Oxmain was guilty of that, and his relatives must pay a heavy fine for the murder. But he said that Grettir was an outlaw when he slew Thorbiorn. Now being an outlaw he was outside the cognizance of the law, he was as one not a native of the country, as one over whom the law had no longer jurisdiction; that, therefore, his slaying of Thorbiorn could not count as expiation of the slaying of Atli; that, moreover, no suit against an outlawed man could stand—it was illegal: that the only way in which Grettir could be brought into court was by the removal of the sentence of outlawry, when at once he could be prosecuted.

Thorod was disconcerted at this; for he could not bring an action against Grettir, and the Biarg people did now bring an action against him for the slaying of Atli, and the court gave sentence that he should pay down two hundred ounces of silver as blood fine for Atli.

Now, at this court, Snorri the judge proposed a compromise. He suggested that the fine should be let drop, and that Grettir should be held scatheless, that the outlawry should be set aside, and the slaying of Thorbiorn be put against the slaying of Atli, and so reconciliation be made.

Thorod did not at all want to pay down two hundred ounces of silver, and the Biarg family were very willing to have the outlawry done away with; so both parties were quite willing to accept this compromise, but Thorir of Garth had to be reckoned with. Grettir was outlawed at his suit for the burning of his sons, and he must be brought to consent, or this arrangement could not take place.

But Thorir was not to be moved. In vain did the law-man Snorri urge him, and represent to him that Grettir, at large, an outlaw, was a danger menacing the country, that he was driven to desperation, Thorir absolutely refused to allow the sentence to be withdrawn. Not only so, but he said he would set a higher price on his head than had been set on the head of any outlaw before, and that was three marks of silver. Then Thorod, not to be behind with him, offered three more.

Grettir resolved to get as much out of the way of his enemies as he could, so he went into that strange excrescence, like a hand joined on by a narrow wrist to Iceland, that extends to the north-west. In this peninsula are two great masses of snow and glacier mountain, called Glam-jokull and Drang-jokull. They do not rise to any great height, hardly three thousand feet, but they are vast domes of snow, with glaciers sliding from them to the firths, and these fall over the edges of the precipitous cliffs in huge blocks of ice that float away on the tide as icebergs. The largest of all the fiords that penetrates this region is called the Ice-firth, and it runs between these great mountains of snow and glaciers. At the extremity of the estuary the valleys are well-wooded—that is to say, well-wooded for Iceland—with birch-trees, for their valleys are very sheltered, and the sea-water that roll in bears with it a certain amount of heat, for it has been affected by the Gulf-stream.

One of these valleys is called Waterdale, and at the time of our story there lived there a man named Vermund the Slim, and his wife's name was Thorbiorg; she was a big, fine woman. Another valley is Lang-dale. Grettir went to Lang-dale—there he demanded of the farmers whatever he wanted, food and clothing, and if they would not give him what he asked, he took it. This was not to their taste at all, and they wished that they were rid of Grettir. He could not remain long in one place, so he rode along the side of the Ice-firth demanding food, and sleeping and concealing himself in the woods. So in his course he came to the upland pastures and dairy that belonged to Vermund Slim, and he slept there many nights, and hid about in the woods.

The shepherds on the moors were afraid of him, and they ran down into the valleys and told the farmers everywhere that there was a big strange man on the heights, who took from them their curd and milk, and dried fish, and that they were afraid to resist his demands. They did not quite know what he was, whether a man or a mountain spirit.

So the farmers gathered together and took advice, and there were about thirty of them. They set a shepherd to watch Grettir's movements, and let them know when he could be fallen upon. Now, it fell out one warm day that Grettir threw himself down in a sunny spot to sleep. The glistening beech leaves were flickering behind him, the rocks were covered with the pale lemon flowers of the dry as, and between the clefts of the stones masses of large purple-flowered geranium stood up and made a glow of colour deep into the wood.

It is a mistake to suppose that Iceland is bare of flowers; on the contrary, there are more flowers there than grass. Beneath Grettir the turf was full of tiny deep-blue gentianellas, just as if the turf were green velvet, with a thread of blue in it coming through here and there.

The shepherd stole near enough to see that Grettir really was fast asleep, and then he ran and told the bonders, who came noiselessly to the spot. It was arranged among them that ten men should fling themselves on him, whilst the others fastened his feet with strong cords.

They made a noose, and cautiously without waking him managed to get it about his legs; then, all at once, ten of them threw themselves on his body, and tried to pin down his arms. Grettir started from his sleep, and with one toss sent the men rolling off him, and he even managed to get to his knees. Then they pulled the noose tighter and brought him down, he, however, kicked out at two, whom he tumbled head over heels, and they lay stunned on the earth. Then one after another rushed at him, some from behind. He could not get at his weapons, which they had removed, and though he made a long and hard fight, and struggled furiously, they were too many for him, and they overcame him in the end, and bound his hands.

Now, as he lay on the grass, powerless, they held a council over him what should be done. The chief man of that district was Vermund Slim, but he was from home. So it was settled that a farmer named Helgi should take Grettir and keep him in ward till Vermund came home.

"Thank you gratefully," said Helgi; "but I have other business to attend to than to keep sentinel over this man. My hands are fully occupied without this. Not if I know it shall he cross my threshold."

So the farmers considered, and decided that another man who lived at Giorvidale should have the custody of Grettir.

"You are most obliging," said he; "but I have only my old woman with me at home, and how can we two manage him? Lay on a man only such a burden as he can bear."

They considered again, and came to the conclusion that one Therolf of Ere should have the charge of Grettir.

But he replied, "No, thank you, I am short of provisions, there is hardly food enough at my house for my own party."

Then they appointed that he should be put with another farmer; but he said, "If he had been taken in my land, well and good, but as he has not, I won't be encumbered with him."

Then every farmer was tried, and all had excuses why they should not have the care of Grettir; and consequently, as no one would have him, they resolved to hang him. So they set to work and constructed a rude gallows there in the wood, and a mighty clatter they made over it.

Whilst thus engaged, it happened that Thorbiorg, Vermund's wife, was riding up to her mountain dairy, attended by five servants. She was a stirring, clever woman, and when she saw so many men gathered together and making such a noise, she rode towards them to inquire what they were about.

"Who is that lying in bonds there?" she asked.

Then Grettir answered and gave his name.

"Why, now, is it, Grettir," she said, "that you have given so much trouble in this neighbourhood?"

"I must needs be somewhere," he answered. "And wherever I am, there I must have food."

"It is a piece of ill-luck that you should have fallen into the hands of these bumpkins," said she. Then turning to the farmers she asked what they purposed doing with Grettir.

"Hang him," answered they.

"I do not deny that Grettir may have deserved the rope," said Thorbiorg; "but I doubt if you are doing wisely in taking his life. He belongs to a great family, and his death will not be to your quietness and content if you kill him." Then she said to Grettir, "What will you do if your life be given you?"

"You propose the conditions," said he.

"Very well, then you must swear not to revenge on these men what they have done to you to-day, and not to do any violence more in the Ice-firth."

Grettir took the required oath, and so he was loosed from his bonds. He said afterwards that never had he a harder thing to do than to control his temper, when set free, and not to knock the farmers' heads together like nuts and crack them, for what they had done to him.

Then Thorbiorg invited him to her house, and he went with her to the Water-firth, and there abode till her husband returned, and when Vermund heard all, then he was well pleased; and deemed that his wife had acted with great prudence and kindness. He asked Grettir to remain there as long as was consistent with his safety, and Grettir accepted his hospitality, and continued there as his guest till late in the autumn, when he went south to Learwood, where was Kuggson, with whom he purposed spending the winter. However, he was not able to stay there, for it soon became known where he was, and his enemies prepared to take him. He accordingly left and went to a friend in another fiord, and remained a short while with him, but was obliged for the same reason to fly thence also; and so he spent the winter dodging about from place to place, never able to remain long anywhere, because his enemies were so resolved on his death, and were on the alert to fall on him wherever they heard he was sheltering.

XXVI: IN THE DESERT

The island of Iceland is one-third larger than Ireland, but then the population is entirely confined to the coast. All the centre of the island is desert and mountain. One mighty mass of mountain covered with eternal snow and ice occupies the south of the island and approaches the sea very closely in the south-east. Much of this is unexplored; it has of recent years been traversed once, across the great Vatna-jokull, but there are passes west of the Vatna. The mountain masses are broken into three main masses. The vast Vatna-jokull is to the east, then comes a pass, and next the circular Arna-fells-jokull, then another pass, and lastly the jumble of snow mountains that form the Ball-jokull and the Lang-jokull, the Goatland and the Erick's-jokull. North of the Vatna-jokull is a vast region, as large as a big county, covered with lava broken up into bristling spikes and deep clefts of glass-like rock, which no one can possibly get across. In the midst of it, inaccessible, rise the cones of volcanoes that have poured forth this sea of molten rock. East and west of this mighty tract of broken-up lava come extensive moors also quite desert, covered with inky-black sand which has been erupted by volcanoes, burying and destroying what vegetation there was. The extent of desert may be understood when you learn that there are twenty thousand square miles of country perfectly barren and uninhabitable, and only partially explored. There are but four thousand square miles in Iceland that are inhabited; the rest of the country is a chaos of ice, desert, and volcanoes. The great lava region mentioned north of the Vatna covers one thousand one hundred and sixty square miles, and the Vatna envelopes three thousand five hundred square miles in ice. Now, here and there in this vast region there are certain sheltered spots where some grass grows, valleys that have escaped the overflow of the molten rock, or the thrust of the glacier; and during the ninety years that Iceland had been inhabited, every now and then a churl who got tired of service, or a murderer afraid of his life, ran away into the centre of the island, and lived a precarious existence on the wild birds, their eggs, and on the fish that abounded in the countless lakes. Probably also they stole sheep, and carried them away to the mysterious recesses of the desert where they had made for themselves homes. They lived chiefly in caverns, of which there are plenty thus formed:—When the lava poured as a fiery stream out of the volcanoes, in cooling great bubbles were formed in it, sometimes these bubbles exploded, blew the fragments into the air, which fell back and made a mass of broken bits of rock like an exploded soda-water bottle; but all the bubbles did not burst, and such hardened when the rock became cool. These bubbles remain as great domed halls, and some of them run deep underground, forming a succession of chambers. I have explored one where a band of outlaws once lived, and found numbers of sheep-bones frozen up in ice in the place where, after they had eaten the mutton, they threw away what they could not devour. At the end of the cave they had erected a wall so as to inclose a space as a store chamber.

These men, living in the desert and rarely seen, were the subject of many tales, and it was not clearly known who and what they really were, whether altogether human, or half mountain-spirits. Imagination invested them with supernatural powers.

When spring came and the snows melted, then Grettir left the farmhouse where he had been last in hiding, and went into the desert, to find food and shelter for himself.

One day he saw a man on horseback alone riding over a ridge of hill. He was a very big man, and he led another horse that had bags of goods on his back. The man wore a slouched hat so that his face could not clearly be seen.

Grettir looked hard at the horse and the goods on the pack-saddle, and thought he would probably find some of these latter serviceable to him, and in his need he was not particular how he got those things which he wanted. So he went up to the rider and peremptorily ordered him to stand and deliver.

"Why should I give you things that are my own?" asked the stranger. "I will sell some of my wares if you can pay for them."

"I have no money," answered Grettir, "what I want I take. You must have heard that by report."

"Then I know with whom I have to deal; you are Grettir the outlaw, the son of Asmund of Biarg." Thereat he struck spurs into his horse and tried to ride past.

"Nay, nay! We part not like this," said Grettir, and he laid his hands on the reins of the horse the stranger rode.

"You had better let go," said the mounted man.

"Nay, that I will not," answered Grettir.

Then the rider stooped and put his hands to the reins above those of Grettir, between them and the bit, and he dragged them along, forcing Grettir's hands along the bridle to the end and then wrenched them out of his grasp.

Grettir looked at his palms and saw that the skin had been torn in the struggle. Then he found out that he had met with a man who was stronger than himself.

"Give me your name," said he. "For, good faith! I have not encountered a man like you."

Then the horseman laughed and sang:

"By the Caldron's side
Away I ride,
Where the waters rush and fall
Adown the crystal glacier wall
There you will find a stone
Joined to a hand—alone."

This was a puzzling answer. The meaning was that he lived near a waterfall that poured out of the Ice mountain, and that his name was Hall-mund, hall is a stone and mund is the hand.

Grettir and he parted good friends; and as he rode away Hall-mund called out to Grettir that he would remember this meeting, and as it ended in friendliness he hoped to do him a good turn yet,—that when every other place of refuge failed he was to seek him "by the Caldron's side, where the waters rush and fall, adown the crystal glacier wall" under Ball-jokull, and there he would give him shelter.

After this Grettir went to the house of his friend the law-man Skapti, and asked his advice, and whether he would house him for the ensuing winter.

"No, friend," answered Skapti, "you have been acting somewhat lawlessly, laying hands on other men's goods, and this ill becomes a well-born man such as you. Now, it would be better for you not to rob and reive, but get your living in other fashion, even though it were poorer fare you got, and sometimes you had to go without food. I cannot house you, for I am a law-man, and it would not be proper for me who lay down the law to shelter such a notorious law-breaker as yourself. But I will give you my advice what to do. To the north of the Erick's-jokull is a tangle of lakes and streams. The lakes have never been counted they are in such quantities, and no one knows how to find his way among them. These lakes are full of fish, and swarm with birds in summer. There is also a little creeping willow growing in the sand, and some scanty grass. It is only one hard day's ride over the waste to Biarg, so that your mother can supply you thence with those things of which you stand in absolute need, as clothing, and you can fish and kill birds for your subsistence, and will have no need to rob folk and exact food from the bonders, thereby making yourself a common object of terror and dislike. One more piece of advice I give you—Beware how you trust anyone to be with you."

Grettir thought this advice was good—only in one point was it hard for him to follow. He was haunted with these fearful dreams at night which fol-lowed the wrestle with Glam, and in the long darkness of winter the dreadful eyes stared at him from every quarter whither he turned his, so that it was unendurable for him to be alone in the dark.

Still—he went. He followed up the White River to the desert strewn with lakes from which that river flowed, and there found himself in utter solitude and desolation.

A good map of Iceland was made in 1844, and on that fifty-three lakes are marked, but the smaller tarns were not all set down. In such a tangle of water and moor Grettir might be in comparative security. He settled himself on a spot of land that runs out into the waters of the largest of the sheets of water, which goes by the name of the Great Eagle Lake, and thereon he built himself a hovel of stones and turf, the ruins of which remain to this day, and I have examined them.

XXVII: ON THE GREAT EAGLE LAKE

Grettir was settled now on the Great Eagle Lake. This lake is shaped like the figure 8, only that the spot of land between the upper and lower por-tion of the lake does not run quite across. On one side of this spot the rock falls away precipitously into the water, whereas it slopes on the other. If I had had a spade and pick, and if there had been more grass on the moor so as to allow of a longer stay, I would have dug about the foundations of Gret-tir's hut, and, who can tell! I might perhaps have found some relic of him. There is no record of anyone else having inhabited it since he was there, and in the middle of the 13th century, when the Saga of Grettir was committed to writing, there remained the ruins of his hut, but no one lived at the place. Now there is no human habitation for many miles; the lake was a day's journey on horseback from the nearest farm, where I had spent the night. You must get some idea of the place where now for some years Grettir was to live.

The moor is made up of rock split to fragments by the frost, and with wide tracts between the ridges of rock strewn with black volcanic ash and sand. It lies high; when I camped out there at the end of June, there was no grass visible, only angelica shoots, and a little trailing willow, so that my horses had to feed on these. The willow does not rise above the surface of the ground, but its roots trail long distances under the surface, groping for nutriment; and for fuel one has to dig out these roots with one's fingers, and employ those which are dryest. Every dip in the moor is filled with a lake, and every lake has in it a pair of swans; in addition there are abundance of other wild fowl, and on the moor are ptarmigan that live on the flowers of the whortle or blae-berry.

Above the rolling horizon of moor, to the south rises the great snowy dome of Erick's-jokull. This is in reality a huge volcano, with precipitous sides of black lava towering up like an immense giant's castle. The great crater has been choked up with the snow of centuries, and the snow in falling had piled up a vast cupola of snow and ice standing high above the black walls, and sliding and falling over the edges in a succession of avalanches. When, at eleven o'clock at night, I looked out of my tent at Erick's-jokull, the scene was sublime. The sun had just gone under the northern horizon of snow and hill, but shone on the great dome of Erick's-jokull, turning it to the purest and most delicate rose colour, and the walls of upright basalt that sustained the dome were of the purple of a plum. Grettir obtained nets and a boat from home, and such things as he wanted for his hut. One great advantage of his present situation was that three different roads or rather tracks led to it from Biarg, so that those who wanted to come to him from home could select their way and avoid observation, till they got among the lakes, when they were in a labyrinth in which anyone might easily be lost, and any one could escape a pursuer. It is true that it was a long and arduous day's ride from Biarg to the Eagle Lake, but the whole of the course along each of the ways lay through uninhabited land.

Now, when other outlaws heard that Grettir was on the Eagle Lake Heath, they had a mind to join themselves to him, and Grettir was not unwilling to have a companion, so lonely did he feel on this waste, and also so fearful was he of being by himself in the dark.

There was a man called Grim, who was an outlaw; and Grettir's enemies made a bargain with him, that he should go to the Eagle Lake Heath, pretend to be friends with Grettir, seek opportunity, and kill him. They on their side undertook, if he would do this, to get his sentence of outlawry reversed, and to furnish him liberally with money.

Accordingly he went to the moor, and after some trouble, found Grettir, and asked if he might live with him.

Grettir replied, "I do not much relish such company as yours, for you have got into outlawry through very infamous deeds. I mistrust you; nevertheless I will suffer you to remain if you work hard and be obedient. I do not want idle hands here."

Grim said he was willing, and prayed hard that he might dwell there, and carried his point. He remained with Grettir the whole of the winter; there was not much friendship between them. Grettir mistrusted him all along, and was never parted from his weapons, night or day, and Grim did not venture to attack him whilst he was awake.

But one morning, when Grim came in from fishing, he went into the hut and stamped his foot and made a noise, seeing that Grettir lay in his bed asleep; and he was desirous to know how soundly he slept. Grettir did not start and open his eyes, but lay quite still. Then Grim made more noise, thinking that if Grettir were awake he would chide him; but Grettir made no motion. Then Grim made sure that he was fast asleep, and he stepped to his side. Now, the short sword that had been taken out of the barrow of Karr the Old hung above the bed-head. Grim leaned over Grettir and laid hold of the sword, and put both hands to it to draw it out of the sheath. At that instant Grettir started up, caught Grim round the waist and flung him backwards so that he was stunned, and the sword fell from his hand. So Grettir made him confess that he had been bribed to set on him and murder him. And then Grettir would have no more of him, and resolved to live entirely alone. Yet—directly he was alone, his dreams, and his horror of the dark, returned on him. Now, Thorir of Garth heard of an outlaw named Thorir Redbeard, a very big man, who for murder had been outlawed, and was therefore in hiding somewhere. Thorir of Garth sent out messengers in search of him, and at last brought about a meeting, and then he offered him a great deal of money if he would kill Grettir. Redbeard said it was no easy task, for that Grettir was wise and wary.

"It is because it is no easy task that I set you to do it," said Thorir of Garth. "You are no milksop to do easy jobs."

This flattered Redbeard, and he undertook to do what was required. He came out on the Eagle Lake Heath in the autumn after that winter when Grim had been with Grettir and made the attempt on his life. Grettir was feeling uneasy and troubled, as the days grew shorter, with the eyes that he thought stared at him from every quarter, and although his judgment prompted him to refuse hospitality to Redbeard, yet his dread of being alone in the dark induced him to disregard his doubts. So he reluctantly admitted Redbeard to be an inmate of his cot.

"Now, mind this," said Grettir. "I let a man be with me here last winter, and he lay wait for my life. If I find that you are false, then I shall not spare you."

Redbeard said he wished for nothing else; and so Grettir received him, and found him to be a very powerful man, and so energetic that he was of the greatest assistance to Grettir.

Redbeard was with him all that winter (1019-1020) and found no occasion on which he could take Grettir unawares. Then set in the next winter 1020-1021, and Redbeard had begun to loathe his life on the heath, and no wonder, for he saw no one save Grettir; the cold and desolation of the spot was surpassingly wretched. Now he became impatient to kill Grettir and get away.

One night a great storm broke over the moor whilst he and Grettir were asleep. The roar of the wind woke Redbeard and he ran outside the hut, down to the water-side, and with a huge stone he smashed the fishing-boat, so that it sank; and the oars and bits he had broken off he threw away into the lake. So did he with the nets.

When he came in Grettir was awake also, and he asked how fared the boat.

"She has broken from her mooring," answered Redbeard, "and has been dashed to bits on the rocks."

Then Grettir jumped up, and taking his weapons ran out to the end of the spit of land on which his hut was built, and saw how the nets were drifting in the waves and were entangled with the oars.

"Jump in, swim out, and bring them to shore," said he to Redbeard. The man shook his head and answered:

"I can do anything save swim. I have not held back from any other work you have set me, but swim I cannot."

Then Grettir laid his weapons down by the waterside and prepared to jump in. But he mistrusted Redbeard, so he said, "I will get in the nets, as you cannot; but I trust you will not deal treacherously by me."

Redbeard answered, "I should be a base fellow and unworthy to live if I were false to you now—after you have housed me so long."

Then Grettir put off his clothes, and went into the water, and swam out to the nets.

He swept them up together and brought them towards the land, and cast them up on the bank; but the moment he attempted to land Redbeard caught up the short sword, drew it hastily and ran at Grettir and smote at him, just as he was heaving himself up out of the water. The blade would have cut into his neck, or between his shoulder-blades, had not Grettir instantly let go, and fallen backwards into the water and sunk like a stone. Sinking thus headlong he reached the bottom, and instead of rising to the surface again he clung to the rocks under water, and groped his way along as close as he could to the bank, so that Redbeard might not see him till he had reached the back of the creek and got aland.

Now, Redbeard stood at the end of the promontory, looking into the water, much puzzled. He had not cut Grettir with the sword, and yet Grettir was gone down, and did not rise. He thought he must have struck his head against a stone, and so have sunk, and he looked out into the water wondering where and when he would rise. Meanwhile Grettir had come ashore behind him and was approaching stealthily. Redbeard was unaware of his danger till Grettir had his arms about him, had heaved him over his head and dashed him down on the rocks, so that his skull was broken. After that Grettir resolved not to take another outlaw into his house, though he could hardly endure to be alone.

Thorir of Garth did not hear of the death of Redbeard till next summer at the great assize; and then he was so angry, and so resolved to make an end of Grettir, that he collected a body of resolute men, his servants and others whom he hired for the purpose, to the number of nearly eighty, to sweep the Eagle Lake Heath and take and kill Grettir.

One day, when Grettir was out on the moor, he saw a large body of armed men riding towards the lake. He had time to fly to a hill that rises at a little distance, where there is a rift in the rock that traverses the top of the hill. When I read the account in the saga I could not quite understand what follows, but no sooner was I on the spot than all appeared quite clear. One could see, at once, that Grettir, taken by surprise, would run to this very spot and no other. It was the nearest available place of vantage, with stone and crag. The situation was not the best that might have been chosen, as it left Grettir's back unprotected; however, he had no time to seek a better.

Thorir came with his men to the bottom of the hill, and shouted to Grettir and taunted him.

Grettir replied, "Though you may have put the spoon to your lips you have not swallowed the broth."

Then Thorir egged on his men to go up the slope at Grettir, but this was not easy. It was steep, and the rocks were close on either side so that Grettir could not be surrounded. Only one man could get at him from before at once. Several attempts were made, but all failed; some of the assailants were killed, some wounded. Then Thorir broke up his party into two, and sent one detachment round to the back of the rocks, to fall on Grettir from behind.

Grettir saw the manoeuvre, and did not see how to meet it. All he could do would be to sell his life dearly. He could not hold out long when assailed simultaneously from before and behind.

Thorir bade the attack slacken till he thought those sent to the rear would be ready, and then he ordered a grand, and, as he believed, a combined assault. Grettir fought with desperation, expecting every moment to be cut down from behind, but to his surprise and that of Thorir he was left unmolested in the rear.

Thorir called off his men, and went round the hill to inquire why the attack from behind had not taken place. To his amazement he came on a discomfited party bleeding, faint, and baffled, and to find that twelve men had fallen in it.

Then he bade a retreat. "Oft," he said, "have I heard that Grettir is a man of marvel for prowess, but I never knew before that he was a wizard, and able to kill as many at his back as he does in front of him."

When he numbered his men, Thorir found that he had lost eighteen. Then he and his retinue rode away, and they carried on them many and grievous wounds.

Now Grettir was no less perplexed with the event than was Thorir, and when the latter had withdrawn he went through the rift in the rocks to see why he had not been fallen on from the rear,—and he lighted on a tall strong man leaning against the rocks, sore wounded.

Grettir asked his name, and the tall man replied that he was Hallmund.

"Do you remember meeting me on the heath one day?" asked the wounded man, "when you tried to stop my horse, and I pulled the reins through your hands so as to skin the palms'? Then I promised if I had the chance to back you up."

"Indeed," said Grettir, much moved, "I remember that right well, and now I thank you with all my heart, for this day you have saved my life."

Then Hallmund said, "You must now come with me, for time must drag with you solitary here on the heath."

Grettir said he was glad to accept the offer; so they went together south to the Ball-jokull, and there Hallmund had a great cave, and his daughter, a big muscular girl, lived there with him; there the girl applied plasters to the wounds of her father and healed him.

Grettir remained with them in the cave all the ensuing summer. But when summer came to an end, he wearied of being so long in the desert, and longed to see and be with his fellow-men in inhabited parts once more; so he bade farewell to Hallmund, and went away to the west to Hit-dale that opens on the Marshland, through which six or seven large rivers flow. Here he had a friend named Biorn living at Holm.

XXVIII: ON THE FELL

Biorn when asked by Grettir to give him shelter declined to do so, not that the will was lacking, but that he had not the power to protect him. "You have made," he said, "enemies on all sides, and if I were to take you under my roof all your enemies would become mine also, and I would be involved in endless and bitter quarrels. I cannot give you direct assistance and shelter, but indirectly I will do what I can for you. There is a long hill, called Fairwood Fell, that runs in front of my house on the other side of the river, and ends just above the marshes. Now, in one place there is a steep shale slide, and above this is a hollow through the mountain, that might very well be made into a dry and comfortable place of abode. From the entrance every one who passes along the highway, all who come across the marshes, can be seen. I can supply you with a few necessaries to fit the place up, but when there you must shift for yourself. I must not risk too much by supporting you."

Grettir consented to this. So he went up to Fairwood Fell and built up the cave, and hung gray wadmal before the entrance, so that no one below could notice that there was anything peculiar or anyone living there. In this eagle's nest among the rocks Grettir spent the time from the autumn of 1022 to the spring of 1024, that is, two winters. Whatever fuel he wanted, all he had to eat, everything he wanted, had to be carried up this slippery and steep ascent by him. Down the shale slide he came when short of provisions, and went over the marshes to this or that farm and demanded or carried off, sometimes a sheep, sometimes curds, dried fish, in a word what he required; and a very great nuisance the men of the district found him. Heartily did they wish they were rid of him, yet they could not drive him from his place of abode, for it was so difficult of access and so easy of defence.

Now, some years ago, in the summer of 1862, the year after I was in Iceland, a very similar lair which Grettir inhabited a little later in the east of Iceland was explored by an Icelandic farmer. This is his description of it: "The lair stands in the lower part of a slip of stones beneath some sheer rocks. It is built up of stones, straight as a line 4-3/4 ells long and 10 inches wide, and is within the walls 7/8 of an ell deep. Half of it is roofed over with flat stones, small thin splinters of stone are wedged in between these to fill up the joints, and these are so firmly fixed that they could not be removed without tools. One stone in the south wall is so large that it requires six men to move it. The north wall is beginning to give way. On the outside the walls are overgrown with black lichen and gray moss."

Something like this was the den of Grettir on the Fairwood Fell, but it was less built up, as he had the natural rock for two of the sides and for the roof.

Whilst Grettir was there, there came a ship into harbour, in which was a man named Gisli, a merchant, very fond of wearing smart clothes, and an inordinately vain man. He heard the farmers talking about Grettir, and what a vexation it was to them to have him in their neighbourhood.

"Don't talk to me about Grettir," said Gisli; "I've had battles with harder men than he. I hope he may came in my way, that I may dress his skin for him."

The farmer to whom he said this shook his head. "You don't know of whom you are speaking. If you were to kill him you would be well off,—six marks of silver were set on his head, and Thorir of Garth has added three more, so that there stand on him nine marks of silver."

"All things can be done for money," said Gisli; "and as I am a merchant I'll see to it. And when we meet—I'll dress his skin for him."

The farmer said it would be well not to talk about the matter. Gisli agreed. "I will abide this winter in Snowfell-ness," he said. "If his lair is on my road thither I'll look out for him, and dress his skin as I go along."

Now, whether he talked in spite of the caution given him, or whether some one overheard what he said, who was a friend of Biorn of Holm, is uncertain. Any how Gisli's threat reached the ears of Biorn, who at once warned Grettir to be on his guard against the merchant.

"If he comes your way," said Biorn, "teach him a lesson; but don't kill him."

"No," said Grettir with a grim smile, "I'll merely dress his skin for him."

Now it happened one day that Grettir was looking out of the entrance to his lair, when he saw a man with two attendants riding along the highway. His kirtle was of scarlet, and his helmet and shield flashed in the sun. Then it occurred to him that this must be the dandified Gisli, of whom he had heard, so he came running down the shale descent to the road. He reached the man, and at once he went to his horse, clapped his hand on a bundle of clothes behind the saddle, and said, "This I am going to take."

"Nay, not so," answered Gisli, for it was he. "You do not know whom you are addressing."

"Nor do I care," said Grettir. "I have little respect for persons. I am in poor and lowly condition myself, so low that I am driven to be a highway robber."

Then Gisli drew his sword, and called to his men to attack Grettir, who gave way a little before them. But he soon saw that Gisli kept behind his servants, and never risked himself where the blows fell; so Grettir put the two churls aside with well-dealt strokes, and went direct upon the merchant, who, seeing that he was menaced, turned and took to his heels. Grettir pursued him, and Gisli in his fear cast aside his shield, then, a little further, threw away his helmet, and so as he ran he cast away one thing after another that he had with him. There was a heavy purse of silver at his girdle. This encumbered him, and as he ran he unbuckled his belt and dropped it and the purse with it. Grettir did not purposely come up with him; he could have outstripped him had he willed, but he let the fellow run a couple of horse lengths before him. The end of the Fell is above an old lava bed that has flowed from a crater called Eldborg or the Castle of Fire, and like an old ruined castle it looks. Gisli ran over this lava bed, jumping the cracks, then dived through a wood of birch that intervened between the lava and the river Haf. The stream was swollen with ice, and ill to ford. Gisli halted hesitating before plunging in, and that allowed Grettir to run in on him, seize him and throw him down.

"Are you the Gisli who were so eager to meet Grettir Asmund's son?" asked the outlaw.

"I have had enough of him," gasped the fallen man. "Keep my saddle-bags and what I have thrown away, and let me go free."

"Hardly yet," said Grettir grimly. "I think something was said about skin-dressing, that is not to be overlooked."

Then Grettir drew him back to the wood, took a good handful of birch rods, pulled Gisli's clothes up over his head, and laid the twigs against his back in none of the gentlest fashion. Gisli danced and skipped about, but Grettir had him by his garments twisted about his head and neck, and continued to flog till the poor fellow threw himself down on the ground screaming. Then Grettir let go, and went quietly back to his lair, picking up as he went the purse and the belt, the shield, casque, and whatever else Gisli had thrown away, also he had the contents of his saddle-bags.

Gisli never came back to Fairwood Fell to ask for them. When he got on his legs he ran up the river to where it was not so dangerous, swam it, and reached a farmhouse, where he entreated to be taken in. There he lay a week with his body swollen and striped; after which he went home, and much was he laughed at for his adventure with Grettir.

XXIX: THE FIGHT ON THE RIVER

Now, whilst Grettir was on Fairwood Fell, favoured by Biorn of Hitdale, his presence after a while became unendurable to the bonders who lived in the marshes. He had been for two winters in his den on the hill, and when they saw that he intended to remain there a third winter, and rob them of sheep and whatever he needed, then they took counsel together how they might rid themselves of the annoyance.

One day in the winter of 1023, Grettir came down from his place of vantage, and went over the marshes to a farm called Acres, and drove away from it two bullocks fit for slaughtering, and several sheep, and he had got on with them some way over the marshes, on his way to his lair, before the farmer at Acres was aware of his loss; he had taken six wethers beside from another farm named Brookbend. This angered the farmers greatly, and they sent a message to the chief man of the district, Thord at Hitness, and urged him to waylay Grettir before he could reach his den. Thord shrank from doing anything; however, they pressed him so much that at last he consented to let his son Arnor go with them. Then messengers were sent throughout all the country side, to every farmer who was concerned. And it was so planned that two bodies of men should march to the taking of Grettir, one on the right, the other on the left bank of the Hit River, so as to take him for certain.

Grettir was soon aware that the country was roused. He was not alone, he had two men with him—one the son of the farmer at Fairwood Fell, with whom he was on good terms, the other a farm-servant. They advised him to desert the cattle and sheep and run for it, cross the river and take refuge in his place of vantage; but this Grettir was too proud to do.

Presently he could see coming on behind him a large band of men, about twenty in all, under Thorarin of Acres and Thorfin of Brookbend. Now, as these were pursuing him over the marshes, up the opposite side of the river came Arnor, the son of Thord of Hitness, and with him a farmer named Biarni of Jorvi.

Grettir managed to reach the river before his enemies came up with him, and he had also time to secure a place of vantage. This was a ness of rock that ran out into the river, or round which the river swept, so that he was protected by the water on all sides but one. Grettir said to the two men with him, that they must guard his back, see that none came up the sides in his rear, and then he took his short-sword in both his hands, planted his feet wide apart on the rock, and prepared to sell his life dear.

The party headed by Thorarin of Acres and Thorfin of Brookbend came up, twenty in all,—but more were coming, for Thorarin had begun the pursuit before all the farmers were collected, and he knew that a body of some twenty or thirty more would arrive before long. Thorarin himself was an old man, and he did not enter into the fray, but urged on his men.

The fight was hard. Grettir was not easily reached where he stood, and he smote at all who approached. Some of the Marshmen fell, and several were wounded. In vain did they attempt to dislodge him by combined rushes, he drove them over the edge into the water, or cut them down with his sword. At last his arm was weary, and he called to the farmer's son to step into his place. He did so, and held the ground valiantly, whilst Grettir rested. Then the party drew back, discomfited. At that moment up came the fresh body of men under Thrand, the brother of Thorarin of Acres, and Stonewolf of Lavadale. These egged on their men eagerly, and they thought they would obtain an easy victory, for Grettir had been fighting for some time, and was weary.

Then Thorarin of Acres called out and advised delay.

"For," said he, "the third party of men under Arnor and Biarni of Jorvi have not come up on the other side of the river."

This piece of advice was rejected by the newcomers. What did they want with more men? They were a large party, fresh and untired, and Grettir had but two men with him, and they were wearied with fighting. So the signal was given for the onslaught.

Then Grettir saw that he must either jump into the river, swim across, and desert the sheep and bullocks he had driven there, or use almost superhuman exertions to defend himself.

His position was, indeed, desperate; for, even if he did hold his own against this second body of men, a third was on its way up the other bank of the river to intercept him on his way up to the Fell. For one moment he hesitated, and then was resolved. No, he would not run. He would die there, and die only after having strewn the ground with his foes. Foremost among his assailants was Stonewolf of Lavadale, and Grettir made a sudden rush at him, and with a tremendous stroke of his sword he clove his head down to the shoulders. Thrand, who sprang forward to avenge him, Grettir struck on the thigh, and the blow took off all the muscle, and he fell, crippled for life. Then Grettir fell back to his place of safety, and dared others to come on. They sprang out on the neck of rock, but would not meet his weapon, one after another fell or was beaten back.

Then Thorarin cried out, and bade all draw off.

"The longer ye fight," said he, "the worse ye fare. He picks out what men among you he chooses."

The party withdrew, and there were ten men fallen, and five had received mortal wounds, or were crippled; and hardly one of the two parties was without some hurt or other.

Grettir, moreover, was marvellously wearied, but had received no wounds to speak of.

Now, hardly had the men withdrawn, carrying their dead and wounded, than up came the third detachment under Arnor and Biarni, on the other side of the river. There can be no question but that, had they crossed and fallen on Grettir, he could not have defended himself longer, so overcome was he with weariness; but Arnor knew that his father had entered on the matter reluctantly, and he was discouraged by the ill-success of the other companies. Consequently, he neither waded through the river at the ford, a little higher, nor did he maintain his ground and cut off Grettir's retreat. Instead, he withdrew with all his men, and left Grettir to recover his strength, and cross and escape to the Fell. This conduct of Arnor provoked much comment; and he was accused of cowardice, an accusation that clung to him through life. Even his father rebuked him, for the father saw what discredit he had brought upon himself.

The point on the river Hit where this affray took place is still shown; and is called Grettir's-point to this day.

When the fight was over Grettir and the two men went to the Fell, and as they passed the farm the farmer's daughter came out of the door, and asked for tidings.

Then Grettir sang:—

"Brewer of strong barley-corn,
Pourer forth of drinking-horn,
Lo! to-day the Stonewolf fell,
Ne'er again his head be well.
Many more have got their bane,
Many in their blood lie slain;
Little life has Thorgils now,
After that bone-breaking blow.
Eight upon the river's bank
In their gore expiring sank."

XXX: A MYSTERIOUS VALE

In the spring of 1024 Grettir went away from Fairwood Fell; for he had been there so long, and had preyed for such a time on the bonders of the marshes, that he himself saw that it would be best for him to remove into quite another part of the island. So he visited his friend Hallmund once more, under the ice of Ball-jokull, and Hallmund advised him where to go. He could not give him hospitality himself that winter, because his stock of goods was run so short that it would hardly suffice for his daughter and himself; but he told him of a valley unknown to anyone, save a friend of his called Thorir and himself. And he informed him how it was to be reached.

Now, as already said, there are passes in Iceland between the several blocks of ice mountains, and such a pass exists between Goatland-jokull and a curious domed snowy mountain called Ok. The pass is called the Cold Dale, because it lies for many hours ride between ice mountains, and under the precipitous Goatland-jokull, whose rocks are crowned with green ice that falls over incessantly in great avalanches. It is seven hours' ride from one blade of grass to another through that dale. I went through it on midsummer-day, and saw the bones of horses lying about that had died unable to get through; perhaps becoming lame or exhausted on the way.

Half through this long trough of the Cold Dale stands up a buttress of rock, or rather a sort of ness, projecting from Goatland-jokull, so precipitous that hardly any snow rests on it, and this is called the Half-way Fell.

Now, Hallmund told Grettir he must go through the Cold Dale till he reached the Half-way Fell, and there he must strike up over the snow and glaciers of Goatland-jokull, due south, and he would all at once drop into a valley known to few.

So Grettir went up the moor till he struck the White River, that flowed out of the Eagle Lakes he knew so well, and under the cliffs and icy crown of Erick's-jokull, then he climbed over broken trachyte rocks for several hundreds of feet, till he found himself in the Cold Dale, and along that he trudged till he had reached Half-way Fell, standing up like a wall as though to stop the pass. There he turned to the left, and as at this point Goatland is no longer precipitous, but slopes in a series of steps to the Cold Dale, he climbed up through the snow, a long and tedious ascent, till he stood on the neck of the mountain, and there he saw that the snow slopes fell away rapidly to the south, and he descended and soon beheld before him a valley in which were a great many boiling springs that threw up clouds of steam, and he saw also, what greatly pleased him, that there was rich and abundant grass in this valley. This is what the saga says: "The dale was long and somewhat narrow, locked up by glaciers all round, in such a manner that the ice walls overhung the dale. He scrambled down into it, as best he could, and there he saw fair hillsides grass-grown and set with bushes. Hot springs were there, and it appeared to him that it was the earth-fires which prevented the ice walls from closing in on the valley. A little river ran down the dale, with level banks. The sun rarely shone into the valley; but the number of sheep there could hardly be reckoned, they were so many; and nowhere had he seen any so fat and in such good condition."

Grettir did not see Thorir, Hallmund's friend, at first; so he built himself a hut of such wood as he could get, and with turf. He killed the sheep he wanted, and found that there was more meat on one of them than on two elsewhere.

The Saga says:—

"There was one ewe there, brown mottled, with a lamb, and she was a beauty. Grettir killed the lamb, and took three stone of suet off it, the meat was some of the best he had ever eaten. But when the mottled ewe missed her lamb, she went up on Grettir's hut every night, and bleated so plaintively as to trouble his sleep, and made Grettir quite troubled that he had killed her lamb."

Now Grettir noticed that at evening the sheep ran in one direction, and once or twice he heard a call; so he went after the sheep one evening, and was led by them to the hut where Thorir dwelt. He was a strange man, who had spent so many years away from the society of his fellow-men as not to care any more to meet them, so he did not welcome Grettir very warmly. However he had three daughters, and they were glad to have someone to talk to, and as the winter crept on Thorir himself became more amiable, and so the winter did not pass as drearily as Grettir had feared it would. He sang his songs and related stories, and the party played draughts with knuckle-bones of sheep.

When spring came, however, he was fain to go; and he did not leave by the way he came, but followed the little river, and it led him out between rock and glaciers into a piece of desert, covered with lava beds that have poured out of a volcano, or rather two that stand opposite this entrance to Thorir's valley. These two volcanoes are quite unlike each other, though side by side, one, called Hlothu-fell has upright walls, like Erick's-jokull, and a crater filled up and brimming over with ice; but the other Skialdbreith, or the Broad-shield, is like a conical round silver shield laid on the ground. The entrance to Thorir's Dale is completely hidden by a round snowy mountain that blocks it, and then a second snowy mountain stands further out in front of the opening, so that not a sign of any valley can be seen from anywhere.

So difficult did Grettir think it would be to find it, that he ascended on Broad-shield and set up a stone there with a hole in it, so that anyone looking through this hole would see directly into the narrow entrance of Thorir's Dale. This stone still stands where Grettir had placed it; but has sunk on one side, so that by looking through the hole the eye is no longer directed to the entrance.

No one had ever visited Thorir's Dale since Grettir left it till the year 1654, when it was explored by two Icelandic clergymen, and an account of their expedition in Icelandic is to be found in the British Museum. The valley as far as I know has not been explored since. It is marked on the map of Iceland, but apparently from the description left by the two clergymen, not from any visit made to it by the map-maker.

When the two men visited the valley they went to it in the same way as did Grettir. They found no hot springs, and the valley was utterly barren; but then they had no time to descend it, they only looked down on it from above. They found the cave with a door, and a window to it, which was probably the habitation of Thorir and his daughters.

XXXI: THE DEATH OF HALLMUND

Now, there was a man called Grim, who was an outlaw for his ill-deeds, and he thought that as Grettir no longer abode in his hut on the Eagle Lake, he might go there and occupy it. This did not please Hallmund, for Grettir had left him his nets, and he was wont to fish in the lake.

Grim had supplied himself with nets, and he one day caught a hundred char, large red-fleshed fish, delicious eating; so he piled them up outside his hut. Next morning to his great surprise all his char had disappeared. Then he went fishing again, and caught even more fish, and he brought them to land, and heaped them up as before.

Next morning they also had disappeared.

He could not understand it; so he fished again, and had on this occasion extraordinary luck: he must have netted nearly three hundred fish. He brought them home, and put them in the same place as before; but he did not go to sleep this time: he remained within, and watched his store through a peep-hole in the door.

During the night he heard someone who trod heavily coming along the ness, and then he saw a man picking up his fish, and putting them into a basket he had on his back. Grim watched till he had filled the basket, which he now heaved upon his shoulders. Instantly Grim threw open the door, rushed out, and whilst the man was still stooping adjusting his load, he swung up a very sharp axe he held, holding it in both hands, and smote at the man's neck. The axe hit the basket, and that somewhat broke its force, but it glanced aside and sank into the shoulder. Then the man started aside, and set off running with the basket to the south, skirting a lava field that had flowed out of Erick's-jokull, and which now goes by the name of Hall-mund's Lava-bed.

Grim ran after him, and saw that he was making for Ball-jokull; but the man, who was of great size and strength, though wounded and losing blood, ran on, and did not stay till he reached a cave in the face of the cliff, above which was the ice, and with long icicles hanging over the front. Into this he entered. There was a fire burning inside, and a young woman sitting by it.

Grim heard her welcome the man, and call him her father, and name him Hallmund. He cast his basket of fish down, and groaned aloud.

Then the girl saw that blood was flowing from him, and she asked him what had happened.

Hallmund told what had befallen him, and said that he was wounded to the death, and that he trusted Grettir would avenge him, for he had no other friend to do so.

After that Hallmund began a lay, and sang the history of his life, the achievements he had wrought, and he sang on till his breath failed, and either he was unable to finish his lay, or Grim could not remember all of it. A good deal, however, of Hallmund's death-song has been retained and is given in the saga.

But Hallmund's hope or expectation that Grettir would avenge him was disappointed, for Grim managed to get away from Iceland, and did not return to it again during the lifetime of Grettir.

XXXII: OF ANOTHER ATTEMPT AGAINST GRETTIR

Now, during the summer, tidings came to Thorir of Garth that Grettir was somewhere about on Reekheath in the north-east. There was his lair which was examined a few years ago, and which remains in tolerable condition, as already mentioned when his lair at Fairwood Fell was described. Now, Thorir of Garth, when he got this tidings was resolved to make another attempt to kill him; and no wonder, for with singular audacity Grettir had come into his neighbourhood. Grettir no doubt thought that he had preyed long enough on men who had not harmed him, and that now he would prey on the goods and cattle of the man who had made an outlaw of him, and who pursued him with such remorseless hostility. Thorir gathered a number of men together and went in pursuit of Grettir. Grettir was not at that time in his den but out on the moor, and he was near a mountain-dairy that stood back somewhat from the wayside, and there was another man with him, when they spied the party of Thorir, all armed, coming along. They had not been observed, so they hastily led their horses into the shed attached to the dairy, and concealed themselves. Thorir came along, went to the dairy, looked about to see if anyone were there who could inform him if Grettir had been seen, noticed only a couple of horses tied up, but supposed they belonged to the farmer whose summer dairy this was, and, without looking further, went on.

As soon as Thorir and his band had gone out of sight, Grettir crept from his place of hiding, and said to his companion:

"It is a pity they should have come such a ride to see me, and should be disappointed. You watch the horses, and I will go on and have a word with them."

"You surely will not be so rash?" exclaimed the other man.

"I cannot let them come all this way without exchanging words with me," said Grettir, and leaving the horses under the care of his comrade, he strode away over the moor to a place where he was sure he could be observed. Now, Grettir had a slouched hat on and a long staff in his hand, and at the dairy he had found some clothes belonging to the herdsman usually there, and these he had put on.

Directly Thorir and his party saw a man with a staff striding about on the moor they rode to him. None of them knew Grettir's face, for, indeed, they had not been given the chance. So they thought this great rough man was the herdsman, and they asked him if he had seen the outlaw Grettir.

"What sort of man is he?" asked Grettir. "Is he armed?"

"Armed indeed is he, with a casque on his head, a long sword, and also a short one in his girdle."

"Is he riding?"

"Most certainly he is."

"Then," said Grettir, "you had better get you along after him due south; he has gone that way not so long agone."

When they heard this Thorir and his party struck spurs into their horses, put them into a gallop, and away they went as hard as they could in the direction indicated. Now, Grettir knew the country very well, and he was well aware that south of where he stood were impassable bogs. Thorir and his fellows were too eager in pursuit to attend to the nature of the ground over which they rode; besides, they thought that if Grettir had ridden that way they could ride it as well. They were speedily mistaken, for in they floundered into a bottomless morass; some of the horses were in to their saddles; the men got off and got out with difficulty, and they had much ado to get their horses out at all. Indeed, some were wallowing there more than half the day. Many curses were heaped on the churl who had befooled them, but they could not find him when the went after him to chastise him.

Grettir hastened back to the dairy, mounted his horse, and rode to Garth itself, whilst the master was floundering in the bog. As he came to the farm he saw a tall, well-dressed girl by the door, and he asked who she was. He was told this was Thorir's daughter. Then Grettir sang a stave to her, the meaning of which was that he who came there was the man whom Thorir was vainly pursuing.

Much laughter was occasioned by this failure of Thorir to take Grettir when he was in his own neighbourhood, and by his being so deceived and befooled by Grettir when he had him in his power.

XXXIII: AT SANDHEAPS

The summer was passing away, and Grettir could not remain without shelter through the winter; so he considered what was best to be done. He could not ask any farmer in the north-east to shelter him, because they were all afraid of Thorir of Garth, who would have pursued with implacable animosity the man who befriended and housed the outlaw. Moreover, Thorir had his spies everywhere, and Grettir found he had to shift quarters repeatedly to escape his deadly enemy.

Now, when the first snows fell Grettir sent his man away with his horses across country to Biarg, and he went further away from where Thorir was; but never stayed long anywhere, nor gave his real name. He had no relatives in this part of the island, and no friends.

Now, a little before Yule—that is Christmas—he came to a farm called Sandheaps, on that river which is called the Quivering Flood. This farm belonged to a widow woman called Steinvor, who had recently lost her husband.

Grettir came and offered his services; he said his name was Guest, that he was out of work, and that he had come there because he heard she was short of hands.

Steinvor looked at him, and saw that he was a very powerfully-built man, and that there was a certain dignity and nobility in his face; so she accepted him, against the opinion of the rest in the house, who were frightened at the appearance of Grettir, and did not know what to make of him, whether he were an ordinary human being or a wild man, half mountain-goblin or troll.

It came to pass on Christmas-eve that the widow Steinvor was very desirous to go to church, but the church was on the further side of the river, and there was no bridge.

Grettir heard Steinvor lament that she could not go to church, so he said bluntly: "You can go. I will attend you and see you over the water."

Then she made ready for worship, and took her little daughter with her. Now, at times the river froze hard across, and then it was possible to cross on the ice. At other times it might be traversed at a ford. But when Grettir came to the side of the Quivering Flood, it was plain to him that by the ice the water could not be crossed. For there had been a rapid thaw, and now the river was overflowed and very full of water; and, moreover, it was rolling down great masses of ice.

When Steinvor saw the condition of the river, she said, "There is plainly no way across for horse or man."

"I suppose there is a ford somewhere," said Grettir.

"Yes," answered Steinvor, "there is a ford at this place; but I do not see how it is to be traversed."

"I will carry you across," said Grettir.

"Carry over the little maiden first," said the widow. "She is the lightest."

"I don't care about making two journeys when one will suffice," answered Grettir. "Come, jump up; I will carry you in my arms."

The widow crossed herself, and said, "That will never do. How can you manage such a burden?"

But without more ado Grettir caught up Steinvor on his arm, and then he picked up the little girl and set her on her mother's lap, and strode into the water; they were on his left arm, but he kept the right free. They were so frightened that they durst not cry out. He waded on in the river, and the water foamed up to his breast; and then he saw a great ice-floe coming bearing down upon him. He put out his right hand, gave the mass of ice a thrust, and it was whirled past them by the current. Then he waded further, and the water washed about his shoulders, and that was the deepest point. After that the river shallowed, and he bore the mother and child safely to the shore and set them down.

Now Grettir turned to go back, and he took up a great stone and set it on his head, and so waded back. If he had tried to go through the water without a stone he would have been washed away; but the great stone on his head enabled him to stand firm and resist the current of the water. Those who have not been through an Icelandic river can hardly imagine the intensity of the cold. I have ridden through these rivers, my horse swimming under me, and when I reached the further side have thrown myself off and lain on the sand for a quarter of an hour before I could recover from the numbness caused by the deadly cold; for some of these rivers are as broad as the Thames at London Bridge, and the water is milky because full of undissolved snow.

When Steinvor reached the church every one was astonished to see her, and asked how she had managed to get across the Quivering Flood. But when the priest heard the story, he called Steinvor aside, and said:

"Mind and do not say too much about your new man; do not talk about his strength, and set folk a-wondering who he may be. I have my own opinion, and I think you will do well to house him, and say nothing to anyone about his being in any way remarkable."

And now there comes into the saga of Grettir a story which is certainly untrue, but how it comes in can be made out pretty easily.

The real truth was, as the saga writer confesses, that Grettir remained hidden at Sandheaps all that winter, and no one in the country round knew that he was there. But then, the saga writer did not feel satisfied with such a dull winter, in which nothing happened; so, to fill out his story and say something interesting, he worked into his history a wonderful tale. The story, which I tell in my own words, is this:—

The Story of the Stream-Troll

There is on the Quivering Flood some miles below Sandheaps a mighty foss, or waterfall. The whole river pours over a ledge in a thundering, magnificent cascade. The stream in the middle is broken by an island. You can hear the roar of the falling water for a long way around, and see the spray thrown up from the fall like a cloud or column of steam rising high into the air. This waterfall is called Goda-foss, and was long supposed to be the finest in the island; but there is another, which I was the first to see, on the Jokull-river, called Detti-foss, which is infinitely finer, but which is in a region of utter desert of sand and volcanic crater, many miles from any human habitation.

It happens that there is a curious black lava rock standing near the river, higher up than the fall, which bears a quaint resemblance to an old woman, and this stone is called The Old Hag; and the story goes that it is a troll-woman turned to stone.

Now, you must know that throughout Norway and Iceland, and, indeed, wherever the Scandinavian race is found, a superstition exists that every river has its spirit, that lives in the river; and it was held that these river-spirits demanded a sacrifice of a human life, at least once a year. If a sacrifice were not given to them, then they took some man or woman, when crossing the water, and carried the victim away. And in heathen times there can be no doubt whatever that human sacrifices were offered to every river; generally an evildoer or a prisoner was thrown in and drowned, to propitiate the Stream-churl, as he was called, so that he should not snap at and carry off other and more valuable lives. Wherever there was a cataract, there the Stream-churl was believed to live, hidden away behind the curtain of falling water. If the stream was small, then this spirit or demon was small; if, however, it were a mighty river, then the spirit was a great troll or giant. Even to this day in Iceland and Norway, the ignorant and superstitious believe that there are these Stream-churls, and tell stories about them, and cannot but suspect that, when anyone is drowned, it is the Stream-churl exacting his toll.

Now, it is quite certain that Steinvor, although she was a Christian, believed in there being a great Stream-churl living under Goda-foss; and as she had lost her husband and one of her servants who had been drowned in the

Quivering Flood, she held that they had been carried off by the Troll of the waterfall.

There had been, as it happened, something mysterious about the death of Steinvor's husband. Two years before Grettir came to Sandheaps, on Christmas-eve, he had disappeared. She had gone off to see some friends at a distance, and when she returned home next day she heard that her husband had not been seen—he was gone, and not a trace of him remained. It occurred to her that in all probability he had gone across the river to church, and had been carried off by the river—that is, by the Stream-churl. But she could be certain of nothing, and she was greatly distressed because she could not give his body burial. A year passed and not a word about her husband could she hear. His body had not be found anywhere washed up by the river, supposing he had been drowned.

Next year she lost one of her men-servants in the same way. He vanished, and none knew how or whither he had gone. If he had run away, she would probably have had tidings of him; but she heard none, and his body was also never found.

I have no doubt that she told Grettir about this, and also that she believed that the Stream-churl who lived under Goda-foss had carried off both her husband and the servant. I believe also that, to satisfy her, Grettir undertook to look, and that he actually dived under the fall, and came up and searched between the sheet of falling water and the rock, and found—nothing.

That is the foundation of a wonderful story which has found its way into the saga. It did not satisfy those who told the tale of Grettir that he should have spent the winter at Sandheaps and done nothing—that he should have dived under Goda-foss and found nothing.

So by degrees old nursery tales got mixed up with this incident about Grettir's search for the Stream-churl, and all was worked into a wonderful story, which you shall hear.

On that night on which Grettir had carried Steinvor across the river, he returned to the farm, and lay down in his bed.

When midnight arrived, then a great din was heard outside, and presently the hall door was thrown open and in through it came a gigantic woman, a Troll-wife, with a trough in one hand and a huge chopper in the other.

As she entered she peered about her, and saw Grettir where he lay, and she ran at him. Then he jumped up and went to meet her, and they fell a-wrestling terribly, and struggled together so furiously, that all the panelling of the hall side was broken.

She was the stronger, and she dragged Grettir towards the door, and forth towards the entrance, in spite of all his efforts. She had got him as far as the entrance, when there he made a final struggle, and in the struggle the door-posts and fittings were torn from their place, and fell outwards.

Then the Troll-woman laboured away with him towards the river, and right down towards the gulfs.

Grettir was exceedingly weary, yet he saw that his only chance was to make a last effort, or be flung by her over the edge into the deep, boiling river.

All night they contended in such fashion, and ever was he drawing nearer to the edge. But just as she was preparing to fling him into the water, he got his right hand free, and he swiftly seized his short-sword, and struck off her arm; and at that moment the sun rose, and the Troll-woman was turned into stone. There she stands with her amputated arm-socket, as a mass of black basalt or lava to this day.

If the reader will recall the story of Grettir's struggle with Glam at Thorod's-stead, in the valley of Shadows, he will see that this is only the same story over again almost in every particular,—except that the first fight was with a man, and this is with a woman. The reason why this story was concocted and put in here, was to account for the stone figure which stands by the river, and which is called the Troll-wife. So far the story carries its character on its face.

Now we will go on to the next part of the tale. It did not satisfy people that Grettir should have dived under Goda-foss and found nothing, so the story was thus told:

When the goodwife, Steinvor, came from church, she thought that her house had been rudely handled; so she went to Grettir and asked him what had occurred. Then he told her all, and she prayed him to go and make a search for her husband's bones, under Goda-foss.

Grettir consented, but he asked that the priest might be sent for. His name was Stone. Steinvor sent for him, and Stone was curious to know whether his suspicions about this stranger were true. So he asked him questions, but Grettir answered that if the priest wanted to know who he was, he must find out. The priest laughed at the story of the Troll-wife, and said he did not believe a word about the struggle.

Then Grettir said, "Well, priest, I see that you have no faith in my tale; now I propose that you accompany me to Goda-foss, and we will search for the Troll himself, and see if we can recover the bones of Steinvor's husband."

The priest, Stone, agreed, and they went together to the side of the waterfall, and they had a rope with them.

Stone shook his head, and he said, "It would be too risky for anyone to venture down there."

"I will go," said Grettir. "But you mind the rope."

The priest drove a peg into the sward on the cliff, and heaped stones over it, so as to make the end firm, and then he seated himself by the heap.

Then Grettir made a loop in the end of the rope, and put a stone through the loop, and threw the stone down, and the end of the rope went to the bottom of the gulf.

"How are you going down?" asked Stone.

"I shall dive," said Grettir.

Then he stripped, but girt on a short-sword, and so leaped off the cliff into the foss. The priest saw only the soles of his feet as he went into the water, and then saw no more.

Now, Grettir had gone in below the fall, and he dived and went under the curtain of water and came up near the rock. The whirlpool below the falls was so strong that he had a desperate struggle with the water before he could reach the rock.

When he rose, he saw that the water fell over a lip of rock, quite clear, and that in the face of the rock was a cavern, and that smoke issued from this cave, and mingling with the spray and foam passed away, and was not discerned beyond.

Grettir climbed over the stones into the cave, and there he saw a great fire flaming from amidst brands of drift-wood; and there was the Stream-churl seated there, a great Troll with a hideous face. When he saw Grettir he roared and jumped up, and caught a glaive that was near him, and smote at the newcomer. Grettir hewed back at him with his short-sword, and smote the handle of the glaive and broke it. Then the giant stretched back for a sword that hung up to a peg against the side of the cave, but as he was thus leaning back Grettir smote him across the breast, and cut through to the ribs, and gashed open his belly. The blood poured forth out of the cave and mingled with the stream. When the priest saw the bloody foam beneath the fall, he was so frightened that he ran away, for he made sure that Grettir was dead.

Grettir remained in the cave, standing across the giant, till he had killed him. Then he took up a flaming brand and searched the cave through. He found nothing more than dead men's bones, and these he put together into a bag, threw that over his shoulder, and went again into the water.

He rose beyond the foss and looked up, but could see nothing of the priest; so he caught the rope, and by means of that he swarmed up to the top of the cliff.

Then he sat down, and with a sharp knife he cut runes on a staff. And what he wrote was this:

"Down into the gulf I went,
Where the rocks are widely rent;
Where the swirling waters fall
O'er the black basaltic wall;
Where, with voice of thunder, leap
In the foaming darkling deep.
There the stream with icy wave
Washes the grim giant's cave."

He had cut as much as he could on one stick, so now he took another, and on that he cut:

"Dreadful dweller in the cave
Underneath the falling wave,
Fierce at me he brandished glaive;
Full of rage at me he drove,
Desperate we together strove.
Lo! I smote his halft in twain,
Lo! I smote and he was slain,
Bleeding from each riven vein."

Then Grettir carried the bag of bones and the staves to the church, and laid them in the porch.

Next morning when the priest came to the church he found the bag of bones and the staves.

Such is the story.

Now, it is clear that a good bit of it is simply transferred from the story of Grettir going down into the cairn of Karr the Old.

The real truth of the tale is no more than what has been stated, that Grettir went under the waterfall and found nothing. It is, of course, possible that he may have hoaxed the priest; but I think it more probable that all this marvellous matter is simply tacked on to one simple fact, and that it was taken, partly from the story of Grettir in the barrow of Karr, and partly from that of his struggle with Glam.

What the saga writer does admit is that the versions of the story do not quite agree, and that—in spite of this wonderful achievement, folks did not know that Grettir was at Sandheaps that winter.

XXXIV: HOW GRETTIR WAS DRIVEN ABOUT

After a while rumours reached Thorir of Garth that either Grettir, or someone very like Grettir,—a tall, powerful man with reddish hair, and one who gave no account of whence he came,—was lodging at Sandheaps, and Thorir made ready to go there after him. Fortunately Grettir, or rather the housewife Steinvor, heard of his intention, and so Grettir made off out of the valley of the Quivering Flood before Thorir came there in quest of him.

He escaped to Maddervales, in the Horg-river Dale. This is a noble valley of the Horg River, with chains of snowy peaks on each side, of peculiar shape, barred with precipices of basalt, on which lie slopes of snow.

Some way up this valley are some very remarkable spires of basaltic rock, one of which that is like a needle is said to have been climbed by Grettir whilst staying in this valley. It is not so said in the saga, but I was told so on the spot, and the tale goes that when he climbed to the top he slipped his belt round the needle, and there it hangs round it still—but no one has been up since to find if it be there where he left it.

He could not remain long there, for Gudmund the Rich, who was farmer at Maddervales, was afraid to house him for long. Thorir of Garth would come and burn his house if he harboured Grettir. However, he kept him for some little while, and then he gave him advice what he should do.

It had come to such a pass with Grettir now that no one dared to shelter him for long, and Thorir had spies everywhere to inform him where Grettir was.

Gudmund the Rich said to Grettir: "You can find no safety anywhere that men dwell; for if there be not treachery, yet the news flies about that you are there. So I advise you to go where you shall be alone."

"Where shall I go?" asked Grettir. "I am hunted like a dog."

"There is an island," answered Gudmund, "lying in the Skagafirth, called Drangey. It is a place excellent for defence, as no one can reach it without a ladder. If you could get upon Drangey, no one could come on you unawares. You would see anyone who came by boat to the island, and you could pull up a rope-ladder, without which no one would be able to ascend."

"I will try that," said Grettir; "but I have become so fearsome in the dark that not even at the risk of my life can I endure to be alone."

"Well," said Gudmund, "that is my counsel. Trust none but yourself. Treachery lies where least expected."

Grettir thanked him for his advice, and went away west to see his mother. And he was most joyfully welcomed by her and his young brother Illugi at Biarg. There he remained some nights—not many; for Ramsfirth was only over a brow of hill, and the tidings of his return home was sure in a few days to reach the relatives of Oxmain, when he would again be set on.

I said, after giving an account of Grettir's adventure at Thorhall's-stead with Glam, that there must have been something of fact in that story, and not pure fiction; and now it has been seen how that event coloured and affected his whole after life, leaving his nerves so shaken, that he could not drive off the impression then made on him, and he was ready to run serious risks rather than be subject to the terrors that came on him in the dark when alone.

He told his mother and Illugi how it was with him, and how that he had been advised to go to Drangey, but that he could not; he dare not, in the long winter night, be on that lonely islet by himself.

Then Illugi his brother said, "Grettir, I will be with you."

"Brother holds to brother as hand clasps hand," answered Grettir, and so they parted. All that summer he wandered about in wild places, shifting his quarters repeatedly, and living how he could.

XXXV: ON THE ISLE

When summer was now over, and the first snow of winter began to fall, when the days were rapidly shortening, and the sun had gone out of the north to the south, where it began to move in a rapidly narrowing arc, Grettir returned to Biarg and remained there a while. "But," says the saga, "so great grew his fear in the dark that he durst go nowhere as soon as dusk set in." We can see that the many years strain on his nerves had broken them. Hunted about as a wild beast, always forced to be on his guard, never able to sleep without fear of being murdered in his sleep, the trial had told on him. This was now the winter of 1028. He was aged but thirty-one; his strength of body was not abated, only his nervous force. He had been in outlawry altogether fifteen years, three for the slaying of Skeggi, then he had been outlawed by King Olaf in 1016. On his return to Iceland he had been outlawed in 1017; this was the eleventh year of his outlawry at the suit of Thorir of Garth, an outlawry not only unjust, but according to general opinion illegal, because he had been tried and sentenced in his absence, and without any witnesses having been called to establish his guilt—condemned on hearsay evidence, and he never allowed to defend himself.

Now Illugi, Grettir's sole surviving brother, was aged fifteen, and was a very handsome, honest-looking boy.

"Grettir," said he, "you know what I said. I will go with you to Drangey, if you will take me. I know not that I will be of much help to you, but this I know, that I will be ever true to you, and will never run from you so long as you stand up. Besides, I shall like to be with you, for here at home we are ever in anxiety for news about you, always fearing the worst; but if I am at your side, I shall know how you fare."

"I would rather have you with me than anyone else," answered Grettir. "But I cannot take you unless our mother consent."

Then said Asdis, "Now I can see that I have the choice of evils. I can ill spare Illugi; yet I know your trouble, Grettir, and that something must be done for you. It grieves me, my sons, to see you both leave me; yet I will not withhold my youngest from you, Grettir. It is right that brother should help brother."

That rejoiced Illugi. Then Asdis gave her sons what things she thought they might want on the island, and they made them ready to depart.

She led them outside the farm inclosure, and then she took farewell of them, saying, "My two sons! There you depart from me, and I dreamed last night that you left me for ever, and would fall together. What is fated none may fly from. Never shall I see you again, either of you. Be it so, that one fate overtake you both. In my dream I saw your bones whitening on Drangey. Be careful and watchful. My dreams have troubled me greatly. Above all beware of witchcraft. None can cope with the craft of the old."

When she had said this she wept sore.

Then said Grettir, "Weep not, mother, for if we be set on with weapons it will be said of thee that thou hadst men and not girls for thy children. Live on well, and be hale."

So they parted. Grettir and Illugi went to their relatives and visited them, never, however, staying long in any place, and so on by Swine Lake, a long sheet of water in a shallow basin, to the Blend River. This river is of the colour of milk and water, because it is so full of undissolved snow, and milk and water is called Bland, i.e. Blend, in Icelandic. Another river enters it that is called the Black Stream, because of the dark colour of the water. Grettir turned up the valley of the Black River and then over a pass by a pretty lake lying in a mountain lap, down into a broad marshy valley in which are three or four rivers, and boiling springs pouring forth clouds of steam on the hill-slopes. The valley is commanded by a beautiful mountain peak, called the Measuring Peak, because the natives thereabouts reckon distances from it.

Grettir and Illugi went down this valley till they reached the sea, and now there opened before them a glorious view of the fiord, extending out north about forty miles, and from ten to fifteen miles across, between mountains and precipitous cliffs. A little way back from the eastern shore stood up the Unadals Jokull, crowned with perpetual snows and with glaciers rolling down the sides, and on the west, close to the sea, seeming to rise in a wall out of it and running up into fantastic peaks, was the range of Tindastoll, famous for its cornelians and agates and other precious stones. In the offing, fifteen miles out, right in the midst of the fiord, stood up the isle of Drangey with sheer cliffs, about which the sea perpetually danced and foamed.

Grettir and Illugi skirted the shore on the west. The wind was blowing cold, and snow was driving before it, as they passed a farm. The farmer stood in his door, and saw a great man stride by with an axe over his shoulder, his hood thrown back, and his wild red hair blowing about in the gale. "Verily," said the farmer, "that must be a strange fellow not to cover his head with his hood in such weather as this." Near this little farm the brothers stumbled upon a tall, thin man, dressed in rags and with a very big head. They asked each other's names, and the fellow called himself Glaum. He was out of work, and he went along with the brothers chatting, and telling them all the gossip of the neighbourhood. Then Glaum asked if they were in want of a servant, and Grettir gladly accepted him, and the man became thenceforth his constant attendant. But the fellow was a sad boaster, and most people thought him both a fool and a coward. He was not fond of work, and he spent his time strolling about the country picking up and retailing news.

Grettir and his brother and Glaum reached a farm called Reykir as the day closed in, where was a hot spring in the farm paddock. The farmer's name was Thorwald; and Grettir asked him to put him across in a boat to Drangey. Thorwald shook his head and said, "I shall get into trouble with those who have rights of pasturage on the island. I had rather not."

Then Grettir offered him a bag of silver which his mother had given him, and at the sight of this, Thorwald raised his eyebrows and thought that he might perhaps do what was asked. The distance was just five miles.

So on a moonshiny night Thorwald got three of his churls and they rowed Grettir and the two who went with him over. On reaching his destination Grettir was well pleased with the spot, for it was covered with a profusion of grass, and the sides were so precipitous that it seemed a sheer impossibility for anyone to ascend it without the aid of the rope-ladder that hung from strong staples at the summit. In summer the place would swarm with sea-birds, and at the time there were eighty sheep left on the island for fattening.

A good many farmers had rights of pasturage on the island. Hialti of Hof was one, whose brother's name was Thorbiorn Hook, of whom more hereafter. Another was Haldor, who lived at Head-strand; he had married the sister of these brothers. Biorn, Eric, and Tongue-stone were the names of three others.

Thorbiorn Hook was a hard-headed, ill-disposed fellow. His father had married a second time, and there was no love lost between the stepmother and Thorbiorn. It is said that one day as The Hook was sitting at draughts, she passed, and looking over his shoulder laughed, because he had made a bad move. Thorbiorn Hook thereupon said something abusive and insulting; this so enraged her that she snatched up a draught-man, and pressing it against his eye-socket, drove the eyeball out. He started to his feet, and with the draught-board struck her over the head such a blow that she took to her bed, and died of the injury. The Hook now went from bad to worse, and leaving home settled at Woodwick on the fiord, a small farm. It will be understood from this story that he was a violent and brutal fellow, and that, indeed, the life in his father's house had not been of an orderly description.

As many as twenty farmers claimed rights to turn out their sheep on Drangey in summer. The way they managed it is the way still employed by their successors. They take the sheep out in boats, and then put them over their shoulders, with the feet tied under their chins, and so they climb the rope-ladder, carrying the sheep up on their backs. Though all these farmers claimed rights on Drangey, The Hook and his brother had the largest share, that is to say, the right to turn out more sheep than the rest.

Now, about the time of the winter solstice, that is just before Yule, the bonders made ready to visit the island, and bring home their sheep for slaughtering for the Christmas feasting. They rowed out in a large boat, and on nearing the island were much surprised to see figures moving on top of the cliffs. How anyone had got there without their knowledge puzzled them, for Thorwald had kept his counsel, and told no one what he had done for Grettir. They pulled hard for the landing-place, where hung the ladder, but Grettir drew it up before they landed.

The bonders shouted to know who were on the crags, and Grettir, looking over, told his name and those of his companions. The farmers then asked how he had got there? who had put him across?

Grettir answered, "If you very much wish to know, it was not one of you below now speaking to us. It was someone else, who had a good boat and a pair of lusty arms."

"Let us fetch our sheep away," called the bonders, "then you come to land with us. We will not make you pay for the sheep you have eaten, and we will do you no harm."

"Well offered," answered Grettir; "but he who takes keeps hold; and a bird in the hand is worth two in the bush. Believe me, I will not leave this island till the time of my outlawry is expired, unless I be carried from it dead."

The bonders were silenced, it seemed to them that they had got an ugly customer on Drangey, to get rid of whom would be no easy matter; so they rowed home, very ill-satisfied with the result of their expedition.

The news spread like wildfire, and was talked about all through the neighbourhood. Thorir of Garth was the more embittered, because he could see no way in which Grettir could be reached and overmastered in this inaccessible spot.

XXXVI: OF GRETTIR ON HERON-NESS

Winter passed, and at the beginning of summer the whole district met at an assize held on the Herons'-ness, a headland in the Skaga-firth, between the rivers that discharge into the fiord. It is, in fact, the seaward point of a large island in the delta of the river that divides about eight miles higher up, inland. The gathering was thronged, and the litigations and merry-makings made the assize last over many days. Grettir guessed what was going on by seeing a number of boats pass to the head of the fiord. He became restless, and at last announced to his brother that he intended being present at the assize, cost what it might. Illugi thought it was sheer madness, but Grettir was resolute. He begged his brother and Glaum to watch the ladder and await his return.

Now, Grettir was on very good terms with the farmer at Reykir, and with some others on that side of the firth, and they were not unwilling to help him. Sometimes his mother sent things to the brothers that she thought they would need, and then there were not wanting men to take these over to the island. So Grettir got put across by his friend Thorwald to the mainland, and he borrowed of him a set of old clothes, and thus attired he went along the coast boldly to Heron-ness. He had on a fur cap, which was drawn closely over his eyes, and concealed his face, so that no one might recognize him. Now, in parts of Iceland, the flies are such torments that men have to wear literally cloth helmets, with only nose and eyes showing, the cloth fitting tight to the head, and round over the ears and neck, exactly like a helmet, or a German knitted sledging cap. When I was in Iceland, when the flies were troublesome, I put my head into a butterfly net, and buckled it round my neck tightly with a leather strap. Now, Grettir's cap was something like those I have described, and no one was surprised at his wearing it, as the whole of that valley is one vast marsh, and is infested with flies that blacken the air and madden men and beasts.

Grettir thus attired sauntered between the booths erected on the headland, till he reached the spot where games were going on.

Now, Hialti and Thorbiorn Hook were the chief men in these sports. Hook was specially noisy and boisterous, and drove men together to the sports, and whether men liked it or not, he insisted on their attendance. He would take this man and that by the hands and drag him forth to the field, where the wrestling and other games went on.

Now, first wrestled those who were weakest, and then each man in turn, and great fun there was. But when most men had tried their strength except the very strongest, it was asked who would be a match for Hialti and The Hook. These two being the strongest and the roughest of all, went round inviting each man in turn to wrestle with them, but all declined.

Then Thorbiorn Hook, looking round, spied a tall fellow in the shabbiest and quaintest of suits, sitting by himself, speaking to no one. Thorbiorn walked up to him, laid his hands on his shoulders and asked him to wrestle.

The man sat still, and The Hook could not drag him from his seat.

"Well!" exclaimed The Hook, "no one else has kept his place before me to-day. Who are you?"

"Guest," answered Grettir shortly.

"A wished-for guest thou wilt be, if thou furnish some entertainment to the company," said Thorbiorn Hook.

Grettir answered, "I am indisposed to make a fool of myself before strangers. How am I to know, supposing that I give you a fall, that I shall not be set upon by you or your kindred, and be unfairly treated?"

Then many exclaimed that there should be fair play.

"It is all very well your saying Fair-play now; but will you say Fair-play, and stick to it, supposing I get the better of this man. You are all akin, or friends, and I am a stranger to you all."

Again he was assured that no one would resent what he did.

"But see," said Grettir, "I have not wrestled for many years, and have lost all skill in the matter."

Yet they pressed him the more.

Then he said, "I will wrestle with whom you will, if you will swear to show me no violence so long as I am among you as a guest."

This all agreed to, and an oath of safe conduct was made, the form of which is so curious that it must be given.

A man named Hafr recited the terms of the oath, and the rest agreed to it.

"Here set I peace among all men towards this man Guest, who sits before us, and in this oath I bind all magistrates and well-to-do bonders, and all men who bear swords, and all men whatsoever in this district, present or absent, named or unnamed. These are to show peace to, and give free passage to the aforenamed stranger, that he may sport, wrestle, make merry, abide with us and depart from us, without stay, whether he go by land or flood. He shall have peace where he is, in all places where he may be till he reaches his house whence he set out, so long and no longer.

"I set this treaty of peace between him and us, our kinsmen male and female, our servants and children. May the breaker of this compact be cast out of the favour of God and good men, out of his heavenly inheritance and the society of just men and angels. May he be an outcast from land to its farthest limits, far as men chase wolves, as Christians frequent churches, as heathen men offer sacrifices, as flame burns, earth produces herb, as baby calls its mother, and mother rocks her child; far as fire is kindled, ships glide, lightnings flicker, sun shines, snow lies, Finns slide on snow-shoes, fir-trees grow, falcons fly on a spring day with a breeze under their wings; far as heaven bends, earth is peopled, winds sweep the water into waves, churls till corn; he shall be banished from churches and the company of Christian men, from heathen folk, from house and den, from every house— save hell! Now let us be agreed whether we be on mountain or shore, on ship or skate, on ground or glacier, at sea or in saddle, as friend with friend, as brother with brother, as father with son, in this our compact. Lay we now hand to hand, and hold we true peace and keep every word of this oath."

Now, this formula is very curious. It must have been brought by the Icelandic settlers with them from Norway, for parts of it are inappropriate to their land. There are no Finns there, nor do fir-trees grow there, nor is any corn tilled. But all that about Christians is of later origin.

After a little hesitation the oath was taken by all.

Then said Grettir, "You have done well, only beware of breaking your oath. I am ready to do my part, without delay, to fulfil your wishes."

Thereupon he flung aside his hood and garments, and the assembled bonders looked at each other, and were disconcerted, for they saw that they had in their midst Grettir Asmund's son. They were silent, and thought that they had taken the oath somewhat unadvisedly, and they whispered the one into another, to find if there were not some loophole by which they might evade the obligation to observe the oath.

"Come now," said Grettir, "let me know your purpose, for I shall not long stand stripped. It will be worse for you than for me if you break your oath, for it will go down in story to the end of time that the men of Heron-ness swore and were perjured."

He received no answer. The chiefs moved away; some wanted to break the truce, and argued that an oath taken to an outlaw was not legally bind-ing; others insisted that the oath must be observed. Then Grettir sang:

"Many trees-of-wealth (men) this morn,

Failed the well-known well to know,
Two ways turn the sea-flame-branches (men),
When a trick on them is tried;
Falter folk in oath fulfilling,
Hafr's talking lips are dumb."

Then Tongue-stone said, "You think so, do you, Grettir? Well, I will say this of you, you are a man of dauntless courage. Look how the chiefs are deep in discussion how to deal with you."

Then Grettir sang:

"Shield-lifters (men) rubbing of noses,
Shield-tempest-senders (men) shake beards,
Fierce-hearted serpent's-lair-scatterers (men),
Lay their heads one 'gainst another,
Now that they know, are regretting
The peace they have sworn to to-day."

In these staves a number of periphrases for men or warriors are used—and the use of these periphrases constitute the charm of these verses.

Then Hialti of Hof burst away from the rest, and said, "No, never, never shall it be said of us men of Heron-ness, that we have broken an oath because we have found it inconvenient to keep it. Grettir shall be at full liberty to go to his place in peace, and woe betide him who lays hand on him, to do him an injury. But an oath no longer binds us should he venture ashore again."

All except Thorbiorn Hook, Hialti's brother, agreed to this, and felt their minds and consciences relieved, that he had spoken out as a man of honour. And thus was seen how of those two brothers, rude and violent though both were, Hialti had some nobleness in him that was lacking in the other.

The wrestling began by Grettir being matched with Thorbiorn Hook, and after a very brief struggle Grettir freed himself from his antagonist, leaped over his back, caught him by the belt, lifted him off his legs, and flung him over his back. This is a throw called "showing the white mare," among Cornish wrestlers of the present day, and a very dangerous throw it is, for it sometimes breaks the back of the man thrown. The Hook, however, picked himself up, and the wrestling continued with unabated vigour, and it was impossible to tell which side had the mastery, for, though Grettir was matched against both brothers, and after each bout with one brother fell to with the other, he was never thrown down. After all three were covered with blood and bruises the match was closed, the judges deciding that the two brothers conjointly were not stronger than Grettir alone, though they were each of them as powerful as two ordinary able-bodied men.

Grettir at once left the place of gathering, rejecting all the entreaties of the farmers that he would leave Drangey. And, so, after all but The Hook had thanked him for his wrestling and praised his activity and strength, he departed. He was put across from Reykir to his island, and was received with open arms by Illugi.

There now they abode peaceably, and Grettir told his brother and his churl Glaum the story of what had taken place at the assize, and thus the summer wore away.

There was much talk through the island of Iceland about this adventure, and all good men approved the conduct of the men of the Skagafiord that they had kept the oath they had so inconsiderately taken.

XXXVII: OF HŒRING'S LEAP

The smaller farmers began seriously to feel their want of the islet Drangey for pasture in summer, and, as there seemed no chance of their getting rid of Grettir, they sold their rights to Thorbiorn Hook, who set himself in earnest to devise a plan by which he might possess himself of the island.

When Grettir had been two winters on the island, he had eaten all the sheep except one piebald ram, with magnificent horns, which became so tame that he ran after them wherever they went, and in the evening came to the hut Grettir had erected and butted at the door till let in.

The brothers liked this place of exile, as there was no dearth of eggs and birds, besides which, some drift-wood was thrown upon the strand, and served as fuel.

Grettir and Illugi spent their days in clambering among the rocks, and rifling nests, and the occupation of the thrall was to collect drift timber and keep up the fire in the hut. He was expected to remain awake and watch the fire whilst the others slept. He got very tired of his life on the islet, became idle, morose, and reserved. One night, notwithstanding Grettir's warnings to him to be more careful, as they had no boat, he let the fire go out. Grettir was very angry, and told Glaum that he deserved a sound thrashing for his neglect. The thrall replied that he loathed the life he led; and that it seemed it was not enough to Grettir that he should keep him there as a prisoner, he must also maltreat him.

Grettir consulted his brother what was best to be done, and Illugi replied that the only thing that could be done was to await the arrival of a boat from the friendly farmer at Reykir.

"We shall have to wait long enough for that," said Grettir. "The bonders have taken it ill that he has favoured us, and he is now unwilling to be seen visiting Drangey. The only chance is for me to swim ashore and secure a light."

"Do not attempt that!" exclaimed Illugi. "That is what you did in Norway, and that led to all your misfortune."

"This case is different," answered Grettir. "Then I brought fire for ill-conditioned men, now it is for ourselves. Then I knew not who was on the other side, but now I can get the fire for the asking from Thorwald."

"But the distance is so great!" remonstrated Illugi.

"Do not fear for me," said Grettir; "I was not born to be drowned."

From Drangey to Reykir is, as already said, about five English miles.

Grettir prepared for swimming, by dressing in loose thin drawers and a sealskin hood; he tied his fingers together, that they might offer more resistance to the water when he struck out.

The day was fine and warm. Grettir started in the evening, when the tide was in his favour, setting in; and his brother anxiously watched him from the rocks. At sunset he reached the land, after having floated and swum the whole distance. Immediately on coming ashore, he went to the warm spring and bathed in it, before entering the house. The hall door was open, and Grettir stepped in. A large fire had been burning on the hearth, so that the room was very warm; Grettir was so thoroughly exhausted that he lay down beside the hot embers, and was soon fast asleep. In the morning he was found by the farmer's daughter, who gave him a bowl of milk, and brought her father to him. Thorwald furnished him with fire, and rowed him back to the island, astonished beyond measure at his achievement, in having swum such a distance.

Now, the farmers on the Skagafiord began to taunt Thorbiorn Hook with his unprofitable purchase of the island, and Hook was greatly irritated and perplexed what to do.

During the summer, a ship arrived in the firth, the captain of which was a young and active man called Hœring. He lodged with Thorbiorn Hook during the autumn, and was continually urging his host to row him out to Drangey, that he might try to climb the precipitous sides of the island. The Hook required very little pressing; and one fine afternoon he rowed his guest out to Drangey, and put him stealthily ashore, without attracting the notice of those on the height. For in some places the cliffs overhung, so that a boat passing beneath could not be seen from above. Now Hœring had lain in the bottom of the boat, covered with a piece of sailcloth, so that the brothers saw nothing of him as the boat was approaching the islet.

They saw and recognized Thorbiorn Hook and his churls, and at once drew up the ladder. Now it was whilst they were watching at the landing-place that Thorbiorn put Hœring out on another point, where the cliffs seemed possible to be climbed by a very skilful man, and then came on to the usual landing place, and there shouted to Grettir. Grettir replied, and then Thorbiorn began the usual arguments to persuade the outlaw to leave the isle. He promised to give him shelter in his house the winter, if he would do so. All was in vain. What he sought was to divert Grettir's attention so as to allow time and occasion for Hœring to climb the cliffs unobserved and unresisted.

The discussion went on but led to nothing. In the meantime Hœring had managed most cleverly to get up by a way never ascended by man before or after; and when he came to the top and had his feet on the turf, he saw where the brothers stood with their backs turned towards him, and he thought that now an opportunity had come for him to make himself a great name. Grettir suspected nothing, and continued talking to Thorbiorn, who was getting, or feigning to get, angry, and used big and violent words.

Now, as luck would have it, Illugi chanced to turn his head, and he saw a man approaching from behind.

Then he cried out, "Brother! Brother! Here comes a man at us with uplifted axe!"

"You go after him," said Grettir. "I will watch at the ladder."

So Illugi started to his feet and went to meet Hœring, and when the young merchant saw that he was discovered, he fled away across the islet, and Illugi went after him. And when Hœring came to the edge he leaped down, hoping to fall into the sea; but he had missed his reckoning, and he went upon some skerries over which the waves tossed, and broke every bone in his body, and so ended his life. The spot is called Hœring's Leap to this day.

Illugi came back, and Grettir asked him what had been the end of the encounter. Illugi told him.

"Now, Thorbiorn," shouted Grettir; "we have had enough of profitless talk. Go round to the other side of the island and gather up the remains of your friend."

The Hook pushed off from the strand and returned home, ill pleased with the result of the expedition, and Grettir remained unmolested on Drangey the ensuing winter.

XXXVIII: OF THE ATTEMPT MADE BY GRETTIR's FRIENDS

The ensuing summer, that is to say, the summer of 1031, at the great annual assize at Thingvalla, all Grettir's kin and friends brought up the matter of outlawry, and contended that he ought to have his sentence done away with. They said that no man could be an outlaw all his life, that was not a condition contemplated by their laws. They said that he had been outlawed first in 1011 for the slaying of Skeggi, and that he had been in outlawry ever since, which made nineteen years.

The old law-man was dead, and now there was another at the assize, whose name was Stein. He laid down that no man might by law be in outlawry more than twenty years. Now, when they came to reckon since 1011 it was nineteen years. It was true that he had been outlawed thrice, once for Skeggi, then by King Olaf, and lastly by the court for the burning of the sons of Thorir of Garth, still—the fact remained that for nineteen years he had been an outlaw, and Stein laid down that by next assize, that is to say in one year, his outlawry would have expired.

Thereat Grettir's kinsfolk were pleased, for they thought that he would only have to spend one winter more on Drangey, and afterwards his troubles would be at an end; Thorir of Garth and his other foes could no more pursue him, and the price set on his head would fall away.

But on the other hand, Thorir of Garth, who had not become more charitable and forgiving as he grew old, became still more incensed and impatient to have Grettir killed before this year would expire, also Thorbiorn Hook cast about how he might be avenged for the deprivation of his rights over Drangey. The men who had sold their claims came to Thorbiorn, and told him he must do one of two things: get rid of Grettir and assert his rights by turning out sheep on the islet, or they would regard the sale as quashed, by his non-usance of the pasture, and they would reclaim their shares of the island as soon as Grettir's outlawry was at an end, and he left the place.

XXXIX: OF THE OLD HAG

Now it was so, that Thorbiorn Hook had a foster-mother, a woman advanced in age, and of a very malicious disposition. When the people of Iceland accepted Christianity, she, in her heart, remained a heathen, and would not be baptized and have anything to do with the new religion. She had always been reckoned a witch, but with the introduction of Christianity witchcraft had been made illegal, and anyone who had recourse to sorcery was severely dealt with. The old woman had not forgotten her incantations and strange ceremonies, whereby she thought to be able to conjure the spirits of evil, and send ill on such as offended her.

When Thorbiorn Hook found that he could contrive in no way to get Grettir out of Drangey, and when he saw that if his expulsion were delayed, and Grettir left of his own accord, he would forfeit the money he had paid for the rights of pasturage on the island, he went to his foster-mother, and told her his difficulty, and pretty plainly let her understand that as he could get help nowhere else, he did not mind having recourse to the black art.

"Ah!" cackled she, "I see how it is, when all else fails, man's arms and man's wit, then you come to the bed-ridden crone and seek her aid. Well, I will assist you to the best of my power, on one condition, and that is, that you obey me without questioning."

The Hook agreed to what she said, and so all rested till August without the matter being again alluded to.

Then one beautiful day the hag said to Thorbiorn, "Foster-son, the sea is calm and the sky bright, what say you to our rowing over to Drangey and stirring up the old strife with Grettir? I will go with you and hear what he says, then I shall be able to judge what fate lies before him, and I can death-doom him accordingly."

The Hook answered, "It is waste of labour going out to Drangey. I have been there several times and never return better off than when I went."

"You promised to obey me without questioning," said the crone. "Follow my advice and all will be well for you and ill for Grettir."

"I will do as you bid me, foster-mother," said Thorbiorn, "though I had sworn not to go back to Drangey till I was sure I could work the bane of Grettir."

"That man is not laid low hastily, and patience is needed; but his time will come, and may be close at hand. What the end of this visit will be I cannot say. It is hid from me, but I know very well that it will lead to his or to your destruction."

Thorbiorn ran out a long boat, and entered it with twelve men. The hag sat in the bows coiled up amongst rugs and wadmal. When they reached the island, at once Grettir and Illugi ran to the ladder, and Thorbiorn again asked if Grettir would come to his house for the winter.

Grettir made the same reply as before, "Do what you will, in this spot I await my fate."

Now Thorbiorn saw that this expedition also was likely to be resultless, and he became very angry. "I see," he said, "that I have to do with an ill-conditioned churl, who does not know how to accept a good offer when made. I shall not come here again with such an offer."

"That pleases me well," said Grettir, "for you and I are not like to come to terms that will satisfy both."

At that moment the hag began to wriggle out of her wraps in the bows. Grettir had not perceived her hitherto. Now she screamed out, "These men may be strong, but their strength is ebbing. They may have had luck, but luck has left. See what a difference there is between men. Thorbiorn makes good offers, and such they blindly, foolishly reject. Those who are blinded and cast away chances do not have chances come to them again. And now Grettir"—she raised her withered arms over her head—"I doom you to all ill, I doom you to loss of health, to loss of wisdom and of foresight. I doom you to decline and to death. I doom your blood to fester, and your brain to be clouded. I doom your marrow to curdle and chill. Henceforth, so is my doom, all good things will wane from you, and all evil things will wax and overwhelm you. So be it." As she spoke a shudder ran over Grettir's limbs, and he asked who that imp was in the boat. Illugi told him he fancied it must be that old heathen woman, the foster-mother of Thorbiorn Hook.

"Since the powers of evil are with our foes," said Grettir, "how may we oppose them? Never before has anything so shaken me with presentiment of evil as have the curses of this witch. But she shall have a reminder of her visit to Drangey."

Thereupon he snatched up a large stone and threw it at the boat, and it fell on the bundle of rags, in the midst of which lay the old hag. As it struck there rose a wild shriek from the witch, for the stone had hit and broken her leg.

"Brother!" exclaimed Illugi, "you should not have done this."

"Blame me not," answered Grettir gloomily. "It had been well had the stone fallen on her head. But I trow the working of her curse is begun, and what I have done has been because my understanding and wit are already clouded."

On the return of Thorbiorn to the mainland the crone was put to bed, and The Hook was less pleased than ever with his trip to the island. His foster-mother, however, consoled him.

"Do not be discouraged," she said. "Now is come the turning-point of Grettir's fortunes, and his luck will leave him more and more as the light dies away up to Yule. But the light dies and comes again. With Grettir it will not be so, it will die, and die, till it goes out in endless night."

"You are a confident woman, foster-mother," said Thorbiorn.

When a month had elapsed, the old woman was able to leave her bed, and to limp across the room.

One day she asked to be led down to the beach. Thorbiorn gave her his arm, and she had her crutch, and she hobbled down to where the water was lapping on the shingle. And there, just washed up on the beach, lay a log of drift-timber, just large enough for a man to carry upon his shoulder. Then she gave command that the log should be rolled over and over that she might examine each side. The log on one side seemed to have been charred, and she sent to the house for a plane, and had the burnt wood smoothed away.

When that was done she dismissed every one save her foster-son, and then with a long knife she cut runes on the wood where it had been planed— that is to say, words written in the peculiar characters made of strokes which Odin was supposed to have invented. Then she cut herself on the arm, and smeared the letters she had cut with her blood. After that she rose and began to leap and dance, screaming a wild spell round the log, making the most strange and uncouth contortions, and waving her crutch in the air, making with it mysterious signs over the log. Presently, when the incantation was over, she ordered the log to be rolled back into the sea. The tide was now ebbing, and with the tide the log went out to sea further and further from land till Thorbiorn saw it no more.

XL: HOW THE LOG CAME TO DRANGEY

In the meantime Grettir, Illugi, and the churl Glaum were on Drangey catching fish and fowl for winter supplies. The fish in Iceland are beaten hard with stones and then dried in the wind, that makes them like leather; but it preserves them for a very long time, and they form the staple of food, as the people have no corn, and consequently no bread. They put butter on these dry fish, and tear them with their teeth. What Grettir did with the fowl he caught was to pickle them with salt water from the sea, and when the frost and snow came on then he would take them out of pickle and freeze them. Now, the whole of the sheep had been eaten some time ago, except the old mottled ram, which Grettir could not find in his heart to kill; and, as may be supposed, he and his brother suffered from want of change of food. Especially deficient were they in any green food; and we know, though he did not, that the eating of green food is a very essential element of health. He had nothing for consumption but salted birds and dried fish—no milk, no bread, no vegetables. Such a diet was certain to disorder his health.

The day after that on which the hag had charmed the piece of timber, the two brothers were walking on the little strand to the west of the island looking for drift-wood.

"Here is a fine beam!" exclaimed Illugi. "Help me to lift it on to my shoulder, and I will carry it up the ladder."

Grettir spurned the log with his foot, saying, "I do not like the looks of it, Little brother. Runes are cut on it, and what they portend I do not know. There may be written there something that may bring ill. Who can tell but this log may have been sent with ill wishes against us." They set the log adrift, and Grettir warned his brother not to bring it to their fire.

In the evening they returned to their cabin, and nothing was said about the log to Glaum. Next day they found the same beam washed up not far from the foot of the ladder. Grettir was dissatisfied, and again he thrust it from the shore, saying that he hoped they had seen the last of it, and that the stream and tide would catch it and waft it elsewhere. And now the equinoctial gales began to rage. The fine Martinmas summer was over. The weather changed to storm and rain; and so bad was it that the three men remained indoors till their supply of firewood was exhausted.

Then Grettir ordered the thrall to search the shore for fuel. Glaum started up with an angry remonstrance that the weather was not such as a dog should be turned out in, with unreason, not considering that a fire was as necessary to him as to his master. He went to the ladder, crawled down it, and found the same beam cast at its very foot.

Glad not to have to go far in his search, Glaum shouldered the log, crept up the ladder, bore it to the hut, and throwing open the door, cast it down in the midst.

Grettir jumped up, "Well done," said he, "you have been quick in your quest."

"Now I have brought it, you must chop it up," said Glaum. "I have done my part."

Grettir took his axe. The fire was low and wanted replenishing, and without paying much attention to the log, he swung his axe and brought it down on the log. But the wood was wet and greasy with sea-weed, and the axe slipped, glanced off the beam, and cut into Grettir's leg below the knee, on the shin, with such force that it stuck in the bone.

Grettir looked at the beam; the fire leaped up, and by its light the runic inscription on it was visible. Grettir at once saw evil. "The worst is come upon us," he said sadly, as he cast the axe away, and threw himself down by the fire. "This is the same log that I have twice rejected. Glaum, you have done us two ill turns, first when you neglected the fire and let it go out, and now in that you have brought this beam to us. Beware how you commit a third, for that I foresee will be your bane as well as ours."

Illugi bound up his brother's wound with rag; there was but a slight flow of blood, but it was an ugly gash. That night Grettir slept soundly. For three days and nights he was without pain, and the wound seemed to be healing healthily, the skin to be forming over it.

"My dear brother," said Illugi, "I do not think that this cut will trouble you long."

"I hope not," answered Grettir. "But none can see where a road leads till they have gone through to the end."

On the fourth evening they laid them down to sleep as usual. About midnight the lad, Illugi, awoke hearing Grettir tossing in his bed as though suffering.

"Why are you so uneasy?" asked the boy.

Grettir replied that he felt great pain in his leg, and he thought, he said, that some change must have taken place in the condition of the wound.

Illugi at once blew up the embers on the hearth into a flame, and by its light examined his brother's leg. He found that the foot was swollen and discoloured, and that the wound had reopened, and looked far more angry than he had seen it yet. Intense pain ensued, so that poor Grettir could not remain quiet for a moment, but tossed from side to side. His cheeks were fevered, and his tongue parched. He could obtain no sleep at all.

Illugi never left him, he sat beside him holding his hand, or bringing him water to slake his unquenchable thirst.

"The worst approaches, and there is no avoiding it," said Grettir. "This sickness is sent by the old witch in revenge for the stone I had cast at her."

"I misliked the casting of that stone," said Illugi.

"It was ill that it did not fall on her head," said Grettir. "But what is done may not be undone." Then he heaved himself up into a sitting posture and sang, supporting himself against his brother's shoulder, a lay, of which only fragments have come down to us. A good deal of the lay refers to incidents in Grettir's life, of which no record remains in the saga, and many staves have fallen away and been lost. So we give but a few verses:—

"I fought with the sword in the bye-gone day,
In the day when I was young;

When the Rovers I slew in old Norway,
The land with my action rung.

"I entered the grave of Karr the Old,
I rived his sword away;

I strove with the Troll at Thorod's-stead,
Before the break of day.

"With Thorbiorn Oxmain in the marsh
I fought, and his blood I shed;

Against Thorir of Garth have I stood in arms,
Who long would have me dead.

"For nineteen years, I a hunted man,
On mountain, on moor, and fen;

For nineteen years had to shun and flee
The face of my fellow men.

"For nineteen years all bitter to bear
Both hunger and cold and pain;

And never to know when I laid me down,
If I might awake again.

"And now do I lie with a burning eye,
As a wolf is fain to die;

Whilst the skies are dripping and ocean roars,
And the winds sob sadly by—"

The song was probably composed before, as otherwise it is not easy to account for its preservation. His head was burning, his thoughts wandered, and he ceased singing. He seemed to be dozing off. But presently he started and shivered, and looked hastily about him.

"Let us be cautious now," he said, "for Thorbiorn Hook will make another attempt. To me it matters little—but to you, brother. Glaum, watch the ladder by day, and draw it up at night. Be a faithful servant, for now all depends on you. Illugi will not leave me, so we are in your hands."

XLI: THE END OF THE OUTLAW

The weather became daily worse, and a fierce north-east wind raged over the country, bearing with it cold and sleet, and covering the fells with the first snows of winter. Grettir inquired every night if the ladder had been drawn up, according to order. Glaum answered churlishly, "How can you expect folk to live out in such a storm as this? Do you think they are so eager to kill you that they will jeopardize their lives in trying to do this? It is easy to see that a little cut was all that lacked to let your courage leak out."

Grettir answered, "Go! and do not argue with us; guard the ladder as you have been bidden!"

So Illugi drove the churl from the hut every morning, notwithstanding his angry remonstrances; and Glaum was in the worst of humours.

The pain became more acute, and the whole leg inflamed and swollen, signs of mortification appeared, and wounds opened in different parts of the limb, so that Grettir felt that the shadow of death hung over him. Illugi sat night and day with his brother's head on his shoulder, bathing his forehead, and doing his utmost to console the fleeting spirit. A week had elapsed since the wound had been made.

Now, Thorbiorn Hook was at home, ill-pleased at the failure of all his schemes for dispossessing Grettir of the island.

One day his foster-mother came to him, and asked whether he were ready now to pay his final visit to the outlaw?

Thorbiorn replied that he had paid quite as many visits to him as he liked, and that he should not go to Drangey again till Grettir left it; and then, with a sneer he asked his foster-mother whether she wanted to have her second leg broken, and was not satisfied with the fracture of one.

"I will not go to Drangey myself," answered the old woman. "That is unnecessary. I have sent him my salutation, and by this he has received it. Speed away now to Drangey, and find how he relishes my message. But I warn you, you must go now or you will be too late."

Thorbiorn would not listen; he said that her advice last time had led to no advantage when he followed it, and that the weather was too bad to go out in.

"You need go but this once," said the crone. "The storm is of my sending, and is sent to work my ends."

Finally he allowed himself to be persuaded. So he got together men, and asked his neighbours to help him; and a large vessel was manned. That is to say, the other farmers consented to lend him men, but none of them would accompany him themselves. The Hook took twelve of his own men; his brother, Hialti, lent him three; Erick of Gooddale sent one man; Tongue-stone furnished him with two; another, named Halldor, let him have six. Of all these, the only two whose name need be mentioned are Karr and Vikarr.

Thorbiorn got a large sailing-boat for his purpose, and started from Heron-ness. None of the men were in good spirits, as the weather was bad; moreover, they had no liking for their leader. By dusk the boat was afloat, the sail spread, and they ran out to sea. As the wind was from the north-east, they were under the lee of the high cliffs, and were not exposed to the full violence of the storm.

Heavy scuds of rain and sleet swept the fiord; the sky was overcast with whirling masses of vapour, charged with snow, and beneath their shadow the waters of the firth were black as ink. For one moment the clouds were parted by the storm, the rowers looked up, and saw the heavens tinged with the crimson rays of the northern light. A flame ran along the cordage, and finally settled on the masthead of the vessel, swaying and dancing with the motion of the boat. It was that electric spark, which is called in the Mediterranean S. Elmo's fire.

A line of white foam marked the base of Drangey; and now and then a great wave from the mouth of the fiord boomed against the crags, and shot in spouts of foam high into the air. Along the western shore of the firth, which was exposed to the full brunt of the gale, the mighty billows were beaten into white yeasty heaps of water. From the top of Drangey one tiny spark shone from the window of the hovel where lay the dying outlaw.

Now let us look again at Grettir.

He had been in less pain that day. Illugi had not left him, but remained faithful at his post.

The thrall, Glaum, had been sent out as usual to collect fuel and to watch the ladder, and to draw it up at nightfall. But instead of doing as he was bidden, the fellow laid himself down at the head of the steps, under a shelter-hut of turf that had been there erected, and went to sleep.

When Thorbiorn and his party reached the shore, they found to their content that the ladder had not been removed.

"Good luck attends on those who wait," said The Hook "Now, my fellows! the journey will not prove as bootless as you expected. Up the ladder with you! and let us all be cautious and bold!"

So they ascended, one after the other, The Hook taking the lead. On reaching the top he looked into the shelter-hut, and there found Glaum, asleep and snoring. Thorbiorn struck him over the shoulders, and asked him who he was.

Glaum turned on his side, rubbed his eyes, and growled forth, "Can you not leave a poor wretch alone? Never was a man so ill-treated as am I. I may not even sleep out here in the cold."

The Hook then knew who this was. "Fool!" shouted he. "Look up, and see who are come. We are your foes, and intend to kill every one of you."

Glaum started now to his feet full awake, and shrieked with dismay when he saw the black figures crowding up from the ladder and surrounding him.

"Make no noise," said Thorbiorn Hook. "I give you the choice of two things; answer the questions I put to you truthfully, or die at once."

The churl answered sullenly that he would speak, and he had nothing to conceal.

"Then tell me where the brothers are?"

"In the hovel I left them, where there is a fire. Not out in the cold. Grettir is sick and nigh on death, and Illugi is with him."

The Hook asked for particulars, and then Glaum told him about the log, and how Grettir was wounded. Thereat the Hook burst out laughing, and said, "Woe to the man that leans on a churl! That is a true proverb. Shamefully have you betrayed your trust, Glaum."

Thereupon Glaum was dragged along to the cabin where Grettir lay, and they treated him so roughly, that what with their blows and what with fear, he was nearly senseless when he reached it.

Illugi had been sitting by the fire with his brother's head in his lap, whilst Grettir lay in some sheepskins beside the hearth. All that evening the sick man's eyes had been wandering about the roof, watching the light play among the rafters, as the firewood blazed up or smouldered away. Illugi saw that his fingers plucked at the wool of the sheep-skins, riving it out, and that he knew was a bad sign. He felt sure that Grettir would die that night, and he watched his face intently, and could not bear to withdraw his eyes from him, for he loved him dearly. Presently Grettir turned his head, and smiled when he saw how he was watching him, and said that he felt easier, and would sleep. In a few moments his eyes closed.

As he dozed, his face became calmer than Illugi had seen it before; the muscles relaxed, and the wrinkles furrowed in his brow by care and suffering were now smoothed quite away. Grettir's face was never handsome, but it was grave and earnest, and the sorrow and trial he had passed through had left its trace on his features. His breath now came more evenly in sleep.

All at once there sounded a crash at the door, and the sleeper opened his eyes dreamily.

"It is only the old ram, brother," said Illugi. "He is butting, because he wants to come in."

"He butts hard! he butts hard!" muttered Grettir, and at that moment the door burst open. They saw faces looking in.

Illugi was on his feet in a moment. He seized his sword, flew to the doorway and defended it bravely, so that no one could pass through.

Thorbiorn called to some of the men to get upon the roof, and he was obeyed. The hovel was low, and in a moment four or five were on top of it tearing off the turf that covered it. Grettir tried to rise to his feet, but could only stagger to his knees. He seized his spear and drove it through the roof, so that it struck Karr in the breast, and the wound was his death.

Thorbiorn Hook called to the men to act more warily—they were twenty-five in all against two men, and one dying.

So the men pulled at the gable ends of the house and got the ridge-piece out, that it broke and fell, and with it a shower of turfs, into the hut.

Grettir drew his short-sword—the sword he had taken from the barrow of Karr the Old—and smote at the men as they leaped upon him from the wall. With one blow he struck Vikarr over the left shoulder, as he was on the point of springing down. The sword cut off his arm. But the blow was so violent, that Grettir, having dealt it, fell forward, and before he could raise himself Thorbiorn Hook struck him between the shoulders, and made a fearful wound.

Then cried Grettir, "Bare is the back without brother behind it!" and instantly Illugi threw his shield over him, planted one foot on each side of him as he lay on the floor, and defended him with desperate courage.

The mist of death was in Grettir's eyes; he attempted in vain to raise himself, but sank again on the sheep-skins, which were now drenched in blood.

No one could touch him, for the brave boy warded off every blow that was aimed at his brother.

Then Thorbiorn Hook ordered his men to form a ring round and close in on them with their shields and with beams. They did so, and Illugi was taken and bound; but not till he had wounded most of his opponents, and had killed three of Thorbiorn's men.

"Never have I seen one braver of your age," said The Hook. "I will say that you have fought well."

Then they went to Grettir, who lay where he had fallen, unable to resist further, for he had lost consciousness. They dealt him many a blow, but hardly any blood flowed from his wounds. When all supposed he was dead, then Thorbiorn tried to disengage the sword from his cold fingers, saying that he considered Grettir had wielded it long enough. But the strong man's hand was clenched around the handle so firmly that his enemy could not free the sword from his grasp.

Several of the men came up, and tried to unweave the fingers, but were unable to do so. Then the Hook said, "Why should we spare this wretched outlaw? Off with his hand!" And his men held down the arm whilst Thorbiorn hewed off the hand at the wrist with his axe.

After that, standing over the body, and grasping the hilt of the sword in both hands, he smote at Grettir's head; the edge of the blade was notched by the blow.

"Look!" laughed Thorbiorn. "This notch will be famous in story for many generations; for men will point to it and say, 'This was made by Grettir's skull.'" He struck twice and thrice at the outlaw's neck, till the head came off in his hands.

"Now have I slain a notable man!" exclaimed Thorbiorn. "I will take this head with me to land, and claim the price that was set on it; and none shall deny that it was my hand that slew that Grettir whom all else feared."

The men present said he might say what he liked, but that they believed Grettir was already dead when he smote him.

Thorbiorn now turned to Illugi, and said, "It is a pity that a brave lad like you should die, because you are associated with outlaws and evildoers."

"I tell you this," said Illugi, "that I will appear before you at the great assize, and there will charge you with having practised witchcraft to effect my brother's death."

"You hearken to me, boy," said Thorbiorn. "Put your hand to mine, and swear that you will not seek to avenge the death of your brother, and I will let you go; but if you will not take this oath, you shall die."

"And hearken to me, Thorbiorn," said Illugi. "If I live, but one thought shall occupy my heart night and day, and that will be how I may best avenge my brother. Now that you know what to expect of me—take what course you will."

Thorbiorn drew his companions aside to ask their advice; but they shrugged their shoulders, and replied that, as he had planned the expedition, he must carry it out as he thought best.

"Well," said The Hook, "I have no fancy for having the young viper lying in wait to sting me wherever I tread. He shall die."

Now, when Illugi knew that they had determined on slaying him, he smiled and said, "You have chosen that course which is best to my mind. I do not desire to be parted from my brother."

The day was breaking. They led Illugi to the east side of the island, and there they slew him.

It is told that they neither bound his eyes nor his hands, and that he looked fearlessly at them when they smote him, and neither changed colour nor even blinked.

Then they buried the brothers beneath a cairn in the island, but they took the head of Grettir and bore it to land. On the way they also slew the thrall Glaum.

Had the old hag, Thorbiorn's foster-mother, any hand in the death of Grettir? Certainly none. It was true that Grettir was wounded in the way described, by his own axe, but the condition of the wound was due to the scorbutic condition of his blood, through lack of green food. This the Icelanders did not understand; they could not comprehend how a wound could seem to be healing well and then break out and mortify afterwards, and they supposed that this was due to witchcraft. Then, again, Grettir's kin could not take the case of Grettir's murder into court, because Thorbiorn had acted within the law when killing him; but by charging him with the practice of witchcraft they made him amenable to the law. So, partly, no doubt, in good faith, they trumped up against Thorbiorn the accusation of having effected Grettir's death by witchcraft.

Now, it must be told how that, one day after the slaying of Grettir, Thorbiorn Hook at the head of twenty armed men rode to Biarg, in the Midfirth-dale, with Grettir's head slung from his saddlebow. On reaching the house he dismounted and strode into the hall, where Grettir's mother was seated with a servant. Thorbiorn threw her son's head at her feet, and said: "See! I have been to the island and have prevailed."

The lady sat proudly in her seat, and did not shed a tear; but lifting her voice in reply, she sang:

"Milk-sop—as timid sheep
Before a fox all cow'ring keep;
So did you—nor could prevail
So long as Grettir's strength was hale.
Woe is on the Northland side,
Nor can I my loathing hide!"

After this The Hook returned home, and folk wondered at Asdis, saying that only a heroic mother could have had sons so heroic. When Yule was over The Hook rode east away to Garth, and told Thorir what he had done, and claimed the money set on Grettir's head.

But Thorir was crafty, and just as the Biarg folk sought a charge against Thorbiorn for his deed, so did Thorir, that he might escape having to pay the silver. He answered, "I do not deny that I offered the money on Grettir's head, promising it to whomsoever should slay Grettir, but I will pay nothing to him who compassed his death by witchcraft; and if what the men who went with you say be true, you did not slay him with a sword, but hacked off his head after he was dead."

This made Thorbiorn Hook very angry, and when summer came he brought his suit against Thorir for the money. But simultaneously Grettir's kin brought a charge against Thorbiorn for having practised witchcraft. Also they had a summons against him for the slaying of Illugi. Now, the case was tried, and hotly discussed, and it ended this way:—It was judged that Thorbiorn had struck off the head of a man who was already dead, and that he had brought about the death of that man by witchcraft; thereupon it was judged that he should receive nothing of the money, and that he should be outlawed from Iceland.

So he went away and never returned.

Now, Grettir and Illugi were brought to land, and their bones lie at Reykir, where was the friendly farmer who had helped them when they were at Drangey. But Grettir's head was buried at Biarg. There is now no church or churchyard there, but there is a mound in the tún where his head is said to lie. I obtained leave to dig there, and I examined the spot, but found only a great stone under the turf, and this we had not the appliances to move. And perhaps it was as well; for if Grettir's head be there, it were better that there it should rest undisturbed.

XLIII: HOW DROMUND KEPT HIS WORD

Now, after that Thorbiorn Hook had been outlawed, he found that he had gotten to himself no advantage, but great harm by what he had done upon Drangey. He was forced to leave Iceland; and he saw, withal, that never again might he set foot therein again with safety, for all the relatives of the Biarg family would seek his life. Accordingly he made over his farm at Woodwick to his brother Hialti, and also all his rights over the island of Drangey, such as they were. Then he collected together what moveable goods he had, and went on board ship and sailed for Norway.

On reaching Norway he bragged much of what he had done in having slain Grettir, of whom tales were told in Norway; and, as may well be understood, he told the tale of the slaying of Grettir in his own way, magnifying his heroism, and saying nothing about such matters as lessened the greatness of his deed.

During the early winter tidings reached Thorstein Dromund at Tunsberg that his brother Grettir was dead, and also that the man who slew him was in the north of the country. When Dromund heard the tidings he was very sorrowful, and he called to mind the words he had said to Grettir when they showed each other what sort of arms they had. Dromund considered that he was bound to avenge his brother's death on his murderer.

Thorbiorn Hook also was aware that there was a half-brother of Grettir in Norway, and when he knew that he was wary, for he suspected that Dromund would seek his life. And, indeed, Thorstein Dromund sent spies to watch Thorbiorn Hook; but the latter was so careful of himself that Dromund was not able to attempt anything against him all that winter. No sooner did the soft, warm, spring breezes begin to blow, than The Hook got away out of Norway by the earliest opportunity. He had heard much talk how that the Emperors of the East, at Constantinople, kept a guard of Norsemen about them, and paid them well, and how that this guard was held in high esteem. So Thorbiorn Hook considered he could not do better than go to Constantinople, and try his fortune there. But before he left Norway he talked of his intention, and this was reported to Dromund at Tunsberg. So Dromund put his lands and affairs into the hands of his kinsmen, and got ready for journeying in search of Hook, whom he had never seen.

He sailed away after him, and wherever he came he made inquiries after the ship in which Thorbiorn Hook had been, and he was always just too late. He never could catch the ship up. And then finally Thorbiorn left the vessel and journeyed overland, and Thorstein lost his traces.

However, Dromund knew that Thorbiorn Hook was going to Constantinople, so he travelled thither also, and reached the imperial city. Now there were a great many Norsemen and Icelanders there in the company called the Varangians, who acted as a bodyguard to the Emperor, and among these men were some twenty or more called Thorbiorn, and which among them was the murderer of Grettir, Thorstein Dromund did not know. The Hook, as may well be imagined, did not tell anyone what his nickname was; not that he imagined he was pursued, but because it was not a pretty and flattering name. Thorstein also offered himself as a soldier in the guard, and was enrolled. He also merely gave his name as Thorstein, and told no one of his nickname of Dromund, lest the man he pursued should take alarm and leave.

So time passed, and Thorstein Dromund could not find out his man; and he lay awake in bed many nights musing on what he had undertaken, on the sad lot of Grettir, and on his ill-success in finding the murderer of his half-brother. Now, it fell out that on a certain day the order came to the Varangian guard that they were to be ready, as they were about to be sent on an expedition of importance.

It was usual, before any such an expedition, that all the men of the guard should burnish up their weapons and armour, and show them, that they were in condition.

So was it on this occasion also. They were assembled in the guard-room, and each produced his weapon. Then Thorbiorn held forth his short-sword—the very weapon that Grettir had taken from the tomb of Karr the Old, the sword with which he The Hook had hewed off Grettir's head.

Now, when Thorbiorn held forth the sword all the other guardsmen praised it, and said it was an excellent weapon; but it had one grievous blemish, for that there was a notch in the edge.

"Oh!" laughed Thorbiorn, "that notch is no blemish at all. It is a memorial of one of my greatest achievements."

"What was that?" asked one of the Varangians.

"With this sword," answered Thorbiorn, "I slew the man who was esteemed the greatest and most powerful champion of his time; a man who was in outlawry for twenty years, who had in his time fought and beaten off as many as thirty or forty who attacked him. But I was too much for him. When I went against him, then he had to give way. We fought for an hour without flagging, and finally I smote him down. Then I took from him his own sword, and with it I smote off his neck; and thus got the sword its notch."

"And his name?" asked Thorstein Dromund.

"His name was Grettir the Strong."

There was a pause; and in that pause the sword was handed to Dromund for him to look at.

"Thus is Grettir avenged!" suddenly exclaimed Dromund. He struck across the table at Thorbiorn with Grettir's own sword; and so great was the stroke that it smote through his skull to the jaw-teeth, and The Hook fell without a word, dead.

It was said, in after times, that Grettir was wonderful in his life, and wonderful in his death—for in life no man had been his equal in strength, and had had a sadder span of life; and in death he was wonderful—for of all Icelanders he was the only one who was avenged far away from home by the shores of the Bosphorus, in the City of the Emperors.

EPILOGUE

In the Icelandic annals the death of Grettir is set down as having occurred in 1033, but the dates are not quite correct, and the real date should be 1031.

Grettir is mentioned in other Icelandic sagas. He is spoken of and his pedigree given in the Landnama Book, the Icelandic Domesday, the most reliable book for history they have. The persons spoken of in the saga of Grettir are heard of in several other quite independent sagas, and in no case is there any serious anachronism.

Grettir, it will be recalled, was taken by the farmers in the Ice-firth. This incident is also related in the saga of the Foster-brothers; so is another incident about a contest concerning a dead whale I have not related, as likely to break the continuity of the history. In the saga of Thord, the hero is said to have blessed the Middle-firth in these words: "Let the man who grows up in this vale never be hung." And this blessing was thought to have had something to do with the saving of Grettir's neck in the Ice-firth. The story of Gisli has been told whom Grettir whipped. Now, in the Viga-styr saga, the most ancient of all Icelandic sagas, we hear of this same Gisli, and his character is painted in the same colours as in the saga of Grettir, but no mention is made of the whipping administered by Grettir. The murder of Atli, the brother of our outlaw, and the consequent slaying of Thorbiorn Oxmain is spoken of in the saga of Bard. The circumstance of Grettir having lived in a cave on the farm in Hit-dale is spoken of in the saga of Biorn. In the history of Grettir mention is made of the strife which took place between Biorn and Thord, but the full particulars of what is there alluded to casually are given in the saga of Biorn of Hit-dale. In our saga, Grettir is spoken of as meeting Bard wounded after a hard fight, in which he had avenged the death of his brother, but no particulars are given. In the saga of the Heath-fights we recover the whole story. Thus one saga explains and supports another.

It is therefore impossible to set down the story of Grettir as fabulous. It is historical; but the history has been somewhat embellished, partly by family vanity which led to the undue glorification of their hero, and partly by superstition which imagined the marvellous where all was really natural.

THE END

Greek and Northern Mythologies - A Comparison by Hélène Adeline Guerber

During the past fifty years learned men of many nations have investigated philology and comparative mythology so thoroughly that they have ascertained beyond the possibility of doubt "that English, together with all the Teutonic dialects of the Continent, belongs to that large family of speech which comprises, besides the Teutonic, Latin, Greek, Slavonic, and Celtic, the Oriental languages of India and Persia." "It has also been proved that the various tribes who started from the central home to discover Europe in the north, and India in the south, carried away with them, not only a common language, but a common faith and a common mythology. These are facts which may be ignored but cannot be disputed, and the two sciences of comparative grammar and comparative mythology, though but of recent origin, rest on a foundation as sound and safe as that of any of the inductive sciences." "For more than a thousand years the Scandinavian inhabitants of Norway have been separated in language from their Teutonic brethren on the Continent, and yet both have not only preserved the same stock of popular stories, but they tell them, in several instances, in almost the same words."

This resemblance, so strong in the early literature of nations inhabiting countries which present much the same physical aspect and have nearly the same climate, is not so marked when we compare the Northern myths with those of the genial South. Still, notwithstanding the contrast between Northern and Southern Europe, where these myths gradually ripened and attained their full growth, there is an analogy between the two mythologies which shows that the seeds from whence both sprang were originally the same.

In the foregoing chapters the Northern system of mythology has been outlined as clearly as possible, and the physical significance of the myths has been explained. Now we shall endeavour to set forth the resemblance of Northern mythology to that of the other Aryan nations, by comparing it with the Greek, which, however, it does not resemble as closely as it does the Oriental.

It is, of course, impossible in a work of this character to do more than mention the main points of resemblance in the stories forming the basis of these religions; but that will be sufficient to demonstrate, even to the most sceptical, that they must have been identical at a period too remote to indicate now with any certainty.

The Beginning of Things

The Northern nations, like the Greeks, imagined that the world rose out of chaos; and while the latter described it as a vapoury, formless mass, the former, influenced by their immediate surroundings, depicted it as a chaos of fire and ice—a combination which is only too comprehensible to any one who has visited Iceland and seen the wild, peculiar contrast between its volcanic soil, spouting geysers, and the great icebergs which hedge it round during the long, dark winter season.

From these opposing elements, fire and ice, were born the first divinities, who, like the first gods of the Greeks, were gigantic in stature and uncouth in appearance. Ymir, the huge ice giant, and his descendants, are comparable to the Titans, who were also elemental forces of Nature, personifications of subterranean fire; and both, having held full sway for a time, were obliged to yield to greater perfection. After a fierce struggle for supremacy, they all found themselves defeated and banished to the respective remote regions of Tartarus and Jötun-heim.

The triad, Odin, Vili, and Ve, of the Northern myth is the exact counterpart of Jupiter, Neptune, and Pluto, who, superior to the Titan forces, rule supreme over the world in their turn. In the Greek mythology, the gods, who are also all related to one another, betake themselves to Olympus, where they build golden palaces for their use; and in the Northern mythology the divine conquerors repair to Asgard, and there construct similar dwellings.

Cosmogony

Northern cosmogony was not unlike the Greek, for the people imagined that the earth, Mana-heim, was entirely surrounded by the sea, at the bottom of which lay coiled the huge Midgard snake, biting its own tail; and it was perfectly natural that, viewing the storm-lashed waves which beat against their shores, they should imagine these to be caused by his convulsive writhing. The Greeks, who also fancied the earth was round and compassed by a mighty river called Oceanus, described it as flowing with "a steady, equable current," for they generally gazed out upon calm and sunlit seas. Nifl-heim, the Northern region of perpetual cold and mist, had its exact counterpart in the land north of the Hyperboreans, where feathers (snow) continually hovered in the air, and where Hercules drove the Ceryneian stag into a snowdrift ere he could seize and bind it fast.

The Phenomena of the Sky

Like the Greeks, the Northern races believed that the earth was created first, and that the vaulted heavens were made afterwards to overshadow it entirely. They also imagined that the sun and moon were daily driven across the sky in chariots drawn by fiery steeds. Sol, the sun maiden, therefore corresponded to Helios, Hyperion, Phœbus, or Apollo, while Mani, the Moon (owing to a peculiarity of Northern grammar, which makes the sun feminine and the moon masculine), was the exact counterpart of Phœbe, Diana, or Cynthia.

The Northern scalds, who thought that they descried the prancing forms of white-maned steeds in the flying clouds, and the glitter of spears in the flashing light of the aurora borealis, said that the Valkyrs, or battle maidens, galloped across the sky, while the Greeks saw in the same natural phenomena the white flocks of Apollo guarded by Phaetusa and Lampetia.

As the dew fell from the clouds, the Northern poets declared that it dropped from the manes of the Valkyrs' steeds, while the Greeks, who observed that it generally sparkled longest in the thickets, identified it with Daphne and Procris, whose names are derived from the Sanskrit word which means "to sprinkle," and who are slain by their lovers, Apollo and Cephalus, personifications of the sun.

The earth was considered in the North as well as in the South as a female divinity, the fostering mother of all things; and it was owing to climatic difference only that the mythology of the North, where people were daily obliged to conquer the right to live by a hand-to-hand struggle with Nature, should represent her as hard and frozen like Rinda, while the Greeks embodied her in the genial goddess Ceres. The Greeks believed that the cold winter winds swept down from the North, and the Northern races, in addition, added that they were produced by the winnowing of the wings of the great eagle Hræ-svelgr.

The dwarfs, or dark elves, bred in Ymir's flesh, were like Pluto's servants in that they never left their underground realm, where they, too, sought the precious metals, which they moulded into delicate ornaments such as Vulcan bestowed upon the gods, and into weapons which no one could either dint or mar. As for the light elves, who lived above ground and cared for plants, trees, and streams, they were evidently the Northern equivalents to the nymphs, dryads, oreades, and hamadryads, which peopled the woods, valleys, and fountains of ancient Greece.

Jupiter and Odin

Jupiter, like Odin, was the father of the gods, the god of victory, and a personification of the universe. Hlidskialf, Allfather's lofty throne, was no less exalted than Olympus or Ida, whence the Thunderer could observe all that was taking place; and Odin's invincible spear Gungnir was as terror-inspiring as the thunderbolts brandished by his Greek prototype. The Northern deities feasted continually upon mead and boar's flesh, the drink and meat most suitable to the inhabitants of a Northern climate, while the gods of Olympus preferred the nectar and ambrosia which formed their only sustenance.

Twelve Æsir sat in Odin's council hall to deliberate over the wisest measures for the government of the world and men, and an equal number of gods assembled on the cloudy peak of Mount Olympus for a similar purpose. The Golden Age in Greece was a period of idyllic happiness, amid ever-flowering groves and under balmy skies, while the Northern age of bliss was also a time when peace and innocence flourished on the earth, and when evil was as yet entirely unknown.

The Creation of Man

Using the materials near at hand, the Greeks modelled their first images out of clay; hence they naturally imagined that Prometheus had made man out of that substance when called upon to fashion a creature inferior to the gods only. As the Northern statues were hewn out of wood, the Northern races inferred, as a matter of course, that Odin, Vili, and Ve (who here correspond to Prometheus, Epimetheus, and Minerva, the three Greek creators of man) made the first human couple, Ask and Embla, out of blocks of wood.

The goat Heidrun, which supplied the heavenly mead, is like Amalthea, Jupiter's first nurse, and the busy, tell-tale Ratatosk is equivalent to the snow-white crow in the story of Coronis, which was turned black in punishment for its tattling. Jupiter's eagle has its counterpart in the ravens Hugin and Munin, or in the wolves Geri and Freki, which are ever crouching at Odin's feet.

Norns and Fates

The close resemblance between the Northern Orlog and the Greek Destiny, goddesses whose decrees the gods themselves were obliged to respect, and the equally powerful Norns and Mœræ, is too obvious to need pointing

470

out, while the Vanas are counterparts of Neptune and the other ocean divinities. The great quarrel between the Vanas and the Æsir is merely another version of the dispute between Jupiter and Neptune for the supremacy of the world. Just as Jupiter forces his brother to yield to his authority, so the Æsir remain masters of all, but do not refuse to continue to share their power with their conquered foes, who thus become their allies and friends.

Like Jupiter, Odin is always described as majestic and middle-aged, and both gods are regarded as the divine progenitors of royal races, for while the Heraclidæ claimed Jupiter as their father, the Inglings, Skioldings, etc., held that Odin was the founder of their families. The most solemn oaths were sworn by Odin's spear as well as by Jupiter's footstool, and both gods rejoice in a multitude of names, all descriptive of the various phases of their nature and worship.

Odin, like Jupiter, frequently visited the earth in disguise, to judge of the hospitable intentions of mankind, as in the story of Geirrod and Agnar, which resembles that of Philemon and Baucis. The aim was to encourage hospitality; therefore, in both stories, those who showed themselves humanely inclined are richly rewarded, and in the Northern myth the lesson is enforced by the punishment inflicted upon Geirrod, as the scalds believed in poetic justice and saw that it was carefully meted out.

The contest of wit between Odin and Vafthrudnir has its parallel in the musical rivalry of Apollo and Marsyas, or in the test of skill between Minerva and Arachne. Odin further resembled Apollo in that he, too, was god of eloquence and poetry, and could win all hearts by means of his divine voice; he was like Mercury in that he taught mortals the use of runes, while the Greek god introduced the alphabet.

Myths of the Seasons

The disappearance of Odin, the sun or summer, and the consequent desolation of Frigga, the earth, is merely a different version of the myths of Proserpine and Adonis. When Proserpine and Adonis have gone, the earth (Ceres or Venus) bitterly mourns their absence, and refuses all consolation. It is only when they return from their exile that she casts off her mourning garments and gloom, and again decks herself in all her jewels. So Frigga and Freya bewail the absence of their husbands Odin and Odur, and remain hard and cold until their return. Odin's wife, Saga, the goddess of history, who lingered by Sokvabek, "the stream of time and events," taking note of all she saw, is like Clio, the muse of history, whom Apollo sought by the inspiring fount of Helicon.

Just as, according to Euhemerus, there was an historical Zeus, buried in Crete, where his grave can still be seen, so there was an historical Odin, whose mound rises near Upsala, where the greatest Northern temple once stood, and where there was a mighty oak which rivalled the famous tree of Dodona.

Frigga and Juno

Frigga, like Juno, was a personification of the atmosphere, the patroness of marriage, of connubial and motherly love, and the goddess of childbirth. She, too, is represented as a beautiful, stately woman, rejoicing in her adornments; and her special attendant, Gna, rivals Iris in the rapidity with which she executes her mistress's behests. Juno has full control over the clouds, which she can brush away with a motion of her hand, and Frigga is supposed to weave them out of the thread she has spun on her jewelled spinning wheel.

In Greek mythology we find many examples of the way in which Juno seeks to outwit Jupiter. Similar tales are not lacking in the Northern myths. Juno obtains possession of Io, in spite of her husband's reluctance to part with her, and Frigga artfully secures the victory for the Winilers in the Langobarden Saga. Odin's wrath at Frigga's theft of the gold from his statue is equivalent to Jupiter's marital displeasure at Juno's jealousy and interference during the war of Troy. In the story of Gefjon, and the clever way in which she procured land from Gylfi to form her kingdom of Seeland, we have a reproduction of the story of Dido, who obtained by stratagem the land upon which she founded her city of Carthage. In both accounts oxen come into play, for while in the Northern myth these sturdy beasts draw the piece of land far out to sea, in the other an ox hide, cut into strips, serves to enclose the queen's grant.

Musical Myths

The Pied Piper of Hamelin, who could attract all living creatures by his music, is like Orpheus or Amphion, whose lyres had the same power; and Odin, as leader of the dead, is the counterpart of Mercury Psychopompus, both being personifications of the wind, on whose wings disembodied souls were thought to be wafted from this mortal sphere.

The trusty Eckhardt, who would fain save Tannhäuser and prevent his returning to expose himself to the enchantments of the sorceress, in the Hörselberg, is like the Greek Mentor, who not only accompanied Telemachus, but gave him good advice and wise instructions, and would have rescued Ulysses from the hands of Calypso.

Thor and the Greek Gods

Thor, the Northern thunder-god, also has many points of resemblance with Jupiter. He bears the hammer Miölnir, the Northern emblem of the deadly thunderbolt, and, like Jupiter, uses it freely when warring against the giants. In his rapid growth Thor resembles Mercury, for while the former playfully tosses about several loads of ox hides a few hours after his birth, the latter steals Apollo's oxen before he is one day old. In physical strength Thor resembles Hercules, who also gave early proofs of uncommon vigour by strangling the serpents sent to slay him in his cradle, and who delighted, later on, in attacking and conquering giants and monsters. Hercules became a woman and took to spinning to please Omphale, the Lydian queen, and Thor assumed a woman's apparel to visit Thrym and recover his hammer, which had been buried nine rasts underground. The hammer, his principal attribute, was used for many sacred purposes. It consecrated the funeral pyre and the marriage rite, and boundary stakes driven in by a hammer were considered as sacred among Northern nations as the Hermæ or statues of Mercury, removal of which was punishable by death.

Thor's wife, Sif, with her luxuriant golden hair, is, as we have already stated, an emblem of the earth, and her hair of its rich vegetation. Loki's theft of these tresses is equivalent to Pluto's rape of Proserpine. To recover the golden locks, Loki must visit the dwarfs (Pluto's servants), crouching in the low passages of the underground world; so Mercury must seek Proserpine in Hades.

The gadfly which hinders Jupiter from recovering possession of Io, after Mercury has slain Argus, reappears in the Northern myth to sting Brock and to endeavour to prevent the manufacture of the magic ring Draupnir, which is merely a counterpart of Sif's tresses, as it also represents the fruits of the earth. The fly continues to torment the dwarf during the manufacture of Frey's golden-bristled boar, a prototype of Apollo's golden sun chariot, and it prevents the perfect formation of the handle of Thor's hammer.

The magic ship Skidbladnir, also made by the dwarfs, is like the swift-sailing Argo, which was a personification of the clouds sailing overhead; and just as the former was said to be large enough to accommodate all the gods, so the latter bore all the Greek heroes off to the distant land of Colchis.

The Germans, wishing to name the days of the week after their gods, as the Romans had done, gave the name of Thor to Jove's day, and thus made it the present Thursday.

Thor's struggle against Hrungnir is a parallel to the fight between Hercules and Cacus or Antæus; while Groa is evidently Ceres, for she, too, mourns for her absent child Orvandil (Proserpine), and breaks out into a song of joy when she hears that it will return.

Magni, Thor's son, who when only three hours old exhibits his marvellous strength by lifting Hrungnir's leg off his recumbent father, also reminds us of the infant Hercules; and Thor's voracious appetite at Thrym's wedding feast has its parallel in Mercury's first meal, which consisted of two whole oxen.

The crossing of the swollen tide of Veimer by Thor reminds us of Jason's feat when he waded across the torrent on his way to visit the tyrant Pelias and recover possession of his father's throne.

The marvellous necklace worn by Frigga and Freya to enhance their charms is like the cestus or girdle of Venus, which Juno borrowed to subjugate her lord, and is, like Sif's tresses and the ring Draupnir, an emblem of luxuriant vegetation or a type of the stars which shine in the firmament.

The Northern sword-god Tyr is, of course, the Greek war-god Ares, whom he so closely resembles that his name was given to the day of the week held sacred to Ares, which is even now known as Tuesday or Tiu's day. Like Ares, Tyr was noisy and courageous; he delighted in the din of battle, and was fearless at all times. He alone dared to brave the Fenris wolf; and the Southern proverb concerning Scylla and Charybdis has its counterpart in the Northern adage, "to get loose out of Læding and to dash out of Droma." The Fenris wolf, also a personification of subterranean fire, is bound, like his prototypes the Titans, in Tartarus.

The similarity between the gentle, music-loving Bragi, with his harp, and Apollo or Orpheus, is very great; so is the resemblance between the magic draught Od-hroerir and the waters of Helicon, both of which were supposed to serve as inspiration to mortal as well as to immortal poets. Odin dons eagle plumes to bear away this precious mead, and Jupiter assumes a similar guise to secure his cupbearer Ganymede.

Idun, like Adonis and Proserpine, or still more like Eurydice, is also a fair personification of spring. She is borne away by the cruel ice giant Thiassi, who represents the boar which slew Adonis, the kidnapper of Proserpine, or the poisonous serpent which bit Eurydice. Idun is detained for a long time in Jötun-heim (Hades), where she forgets all her merry, playful ways, and becomes mournful and pale. She cannot return alone to Asgard, and it is only when Loki (now an emblem of the south wind) comes to bear her away in the shape of a nut or a swallow that she can effect her escape. She reminds us of Proserpine and Adonis escorted back to earth by Mercury (god of the wind), or of Eurydice lured out of Hades by the sweet sounds of Orpheus's harp, which were also symbolical of the soughing of the winds.

Idun and Eurydice

The myth of Idun's fall from Yggdrasil into the darkest depths of Niflheim, while subject to the same explanation and comparison as the above story, is still more closely related to the tale of Orpheus and Eurydice, for the former, like Bragi, cannot exist without the latter, whom he follows even into the dark realm of death; without her his songs are entirely silenced. The wolf-skin in which Idun is enveloped is typical of the heavy snows in Northern regions, which preserve the tender roots from the blighting influence of the extreme winter cold.

Skadi and Diana

The Van Niörd, who is god of the sunny summer seas, has his counterpart in Neptune and more especially in Nereus, the personification of the calm and pleasant aspect of the mighty deep. Niörd's wife, Skadi, is the Northern huntress; she therefore resembles Diana. Like her, she bears a quiver full of arrows, and a bow which she handles with consummate skill. Her short gown permits the utmost freedom of motion, also, and she, too, is generally accompanied by a hound.

The story of the transference of Thiassi's eyes to the firmament, where they glow like brilliant stars, reminds us of many Greek star myths, and especially of Argus's eyes ever on the watch, of Orion and his jewelled girdle, and of his dog Sirius, all changed into stars by the gods to appease angry goddesses. Loki's antics to win a smile from the irate Skadi are considered akin to the quivering flashes of sheet-lightning which he personified in the North, while Steropes, the Cyclops, typified it for the Greeks.

Frey and Apollo

The Northern god of sunshine and summer showers, the genial Frey, has many traits in common with Apollo, for, like him, he is beautiful and young, rides the golden-bristled boar which was the Northern conception of the sunbeams, or drives across the sky in a golden car, which reminds us of Apollo's glittering chariot.

Frey has some of the gentle Zephyrus's characteristics besides, for he, too, scatters flowers along his way. His horse Blodug-hofi is not unlike Pegasus, Apollo's favourite steed, for it can pass through fire and water with equal ease and velocity.

Fro, like Odin and Jupiter, is also identified with a human king, and his mound lies beside Odin's near Upsala. His reign was so happy that it was called the Golden Age, and he therefore reminds us of Saturn, who, exiled to earth, ruled over the people of Italy, and granted them similar prosperity.

Freya and Venus

Gerda, the beautiful maiden, is like Venus, and also like Atalanta; she is hard to woo and hard to win, like the fleet-footed maiden, but, like her, she yields at last and becomes a happy wife. The golden apples with which Skirnir tries to bribe her remind us of the golden fruit which Hippomenes cast in Atalanta's way, and which made her lose the race.

Freya, the goddess of youth, love, and beauty, like Venus, sprang from the sea, for she is a daughter of the sea-god Niörd. Venus bestowed her best affections upon the god of war and upon the martial Anchises, while Freya often assumes the garb of a Valkyr, and rides rapidly to earth to take part in mortal strife and bear away the heroic slain to feast in her halls. Like Venus, she delights in offerings of fruits and flowers, and lends a gracious ear to the petitions of lovers. Freya also resembles Minerva, for, like her, she wears a helmet and breastplate, and, like her, also, she is noted for her beautiful blue eyes.

Odur and Adonis

Odur, Freya's husband, is like Adonis, and when he leaves her, she, too, sheds countless tears, which, in her case, are turned to gold, while Venus's tears are changed into anemones, and those of the Heliades, mourning for Phaeton, harden to amber, which resembles gold in colour and in consistency. Just as Venus rejoices at Adonis's return, and all Nature blooms in sympathy with her joy, so Freya becomes lighthearted once more when she has found her husband beneath the flowering myrtles of the South. Venus's car is drawn by fluttering doves, and Freya's is swiftly carried along by cats, which are emblems of sensual love, as the doves were considered types of tenderest love. Freya is appreciative of beauty and angrily refuses to marry Thrym, while Venus scorns and finally deserts Vulcan, whom she has been forced to marry against her will.

The Greeks represented Justice as a goddess blindfolded, with scales in one hand and a sword in the other, to indicate the impartiality and the fixity of her decrees. The corresponding deity of the North was Forseti, who patiently listened to both sides of a question ere he, too, promulgated his impartial and irrevocable sentence.

Uller, the winter-god, resembles Apollo and Orion only in his love for the chase, which he pursues with ardour under all circumstances. He is the Northern bowman, and his skill is quite as unerring as theirs.

Heimdall, like Argus, was gifted with marvellous keenness of sight, which enabled him to see a hundred miles off as plainly by night as by day. His Giallar-horn, which could be heard throughout all the world, proclaiming the gods' passage to and fro over the quivering bridge Bifröst, was like the trumpet of the goddess Renown. As he was related to the water deities on his mother's side, he could, like Proteus, assume any form at will, and he made good use of this power on the occasion when he frustrated Loki's attempt to steal the necklace Brisinga-men.

Hermod, the quick or nimble, resembles Mercury not only in his marvellous celerity of motion. He, too, was the messenger of the gods, and, like the Greek divinity, flashed hither and thither, aided not by winged cap and sandals, but by Odin's steed Sleipnir, whom he alone was allowed to bestride. Instead of the Caduceus, he bore the wand Gambantein. He questioned the Norns and the magician Rossthiof, through whom he learned that Vali would come to avenge his brother Balder and to supplant his father Odin. Instances of similar consultations are found in Greek mythology, where Jupiter would fain have married Thetis, yet desisted when the Fates foretold that if he did so she would be the mother of a son who would surpass his father in glory and renown.

The Northern god of silence, Vidar, has some resemblance to Hercules, for while the latter has nothing but a club with which to defend himself against the Nemean lion, whom he tears asunder, the former is enabled to rend the Fenris wolf at Ragnarok by the possession of one large shoe.

Rinda and Danae

Odin's courtship of Rinda reminds us of Jupiter's wooing of Danae, who is also a symbol of the earth; and while the shower of gold in the Greek tale is intended to represent the fertilising sunbeams, the footbath in the Northern story typifies the spring thaw which sets in when the sun has overcome the resistance of the frozen earth. Perseus, the child of this union, has many points of resemblance with Vali, for he, too, is an avenger, and slays his mother's enemies just as surely as Vali destroys Hodur, the murderer of Balder.

The Fates were supposed to preside over birth in Greece, and to foretell a child's future, as did the Norns; and the story of Meleager has its unmistakable parallel in that of Nornagesta. Althæa preserves the half-consumed brand in a chest, Nornagesta conceals the candle-end in his harp; and while the Greek mother brings about her son's death by casting the brand into the fire, Nornagesta, compelled to light his candle-end at Olaf's command, dies as it sputters and burns out.

Hebe and the Valkyrs were the cupbearers of Olympus and Asgard. They were all personifications of youth; and while Hebe married the great hero and demigod Hercules when she ceased to fulfil her office, the Valkyrs were relieved from their duties when united to heroes like Helgi, Hakon, Völund, or Sigurd.

The Cretan labyrinth has its counterpart in the Icelandic Völundarhaus, and Völund and Dædalus both effect their escape from a maze by a cleverly devised pair of wings, which enable them to fly in safety over land and sea and escape from the tyranny of their respective masters, Nidud and Minos. Völund resembles Vulcan, also, in that he is a clever smith and makes use of his talents to work out his revenge. Vulcan, lamed by a fall from Olympus, and neglected by Juno, whom he had tried to befriend, sends her a golden throne, which is provided with cunning springs to seize and hold her fast. Völund, hamstrung by the suggestion of Nidud's queen, secretly murders her sons, and out of their eyes fashions marvellous jewels, which she unsuspectingly wears upon her breast until he reveals their origin.

Myths of the Sea

Just as the Greeks fancied that the tempests were the effect of Neptune's wrath, so the Northern races attributed them either to the writhings of Iörmungandr, the Midgard snake, or to the anger of Ægir, who, crowned with seaweed like Neptune, often sent his children, the wave maidens (the counterpart of the Nereides and Oceanides), to play on the tossing billows. Neptune had his dwelling in the coral caves near the Island of Eubœa, while Ægir lived in a similar palace near the Cattegat. Here he was surrounded by the nixies, undines, and mermaids, the counterpart of the Greek water nymphs, and by the river-gods of the Rhine, Elbe, and Neckar, who remind us of Alpheus and Peneus, the river-gods of the Greeks.

The frequency of shipwrecks on the Northern coasts made the people think of Ran (the equivalent of the Greek sea-goddess Amphitrite) as greedy and avaricious, and they described her as armed with a strong net, with which she drew all things down into the deep. The Greek Sirens had their parallel in the Northern Lorelei, who possessed the same gift of song, and also lured mariners to their death; while Princess Ilse, who was turned into a fountain, reminds us of the nymph Arethusa, who underwent a similar transformation.

In the Northern conception of Nifl-heim we have an almost exact counterpart of the Greek Hades. Mödgud, the guardian of the Giallar-bridge (the bridge of death), over which all the spirits of the dead must pass, exacts a tribute of blood as rigorously as Charon demands an obolus from every soul he ferries over Acheron, the river of death. The fierce dog Garm, cowering in the Gnipa hole, and keeping guard at Hel's gate, is like the three-headed monster Cerberus; and the nine worlds of Nifl-heim are not unlike the divisions of Hades, Nastrond being an adequate substitute for Tartarus, where the wicked were punished with equal severity.

The custom of burning dead heroes with their arms, and of slaying victims, such as horses and dogs, upon their pyre, was much the same in the North as in the South; and while Mors or Thanatos, the Greek Death, was represented with a sharp scythe, Hel was depicted with a broom or rake, which she used as ruthlessly, and with which she did as much execution.

Balder and Apollo

Balder, the radiant god of sunshine, reminds us not only of Apollo and Orpheus, but of all the other heroes of sun myths. His wife Nanna is like Flora, and still more like Proserpine, for she, too, goes down into the underworld, where she tarries for a while. Balder's golden hall of Breidablik is like Apollo's palace in the east; he, also, delights in flowers; all things smile at his approach, and willingly pledge themselves not to injure him. As Achilles was vulnerable only in the heel, so Balder could be slain only by the harmless mistletoe, and his death is occasioned by Loki's jealousy just as Hercules was slain by that of Deianeira. Balder's funeral pyre on Ringhorn reminds us of Hercules's death on Mount Œta, the flames and reddish glow of both fires serving to typify the setting sun. The Northern god of sun and summer could only be released from Nifl-heim if all animate and inanimate objects shed tears; so Proserpine could issue from Hades only upon condition that she had partaken of no food. The trifling refusal of Thok to shed a single tear is like the pomegranate seeds which Proserpine ate, and the result is equally disastrous in both cases, as it detains Balder and Proserpine underground, and the earth (Frigga or Ceres) must continue to mourn their absence.

Through Loki evil entered into the Northern world; Prometheus's gift of fire brought the same curse upon the Greeks. The punishment inflicted by the gods upon the culprits is not unlike, for while Loki is bound with adamantine chains underground, and tortured by the continuous dropping of venom from the fangs of a snake fastened above his head, Prometheus is similarly fettered to Caucasus, and a ravenous vulture continually preys upon his liver. Loki's punishment has another counterpart in that of Tityus, bound in Hades, and in that of Enceladus, chained beneath Mount Ætna, where his writhing produced earthquakes, and his imprecations caused sudden eruptions of the volcano. Loki, further, resembles Neptune in that he, too, assumed an equine form and was the parent of a wonderful steed, for Sleipnir rivals Arion both in speed and endurance.

The Fimbul-winter has been compared to the long preliminary fight under the walls of Troy, and Ragnarok, the grand closing drama of Northern mythology, to the burning of that famous city. "Thor is Hector; the Fenris wolf, Pyrrhus, son of Achilles, who slew Priam (Odin); and Vidar, who survives in Ragnarok, is Æneas." The destruction of Priam's palace is the type of the ruin of the gods' golden halls; and the devouring wolves Hati, Sköll, and Managarm, the fiends of darkness, are prototypes of Paris and all the other demons of darkness, who bear away or devour the sun-maiden Helen.

Ragnarok and the Deluge

According to another interpretation, however, Ragnarok and the consequent submersion of the world is but a Northern version of the Deluge. The survivors, Lif and Lifthrasir, like Deucalion and Pyrrha, were destined to repeople the world; and just as the shrine of Delphi alone resisted the destructive power of the great cataclysm, so Gimli stood radiant to receive the surviving gods.

Giants and Titans

We have already seen how closely the Northern giants resembled the Titans. It only remains to mention that while the Greeks imagined that Atlas was changed into a mountain, so the Northmen believed that the Riesengebirge, in Germany, were formed from giants, and that the avalanches which descended from their lofty heights were the burdens of snow which these giants impatiently shook from their crests as they changed their cramped positions. The apparition, in the shape of a bull, of one of the water giants, who came to woo the queen of the Franks, has its parallel in the story of Jupiter's wooing of Europa, and Meroveus is evidently the exact counterpart of Sarpedon. A faint resemblance can be traced between the giant ship Mannigfual and the Argo, for while the one is supposed to have cruised through the Ægean and Euxine Seas, and to have made many places memorable by the dangers it encountered there, so the Northern vessel sailed about the North and Baltic Seas, and is mentioned in connection with the Island of Bornholm and the cliffs of Dover.

While the Greeks imagined that Nightmares were the evil dreams which escaped from the Cave of Somnus, the Northern race fancied they were female dwarfs or trolls, who crept out of the dark recesses of the earth to torment them. All magic weapons in the North were said to be the work of the dwarfs, the underground smiths, while those of the Greeks were manufactured by Vulcan and the Cyclopes, under Mount Ætna, or on the Island of Lemnos.

The Volsunga Saga

In the Sigurd myth we find Odin one-eyed like the Cyclopes, who, like him, are personifications of the sun. Sigurd is instructed by Gripir, the horse-trainer, who is reminiscent of Chiron, the centaur. He is not only able to teach a young hero all he need know, and to give him good advice concerning his future conduct, but is also possessed of the gift of prophecy.

The marvellous sword which becomes the property of Sigmund and of Sigurd as soon as they prove themselves worthy to wield it, and the sword Angurvadel which Frithiof inherits from his sire, remind us of the weapon which Ægeus concealed beneath the rock, and which Theseus secured as soon as he had become a man. Sigurd, like Theseus, Perseus, and Jason, seeks to avenge his father's wrongs ere he sets out in search of the golden hoard, the exact counterpart of the golden fleece, which is also guarded by a dragon, and is very hard to secure. Like all the Greek sun-gods and heroes, Sigurd has golden hair and bright blue eyes. His struggle with Fafnir reminds us of Apollo's fight with Python, while the ring Andvaranaut can be likened to Venus's cestus, and the curse attached to its possessor is like the tragedy of Helen, who brought endless bloodshed upon all connected with her.

Sigurd could not have conquered Fafnir without the magic sword, just as the Greeks failed to take Troy without the arrows of Philoctetes, which are also emblems of the all-conquering rays of the sun. The recovery of the stolen treasure is like Menelaus's recovery of Helen, and it apparently brings as little happiness to Sigurd as his recreant wife did to the Spartan king.

Brunhild

Brunhild resembles Minerva in her martial tastes, physical appearance, and wisdom; but her anger and resentment when Sigurd forgets her for Gudrun is like the wrath of Œnone, whom Paris deserts to woo Helen. Brunhild's anger continues to accompany Sigurd through life, and she even seeks to compass his death, while Œnone, called to cure her wounded lover, refuses to do so and permits him to die. Œnone and Brunhild are both overcome by the same remorseful feelings when their lovers have breathed their last, and both insist upon sharing their funeral pyres, and end their lives by the side of those whom they had loved.

Sun Myths

Containing, as it does, a whole series of sun myths, the Volsunga Saga repeats itself in every phase; and just as Ariadne, forsaken by the sun-hero Theseus, finally marries Bacchus, so Gudrun, when Sigurd has departed, marries Atli, the King of the Huns. He, too, ends his life amid the flames of his burning palace or ship. Gunnar, like Orpheus or Amphion, plays such marvellous strains upon his harp that even the serpents are lulled to sleep. According to some interpretations, Atli is like Fafnir, and covets the possession of the gold. Both are therefore probably personifications "of the winter cloud which broods over and keeps from mortals the gold of the sun's light and heat, till in the spring the bright orb overcomes the powers of darkness and tempests, and scatters his gold over the face of the earth."

Swanhild, Sigurd's daughter, is another personification of the sun, as is seen in her blue eyes and golden hair; and her death under the hoofs of black steeds represents the blotting out of the sun by clouds of storm or of darkness.

Just as Castor and Pollux hasten to rescue their sister Helen when she has been borne away by Theseus, so Swanhild's brothers, Erp, Hamdir, and Sörli, hasten off to avenge her death.

Such are the main points of resemblance between the mythologies of the North and South, and the analogy goes far to prove that they were originally formed from the same materials, the principal differences being due to the local colouring imparted unconsciously by the different races.

CPSIA information can be obtained
at www.ICGtesting.com
Printed in the USA
BVHW040824271218
536511BV00012B/133/P